Swordsmen of Gor

Gorean Saga

01 - TARNSMAN OF GOR
02 - OUTLAW OF GOR
03 - PRIEST-KINGS OF GOR
04 - NOMADS OF GOR
05 - ASSASSIN OF GOR
06 - RAIDERS OF GOR
07 - CAPTIVE OF GOR
08 - HUNTERS OF GOR
09 - MARAUDERS OF GOR
10 - TRIBESMEN OF GOR
11 - SLAVE GIRL OF GOR
12 - BEASTS OF GOR
13 - EXPLORERS OF GOR
14 - FIGHTING SLAVE OF GOR
15 - ROGUE OF GOR
16 - GUARDSMAN OF GOR
17 - SAVAGES OF GOR
18 - BLOOD BROTHERS OF GOR
19 - KAJIRA OF GOR
20 - PLAYERS OF GOR
21 - MERCENARIES OF GOR
22 - DANCER OF GOR
23 - RENEGADES OF GOR
24 - VAGABONDS OF GOR
25 - MAGICIANS OF GOR
26 - WITNESS OF GOR
27 - PRIZE OF GOR
28 - KUR OF GOR
29 - SWORDSMEN OF GOR
30 - MARINERS OF GOR
31 - CONSPIRATORS OF GOR
32 - SMUGGLERS OF GOR

Swordsmen of Gor

John Norman

978-1-4976-4874-6

This edition published in 2014 by Open Road Integrated Media, Inc.
345 Hudson Street
New York, NY 10014
www.openroadmedia.com

Swordsmen of Gor

Chapter One

What Occurred at the Edge of the Forest

"I had not dreamed it so," she said. "How could it be so beautiful?"

She stood on the beach, Thassa, calm, the sea, before her, the forest behind her.

We watched the ship of Peisistratus ascending, almost vertically, and then vanishing, far off, a sparkle, in the bright, blue sky.

"You had seen only Earth," I said, recalling that distant, desecrated, half-ruined world from my past, "and the Steel World, once ruled by Agamemnon." The name 'Agamemnon' was not the actual name of he who was once a Steel-World master, but it was chosen, it seems, for obscure associations. In any event, the actual name, being in Kur, could not be well rendered into phonemes accessible to the human throat.

In any event, we need not concern ourselves with Agamemnon as he had been dethroned, removed from the Steel World in question, and brought to Gor by exiled, devoted liegemen. Too, without a body, he was little to be feared.

The Steel Worlds are not visible to the naked eye, nor even to relatively sophisticated telescopic instrumentation. Too, they lurk, like wolves, muchly concealed, amongst the scattered stones, some small, many mighty, of what, on Earth, is commonly referred to as the asteroid belt, on Gor, by those familiar with the Second Knowledge, as the reefs of space.

Ramar, the sleen, lame, rubbed against my thigh.

"You can live in this place," I told him. "I do not even know where we are."

To be sure, I knew we were somewhere in the vicinity of the northern forests, north of the Tamber gulf, east of Thassa, well south of Torvaldsland. This mode of orientation is not Gorean, the common compass of which, with its eight cardinal points, is oriented to the Sardar, the dark, walled, mountainous abode of Priest-Kings, but founded on the Gorean poles. I am utilizing this manner of speaking, as it seems to me not only convenient but suitable. Should this record, then, which is written in English, and will thus be unintelligible to most Goreans, this often a boon to the writer, assuring as it does a modicum of privacy, indeed, it commonly amongst Goreans counting as a suspect, secret writing, come into the hands of any who might be familiar with English, these directions will be reasonably well understood. I write in English because it is easiest for me. Although I speak Gorean fluently, I can read it and write it only with difficulty. This is not unusual with those of my caste, many of whom, by choice, are contemptuously, pridefully illiterate, holding themselves superior to what they despise as trivial, vulgar learning. The business of their caste, then, in their view, is not with the pen but with steel, not with ink, but blood. Let scribes, they say, be adept with letters, and such, for that is their business, little scratches and marks on scrolls, and such. But this is not for them, not for the Scarlet Caste. But, too, should not each caste concern itself with its own business, the metal worker with metals, the peasant with the soil, the mariner with the sea, and so on? I do not commend this view, but report it. Too, in all honesty, it is not that unusual to find refined, literate members of my caste. Some members of my caste are educated gentlemen, educated, distinguished, dangerous gentlemen. Gorean, incidentally, is written "as the bosk plows," which requires an alternating laterality, the first line read from left to right, the second from right to left, and so on. I might also mention that certain measures, of, say, length and weight, and such, will be approximated in English, in terms of pounds, yards, inches, and such, rather than in terms of stones, paces, horts, and such. The Gorean pace is very close to the English yard, but the stone is well over a pound and the hort is somewhat longer than an inch. I think this way of doing things will be helpful to an English reader. An exception, though perhaps not the only one, is the "pasang," a convenient, often-encountered linear measure, easily graspable, I think. It is, as nearly as I can determine, having paced it out long ago, between pasang stones in the vicinity of Ko-ro-ba, some seven tenths of an English mile.

"The air," she said, "exhilarates me!"

"The air has not been fouled," I said. "Goreans love their world."

"It is all so beautiful," she breathed, wonderingly.

"Earth," I said, "was doubtless once much like this."

"The gravity," she said, "is much like that of the Steel World."

"It should be identical," I said. "The rotation of the Steel Worlds, which produces their surrogate gravity, is arranged to simulate that of Gor."

"There is a purpose in that?" she said, uneasily.

"Certainly," I said. "The Kurii want Gor. Would you not want Gor, as well?"

"Given the fall of Agamemnon," she said, "Gor has nothing to fear."

"That is false," I said. "Agamemnon wished to act unilaterally, and have Gor for himself. Many others, and even many in his own world, found that ambition unacceptable, or, at least, unrealistic. The denizens of the Steel Worlds, on the whole, wish to obtain Gor cooperatively, and, after that, they can dispute it amongst themselves."

"And would?"

"Of course," I said. "They are Kur."

"I suppose humans might, as well," she said.

"That explains much of the history of Earth," I said, "competition for territory, resources, and such."

"And women?" she said.

"Certainly," I said, "women are highly desirable resources."

"As loot, as properties, and slaves," she said.

"Of course," I said. "They are always valuable, as counters of wealth, and such."

"And, one supposes, as helpless, vulnerable vessels of pleasure," she said.

"Yes," I said, "as helpless, vulnerable vessels of pleasure, vessels of inordinate pleasure."

"As animals, whom you use as you wish?" she said.

"Of course," I said.

"Men are beasts," she said.

"They are what they are," I said. "And on Gor they do not pretend to be what they are not."

Her hand went, inadvertently, not really thinking much about it, to her throat. She could not remove the light, flat, slender metal band which encircled it, attractively, closely.

"Gor is lovely," I said.

"Yes," she said, looking out, over the sea.

"Sometimes the Priest-Kings," I said, "as a most cruel punishment, condemn an individual to Earth."

"Condemn?"

"Precisely."

"Those of Earth are unaware of the nature of their world," she said.

"They do not much mind it," I said, "for they have known nothing else, nothing better. But the poor man, or woman, who is sent to Earth from Gor, they well understand the harshness of their sentence."

"I suppose they, their lesson learned, must hope in time for mercy, a pardon, a reprieve?" she said.

"Some are sentenced for life," I said.

"I am much pleased to be here," she said.

"Even as you are?" I asked.

"Certainly," she said.

She was well legged, sweetly hipped, narrow waisted, and well breasted. I did not think she would need be disappointed at the price that would be likely to take her off the block.

She was the sort of woman who was eminently purchasable.

The block was designed with such as she in mind.

"Even as what you are?"

"Oh, yes," she said. "Yes! Yes! Extremely so! And particularly and appropriately so!"

"It is right for you?"

"Yes, and perfectly so!" she said.

"Perfectly so?"

"Yes, absolutely, perfectly so!"

"On Earth you did not anticipate it," I said.

"Certainly not," she said, "though I now realize how pathetically, and needfully, half consciously, sometimes fully consciously, I longed for it."

"I see," I said.

"I did not realize then what it was, what it would be, to be overwhelmed, owned, and mastered."

"You are content?" I said.

"Yes," she said, "joyfully so."

"But it does not matter," I said, "one way or the other."

"No," she said, "I know that. It does not matter, one way or the other."

I looked out to sea.

No sails were seen.

The horizon was clear.

"You, and others," she said, "fought against Agamemnon, furthering the ends of other Kurii, those opposed to him. Are not you, then, and your colleagues, friends, allies, with them?"

"For a moment, we were," I said. "It was a brief intersection of interests, a moment when we traveled a single road."

"And that road has forked?" she said.

"I think so," I said. "Kurii are intent, and steadfast."

"But we have been brought here, and put here, alive."

"Doubtless in virtue of an arrangement with Priest-Kings," I said.

"Who are Priest-Kings?" she asked. "What are Priest-Kings?"

"Do not concern yourself with the matter," I said.

"Curiosity," she said, "is not for one such as I?"

"No," I said. "Such as you are for other things."

"'Other things'?" she said.

"Certainly," I said.

"I can no longer see the ship of Peisistratus," she said, looking after the path of the ship, shading her eyes.

"I gather it is to make landfall within territories under the hegemony of Ar, and there disembark the Lady Bina and her cohort, and guard, Lord Grendel."

"To what purpose?"

"I know not," I said.

"She expects to become a Ubara," she said.

"She is clever, and beautiful," I said, "but the thought is madness."

"But she was put there, with her guard, Lord Grendel. Do you think this is a guerdon for obscure services she rendered, or a gift to Lord Grendel?"

"It seems unlikely," I said.

"If you have been placed here, in this verdant wilderness, at the will of Priest-Kings, whoever or whatever they may be, might not the Lady Bina and Lord Grendel have their purposes, as well?"

"I do not know."

"Why have you been put here?"

"I do not know," I said.

"I see nothing about," she said.

"Nor I," I said.

"You have your bow, some arrows, a sword, a knife," she said.

"Rejoice," I said, looking about.

"It does not seem we were put here to perish," she said.

"No," I said, looking back to the forest, "but we may perish."

"There are animals?" she said.

"Doubtless," I said.

"Men?" she asked.

"One does not know," I said.

"We have some provisions," she said, "bread, a bota of ka-la-na."

"I will hunt," I said. "We will seek water."

"When Peisistratus disembarks Bina—" she said.

"*Lady* Bina," I said, sharply, narrowly.

"Yes," she said, quickly, "*Lady* Bina."

I wondered if she were testing me. That would have been unwise on her part. No love was lost between her and the beauteous Lady Bina, but that was no excuse for an impropriety in this matter, however inadvertent or slight. There were forms to be observed. Too, a chasm, a world, separated her from the Lady Bina. The gulf between a tarsk and a Ubara was less than the gap between one such as she and one such as the Lady Bina. To be sure, I had often thought that the Lady Bina would herself look quite well in a collar.

How did she expect to become a Ubara?

She did not even have a Home Stone.

And there was a Ubara in Ar, if only a Cosian puppet on the throne, Talena, a traitress to her Home Stone, Talena, once the daughter of the great Ubar, Marlenus of Ar, whose whereabouts, as far as I knew, were unknown.

"When Peisistratus disembarks the Lady Bina and Lord Grendel," she said, "whence then he?"

"He will undoubtedly continue his work," I said. I did not elaborate on the nature of his work, but she was substantially familiar with it. Peisistratus, and his crews, were in their way mariners and merchants. He doubtless had one or more bases, or ports, on Earth, and one or more on Gor, and I knew he had one on the Steel World from which we had been brought, that now under the governance of Arcesilaus, now theocrat of that world, and now, claimedly, Twelfth Face of the Nameless One.

"He is a slaver," she said.

"He doubtless deals in various commodities, in various forms of merchandise," I said.

"He is a slaver," she said.

"Yes," I said, "certainly at least that."

"Predominantly that," she said.

"Perhaps," I said. "I do not know."

"I saw the capsules on the ship," she said.

"He is a slaver, certainly," I said.

"Perhaps he thinks he is rescuing women from the ravages of Earth," she said.

"That seems unlikely," I said.

"At a price, of course," she said.

"Oh?" I said.

"A rag, if that, and a mark, a collar," she said.

"I doubt that his motivations are so benevolent, so thoughtful," I said, "even mixedly so. And, on the other hand, his motivations are certainly not villainous, or malevolent. Do not think so. You know him too well for that. I think of him primarily as a business man, obtaining, transporting, and selling, usually wholesale, wares of interest."

"Women," she said.

"Perhaps an occasional silk slave, to delight a free woman," I said.

"Mostly women," she said.

"Almost always," I said.

"They sell better," she said.

"Of course," I said. "They are the most fitting, appropriate, and natural form of such merchandise."

"'Merchandise'?" she said.

"Yes," I said.

"Goods?"

"Of course."

"They view us as animals, as cattle," she said.

"There is nothing personal in it, or usually not," I said. "To be sure, one might take a particular female who has displeased one, in one fashion or another, and have her brought to Gor, to keep her, or see her sold off to the highest bidder, that sort of thing."

"As cattle!" she said.

"No," I said, "as less, as females."

"It seems I have an identity, and a value," she said.

"Certainly," I said.

"But I was not brought to the Prison Moon by him, or by one such as he," she said.

"No," I said. "But do not be distressed, for he assured you that you would have been well worthy of selection and transportation, that you were exactly the sort of goods which would have been well enclosed, so to speak, in one of the capsules."

I had found myself, months ago, imprisoned in a container on the Prison Moon, sharing the container with two individuals, a young Englishwoman, Miss Virginia Cecily Jean Pym, and a lovely Kur Pet, who had later come to be the Lady Bina. These were both free women and I, who had seemingly displeased Priest-Kings had been, apparently, enclosed with them as an insidious punishment, that, sooner or later, as I weakened, becoming more bitter, frustrated, outraged, and needful, my honor would be compromised, or lost. And, after that, I do not know what fate they might have planned for me, perhaps a hideous death, perhaps a wandering life of exile, beggary, and shame. One does not know. Both were, at the time, though without Home Stones, yet free women, you see, and thus, given the nobility of their status, not to be lightly put to one's pleasure, certainly not without suitable provocation. It is difficult to convey the dignity, importance, and social standing of the Gorean free woman to one with no first-hand awareness of the matter. They have a position and elevation in society which far transcends that of, say, the free woman of Earth who is usually not so much free as merely not yet enslaved. The analogy is imperfect but suppose a society of rigid status, of severe hierarchy, and the rank and dignity that might be attached to the daughter of, say, a royal or noble house. One in such a society would not be likely to think of bedding such an individual, at least as a serious project. To be sure, a Goth, a Turk, a Saracen, a Dane might have fewer inhibitions in such a matter.

Kurii had raided the Prison Moon, freed me, and brought me to what was then the Steel World of Agamemnon.

But this event and various ensuing events, as I understand it, have been elsewhere chronicled.

"What are you doing?" she asked.

"Ramar," I said, "must be freed."

"Is that wise?" she asked.

"I do not know," I said. "But it was for this reason that I had him brought to Gor."

I had first seen Ramar in an arena on the Steel World, a milieu in which his ferocity, might, and cunning, in virtue of dozens of bloody victories, were renowned. Bred for dark sports, trained to hunt and kill, he was a prize of his breed, a champion of his kind. Later, in the insurrection, he, and other sleen, as Agamemnon grew more desperate, uncertain, and frightened, had been freed, that they might hunt down, destroy, and devour his foes, in particular ill-armed humans who might be party to the rebellion. A Kur, unarmed, is a match for a sleen. A Kur, armed, has little to fear, unless taken unawares. In turn, the revolutionaries, primarily the rebel Kurii, primarily on behalf of their human allies, had set a number of heavy, metal traps, more than two-hundred pounds in weight, baited with haunches of tarsk, traps fastened by heavy chains to large stakes sunk deeply into the ground, and in one such trap this beautiful animal, this great, fierce, dangerous, six-legged, sinuous monster, Ramar, had been caught. In this trap, held by its steel teeth, clamped deeply into his left rear leg, to the bone, bleeding and tortured, jerking against the stake and chain, then quiescent and silent, he would have died, of prolonged pain, or thirst. He was a large, noble animal, and beautiful in the hideous way in which a sleen can be beautiful, and it did not please me that such a creature should perish so miserably. Doubtless unwisely, I managed, with great difficulty, to open the trap, and the beast, freed, withdrew, vanished, limping, into the brush. He had not attacked me. Perhaps it had not occurred to him to do so. Later, we had encountered one another now and again. I think some record of this is elsewhere available. Following the denouement of the insurrection on the Steel World in question and, seemingly, in virtue of some interaction or agreement between Priest-Kings and victorious Kurii, it was determined that I, and others, were to be returned to Gor. Might we have hoped that our labors on the Steel World had pleased, or, at least, appeased, Priest-Kings? Could such forms of life be mollified? And could they not then have been satisfied, at last, and have seen fit, in their wisdom, to free us from their interests? Certainly we had, or some of us, however unintentionally or inadvertently, served them. Surely they now had less to fear from one of the greatest and most dangerous of the Kurii, Lord Agamemnon, an ambitious, skilled, determined, brilliant, gifted, implacable foe. In any event I had not been slain, or returned to the horrors of the Prison Moon. I now found myself again on Gor. I had then little hope that Priest-Kings had finished with me, as I would have fervently desired. Had that been so should I not have been returned, liberated and thanked, perhaps even bountifully rewarded, to my holding in Port Kar? But I was here, somehow, on this remote beach, the forest behind me. In leaving the Steel World I had brought Ramar with me. He deserved, I thought, the woods or forests, the plains or mountains, the openness and freedom, of Gor, not the steel platings and inserted gardens, the contrived geography, of a Steel World. Let him live as a sleen, in a world fit for him. Indeed, let men live in worlds fit for them. Too many live in their own Steel Worlds, and know not this, know not their prisons.

"He will turn wild," she said.

"He is wild," I said.

"He will become dangerous," she said.

"He is dangerous now," I said.

I unbuckled the thick, spiked collar from the throat of the giant, lame sleen, Ramar, and pointed behind us, to the forest. The large, round eyes regarded me, as though quizzically.

"Yes," I said, "friend. Go."

A protestive growl emanated from the throat of the beast. It wound its body about me, moving, curling about me. I thrust the heavy body from me.

"Go," I said, sternly. "Yes, it is my wish."

"He does not want to go," she said.

"Go," said I, to the sleen.

I then, impulsively, knelt down and seized the massive body about the neck, and buried my face in the fur of his shoulder.

"You are crying," she said.

"No," I said.

I then stood, and wiped my eyes with the back of my forearm.

"You are crying," she said.

I scorned to respond to so foolish an allegation.

Ramar whimpered.

"The forest is there!" I said to him, turning his head with my hand toward the forest. "That is your world!" I said, pointing. "Go! Go!"

I watched the sleen take its leave, its left, hind foot marking the sand, where he dragged it behind him.

Then he was gone.

I then turned to regard her.

"Wipe the tears from your cheek," I told her.

She obeyed.

To be sure, emotion is acceptable for women, and certainly for such as she, the sort which, though the least, is the most female of all women.

She had been one of the two women who had been enclosed with me in the small, transparent container on the Prison Moon, two who had been deliberately, carefully selected by Priest-Kings, with all their shrewdness and science, with all their malevolent expertise, to constitute exquisite temptations for me, who were intended to be such as would prove irresistible to me, either of them a suitable engine to accomplish in time the destruction of my honor, either one of which was a banquet to lure me, tormented and starving, inevitably, sooner or later, from the rigors of my codes.

I regarded her.

She who had become the Lady Bina had been, at that time, long ago, in the container, no more than a Kur pet, a human pet of a superior life form, the Kurii, one at that time not even speeched, one at that time no more than a simple, naive, luscious, appetitious little animal. Surely the little beast was exquisitely desirable, who could deny that, but even then the other, the dark-haired captive, the English girl, Miss Virginia Cecily Jean Pym, clearly the product of a pathological culture, inhibited, unpleasant, arrogant, nasty, with such clearly ambivalent feelings toward men, even hostility toward males, was the one on whom I most wished to lay my hands, she whom I most desired to seize and subdue, whom I thought it would be most amusing to have in my arms, and force to buck and squirm, and whimper and plead, and cry out and beg, and weep in my arms her helpless, unconditioned, grateful, rapturous submission, that of the shattered, devastated, begging female to the will of the possessive, uncompromising, owning male. I do not think that she was objectively superior to the Kur pet, and might even have brought a lower price than the Kur pet in most markets, but she was somehow very special to me. Indeed, I have little doubt that she had been selected for me, with great care and skill, perhaps from amongst thousands, that she had been matched expertly to my inclinations, preferences, and needs, inclinations, preferences, and needs of which I might not even have been aware. Two other factors, too, I suspect, were involved. As she had been matched to me, I suspect that I had been matched to her, as well. The Priest-Kings, I suspect, had, so to speak, fitted us together. Had she no need of such as I, the temptation would have been primarily mine, and it would have failed of its devastating symmetricality. But I, so desiring her, how helpless I would have been, had she been, sooner or later, similarly distressed and tormented. How could we have then failed to embrace, and therewith comply with the will and intrigues of Priest-Kings?

Do they not use us as their pawns, their dupes, and instruments? Using our congruent natures how could we, so subtly manipulated, have failed to dance upon their strings?

The other factor involved was one I sensed early, the deep nature of the lovely English female, but had confirmed only after the rupturing of the Prison Moon, after the destruction and melting of a steel gate, and the opening of the container, these events implicated in the Kur raid, in their hurried, transitory seizure of an artificial moon, or a portion thereof, in that fearful traversing of forbidden borders, an act of perhaps unwise transgression, the fruit perhaps of a strange wager, one in which the winnings, seemingly the liberation of a single, imprisoned warrior, and one commonly their foe, would seem small, put against the risks of loss, the possible retribution and reprisal of Priest-Kings, masters of Gor and her space.

Surely much was rushed for time was short.

Presumably within Ehn, so shortly, the ships of Priest-Kings might come to investigate, to succor, to retaliate, to recover their threatened, violated sphere, the Prison Moon.

Squirming in terror on the flooring outside the container, on its metal plating, amongst the clawed feet of Kur raiders, fearing to be destroyed, even eaten, by what to her were fierce and incomprehensible beasts, she had cried out "Masters!"

This had surprised me.

I had been startled, though I had sensed even in the container something of the deep nature, the hidden reality, of the lovely, petty, snobbish, supercilious Miss Pym.

Who knows the secret thoughts locked in the diary of a woman's dreams? And how few of them would dare to open the pages of that intimate journal to a stranger's perusal.

How tragically alone such women are!

And how natural it is that they should fear, at first, not to be alone!

Many fear even to speak to themselves, let alone another.

In her extremity, her elections of certain utterances were, of course, not to be unexpected in a female.

They are common in the history of worlds.

What have they to bargain with, save their beauty?

And will it be enough?

Is it sufficient? Is it enough that they will be spared, to be brought, perhaps rather sooner than later, to the sales block?

But such a cry was to be expected, not only in any woman at the feet of males, but particularly from one such as she, who, in a thousand ways, I discerned, sensed the fittingness of her position, her prostration.

Had she not been so, in one way or another, in her dreams, on the smooth, scarlet tiles of a conqueror's palace, on the deep-piled rug within the tent of a desert chieftain, on the deck of a pirate's vessel?

In a pathological culture, of course, many things are kept concealed, often those which are most illuminating and meaningful, most important.

She had shortly thereafter explicitly proposed herself as a slave, indeed had pathetically begged bondage. Indeed, a moment later, she had clearly, explicitly, pronounced herself slave.

These words, "I am a slave," were cried out in full consciousness. They came from the subterranean depths of her, as a quaking, helpless, unexpected eruption of truth from the volcano of her being.

What a moment of release, of emotion, that must have been for her!

In that moment she had grasped her womanhood, only, to be sure, to soon desire to repudiate it, again.

But it was too late.

With those words, she had, by her own deed, become a slave.

And such words cannot be unspoken.

It is done.

She is then helpless to qualify, reduce, diminish, or revoke the words, for she is then a slave.

All that remains is that she be claimed.

That had been done later, weeks later, in the Pleasure Cylinder, a small adjunct or auxiliary world to the Steel World at that time ruled by Agamemnon, Theocrat of the World, Eleventh Face of the Nameless One. Three other such related worlds were the Hunting World, used for Kur sport, the Industrial World, in which its manufacturing was accomplished, and the Agricultural World, in which a variety of crops were raised under controlled conditions, largely by automation. Kurii are naturally carnivorous, but in the limited environments of the Steel Worlds a number of processed foods have been developed, with which they may be nourished. Humans, and other animals, too, of course, were commonly raised for food. Following the services of a number of human allies in the rebellion, however, humans are no longer eaten in the Steel World in question, and, I understand, in certain of the others. The "cattle humans" who were raised specifically for meat are herded about and cared for, or relocated, but no longer eaten. It is supposed they will eventually disappear as they are large, clumsy, lumbering beasts disinclined to mate. Their numbers in the past were increased by means of artificial insemination. The ships of Peisistratus, incidentally, were docked within the Pleasure Cylinder. It was from one of its locks that his ship had exited, and sped to Gor.

"Ramar is gone," she said, looking toward the forest.

"Yes," I said.

"You freed him," she said.

"Of course," I said. "He should be free."

"Should I not be free?" she asked.

"No," I said.

"I do not mind being as I am," she said.

"It does not matter whether you do or not," I said.

"I see," she said. "My will is nothing."

"Precisely," I said.

"You would keep me as I am?"

"Of course."

"Why?" she asked.

"You are a female," I said.

"Many females are free," she said.

"True," I said.

"Do you think that women should be slaves?"

"The most desirable ones, of course," I said. "They are of the most interest. The others do not matter."

"I have heard that Goreans believe all women should be slaves," she said.

"You could probably find a Gorean free woman who does not accept that, but then she has not been in the collar."

"If she were in the collar, she would change her mind?"

"If she were in the collar," I said, "it does not matter whether she changed her mind or not."

"She would still be in the collar."

"Of course."

"I suppose that Gorean men," she said, "believe all women should be slaves."

"I would not know what all Gorean men believe," I said, "but many Gorean men believe that all women *are* slaves, only that not all of them are in collars, as they should be."

"I see," she said.

I looked upon her, as one such as she may be looked upon.

She straightened her body.

"Shall I strip and assume inspection position?" she inquired.

I did not respond to her. I recalled she had earlier referred to the Lady Bina, but had omitted her title, as "Lady." That title is given only to free women, unless it might be, in virtue of its inappropriateness, bestowed in such a way as to terrify one such as she.

In inspection position one such as she would normally be stripped, and standing with her feet spread, and her hands clasped either behind the back of her neck, or behind her head. In this way the breasts are lifted nicely, and, given the position of the hands, one has no interference to one's vision, and, similarly, one may, perhaps walking about her, test her for firmness, and for vitality, and such things. Teeth are often examined, as well. A barbarian girl, brought from Earth, often can be told from fillings in the teeth. Another common mark is a vaccination mark, usually thought by Goreans to be an Earth brand. Goreans prefer, of course, Gorean brands, which are commonly clear, tasteful, unmistakable, and beautiful.

"You are no longer on the Steel World," I said. "Here is a planet, with openness. You are not now encircled with curving walls of steel. Perhaps you think things will be different for you here."

"Doubtless in some respects," she said.

"Essentially?"

"I do not know," she said.

"They will not be," I said. "This is Gor."

"I wear a collar," she said.

"Precisely," I said.

"Collar!" I snapped.

Instantly she faced me, holding her hands slightly behind her, and lifted her chin.

She had received, I saw, some training in the Pleasure Cylinder. This would have occurred before she had been claimed.

It was appropriate, of course, that she should have been apprised of such things, or several such things, even before her claiming.

In such a way, in so simple a manner, may be precluded various instructions with the leather.

In this position the collar may be conveniently read.

I held the collar with two hands.

"What does the collar say?" I asked.

"I cannot read," she said. "I am told it says 'I am the property of Tarl Cabot.'"

"That is correct," I informed her. "Who am I?"

"Tarl Cabot," she said.

"Then whose property are you?" I asked.

"Yours," she said, "—*Master*."

"You are a slave," I said.

"Am I?" she asked.

"Yes," I said.

"Even here?" she said.

"Yes," I said.

"Do you wish to be freed?" I asked.

"There is nowhere to go," she said. "I could not live."

"Do you wish to be freed?" I repeated.

"No," she said.

"Why not?"

"I beg not to be made to speak," she said.

"You are clad as a slave," I said.

"Yes," she said.

She wore a Gorean slave tunic.

It was a brief, gray shipping tunic, from the ship of

Peisistratus. It had a number inscribed on the upper left side, "27." This number, as others, had been correlated with the numbers of a set of chaining rings, number 1 with ring 1, and so on. She with others of her sort had thus been chained in an orderly fashion, serially, in one of the ship's corridors. By means of the numbers a girl, if removed from her chaining ring, can be returned to the same ring. Order, discipline, and precision are important in the closed environment of a ship. I had removed her from her ring several times during the voyage. The Lady Bina, on the other hand, had been accorded quarters, as she had insisted, in the cabin of Peisistratus himself, the captain, who then, with her guard, Grendel, had bunked with his men. It must not be thought surprising that the Lady Bina had been deferred to, for she was a free woman.

The girl before me was fetching in the shipping tunic, but that was not surprising as such tunics, even such as hers, a shipping tunic, are not designed to conceal the charms of their occupant.

The Gorean slave tunic, incidentally, is a form of garment with several purposes. In its revealing brevity and lightness it well marks the difference between the slave and the free woman, a difference of great consequence on Gor. From the point of view of the free woman it supposedly humiliates and degrades the slave, reminding her of her worthlessness, and that she can be bought and sold, that she is no more than a domestic animal, an article of goods, and such. The slave, on the other hand, as she grows accustomed to her status, and its remarkable value in the eyes of men, tends to revel in its enhancement of her charms, a pleasure which is likely to be seriously begrudged her by the more heavily clad free woman. Few women, of course, object to being found appealing, even excruciatingly desirable, by males. Do not even free women sometimes inadvertently disarrange their veils? So, many slaves, at least in the absence of free women, before whom they are likely to grovel and cower, and wisely, to avoid being beaten, luxuriate and rejoice in their beauty and its display. A slave tunic, you see, leaves little to the imagination. Other advantages, too, adhere to such garments. For example, as they commonly lack a nether closure, with the exception of the

Turian camisk, the slave is constantly, implicitly, advised of her delicious vulnerability as a property, and reminded of one of her major concerns, which is to please the master, instantly and without question, to the best of her ability, in any way he may wish. The slave, on her part, too, cannot help but find such garments arousing. In their way they serve to ignite and stoke the slave fires in her lovely belly. It is no wonder slaves often find themselves at the feet of their master, kneeling, and begging. Too, such garments are supposed to make it difficult to conceal weapons. There is no place in such a garment, for example, for a dagger. To be sure, it can be a capital offense for a slave to touch a weapon without a free person's permission, so there is little danger of the slave's attempting to conceal a weapon in the first place. But the garment, too, makes it difficult, or impossible, to conceal a roll, a purloined larma, or such. When the slave shops, if she is permitted to use her hands, and is not sent out back-braceleted with a coin sack tied about her neck, she commonly holds the coins clenched in her fist, or, not unoften, either, holds them in her mouth. Such garments are cheap, too, of course, and require little cloth. Too, many are designed with a disrobing loop, by means of which the garment may be easily removed, to be swept from her, or dropped, to fall about her ankles, depending on the garment. The loop is usually at the left shoulder, as most masters are right-handed.

She turned away from me.

"We are now out of the Steel World," she said.

"So?" I said.

"You freed Ramar," she said.

"Yes," I said.

"Will you not now free me?" she asked.

"No," I said. "Do not be absurd. You are not a sleen. You are nothing, only a human female."

"And one who belongs in a collar?"

"Obviously," I said.

"In your collar?"

"In a collar," I said, "whomsoever's it might be."

"In any man's?" she said.

"In some man's," I said.

"Yours?"

"Not necessarily," I said, "but in some man's collar."

"I belong in a collar?"

"Of course," I said.

"I gather," she said, "that female slavery exists on this world?"

"That is true," I said, "and male slavery, as well."

"But most slaves are female, are they not?"

"Yes," I said. "Slavery is a misfortune for the male, for the male, or most males, are naturally free, and master, but bondage is apt for the female."

"Females are not the same as males?" she said.

"No," I said. "They are quite different, profoundly, radically different."

"The male is to own, and the female is to be owned?"

"The female, as a female," I said, "can find her total fulfillment only in bondage, only at the feet of a powerful male, who will see her and treat her as the property she wishes to be, and nature intended her to be."

"I see," she said.

"It does not matter whether you do or not," I said.

"I am in a collar."

"Yes."

She looked away.

"I suppose female bondage has a justification," she said.

"Yes," I said.

"Nature," she said.

"Certainly," I said. "Nature. Let her tell you of the rightfulness of your collar."

She spun about, tears in her eyes. She clutched her collar. "She has told me!" she cried.

"I know," I said.

"But we are no longer in the Steel World," she said. "Here, surely, whether I will it or not, you will free me!"

"If you are testing me, trying my patience," I said, "I do not care for it."

"But we are alone," she said. "You need not now, nor could you, continue to hold me in bondage!"

"Do you wish to be freed?" I asked.

"No," she cried. "I do not wish to be free! But you must free me! You are not Gorean! You are of Earth, of Earth! You have no choice but to free me!"

"I do not understand," I said. Did she not know she stood on the soil of Gor, and was collared?

"You must take me away from myself!" she sobbed. "You must rob me of myself!"

"I do not understand," I said.

"You are of Earth, of Earth!" she said. You have no choice but to free me! You must free me!"

"You think so?" I asked.

"Certainly," she wept.

"Certainly?" I inquired.

"Certainly," she said.

"Remove your clothing," I said, "and approach me, with your wrists crossed, before your body."

"What?" she said.

"Now," I said.

In a moment I lashed her wrists together before her body. I then drew her, stumbling, by the loose end of the strap to the edge of the forest. There I thrust her against a tree, belly against the bark, and flung the free end of the strap over a branch. "Master!" she cried. I then drew her crossed, bound hands up, high, unpleasantly so, over her head, and fastened them in place, that by means of the same strap, it now tied beneath the straps on her wrist.

"Master!" she wept.

She was stretched, on her tiptoes.

"You have not been pleasing," I informed her.

"Forgive me, Master!" she cried.

I removed my belt.

In a moment I was through with her, but it had been enough.

"Do you think you will be freed?" I asked.

"No, Master!" she wept.

"Perhaps I will sell you," I said. The former Miss Virginia Cecily Jean Pym had not been pleasing.

"Please do not sell me!" she begged.

I replaced my belt, freed her and turned away.

In moments she had followed me, and was on her belly on

the pebbled sand, naked, sobbing, licking and kissing my feet, in piteous supplication.

"Do you think you will be freed?" I asked.

"No, Master!" she wept. "No, Master!"

"I am Gorean," I said.

"Yes, Master!" she said.

"Do you understand that, Earth female?" I said. "You are owned—*owned by a Gorean.*"

"Yes, Master!" she said.

"Do you understand the meaning of that?"

"Yes, Master!" she said. "I am a slave, only a slave, and no more!"

"The most abject, worthless, and meaningless of slaves," I said.

"Yes, Master!" she wept.

"What a miserable lot is yours," I said, "that of helpless, abject bondage."

"Yes, Master," she said.

"Perhaps you understand better now the peril and degradation of your condition?"

"Yes, Master!"

"Do you still wish to be a slave?" I asked.

"Do not make me speak!" she begged.

"Speak," I said.

"Yes, Master!" she sobbed. "Yes, Master!"

"Why?" I demanded.

"For then," she said, "as a woman, I am wholly myself!"

"Do you think you will be kept as a slave for any reason of yours?" I asked. "Perhaps because you wish to be a slave?"

"Master?" she said.

"What you might wish is not only unimportant," I said, "but meaningless, absurdly irrelevant."

She looked up at me, from her belly, tears in her eyes.

"It is irrelevant," I said, "whether or not you want to be a slave, or desire to be a slave, or need to be a slave."

"Master?" she said.

"You will be kept as a slave," I said, "because you are a slave, and should be a slave, and it pleases men that such as you should be owned."

"Yes, Master," she sobbed.

"Your will is nothing," I said.

"Yes, Master," she said.

"You were less than fully pleasing," I informed her. "A slave is to be fully pleasing."

"Yes, Master!" she wept.

"I think I will sell you," I said.

"Please, no, Master!" she wept. "I will try to please you, Master, fully, Master, fully, fully, perfectly, in all ways! Please do not sell me, Master! Keep me, I beg you!"

"I will do as I wish," I informed her.

"Yes, Master," she wept.

"Perhaps you now better understand what it is to be a slave?"

"Yes, Master," she whispered. "Yes, Master."

She looked up at me, mine, her face run with tears.

I regarded her.

Her lips trembled with emotion.

Her face was sensitive, soft, and beautiful. It was nicely framed in glossy, dark hair, still a bit short, perhaps, but it would grow. Long hair, as is well known, is favored in such as she. Much may be done with it, aesthetically, and in the furs. Too, it might be noted, in passing, that the female was highly intelligent. That much improves a girl's price. That would be important if I chose to sell her. Such women make the best slaves. They quickly learn what they now are. Too, compared to the more ordinary, or average, woman, they tend to be, at least initially, more in touch with, and more aware of, and more open to, their own deepest needs, and desires. They come into the collar, thus, half-prepared for bondage.

Gorean slavers do not bring stupid women to Gor. They do not sell well.

I looked down upon her.

I liked her as she was, at my feet, collared, naked.

She belonged there.

"Now," I said, "we must welcome our visitor."

She looked up at me, wildly.

"Clothe yourself, girl," I said.

She scrambled on her knees to her discarded garment,

hastily pulled it on, over her head, and turned, on her knees, to face the visitor.

She would remain kneeling until given permission to rise, as she was a slave in the presence of free men.

"Tal," said the fellow, standing back, amidst the trees, in the shadows.

"Tal," I rejoined.

Chapter Two

Pertinax; A Vessel Will Not Beach

"Come forward," said the fellow, gesturing toward the forest.

"You come forward," I said, motioning him down, toward the beach. I did not know what might lurk in the forest.

"You want me within the circuit of your steel," he remarked.

"You need not approach that closely," I said. "Too, my blade is sheathed."

"That seems unwise," he said, "when greeting a stranger."

"You do not appear to be armed," I said.

I wondered if he realized how swiftly a blade might be unsheathed.

"Are you one of them?" he asked.

"One of whom?" I asked.

"I saw no ship," he said.

"From the sky," I said. "Do you know such ships?"

He wore a mottled tunic, irregularly green and brown. It would match in well with the background, with attendant shadows.

He did not have the blue and yellow chevrons which sometimes characterizes the lower-left-hand sleeve of the slavers, different, of course, from their more formal regalia, or robes, commonly blue and yellow, their colors. Some view the Slavers as a caste, others as a subcaste of the Merchants. The colors of the Merchants are yellow and white, or gold and white.

Had he been a slaver it was possible he might have been aware of the sky ships, so to speak, such as the disklike vessel of Peisistratus. On the other hand, the greater numbers, indeed, the vast majority, of Gorean slavers, one supposes, as Goreans of other sorts, had never seen such a ship. Indeed, many Gorean slavers, as many Goreans, might not even believe in the existence of such ships. They, of course, as most Goreans, would be well aware of the existence of Earth girls, from the markets, if from no other source, but they, as many Goreans, might suppose that Earth was somewhere on Gor, though doubtless far away. Much of Gor, you see, even from the point of view of Goreans, is, so to speak, *terra incognita*. Gor is somewhat smaller than Earth but having missed the cataclysm that drew, say, a sixth of Earth into space to form her magnificent single moon, leaving behind a mighty basin to become in time a vast ocean, her land area is quite possibly more extensive than that of Earth. In any event, much of Gor, to most Goreans, is unexplored, and consequently uncharted. There is thus no great difficulty in supposing the existence of unknown lands, even many of them, and one, perhaps, might be called "Earth." And most Goreans, even today, would be as unacquainted with, and as skeptical of, the possibility of space travel as men of Earth might have been a thousand or more years ago.

The fellow, observing me carefully, came forward, some yards down the beach.

He was a tall man.

He glanced at the slave. "Her name is '27'?" he asked.

"You can read," I said.

"Passably," he said.

"'27' was a ring number," I said. "Her name is Cecily."

"That is a strange name," he said.

"She is from Earth," I said.

"That is far away," he said.

"Yes," I said.

"I am not unfamiliar with such women," he said. "Some have been brought here, to content us."

"There are others then," I said.

"A few," he said.

Gorean men need women, and by "women" they commonly understand the most luscious and desirable of women, the female slave. To be sure, the forests are dangerous, and what free woman would care to frequent them? Girls brought on chains, of course, have little to say about such things.

"She is pretty," he said.

"She is not muchly trained," I said, "and there are doubtless thousands who would bring higher prices."

"Still, she is very pretty," he said.

"Do you wish to challenge for her?" I asked.

"No," he said. "I have a better."

Unless there should be some misunderstanding here, one might observe that such challenges are not frequent, and normally require almost a ritual of circumstances. For example, aside from the usual impropriety of challenging one with whom one might share a Home Stone, Gorean honor militates against, if it does not wholly preclude, casual or unprovoked challenges. Obviously a skilled swordsman would have an advantage in such matters, which it would be inappropriate, and perhaps dishonorable, to press. Normally challenges would take place to recover a stolen slave, to protect a mortally endangered slave, perhaps to obtain a slave once foolishly disposed of, without which one cannot then bear to live, such things. Too, there may be economic constraints, as well, for if the challenge is not accepted, one is sometimes expected, depending on the city, the castes, and circumstances, to pay for the slave, with a purse several times her value. Few potential challengers then care to risk a refused challenge, as it is likely they cannot afford the slave, and must then retire in embarrassment. Many other possibilities enter into these things, but these remarks, hopefully, will give any who might chance to peruse these several sheets a sense of some of the prevailing customs in these matters. To be sure, brigands, pirates, enemies, and such, are not likely to concern themselves with challenges, but are rather the more likely, as they see fit, to attack, and kill. Similarly, in raids, and wars, it is understood that the property of the enemy, or quarry, or target, including not only his livestock and slaves, but even his free women, is legitimate booty. A proper challenge, on the other hand, is more akin to a duel, sometimes even to the setting of a time and place.

"You are a forester?" I said.

"Yes," he said. "You are in the precincts of the reserves of Port Kar," he said.

"I did not know that," I said.

The great arsenal at Port Kar has its shipyards, as well as its warehouses and wharves. To guarantee a supply of valuable, suitable timber, for example Tur trees for strakes, keels, and planking, needle trees for masts, and tem wood, the rare yellow tem wood, for oars, the arsenal claims and badges selected trees within given ditched areas in the northern forests, which supplies, largely in a raw state, together with others, more processed, such as tars, resins and turpentines, items primarily suitable for naval stores, are transported southward on Thassa to the Tamber gulf. Occasionally, it is rumored, the precincts set aside by Port Kar are raided, or exploited, or poached upon, by other naval powers, particularly those of Tyros and Cos. On the other hand, I frankly doubt that this is true. Both of those formidable maritime ubarates have their own reserves, and extensively so, as does Port Kar. Indeed, predictably, there are similar rumors abroad, I understand, that Port Kar predates on the precincts of Tyros and Cos, and other maritime ubarates. I take these rumors to be false, as well. The last thing Port Kar, or these other powers, needs is a land war, which would have to be primarily conducted by mercenaries. Cos is already overextended in this manner in the south, at Ar. Indeed, there now tends to be little interaction, at least ashore, amongst these powers. Much contest, however, is done for the mastery of certain sea lanes, particularly toward the south, and towards Tabor and Asperiche, and even as far south as Bazi, Anango, and Schendi. If the forests were less abundant, one supposes, of course, that wars would be fought for scarce, possibly dwindling resources. On the other hand the environed trees, and, in particular, those marked or badged, tend on the whole to be left unmolested, in the various precincts.

I was soon to learn, however, that these surmises, however sound in principle, required certain qualifications.

"Your Home Stone," I said, "is that of Port Kar?"

"Yes," he said, "but I have not seen her for years."

"You were not born in the forests?"

"No," he said. "There are few free women in the forests."

Slaves are commonly used for work and pleasure. They may be bred, of course, as the livestock they are, at their master's will. There are slave farms here and there, but they are rare, and often specialize in exotics of various sorts. It is expensive and time consuming to raise female slaves from infancy. It is easier and less expensive to allow others to raise them, so to speak, and then, when convenient, attend to their harvesting and collaring. There are many female slaves on Gor and it is often, to the irritation of venders, and the mortification and chagrin of the slaves, a buyers' market. Almost all Gorean slaves are captures, having once been free women. The bred slave, other than in the sense that all women are bred slaves, is rare.

One might mention, at this point, a word or two about the stabilization serums, which were developed centuries ago by the green caste, that of the Physicians. By means of these serums a given phase of maturation, say, beauty in a woman, strength in a man, and so on, may be retained indefinitely. The caste of Physicians, long ago, construed ageing as a disease, the "drying and withering disease," and not as an inevitability or fatality, and so set to work to effect, so to speak, its cure. Scientists of Earth, as I understand it, are only now beginning to sniff about the edges of this problem. A radical shift in perspective, of course, is necessary. And such conceptual reformulations, as is well known, are difficult, rare, and, oddly, often unwelcome. Major truths, no matter what the evidence in their favor, are often, in the beginning, denied, then ridiculed, then battled, and then, if the cultural situation permits, and insufficient numbers of the heretics, or proponents, of the new views are imprisoned or executed, grudgingly accepted, and then, later, hailed as obvious, and those originally most adamant in their opposition, perhaps having run out of penitentiaries and firewood, will claim credit for the discoveries to which they have so reluctantly succumbed. Indeed, can they not find passages in their texts which hint of those very secrets, and other passages which allude to them in now-transparent metaphors?

Claims to the effect, say, that ageing is, or is not, a disease are at least cognitive. One can be right or wrong about them. They should be distinguished from claims, or seeming claims, which are noncognitive, namely, which lack either truth or falsity. For example, it is impossible to confute nonsense for it is neither true nor false, and that which is neither true nor false cannot be shown to be either. The truth or falsity of such things is not hiding. It just does not exist. It must not be lost sight of in these matters, of course, that nonsense is often well armed. Consider poison. It, too, is neither truth nor false, but it is dangerous, and it can kill.

Please forgive the above digression.

I thought it germane to the narrative, however, to refer to the stabilization serums, because of the reference to the rare "bred slave." Two characteristics of the economic condition, as is well known, are the scarcity of resources and the disutility of labor. Both of these conditions militate against the breeding of slaves, except in special cases, usually exotics, where the rarity is thought to justify the attendant expenditures. It is expensive and troublesome to raise a slave from infancy at one's own expense and that is why slaves are seldom bred, at least on a wide scale. It is much more convenient to acquire them when they are ready for plucking, so to speak. Why raise the grapes when they are about, and one may pick them, as one sees fit, when they are nicely ready and ripe? To be sure, there are some slave farms which, after a few years, produce their annual crop, so to speak. On the other hand, these enterprises usually require a large initial investment, say, large physical facilities, and hundreds of breeding slaves, male and female, to be carefully matched and crossed, and it normally takes years for the first crop to be readied for market. And such farms, too, commonly deal in exotics. The most common exotic is the virgin slave who has been raised without the knowledge that men exist. Slaves, too, of course, may be bred for a diversity of colors, peltings, facial features, and such.

There is a technique, incidentally, based on a variation of the stabilization serums, for hastening physical maturation, but this is little used because one has then to show for one's pains only an unusual child. Much can be done with the body, it seems, but little with the mind, saving, perhaps, by Priest-Kings in the recesses of the Sardar. Gorean men are not interested in children, even if they have the bodies of women. They find them uninteresting. Nor will they be of interest until several years have passed. Then they may be interesting, perhaps quite interesting. Humanity, one notes, exceeds physiology. Unfortunately, too, several of these children will suffer confusing stress, as they lack the emotional maturation to relate comprehensibly to the needs and demands of their grown bodies, bodies hastened beyond the horizons of a child's understanding. Accordingly, this application of the stabilization serums is frowned upon in Gorean society, and in many cities is illegal. A much more benign, or, at least, more acceptable, application of the stabilization serums is founded on a related, and accepted, but opposing principle, the reversibility of all physical processes. In this application, within limits, adjustments to the serums may effect the restoration of youth. The usual application of this technique, as would be expected, is to return a middle-aged, or older, female, to her youth, health, energy, and beauty. As I understand it, this is normally done only with particularly selected women, ones whose once remarkable beauty, this usually determined from old drawings, paintings, and photographs, has faded. Brought to Gor, restored to their earlier vitality and beauty, and collared, they will find themselves, not surprisingly, of great interest on the block. All beauty, of course, is not confined to a particular generation. Would it not be nice to see Thais, Phyrne, Cleopatra, and such on the block?

The usual thing, of course, at least where girls from Earth are concerned, as free Goreans have access to these serums as a matter of course, is to pick out young, superb, slave fruit, and then bring it to the chains of Gor, and here, in the pens, or, at any rate, early in its bondage, subject it to the stabilization serums, that it may be protected from the ravages of alteration and deterioration. Gorean masters, predictably, tend to favor young, luscious, female slaves. Slavers, too, who wish to buy and sell them, wish them to stay this way, as their value is maintained and, in many cases, improved. Cecily, whom we have met in the preceding pages, was subjected to the serums not on Gor but in the Pleasure Cylinder associated with the Steel World ruled at that time by Agamemnon, Eleventh Face of the Nameless One. Though she was far from immortal, and might even be fed to sleen, she would retain her youth and beauty. To be sure, it would wear a collar.

Doubtless a value judgment is involved in such things.

One might balance, say, freedom, misery, and death, against bondage, happiness, and life.

One might consider two lives. In one, we might suppose a given woman who, with some good fortune, might live a life of, say, some eighty to ninety years, and live to watch her interest and beauty fade, and observe her once lovely body submit to the slow degradations of age, watch it dry, wither, suffer, decay, and weaken until it subsides into an infantile helplessness, characterized by misery and pain, or perhaps a semi-comatose, bedridden state in which, indifferent and drugged, she waits for an encroaching end which she no longer even understands. Conceivably that could be the choice of a given woman. Does it fulfill her? Does it make her happy? Has her life been a good life? Let us hope so. Then let us consider another life. Let us suppose a young woman is brought to Gor, to be collared and sold like meat off a block. She will learn she is property, and a slave. She will find herself at the feet of men, subject to discipline, chains, and the whip. She will find herself the most degraded and despised, and the most valued and sought-after, of women. She will be expected to kneel and obey. She will be dressed in revealing fashions. She will learn to labor. She will learn what it is to be roped, to wear a chain, perhaps to crouch in a tiny, locked cage. She will learn a life of radical and profound sexuality, in which she will be expected to perform for, and well please, a master, in ways which might have been beyond her hopes, dreams, and ken as a mere female of Earth. She will learn what it is, for the first time in her life, to breathe good air, to look into a blue sky, to see an unpolluted sunset or sunrise, to eat fresh and natural foods, to relish the taste of fresh bread, to be grateful for a piece of meat fed to her by a master's hand, to put her tongue, if permitted, to a wine beyond what she thought might exist. The purpose of her life will be to please her master. She may fall in love with him, but she should be wary of letting him suspect this, and surely should not speak of it, lest she be peremptorily sold. And in this degradation she may live indefinitely. She learns to understand men and herself. She is likely, in most cases, to be rapturously content, and is likely to live in joy, but she is, of course, when all is said and done, only a slave. She is in a collar. It gives her security, and meaning, and happiness, and identity. Perhaps it is right for her. Could that be? But whether it is right for her or not, she cannot remove it. She is slave.

"How is it that a forester," I said, "claims as his the Home Stone of Port Kar?"

"I once lived there," he said, "before I took caste. At that time, long ago, there were few, if any, castes in Port Kar. She had no Home Stone. She was a den of thieves, as it was said, a lair of cutthroats, and such, a stinking maze of canals at the marshes, squalid and foul, and malignant."

"And without honor," I said.

"Yes," said he, "and without honor."

"I think once she had no Home Stone," I said.

"That is true," he said. "Can you conceive of a city, a town, a village, a hamlet, without a Home Stone?"

"There are probably such places," I said.

"Then," said he, "that changed. In a moment of crisis, in a time of confusion and terror, when a vulnerable Port Cos awaited the onslaught of the combined fleets of Tyros and Cos, the word spread, the startling mysterious word, a word like the flash of lightning, a word striking through the darkness, a word as mighty as the rallying of a thousand battle horns, as swift as the flight of a tarn, that there was now a Home Stone in Port Kar."

"Jewel of Gleaming Thassa," I said.

"Tatrix of the Sea," said he.

"So you chose caste, that of the foresters, and came here, to serve the Home Stone hundreds of pasangs away?"

"The Home Stone of Port Kar may be served here as well as at the gulf, as well as in the shops of the arsenal, as well as on the wharves, as well as on the decks and benches of her ships."

"True," I said.

"I am fond of the forests," he said. "Most are born to their caste. I chose mine."

"Some do," I said. To be sure, it is not easy to change caste, nor is it frequently done. Indeed, few would wish to do it. Goreans tend to be extremely devoted to their castes. In a sense they belong to their caste. It is surely part of their self-identity, and not only in their own eyes, but in the eyes of others, as well. And, indeed, there are few caste members who are not convinced that their caste, somehow, is especially important, even that it may be, in some way, the most essential or the most estimable of all. Surely the peasants, supposedly the lowest of all the castes, have this view. They regard themselves as the "ox on which the Home Stone rests," and, in a sense, they may be right. On the other hand, where would any of the other castes be, or civilization itself, were it not for my own caste, that of the Warriors?

"You are pleased with the forests?" I said.

"Yes," he said. "When you see them," he said, "you will understand."

"Perhaps," I said.

I was not clear why the Priest-Kings had arranged my being in this place at this time. I did suspect, however, that they had their reasons. Little took place in the Sardar which was not planned without an end in view, their own end.

"What is your Home Stone?" he asked.

"It is not that of Cos, or Tyros," I said.

"No," he said. "Your accent is different."

As he was of Port Kar, or claimedly so, I thought it well to establish this matter. A state of war exists between Port Kar and the maritime ubarates of Cos and Tyros. To be sure, sometimes enemies meet affably enough.

"My sword, once, long ago," I said, "was pledged to the Home Stone of Ko-ro-ba."

"Long ago," he said.

"I have served Port Kar," I said.

"Were you there on the 25th of Se'Kara?" he asked.

"Yes," I said. "Were you?"

"Yes," he said.

On the 25th of Se'Kara, in Year One of the Sovereignty of the Council of Captains, a great naval a battle was fought between Port Kar and the fleets of Cos and Tyros. Port Kar, on that occasion, was victorious. In the chronology of Ar, this battle took place in 10,120 C.A., that is "Contasta Ar," or "From the Founding of Ar." To be sure, I doubt that anyone really knows when Ar was founded.

"We are then in our way, are we not, 'trust brothers,'" he said.

"It would seem so," I said.

Certainly a bond would forever unite those who had been at sea on the 25th of Se'Kara, who had met Tyros and Cos that day.

From that day on they would be different.

"Were you there?" one seaman might ask another in the taverns of Port Kar, over kaissa or paga, the girl of his choice lying bound hand and foot by his table, waiting to be carried over his shoulder to an alcove, at his convenience, or wherever two fellows of that unusual polity might meet, perhaps even on a remote beach, by forests, and one need never ask "Where?"

But he had asked, in a way, had he not, for he had specified the date.

"Have you ever seen the Home Stone of Port Kar?" he asked.

"How is it that I, one not of Port Kar, should have seen her Home Stone?" I asked. "Have you?"

"Of course," he said.

"I have heard," I said, "that it is large and well-carved, and inlaid with silver."

"With gold," he said.

"I am not surprised," I said. "In the cupboards of Port Kar, it is said, one is as likely to find gold as bread." It was a saying. The corsairs of Port Kar venturing at sea, prowling the merchant routes, unannouncedly visiting coastal towns, and such, often returned to port well freighted with various assortments of goods, fruits and grains, weapons, vessels, tools, leathers, viands and wines, precious metals and stones, diverse jewelries, unguents, perfumes, silks, women, and such. These women are often wholesaled, given their numbers. Not infrequently they are wholesaled south to Schendi, for those of Schendi are fond of white-skinned female slaves. Slavers, of course, come from various cities to bid. Port Kar is well known for the high quality of her "fresh collar meat." Many of these women, of course, on the other hand, are distributed as gifts by the captains or, more likely, retailed locally, for example sold to various local taverns. The women are usually of high quality or they would not be taken. When they are stripped, if ashore, before embarking, before returning to port, it is determined whether or not they are, as the saying is, "slave beautiful." If they are not, they are freed and dismissed. If they are, they are taken aboard and chained, sometimes on deck, sometimes in the hold. If at sea, those who are less than "slave beautiful" are separated from the others, as though they might contaminate them, and kept for pot girls, laundresses, kettle-and-mat girls, and such. Interestingly, a kettle-and-mat girl, or such, in the collar, often becomes beautiful. In my view this far exceeds the matter of diet and exercise. In bondage a woman, even a beautiful woman, becomes more beautiful. The collar, it seems, has a remarkable and lovely effect on a woman. It softens her and, in it, in her place in nature, she becomes, as she must, doubtless for the first time in her life, a total woman. Mastered, at a man's feet, she discovers fulfillments which were beyond her ken as a free woman. She finds an inward meaning and happiness and this is inevitably expressed in her features, bodily attitudes, and behaviors.

The free woman is to be sought and wooed; the slave is to be summoned, and instructed.

"It is surprising to encounter one here, for the beach is lonely," I said.

"I was passing," said he, "and noted you."

"And one from Port Kar," I said, "as well."

"That is not so surprising," he said, "for one of the major precincts of Port Kar is close, one of her major timber reserves."

"Of course," I said.

The ship of Peisistratus, I was sure, had not set us ashore at random. Coordinates would have been supplied, presumably as long ago as the Steel World.

"What is your name?" he asked.

"Tarl," I said.

"A Torvaldslander name," he said.

"It is a name not unknown in Torvaldsland," I said.

"My name," said he, "is Pertinax."

"Alar?" I said.

"Perhaps in origin," he said. "I do not know."

"Is there a village nearby?" I asked.

"Some huts," he said, "foresters, guards."

"Why are you not armed?" I asked.

"The huts are nearby," he said.

Whereas brigands, assassins, and such will strike an

unarmed man, the common Gorean would not be likely to do so. It seemed clear to me that his unarmed approach was not then merely to reassure me but, in a way, to diminish, if not preclude, the possibility of himself being attacked. In Gorean there is only one word for "stranger" and "enemy." Too, in the codes there is a saying that he who strikes first lives to strike second.

"What are you doing here?" he asked.

"I do not know," I said.

"You were put ashore, marooned?" he asked.

"Perhaps I am to be met," I said.

"Here?"

"Yes."

He looked about warily.

"You asked earlier, if I were 'one of them.' Who are they?"

"Brigands, assassins, mercenaries," he said. "I think they are from the wars, from the south, even from Ar. Hundreds have come, in many ships."

"To this remote place?" I asked.

"Yes," he said.

"They cannot be from Ar," I said. "Ar has fallen, and been garrisoned by Cos and Tyros. Ar lies under the heel of Chenbar of Tyros and Lurius of Jad, of Cos. Ar is looted, bled, and chained. Ar is beaten, subdued, and helpless. Her riches are carted away. Many of her women are led naked in coffles, to Brundisium, to be put on slave ships bound for Tyros, Cos, and the islands. Myron of Temos, of Cos, is *polemarkos* in Ar. On the throne of Ar sits an arrogant puppet Ubara, a traitress to her Home Stone, a woman named Talena, a hypocrite and villainess, a female once the daughter, until disowned, of the great Marlenus of Ar himself."

"Perhaps things have changed in Ar," he said.

"Impossible," I said. I had been in Ar. I had seen her helplessness and degradation, even how her citizenry was being taught to acclaim their conquerors, to blame themselves for the faults of others, to seek forgiveness for crimes of which they themselves were the victims. Wars could be fought with many weapons, and one of the most effective was to induce the foe to defeat himself. And so men, defeated and disarmed, must learn to rejoice in their weakness, and commend it as virtue. Every society has its weaklings and cowards. But not every society is taught to celebrate them as its wisest and noblest, its boldest and bravest.

"The strangers, hundreds of them, disembarked, from ship after ship, trek in long lines through the forest," he said. "They are the dregs and rogues of Gor. I do not know their destination."

"You," I said, "have not come to meet us?"

"Certainly not," he said. "And if others are to be here, to meet you, I am apprehensive."

"You are afraid?"

"Yes," he said.

"But you do not fear me?"

"No," he said. "Were we not together on the 25th of Se'Kara?"

"Give me your hand on that," I said.

"No," he said. "I fear my hand is harsh, from the ax."

"Forgive me," I said.

"You will share my hospitality, of course," he said, "for the 25th of Se'Kara?"

"With pleasure," I said.

He who designated himself as Pertinax then smiled, and looked upon the kneeling slave, who, as was suitable, had been silent, as she had been unaddressed, and in the presence of free persons.

"Can she speak?" he asked.

"She has a general permission to speak," I said. Such a permission, of course, at a word or gesture, may be revoked.

"You are generous with a slave," he said.

"Many allow their girls that liberty," I said. To be sure, the slave is to speak as a slave, and act as a slave, with suitable deference in words, tone of voice, physical attitude, and such. They are not free women. Sometimes a new slave thinks she may hint at insolence, or even manifest the barest glimmering, or thought, of disobedience, say, in a tone of voice, or a tiny gesture, or fleeting expression, but she is seldom going to repeat this infraction, even in the most transitory and petty manner. She is likely to find herself instantly under the switch or whip, put in lock-gag, be forbidden human speech, be put in the discipline of the she-tarsk, or worse.

"Girl," said Pertinax to the slave.

"Yes, Master," she said.

"I understand your name is Cecily," he said.

"Yes, Master," she said, "if it pleases master."

"If it pleases your master," he said.

"Yes, Master," she said, putting her head down.

"You are very pretty Cecily," he said.

"Thank you, Master," she said.

"Cecily," I said.

"Yes, Master," she said, lifting her head.

"You are in the presence of a free man," I said. "Show him deference. Go to him, put your head down, and lick and kiss his feet, and then kneel before him and take his hands and lick and kiss the palms of his hands, gently, softly, moistly, tenderly."

"Yes, Master," she said.

"Yes," said Pertinax, after a time. "She is a lovely slave."

The kneeling, and kissing and licking the male's feet, is a common act of deference in the female slave. Too, the holding of the hands, and putting one's lips, and tongue, to the palms, humbly and gratefully, and kissing and licking them, is a lovely gesture. It can also, of course, ignite male desire. The slave is caressing the very hands which, if she be displeasing, may cuff and strike her. Interestingly, this same act can be quite arousing for the slave herself. So, too, of course, is something as simple as kneeling before the male.

"Back, girl," I said. "Position."

I did not think it wise to let her prolong such ministrations to a Gorean male.

Cecily drew back and knelt beside me, to my left.

"A Pleasure Slave," said Pertinax, approvingly.

"Yes," I said. "She is from Earth, as noted earlier. In that place, she is from a place called England."

"I have never heard of it," said Pertinax. "Was she free there?"

"Yes," I said.

He regarded her, appraisingly, as a Gorean may look upon a slave. "Absurd," he said.

"Yes," I said.

"Is she any good?" asked Pertinax.

"She now knows she is in a collar," I said.

"Good," he said.

I thought Cecily would look nice in a camisk, a common camisk. The camisk is much more revealing than the common slave tunic. It is a one-piece, extremely simple, suitable for slaves, narrow, poncholike garment. It is slipped over the head. It is usually belted with a loop or two of binding fiber. One may use the binding fiber to bind the slave. It is tied with a slip knot, which may be loosened with a casual tug, at the left hip, as most masters are right-handed. The common camisk is seldom worn publicly, in cities. One supposes the reasons for that are clear.

"Women make lovely slaves," he said, wistfully, I thought.

"As you would know from yours," I said.

"Of course," he said.

"They are bred for the collar," I said, "and they are not whole until they are within it."

"True," he said.

"Ai!" he said, suddenly, and, shading his eyes, looked out to sea. I turned, too. The slave started, but remained in position, not daring to turn about.

"A sail," I said.

It was far off, a lateen-rigged sail, so presumably from the south, not the north. In Torvaldsland the common sail is square. Too, their ships commonly are clinkerbuilt, with overlapping planks, to allow more elasticity in hard seas. Most of the southern ships are carvelbuilt, so they ship less water. The northern ships commonly have a single steering board, whereas most of the southern ships are double helmed.

"Come back, into the trees," said Pertinax, anxiously.

"I do not think they can see us from there, not yet," I said, "but we will join you momentarily." I bent to gather up the small bit of supplies with which we had disembarked the ship of Peisistratus. The girl came to assist me.

"The palms of our friend's hands?" I said to her.

"Soft, smooth," she said.

"He is not a forester," I said.

"Who is he, Master?" she asked.

"I do not know," I said. "He is, however, a liar and a hypocrite."

"Master?" she said.

"Pretend something has been dropped, and you are looking for it, in the sand," I said.

She began to feel about, in the sand.

"He has never seen the Home Stone of Port Kar," I said. "It is not well-carved, inlaid with gold, and such. It is rough, and of common rock. It is not large, only a bit larger than a man's fist. It is gray, heavy, granular, nondescript, unimposing. The initials of Port Kar, in block script, are scratched into its surface. It was done with a knife point."

"How do you know?" she asked.

"I did it," I said.

"He is not of Port Kar?" she said.

"I do not think so," I said. "Certainly he did not speak of the 25th of Se'Kara as would one of Port Kar. He was probably not abroad upon turbulent, green Thassa on that remarkable and unusual day."

"Then he is not a 'trust brother'," she said.

"He is no more a trust brother of mine," I said, "than Myron, *polemarkos* of Temos."

"I am afraid," she said.

"Do not show fear," I said. "Too, although we know he is a liar and a hypocrite, he may be a benign liar and hypocrite."

"Master?" she said.

"I think he was to meet us," I said. "Things would not make much sense otherwise."

"But for whom does he work, whom does he serve, Master?" she asked.

"I would suppose the Priest-Kings of Gor," I said.

"There is no other possibility?" she said.

"There is one other possibility," I said.

"Master?"

"Kurii," I said. "But not those with whom we were allied. Others. Others might have had the coordinates."

"Former minions of Agamemnon?" she asked.

"Or of others," I said.

"You have now found what you were looking for," I said. "Put it in the sack."

She obediently executed this small charade.

I rose to my feet, and she stood, too, beside me. I looked back, at the horizon. The sail was larger now.

"Hurry! Hurry!" called Pertinax, back amongst the trees.

We joined him in the shadows.

The ship, a common Gorean ship, small, light, oared, straight-keeled, ram-prowed, shallow-drafted, would be drawn up on the sand, if the night was to be spent here. It swung athwart, however, some yards from shore.

"Come," said Pertinax. "It is dangerous to remain here."

Men, some clambering over the side, lowering themselves, others leaping, entered the water, which at that point was waist to chest high. They began to wade ashore. These men were armed variously. Most had sacks slung about them. These tended to buoy upward in the water. More than one fellow steadied his approach with the butt of a spear.

"Who are these men?" I asked. They seemed a nondescript, but dangerous lot. There were some fifty men.

"Bandits, mercenaries, assassins, outcasts, men without captains, strangers, all strangers," he said.

"What are they doing here?" I asked.

"I do not know," said Pertinax. "Do not let them see you."

"Where do they go?" I asked.

"They follow the blazings, the flags," he said.

"To where?" I asked.

"I do not know," he said. "Somewhere deep in the forest, perhaps to the headwaters of the river, well south and east of the reserves."

"What river?" I asked.

"The Alexandra," he said.

"I know it not," I said.

"It is not a large river," he said.

"And why might they go to the headwaters of that river?" I asked.

"I do not know," he said.

"The river, I gather," I said, "is narrow, but deep, sheltered by rock, as might be a fjord."

"I thought you said you knew not the river," he said.

"I do not," I said, "but certain things would be needful, if certain purposes were to be served."

"The men are unlawed, and dangerous," he said. "Come away."

He then withdrew silently into the woods, and I, and a slave, followed him.

I turned back, once.

The ship had swung about. Water fell from the oars. The ship would not beach.

It was growing dark.

Chapter Three

We Sup with Pertinax; Constantina

"Is she First Girl, Master?" asked Cecily, angrily.

"No," I said. "If she were I would have you at her feet."

"Hear that?" asked Cecily, angrily, of the other girl.

"Stir the soup," snapped the other girl.

"Do not quarrel," said Pertinax, affably.

Masters seldom interfere in the squabbles of slaves.

His slave, Constantina, cast him a dark look. I found that interesting. One had the sense she was not pleased with chores. Certainly she had done little, and had seen to it that Cecily had done much, even to the gathering of firewood.

Pertinax and I were sitting, cross-legged, waiting to be served.

His slave, Constantina, seemed to me unpleasant, irritable, even surly. Perhaps it was because of Cecily. It is not unusual when one attractive slave encounters another attractive slave in the vicinity of her master that certain frictions may occur. Both know, so to speak, that they are meaningless, and no more than luscious toys for men, toys which, to their misery, and fear, may easily be discarded or replaced, and, accordingly, they tend to be acutely jealous of the attentions of their masters.

Slave girls are not unaware of their effect on men, or of those of other slaves.

They are well aware that it is not only they, but others of their kind, as well, which constitute delectable, tempting morsels for any male appetite.

The female slave cast amongst strong men is not unlike steaming, juicy, roasted meat cast among ravening sleen.

Indeed, few females of Earth, from their experiences on their native world, have any understanding of what it would be to be a female amongst men such as those of Gor; few such females would be prepared in the least for the possessiveness and power, the virility and lusts, of such men, natural men, and masters; and few would anticipate how exquisitely desirable they would appear to such men, and few would suspect how helpless and vulnerable, too, they would find themselves in the midst of such men, particularly were their necks clasped in the collar of a slave.

And yet I had the sense that Constantina's attitudes might not be typical of the common slave, fearing for the loss of the interest or attentions of her master.

Indeed, she seemed to show not only myself, a stranger, but her master little deference. I found it of interest that he, for his part, seemed to accept this. I found this tolerance on his part surprising, and her laxity incomprehensible. I could not have expected this in a Gorean domicile, and if, unaccountably, it had occurred, I would have expected the slave to have been subjected to a sharp, immediate discipline, that presumably to be followed by a period of punishment, perhaps being chained uncomfortably for several Ahn, perhaps being housed in a tiny slave box for a day and a night, perhaps being smeared with honey and then being staked out, naked, spread-eagled, for insects, or such. I wondered if our host were Gorean.

Her behavior, too, had seemed untypical, at least of a slave, when her master had arrived with company. Initially, I had wondered if her response might not have been more to be expected of an ill-tempered, unhappy wife of Earth, a common form of contractual partner, or a Gorean free companion, a pledged partner, should her husband, or companion, appear at supper time with unannounced, unexpected guests. But it had soon seemed to me that her annoyance was less that of being taken unawares, or unprepared, and finding herself at a loss, and being thusly embarrassed, as a simple disinclination to the work itself. It was less a social contretemps, it seemed, than an imposition, that she might be expected to work, at all. I had the distinct impression that she was such as to not only evade and resent the performance of various domesticities, even those that might be commonly expected of her, but was literally unaccustomed to them, as well. Perhaps, I thought, she is new to her collar. I wondered if Pertinax was Gorean. It is unusual for a Gorean male to accept laxity in a female slave.

I thought she might profit from a bout with the whip.

That implement is ideally suited to reminding a slave that she is a slave.

I wondered that he did not strip and tie Constantina, and then let her squirm, jerk, and weep, under the implement.

I thought she would profit muchly from its attentions.

Constantina seems a rather fine name for a slave, I thought. It is not unknown, of course, as a free woman's name. It did seem pretentious for a slave.

Her tunic seemed a bit ample for that of a slave, as the hem of its skirt came to her knees, and the neckline was modestly high, though open enough to show the collar.

The tunic itself was heavier and richer, and more closely woven, than was typical of such garments.

It was almost as though she might have designed it not so much as the garment of a slave, as a garment designed to resemble that of a slave.

She seemed to have excellent legs. I wondered that her master had not then, in his vanity, chosen to show them off. Gorean masters tend to be very proud of their slaves, rather as men of Earth are proud of their dogs and horses.

I thought she was nicely figured, though the size, weight and texture of the tunic tended to conceal this to some extent.

The tunic would be slipped on, over the head. There was, accordingly, no disrobing loop at the left shoulder.

On the other hand the "strip" command may be obeyed, even so, with grace and alacrity. The garment is usually slipped back over the head as the girl kneels.

Even in response to a simple, direct command, as suggested, the girl is expected to be graceful. Clumsiness is not acceptable in a slave; she is not a free woman. She is quite different, you see; she is a slave.

There are, of course, a number of disrobing commands in Gorean, which are less curt and brutal than the direct, blunt, unadorned "Strip." For example, one might hear "Remove your clothing," "Bare yourself," "Disrobe," "Show me a slave," "I would see my slave," "Why are you clothed before me?" "Exhibit my property," "Display yourself," "You need not wear your tunic at the moment," "Remove the impediments to my vision," "You are lovelier stripped than clothed, are you not?" "What do I own?" "To the collar and brand, girl," "How were you on the block?" And so on.

There was, as noted, a collar on her neck.

I wondered if it was locked.

I supposed so.

If locked, I wondered who held the key.

Surely not she, as she was a slave.

In her way, she was not unattractive, but that was to be expected, in one who was a slave, or expected to pass as a slave.

Personally, on the other hand, I thought most Goreans would not have bid on her, as, clearly, she was not yet slave soft, or slave ready. There are enormous differences among women in these matters.

Although, as I have suggested, she was not unattractive, it must be understood that this was in an Earth sort of way, the way in which many Earth females may be accounted attractive, attractive more in the sense of what they might become, how perhaps they might be, rather than in the sense of what they currently are. By this I mean, despite certain suitabilities of face and figure, she had something of the tightness, the apparent inhibitions, the uncertainties, and confusions, masked with the compensatory arrogance, nastiness, and insolence, of many Earth females, afflicted with the customary ambivalences toward their sex, comprehensible enough, one supposes, given their backgrounds, educations, and conditionings, their subjection to an environment seemingly engineered to produce, depending on a variety of circumstances, and the person, symptoms or tortures ranging from anxiety and neurosis to ill temper, misery, nastiness, pettiness, boredom, and depression.

"The soup is hot," said Constantina. "Surely you can tell that, stupid slave. Hurry, wrap the tabuk strips on their skewers, and put them to the fire. Are the suls and turpah ready?"

"If my eyes do not deceive me," said Cecily, testily, "my neck is not the only neck which is encircled with a slave band."

Constantina drew back her hand, as though to strike Cecily, but she stopped, suddenly, angrily, as Cecily, eyes flashing, was clearly prepared to return the blow, or worse. Fights amongst slave girls can be very disagreeable, with rolling about, clawing, biting, scratching, and such. One is reminded somewhat of the altercations that sometimes take place between sleen, in territorial disputes, mate competition, the contesting of a kill, and so on. In such frays, in the tangling, snarling, twisting, and swirling about, it is sometimes difficult to tell where one beast leaves off and the other begins. It can be worth an arm to try to separate fighting sleen.

"Why not have her serve naked," said Constantina. "Is that not commonly done with collared sluts?"

"Why not have them both serve naked?" I suggested.

Constantina turned white. Had she never served so, humbly, hoping to please, fearing the switch if she did not?

"No, no," said Pertinax, soothingly.

Constantina's color returned. She seemed shaken. I found this of interest. Did she not know that, as a slave, she was a domestic animal, as much as a verr or tarsk, and was not permitted modesty?

Cecily seemed pleased at this slight turn of events.

Constantina's hair was blonde and her eyes were blue. Cecily was a dark-eyed brunette. Constantina's hair was longer than Cecily's hair, and Constantina was a bit taller than Cecily, and a bit thinner than Cecily. Both would look well at the end of a man's chain. I supposed Constantina's hair must be a natural blonde, as Goreans tend to be very strict about such things. Few slavers will try to pass off a girl as being, say, blonde or auburn-haired, if that is not the natural hair color of the slave. In some cases their stock has been confiscated by the city and their establishment burned to the ground. If a girl with dyed hair is brought to Gor her head is normally shaved in the pens, that it may grow back in its natural color. Most slaves, like Cecily, are brunette, except in the north, where blondes are more common. I wondered if Constantina had been purchased in the light of someone's notion of what might constitute an attractive slave. If this were the case, I was surprised an auburn-haired girl had not been chosen, as auburn hair tends to be prized in most markets. I wondered if Constantina's buyer had been aware of that. To be sure, he might have found such women appealing, blondes, personally, for some reason. There is a supposition amongst some buyers that blonde slaves tend to be more sexually inert, and less pathetically needful in the furs, than dark-haired slaves, but this supposition is mistaken. Whatever the case may be initially, once the slave fires have been lit in a woman's belly, whatever her coloring, and such, you have a slave at your feet. The blonde can whimper, beg, and crawl as needfully as any other slave.

It is pleasant to have women so, at one's feet.

To be sure, a woman whose slave fires have not been ignited may have little understanding of this sort of thing, little understanding of the needs, sensations, miseries, and torments to which their embonded sisters are subject.

It is little wonder then that free women commonly hold female slaves in contempt, despising them for their needs.

How weak they are, they think.

But how alive they actually are!

And how the free woman, fearing to explore the edges of her consciousness, uneasily, perhaps angrily, perhaps inconsolably, senses how much she is missing, herself, to be found only in the arms of a dominant male, a master!

I glanced about the hut. I saw no slave whip on its convenient peg. This seemed an odd omission in a Gorean dwelling, at least one in which there was a slave, or slaves. It is not that the whip is often used. Indeed, normally, it is seldom, if ever, used, for there is no call for it. The girl knows it will be used if she is in the least bit displeasing, and so there is seldom a call for it. That it is there, and it will be used, if the master sees fit, is usually all that is necessary to keep it securely on its peg.

I had the sense that his slave, Constantina, was surly. It was almost as though she were distempered, to be expected to attend to her duties. I wondered if she attended to the hut, the firewood, and such, at all. Did Pertinax himself, our supposed forester, attend to such things? Were there other slaves about?

"I suppose," I said to Pertinax, "you obtain little news here, so far from Port Kar."

"One hears things occasionally," he said. "Transients, like yourself, a coastal peddler, the arrival twice yearly of an inspector and scribe, to review the trees, to inventory the reserves."

"You suggested earlier," I said, "that things might have changed in Ar?"

"Did I?" he asked.

"I think so," I said.

"A surmise," he said, "based on the appearance of many intruders."

"Surely harvesters, loggers, and such, come occasionally to cull the forests."

"Of course," he said, uneasily I thought.

"When will they be due?" I asked.

"One does not know," he said. "It is intermittent, depending on the needs of the arsenal, of the fleet."

"The fellows who disembarked from the ship," I said, "did not seem harvesters, loggers, or such."

"No," he said. "Not they."

"Who are they?" I asked. "What is their business?"

"I do not know," he said.

"The logs must be taken to the coast, for shipment," I said.

"Of course," he said.

"I saw no track amidst the trees, no road," I said.

"It is elsewhere," he said.

"I saw no stables for draft tharlarion," I said.

"They are elsewhere," he said.

"I am surprised there are no crews here, sawyers and carpenters, to dress and shape the wood, to cut planks and joints, such things."

"It is not the season," he said.

"I see," I said.

I had then more evidence that our friend, Pertinax, and perhaps his slave, Constantina, were not what they pretended to be. For one who did not know the ways of Port Kar, it would be a natural assumption, one I pretended to make, that dressing crews would shape and plank a great deal of the wood before shipping it to the south. Indeed, I had often thought that that would be a sensible practice. On the other hand, the artisans of the arsenal, under the command of the master shipwrights, attended to these matters in the arsenal itself. The rationale for this, as it had been explained to me, was that each mast, each strake, each plank, each article of the ship, was to be shaped and customized under the supervision of the arsenal's naval architects. Accordingly, it would be rare, if it was allowed at all, given the practices of Port Kar, and perhaps the vanity and arrogance of her craftsmen, intending to control to the greatest extent possible every detail of their work, to allow this carpentry to take place in a remote venue in which they had no direct supervision.

I would learn later, however, something earlier suspected, that something along these lines was taking place within the forest itself, outside the reserves, some pasangs to the south.

It had to do with the intruders, and the river, the Alexandra.

And it had little to do, I conjectured, even then, with the reserves of Port Kar and the needs of her arsenal.

"Foresters," I said, "normally cluster their huts, in small palisaded enclaves, but I saw no other huts here, nor a palisade."

Constantina cast a swift glance at me, and Pertinax looked down.

"The village is elsewhere," he said. "This is an outpost hut, near the coast, where we may watch for round ships."

"I see," I said.

The "round ships" are cargo ships.

The Gorean "round ship" is not round, of course, though the Gorean would translate as I have it. It is merely that the ratio of keel to beam is greater in the long ship, or ship of war, more length of keel to width of beam, than in the "round ship."

The round ship is designed for the carrying of cargo. The long ship is designed for speed and maneuverability. It is like a knife in the water.

"You are of the warriors, I take it," said Pertinax.

"Why should you think so?" I asked.

"You carry yourself as a warrior," said Pertinax. "Also, your weapon seems such as theirs."

It was the Gorean short sword, or *gladius*, light, easily unsheathed, convenient, designed for wickedly close work, to move behind the guard of longer, heavier weapons, to slip about buffeted shields or bucklers. It was pointed for thrusting, double-edged for slashing. Lifted and shaken it could part silk.

"I have fought," I said.

"You could be a mercenary," he said.

"Yes," I said.

"But I think you are of the warriors," he said.

"Perhaps of the assassins," I said.

"You do not have the eyes of an assassin," he said.

"What sort of eyes are those?" I asked.

"Those of a fee killer, an assassin," he said.

"I see," I said.

"You are a tarnsman, are you not?" asked Pertinax.

"I have not said so," I said.

"But you are, are you not?"

"I have ridden," I said.

"Those who know the tarn are not as other men," he said.

"They are as other men," I said. "It is merely that they have learned the tarn."

"Then they are different afterwards," he said.

"Perhaps," I said.

"If they have survived," he said.

"Yes," I said.

Many have died learning the tarn. The tarn is a dangerous bird, aggressive, carnivorous, often treacherous. The wingspan of many tarns is in the neighborhood of forty feet. Humans are small beside them. Many human beings will not approach them. It, like many wild beasts, can sense fear, and that stimulates its aggression. In facing a tarn a human being has little but will to place between himself and the beak and talons. To be sure many tarns are domesticated, so to speak, raised from the egg in the vicinity of humans, taught to expect their food from them, accustomed to harnessing from the age of the chick, and so on. In the past domestic tarns were sometimes freed, to hunt in the wild, and later to return to their cots, sometimes to the blasts of the tarn whistle. That is seldom done now. A hungry tarn is quite dangerous, you see, and the reed of its domesticity is fragile. There is no assurance that its strike will be directed on a tabuk or wild tarsk, or verr. Too, it is not unknown for such tarns to revert, so to speak. I think no tarn is that far from the wild. In their blood, it is said, are the wind and the sky.

I thought of a tarn once known, a sable monster, whose challenge scream could be heard for pasangs, Ubar of the Skies.

There had been a woman, Elizabeth Cardwell, whom I, for her own good, had hoped to rescue from the perils of Gor, and return to Earth, but she had fled with the tarn, to escape that fate. When the tarn returned I drove him away in a foolish rage. I had encountered the tarn again, years later, in the Barrens, and we had again been one, but at the end of local wars I had freed him again, that he might again take his place as the master of a mighty flock, that he might be again awing in broad, lonely skies, be again a prince amongst clouds, a lord amongst winds, that he might be again regent and king ruling over the vast grasslands he surveyed.

The woman, predictably, had fallen slave.

Encountering her I had left her slave.

I had encountered her again, later, in the Tahari.

Once, I would have given her the gift of Earth, returning her to the liberties, such as they are, of her native world, but she had fled. She had chosen Gor. It had been her choice.

Where was she now?

She was now in a collar, where she belonged.

I supposed I should sell her, perhaps to the mercy of Cosians, or into the beaded leather collars of the Barrens, or perhaps south to Schendi. Those of the Barrens and Schendi know well what to do with white female slaves.

She had made her choice.

She had wagered. She had lost.

She looked well, as other women, in her collar.

"But you are a tarnsman, are you not?" persisted Pertinax.

"I have ridden," I said. I was not clear why this might be important to him.

"I think the tabuk strips, the suls and turpah, the soup, all, must be ready," said Pertinax. "Let us have supper."

The hut was now redolent with the odors of which, for a forester, at least, must have seemed a feast.

"There is paga," said Pertinax.

"Of the brewery of Temus of Ar?" I asked.

"Yes," said Pertinax.

"It must be rare in the forests," I said.

"Yes," said Pertinax.

"It is my favorite," I said.

"I am glad to hear it," said Pertinax.

"Serve the men, slave," said Constantina.

Cecily looked at her, startled.

"Surely you will both serve," I said.

"He is right," said Pertinax, cautiously. It seemed he might be afraid to incur the displeasure of the slave.

Angrily, Constantina went to the side to fetch trenchers and utensils, to assist Cecily, who was already, ladle in hand, at the kettle, apportioning servings into two bowls, forward. Two other bowls were in the background, which might do for the slaves, later, were they given permission to eat. The first food or drink is always taken by the master, but, commonly, following this, the slave receives permission to share in the meal.

Cecily, kneeling, head down, placed one of the bowls before Pertinax, which was proper, as he was the host. I was then similarly served.

Constantina, irritably, was placing food on the trenchers, flinging it onto the simple, wooden surfaces. I noted that she was sharing out, already, four trenchers. How did she know she would be given permission to eat? I noticed she put very little on one of the trenchers. I supposed that was the one for Cecily. This irritated me. Cecily after all, was the slave of a guest. I don't think Cecily noticed, at the time. She did later.

"You have a Home Stone here somewhere?" I said to Pertinax. Usually the Home Stone is displayed in a place of honor. I did not, however, detect its presence. In his own hut, if it has a Home Stone, it is said that even a beggar is a Ubar.

"This is an outpost hut," said Pertinax, "a temporary place, a mere domicile of convenience. I have no Home Stone here."

"But elsewhere?"

"My Home Stone," he said, "is the Home Stone of Port Kar."

"Of course," I said.

I noted Constantina take a bit of meat from one of the trenchers, presumably her own. Cecily had carefully, earlier, removed the tabuk strips from their skewers and had laid them on a plate to the side. From that location Constantina had selected hers, and later, those for others. The suls and turpah, too, had been put to the side, for servicing onto the trenchers.

Constantina must have noticed my eyes on her. She put down her trencher, on a small stand to the side, and, bending down, handed a trencher to Pertinax.

"Thank you," he said.

That was interesting, I thought. He had thanked one who was merely a slave.

She then fetched another trencher, mine, it seems, and brought it to my place, and, bending down, put it toward me, for me to take it. I did not, however, take it.

She looked at me, puzzled, irritated.

"On your knees," I said to her, unpleasantly.

She cast me a look of fury.

"Kneel," I said to her.

She looked at Pertinax, angrily, but he merely smiled.

"Now," I said.

Angrily she knelt beside me, clutching the trencher. Her knuckles were white.

I had repeated a command. It should not be necessary to do that. Such is cause for discipline. Cecily looked frightened. Slaves, of course, are to obey immediately, and unquestioningly. Exceptions to this practice should occur only if the slave has not heard the command or does not understand it. If the masters should ask, "Must a command be repeated?" the slave knows that she is in jeopardy; at the least, the master is thinking, "Whip." At such a point, the slave will doubtless do her best to make it clear to the master, honestly, that she did not hear the command or does not understand it. "Please be merciful, Master," she might plead. "I did not hear Master." Or, say, "Your girl desires to please, but she does not understand what she is to do. Please tell her, Master." The girl might, of course, honestly suspect that the master did not say himself as he intended. An inquiry in such a case, is simple, and should clarify matters. She might, of course, beg permission to speak, and attempt to discuss or review the command, perhaps if she fears the command might have been ill considered, perhaps contrary to the master's own best interests. For example, it would not be regarded, or, perhaps better, should not be regarded, as a breach of discipline if the slave were to remonstrate against, or at least question, the advisability of a master's putting his own life or welfare in jeopardy. Few slaves will happily bring a master his cloak if he is in no condition to walk the high bridges, or, more dangerously, enter for some reason unarmed amongst enemies. In the end, of course, the master's will is definitive. It is for the slave to hear and obey. In all such matters, ideally, however, common sense and judgment should hold sway.

"Head down," I said to Constantina.

She put her head down, before me.

I waited for a few moments, and then took the trencher. "Draw back," I said to her. "And wait, kneeling."

She moved back a little, regarding me with fury, but obeyed.

"You look well on your knees," I said.

She made a tiny, angry noise, but remained as placed.

I glanced to Pertinax, to see if he objected to my treatment of the slave. But his eyes were alight. I wondered if he had never seen his own slave so.

I wondered if she were a slave.

Pertinax was not a forester.

"Perhaps the slaves may now feed," said Pertinax.

"Surely," I said.

It was at that time that Cecily, regarding her trencher, first became aware of its lightness. Constantina had given her little, and, I suspected, that little was not of the best.

After a bit I snapped my fingers that Cecily should approach me, and then, bit by bit, as she knelt by me, and extended her head, delicately, I fed her. She was not to use her hands, of course. Such homely practices remind the slave that she is dependent on the master for all things, not only for her collar, her clothing, if any, and her life, but even the tiniest morsel of food. Bit by bit I fed Cecily and watched her take the food gently, delicately, between her small, fine white teeth. Some of the sul I let her lick from my fingers.

I stole a glance at Pertinax, and noted that he, as I had suspected would be the case, was almost aflame with admiration and awe, with delight and envy. To have a beautiful woman so at one's mercy, so much in one's power, so much one's own, fills a man with triumph and joy, even with exultation. He then begins to understand what it can be, to be what he is, a man. To be sure, Goreans take this sort of thing much for granted.

Cecily took the food gratefully from me, and seemed almost dreamily content. Sometimes, head down, she kissed softly at my hand, and fingers.

"Slave, slave!" hissed Constantina.

"Yours, Master," Cecily whispered to me.

"Slave!" cried Constantina.

"Perhaps," I said to Pertinax, "you might similarly feed your girl."

"Never!" said Constantina.

"That will not be necessary," said Pertinax.

"Perhaps it is time for paga," I said.

Pertinax made as though to rise, but I motioned him to remain as he was, and he, with a glance at Constantina, a glance almost apologetic, resumed his position.

"Cecily," I said.

She rose, and went to the side. In a moment she had removed the lid from the vessel, set it aside, and half-filled two goblets. One she placed where Constantina might reach it, and the other she brought to my place, holding it, and knelt there. She lifted her eyes to me, to see if the serving ritual might begin, but my eyes cautioned her to wait.

I glanced back at Constantina, where she knelt, seething with rage, with humiliation.

"Is she a pleasure slave?" I asked Pertinax.

"Scarcely," he said, almost laughing, as though the idea were somehow preposterous.

Constantina cast him an ugly glance.

I had told from her manner of kneeling, of course, that she was not a pleasure slave. There are a variety of ways in which a pleasure slave may kneel, but the most common is back on her heels, knees spread, back straight, head up, the palms of her hands down, on her thighs. Sometimes, when her needs are muchly upon her, she may kneel muchly like that, save that her head may be lowered humbly, daring not to meet the eyes of the master, and the backs of her hands, not the palms of her hands, may be down on her thighs, which exposes the delicate palms of the hands to the master, a lovely hint of hope and petition. As is well known the small, soft palms of a woman's hands are sensitive and alive with nerve tissue, though far less so than what they are symbolizing, the moist, pleading tissues of her begging, heated belly.

"Any woman can be made a pleasure slave," I informed Pertinax.

"I should like to think so," he said.

A tiny, angry noise escaped Constantina.

"Where is your whip?" I asked Pertinax.

"I have none," said Pertinax. "It is not necessary."

"You are mistaken," I said.

"Would you dare to whip me?" asked Constantina.

"Were you given permission to speak?" I inquired.

"She has a standing permission to speak," said Pertinax, hastily.

"In her case, that may be a mistake," I said.

Pertinax was silent, and looked away.

"Would you dare to whip me?" persisted Constantina.

"That is for your master to do," I said.

"He dares not do so," she said, haughtily.

"Why not?" I asked.

"Let us have paga," said Pertinax, quickly, affably.

"Serve your master," I said to Constantina.

She seemed startled, but no more so, I think, than Pertinax.

I gathered that this relationship, the ritual serving of drink to the master by a slave, was unfamiliar to them.

By now it was overwhelmingly clear that Constantina's relationship to Pertinax was not that of a slave to her master, even should she be a slave, perhaps in some legal sense.

She picked up the goblet.

"Both hands," I informed her.

She put both hands on the goblet.

The justification for this grasp is practical and aesthetic, practical in the sense of assuring greater control of the vessel, and aesthetic, having to do with symmetry, and a framing of the slave's beauty. But, too, in this fashion the position of the slave's hands is clear. No hand is free, for example, to grasp a dagger, or slip powder into the drink. Long ago, in Turia, it is said that a free woman, armed with a dagger, disguised as a slave, attempted to assassinate a Ubar in his cups. Fortunately for the Ubar the attack was botched. Unfortunately for the would-be assassin, she failed to make her escape. It seems her anonymous employers had had no intention that she should escape, as arrangements for such a withdrawal might have been dangerous, and might have resulted, should confederates be captured, in the exposure of their identities. Fleeing, she had found doors locked before her. Captured and put under the iron, the Ubar would later find much pleasure in her. Too, as she had been of high family in Turia, her public bondage, exposure in triumphs, and such, afforded the populace much delight. No longer carried in her sedan chair by slaves, for whom citizens must make way, she was now less than a tarsk in the city. Surely she had been chained in more than one paga tavern. One wonders why a woman would have risked so much. One wonders if there are secret wheels, and springs, and engines, deep in the mind and heart, which impel one to travel fearful, beckoning roads. One wonders why some women place themselves at risk, why they undertake hazardous journeys and voyages, why they walk the high bridges at night, such things. Perhaps she was, in her way, courting the collar. If so, she found it. It is hard to understand the mind, and even harder, one supposes, to understand the heart.

In any event, both hands are to be on the goblet.

She rose to her feet, holding the goblet with both hands. She approached Pertinax. She bent down, and, irritably, extended the goblet to him.

"On your knees," I told her.

Angrily she knelt.

Pertinax much enjoyed, I could tell, having her on her knees before him. How right she looked.

I wondered if, somewhere, there might not be a man in Pertinax.

Again, she extended the goblet to Pertinax.

"No," I said to her.

"I am on my knees," she snapped. "What more do you want?"

"Have you never served wine or paga to a man?" I inquired.

"What do you want?" she asked.

"Cecily," I said, "it seems we have here an ignorant slave. Instruct her."

"I, too, Master," she said, "am ignorant. I am little trained."

"That is true," I said, "but do what you can."

"I will not be instructed by a slave," said Constantina, adding, quickly, "such a slave."

"Then you will be stripped and instructed by my belt," I said.

"I protest," said Pertinax.

"You have no Home Stone here," I said.

"It is my hut," he said.

"I am not sure of that," I said.

"You are not my master," she said. "You cannot whip me!"

"Are you sure of that?" I asked.

"No," she said. She then looked at me uncertainly. Perhaps for the first time she sensed she was looking into the eyes of a man who could bring the whip to her back and legs. I saw she was trying to deal with this thought. Too, I saw a flicker in her eyes, perhaps of fear, but, too, perhaps of something else, as well.

She had never before been, I suspected, subject to a male.

Certainly one does not go about punishing the slaves of others, though free women tend to be rather free in this regard, and most Goreans are not above reprimanding errant slaves, whether their own or those of others. An errant slave girl is not above being, say, knelt and cuffed by a free person. Do not all slaves call free men "Master," and free women "Mistress"?

Too, Constantina was clearly in need of discipline, and I suspected I might be willing to make an exception to my general reservations in her case.

To be sure, if she were a free woman, the whip would not do at all. Free women on Gor, as on Earth, are free to do much what they wish, with little or no fear of consequences. They are free to do almost anything, without fear of punishment. This indulgence and latitude are not extended, of course, to the slave.

"Master?" asked Cecily.

"Begin," I said to her.

"You are before your master," said Cecily. "Split your knees."

I sensed Cecily would enjoy this.

"Never!" said Constantina.

"Now, slave!" snapped Cecily.

Constantina threw me a pleading glance, but I fear she found little comfort in my gaze.

"Ai!" said Pertinax, softly.

Constantina knelt before him, her knees spread, in the position of a Gorean pleasure slave. I gathered he had never had this woman so before him.

Obviously he, if not Constantina, was muchly pleased.

"Press the metal of the goblet to your belly," said Cecily. "Press it in there, so that you can feel it. Really feel it, the metal against your belly. Surely you understand this, the metal against your belly. More. Better. More. Good. Now, to your breasts, softly but firmly. Feel the metal."

There was a change in the breath of Constantina. She cast me a glance, almost piteously. I think she did not understand her sensations.

"Look at your master, not mine," said Cecily, unpleasantly.

Constantina turned to Pertinax, unwillingly, it seemed, the goblet at her breasts.

"Now," said Cecily, "lift the goblet to your lips, and, gazing over the rim at your master, kiss the goblet, tenderly, and lick it, lovingly, lingeringly, for he is your master, and he is permitting you, a mere slave, to serve him. Keep your eyes on your own master, slave!"

Constantina turned back to Pertinax.

Then she put down her head, frightened, for perhaps it was the first time she had seen him regard her as what she was, or supposedly was, a slave.

"Now," said Cecily, "extend your arms, holding the cup, to your master, and put your head down, humbly, between your extended arms."

This is, of course, a beautiful sight.

Pertinax, it seemed, would almost forget to accept the cup. Perhaps he was unwilling to let the moment go. Then he accepted the cup, and drank.

"Thank you," he said.

"You do not thank her," I informed him. "It is a great honor and privilege for a slave to be permitted to serve her master. Too, it is what she is for."

"True," said Pertinax.

"That was not so hard, was it, girl?" I asked Constantina.

"No," she said.

"No, what?" I asked.

"No," she said, "*—Master*."

"You may now draw back," I said, "but you will remain in the vicinity, kneeling. You may be required later."

"'Required'," she said, uncertainly.

"For further serving," I said.

"Yes," she said, "—Master."

Pertinax seemed unable to take his eyes from her. I wondered what their relationship might be.

"May I serve Master paga?" inquired Cecily.

"Yes," I said, and she served me paga, and well. I trusted Constantina was attentive.

How incredibly beautiful was the former Miss Virginia Cecily Jean Pym!

Then she withdrew, a bit, to kneel in the background, where, unobtrusively, she would be at hand, should she be needed, or wanted, or desired. The slave does not withdraw from the master's presence without permission.

I finished the paga and set down the goblet.

"I thank you for your hospitality," I said to Pertinax.

"It is nothing," he said. "I hope you will stay the night."

"The others, I gather," I said, "have not yet arrived."

"What others?" he said.

"I do not know," I said.

"I do not understand," he said.

"Perhaps we should talk," I said to Pertinax.

"Remain as you are," I said to Constantina, for it seemed she stirred, and would have risen to her feet.

She was not accustomed, it seemed, to obeying men. I found this odd, as she had a collar on her neck.

"By all means," said Pertinax, uncertainly. "But talk of what?"

At that moment, far over the roof, high, outside the hut, far overhead, there was a thunderous noise. It was like a sudden, passing surf, a storm in the sky. It lasted no more than a part of an Ehn.

"Master?" said Cecily, startled.

Constantina seemed frightened.

Perhaps she had at one time seen tarns.

I did not leave my place.

"Migratory tarns," said Pertinax.

"The tarn is not a migratory bird," I said.

"Forest tarns," he said.

"Tarns are of the mountains and the plains," I said. "They

do not frequent the forests. They cannot hunt in them, for the closeness of the trees."

"Perhaps it was thunder," he said.

"You may be unfamiliar with the sound," I said, "but I am not. That was the passage of several tarns, perhaps a tarn cavalry."

"No," he said, "not a cavalry."

"Not one disciplined, at any rate," I said.

In a tarn cavalry the wing beats are synchronized, much as in the pace of marching men. Normally this is facilitated, unless surprise is intended, by the beating of a tarn drum, which sets the cadence. One of the glorious sights of Gor is the wheeling, the maneuvering and flight, of such cavalries in the sky, a lovely sight, in its way not unlike that of a fleet of lateen-rigged galleys abroad on gleaming Thassa, the sea.

"A very large band of mercenary brigands?" I suggested.

"They are not mounted," said Pertinax.

"I do not understand," I said.

"Do not speak," snapped Constantina. "Be quiet, you fool!"

Pertinax subsided, and looked down.

I rose to my feet and went to my things, gathering in some few articles, and then returned to face Constantina, where she knelt. I took her by the hair and, as she cried out, twisted her about and threw her to her back, and knelt across her body. She squirmed, helpless, pinioned. She looked up at me, wildly, protestingly, frightened, as I thrust the wadding into her mouth, and then, turning her to her belly, secured it in place behind the back of her neck. I then, with binding fiber, as she lay on her belly, lashed her wrists together behind her back, tightly, and so served her ankles, as well, which I then bound, high, to her wrists. Such a tie is very unpleasant. I then lifted her in my arms, carried her outside, and threw her to the leaves, in the darkness, some feet from the hut entrance. I then returned to the hut, and resumed my place, cross-legged, across from Pertinax.

"I have no interest in killing you," I said to Pertinax, "but I think we should talk."

"By all means," he said.

"I doubt that you are Gorean," I said. "Certainly you are not of Port Kar, and you are not a forester. My slave and I were set down on the beach, doubtless to be met. You arrived, supposedly, as a matter of coincidence. I do not believe that. Whom do you serve?"

"Men," he said.

"Priest-Kings? Kurii?" I asked. Certainly Priest-Kings knew the coordinates for the landing of the ship of Peisistratus, but, so, too, it seemed possible, did Kurii. Certainly the coordinates had been transmitted through Kurii to Peisistratus.

"I know nothing of Priest-Kings and Kurii," said Pertinax. "Are they not mythical?"

"No," I said.

"Men," repeated Pertinax.

"Men who serve Priest-Kings, or Kurii?" I asked.

"Men," he said. "I know nothing more."

"I think you do not fear the intruders in the forest, those who come in ships," I said. "I think you understand them."

He said nothing.

"Explain to me the tarns," I said.

"They are from Thentis," he said, "most of them, some from elsewhere."

Thentis is a high Gorean city, east and north of Ko-ro-ba. It is famed for its tarn flocks.

One thinks of "Thentis, Famed for her Tarn Flocks," rather as one thinks of "Glorious Ar," of "Ko-ro-ba, the Towers of the Morning," of "Port Kar, Jewel of Gleaming Thassa," and so on.

"How do you know they were not mounted?" I asked.

"They are raised, but are young, and not trained," he said. "Few but hardy tarnsters, or tarnsmen themselves, would dare to approach them in their present state. They are linked together by long ropes. They are being delivered to a rendezvous, in the forest."

"Near the Alexandra," I said.

"Yes," he said, startled.

"There is a mystery here," I said. "What is its nature?"

"I know little of it," said Pertinax, "but I can link you with those who do."

"As you did not discourse with me of these things," I said, "I gathered that there were others who could, for whom you were waiting."

"They are in the forest," he said. "They will not be coming here. I will take you to them, in two days."

"Your slave," I said, "is badly in need of discipline."

"As she has been treated this evening," he said, "I think she is more aware than hitherto that she is a female."

"It is unfortunate," I said, "that some women must be reminded of that."

"She thinks of herself as a man," he said.

"She is mistaken," I said. "Her thinking must be corrected."

One could see clearly she was woman, even if she did not understand that, except perhaps in some peripheral sense.

Certainly she was nicely shaped. And I thought she might, given some instruction, and a sense of what it was to be a slave, sell well.

It is interesting, I thought, the Book of Woman. How few have opened that book. Is the seal, I wondered, so securely fastened? Is it truly so hard to break? How many women themselves have feared to open that book and read what is written there. But some do open the book, with whatever trepidation, and read what is written there. And then, page by page, they peruse the ancient text, and in it, ever more deeply, page by turning page, discover themselves, and I think there is no final page for that book, for the book is without an end, for it is the Book of Woman.

"She is from Earth, is she not?" I said.

"Yes," he said.

"As are you?"

"Yes," he said. "But so, too, I gather, are you, and your slave. Your accents."

"English," I said.

"It seemed so," he said.

"You are Canadian, or American?" I surmised.

"Canadian," he said.

"Your slave," I said, "is Canadian?"

"No," he said. "She is American, from the eastern seaboard of America."

"An excellent area for slaving, I understand," I said.

"Perhaps," he said. "I would not know."

I recalled Peisistratus, who had sampled women from various nations and continents, had spoken highly of several areas, Canada, Australia, England, France, Germany, Japan, Taiwan, Hawaii, the southwest of the United States, its west coast, its eastern seaboard, and such. It was pleasant, he had remarked, to take beautiful, highly intelligent, sophisticated, civilized women, so often unhappy, some even stupidly at war with their sex, and teach them their collars.

"She is from New York City," said Pertinax.

"Not originally," I said. "Her accent is different. I lived there for a time."

"Then from elsewhere," he said.

"An immigrant to that metropolis," I said, "perhaps from Cleveland, Cincinnati, Chicago, Los Angeles, San Francisco, or somewhere."

"I do not know," he said.

"Perhaps one determined and ambitious, and one not too scrupulous, one intending to achieve wealth and success at any cost."

He smiled. "Yes," he said.

"As many others," I said.

"Yes," he said.

"And now," said I, "she is in a collar on Gor."

"Yes," he said.

"But it seems she does not yet know the meaning of her collar," I said.

"No," he smiled.

"Teach it to her," I said.

"You do not understand," he said. "She is my superior. There are riches behind her. It is she who recruited me."

"A slave has such power?" I asked.

"It would seem so," he said.

"In two days, as I understand it, you are prepared to unravel this mystery for me?"

"We will leave in two days," he said. "There is to be a rendezvous. I will conduct you to the place."

"You think you will then be through with the matter?" I asked.

"Surely," he said.

"You are entangled here," I said.

He regarded me, uneasily, startled.

"No," he said.

"We shall see," I said.

"Should we not free Constantina?" he asked.

"Leave her where she is," I said. "Let her squirm in the darkness and leaves, for a time. It will do her good."

"Is that appropriate?" he asked.

"Quite," I said, "as she is a slave."

"Perhaps she will work herself free," said Pertinax.

A small sound of mirth escaped Cecily.

Pertinax looked at her, puzzled.

"She was bound by a warrior," I explained.

"I see," said Pertinax.

"She might, of course," I said, "be stolen, say, by some of the brigands to whom you have occasionally alluded, or, say, be dragged away, by a sleen, to be eaten in some secluded place."

"We must bring her in, instantly," said Pertinax, "and free her!"

"Shortly," I said. "You know who I am, I take it."

"You are a tarnsman," he said, "one known as Tarl Cabot."

"You have read my girl's collar?" I inquired.

"No," he said.

"You have been waiting for me," I said.

"Yes," he said.

"I am Tarl Cabot," I said. "That is of less interest, I take it, than the fact that I have ridden."

"That you are a tarnsman, yes," he said. "I think so."

"Master!" said Cecily. "I hear a stirring outside."

"Yes," I said, "it is a sleen."

"Master!" she cried.

"It has been there for a time," I said.

"I cannot go out," said Pertinax, turning white. "I am no hunter, no sleen master. I am no match for a sleen. It would kill me!"

"Do not be concerned," I said. "I saw it when I went out. The sleen is a tenacious hunter. It clearly had another trail in which it was interested. At the most it will investigate your Constantina, poking her a bit with its snout, or such. In its hunt she will be no more than an inconvenience or distraction. It might not even be hungry. It is probably gone by now."

"Bring her in," said Pertinax. "I beg you!"

"She is only a slave," I reminded him.

"Please!" he said.

"To be sure," I said, "she will not be worth much on the block if she has been mauled by a sleen."

"Please!" he insisted.

"I saw the beast," I said. "I watched it. There is no danger."

"Please!" he insisted.

"It was otherwise occupied," I said.

"There might be another," he said.

"The sleen is territorial," I said. "It is unlikely there would be another in the vicinity."

"Please! Please!" he said.

"Very well," I said. I then left the hut and went to where I had left the girl. The sleen was gone, as I had anticipated. I could see a little, from one of the moons, which was ascendant, but not yet full. The leaves about her were muchly crushed, which suggested she had done, at least at first, a good deal of squirming and, as she could, rolling about. I also saw sleen tracks near her, and could smell sleen on the leaves. She had been unable to call attention to what she must have deemed her harrowing predicament, given the gag. One might have heard something if one were quite close to her. When I came to her she had fainted. I picked her up, and carried her into the hut, and Pertinax, gratefully, closed and bolted the door. I removed the bonds and gag from the unconscious girl and replaced the binding fiber in my pouch, and left the gag out, to dry. She murmured then, in misery, and, half-conscious, huddled, trembling, on the floor of the hut.

"Let us see more of her legs," I suggested.

"No!" cried Pertinax.

I thrust up the tunic so that I could see more of her legs. She was nicely legged, but one expects that in a slave.

The girl whimpered, but, terrified, made no effort to readjust her tunic. It was as though she realized that various things might be done to her as others might please, and that she must abide their will.

Pertinax regarded her with visible excitement. Had he never seen a slave?

"It is late," I suggested. "Perhaps we should retire."

"There are blankets," said Pertinax.

"Good," I said.

"And there are two mattresses, filled with grass," he said.

"Why do you have two?" I asked.

Pertinax did not respond.

"Cecily and I," I said, "if you have no objection, will share this mattress."

"Certainly," said Pertinax.

"Surely you should have the mattress, Master," said Cecily, "and I should sleep at your feet."

What she had in mind was doubtless a common arrangement in a Gorean dwelling, of which she had been apprised by other slaves while in the Pleasure Cylinder associated with the Steel World from which we had recently departed. It is common for the slave to be slept at the foot of the master's couch, chained there to a slave ring. But in such a situation she is likely to have at least a mat and, commonly, deep, luxurious furs on which to recline. Indeed, the slave is often put to service on such furs, which are commonly spoken of as "love furs." If she has been displeasing, of course, she may be slept naked at the foot of the couch, on her chain, on the bare tiles or stones of the floor. That is not so pleasant, and, of course, it gives the slave some time to consider how she might endeavor to be more pleasing to the master. It is a sign of favor with the master for a slave to be allowed to share the surface of the couch. On the other hand, I suspect it is commonly done, except perhaps in a house with many slaves. Certainly it is pleasant to have a slave at one's side, of whom one may make use at any Ahn of the night or morning. It is a cusp in a slave's bondage when she is first permitted to the surface of the master's couch.

"Later, perhaps," I said. "I have not had you in more than twenty Ahn."

"Yes, Master," she said, pleased.

Pertinax crouched down beside Constantina.

She lay still, as though frightened, disbelieving, or numb.

"Let me help you to your couch," he said.

"No," I said, standing up, approaching them. "You, Pertinax, are master. It is you who will have the couch, and not the slave. She will sleep at the foot of the couch, on the floor, or outside."

"Surely not," protested Pertinax.

I nudged the slave with my foot, not gently, and she reacted, and whimpered. "Do you understand, slave?" I asked.

"Yes," she said, "Master."

"Then crawl to your master," I said, "kiss his feet, and beg to be permitted to sleep at the foot of his couch."

Constantina, on all fours, head down, her long hair to the floor, crawled to Pertinax, bent down, and kissed his feet. "I beg to be permitted to sleep at the foot of your couch, Master," she said.

"Ai!" cried Pertinax, half in consternation, half in delight.

"Well?" I asked Pertinax. "A slave awaits an answer to her petition."

"You may do so," said Pertinax, his voice unsteady.

"Thank you, Master," she said, and went to her place.

Cecily drew away her tunic, like the beautiful, uninhibited, shameless little animal she was, and knelt beside the mattress, at its lower left side, and lifted it a bit, and kissed it. She looked at me, expectantly, hopefully, to learn my will, and I reached down and seized her by the hair and, as she winced, in pain and delight, I drew her beside me on the mattress.

Even in the Pleasure Cylinder the slave fires had been well lit in Cecily's lovely, helpless, vulnerable little belly, and she had soon found herself, as is common with female slaves, their victim and prisoner.

How the flames of their needs goad slaves to the feet of masters, even to the feet of those they may loathe.

I did not begrudge Cecily her ecstasies, nor would I hinder them. Some masters try to shame their slaves for what they cannot help, indeed for responses for which the master himself may have been significantly responsible, particularly if they have known them as lofty, frigid free women, now, by their will, reduced to begging animals. That, however, seems to me cruel. It does help the slave, of course, to see herself as a slave, in misery and shame, as she recalls her former contempt for such things in slaves. Now she herself understands what it is to be in the throes of being mastered.

And at a given point she throws her head back and says, "Yes, yes!" to the collar, and is whole.

Cecily, in her yieldings, was muchly pleasured, and her master, too, if it must be known, was well pleased with his slave.

Constantina had risen to her knees and was looking, hollow-eyed, dry-eyed, across the hut at us. There was a little light, from the embers of the fire.

"She is a slave, a slave!" said Constantina.

"Yes, yes, yes," gasped Cecily, beside herself with collar rapture.

"Disgusting! Disgusting!" said Constantina.

"Pertinax," I said, "take your slave, and put her to use."

"No, no!" said Pertinax, frightened.

I then rolled to the side, and struggled with the vital thing in my arms, kissing, and licking me, gasping, wanting more, and more.

Later, an Ahn or more later, Cecily was asleep, and, I gathered, so, too, was Constantina. I lay awake, looking up at the beams and thatch of the hut's roof. Who was I to meet in two days, or so?

"Cabot," I heard.

"Yes," I said, softly.

"You spoke of entanglement," said Pertinax.

"Yes," I said.

"I am to be paid," he said, "and then I am done with matters."

"I do not think so," I said.

"What of her?" he asked.

"The slave?"

"Constantina," he said.

"She, too, is entangled," I said.

I was now confident that his employers were not representing Priest-Kings, but others, perhaps brigands, or merchants, somehow associated with Kurii. Some Kurii, I was sure, from the Steel World, would have had the coordinates for our landing. Certainly they had been transmitted through Kurii, and the security may have been lax, or deliberately compromised. It was a common practice for Kurii to recruit agents on Earth, usually through confederates, often slavers. There were doubtless several possible networks involved in such matters. Diverse and subtle are the tentacles of the Steel Worlds.

My convictions in this matter had primarily to do with Constantina. It seemed to me quite unlikely that she would have been recruited by Priest-Kings. What need had they, in their plenitude of power, of such instruments? She was, on the other hand, exactly the sort of woman whom slavers, abetting the schemes of Kurii, would choose to recruit. When their services were no longer required there were always other things that could be done with them. There was always the block, and collar. Such women, vain and egotistical, self-serving, greedy and deceitful, dazzled by dreams of riches and power, would think little of betraying others, but it seldom occurred to them, for some reason, that they might, in their turn, be betrayed as easily.

Expecting to be returned to Earth, to power and riches, they would commonly find themselves incarcerated, perhaps thrust into tiny cages, bewildered, grasping the bars, awaiting their sale.

Why not?

They had served their purpose.

Let them now be good for a little something further, say, whatever handful of coins they might bring on the block.

"What are we to do?" asked Pertinax.

"Link me with those who hired you," I said.

I do not know if he slept then.

For my part, I knew that the Priest-Kings, for some reason, had arranged to have me set down on the beach, which was not far away, no more than a quarter of a pasang from this hut.

I was then certain that another was to meet me, one who truly stood in the service of Priest-Kings.

On the morrow, I would go again to the beach, to the point where I had been landed.

It was there, surely, I was to be met.

It rained heavily that night, the storm coming in from Thassa. I supposed that the seas might have been high for two or three days, perhaps for hundreds of pasangs offshore. That might delay the arrival of a ship, one approaching from the west, say, from Tyros or Cos. Gorean vessels, incidentally, are usually shallow-drafted, and usually tend to keep in sight of land. Few would risk the open sea in an inauspicious season. In storms, many would beach. On the other hand, ships from Tyros and Cos, if they were to reach shores to their east, could not coast, but must address themselves to the open sea, and for days.

I decided that on the morrow I would return to the beach.

Chapter Four

A Sail

I stood back amongst the trees, looking out to sea.

It was early morning.

I had left the hut of Pertinax a few Ehn earlier.

It was very pleasant near the shore, with the smell of Thassa, with the cool, penetrant air, the sense of the salt of her churning waves, the sound of the surf, the incoming tide, the wash of sea weed on the shore, the water with its soft, fluid rush across the sand and amongst the stones, and then its circuitous return, and then its advance, and then again its return, and the wheeling and intermittent crying offshore of broad-winged coast gulls. Too, as it had rained the preceding night, the higher rocks and the sand above the tide line were still dark with damp. The forest, too, with its moist soil and its glistening, rustling canopies of wet, dripping leaves, shaken in the wind, had about it its sweetness of life.

I wondered if human beings were good for such a world.

Yet if they did not inhabit her would such a world not have been something of a waste, for who, then, would know how beautiful she was?

The Gorean, incidentally, is not a soiling and a plague upon his world, nor is he so arrogant as to deem himself superior to it, its guardian or steward. He regards himself, rather, as a part of her, as much so as a leaf, or tree, but an unusual part, of course, a part which knows itself a part. He is a partaker of its warmth and cold, its winters and summers, its light and darkness, its day and its night, its storms and serenities. He loves his world but he does not understand it for what it is not. It is beautiful but, too, it is awesome and terrible. With equanimity, not caring, it brings forth life and death, flourishing and destruction, growth and decay. It is a world that contains not only the beauty of grass and the blossoming of the talendar but the fangs of the ost, the coils of the hith, the jaws of the larl, the frenzies of flocking, feeding jards, the sudden, wrenching, twisting strike of the nine-gilled shark, the claws of the sleen, the beak and talons of the tarn.

The beach seemed deserted.

No furrows marked where the keel of a long ship might have been drawn ashore.

The horizon seemed clear, gray, and cool, but clear.

It had seemed likely to me that I would have been met by agents of Priest-Kings, but I had encountered only Pertinax, and a woman called 'Constantina'. These, I was sure, stood in place of Kurii, some Kurii. How much they knew of their role in these matters I was not sure. The human agents of Kurii were seldom enlightened, I supposed, as to the ramifications and depths of the plans of their employers, nor the remote objectives of such plans. I was aware of the usual dispositions of their female agents, once they had fulfilled their purposes. They would not be returned to Earth, with the promised emoluments of their service, riches, at least. This might lead to complications, a request for explanations, inquiries, and such. Kurii, as many predators, are fond of concealment, until they act. Too, their female agents could not be well integrated into Gorean society, with its orderings, its clan and caste arrangements, its rank, distance, and hierarchy. Such women did not even have the protection of a Home Stone. Too, they were, like slaves, selected for their beauty, and this placed them in jeopardy in a world such as Gor. A tabuk doe, so to speak, amongst larls, will not be long without her collar. Gorean males are not men of Earth. I was less certain of the fate of male agents, such as Pertinax. It seems there would be little point in sending them to the quarries or mines. Perhaps they would simply be killed. Certainly they would not be allowed to withdraw from the services of Kurii. That would be highly unlikely. I supposed they might be kept, then, to be used again. Knowing a native language of Earth they might be of continuing value as agents. Too, they could be rewarded on Gor, if not on Earth, where curiosity might be aroused, and in ways which would be unlikely on Earth, but appealing to males. Indeed, many males, one supposes, might prefer Gorean rewards to those of Earth, for example gold, power, slaves, and such.

In moving to the beach I had, as was my training, been alert to a variety of particulars, movements and shadows, the integrity of brush, the branches overhead, the nature of the ground underfoot, was a leaf pressed down here and there, was that a pebble possibly dislodged, such things. There was nothing unusual in this, and the circumspection and alertness involved, the care taken in one's passage, would have been typical of one of my caste, and certainly in negotiating an unfamiliar and perhaps dangerous terrain. Too, I suspected there might be another, or others about. Was I not to be met?

But no rendezvous had taken place, not with agents of Priest-Kings.

It occurred to me that such an agent, or agents, might have been waiting, and had been killed.

On the other hand, I had detected little or no uneasiness on the part of Pertinax or his slave, Constantina, which might have appertained to such a deed.

To be sure, they might know nothing of it. Kurii might know. But why would Kurii have agents of theirs meet me here at all?

It would have to do, one supposed, with the intruders, with flights of tarns, but I understood nothing of this.

Or had such things to do with Priest-Kings, and their plans?

And were Kurii here intent on turning something to their own advantage?

From the shelter of the trees, I looked across the water.

The horizon was still clear.

When I had left the hut of Pertinax, or the hut he utilized, he, and Cecily, had been asleep. I did not think Constantina had been asleep. To be sure she appeared to be asleep.

It interested me that Pertinax had identified Constantina as his superior. Indeed, he had informed me that she had recruited him.

It seemed unlikely a slave would be so charged, so privileged.

I heard the tiny sound a few yards away.

I had been waiting for it.

Constantina, you see, had not truly been asleep. I had been reasonably sure of that.

In approaching the shore, I had left an easy trail leading to the beach, but had then doubled back, and waited in the shelter of some trees, a few yards back, and to the side, from which point of relative concealment I could both survey the beach and monitor my original trail.

As I expected, Constantina was moving toward the beach. Interestingly, she did not seem to be following the trail I had left, quite obviously, I had thought. Rather she was just moving cautiously, directly, toward the beach. I had little doubt she was trying to spy on me, though, given her clumsiness, and her apparent lack of awareness of the trail I had left, the word is perhaps more complimentary than it needed be.

Kurii would know, of course, that the coordinates of my landing would be known to Priest-Kings. Indeed, they were specified by Priest-Kings.

These coordinates, too, or, better, the locale in question, would have been made clear to Pertinax and Constantina.

The agent, or agents, of Priest-Kings, it seemed, then, were either late for their appointment, or had been killed, and their bodies disposed of. That Constantina had come to the beach, to spy on me, suggested to me that either the agent, or agents, of Priest-Kings had not yet arrived, and Constantina was concerned to detect their presence, or, if they had arrived, and been disposed of, Constantina was unaware of that fact.

As indicated earlier, I was reasonably sure that neither Constantina nor Pertinax were harboring any surreptitious knowledge of murders recently wrought. If such murders had taken place I did not think that Kurii would have risked entrusting Constantina or Pertinax with a cognizance so dreadful and solemn, lest it be betrayed by some careless word, some inadvertent expression, a surprising hesitation, some gauche, unwary phrase, or pause.

There had been a storm last night, and it had moved in from the west, from Thassa. That might have delayed a ship, as she hove to, or was blown off course. Too, who knew what weathers might have prevailed in the last several days.

Priest-Kings, you see, seldom use their own ships in the vicinity of Gor's surface. They tend to protect their mystery or privacy zealously. The dark, palisaded Sardar itself, the abode of Priest-Kings, is sealed away. It is sacred, and forbidden. Accordingly, the agents of Priest-Kings, on the surface of Gor, tend to move as Goreans would move, and commonly appear indistinguishable from ordinary Goreans. The sight of large metal vessels, coming and going, might make the Priest-Kings seem too comprehensible, remarkable, and powerful, but comprehensible. Humans are likely to fear best what they cannot see; what they can see they may investigate. Too, the caste of Initiates, which claims to mediate between humans and Priest-Kings, with their sacrifices, and such, would obviously prefer for Priest-Kings to remain as invisible and mysterious as possible. Thus they can interpret their "will" as they please, as the wind blows, so to speak, or, perhaps more accurately, as the gold depresses the scales. To be sure, many Initiates doubtless take themselves seriously.

Constantina was quite near now.

She was doing her best to move stealthily. Whatever her various qualities, properties, values, and virtues might be, which might make her of interest to a man, her strong suite was obviously not woodcraft. She was looking toward the beach, and, forward, from side to side. She seemed puzzled, that she did not see me.

Where could I be?

Suddenly she stiffened, pulled back, against me, her cry stifled by my hand across her mouth.

"Tal," I said to her.

She squirmed, helpless.

I held her for a time, until her struggles subsided, until she knew herself my prisoner. I then removed my hand from across her mouth, but held her by the arms, from behind.

"What are you doing here, girl?" I asked.

"'Girl'!" she said.

"'Girl', 'Slave'," I said.

She struggled, again, in my arms, held from behind, but could not free herself.

"Girl, slave," I said.

"Nothing!" she said.

"I think we should have a talk," I said.

"I was come to fetch water!" she said.

"You cannot drink the water of Thassa," I said. "If there is a spring about, it is not here."

"I lost my way," she said.

"Where is your yoke, with the attached buckets?" I asked. "Doubtless you would look well, carrying water in such a device."

"I was looking for the spring," she said.

I then drew her by the right arm, she stumbling, to the edge of the trees, at the border of the beach.

There I thrust her back against a small tree and, pulling her arms behind her, fastened her wrists together, behind the tree, so that she stood before me, fastened in place.

She pulled at the ropes a bit, futilely.

She looked at me, angrily. "Let me go!" she said.

"Why were you following me?" I asked.

"I was not following you!" she said.

"You are aware that you can be seen easily, from the shore?" I said.

She looked about, frightened. "Yes?" she said.

"There may be intruders about," I said. "I saw several disembarked yesterday. Pertinax tells me that there have been many of them. Some may still be about. Others may arrive."

"I do not understand," she said.

"I thought you might," I said.

"This is Gor," she said. "Do not leave me here, a woman, bound as I am!"

"Then you acknowledge yourself a woman?" I said.

"Of course!" she said.

"And you are not a man?"

"No," she said, "I am not a man—I suppose."

"You suppose?" I asked.

"I am not a man," she said.

"You are quite different?" I said.

"Perhaps," she said, jerking at her bonds.

"Perhaps?" I inquired.

"Yes," she said. "I am quite different!"

"I wonder if you understand that," I said. "That you are

radically different, wholly and absolutely different, wonderfully different."

"Wonderfully different?" she said.

"Yes," I said, "but you have not yet learned your womanhood."

"I hate being a woman!" she said.

"That is because you have not yet been put at the feet of men," I said.

"Untie me," she said.

"I like you as you are," I said.

"Untie me!" she said.

"Free yourself," I said.

"I cannot!" she said.

"Then you will remain as you are," I said.

"I was not following you," she said. "I was fetching water, I lost my way."

"And forgot containers, in which water might be brought?"

She was silent.

"Perhaps, rather," I said, "you wished merely to look upon the sea, in the early morning, to hear the gulls, and such."

"Yes," she said, "that is it!"

"But you feared to be caught, unengaged in labors, lest Pertinax, your master, beat you for dalliance?"

"You have found me out," she said, sadly. "Please do not inform my master."

"Your severe master?"

"Yes," she said, head down, "I do not wish to be beaten."

"You have never been beaten in your life," I said.

She looked up, angrily.

"It is hard to know whether there is a man in Pertinax or not," I said. "If there is, it is hard to see, for the spineless urt."

A flicker of a smile crossed her countenance.

How she despised him!

Women despise men for weakness, and fear them for strength.

"And I doubt you have ever looked on anything," I said, "without considering how it might be put to your advantage."

"That is not true!" she said.

"Perhaps when you were younger," I said.

"Let me go!" she said.

"You are a mercenary, of sorts," I said.

"I am a mere, worthless slave," she said, humbly, "only a Gorean slave girl."

"We are going to have a talk," I said.

"Release me!" she demanded.

I stood back, and, for a time, regarded her.

"Do not look at me like that!" she said.

"Why should I not do so?" I inquired.

"It, it makes me uncomfortable!" she said.

To be sure, the tunic was a bit long, and heavy, but her arms, at any rate, were bared.

"Please," she said.

"A slave," I said, "should hope that she would be so looked upon, and should hope that she would find favor in a man's eyes."

"Beast!" she said.

"You are a slave, are you not?" I asked.

"Certainly!" she said.

"And your master is Pertinax?" I said.

"—Yes!" she said.

"What is your brand?" I asked.

"I am not branded!" she said. "That is a cruel thing to do, and Pertinax, my master, has not had it done to me."

"A slave should be branded," I said.

"I am not branded," she said.

"Do I have your word on that?" I asked.

"Certainly!" she said.

I then went to her tunic, and, on the left side, lifted the tunic to the hip.

"Monster!" she wept, and pulled at the ropes.

The common branding site is the left thigh, just under the hip. The common tunic, of course, covers the brand. A side-slit tunic makes the brand easily detectible, and certain other garments, as well, for example the common camisk.

"Do not!" she said, pulling away.

Some masters, after all, are left-handed.

"Beast, beast!" she said.

I smoothed down the tunic, on both sides, and she pressed back, against the slim trunk of the tree, and turned her head, angrily, and looked to the side.

"You are not branded," I said, "at least not obviously."

"I told you that," she said, angrily.

"I thought you might be lying," I said.

"I was not," she said.

"A slave should be branded," I said. "It is an explicit recommendation of Merchant Law."

"My master is too kind to brand me," she said.

"It is not a matter of kindness," I said. "It is simply something to be done with a slave, routinely."

"Well, I am not branded," she said, turning to look at me, angrily.

"You are sure you are a slave?" I asked.

"—Certainly," she said. "If you look closely, perhaps you can see that I am in a collar!"

"Do you like your collar?" I asked.

"Of course not," she said. "It is humiliating, degrading, and hateful."

"Is it uncomfortable?" I asked.

"No," she said.

"Most slave girls love their collars," I said. "Many would not trade them for the world."

"I see," she said.

"They are certificates of their attractiveness, that they are of interest to men, that they have been found worth collaring."

"I see," she said.

"Collar!" I snapped.

"What?" she said.

She had not lifted her head, exposing her throat and the encircling collar.

I approached her and examined the collar. "This collar is not engraved," I said. "Should it not identify you as the property of Pertinax, of Port Kar?"

"It is a plain collar," she said.

"Doubtless it is locked," I said.

"Certainly," she said. "I am a slave."

I turned the collar, and tested the lock, and then turned it, again, so that the lock was at the back of the neck.

"You see!" she sniffed.

That she seemed so calm about this convinced me that she

had access to the key, that either it would be within the hut, or, perhaps, more likely, on her person. It seemed clear to me, from what I had seen of her relationship with Pertinax, her supposed master, he would not have it.

I was reasonably certain she would be terrified if the key were not in her own possession.

In the hut, it might be available to others.

I supposed, then, that the key would be about her person, somewhere.

"What are you doing?" she said.

"Here," I said, "at the hem."

"Do not!" she wept, trying to pull away.

It was a moment's work, with the point of my knife, to free the key, which I then held before her.

She averted her head, in misery.

I wondered if she knew the penalties to which a Gorean slave might be subject, for such a crime.

I supposed not.

"Come back!" she cried.

I had turned about and walked down, toward the shore, and stood there, my ankles in the lapping water.

"No!" she begged.

I spun the key far out into the waves.

"No, no!" she called.

I then returned to where I had left her.

"The collar is locked!" she said. "I cannot take it off!"

"That is common with female slaves," I said.

"You do not understand!" she hissed.

"What do I not understand?" I asked.

"Nothing, nothing," she said, sullenly.

"Do not fear," I said. "With proper tools the collar may be easily removed. Any metal worker, with the proper tools, could manage the business without difficulty."

"Beast!" she said.

"How does it feel to be collared, truly collared?" I asked.

"I hate you!" she said.

"Now that you are truly collared," I said, "I think certain other adjustments would be in order."

"Stop!" she said.

But, tied, as she was, she could not deter my work, and I carefully, without being extreme, or excessive, in the matter, shortened the skirt of her tunic in such a way that it would be more typical in length for that of a Gorean slave girl.

"Beast, monster!" she hissed.

"I do not think Pertinax will mind," I said. "And if he wishes to shorten it further, to make it truly 'slave short,' or 'slave delightful,' he is free to do so."

"Do you not understand!" she exclaimed. "If someone sees me like this, they will take me for a slave!"

"You are a slave, are you not?" I asked.

"—Yes, yes," she whispered.

"And I did not slit the skirt at the left thigh," I said, "so Goreans will assume it is branded. If it were discerned that it lacked the brand, they would doubtless soon see that the oversight, one scarcely pardonable, was remedied."

In her distress I do not think she even understood what I was saying.

I then fastened my hands at the neckline of the tunic.

"No," she said. "No!"

"Why not?" I asked.

"I am not a slave!" she said. "I am a free woman!"

"Perhaps you are a slave and do not even know you are a slave," I said.

"No, no!" she said. "I am free, free!"

I did not remove my hands from the neckline of the tunic.

"Speak!" I said.

"I was hired!" she said.

"You and Pertinax," I said.

"Yes!" she said.

"To whom are you in fee?" I inquired.

"Men," she said, "anonymous. I was approached on Earth, and it was I who recruited he whom you know as Pertinax."

"Your Gorean is acceptable," I said.

"We were given weeks of intensive training on Earth," she said, "and more on Gor."

"Continue," I said.

"I was given a retainer of one hundred thousand dollars,"

she said, "and so, too, was Pertinax, and we are to receive one million dollars each at the accomplishment of our mission."

"The deposit was seemingly made to a given bank, one selectively chosen, and you were furnished with what appeared to be documentation of this," I said. "But I am confident the money was never in actuality deposited."

She regarded me, wildly.

"To be sure," I said, "you were doubtless given funds, which led you to believe the business was in earnest."

"More than five thousand dollars," she said.

"I see," I said.

"I shall collect the rest when I am returned to Earth," she said.

"Of course," I said.

"I shall return to Earth shall I not?" she said.

"You are on Gor, girl," I said, "and on Gor you will remain."

"No," she said. "No!"

"And there will be others," I said, "as greedy, and foolish, as you."

Wide were her eyes.

"You are, doubtless unknowingly, a minion of a life form known as Kurii," I said. "Kurii, however one views them, have a sense of honor, a sense of what is appropriate, of what is proper. I assure you they have little respect for traitresses."

"I do not believe you!" she said.

"As you wish," I said.

"What would be my fate?" she asked.

"You are nicely faced, and figured," I said.

"No!" she said.

"It would amuse Kurii," I said, "that you would sell for a handful of coins."

"You are trying to frighten me," she said.

"You were not to be trusted," I said. "Why should you expect that others were to be trusted?"

"I will not be frightened!" she insisted.

"When the iron is put to your thigh," I said, "you will know what you are."

"No!" she said.

"Then you will finally be worth something. Someone will get some good out of you."

"No!" she said.

"Continue to improve your Gorean," I said. "You may be well whipped for errors."

"Let me go!" she said.

"But we have not finished our chat," I said.

"Release me," she said. "What if someone should see me as I am?"

"What is your role here?" I asked.

"Surely you do not expect me to speak," she said.

"As you wish," I said.

My hands tightened at the neckline of her garment.

"Do not!" she said. "You are of the warriors. You have codes. I am free, a free woman! I am not to be touched! I am to be treated with respect and dignity! I am not a slave! I am a free woman!"

I removed my hands from her garment, and stepped back.

"Now untie me," she said.

I left her bound.

She did have nice legs. Such women put a strain on the codes.

"I think," I said, "that you are indeed a free woman, but, you must remember, you are one of Earth, not Gor. There is a considerable difference. For example, you have no Home Stone."

"What is a Home Stone?" she said.

"Surely you have heard of them," I said.

"Yes," she said, "but I do not understand them."

"I am not surprised," I said.

She pulled at the bonds.

"Do not look at me like that!" she said.

"Do you not know how appealing to a man is the sight of a bound woman?" I asked. "Masters not unoften bind their slaves and order them to squirm. The slave then is well reminded of her dependency and helplessness. And the master, for his part, now knows the slave is wholly his, prostrate at his mercy, and he finds this pleasant, and stimulating. Too, the woman is aroused, as well, and knowing herself helpless, and wholly in the master's power, is soon beside herself with readiness. This has much to do with dominance/submissive ratios, which are pervasive in nature. Too, much can be accomplished along these lines by merely dressing the woman as one pleases, and seeing to her obedience and service. The master/slave relationship is extensive and complex. It is not all a matter of putting the slave to one's pleasure, though, to be sure, without that it is nothing."

She then stood very still.

"Yes," I said. "Women such as you strain the codes."

"I am free," she said. "Free!"

"Yes," I said, "you are a free woman, but one of Earth. You do not have the status of a Gorean free woman. Compared to a Gorean free woman, sheltered by her Home Stone, secure within her walls, complacent in the unquestioned arrogance of her station, the women of Earth do not even understand what it is to be free. The Gorean free woman is glorious in her freedom. The free women of Earth are no more than the sort of women that Gorean slavers think nothing of enslaving. They see the women of Earth not as free women, but only as slaves who have not yet been put in their collars."

"I am a woman of Earth!" she said.

"Precisely," I said.

"Monster!" she said.

"But it is true," I said, "that you are a free woman of Earth, at least as far as those women can be free, and thus that my codes, though the matter is controversial, much depending on interpretations, do suffice to give me pause."

"Excellent," she said. "Now release me."

"But you have not yet explained your role here," I said, "nor that of Pertinax."

"Nor is it my intention to do so," she said.

"Very well," I said.

"Untie me," she said.

I turned about, and looked out to sea. I was now sure of it. What had been hitherto no more than a dot on the horizon, perhaps no more than a sea bird resting on the waves, even sleeping, as they do, was now clearly, though still small, and far off, a sail.

"There is a ship," I said, shading my eyes.

"There have been such ships," she said, straining her eyes, pulling against her bonds, looking outward, toward the horizon.

"One came in yesterday," I said, "from which were disembarked, following the surmises of Pertinax, your subordinate, and not master, bandits, brigands, or such."

"Untie me! Untie me, swiftly!" she begged.

I wondered if an agent, or agents, of Priest-Kings might be aboard that vessel, now so far off, now seeming so tiny.

"Untie me, now!" she cried.

"As you are a free woman," I said, "even though one of Earth, I have treated you with some circumspection. In the codes such matters are gray, for it is commonly supposed that a Home Stone would be shared. If you were a slave, of course, whether of Earth or not, the matter would not even come up. Too, as you may not understand, even a Gorean free woman is expected to show a fellow respect, as another free person. If she insults him, belittles him, ridicules him, or treats him in any way which he deems improper or unbecoming, sometimes even to the glance, depending on the fellow, she is considered as having put away the armor of her status, and may be dealt with as the male sees fit. This is particularly the case if there is no shared Home Stone. Other situations are also regarded as ones in which the woman has voluntarily, or inadvertently, divested herself of the social and cultural mantles usually sufficient to protect her freedom and honor, such as walking the high bridges at night, undertaking dangerous expeditions or voyages, traversing lonely areas of a city, entering into a paga tavern, and so on."

"There is a ship there!" she said. "I can see it clearly!"

"Yes," I said.

"Can they see us?" she asked, desperately.

"Perhaps," I said. "They may have a glass of the Builders."

"If they see me here," she cried, "half naked, bound, collared, what will they do with me?"

"Put you on a chain, of course," I said.

"But I am free!" she said.

"Perhaps for the better part of an Ahn, or so," I said.

"I am free," she said. "Your codes! Your codes! You must protect me!"

"My codes do not require that," I said.

"You would not leave me here as I am!" she cried.

"You are mistaken," I said. "That is precisely what I will do."

I then turned away, to withdraw into the forest.

"Wait!" she begged. "Wait!"

I turned to face her.

"I will speak, I will speak!" she cried.

"As you will," I said.

"Untie me!" she cried. "Let us hide! They can see us here. They may have already seen us here."

"Possibly," I said.

"Untie me!" she begged, wildly.

"Speak first," I said.

"We were brought here, Pertinax and I, by a disk craft, and told to wait for you," she wept. "We were to encounter you, and show you hospitality, and then conduct you into the forest, to a rendezvous. Pertinax knows the place. He has been there. The trail is marked."

"What sort of rendezvous," I asked, "with whom, and to what purpose?"

"I know little," she said, "save that they would enlist your services."

"My services are not easily enlisted," I said.

"They will have a hold over you," she said. "A woman."

"What woman?" I asked.

"I do not know!" she cried.

"I understand little of this," I said.

"It has to do with tarns, and a ship, a great ship," she said.

"What woman?" I asked. "What woman?"

"I do not know," she said.

I untied her hands and she pulled away from the tree, weeping, and fled back some yards into the forest. There I saw her stop for a moment and tear wildly, hysterically, at her collar. She could not, of course, remove it. It was nicely on her, a typical Gorean collar of the higher latitudes, sturdy, flat, close-fitting. She tried to jerk down the hem of the shortened tunic, on both sides, but it sprang upward again. She then cried out in misery, and disappeared into the trees, presumably to warn Pertinax.

Presumably he would see her differently now, given the alterations to her tunic. And he would note, too, from its shortening, and the ragged lower edges, that the key was no longer in its place.

Yes, I thought, he would doubtless see her differently now.

And doubtless she would be well aware that she would now be being seen differently.

To be sure, I did not think she had anything to fear from Pertinax. It would be quite different, of course with a Gorean male.

I then turned to note the ship, now something like a hundred yards off shore.

It was a round ship, more deeply keeled, more broadly beamed, than the long ship.

It would not beach.

A longboat was being put in the water.

It had four rowers and a helmsman, and one individual forward.

The individual forward, I supposed, would be he for whom I had been waiting, the agent of Priest-Kings.

I suspected that Constantina would by now be at the hut, begging, perhaps on her knees, in her desperation, and as she was now clothed, Pertinax to flee.

To be sure, it mattered little to me that she might observe the arrival of the newcomer.

Chapter Five

An Old Acquaintance Is Renewed; A New Ship Arrives, and Discharges Passengers and Cargo; I Obtain Considerable Intelligence, but Not Enough

He waded ashore.

The longboat did not beach.

"You?" I said.

"From the time of the Five Ubars, in Port Kar," he said.

"Before the ascendancy of the Council of Captains," I said.

"It has been a long time," he said.

"Do not approach too closely," I said.

"I am unarmed," he said, opening his hands and holding them to the sides. "But others are not."

I did not unsheathe my weapon.

Two of the oarsmen from the longboat were in the water to their waists, and each held a crossbow, with a quarrel readied in the guide.

The other two oarsmen, oars outboard, and the helmsman, his hand on the tiller, nursed the boat, keeping it, as it was turned, muchly parallel to the shore. It could be easily swung about.

"Sullius Maximus," I said.

"Officer to Chenbar, of Kasra, Ubar of Tyros," he said.

"Traitor to Port Kar," I said. "Mixer of poisons."

He bowed, humbly.

"You recall," he said, smiling.

"But you brewed an antidote," I remarked.

"Not of my own free will," he smiled.

He had been infected with his own toxin, which produced, in time, a broad paralysis, that he might prepare, if time permitted, its remedy. His lord, Chenbar, had not approved of poisoned steel, and I had once spared the Ubar's life, on the 25th of Se'Kara. The antidote, proven in the case of Sullius Maximus, had been conveyed to Port Kar.

"I am pleased to see you are looking well," said Sullius Maximus.

"How is it that I find you here?" I asked.

"Surely you know," he said.

"Scarcely," I said.

"Surely you do not think this is some eccentric coincidence," he said.

"No," I said.

"You are waiting for the agent of Priest-Kings," he said.

I was silent.

"I am he," he said.

"No," I said.

"How else would I know of your location?"

"Kurii know," I said.

"Who are Kurii?" he said.

"You do not know?" I said.

"No," he said.

"How is it that you, an agent of Priest-Kings, know not of Kurii?"

"To serve our lords, the masters of the Sardar," he said, "one needs know no more than they deem suitable."

"Perhaps they are your lords," I said. "They are not mine."

"Are they not the lords of us all," he said, "are they not the gods of Gor?"

"And are the Initiates not their ministers and servitors," I said.

"One must allow all castes their vanities," he said.

"Doubtless," I said.

"I understand," he said, "that you have labored, now and then, on behalf of Priest-Kings."

"Perhaps," I said.

"I find their choice of agents strange," he said. "You are a barbarian, more of a larl than a man. You know little of poetry, and your kaissa is commonplace."

"My kaissa is satisfactory," I said, "for one who is not a Player."

"You are not even a caste or city champion," he said.

"Are you?" I inquired.

"Games are for children," he said.

"Kaissa is not for children," I said. Life and death sometimes hung on the outcomes of a kaissa match, and war or peace. Cities had been lost in such matches, and slaves frequently changed hands.

Too, the game is beautiful.

Its fascinations, as those of art and music, exercise their spells and raptures.

"To be sure," he said, "you do have, I gather, a certain audacious expertise in certain forms of vulgar weaponry."

"Less sophisticated and urbane, doubtless," I said, "than the administrations of poisons."

"Do not be bitter," he said. "All that was long ago, and seasons change."

"Seasons, like enmities, and tides, return, do they not?" I asked.

"I come to you in friendship," he said, "as partisans in a common cause."

"I do not think you are an agent of Priest-Kings," I said.

"I find it difficult, too," he said, "to suppose that you are an agent of Priest-Kings."

"I do not think of myself as such," I said.

"But you are here," he said.

"At the will of Priest-Kings, yes," I said, "but I do not know why."

"I am here to inform you," he said.

"How do I know you are an agent of Priest-Kings?" I asked.

"Perhaps I am an unlikely agent," he said. "Who am I to know? One might say the same of you, if you are indeed an agent. Who is to tell Priest-Kings who will be their instruments? Are you privy to their councils, can you read the mists, the fogs and clouds, which hover about the Sardar?"

I supposed it was possible that this man might be an agent of Priest-Kings. Doubtless they selected their human agents with an eye to probity and utility, not nobility, not honor. Too, the moralities of Priest-Kings might not be those of men, or of Kurii. Too, I knew there was a new dynasty in the Nest. The remnants of the older order might, by now, dispossessed and superseded, neglected and scorned, have long ago sought the pleasures of the Golden Beetle.

"You have some token, some sign, some credential, or such, which might testify to your legitimacy here, something which might certify your authenticity?"

"Certainly," he said, reaching within his tunic.

I tensed.

He smiled.

He withdrew a loop of leather from within the tunic, on which loop was fastened a golden ring. This ring was something like two inches in diameter, and the way it hung suggested its weightiness.

The golden circle, incidentally, is taken as the sign of Priest-Kings. Such circles are often carried by high Initiates, on golden chains about their necks. Too, they are likely to appear on the walls, and over the gates, and such, of temples, and, within temples, they invariably surmount altars. Staffs surmounted with this symbol are often carried by Initiates, as well, and such staffs invariably figure in their ceremonial processions. The gold is the symbol of that which is rare, is precious, is constant, and does not tarnish. The circular form is a symbol of eternity, that which has no beginning, that which has no end. The blessings of Initiates are accompanied by the sign of Priest-Kings, a circular motion of the right hand. These blessings, on feast days, may be bestowed on the faithful without cost. Sometimes, of course, such blessings must be purchased. The favor of Priest-Kings is not easily obtained, and Initiates, as other castes, must live.

"Anyone," I said, "might fix a ring of gold on a leather string."

"That is how you know its authenticity," said Sullius Maximus. "For those endeavoring in fraud, to abet a ruse, would surely fix the ring on a chain of gold."

"May I see the ring?" I said.

I was not interested in the ring, of course, but the leather string, for leather can absorb certain substances, such as oil, or the exudates of a communicative organ.

Sullius Maximus cast me the ring, on its leather loop. He did not care to approach me too closely. I did not blame him. Might not a knife swiftly, like a striking viper, dart from its sheath, find its home in a startled heart, and might not the very body of that heart serve an assassin as shield, sheltering the assailant from the vengeance of the crossbows' metal-finned, soon-flighted penetrant iron?

I pretended to examine the gold. I lowered my head respectfully to the symbol, as one might salute the Sardar, but I kept my eyes raised, to keep in view its purveyor. The string, in which I was primarily interested, was bunched in my hand, close to the ring, and I took its scent. Without a translator I had no hope of deciphering the scent, but I recognized the voice, so to speak, of Priest-Kings, who communicate by scent. I had no doubt that that leather had been impressed with the message of Priest-Kings.

But I had no way of reading it.

I did not inquire of Sullius Maximus the location or fate of an appropriate translator, for I was confident he knew nothing of such a device.

It was lighter now, and I examined the string, visibly. On it, in two places, there were reddish brown stains.

"The string is soiled," I said.

"Is it?" he asked.

"Blood," I said.

"Interesting," he said. "It was given to me as it is."

"I do not doubt that it came into your possession rather as it is," I said.

He bowed his head, in assent.

I now knew I would not be met here by an agent of Priest-Kings.

The agent of Priest-Kings had been intercepted.

How then would I know the will of the denizens of the Sardar, even to judge whether or not I should honor it, or endeavor to comply with it?

"You have been to the Sardar?" I asked.

"Yes," he said, looking at me, narrowly.

"Recently?"

"Of course, to be given the ring, and the message."

"What are the Priest-Kings like?" I asked.

"Surely you know," he said.

"Tell me," I said.

"They are like us," he said.

"I am pleased to hear it," I said.

"Only larger, stronger, more powerful," he said.

"Of course," I said.

"As befits gods," he said.

"Of course," I said.

"I recognize, and respect, and honor, your caution," he said. "But now, if you are satisfied, I will execute my charge. I will deliver the message of Priest-Kings, and withdraw."

"You received this message," I said, "from the great Priest-King, Lord Sarm?"

"—Yes," he said.

Sarm, of course, years ago, had succumbed to the pleasures of the Golden Beetle. I was reassured, then, that the Kurii still knew little of the denizens of the Sardar.

It is difficult to do contest with an enemy which is both mysterious and powerful.

I had little love for Priest-Kings, but theirs was the law and the rod which held in check the inventive and indiscreet aggressions of humans on this, their world. Had it not been for the governance of Priest-Kings, and their surveillance, and the enforcement of their prohibitions on technology and weaponry, I had little doubt that the suspicions, fears, and simian ingenuity of my species on Gor would have by now produced lethalities equivalent to, if not superior to, the madnesses which currently threatened the destruction of another world, the ruination of another habitat, the extinction of an indigenous species, my own, on that other world. The paw which first grasped a jagged stone can eventually become the hand which can, with the pressing of a switch, eliminate continents. How easy it is to poison atmospheres, and how easy, soon, to set axes awry, and roll a world into a star's flaming maw. I supposed that the human species was one of the few species with the capacity to render itself extinct. I doubted that the Priest-Kings were overly concerned with the welfare of humans, but it seemed clear that they had no intention of sharing the psychotic pastimes of such a species, or of enduring the consequences of its stupidities, hence their weapon and technology laws. But the shield of Priest-Kings was concerned not only to protect their own world from the potential dangers of an eventually advanced and technologically armed humanity, mostly, originally, brought over millennia to Gor in Voyages of Acquisition for its biological interest, as were many other forms of animal life not native to the world, but, as well, from the incursions of a particularly acquisitive and predatory life form, the Kurii. Too, interestingly, the sheltering wing of the Priest-Kings, her declared protectorate, extended beyond Gor to another world as well, to her sister world, Earth. It, and its resources, were to be protected from Kurii. Let Kurii be denied Earth, with its wealth of water and hydrogen, be denied such a foothold and platform for their projects, so splendid a staging area for an approach to Gor. Let them remain, rather, in their distant, isolated, metal worlds, confined to an alien wilderness, an archipelago of debris between Mars and Jupiter, the Reefs of Space, the Asteroid Belt. It was interesting, I thought, that those of Earth owed so much, their world as they knew it, to an unknown benefactor, a form of life whose very existence was unknown to them. To be sure, I was confident that the motivations of Priest-Kings were self-serving and prudential, not moral, or at least not moral as humans might understand such things. If there were agendas here they were not ours; they were those of the Sardar.

"What is the message of Priest-Kings?" I asked.

"First," said he, "return to me the ring."

"Should I not keep it?" I asked.

"No," he said. "It is meaningless to you. It is important to me. It is my token, my proof, that I speak for Priest-Kings."

"You are to speak further," I asked, "to others, at other times?"

"I do not know," he said. "Put the ring down, on the sand. Step away. I will pick it up."

To be sure, I had no translator, and was, accordingly, unable to read the message. I wondered if Sullius Maximus suspected that some significance, other than that which he had conjectured, might lie within the leather loop of the golden ring. He was a highly intelligent man. That was surely not impossible.

"Did Lord Sarm give you the token," I asked, "in a box, a container, of some sort?"

Sullius Maximus regarded me, suddenly, alertly.

Yes, I thought, he is quite intelligent.

Presumably the agent of Priest-Kings, he who had been intercepted, would have had about himself not only the message but a translator. The translator would presumably, as it was outside the Sardar, open only to a code, and only at a certain time, and for a certain time. Presumably there would have been a schedule or envelope of two or three days in which it might have been utilized. The agent would have been instructed to process the leather band, which was, in effect, a scent tape, only in my presence, or, more likely, supply me with the code, and then withdraw. The scent itself, given its nature, as a covert message, would fade after a time, not having been imprinted permanently on the tape. These would seem fairly obvious security measures.

"There was a box," said Sullius Maximus.

"But it was unusual, was it not?" I asked.

"Quite," said Sullius Maximus.

I was sure that Sullius Maximus, and his presumed fellows, would have supposed the message was in the box, which was, in fact, unknown to them, either the translator, or contained the translator, and would have tried to open it. I did not think they would associate the ring, on its leather cord, with the box itself. I had little doubt that their efforts had been attended with surprising results. I remembered a metal envelope in which I had received a message, years ago, on a solitary camping trip, in the winter, in the White Mountains of New Hampshire. I had neglected to follow the instructions, to discard the envelope. It had burst suddenly into flame. The fearful destruction of the object not only destroyed it, but was such that it might have blinded one in whose hands it lay, or burned them alive. It had been in my knapsack and I had managed to slip it free and let it fall to the snow, which it melted, for yards about.

"In what way?" I asked.

"—Ornate," said Sullius Maximus, "small, crusted with jewels, such things."

"I see," I said.

I wondered if one or more of his confederates had been incinerated. Doubtless the agent of Priest-Kings would have resisted capture, and would have been quickly, brutally slain, it being presupposed that his life would be of small value, that he was the mere carrier of the message, a message presumably in the box, and the token, which they would have supposed was his identification, his certification to be the one to whom the Priest-Kings had entrusted the transmission of the message.

Sullius Maximus, and his fellows, then, would be unaware of the contents of the actual message.

But then, so, too, was I.

To be sure, the actual nature of the message, which might have been suspected by Kurii, and which, in any event, they would not have delivered to me, would be of less interest to them than the message, their message, which they would want delivered to me, as though it were the message of Priest-Kings. The will of Kurii then would be conveyed to me under the pretense that it was the will of Priest-Kings. If their designs held firm, and their deception was successful, I would then, supposing me obedient to Priest-Kings, pursue their design in place of that of the masters of the Sardar.

Given the presumed destruction of the "box," supposed to contain the original message, presumably on its scroll, the Kurii, or their minions, utilizing the "token," not understanding the nature of its imbedded message, and accommodating themselves to the situation as best they might, would deliver their own message orally.

Fortunately for me, they knew little of the Sardar, of Priest-Kings themselves, of their modalities of communication, of their caution, of their security measures.

"The ring, please," said Sullius Maximus.

I put the ring, on its loop, down on the sand, and backed away from it.

Sullius Maximus approached it and, not taking his eyes from me, picked it up.

"My thanks," said he.

"Smell the leather," I said. "It seems to have been perfumed."

"I know," he said. "But I doubt the perfume would be popular in the paga taverns of Kasra."

"Nor elsewhere," I speculated.

He held it briefly to his nose, and then, with an expression of disgust, returned the loop and ring to a concealment within his tunic.

"Perhaps it would do for a free woman," I said, "intent on discouraging the avidity of a suitor."

"No," he said. "Free women are women, and they desire to be desired. It gives them great pleasure to attract, and then deny and torment suitors. They find it gratifying. It is an exercise of power."

"True," I said. Gorean free women were famed for their arrogance and pride. It was little wonder that men often took such things from them. What a terror for a free woman, reduced to bondage, to know that spurned suitors may find her, even seek her out, and buy her. When a woman is stripped and collared, and knelt, and has the whip pressed to her then unveiled lips, she is scarcely any longer in a position to discomfort and torment a fellow. Rather she must then be seriously concerned for her life, and hope that she will be found pleasing, and fully.

"It was much stronger a few days ago," he said. "The scent has faded, significantly."

"Even since yesterday?" I asked.

"Yes," he said, puzzled.

The agent of Priest-Kings was to have contacted me yesterday, I supposed, the day I had arrived on the beach, disembarked from Peisistratus's ship. Instead I had been met by Pertinax.

"If you find it offensive," I said, "you might clean the cord, wipe it free of scent—and blood."

"I will," he said, "now."

"Now?" I said.

"I thought the odor might be pertinent to the authenticity of the token," he said. "I noted that you took the scent."

"You are perceptive," I said.

"But the scent is fading," he said. "If I accept an office anew from Priest-Kings, they will doubtless provide a new signature string, with the appropriate scent."

"Thus you would clean the soiled string?"

"Yes," he said.

"Why not discard it?" I said.

Whereas I was not sure the message was still readable, and I had no translator at my disposal, even if it were readable, I would have been concerned to retrieve the cord.

"No," he said. "I think it best to keep the whole intact, lest inquiries arise."

"I would suppose," I said, "the ring is the token."

"But on a strand of leather, not a golden chain," he said.

"Doubtless you are right," I said.

"Do you think the odor is important?" he asked.

"I do not know," I said. "It might, as you suggest, be relevant to the authenticity of the token."

"You took its scent," he said.

I shrugged. "The odor was odd," I said. "I was curious."

"It meant nothing to you?"

"Little or nothing," I said.

"I speculate," he said, "you know as little of this as I."

"I fear so," I said. Certainly I had no idea what might have been the message of the string.

Then the helmsman in the longboat called out, "Hurry!" He was looking about. I looked out, across the water. A narrow spume of smoke rose from the round ship, near its bow. This was, I supposed, a signal to return to the ship. Such signals are silent, and in waters where it might be wise to be wary, drums or horns would not be used. At night, dark lanterns, shuttered and unshuttered, may be used. Other devices, more common on ships of war, in similar situations, are flags and banners. Needless to say there are codes involved, which may be changed when deemed appropriate.

Sullius Maximus backed away a step or two, looked briefly back, to the round ship, some hundred yards offshore. It had begun now to come about, its bow moving, turning, toward the horizon.

"It is dangerous here," he said. "I must hasten."

"Hurry," called the fellow at the tiller, again. The two oarsmen turned the longboat toward the round ship.

"How, how dangerous?" I asked.

Certainly he had two crossbowmen at his back. And the beach was open several yards behind me. He was beyond a cast of the spear. This was a remote area. To be sure, he was well within the purview of a longbow.

"Attend," said he, "fellow partisan of the plans of Priest-Kings, attend the commands of the Sardar!"

"What is your sudden concern?" I asked.

I saw no new sail on the horizon.

Something, of course, might have been seen from the height of the permanent mast of the round ship. A lookout is often posted there, with a Builder's glass. He stands on a small platform, and is usually roped to the mast, or has his place within a chest-high ring of metal. The masts of the common Gorean warship are commonly lowered before entering battle. This makes the ship more amenable to her oars and less vulnerable to flaming missiles, which might ignite a sail on its long, sloping yard.

I wondered that Sullius Maximus had not been conveyed hither in a long ship. Surely Tyros has one of the most formidable fleets on Thassa.

Perhaps this had little to do with Tyros?

Perhaps a round ship would raise less suspicion?

Perhaps this was the very ship on which the agent of Priest-Kings might have had his passage?

"I speak in the name of Priest-Kings," said Sullius Maximus, swiftly, as though by rote. "You are to attend me intently, and are to obey with perfection."

"I am a free man," I reminded him.

"Hear the will of Priest-Kings!" he said.

And so I prepared to hear the will of Kurii.

"You are to enter the forest," said Sullius Maximus, "and seek out a forester, by name, Pertinax. The hut is nearby. You will know him by name, and by his possession, a blond-haired, blue-eyed slave. She is barbarian. She has tiny bits of metal in two of her teeth, and a tiny brand on her upper left arm. Her name is Constantina. They are to conduct you within the forest, to a rendezvous with a mariner from west of Tyros and Cos."

That interested me, for few ships voyaged to the west of those maritime ubarates. There were, of course, some islands beyond Tyros and Cos, some smaller islands, spoken of, commonly, as the Farther Islands. I supposed, thus, that the "mariner," if he were a mariner, must be from one of the Farther Islands. I was personally unaware of any who had sailed beyond those islands, and returned.

What Sullius Maximus had referred to as a brand on the upper left arm of Constantina was doubtless a vaccination mark. Few, if any, of the maladies which immunization was designed to prevent on Earth existed on Gor. It was natural for Goreans, hence, to suppose that this form of scarring was a brand, a deliberately inflicted mark, though not necessarily one indicative of bondage. Ritual scarring was not unknown on Gor, for example amongst certain of the Wagon Peoples of the southern plains, certain tribes south and east of Schendi, in the vicinity of the Ua, and so on. The girls were, of course, barbarians. Some Goreans supposed the tiny marks were "selection marks," marks identifying choice females, suitable for eventual enslavement. This misunderstanding was presumably fostered by the fact that the great majority of Earth females brought to Gor were, in their variety of ways, choice merchandise or, to speak vulgarly, superb "block meat."

"You are to take your orders from this person, or his superiors," said Sullius Maximus.

"I do not understand what is going on here," I said.

"Your duties will be explained to you," said Sullius Maximus.

"What is the name of this 'mariner'?" I asked.

"Nishida," he said. "Lord Nishida."

"Hurry! Hurry!" called the fellow at the tiller of the longboat.

Sullius Maximus then turned about, and hurried toward the shore.

He waded into the surf and, when he had boarded the small craft, the two fellows with crossbows followed him, and, in moments, their weapons stowed, they, and the other two oarsmen, were propelling the longboat toward the round ship. The fellow at the tiller had a steady hand, and the longboat was soon aside the round ship, and had been hoisted over the gunwales. At the same time the lateen sail was unfurled from its yard, and, swelling, took the wind, and the ship, like a stately bird, was aflight.

Sullius Maximus would have had no way of knowing that

I had already made the acquaintance of Pertinax and Lady Constantina, nor in any event would this have much mattered. The principal point of his contact with me, I supposed, was to convince me that I had now kept my appointment with the agent of Priest-Kings, and had thereby received my instructions from the Sardar. I would be thus relieved of any inclination to await that contact, my possible suspicions having been thusly allayed. Presumably, too, assuming I was compliant to the will of Priest-Kings, I would now naively prosecute the machinations of Kurii, confident that it was in the cause of Priest-Kings that I labored.

What I had learned from Pertinax and Lady Constantina, of course, was rather similar to that which I had learned from Sullius Maximus, which was only to be expected, as they, though perhaps unbeknownst to one another, were in league. From Pertinax I had gathered the rendezvous in the forest might take place tomorrow, or soon thereafter. From Sullius Maximus, I had gathered that it was to take place with a "mariner" called Nishida. That did not sound to me like a Gorean name. Similarly, he had spoken of "Lord Nishida," which suggested that the individual, if a mariner, at all, was not likely to be a common mariner. From Lady Constantina I had learned that a ship was somehow involved, and tarns. She had also suggested that I would be subject to a hold of some sort, presumably something that would guarantee my fidelity to the orders received. This hold, I had gathered, had something to do with a woman. I understood little of this.

Once this rendezvous had taken place it seemed to me unlikely that the Kurii would have further use for Lady Constantina. I rather doubted that she would be given to Pertinax, as he seemed still much of Earth. He did not seem to me a master. Naturally it would be appropriate to give a woman, particularly a good-looking woman, which Constantina was, only to a master.

They know what to do with such women.

I decided to return to the hut of Pertinax.

I supposed he would still be there, even if Lady Constantina would have urged flight. Too, I was sure Cecily would be there, as well. She had not been given permission to leave the area, nor did I think, in fact, she would wish to do so. Once, before, on a Steel World, she had fled. She had, of course, eventually, easily enough, a half-naked slave, branded and collared, been recovered. I had punished the Earth girl well for her indiscretion. She was now, as the saying is, more familiar with her collar. Now, the very thought of attempting to escape, or of even failing to be pleasing, and fully so, would fill her with terror.

Constantina, I had now discovered, was, as I had hitherto suspected, a free woman. I did not think she would inform Pertinax that I now knew her secret. It was, of course, one to which he would be privy. It would be important to her, surely, to try to retain her pretense of bondage, at least before Pertinax, when I was present. She would not be sure, too, of what consequences might accrue to her, from her employers, should they learn of her disclosures at the shore. Better to pretend things were as before. And, indeed, was her disguise not required of her, that she might, in relative safety, arousing little suspicion, negotiate the realms of Gor, her markets and streets, her fields and bridges, her wharves and roads? To Goreans, a free female of Earth would be surprising, at least. Too, there were few, if any, free women in the forests. These were not the locales to which a free woman would be likely to be brought, nor to which they would wish to come.

So now it seemed to me that I might well behave toward Lady Constantina, as before, as though I still accepted her as, and believed her to be, the slave of Pertinax. To be sure, it would now give me special pleasure to treat her as the slave she pretended to be. Let her, a proud, insolent free woman of Earth, used to the men of Earth, such as Pertinax, men whom she despised and might affront with impunity, and upon occasion, in virtue doubtless of wealth and authority, command, have to behave before me, and before Pertinax, as a mere slave.

I wondered if the adjustments I had made to her garmenture, and the fact that she no longer held the key to her collar, and could not now remove it, might help her have to have more of a sense of what it might be, to be a slave.

Certainly she would be uneasy.

I thought I would enjoy this.

And I was sure Cecily, too, would enjoy it.

Cecily, of course, believed her a slave, one, however, surprisingly in need of discipline.

Slaves desire to be kept in order, and certainly expect other slaves to be kept in order, as well. They find infractions of discipline almost incomprehensible, perhaps because they so seldom occur, and when they do, they are usually promptly and sharply punished. A slave expects to be punished if she is not pleasing. Indeed, if she knows herself to have been negligent or omissive, which sometimes occurs, she may beg to be punished, that she may feel that the balance, harmony, and order of her existence, of her very world, has been restored. If a slave is not treated as a slave she may become confused and frightened, for she knows she is a slave, and how she should be treated. Should a master begin to treat the slave as though she might be a free woman, she is likely to throw herself to his feet, and beg not to be sold.

The preciousness of the collar to the slave, and the fulfillments of her bondage, are not to be minimized. Commonly she lives to love and serve the master, to the best of her ability. She knows she is a slave, and how slaves are expected to behave. Accordingly that is how she does behave, as a slave.

Even free women, it seems, have some sense of these remarkable and profound fulfillments, and this accounts, one supposes, for their almost universal hostility toward, and contempt for, their embonded sisters.

The slave, it might be noted, is seldom, if ever, treated with gratuitous or wanton cruelty. She is subject to that, but what would be the point of it? To a Gorean such things would be incomprehensible, or absurd. What is important is the mastery, and firmness, to be sure a mastery and a firmness which is uncompromising and exacting, categorically and absolutely so, but also one which is commonly taken for granted, by both the master and the slave.

When a man has what he wants from a woman, a hot, helpless, grateful slave, one devoted and dutiful, a lovely property, vulnerable in his collar, why should he not be contented, well-disposed, and benevolent?

A man finds himself, a slave at his feet, and a woman finds herself, a slave, at the feet of her master.

And thus speaks the cave, the dances at campfires, and

thongs. And thus, in the enhancements of civilization, speak bracelets, the collar, and the block.

I wondered if I should gather in Cecily, and try to make my way south, eventually to Port Kar.

This might expose me, and my holding, and properties, ships, treasures, slaves, and such, to the reprimand of Priest-Kings, of course.

And if I slipped from the surveillance of Kurii, and their minions, this, too, might place much in jeopardy.

Pertinax, for example, who seemed a nice enough fellow, might be punished for having failed his more remote employers. I doubted that the displeasure of Kurii could be lightly borne.

Primarily, I suppose, I was curious.

I did not know the will of Priest-Kings, and so did not know either how to thwart it, or abet it, even if I wished to pursue one of these objectives. But, similarly, I did not know what project Kurii might have afoot.

But I was curious.

I decided I would remain in the forest.

Sometimes high warriors, city masters, Ubars, generals, and such, play "blind kaissa." Two boards are used, with an opaque barrier between the boards, so neither player can see the pieces of the other. An adjudicator observes both boards and informs the players whether a move is legal, whether a capture has been made, and so on. Thus, in a sense, the game is played in the dark. Gradually, however, from the adjudicator's reports, particularly if one has much experience of this version of kaissa, one begins to sense the positions and strategy of the opponent. This game is intended to intensify and heighten the intuitions of battle. In Gorean warfare, of course, as in much traditional warfare, prior to electronic sophistications, one is often uncertain of the position, strength, and plans of the enemy. Too much in war, and often much of fearful moment, is "blind kaissa."

And so, I thought, perhaps in the northern forests, I might try my hand at "blind kaissa."

I would return to the hut of Pertinax.

It was at this time that I, facing the sea, looked to my left, several hundred yards down the beach, and, too, several yards out to sea.

I now suspected the meaning of the signal smoke near the bow of the round ship, and why she had recalled her longboat, had swung about and unfurled her sail. Presumably, her lookout had espied, far to her starboard, another sail. Gorean ships seldom approach one another, and when they do, it is likely that one or both have piracy or war on their mind.

Yesterday I had gathered from Pertinax that ships, perhaps several, had come to the local shores, and disembarked fellows of a sort whose acquaintance he was not eager to make. Indeed, while I had been with him, yesterday, one such ship had disembarked a number of armed men.

A small ship was there, her sail furled. She had some ten oars to a side; she was smaller than my *Tesephone*. She was of a sort that might be used in messaging, or packet work. She had swung parallel to the shore, her bow south. Several men were spilling over her port side, perhaps twenty or more. Some boxes, too, perhaps supplies, of one sort or another, were cast overboard, and these were being guided by wading men to the shore, where they were drawn up on the beach. I then noted, lastly, another form of cargo, one that had not been on the earlier ship, items strung together, which were then rudely, unceremoniously, disembarked, plunged overboard into the chilly waters. These items then, some immersed, now and again, others trying desperately to hold their heads above the water, were dragged through the surf to the shore, and then, barefoot, stumbling, shuddering, were knelt on the wave-washed pebbled sand, water, coming and going, swirling about their knees and thighs, where they huddled together, heads down, several clutching their arms about themselves for warmth. I counted some fifteen, though it was hard to tell, at the distance, as they were crowded together. Sometimes such properties, so linked, are spoken of as a "slaver's necklace," pretty beads, so to speak, on a common string. In any event they were chained together, by the neck. The chain seemed heavier than necessary, and the collars were high and dark. If the girl kneels upright, her back straight, as slaves are commonly expected to kneel, she cannot well lower her head in such a collar. The head remains lifted to the master, which can be fearful for a slave. She lowers her head by bending at the waist. I surmised they were low slaves. To be sure, even recent free women are sometimes put in such devices, that they become that much the sooner accustomed to their condition, that they are no longer free, but are now goods, now properties, now slaves.

Pertinax would have fled such fellows, I suppose, but I was curious as to their origin, and their business here, in this remote area.

Too, I was armed.

So I approached them, as though I might have been waiting for them.

Doubtless they were to be met, in one way or another, either at the beach, or later, in the forest.

I lifted my hand. "Tal," I said.

"Tal," said a fellow, and then one or two or more.

"You are late," I said.

I had no idea if this were true or not, but the round ship which had recently departed, I was reasonably sure, had been late. Should it not have arrived yesterday, when I had been disembarked from the ship of Peisistratus?

"Adverse winds," said a fellow. "We were much under oars. The sea was high."

That accent, I conjectured, was Tyrian, or Cosian. They are muchly similar.

"How are things in Kasra?" I inquired. "In Jad?" These were, respectively, ports in Tyros and Cos.

One of the fellows looked at me, strangely.

"It is years since I saw Kasra," said a man.

"I have not seen the terraces of Cos since the fall of Ar," said another.

"They are mariners," said the fellow who had first returned my greeting. "Most here are fee fighters, mercenaries."

"You do not appear regulars," I granted him.

I watched the small ship dip her oars and begin to move south. After a time, a hundred yards or so from shore, she dropped her sail.

"There was another ship here," said a man. "We heard the lookout cry her position."

"A round ship," I said. "I could not persuade her to dally."

Several of the men laughed. It was a laugh which would not have reassured Pertinax.

"How are things in Ar?" I inquired.

"Have you not heard?" said a fellow, incredulously.

"No," I said.

"Ar has risen," said another. "Only by forced marches, on which many perished, were we able to elude vengeful citizens."

"Hundreds were captured, tortured, and impaled," said another.

"We, and some hundreds, fought to open the streets which had been barricaded against us, to prevent our egress, to pen us helplessly within that sea of fire and blood," said another, shuddering.

"Some of us," said a man, "apprised of the danger, wary to rumors, took what loot we could, what we had acquired in the occupation, and more, and slipped away, into the night, before the great bars rang the rebellion."

"Those were the fortunate ones," said a fellow, grimly.

"I do not understand," I said.

"You have heard of Marlenus," said a man, "surely?"

"Of course," said I, "Marlenus of Ar, of Glorious Ar, Ubar of Ubars."

"Long was he gone from Ar," said a fellow. "He disappeared, on a hunting trip, in the Voltai."

"As time went on, he was supposed dead," said a man. "Surely you know of the war betwixt Ar, and Tyros and Cos, and other polities?"

"Yes," I said.

A hundred war banners, I feared, had been unfurled.

"Fortunate it was for Tyros, Cos, and their allies," said a fellow, shuddering, "that Marlenus was absent from the city."

I supposed that so.

"Mercenaries, and mercenary bands, were recruited from dozens of states, even from brigand bands, from outlaw leagues, eager for loot."

There was some rueful laughter from several of the fellows about.

"These swelled the ranks of the spears of the island ubarates," said a fellow.

The strength of the maritime ubarates was surely in their fleets, not in their ground forces.

"Ar neglected precautions," said a man, incredulously. I wondered if he might not have been a banished warrior, from some city. I thought the scarlet would not have ill become him. "She failed to arm and deploy her formidable infantries."

"I see," I said.

These things I muchly knew.

I recalled that Dietrich of Tarnburg had fought a tenacious holding action at Torcodino, to delay the advance on Ar, to give her time to meet the avalanche, the swift confluences, of armed men who would descend upon her. But his action had been unavailing, and Ar had remained quiescent, even inert, though surely the screams of the tarns of war must have somehow reached her walls. Could they not heed the plaints of refugees, hear the drums of spearmen, sense the ponderous tread of war tharlarion? It soon became clear to many that conspiracy and treachery reigned within the Central Cylinder, and that the throne itself might now be festooned with the promises and wealth of the island ubarates. Ar, pathetic, confused, disorganized, and distraught, was unable to muster more than the feeblest of resistances, and these were muchly betrayed by commands from the Central Cylinder. Many of the best forces of Ar, her finest troops, her best officers, by intent, to divert them from the defense of the city, had been earlier ordered to the vast delta of the Vosk, to engage there in an alleged punitive expedition against supposed incursions from Cos and Tyros. These troops were deliberately undersupplied and misled. They were deliberately subjected to orders which were obscure or confused, even contradictory, orders the compliance with which would be almost suicidal in the terrain. These troops, as planned, had been decimated in the delta of the Vosk, and largely lost, the prey of heat and insects, of salt water and quicksand, of armed rencers, of serpents and tharlarion. Few, proportionately, had returned home. Some, dazed and starving, half mad, had reached the southern dikes of Port Kar, separating her from the delta. And when some managed to reach Ar, they found her surrendered to the enemy, garrisoned by the foe. Myron, *polemarkos* of the continental forces of Cos, he of Temos, cousin to Lurius of Jad, of Cos, was in command of the city, though he maintained a headquarters outside her *pomerium*. In this fashion it was proclaimed that Ar had been liberated and a new day had come about, one of harmony, peace, and amicability. Meanwhile the citizens of Ar were to believe their loss was a gain, their defeat a victory. They must atone now for the erstwhile glory of Ar, regret her former might, influence, and power. Now they must acknowledge her misdeeds, and celebrate her redemption by her friends and allies, the benign forces of Cos, Tyros, and their allies. And many sang, and congratulated themselves on their newly found virtue, while dismantling their walls to the scornful music of flute girls. Meanwhile, of course, the invaders tightened their controls and, for months, either randomly, as it pleased them, or systematically, in accord with the directives of the *polemarkos*, began to loot Ar of its wealth, its silver and gold, its jewelries and gems, its medical elixirs, its ointments and scents, its pagas and wines, its manufactures, its beasts, its slaves, and, in many cases, its free women, some put in paga taverns and brothels, others stripped and coffled, to be led to foreign markets, and some even, after transport from Brundisium, to Cos and Tyros themselves.

To be sure, all had not gone as smoothly as it might have for the invaders because, eventually, sporadic acts of resistance occurred. These were generally attributed to the work of a small group of resistance fighters, which became known as the Delta Brigade. Because of the vast, triangular spreading of the Vosk river, into dozens of smaller rivers, often mutually interfluent, flowing into the Tamber Gulf, which leads to Thassa herself, the sea, that area is known in Gorean as the Delka, or, better, the Delka of the Vosk. "Delka" is a triangular letter in Gorean, the fourth letter in her alphabet, derived, it seems, from the Greek letter "Delta." The core of the Delta Brigade was surmised to be composed of veterans returned from the misdirected and ill-fated campaign in the Vosk's delta, and thus the term "Delta Brigade."

"Tell me of the rising, the rebellion," I said.

"Woe to Cos and Tyros," said a fellow. "Marlenus returned."

"Where had he been, what had been his fate?" I asked.

"Much is unclear," said one of the fellows. "It seems he was injured in a fall, whilst hunting, lost his sense of self, wandered perhaps, no longer knew himself."

"Some think he might have been captured, and imprisoned in Treve," said a fellow.

"Impossible," said another.

"In any event," said a bearded fellow, "it seems he emerged from the Voltai, thought himself somehow of the Peasants, and labored with them."

"He was eventually recognized, in Ar," said another.

"It was said by a mere slave," said another.

"Interesting," I said.

"A female," said another.

"Was she then freed?" I asked.

Several of the men laughed.

"Forgive me," I said. "I spoke foolishly."

Gorean slaves were seldom freed. Indeed, there is a saying that only a fool frees a slave girl.

"Soon others recognized him, as well," said another.

"Then he was concealed by partisans," said another.

"He recovered his memory," I said.

"It was strange," said another.

"We know only the stories," said another.

"He was like a child, it seems," said another, "a powerful, dangerous child. He listened to what he was told. He learned what had occurred in the city, as it was patiently explained to him. He grew sorrowful, and then, slowly, angry. Then he said, 'But where is Marlenus?'"

"This elated his sheltering partisans," said another, "that he could recall that name. 'Where is Marlenus?' he asked, again, and again. 'He must return,' he was told. 'Where is he?' he asked. 'In the city, it is thought,' he was told."

"He did not know himself Marlenus?" I said.

"No," said one of the men.

"Continue," I said.

"'Who rules in Ar?' he asked," said the bearded fellow.

"'Truly, or in name?' inquired his interlocutor," said another. "And he wished to know in truth who ruled, and he was told Lurius of Jad, in far Cos, but through Myron, the *polemarkos*, with the collusion of Seremides, master of the Taurentians, the palace guard. And then he asked who then ruled in name, and men feared to tell him, that it was she who had once been his daughter, before her dishonoring, and disownment, for the slur she had once cast on his honor."

I knew something of this.

She had once been captured and enslaved by the tarnsman, Rask, of Treve, but he, having become, however unaccountably, enamored of a blond barbarian slave named El-in-or, gave her to Verna, a leader of Panther Girls, who took her to the northern forests. Later, on the northern coast, she was exposed for sale. There she had come within the cognizance of a slaver, Samos, first Captain in the Council of Captains of Port Kar. Eager to escape the toils of her cruel mistresses, and hoping that she might be returned to civilization, and even freed, she had begged him to buy her. And thusly had she performed a slave's act, begging to be purchased, for in this act one acknowledges oneself purchasable, and thus a slave. I, later, at the time unable to walk, and muchly paralyzed by the poison of Sullius Maximus, encountered her in the house of Samos. I had had her freed and returned to Ar. It was by then common knowledge how she had been slave, and in what fashion she had come into the keeping of Samos. The honor and pride of a man such as Marlenus of Ar, Ubar of Ar, Ubar of Ubars, refused to sustain indignities of this enormity. Such affronts could not be brooked by an honor such as his. What an insult, profound and grievous, was this to his blood, and to the throne of Ar! He thus disowned her as his daughter, and had had her sequestered in the Central Cylinder, that her shame might be concealed from the city and the world.

Had she not been free when she was delivered to Ar it is quite probable she would have been whipped and sold out of the city.

Had she, when free, and not slave, been guilty of a stain on the honor of Ar she might well have been publicly impaled.

"But he asked, again, and again, in his slow, childlike way, who now, be it only in name, ruled in Ar," said one of the men on the beach, "and the partisans took council, and decided to risk the disclosure, though they knew not what effect it might have."

"'Talena,' he was told," said another, "'daughter of Marlenus of Ar.'"

"Then," said another, "as the story has it, he lifted his head, and his whole mien changed, and his body seemed to become larger and filled with power, and his eyes took on a strange, fierce, wicked gleam, and he said, quietly, and not in his slow, innocent, puzzled, childlike voice, but in another voice, a voice like iron and ice, 'Marlenus of Ar has no daughter.'"

"The partisans looked to one another, their eyes alight," said a man.

"It is then," said another, "as the story goes, that he stood upright amongst the partisans, like a larl amongst panthers, and said, 'Bring me a banner of Ar.'"

"'Who are you?' he was asked, 'that you dare ask for a banner of Ar?'" said another. "'They have been forbidden,' said a partisan. 'They are concealed.'"

"'Bring me a banner,' he said, 'one large, and broad.' 'Furled or unfurled?' he was asked. 'Furled,' he said, 'that it may then be unfurled.'"

"The partisans then gasped, realizing who it was who then stood amongst them."

"'Who would dare unfurl the banner of Ar?' he was asked."

"'I,' he said, 'Marlenus, Ubar of Ar.'"

The unfurling of a furled banner, in given circumstances, when this is accomplished deliberately, slowly, and ritualistically, is far more than a sign of war; it is a sign of unappeasable purpose, of unmitigated intent, of implacable resolution. More than once the surrender of cities has not been accepted, but they have been leveled and burned, simply because a banner had been unfurled.

"'How many swords have we?' he is said to have asked, and then demanded maps of the city, that he might be shown the locations of intrusive garrisons. The men about him he appointed high officers, by his word alone."

This was possible, as the word of the Ubar takes precedence over councils.

"Had we known Marlenus was in the city," said a man, "we should have withdrawn."

"Word," said another, "was soon in the streets, and it swept from *insula* to *insula,* and to the lesser cylinders."

"But we were not immediately aware of this," said a man. "Surely the great bar had not yet rung, signaling the rising."

"They planned swiftly, and well," said another fellow, shuddering.

"Weapons had been forbidden to the populace," said another, but many had been concealed, and there is little which may not figure as a weapon, axes and hammers, the implements of agriculture, planks, poles and sticks, the very stones of the streets."

I nodded. A tyrant state always wishes to disarm the public, for it understands its secret intents with respect to that public, and wants it at its mercy. This disarming is always, of course, alleged to be in the public's best interest, as though the public would be safest when least capable of defending itself.

"Many of Ar, particularly in the higher, richer cylinders," said a fellow, "had collaborated with us, had abetted the occupation, had shared in the looting of the city."

I supposed that was true. There were always such, in all cities, attentive to the directions of shifting winds.

"Proscription lists had been prepared," said another.

I shuddered.

"It was safer to be in the blue of a Cosian regular," laughed a man, "than in the satin robes of traitors."

I feared then for Talena, arrogant traitress, puppet Ubara, occupant of the throne on the sufferance of invaders, sullier of her Home Stone.

Marlenus had returned!

"We awakened at dawn," said a man, "startled, bewildered, to the ringing of the great bar, and rushed into the streets, to be met with steel and stones. They swarmed from everywhere, struck from everywhere. An arsenal had been seized. The cry of battle, 'For Glorious Ar,' was all about us. We cut down what we could, but they were everywhere, screaming, rushing at us. A fellow would kill two, and have his throat cut by a third."

"We were outnumbered, dozens to one," said a man.

"They were maddened, merciless," said another. "Like starving blood-maddened sleen!"

"They had planned well," said another. "A thousand avenues of escape were closed, even to the spilling of walls into the streets. We lost many, surmounting such obstacles, fighting our way toward the open."

"Luckily," said another, "much of the walling of Ar had been earlier dismantled by her own citizens, or we might have been unable to reach the fields, the marshes, the Viktel Aria."

"What of Myron," I asked, "his troops?"

"He was drunk in his tent," said another, bitterly.

"Many of his troops," said another, "those of the mercenary captains, given the emptying of Ar, and the lessening of loot, had deserted."

"There were regulars, surely," I said.

"Too few," said another man. "It had been thought that Ar was pacified, that she required little attention, that the propaganda of Tyros and Cos had done its work, weakening and confusing Ar, dividing her and turning her against herself. Many troops had been recalled to the island ubarates themselves, others to the Cosian principalities on the Vosk."

"They did engage," said another man, "but not as they would have preferred. They had little time to form, as enraged thousands, many now armed with captured weapons, rushed forth from the city to deal with them."

Commonly a large Gorean military camp is square, or rectangular. It is carefully laid out, and is usually severally gated, which allows for the issuance of forces from the interior in a variety of manners. Too, it is ditched, and palisaded, with lookout towers at the corners of the palisade. Watches are routinely maintained, and not unoften patrols reconnoiter the locality. I recalled, however, from when I had been last in Ar, that many of these provisions had not been supplied by the *polemarkos*. Though Myron had had his weaknesses, for paga, and, occasionally, for a slave, he was not a poor officer. The nonfortifying of the camp had been deliberate, a part of the charade that Tyros, Cos, and their allies, had come to Ar not as conquerors but as liberators.

"We soon heard," said one of the men on the beach, "that a banner had been unfurled."

"And that Marlenus had returned," said another.

"That broke the spirit of hundreds," said another.

It is interesting, I thought, what may be the effect of will, and a given leader, on a course of events, how such things, will and a given leader, as though by magic, can generate storms, can shake the earth, may turn even urts into larls, jards to tarns.

How does the leader know this will occur, I wondered. Or does he know?

"Hundreds escaped with their lives," said a man.

"And thousands did not," said another.

"The streets of Ar ran with blood," said a fellow. "Traitors, hundreds, gathered together from the proscription lists, were taken outside the city and impaled."

"The great road, the Viktel Aria, was lined, on both sides, for pasangs, with the bound, squirming, whimpering bodies," said a man.

I nodded.

The vengeance of a Marlenus, I knew, would be a frightful thing.

"Many bodies were hurled, like beasts, into the marshes, for tharlarion," said a fellow.

"Or into *carnariums*," said another.

These were deep pits outside the city, used for the disposal of filth, of garbage, and such. Occasionally a new one was dug, and an old one covered over. Occasionally one was opened, even generations after its closure, that it might be reused, and the lingering stench might still overcome even a strong man. Usually these pits were tended by male slaves, with shovels, with the lower parts of their faces wrapped in scarves.

"The walls of Ar," I said, "are doubtless being rebuilt."

I must not make my serious concerns too obvious.

"With soaring hearts and singing," said a fellow.

"And the flute girls who so tormented and mocked the earlier dismantlers of the walls?" I asked.

"Collared, naked, sweating, under the lash," said a fellow, "they now struggle to bear stones to the builders."

"They will be distributed later, as officers deem fit," said another.

"Excellent," I said.

I tried to keep my voice steady.

"And what of Talena?" I asked.

"A great price has been put upon her head," said a fellow.

"Ten thousand tarns of gold," said a fellow.

"Tarn disks of double weight," said another.

"Then she escaped the city," I said. "She has not been captured."

"You seem pleased," said a man.

"He is a bounty hunter," laughed a fellow.

"You will not have much of a chance to get your capture rope on her," said another.

"Every bounty hunter on Gor will seek her," said another.

"Where would she go? How would she escape capture?" asked another. "I wager she is already captured, and her hunter is pondering how he might get her safely to Ar."

"He may be negotiating for a better price, even now," said another.

"Perhaps she was concealed, and sped to Cos," I said. "Surely they owe her much. She did them much service."

"Ar has risen," said a man. "If she is in Cos, Lurius will deliver her to Marlenus as a peace offering, as a sign of reconciliation and proposed amity."

"I do not think she is in Cos," said a fellow, "or Tyros, either."

"Where then?" said a man.

"I know not," he replied.

"Where would she go?" asked the fellow who had spoken earlier. "Who would shelter her? She cannot just enter another city, even a village."

I realized the fellow's point. There would be the matter of clan, of caste, of identity, of Home Stone. The veils of anonymity are not easily donned in a closely-knit society.

"Surely she might bribe discretion," said a man.

"And what bribe might she, unthroned and sought, a fugitive, offer to better the bounty of ten thousand tarn disks?" asked a fellow.

"Of double weight!" laughed another.

How much could the fleeing Ubara have taken with her, I wondered, given the suddenness of the turn of events, the surprise of the rising. A handful of economic resources, seized in a moment of panic-stricken flight, would not be likely to last long.

"Might she not have loyal retainers?" I asked. "Men who would die for her?"

"None would stand by her," said a fellow, "once she no longer stood within the palisade of foreign spears."

"She was despised," said another, "even by those welcomed within the chambers of her treason."

Too, I thought, how foolish to look for loyalty amongst the disloyal, to hope for honor from those who were without honor. Would the ultimate motivation of the conspirator not be the sanctity of his own skin? Frightened urts will turn on their fellows and lacerate them. They will kill one another for a drop of blood. Betrayal is a not infrequent behavior, and it is one to which one may easily become habituated.

"It is only a matter of time," said a fellow, "until she is thrown, naked and in chains, to the tiles at the foot of the Ubar's throne."

"Woe to Talena," said a fellow.

"She is a traitress to her Home Stone," said a man.

"True," said the fellow. "Let it then be done to her according to the ways of Gor."

"And the mercy of Marlenus," said another.

At this there was a coursing of rude, cruel, unfeeling mirth amongst the rough fellows on the beach.

And these fellows, I thought, were the very fellows from whom she might have hoped succor, for it had been blades such as theirs which had placed her upon, and protected her upon, the usurped throne of Ar.

But they were Gorean, and she was a female, and one who had betrayed her Home Stone. I did not doubt but what any one of them would have been pleased to have her bound at his feet.

On Gor a traitress is a prize.

Anything may be done with her.

"Are we to make camp here?" asked a fellow.

"No," I said.

The fellows who had disembarked yesterday, even later in the day than the present Ahn, had entered the forest.

Too, I thought their employers, whoever they might be, would not want them to camp in the open.

I had gathered that the arrivals of these mysterious, armed visitors was surreptitious.

Obviously I could not inquire too closely into their business, their expectations, plans, and such, for it would be supposed I knew as much, or more, than they did at this point. I had learned a great deal in the past Ahn, but there was much I still did not know.

I wandered over to the huddled, kneeling cargo which had been rudely disembarked, that put into the water, with the crates, boxes, and such.

Some four or five of the newcomers followed me.

"Form a line," I said to the girls, "facing me."

On all fours, they formed this line, looking up at me.

There were, as I had earlier supposed, fifteen on the chain.

The chain, heavy and black, much heavier than it needed to be, dangled between them. The collars, as noted, were somewhat unusual, rather like punishment collars.

There was a cool breeze sweeping in from Thassa.

The cargo had not been brought much onto the beach and, as they were, on all fours, the cool surf washed up about them, swirling about their feet and knees, and covering their hands to the wrist.

The bodies of the girls glistened with water, from the nature of their arrival. Drops of water clung to their eyelashes. Their hair was soaked. In some cases it fell about their faces. It seemed, too, in some cases to have been hastily, unevenly, cut. Whereas long hair is commonly favored in slaves, it is seldom that a slave is brought to the block with ankle-length hair. On the other hand, Gorean free women often have quite long hair, in which they take great pride. It is not unusual that it might reach to the back of their knees. When they are enslaved it is commonly shortened, considerably. There are various reasons for this, as I understand it, for example, the slave learns that she is no longer a free woman, that her hair, its length, dressing, and such, is now at the disposal of masters, that the distinction between her and the free woman is to be clearly drawn, even in a matter as simple as hair, and that the envy of the free woman is not to be aroused at the sight of hair in a slave which might be the pride of a free woman. Too, the shorn hair is of value in a number of ways, not only for wigs, falls, and such, but, too, interestingly, because it makes the best cordage for catapults, far superior to common hemp, and such. Too, I supposed, if one wished to alter the appearance of a free woman, or, more likely, a former free woman, for some reason, perhaps to afford her something in the nature of a disguise, her hair might be shortened.

Here and there wet sand clung about their bodies.

The chain, and the collars, were dark with water.

One or two of the girls whimpered, with fear, or cold.

They were naked, as this is the way slaves are commonly transported. In this way there is less bother with clothing, its soiling, its cleaning, repair, and such. Too, in this fashion it is easier to keep the girls clean, with cast buckets of water, or forcing them into pools and streams, and such. In slave ships the heads are usually shaved, this reducing to some extent the dangers of insect infestation. Slave dips are not uncommon, too, after transportation, as a precaution against such infestation.

I examined the line. "Not all are branded," I said.

"Not yet," said a fellow.

"Position!" I snapped.

Three of the girls immediately went to position. Others, startled, looked about, in consternation, trying to understand what they must do, or perhaps, even, if "position" was truly to be expected of them.

Many free women, incidentally, have never seen a slave in "position," though they may, to their disgust, or delight and envy, have heard the attitude described. This is not as surprising as it sounds for free women are not allowed in paga taverns, and such places, and would seldom have an opportunity to observe what takes place between a female slave, particularly a pleasure slave, and her master. The female slave, before a free woman, kneels, certainly, but commonly demurely, not as she would, and must, if she is a pleasure slave, before a male.

I called attention to one of the girls. "This is 'position,'" I told the others. The others then, though doubtless some with misgivings, for a woman is extremely vulnerable before a male when she is in "position," attempted, to a greater or lesser extent, to duplicate the posture and bodily attitude of the girl to whom I had called their attention.

I attended then to the line. "Oh!" cried more than one, when I kicked apart her knees.

I called the attention of the men to one of the girls, not branded, who was now, like the others, in position. Her lips were slightly parted. There was a slightly startled expression in her eyes, as of suddenly sensed possibilities and sensations.

"This one," I said to the men, "will be soon heated."

She lowered her eyes, but, in position, because of the collar, she could not lower her head.

"Yes," said one of the fellows.

She shuddered. Was it with cold? Or was it because she had suddenly sensed, however fearfully, or curiously, or eagerly, the long-suspected latencies of her lovely belly?

"Soon enough," said another fellow, "they will all heat quickly."

I nodded. I did not doubt it.

"Some of these are new to the collar," I said, "not even branded. Where did you get them?"

"These are all of Ar," said one of the men. "The three who went immediately to position were taken from a paga tavern, which had purchased them, after their consignment to the collar by the judgment of Talena, then Ubara."

I recalled that several women had been brought publicly, on various days, before the judgment of Talena, in her open-air court on the platform near the Central Cylinder. I supposed that she had been given quotas to fill by her superiors, largely under the pretext of reparations due the invaders, these because of the misdeeds of Ar, but how she filled the quotas might, I supposed, be muchly up to her. It did provide her with a convenient opportunity for evening a variety of scores and such, particularly with free women who might have found her diminishment in Ar, and her sequestration, a matter of some satisfaction or amusement. I recalled she had designated Claudia Tentia Hinrabia, who had been the daughter of a former administrator of Ar, Minus Tentius Hinrabius, for the collar. Claudia, a rival and critic of Talena, was the last of the Hinrabians. She was also a rival in beauty to the Ubara. These other women, however, I had not seen. They were new to me.

"When the fighting began, and it became clear how desperate it was," said a fellow, "and how the city would be lost to us, we sought, in a brief surcease of battle, to sack up what coin we might, and other valuables, and prepared to fight our way toward the *pomerium*."

"That is when we entered a paga tavern, the Kef, to gather in, and take with us, some recollected items of flesh loot," said a man. He pointed, one by one, to the three women with brands, who had instantly gone to position, obedient to my command."

I nodded. These were the women taken from a paga tavern. Perhaps once they had been free women of Glorious Ar but they were now marked-thigh girls, slaves.

All were quite attractive.

But that was not unusual with Gorean slaves.

The "Kef," incidentally, is the first letter of the Gorean expression, *'Kajira'*, which is the most common Gorean word for a female slave. More than one paga tavern is so designated, though not on the same street. There might be, say, a "Kef" on Teiban, another on Venaticus, another on Emerald, and so on. The small, cursive "Kef" is also the most common brand on Gor for a female slave. Each of the three slaves bore it, on the left thigh, high, under the hip.

"They came with us, willingly," said a fellow.

"Quite willingly," laughed another.

"Of course," I said.

Those unfamiliar with the ways of Gor might suppose that a foregone consequence of the liberation of a city would be the freeing of certain slaves, say, those of the city who had been impressed into bondage. That is not, however, how the Gorean sees such things. Many Goreans are fatalists and believe that any woman who falls into bondage belongs in bondage, even that it is the will of Priest-Kings that her throat should be enclosed in the lovely circlet of servitude. Most, however, understand that when a woman has worn the collar, it is quite likely that she, in her heart, even if freed, will always wear the collar. She will need a master, and long for one. She understands herself as something which, ideally, belongs wholly to a man. In her heart, and her belly, she will always treasure the collar. The vanities and inanities of the free woman, with her hypocrisies and pretensions, will no longer satisfy her. She will always remember what it was, to kneel, to be bound, and to love. She will always remember the wholeness and beauty of her life as a slave, and the raptures of the collar. She has been, as it is said, "spoiled for freedom." Too, Gorean honor enters into these things. That, say, a daughter should fall slave, is taken not so much as a lamentable tragedy, as it might be in some cultures, as an intolerable affront to a family's honor. Goreans, after all, are well aware of the many remarkable and fulfilling aspects of female bondage, for they may own slaves of their own. They have little doubt that the embonded daughter will well serve her master. Indeed, she had better do so. But she is then an animal and regarded as lost, and well lost, to her family and Home Stone. Tarsks, verr, kaiila, and such, of course, do not have Home Stones. Thus, the family puts the thought of her aside, for she is now a slave. And, of course, to assuage the family's honor she will be left a slave. To be sure, a woman of a city found enslaved within the city is commonly sold out of the city. Slavers, for example, will seldom sell a woman in what was once her own city. I was not surprised then that the three paga slaves, former free women of Ar, would accompany the mercenaries willingly, even eagerly. It would be far preferable to being pilloried naked, subjected to the blows and abuse of irate citizens, being publicly, ceremoniously, whipped, and then being transported out of the city, naked, standing, wrists lashed to an overhead bar, on a flat-bedded, public slave wagon, to the jeers of free citizens. In such a way, it is supposed, might be wiped away the dishonor which her bondage had inflicted on the city, at least to some extent.

"You knew these women?" I asked.

"They frequently brought us paga," said a man.

"I see," I said.

"We can rent them on leashes," said a fellow. "They will bring good coin in the furs."

"They are hot?" I said.

"A touch will make them beg," said another fellow.

"Excellent," I said.

I looked then to the other women.

"These others, too," I said, "were then designated for the collar by Talena, then Ubara?"

"Not at all," said a fellow. "These were confidantes, even cohorts, of the Ubara, women of high caste, rich, well-placed, favorers of the policies of the occupation, not only condoners but abettors of the predations of Tyros and Cos. Several became rich."

"Collaborators?" I said.

"Precisely," said a man.

"Several, in the fighting, learned they were on the proscription lists, copies of which were posted on the public boards," said another.

"They knew themselves in frightful danger," said another.

"They came to us and flung themselves to our feet, begging to be protected, to be permitted to accompany us in our flight."

"We were in haste," said a fellow, "as you may well suppose. Enemies were at hand, ransacking houses, scouring bridges, searching towers, closing in upon us. Our heads were at stake. We must seize what loot we could and flee for our lives."

"'Take us with you!' they begged!"

"'Remain behind, as befits your crimes,' we told them."

"'No! Mercy!' they cried."

"'Loathsome she-urts, detestable profiteers and traitresses,' we cried, 'remain behind, be hurled to eels, be cast amongst leech plants, be weighted and thrown into *carnariums,* view the city you betrayed from the height of high impaling stakes!'"

"'No, please!' they wept. 'Show us mercy!'"

"'What interest have we in free women?' we asked."

"'In free women?' they said, bewildered."

"'None,' we informed them. We could hear the shouts of foes, nearing our hiding place."

"We gathered what we could, which was little enough."

"'Take us with you!' they wept. They were on their knees, their hands extended to us in piteous, frantic supplication."

"Time was short."

"We turned to face them."

"'Take us with you!' they cried."

"'Why?' we inquired."

"They did not understand this question," laughed a fellow.

"Free women are so stupid," said another.

"'Please, please!' they cried."

"'Remove your veils,' ordered Torgus," said one of the men, indicating a large fellow nearby.

"'Never,' they cried," recalled another fellow, grinning.

"We turned then to leave," said another fellow, "but we heard 'Wait! Please, wait!' When we looked back they begged that we remove their veils, even to the ripping of them from them, as might be done with the insolence, amusement, and scorn of a slaver. But this, in our anger and contempt, we refused to do. 'Remove your own veils,' we told them."

"'Do not so shame us!' they wept."

"But in moments, by their own small, desperate hands, their faces were bared to men, men neither of their families nor companionship."

"By their own hand they had face-stripped themselves," said one of the fellows.

At this moment three or four of the girls on the chain burst into tears.

This is perhaps difficult for those unfamiliar with Gor to understand, one supposes, but the matter is cultural, certainly in the high cities. The face of a free woman, particularly one of high caste, of station, and such, is secret to herself, and to those to whom she might choose to bare it. It is not like the face of a slave, exposed to any herdsman or peddler, any passer-by, who might choose, however casually, to look upon it.

Some of the girls, careful to retain the posture in which they had been placed, lest they be struck, wept. They had not forgotten the moment, it seemed. Later, the sting of that humiliation would fade, and they would rejoice to be freed of the encumbrances of veiling, and revel in the feel of the air on their face, a face whose soft, luscious, inviting, vulnerable lips were now exposed to the sight, and kisses, of men.

Perhaps the closest analogy to this would be a woman of

Earth complying with an order to remove her clothing before imperious strangers.

From the Gorean point of view, the face of a woman, you see, is the key to her self, the face, with its beauty, its softness, its special uniqueness, its myriad expressions, proclamatory of her feelings, her thoughts, and moods. How beautiful is a woman's face, and how its subtlest expressions, even inadvertently, even unbeknownst to herself, may be fraught with the delicious treasures of betraying disclosures! The master reads the face of a slave; he may ponder the thoughts, the motivations, and intentions of the veiled free woman.

How precious is the veil to the free woman; she is not a slave.

The free woman is mysterious; the slave is not; she is at a man's feet.

"'Hurry, hurry!' we were urged," recollected one of the fellows.

"We could hear the men of Ar on the street, doors away," said another.

"'Submit, strip, pronounce yourself slave, hurry to the rope,' barked Torgus to the dismayed, frightened women," said a man.

"In moments," said another man, "each hastened to submit."

Submission may be rendered in a number of ways. The most important thing is that the submission is clear. A common posture of submission is to kneel, lower the head, and extend the arms, wrists crossed, as though for binding. Often a phrase, or formula, is employed, as well, often as simple as "I submit," "I am yours," "Do with me as you will," or such. If one is of the Warriors the codes then require one to either slay the captive or accept the submission. Almost invariably the submission is accepted, as women on Gor are accounted a form of wealth, at least once they are collared. I know of only one exception to this almost invariable acceptance of a submission. A woman submitted and then, later, betrayed the submission, and stabbed he to whom she had submitted. The next time she submitted her head was cut off. It might be noted that the submission, in itself, strictly, does not entail bondage, but captivity. Nonetheless it is almost invariably followed by the captive's enslavement. A woman who submits expects the collar to follow.

"Each then," said a fellow, "divested herself of her robes, stepped from them, declared herself slave, and hurried to Torgus, who knotted a length of a coarse, common rope about her neck."

"We made certain each was block naked," said a fellow.

"Some had foolishly neglected, or forgotten, to remove their sandals or slippers," explained another fellow.

"They were suitably cuffed?" I said.

"Yes," said a man.

This was acceptable, as they were then slaves.

Those were probably the first blows they had ever felt.

"'We are lost,' we thought," said a man. "For the men of Ar were at the door itself."

"'We are fee fighters,' Torgus told us, 'in no uniform. The men outside will not know we are not of Ar. Ar is a great city. Who knows all her citizens? Throw open the door, cry out "For Glorious Ar," in suitable accents, and drag our prizes into the street. Given the length of their hair the men of Ar will assume these are free women, captured, in accord with the proscription lists. Cry out that we are conducting them to the impaling poles.'"

"You are clever," I said to Torgus. "I gather that the ruse was successful."

"For a time," said the large fellow, Torgus.

"Until it became clear we might be fleeing the city," said another.

"This aroused suspicion, and, forced to speak, the foreignness of the accents of some of us, for not all were skilled in the intonations of Ar, unsheathed the swords of men of Ar."

"There was then fierce blade work," said a fellow.

"The slaves lay naked on the ground, on their bellies, covering their heads, moaning, shrieking, while steel flashed about them."

I nodded. They would await the outcome of the fierce altercation. They would affect its outcome no more than tethered kaiila.

They must wait to learn their fate, which would by determined by men.

"Many were trod upon," said a man, "and sparks stung their backs."

"Here, though, in the vicinity of the *pomerium,*" said a man, "we were not overmatched as in the city, and we were fee fighters, and mere citizens were opposed to us."

"We lost men, and so, too, did they, and more, but we cut our way clear to the rubble of the dismantled wall."

"Those opposed to us knew themselves outskilled and drew back, to summon reinforcements."

"We then struggled over the rubble, dragging the slaves with us, and were soon beyond the *pomerium,*" said a man. "The camp of Myron had been overrun, but Cosian regulars, abetted by Tyrian contingents, and some allies, had regrouped and, well disciplined, and orderly, in their squares, had already begun the withdrawal northwest to Torcodino, and would from there march to the great port of Brundisium, where would await them ships of Tyros and Cos."

"We, and hundreds of fugitives, with loot, and baggage, and slaves, attached ourselves to these units, and clung to the perimeters of their camps," said one of the fellows on the beach.

"We lost no time shortening the hair of our detestable traitresses," said a man, "to a length suitable to their new condition, that of slave. We would not want reconnoitering tarnsmen, flighted from Ar, to suspect that they might be refugees from the proscription lists, lest determined efforts be made to recover them."

I supposed the women had no objection to this, despite the shearing of their beloved tresses being in its way a badge of degradation and servitude.

Surely it was better to be shorn of those treasured tresses than be betrayed by them into the hands of vengeful citizens.

And better, surely, the degradations of collars and their fair lips pressed to the feet of masters than the slow, lingering death of the impaling pole.

The three paga slaves had little to fear, of course, for their brands would protect them.

They were attractive, domestic animals.

Yet they, too, would be eager to escape Ar, for its Home Stone had once been their own.

Too, they were now different from what they had been, quite different, for they had known the touch of masters.

"It was a terrible march," said a fellow. "We were afflicted from the air, arrowed by avenging tarnsmen. Sometimes small groups attacked the margins of our march. We knew not whether they were allied with Ar, or merely seeking spoil, or trying to curry favor with great Marlenus."

"We must deal with brigands and thieves, within our own camps," said another. "There were many desertions."

"Bosk, and verr, and tarsks, were driven from our path," said a man. "Fields were burned. Wells were filled in. There was little to eat or drink. They opened and closed the veins of kaiila, draining their blood into flasks. A single urt cost as much as a silver tarsk."

"At last we reached Torcodino," said a man, "and found safety within her walls."

"It was there," said a man, "that we put iron on the necks of our sluts."

"They then well knew themselves slave," said a man.

"Ten days later we accompanied the march to Brundisium," said a man. "The regulars of Tyros and Cos, and their officers and slaves, were soon embarked, and gladly, with songs of joy, for their home islands, but it fared differently with many of us, the gathered mercenaries who had served the island ubarates."

"The port police would not permit us within the walls of Brundisium," said a man. "Refugees were unwelcome. They brought nothing to the city, there was no work for them, they were dangerous, they would be expensive to feed."

"By heralds we were warned away from the walls," said a man.

"'Scatter! Begone!' we were told," said a man.

"Rumors had it that our slaughter was planned," said another.

"It was at that time," said a fellow, "that the strange men contacted us."

"Of course," I said.

I did not understand them, of course, but they would suppose this was all familiar to me. Strange men, at least, would be men, not, say, Kurii. That they spoke of them as "strange" interested me. How would they be strange? In demeanor, in language, in dress? I gathered, whatever might be the case, that they were men of a sort to which they were unaccustomed, men of a sort with which they were unfamiliar.

"Some hundreds of us were then soon within the walls of Brundisium," said a fellow, "and were conducted to the wharves, thence, over several days, to be embarked on various ships, toward points unknown."

"As here," I said.

"It seems so," said a man, looking about the beach, after the departing vessel, then to the looming forest.

"The ships would depart at intervals," I said.

"Hirings and charterings took time," said a fellow.

"I trust," I said, "in the meantime you were comfortably housed."

"In mariners' billets," said a fellow.

"The strange men were generous," said another. "Each of us received, in copper tarsks, the equivalent of a silver stater of Brundisium."

"They were generous, indeed," I said.

"We had several nights to enjoy the taverns," said a fellow.

"What of your slaves?" I asked.

"We chained them in the basement of one of the billets," said a man.

"Apparently you could take them with you," I said.

"Yes," said he, who was called Torgus. "We were told that uses might always be found for such."

"I do not doubt it," I said. I glanced at the slaves, in position, the iron on their necks, the water swirling about their knees. They were soft, pathetic, and fearful. They were helpless. They were owned.

I wondered if Pertinax might have felt sorry for them. But that would have been absurd, for they were slaves. One might as well have felt sorry for a kaiila or tarsk.

A slave is not to be coddled, but mastered.

Yes, I thought, uses might always be found for such. Indeed, wherever there were strong men, uses might be found for such.

They were slaves.

How delicious, and delightful, and lovely, are slaves.

I felt sorry for the men of Earth, so many of whom had never held a slave in their arms.

How different they would be, I thought, if they knew the mastery.

Who could do with a free woman, I wondered, who had once tasted slave?

It is no wonder free women hate their embonded sisters, and treat them with such contempt and cruelty.

"I think," said Torgus, "we ought not to remain too long on the beach."

"Certainly not," I said.

"I have the countersign," he said. "I await the sign."

"It is not yet time," I said.

"I think it is time," he said.

"Who are you?" suddenly asked a fellow.

"Give us the sign," said another.

"A ship arrived yesterday," I said.

"Our ship is the last," said Torgus.

"The sign, I have," I said, "is *'Tarns aflight'*."

"I have no countersign for that," said Torgus, very quietly.

"The countersign," I said, "from yesterday's ship, was *'from Ar'*."

"That is not the sign I was to expect, nor to answer with my countersign."

"I suspect there is a misunderstanding," I said.

I noted I was being ringed with fellows, but space was left, in which weapons might be drawn. Torgus stepped back, to put a few feet between us.

"He must be our contact," said a fellow. "How else would he be here, to meet us?"

"We were warned of strangers," said Torgus.

"Tarns aflight," I said.

"From Ar, from Ar," volunteered a fellow, hopefully.

"Yes," I said, cheerfully, "*'from Ar'*."

I saw the hand of Torgus, and that of several others, move to the hilts of weapons. Their scabbards, on the whole, as mine, were at the left hip, suspended there on a shoulder strap. This is common if conflict is not imminent. If it is, the scabbard is often hung loosely at the left shoulder, where, the blade drawn, it may be instantly discarded. A hand in a shoulder strap, in grappling, for example, may serve to hold an enemy in place for, say, the thrust of a knife.

I did not draw my weapon, nor did any of the others.

Clearly they were undecided as to what to do.

"Your slaves are attractive," I said. "What do you want for them?"

"They have already been purchased, by our employers," said Torgus. "We are merely delivering them."

Several of the girls looked startled at this intelligence. It seems they had not realized they had been sold.

"The sign," said Torgus, "the sign."

"Certainly," I said, looking about. I detected a movement in the forest. "My superior will supply it. Mine was apparently for the ship yesterday. There seems to have been some confusion."

"Apparently," said Torgus.

"Wait a bit," I said. "He will be here."

"Are you not to guide us?" asked a fellow.

"No, my superior," I said.

"How long must we wait?" said Torgus, glancing about. The beach was apparently more open than was to his liking.

I was sure that this ship would be met, and I must endeavor to keep things as they were, and hope that the contact would reveal himself shortly, and the sooner the better. Torgus was tolerant, but he was suspicious, and he was not a fool.

"How long?" asked Torgus.

"Not long," I said. "A few Ehn, perhaps a bit more."

I had seen a movement within the forest and, given the remoteness of the area, I was sure it must be connected with the new arrivals.

After a time, Torgus said, "We have waited long enough."

"Wait a little more," said one of his men, the fellow whom I had earlier conjectured might not have ill worn the scarlet.

Torgus shrugged. It seemed he attended this man, and respected him.

"I shall enter the forest," I said, "and seek out my superior."

"Remain where you are," said Torgus.

"Very well," I said. I thought I might be able to bring down two or three, but then I would have expected to be cut down.

If Cos and Tyros had paid these men good coin for their work in Ar, as I supposed they had, they would be skilled. I recalled how they had, as related to me, cut their way through several fellows of Ar to reach the *pomerium*, from whence they, together doubtless with other remnants of garrisons which had managed to escape the city, had joined in the general retreat from Ar.

"He is a spy," said a fellow. "Kill him."

Torgus drew his weapon.

"We do not know he is a spy," said the fellow who might once have worn the scarlet.

"He is a spy," said Torgus.

"If so," said the fellow, "better to hold him, to bind him, and keep him for questioning."

"Yes," said Torgus, "that is best."

"Who will bring the rope?" I asked.

I stood within the ring.

"He has drawn!" said a fellow.

"I did not see it," said another.

"He is of the Warriors," said a man.

Those of the scarlet are trained in such a draw. One does not indicate that one will draw. One does not glance at the hilt. One does not tense. One's attention seems elsewhere, and the eyes of others will follow. The hand is not noticed. It is, I suppose, in a way similar to a magician's sleight of hand. And then, surprisingly one notes that the weapon is free.

"Ho!" cried a voice, from the edge of the forest.

I had been right.

I could see some fellows amongst the trees.

Attention was then directed upon the newcomers. I stepped back, a little, amongst the fellows on the beach. The new arrivals might have noticed the semblance of a dispute on the sand, but such things might be common amongst fee fighters, rough men, fierce, and dangerous, undisciplined. Such men often adjudicate disagreements with steel. I was not in the scarlet. I might be, for all the newcomers knew, another of the fellows whom they had come to meet. How, at least for a few moments, would they know otherwise?

I sheathed my blade.

"I would leave, if I were you," said the fellow next to me, who had drifted back with me. It was he whom I had thought might once have been of the Warriors. I supposed he might have murdered a man, or betrayed a Home Stone, some such thing. It seemed strange to me that he should be with these other fellows.

"My thanks," I said.

But I did not move.

His accent seemed Cosian.

Mine he could probably not place.

Port Kar, of course, was at war with Cos, but that does not mean one had to keep it constantly in mind. There is a time to kill, a time to play kaissa, a time to share paga, a time to do business, a time to exchange slaves, and so on. As warriors are not politicians, their truces are frequent, their salutations genuine.

Besides, he might not be of Cos.

Many of the islands to the west had similar accents.

I moved forward a little.

One of the newcomers, he in advance of his cohorts, stepped forward, and lifted his hand, addressing Torgus, who had come forward, to meet him.

"Tal," he said.

Torgus returned this greeting.

There might have been twenty fellows with the newcomer. Behind them, back in the trees, I saw seven or eight briefly tunicked slaves. Some carried poles, with coiled ropes. Such poles could be used for portering, the baggage fastened to them by the ropes. Sometimes captured panther girls, small bands of which occasionally roamed hundreds of pasangs to the south, were slung from such poles. They were bound, hand and feet, by their captors, to the poles, as might have been slain or captured panthers, the beasts from which they derive their name. They are fastened to the poles in such a way that they dangle, swinging, from them, their bellies to the pole, their backs to the ground. The poles are carried by female slaves, a great insult to the panther girl for they despise female slaves. And she does not know, of course, to what fate she is being carried. When they are returned to civilization, the captured panther girls, most of whom suffer from repressed sexuality, are stripped, branded, and collared, and taught their womanhood. They sell well, and some men seek them out, in the taverns. Wonders, it is said, may be wrought in such women by a switch, and a master's hand. Supposedly they make superb slaves. And once the slave fires have been ignited in their bellies, they are, of course, as helpless, and needful, as any other slave.

"*Beyond Tyros*!" said the newcomer.

"*Beyond Cos*!" said Torgus.

Several of the fellows on the beach looked uneasily at one another. There was little, as far as we knew, beyond Tyros and Cos, some small islands, of course, usually spoken of as the Farther Islands, but nothing else, lest it be the World's End, the edge of the sea, supposedly the plunge into the abyss, nothing.

Few ships, as far as I knew, had ventured west of the Farther Islands, and of those, as far as I knew, none had returned.

Thassa, it seemed, might be jealous of her secrets.

I moved forward. "Tal," I said to the newcomer.

"Tal," he said.

I had addressed him familiarly. This seemed to convince even Torgus that I knew him, and the newcomer supposed, as I had supposed he would, that I was one of the others, though perhaps one a bit more indiscreet or forward than might have been desirable.

The newcomers were nicely organized, and, in moments, much of the baggage had been lashed to the poles, and the briefly tunicked slaves shouldered the poles with the suspended cargo, and stood ready to depart. They were a good looking set of slaves, and the brevity of their tunics, which is a feature of such garments, left few of their charms to speculation. They stood very straight, but with the grace that is expected of a slave. Clumsiness, awkwardness, stiffness, and such, are not permitted to slaves; they are not free women. I noted that the slaves stole glances at several of the fellows on the beach. They knew they might be given to them. I went behind one of the women, at the aft end of a pole, and carefully turned her collar. She remained absolutely still. The collar was plain. I adjusted it then so that the lock was again at the back of the neck, where it belongs. I had learned nothing.

I then, in order to make myself useful, put the fifteen neck-chained girls, who had arrived on the ship, to their feet, and arranged them in a line, one behind the other. I gathered they had been marched in something like this order before, because of the gradations of height. I put the tallest girl in front, as that is the usual way the slavers arrange their "beads." I then distributed several of the smaller packages, which had been left free, doubtless deliberately, amongst them, the heaviest to the taller, larger girls. Indeed, precisely fifteen such packages had been left, not attached to the poles borne by the fair porters come from the forest. Surely this was not a matter of coincidence. The new girls, too, then, were to carry burdens, perhaps their first.

"Place the boxes on your head," I told them, "steadying them with both hands."

This is a common way in which Gorean slave girls, and, indeed, free women of lower castes, carry boxes, baskets, bundles, and such. This form of lading is particularly lovely in the case of female slaves because the hands are thus fixed in position over their heads, almost as though chained, and the breasts are nicely lifted. Too, they then know themselves, as much as pack kaiila, bearing the burdens of men.

In moments the leader of the fellows from the forest had set out amongst the trees. A march then followed him, first his own men, then the portering slaves, with their poles and baggage, and then Torgus, and the fellows from the ship, and then, bringing up the rear, a lovely coffle, fifteen shapely pack beasts, the girls from the ship.

I thought they looked well on their chain, bearing their burdens.

Then the chain, at the edge of the forest, stopped.

I suspected it was terrified to enter that gloom.

And it was not being supervised. There was no master or switch slave behind them.

That was interesting, I thought.

But then what would they do, where would they go? How would they survive in the forest, naked and chained?

Their very survival depended on masters, and, as they were slaves, on pleasing masters.

The chain was clearly frightened.

All that they knew, and were familiar with, lay behind them.

One girl, the last on the chain, turned to look back at me, almost wildly, her hands steadying her burden.

It was she who had seemed, finding herself in "position," perhaps for the first time in her life, to have come suddenly to a new sense of herself, to a new astonishing awareness of herself. The very assumption of "position" by a woman can have that effect. It is hard to be in "position" and not know oneself a female, and a particular sort of female. It is not only a symbolic posture for a woman, which she well understands, her kneeling, and vulnerability, and such, but it is an arousing posture, as well. I had seen her expression, her surprise, her apprehension, her fear, her curiosity, her incipient readiness. I had little doubt she would heat quickly, and might be the first of the lot to weep in need at the smallest touch of a master.

Then the chain moved, presumably frightened to remain where it was, presumably fearful of falling behind, and, the chain jerking against the side of her neck, she stumbled forward. Then she, with the others, had disappeared into the forest.

The women, I supposed, had not been named yet.

I recalled they had been recently sold, though to whom, or what, I knew not.

In any event, names, if they were to receive them, would be given to them by masters. The slave in her own right has no name, no more than any other animal. As a slave changes hands, she is commonly renamed.

I looked after the departing march.

It was no longer visible.

Then, to my surprise, I heard, from deep within the forest, what was, unmistakably, the roar of a larl.

I found this anomalous.

The larl is not indigenous to the northern forests.

I had let the march proceed without me, and none seemed to be concerned with that.

I was hungry.

I would now return to the hut of Pertinax.

Chapter Six

We Trek the Forest

It was the afternoon of the day following the encounters on the beach, first with Sullius Maximus, and later with Torgus, the fee fighter, or mercenary, and his cohorts.

I was now accompanying Pertinax, deeply into the forest, being led, I supposed, to the alleged rendezvous with one whom I had been led to believe would be an agent of Priest-Kings. I supposed, of course, for reasons earlier suggested, that this individual would not be an agent of Priest-Kings but, most probably, of Kurii.

As it would turn out these matters were darker and deeper than I had suspected, and, in a sense, perhaps unknown to either, both Priest-Kings and Kurii, in a way, were being used.

Agents of both Priest-Kings and Kurii were being applied, unbeknownst to themselves, it seems, to the ends of a third party, or, perhaps it might be better said that three stratagems were afoot, which were occasionally intertwined. Do not dark rivers sometimes flow in the same channel?

The light was mottled, filtering through the foliage of the canopy.

"We are not in the reserves of Port Kar," I said to Pertinax. This was obvious, for the reserves are gardened, or nearly so, shrubbery cleared, trees spaced, and such, that they may grow exuberantly upward, muchly straight, and tall. One nurses, so to speak, the loftiest and best wood, before its harvesting. Too, we had crossed none of the ditches that act as boundaries to a reserve, whether one of Port Kar or of another polity. Here, in this part of the forest, there was a great deal of shrubbery, brush, broken branches, fallen timber, debris of various sorts. Occasionally one waded through leaves, as through thigh-high surf. Here the trees were muchly together, each challenged by the others, leaves competing for sunlight, roots engaged in their subterranean contests to absorb water and minerals.

"No," he said.

"You have not been this way before," I said.

"No," he said.

"The trail, however, is clear," I said.

"You see it?" he said, surprised.

"Yes," I said.

It was not really difficult. I did not know the sign but it appeared here and there, each sign usually visible, some fifty yards or so, from the vantage point of the previous sign. It resembled a yellow stain, such as might have resulted from talendars being rubbed on bark, but, examined closely, given its articulation, it was clearly the product of intelligence, of some intelligence.

"I suspect that we had to come today," I said. I recalled he had been quite clear about the time we would enter the forest.

"Yes," he said.

This confirmed my suspicion that the stain, whatever might be its composition, would be temporary, evaporating, or lapsing from visibility, within twenty or so Ahn. I took this as confirming my view that we were dealing with Kurii, for their science could easily manage such a thing. To be sure, so, too, could that of Priest-Kings. I also suspected that there would be a scent, or a flavor, to such a thing, that it would attract insects who would eliminate any possible residue.

"Oh!" cried Constantina.

I had jerked on the leash.

She could not see, of course, as she was hooded. Too, her wrists had been bound behind her.

Cecily had been similarly served. She, too, was hooded, and her small, lovely wrists fastened behind her.

This morning, to her consternation, I had fashioned a hood for Constantina, from opaque cloth, which artifact, once it was well on her, and completely enclosing her head, I fastened in place with some string about her throat.

I had then tied her hands behind her back, and put her to her knees.

"What are you doing?" had asked Pertinax, uneasily, not that I think he much minded seeing Constantina as she then was.

Certainly I had seen his eyes on her frequently the preceding evening. Her appeal to him had been much enhanced, I gathered, by my judicious amendments to her garmenture.

Doubtless he, too, suspected that she was no longer capable of removing her collar.

That, in itself, can make quite a difference in a man's view of a woman.

All in all, I think he was toying with the thought of her as a slave. What would it be, if she were truly a slave?

Would that not be pleasant for a fellow?

She did not object, of course, to the hooding and binding, as she was desperate to keep up her pretense of bondage before Pertinax. I was not supposed to know that she was a free woman.

"Is it not obvious?" I had asked.

"But, why?" he asked.

"She is a slave," I said. "Why should she know where she is going?"

"I see," he said.

Such practices help to keep the slave helpless, and dependent on the master.

"Hood me, too, Master," begged Cecily.

"I intend to," I told her.

She purred with delight. The slave responds well to restraints, and the uncompromising dominance which she yearns for with all her heart. Obviously she does not wish to be hurt, nor, generally, should she be hurt, unless she has been in some respect displeasing, and punishment is in order, but she does want to know herself slave, owned, and mastered. Accordingly she loves to be in the master's power, whether merely heeding his word, obeying, or realizing, in frustration, that no matter how much she might wish to do so, she is not permitted to speak, or writhing in his bonds, helplessly exposed to his mercy, and caresses, should he choose to bestow them upon her, such things. She responds well to blindfolds, hoods, gags, ropes, straps, collars, slave bracelets, chains, and such. When I tied her hands behind her she put back her head in the hood, lovingly, and pressed against me.

Cecily, I thought, was coming along well.

From rope I had improvised a single leash, a common leash, by means of which, grasped at its center, I might control both girls.

I put them in this.

It was thus that they were being conducted through the forest.

Later unhooded, they would have no idea where they were, or how they had gotten there, nor where Pertinax's hut might be found. The best they might do, given the time of day and the location of Tor-tu-Gor, Light-Upon-the-Home-Stone, the common star of Gor and Earth, would be to reach the coast, but, even so, would the hut of Pertinax lie to the north or south? And, of course, an isolated woman, or women, on Gor, undefended by men, whether collared or not, would be fair game for almost any Gorean male. It would be like picking up shells on the beach.

Constantina had stumbled.

"I beg to be unhooded!" she wept.

I then stopped, and Constantina, sobbing, stood still, waiting to be unhooded. She reached her bound wrists out a few inches from the small of her back. "Please, too," she said, "untie me."

Pertinax seemed pleased that the proud Constantina had begged, and had said "Please."

This was not the Constantina with which he was familiar.

She stood still, waiting to be unhooded, and unbound.

Cecily stood docile, hooded and bound, on the leash, her head lowered. She knew it would be done with her as masters pleased, and she, a slave, wished to be done with as masters pleased.

I located a slender, supple branch, and broke it off.

"Oh!" cried Constantina, stung across the back of the thighs.

"Now," I said, picking up the leash, "let us be on our way."

We then continued our journey.

Chapter Seven

We Reach a Reserve; The Signs Vanish; We Will Wait

After an Ahn we came to the edge of a deep ditch, some twelve feet or so deep, and as wide. It extended for some hundreds of yards to the left and right. We could not see the corners, where it would turn and begin to enclose a large rectangle of ground.

It was a relief to have come through the tangles of our earlier passage. We had been moving largely eastward.

I stood at the edge of the ditch.

"Do not move closer," I told Constantina and Cecily. "There is a drop here."

I thought the reserve, what I could see of it, was awesomely impressive.

"Have you been here before?" I asked Pertinax.

"No," he said.

"The signs continue," I observed.

A wand was nearby, across the ditch and to the left. A ribbon dangled from it. I could see another wand or two, beyond it, to its left, along the ditch, and another to my right, perhaps a hundred yards away. I supposed such wands and ribbons, at intervals, lined the edges of the ditch.

"This is clearly a reserve," I said.

"Clearly," he agreed.

"It may be one of Port Kar," I said.

"Perhaps," he said.

"The ribbons will tell," I said. They were green. That suggested Port Kar. Thassa, the sea, is generally green. Indeed, pirates commonly painted their ships green, to make them less discernible at sea, certainly while under oars, with the masts lowered. Colors in the Gorean high cultures, as in most cultures, have their connotations or symbolisms. Too, in the Gorean high culture, certain colors tend to be associated with certain castes, for example green with the Physicians, red, or scarlet, with the Warriors, yellow with the Builders, blue with the Scribes, white with the Initiates, and so on.

"This is very impressive," I said. "I think I shall unhood Cecily for a moment. You may unhood your slave, too, briefly, if you wish."

"How beautiful it is!" said Cecily.

"Unhood me!" demanded the Lady Constantina.

"Apparently," I said to Pertinax, "your slave wishes one or more additional, corrective strokes of the switch."

"No!" said the Lady Constantina.

She started to move awkwardly, turning about, pulling at her bound wrists, apprehensive, frightened, bewildered and helpless in the hood.

Was I behind her, again, with a switch?

"Be careful," I said to her. "There is a drop."

She stood very still then, whimpering.

"Hold still," said Pertinax. "I will unhood you."

"Wait," I said to Pertinax. "I heard no suitable request."

Constantina straightened her body, angrily. "Please," she said, to Pertinax, in a voice venomous with irony, "unhood me," adding, "—*Master*," in a tone of voice which was more than anything else an insult.

"Of course," he said, fumbling with the strings at her neck.

She would not have addressed me, I was sure, as she did Pertinax. Her contempt for him was in no way disguised. But then he was, of course, her employee, so to speak.

I was angry but would not interfere. She was, after all, a free woman. A slave who had spoken so to a Gorean master would have been instantly subjected to discipline, would have been instantly punished, and grievously, if not slain. She would never again dare to so address her master. In moments, sobbing, she would be at his feet, begging forgiveness. The slave addresses her master, and all free persons, with deference. She is a slave. She does not wish to die.

"It is beautiful," I said, agreeing with Cecily.

"The prospect is not unpleasant," said Constantina, freed of the hood.

The hair of both girls was damp, from the hood.

We stood before a reserve.

The trees were spaced, yards apart, and were lofty. There was a solemnity about the vista, as with colonnades stretching into far shadows, a world of living columns, with capitals of shimmering foliage.

They were Tur trees.

These are used mostly for strakes, keels, beams, and planking.

Needle trees, of which there were none here, are usually used for masts. They are a softer wood, and, less rigid, more flexible, are more inclined to bend with the wind and the yard, and so, under certain conditions, violent conditions, less likely to snap. Too, the wood is lighter and this is useful in the raising and lowering of masts. The yards, too, as would be supposed, are commonly of needle wood. Needle trees, too, come to maturity more rapidly than Tur trees, and may thus be the sooner and the more frequently harvested.

"Rehood your slave," I said to Pertinax.

I was attending to this chore with Cecily.

Constantina jerked angrily, futilely, at her bound wrists and cast Pertinax a look of fury, which seemed to dare him to comply with my instruction.

"Now," I said to Pertinax.

"Do you think it is necessary?" he asked.

"Do it," I said.

"Very well," he said.

Constantina's angry features disappeared within the folds of the hood.

"Oh!" she said.

Pertinax had jerked the strings on the hood against the back of her neck, and had then knotted them snugly under her chin. She then knew herself nicely hooded. I think Pertinax enjoyed that. I thought there might be a man in him, somewhere. Indeed,

I suspected he might now be ready to learn how to handle a slave leash, and I supposed that he would not be displeased to have Constantina on such a leash, a slave leash. Too, to get the girls across the ditch, it would help not to have them on a common leash.

So I cut the leash at the center, so that we had, in effect, two leashes. I then put Cecily over my shoulder, her head to the rear, as a slave is carried.

I was pleased to see Pertinax draw Constantina to him, on the leash.

I think she was surprised.

Perhaps she thought it was I.

When a girl is hooded it is hard for her to know who has her leash.

For example, a girl might be taken out, hooded, leashed, by one fellow, and, later, certain arrangements having previously taken place, arrangements unknown to her, she may, when she is knelt and unhooded, find herself, on her leash, looking up into the eyes of a stranger.

She has been sold.

To be sure, I supposed that Pertinax might at present be still somewhat diffident about leash-mastering a female.

Doubtless there was still much of Earth in him.

He could learn, of course.

I supposed a woman could usually tell, even in a hood, from the way the leash was used, whether or not she was in the custody of one accustomed to the leashing and handling of a woman.

When a woman is put through slave paces she is not unoften on a leash. Sometimes masters have contests with their girls in such a fashion. The winning girl often receives a sweet, the loser, often, two or three strokes of the switch, to encourage her to do better next time.

It is not unusual to leash a slave, for tethering her, for taking her on a walk, and such.

Slaves, on the leashes of their masters, are a common sight in the high cities, in the streets, on the bridges, and so on.

On a leash, a slave is nicely displayed.

"The signs continue," I said. "We will enter the reserve."

Pertinax made ready to lift Constantina in his arms.

"Do you think she is a free woman?" I inquired.

He looked at me, puzzled.

"See how I carry Cecily," I said.

She was over my left shoulder, her head to the rear.

A slave is not likely to be accorded the dignities appropriate to a free woman. The free woman is to be carried, if carried at all, gently, respectfully, nestled in one's arms. For example, one may not wish her to risk soiling the hem of her rich robes, or the brocade of her slippers. Sometimes a free woman will wait, before, say, a rivulet or puddle, even a small one, to be carried to safety by some lucky fellow. The manner of carrying the slave is usually quite different. She is carried as property, as though she might be no more than produce, and her head is to the rear so that, even were she not hooded, she cannot see where she is being carried. That is for the master to know, for the slave to learn. And so, in this way, even in such a small way, even in such a trivial way, we discover yet another way in which a distinction may be drawn between the slave and the free woman. In the manner of small fordings and such the slave will usually wade after the master, the water perhaps to her knees. Free women, of course, may own female slaves, whom they often treat with great cruelty. For example, if a female slave, owned by a free woman, dares to look at a male, she may be whipped. And it is not unusual, in these small fordings, and such, of which we spoke, for the free woman to put her slave into the mire, and use her body as a bridge, in this way protecting her garments and the daintiness of her feet and ankles.

In a moment then Pertinax had scooped up the Lady Constantina and had her over his shoulder, her head to the rear.

In this position even an unbound free woman is helpless.

I had seen more than one so carried, captured in war. She can do little but scream and pound her small fists futilely on a fellow's back, squirm, kick her legs, and such.

I then, with some difficulty, descended into the ditch, and, then, on the other side, slowly, step by carefully placed step, made my way to the level. I was followed, momentarily, by Pertinax. Some dirt slipped, but he was then at my side. The declivity, though deep, was not steep. The ditch was not intended for defense. It was primarily a boundary, but it did, too, discourage the entry of animals into the reserve.

We put the girls on their feet, safely away from the edge of the ditch, into which they might have had a nasty tumble.

"There is the next sign," said Pertinax, pointing.

"Yes," I said.

I went to the nearest wand, and held up the green ribbon, which was dangling from it. I held it in two hands. As I had supposed, there was printing on the ribbon.

"Can you read this?" I asked Pertinax.

"Not well," he said. "What does it say?"

"It is a simple legend," I said. "It says 'These are the trees of Port Kar.'"

"This is the reserve of Port Kar then," he said.

"One of them," I said. "These seem to be Tur trees, all Tur trees."

I went to one of the trees a few yards back and to the left. It was tagged. It wore the badge of Port Kar.

"This beauty," I said, looking upward, "has been marked. It is selected, marked for the arsenal, for the yard of Cleomenes." I supposed it would be harvested in the fall, when it would have finished its season's growth. The time of year, now, as nearly as I could tell, from the vegetation, was late summer. I hoped our business in the area could be finished before the onset of winter. Winters can be quite bitter in the northern forests. The yard of Cleomenes was one of the yards under the aegis of the arsenal of Port Kar, of which yards there were several.

I looked ahead, and some yards to the right, deeper into the reserve, where another sign, in its yellow, indicated our route.

"Let us continue our journey," I said.

Pertinax offered me Constantina's leash.

"Lead your own slave," I said.

I moved ahead, with Cecily.

I heard Constantina gasp, as she was jerked forward.

We had been entered into the reserve now for perhaps the better part of an Ahn when the signs we had been following assiduously could no longer be detected.

I examined the last sign, the one beyond which we noted no other sign. It was clear, and, as yet, showed no sign of fading. It seemed unlikely then that the next sign, if there had been one, would have become undetectable.

"I think this is the last of the signs," I said.

"No!" said Pertinax, alarmed.

"They seem not to continue," I said.

"They must!" insisted Pertinax.

We looked about. Each sign had been reasonably obvious from the vantage point of the preceding sign. This pattern, however, clearly, no longer held.

"I do not understand," said Pertinax, obviously concerned.

"What is wrong!" demanded Constantina.

"Was your slave given permission to speak?" I asked.

"She has a standing permission to speak," said Pertinax, uneasily.

"Surely not when hooded," I said.

"Oh?" said Pertinax.

"No," I said.

"May I speak?" said Constantina, quickly.

Pertinax looked at me, and I nodded.

"Yes," he said.

"Something is wrong!" she said. "What is going on? What is wrong?"

I smiled.

Women are so much at one's mercy, so helpless, when bound, and hooded.

I went behind her and took her by the upper arms and held her. "Nothing is wrong," I told her. "And, besides, curiosity is not becoming in a *kajira*."

"Something is wrong, is it not?" asked Pertinax.

"I do not think so," I said.

"What are we to do?" he asked.

"Wait," I said.

"We have long trekked," he said. "It will soon be dark."

"We have some food, a bota of water," I said.

"It is dangerous here," he said. "There may be animals."

"That is possible," I said, "but I do not think there is much to fear in the reserve. The oddity of the ditch discourages the entrance of animals, and, as there is little grazing here, there would be few herbivores, and there being few herbivores, there will be few carnivores. Too, the human is unfamiliar prey to most carnivores, the panther, the sleen, the larl, and such. They will certainly attack humans, and humans are surely within their prey range, but, given a choice, they will usually choose prey to which they are accustomed, wild tarsk, wild verr, tabuk, and such."

"There are no larls this far north," said Pertinax.

"Yesterday, on the beach," I said, "I heard one."

Pertinax paled.

"We are probably too far north for panthers," I said. "One is more likely to encounter them in the forests to the south."

"Good," said Pertinax.

"Unless, of course, some range this far north, but that is unusual. There should, however, be sleen about."

I recalled one had been in the vicinity of Pertinax's hut, when Constantina, who had annoyed me, had been put outside, gagged and bound, hands tied behind her, feet crossed, pulled up, and fastened closely to her hands, on the leaves.

It is an unpleasant tie.

I hoped she had found it instructive.

The common sleen burrows, and would have its den below the frost line. To be sure it is an adaptive, successful life form. In the vicinity of the Red Hunters, there are snow sleen. In certain waters, there are sea sleen, and so on.

"I wish I had a rifle," said Pertinax.

"It is better that you do not," I said. "If you possessed such a weapon, you would be in violation of the weapon laws of Priest-Kings, and liable to the flame death."

"Surely there would be an inquiry, a trial, or such," he said.

"No," I said.

"At least you have a sword, a knife," he said.

"Such tools would be of little help against large predators," I said. "A spear would be better, or, if one had time, time for several arrows, the great bow."

"I do not like this," said Pertinax.

"Nor I," I said. "Let us unhood the slaves. They know they are in the reserve. Thus, no security will be compromised."

Both girls were then freed of their hoods.

I then sat them down, facing one another. We left the leashes on their necks.

"What are you doing?" asked Pertinax.

"I am tying their ankles together," I said. "Now let us eat. We can feed them later."

After Pertinax and I had fed, I went to Cecily, and knelt down, and she leaned forward, her hands tied behind her. I had some bread for her. She looked at me. I extended my hand. She kissed it, and licked it, the hand of her master. I then, bit by bit, fed her by hand, and then, when I thought she had had enough, I gave her of the bota. I then stood up, my shapely beast having been fed and watered.

"What of me?" demanded Constantina.

"What is done with you is up to your master," I said. "Surely you know that, *slave*."

"Untie me," she said to Pertinax.

"Do not," I said.

"I am hungry!" she said.

"Then you will take food from your master's hand," I said.

"Never!" she said.

"Then you will go hungry," I said.

She tried to rise, but, as her feet, crossed, were bound to those of Cecily, crossed, she fell, and heavily, to her side. She struggled again, then, to her seated position. She realized then she could not rise.

Constantina cast me a look of fury, but, I fear, it was a mild thing compared to that with which she regaled Pertinax, who looked hastily away.

It was then an Ahn later.

Night, by then, was well fallen.

"I am hungry," said Constantina. "Please feed me."

"Are you ready to take food from your master's hand?" I asked.

"Yes!" she said, angrily.

Pertinax, obligingly, approached her, and knelt down beside her.

"Not yet," I told him. "You may beg to be fed," I informed Constantina.

"I beg to be fed," she said.

"Have you not forgotten something?" I asked.

"—*Master*," she said.

Pertinax leaned forward.

"Not yet," I told him. Then I addressed myself to the Lady Constantina. "You should be grateful that your master consents to feed you," I told her.

She looked at me, angrily.

"Extend your hand to your slave," I said to Pertinax. "Good," I said, as he had done so. "Now," I said to the Lady Constantina, "lick, and kiss, his hand, softly, tenderly, gratefully."

"Ai!" said Pertinax.

I gathered that the Lady Constantina must, indeed, be very hungry.

"You may now feed the slave," I informed Pertinax.

I thought this little exercise would do the proud Lady Constantina a world of good.

Certainly, now, she would better understand, even as a free woman, how she was in the power of men, should men choose to exercise their power.

Later, we separated the slaves, and tied the leash of each about a tree. We left their hands bound, but we untied their ankles.

I looked down at the Lady Constantina.

She lay on her side, looking up at me.

I glanced at her legs, and then I asked her, "Have you had slave wine?"

"What is slave wine?" she asked.

"It prevents conception," I said. "Slaves are not to breed randomly. Their crossings are to be decided by masters."

"I have not had slave wine!" she said.

"A pity," I said.

"But I have had what I was told," she said, "was the wine of 'the noble free woman'."

"Strange," I said, "as you are a slave."

"You know I am not a slave!" she whispered.

"Ah, yes," I said, "sometimes, when I look at your legs, I forget."

"Beast!" she hissed.

"As you have had 'the wine of the noble free woman,'" I said, "it does not much matter. The substances, save in the pleasantness of their imbibings, are equivalent. Indeed, both have as their active ingredient sip root."

"Do not touch me!" she said.

"I have no intention of doing so," I said.

"I am a virgin!" she said.

"That surprises me," I said.

"Why do you smile?" she asked.

"It is nothing," I said. In some markets virgins sold well. That always seemed to me a bit strange. In any event, virgin slaves were rare.

"You think I am not attractive?" she asked.

"As a free woman of Earth," I said, "I would think you are quite attractive."

"I am!" she said.

"You are vain?" I asked.

"Perhaps," she said, "but legitimately so. My beauty is obvious. It is a matter of fact."

"I see," I said.

"I am beautiful," she said. "I am extremely beautiful!"

"For a free woman of Earth," I said. "But you have not yet even been opened."

"'Opened'?" she said.

"For the pleasures of men," I said.

"I see," she said, icily.

"But more importantly," I said, "you have not yet been awakened, softened, and sensitized. Your body is not yet a sheet of awareness. Are you even aware of the feel, the exact feel, consider it now, of the straps on your wrists?"

She shuddered.

"There are horizons, and vistas, of your sex," I said, "sensations, feelings, hopes, apprehensions, awarenesses, fears, anticipations, yearnings, longings, of which you are totally unaware. You have not yet begun to learn yourself. You are still a stranger to nature, to yourself, and the world. You do not yet know who you are, or what you are."

"I know very well who I am, and what I am," she said.

"No," I said. "It is only in the collar that women learn themselves. It is only in the collar that the flower of their sex opens, one by one, its vulnerable petals. It is only in the collar that a woman comes to her true happiness, and true beauty."

"Kneeling before a man," she said, angrily, "her lips pressed to his feet!"

"Certainly," I said. "Can you not conceive of yourself so?"

"Yes," she said, "in terror of my life."

"Yes," I said, "it often begins so."

"Leave me," she said.

"What do you think of Pertinax?" I asked.

"He is a despicable weakling," she said.

I then left her, as she had requested. A Gorean male, commonly, complies with the wishes of a free woman.

They are, after all, free.

I turned about, and went to Pertinax. "Take the first watch," I said.

I then went and lay down near Cecily.

"Master," she whispered.

"Yes?" I said.

"My needs are much on me," she said. "Caress me, please."

"No," I said.

The satisfaction of the slave's needs is up to the master. Occasionally one frustrates them. It helps them to keep in mind that they are slaves. On the other hand, the sex lives of slaves are a thousand times richer and deeper than those of a free woman, if the free woman, with her hauteur and grandeur, has anything worth considering a sex life. There is no comparison with that of a free woman. The sexual experiences of slaves, as opposed to those of free women, are lavish, vital, frequent, and prolonged. The sexual experiences of the free woman are usually brief and disappointing. The life of the slave, on the other hand, is essentially a sexual life; sexuality irradiates her entire existence; it does not begin and end with a caress; in the collar she knows she is essentially a sexual creature, a slave, at the master's bidding, and this knowledge imbues her entire life with an erotic glow, a permeating ambience. For the slave, polishing a master's boots, tying his sandals, presenting him with food, greeting him at the door, kneeling, and such, are sexual experiences. Normally, of course, the slave's petitions for attention will be entertained, and usually acceded to, and readily.

This should be easy to understand. It is, naturally, usually quite pleasant to assuage the slave's needs, as anyone who has done so knows. Having a slave at one's mercy and forcing her through the throes, she perhaps jerking at her chains, of a succession of belly-wrenching, belly-rocking orgasms, is gratifying. Who does not want a naked slave, in her collar, sobbing, and bucking and squirming, and begging for more? Also, one usually has, if not a duty to content the slave, for nothing is owed to the slave, an inclination to do so. Surely this is easy to understand. She is so needful, and beautiful! Too, have not men been responsible for the tormenting acuity of those very needs which so distress her? Has it not been men who have seen to it, with an almost cruel intent, that slave fires will rage in her lovely belly? Should not those who have set such tinder alight satisfy the very needs they have done so much to ignite and intensify?

Cecily moaned, softly.

"Be silent," I said to her, softly.

"Yes, Master," she said. "Forgive me, Master."

In several Ahn I knew she would be even more needful and desperate. One of the controls a master has over a slave, as the control of her food, her clothing, and whether or not she is to be permitted clothing, and such, is the control he exercises over her in virtue of her sexual needs. Slave fires, even when extinguished by the mercy of the master, will soon rekindle.

Any woman in whose belly slave fires burn knows herself slave.

Such fires will put her at the mercy of even a hated master.

"Master," said Cecily.

"Yes?" I said.

"The signs have vanished," she said. "Why do we linger in the reserve?"

"Because the signs have vanished," I said.

"I do not understand," she said.

"We will be met," I said. "We will have a guide."

"And signs are not to be risked?" she said.

"Not beyond this point, I gather," I said.

"I see," she said.

Chapter Eight

Tajima; A Woman of Earth Is to Be Presented to Lord Nishida

It was now the next morning.

I had had the second watch.

"Do not disturb him," I said.

"Does he know we are here?" asked Pertinax.

"Certainly," I said. "Sit here, cross-legged, beside me." I looked over my shoulder, to the girls. "Slaves, kneel," I said.

Pertinax assumed the suggested position, and, behind us, Cecily and Constantina knelt down.

They were still bound.

The rope leashes dangled from their necks.

We spoke in whispers.

We were some twenty yards from the fellow, who was engaged, I supposed, in certain martial exercises, certainly of a rather stylized, formal nature. I had never seen anything exactly like this before. He was standing, and sometimes wheeled about, gracefully. He had two hands on an unusual sword, with which he described certain evolutions, thrusts, strokes, a return to guard, and so on. It seemed ritualistic, but he was certainly intent on what he was doing. I had the sense of a severe concentration.

I was reminded somewhat of the Pyrrhic dances of Gorean infantry, particularly of those infantries who specialized in the tactics of the phalanx, rather than the shifting, melting, forming, reforming tactics of the squares. Nothing stood against the phalanx on level ground. The squares, however, were more flexible, and better suited to an uneven terrain. The Pyrrhic dances were used primarily as training exercises, but also figured in parades and martial displays, men shouting, spears clashing rhythmically on shields, the spear hedge rising and falling, wheeling about, a thousand spears in unison, this all to music. It is very impressive. This fellow's exercises, however, were done by a single man and, as nearly as I could determine, from the distance, in silence.

He wore a light, loose, white robe, which came about to his knees. It had wide, but short, sleeves.

"I have been told of such fellows," said Pertinax. "He is Tuchuk."

"I do not think so," I said. He did not look Tuchuk to me. The Tuchuks are, on the whole, short and broad, strong fellows, agile riders. This fellow seemed a bit taller, and certainly thinner, more lithe, more pantherlike.

"Tuchuk," said Pertinax.

"There is no facial scarring," I said.

"Surely not all Tuchuks are disfigured," said Pertinax.

"They do not think of it as disfigurement," I said, "but, if anything, as enhancement."

"Surely they are not all scarred," said Pertinax.

"True," I said. And, indeed, it was true that not all Tuchuks were scarred. The scars were not easily come by. They had to be earned, by success in war, and such.

As noted, I had had the second watch.

In the neighborhood of dawn I had seen him through the trees. He was bare-headed. He carried a single sword. I saw him, and he saw me. We did not exchange a greeting. He determined that most of our camp was asleep, and then withdrew, to wait. He sat cross-legged for a time, facing our camp. Then, after a time, he had risen, unsheathed his unusual sword, and commenced his exercises.

I had the sense he did not wish to disturb the camp, but thought it appropriate to wait until it was awake.

This, I took, somewhat to my surprise, as politeness.

To be sure, it is dangerous to come on a sleeping warrior, which he would presumably take Pertinax to be. Normally one makes certain, if one's intentions are peaceful, that any approached camp is well aware of one's approach, even to one's singing, calling out, pounding on a shield, or such. A surreptitious advance is usually taken as an act of war.

He took little note of the girls, other, I suppose, than to note that their wrists were bound behind them, and each, by the neck, was fastened to a tree. They were, in effect, tethered, as might have been kaiila. From his vantage point, he would not have been much aware of their quality as females, for example, their value as properties. To be sure, Constantina was priceless, as she was a free woman.

When he had begun his exercises I had come forward to the point where I might sit, and watch. I was careful, of course, not to approach too closely.

When Pertinax awakened, he discovered my absence, doubtless to his considerable uneasiness, and had seemingly, swiftly, cast about to locate me, which event took place shortly. He then awakened the girls and freed their rope leashes from the respective trees to which they had been fastened, and approached me, followed by the girls, still bound, but the leashes now dangling from their necks.

After a time, the fellow sheathed his sword, bowed to the southeast, and turned to face us.

He approached to within about fifteen feet of us, and Pertinax and I, which seemed appropriate, rose to our feet. In this way, though I do not think Pertinax was aware of this, we showed him honor. For us to have remained recumbent, so to speak, would have made it seem rather as though he was an inferior, reporting to us. "Remain kneeling," I cautioned the girls. Cecily, of course, well aware that she was in the presence of a male, and one presumably free, had not stirred. Constantina, however, had seemed on the point of rising. At my word, of course, though she was not much pleased about it, she remained on her knees.

I lifted my right hand. "Tal," I said. I hoped he spoke Gorean.

He seemed surprised that I had greeted him first. As he had come, presumably, to render us a service, to conduct us somewhere, his station, quite possibly, would have been subordinate to ours. I had never, however, put great store in protocol. I am English, but I was not derived, as far as I knew, at least recently, from strata in English society where such formalities or precedences much mattered. Too, I had lived for several months in the colonies, so to speak, and, as is well known, they tend be careless in such matters, even to the point of embarrassment. I sensed, however, that proprieties of one sort or another might be not only extremely important to this fellow, but might, to a large extent, govern his life.

"Tal," he said.

"Tal," said Pertinax. "I gather you have come to meet us. You are the first Tuchuk I have met."

The fellow looked puzzled.

I was reasonably certain he was not Tuchuk. The Tuchuk face is commonly swarthy and broad. This fellow's face, a subtle yellowish brown, was narrower than would be common with the Tuchuk. He did have high cheekbones. He did have the epicanthic fold.

I had little doubt this was a fellow of the sort of whom I had heard yesterday on the beach, the sort spoken of as "strange men."

"How are the bosk?" I said to him.

"Some are in the forest," he said, uncertainly, "outside the reserve."

He would be referring to wild bosk, which can be surly and territorial. In forested areas, they are substantially forward horned, and attack, head down, directly. The Tuchuk bosk, on the other hand, usually have wide, spreading horns. When angered they attack, a bit to the side, to tear the enemy. They also hook nicely, and, if one is caught on the horn, one can be hurled a hundred feet. They are large and powerful. The straighter horns of the forest bosk are presumably an adaptation to the arboreal environment. The plains bosk are, as suggested, usually more widely horned.

"Are the quivas sharp?" I asked.

"I do not know the word," he said.

"It is important to keep the axles of wagons greased," I said.

He regarded me, strangely. "I would suppose so," he said. "The wagoners attend to such matters."

"Forgive me," I said to him.

"It is a test?" he said.

"In a way," I said.

He seemed troubled. "Have I failed?" he asked.

"Not at all," I said. "You have done splendidly." I then turned to Pertinax. "He is not Tuchuk," I said.

"Very well," said Pertinax.

Although there can be some variation in these matters I had rehearsed a common formal greeting often exchanged amongst Tuchuks. In response to my first question, a Tuchuk would most likely have informed me that the bosk were doing as well as might be expected; to my second question, that one tries to keep them that way, namely, sharp. The quiva is a Tuchuk saddle knife. Usually there are seven to a saddle. They are balanced, for throwing. In response to my third question, a Tuchuk would have been expected to agree, amicably, with some remark such as, "Yes, I believe so," or "Yes, I think so."

"Is one called Tarl Cabot, a tarnsman, amongst you?" he asked.

"I am Tarl Cabot," I said.

"I am honored," he said, "to greet a two-name person."

I did not respond, as I did not understand what he had in mind.

"I am Tajima," he said. "I am a one-name person, but I hope, one day, to be a two-name person."

"It is my hope, as well," I said, "that you will one day be a two-name person." I was not sure, frankly, what I was doing here, but I gathered it must have been right, for he bowed, graciously. I bowed back, not sure of what was going on.

"We have located Cabot and brought him here," said Pertinax. "Conduct us to your superior."

"I will do the talking," said Constantina, rising to her feet. "Untie me! Take this horrid rope off my neck."

Tajima seemed startled.

"Who is the yellow-haired collar-girl?" he asked.

"I am Margaret Wentworth," she said. "I am in command here. Tarl Cabot has identified himself. My colleague is Gregory White. Untie me! Free me of this disgusting tether."

"She is a free woman?" said Tajima.

"Yes," said he whom I had thought of as Pertinax.

"What of the dark-haired collar-girl?" asked Tajima.

"She is a slave," I informed him.

"She is your slave?" he asked.

"Yes," I said.

"I was told to expect two free men and a slave," said Tajima, "but I find two free men, and two slaves."

"I brought a slave," I said.

"I am not a slave!" said she whom I had thought of as Constantina.

"Lord Nishida," said Tajima, "is fond of yellow-haired collar-girls."

"I am not a collar-girl!" she snapped.

I supposed that, in a sense, Miss Wentworth had been a slave for some time, perhaps from the time she had been entered on certain records, or acquisition lists, at least from the point of view of slavers. They tend to regard such entries as effecting embondment, though, to be sure, there are various details to be later attended to, branding, collaring, and such. If one does not accept the slavers' view of these matters, one would understand, at least, that the selectees had been designated for bondage.

I wondered if this "Lord Nishida" had put in a request for a yellow-haired collar-girl, if one had been included in, say, his "want list."

"Miss Wentworth," said Pertinax, for I shall continue to refer to him by this name, as it is familiar, and convenient, and as it would become his Gorean name, "is in disguise. As free women are apparently seldom, if ever, in this locality, we were advised to conceal her identity, to pretend that she might be naught but a mere, degraded slave, a low-value slave, such as might be brought hither."

"'Low-value'!" said Miss Wentworth.

"Whilst I myself," said Pertinax, "assumed a disguise as a simple forester, assigned to the reserves of Port Kar."

"Release me!" demanded Miss Wentworth.

Pertinax went to untie the wrists of Miss Wentworth.

"Wait, please," said Tajima.

"Wait," I told Pertinax.

"If there is a confusion in this matter," said Tajima, "it will be clarified, three days from today, at the camp."

"'Three days'!" exclaimed Miss Wentworth!

"Two days with men," said Tajima, "three days with females."

"What camp?" I said.

"That of Lord Nishida," he said, "in which men, some men, will learn the tarn."

"'Some men'?" I asked.

"We expect to lose several," he said.

"See here," said Pertinax, who, I am afraid, took the courteous attitude of our guide as timidity or diffidence, and as legitimating an occasion for aggressive, peremptory discourse, "Miss Wentworth and I have discharged our part of the bargain. We have delivered Cabot here, as specified. We are now to return to the coast, be met by a ship, receive our wages, and be returned home, to Earth."

"'Earth'?" said Tajima.

"A place far away," I said. I did not know if Tajima was familiar with the Second Knowledge, or only the First, or, indeed, even if these distinctions were appropriate in his case. In any event, the place, "Earth," as nearly as I could tell at the time, did not seem familiar to him.

"Our home, you fool," said Pertinax.

I detected a brief flicker of displeasure in the eyes of Tajima, but his countenance, almost instantly, resumed its attitude of almost solicitous attention. I did not know Tajima, nor was I familiar with his background, but I sensed that he was of a sort which might be acutely sensitive, perhaps pathologically so, to the way in which he was treated. Rougher, bluffer fellows might have discounted or dismissed Pertinax's rudeness as mere tastelessness or stupidity, or even found it amusing, but I did not think that this would be the case with Tajima. He did not seem to me to be the sort of person whom it would be wise to treat with contempt. Such things might be taken more seriously by him than other fellows, might rankle with him, might fester within him, might eat away at his pride, might not be forgotten, might seem to require attention.

"He is tired, and upset," I said to Tajima. "Please do not mind him. He was thoughtless. He did not mean what he said. I apologize for him, and ask that you forgive him. He is sorry, very sorry." Then I said to Pertinax, in English, "You are asking for your head to be cut off. Apologize, quickly."

"He is a servant," said Pertinax to me, in English.

"No matter," I said to him, in English. I supposed there were formalities to be observed amongst these "strange men," and that amongst them there might obtain extremely complex human relationships, which would be culturally articulated, quite possibly in considerable detail. I suspected he came from a hierarchical society, as that had been suggested by his demeanor, and his concern with one-name and two-name individuals, and so on. In such a society rigid protocols would doubtless obtain between superiors and inferiors, each, in his way, showing due respect, in some mutually understood fashion, to the other. Protocol, and courtesy, I suspected, would be important to them.

"I am sorry," said Pertinax to Tajima. "It is only that I am anxious to return to the coast, meet our ship, and return home. Please forgive me."

"Tell him," I said to Pertinax, in English, "that it is not he who was the fool, but you."

"I am the fool," said Pertinax to Tajima, in Gorean, "not you. You are not a fool. It is I who am the fool, not you. I am sorry."

Tajima, interestingly, looked to me.

"He is sorry, genuinely sorry," I said. "Please accept his apology."

Tajima turned to Pertinax. He inclined his head, briefly.

"Your apology," I said to Pertinax, "has been accepted." I thought it well to be clear on that. If it was not accepted, or was accepted with certain reservations, that would presumably be very important to know. Honor, I was sure, was somehow entangled in these matters.

"I am not a fool," said Tajima to Pertinax.

"Of course not," said Pertinax.

"There is no ship," said Tajima.

"What?" said Pertinax.

"What!" exclaimed Miss Wentworth.

"No ship," said Tajima.

"I do not understand," said Pertinax.

"It is you who are the fools," said Tajima.

"Where is our money, our gold?" asked Pertinax.

"If it exists," said Tajima, "it is being applied elsewhere, otherwise than to fill purses such as yours."

"Take us to your superior!" said Miss Wentworth.

"I shall," said Tajima. "That is why I am here."

"We shall see about this!" said Miss Wentworth. "I have suffered indignities enough. My disguise is now at an end."

"That is possible," said Tajima, politely.

"You are a dolt," said Miss Wentworth. "This will all be explained to you by Lord Nishida. He will clarify everything."

"I am sure he will," said Tajima, politely.

It was interesting to me that Tajima seemed to take no umbrage whatsoever at the attitude and words of Miss Wentworth. It had been quite different with Pertinax. Tajima seemed to consider her insult as nothing to be dealt with within the context of honor, though perhaps, I supposed, it might be dealt with, and suitably, outside of that context, perhaps as one might see fit to deal with the behavior of a small, naughty animal.

"You have been unaccommodating, even insolent," said Miss Wentworth to Tajima. "I will have you punished by Lord Nishida."

"Your dress is quite short," observed Tajima, as politely as ever.

"Beast!" she said.

She then faced me. "You, Cabot," she snarled, "are responsible for much of this! You, too, will answer for my shame, my humiliation! I will inveigh with Lord Nishida to see to it that you, too, are punished. Tie my hands! Hood me! Lead me about, on a leash, like a slave! We shall see about such things! I am a free woman, a free woman!"

I did not respond to her.

I did not think I had much to fear, at least now, from Lord Nishida, whoever he might be. I had been brought to the northern forests for some reason. I was not yet fully clear on what, ultimately, that might prove to be.

"Present me to Lord Nishida, as soon as possible," said Miss Wentworth. "I will be very pleased to see him!"

"I think he will be pleased to see you, as well," said Tajima.

"I hope so," she said, acidly.

"Yes," said Tajima, "I think you should hope that."

"I do not understand," she said, uncertainly.

"It will not go well with you, if he is disappointed," said Tajima.

"I do not understand," she said.

Tajima then turned to Pertinax. "You are no longer needed," he said. "You are free to go."

"Go," said Pertinax. "Where?"

"Anywhere you wish," said Tajima.

"I am unarmed," said Pertinax. "You cannot just leave me here."

He was clearly, and justifiably, alarmed. He was not skilled with weapons, nor in woodcraft, as far as I knew. Gor was a beautiful, but a dangerous, perilous world. Surely it was muchly different from the world he knew, and, in a variety of ways, it could be unforgiving, and merciless. It had to be met on its own terms, with courage, and steel. Too, he was not Gorean. He knew not the ways of Gor. He had no clan, no caste, no Home Stone.

"Accompany us," I said to him.

"Yes, yes!" said Pertinax. "Then we can explain matters to his superior."

"As you wish," said Tajima to Pertinax.

"This prerogative of departure is extended to me, as well, surely," said Miss Wentworth.

"No," said Tajima.

"'No'?" she said.

"No," he said.

Then Tajima turned to me. "Perhaps you would present the girl to Lord Nishida? I am sure he would look kindly on one who presents her."

"You have traveled far," I said. "You are, I take it, a loyal and trusted retainer of Lord Nishida. Therefore it seems to me that it would be more appropriate if it was you who presented her to your lord."

"I serve," said Tajima. "Are you the friend of the one who may go?"

"I wish him no harm," I said.

"Then," said Tajima, "I think it would be well for him to present her to Lord Nishida. Lord Nishida may then look upon him with kindness, perhaps even favor."

"And might be inclined to spare his life?" I said.

"Precisely," said Tajima.

I turned to Pertinax. "Do you agree to present Miss Wentworth to Lord Nishida?"

"—Yes," he said.

"What is going on here?" said Miss Wentworth. "Untie me! Free me!"

I regarded her. She was pretty, in her way, so angry. I wondered if she knew how she looked, so helpless, so futile, so lovely.

"What are you looking at!" she snapped.

It was true. I fear I had not been looking at her in a way appropriate to look at a free woman.

"I agree with our friend," I said. "Your dress is quite short."

"I am a free woman!" she cried. "Untie my hands! Take this degrading rope from my neck!"

"If would be better if they were hooded," said Tajima.

"Yes," I said.

In moments the hoods were in place.

"Turn them about," said Tajima.

This was done, both to the left and right, a number of times, as though randomly.

Soon, almost immediately, long before we were finished, both women were thoroughly disoriented. Neither would have the least idea of where she was being taken. When our destination was reached, wherever it was, neither would know how they had come there, nor where they were.

I picked up Cecily's leash.

"Take Miss Wentworth's leash," I said to Pertinax. "It is, after all, you who are to present her to Lord Nishida."

He picked up the leash.

"You do not mind having her on your leash, do you?" I asked.

"No," he said.

He pulled twice on the leash, and she pulled back, angrily, in indignation.

"Things have muchly changed, have they not?" he asked.

"Yes," I said.

He then drew twice more on the leash, quickly, firmly, and his hooded charge stumbled toward him. They were then standing quite close to one another. She must have sensed his nearness, for she trembled. She was, after all, a woman, quite close to a male. This doubtless made her uneasy. Too, he was a large male, and, indeed, one considerably larger than she. Then she steeled herself, with the stiffness of the free woman. He coiled the leash, and then held it, some four inches from her throat, and jerked her chin up, so that her head was lifted to him. Had she not been hooded and had dared to open her eyes, she would have found herself, close on the leash, looking into his eyes.

"Wait!" she said to him. "Wait! I shall see to it that you are punished, as well."

Pertinax then loosened the leash, and stepped back from her, some seven or eight feet away.

"Yes," she said, sensing his withdrawal, "keep your distance!"

The leash looped up from his hand to her neck.

She stood there, confident, now that he had retreated.

"They are right," said Pertinax to her.

"What?" she said.

"Your dress is quite short," he said.

She cried out with rage.

"She has pretty legs, does she not?" asked Pertinax.

"Yes," I said. "They are very nice." Indeed, that was one of the reasons I had shortened her tunic on the beach. Certainly that would improve her disguise, would it not? Too, slave girls often have lovely legs. That is doubtless one of the things slavers have in mind when they select them.

"We should be on our way," said Tajima.

I joined him, keeping a soft hand on Cecily's leash. I also allowed her a comfortable margin of slack. In this fashion, the slave is nicely guided, and she is, of course, never out of the control of the master. A hard hand on the leash is normally used only with a captured free woman or a new slave. The leash is considerably shortened, of course, if there is danger in the vicinity, say, animals, or uneven ground, or water about, or one is in a crowd, or such. In cities, sometimes display leashes are used, of colored leather, of beaded, even jeweled, leather, or of light, closely meshed lengths of chain, sometimes of silver or gold. Most leashes, on the other hand, are little more than functional, and usually of brown or black leather. Metal leashes are common if one wishes to chain the girl to a slave ring, a convenience with which Gorean buildings and streets are usually well furnished. The typical leash is long enough to permit the binding of the slave, if one should desire to do that. In walking a slave, particularly on the promenades, it is common to make certain that the leash describes a graceful curve, from the master's hand up to the slave's collar.

"You are from Earth," said Tajima.

"Yes," I said. "It is far away."

"It is another planet," he said.

"Yes," I said.

And it was only a moment later that I realized he had spoken in English.

Chapter Nine

The Thatched Hut; Three Tubs

"When are we to be allowed to see someone important?" asked Miss Wentworth.

"I regret my unimportance," said Tajima.

"Go away!" said Miss Wentworth.

With a courteous bow, Tajima withdrew.

The camp was quite large.

I had expected it to lie on the northern bank of the Alexandra, but it did not. It was toward the Alexandra, but well inland.

"Someone will pay for this!" said Miss Wentworth. "I will not be kept waiting!"

"There is no ship," said Pertinax.

"I will see that there is one!" said Miss Wentworth. "Our agreements were clear. The arrangements were clear. We completed our part of the work, and now we must be paid, and returned to Earth, with wealth, wealth!"

"There is no ship," said Pertinax.

"We will not be betrayed!" said Miss Wentworth.

"Are we ourselves so innocent?" asked Pertinax. "Are we not, ourselves, in our way, guilty of betrayal? Did we not engage, enthusiastically and uncritically, in betrayal, pretending to be what we were not, engaging to deliver a stranger, whom we knew not, to an uncertain fate, one we did not understand, and which might, for all we knew, have proven fatal?"

In a sense, I thought, their betrayal was deeper than they understood, for they had labored, however ignorantly, in the cause of beasts, Kurii, who would covet not only Gor, but

Earth, as well. In a sense they had betrayed a world, and a species.

"I think," said Pertinax, "we have been betrayed not so much by others as by ourselves, by greed."

"Absurd!" snapped Miss Wentworth.

"You would do anything for money," said Pertinax.

"So, too, would anyone!" she said.

"I used to think so," said Pertinax. "I am no longer sure of it."

"You are a fool," she said.

"There is no ship," said Pertinax.

"There will be," she said. "I will demand it!"

"Perhaps you will be successful," he mused. "One of your smiles can twist a knife in a man's guts. I know."

"Yes!" she said. She laughed.

I gathered she had had little difficulty in having her way with men.

"Brew me tea," said Miss Wentworth to Cecily.

Cecily looked to me, and I nodded.

"Yes, Mistress," said Cecily. Cecily knew enough to address all free women as "Mistress," and all free men as "Master." On the other hand, having been embonded on a Steel World, that of Agamemnon, later that of Arcesilaus, an unlikely place to encounter free women, she knew little of free women, at least of a Gorean sort. The only free woman with whom she had had contact with on the Steel World had been the Lady Bina, a former Kur pet, who was less a Gorean free woman than a remarkably beautiful, ambitious, vain little animal. I had warned Cecily of free women, but I fear she took my cautions too lightly. She thought my concerns exaggerated, and disproportionate to the likely reality. In my view, however, my concerns and cautions were not excessive, but practical and judicious. She seemed to believe that since the slave and the free woman were both women that there would be a sympathy, an understanding, a rapport, between them. She knew so little. The free woman was a person; the slave was a property, an animal, and an animal which, aside from matters of social advancement, position, wealth, and status, was commonly preferred a thousand times by men to a free woman. But Cecily was highly intelligent, and she would learn quickly, if only under a free woman's switch.

Her safety, of course, would lie with men, and masters, who would to the extent practical, given a free woman's status and prerogatives, protect her.

We were housed in a small, thatched hut.

The door of the hut was open, but it might be fastened, when one wished, with thongs.

Once in the camp, with the license of Tajima, whom we took as our mentor and guide in these matters, we had freed the girls of their impediments, removing the hoods and leashes, and then unbinding their small wrists. The wrists of women look lovely, thonged, or braceleted, or such.

"I am a free woman," had said Miss Wentworth to Tajima, rubbing her wrists. "Bring me some decent clothing, now, and arrange an audience, immediately, with your superior. I do not wish to appear before him, as I am, so shamefully garbed."

"I am sure you will not appear before him so garbed," said Tajima, politely, and left, quietly, as was his wont.

That, however, had been two days ago.

"Go out," said Miss Wentworth, to Pertinax, "and demand an audience with someone, anyone!"

"I think we should wait," I said.

"That would be best, I think," said Pertinax.

"Then I shall go out!" she cried.

"I would not," I said. "There are strong men about, Goreans."

She stamped her small foot, petulantly, and jerked at her collar. It may be remembered that its key had been cast into Thassa, long ago. She could not remove it. To be sure, it might easily be removed with suitable tools.

In the meantime it would remain on her neck.

I had gathered, from earlier conversations between Pertinax and Miss Wentworth, that she had been the employee of a large investment firm and had been primarily utilized to solicit investments from male clients, in which endeavor she had apparently been unusually successful. Her ambitions, however, extended well beyond enticing wealth to her employer's firm, and obtaining thereby the routine emoluments of a salary and commissions. Why should she herself not have the wealth which she so ably diverted into the channels of others, an illusive wealth to whose passage she stood so near but from which she was yet so far? She seemed to me little more than an unimaginative creation of her time, a creature of ambition and egotism set mindlessly upon the pursuit of the dazzling, gleaming bubbles of a meretricious culture. To be sure, she was quite lovely, and that was doubtless what first drew her to the attention of Gorean slavers. Here was a female, however, who would not only look well in shackles, but, first, might be turned to the advantage of purposes extending far beyond the coins she might bring when taken from the block. And so she had been approached. Pertinax had been a minor clerk in the same firm.

The movements of free women on Gor tend to be restricted, and monitored. One is always aware when they are about. They are precious. One pays attention to them. Slaves, on the other hand, are generally free to come and go, as they please, not much noticed. They may have to request their master's permission to leave their domicile, and they may have to return at a stipulated time, subject to discipline, and, indeed, has one not seen them hurrying frantically through the streets hoping to cross their master's threshold before the ringing of the fifteenth bar, but one is used to them, and pays them little attention when they are about in the streets, the alleys, the markets, the plazas, and parks, save, of course, to speculate on their lineaments and wonder how they might look at one's slave ring. Accordingly, it is not unprecedented that a female Kur agent on Gor, to increase her mobility and anonymity, may be dressed as though she were, despite her freedom and importance, no more than a slave. And if that is the case, will she not require a male to complete her disguise, one who will pose as her master?

And, as noted, earlier, free women are rare in certain locales, such as the northern forests. Thus, if a project is afoot in such an area, and one may wish to have a female agent on hand, one who may be useful with respect to its success, it is almost certain that she will be disguised as a female slave, and, if her disguise is to be plausible, she must have one about who will appear to be her master.

Mr. Gregory White, a minor employee at the investment firm, was no more immune to the charms of Miss Margaret Wentworth than a great many other males. Indeed, he had long looked upon her from afar, acutely, and poignantly, well aware of the chasms, social and commercial, which separated him from such a different and special creature. A clever, beautiful young woman, she was well aware of his hapless infatuation, just as she was in the case of a number of other males of no interest or importance to her, whom she scarcely deigned to notice. It gave her great pleasure to be above them, remote, frosty, businesslike, inaccessible, beyond their level, out of their grasp. She was above them; they were beneath her. It was she who could come and go within the doors of the great and powerful, doors they could not even approach. Kur agents, of course, often recruited pairs, primarily, one supposes, for the reasons suggested earlier. When she learned that she might have to disguise herself as a slave, she almost withdrew from the project. She, a slave! How absurd! How disgusting! To be sure, this would have meant only that another would have been sought in her place, and she would have been placed on an acquisition list for a later pick up, not as an agent, of course, but merely as another slave, her beauty perhaps then indistinguishable amongst that of many others. The cages and pens, after all, are filled with beautiful women. When it became clear to her, however, that the offer was to be withdrawn, and her dreams of unusual wealth were fading, she swiftly relented, agreeing that it might be amusing to play such a role, that of a mere slave. She would need, of course, some fellow to pretend to be her master. They were willing to find her one, but, interestingly, for some reason, she suggested White. Presumably she did this because she thought him a typical, diffident man of Earth, one easily manipulated, one easily dominated. Too, of course, she was well aware of his infatuation, and this would add a delicious, exploitable nuance to the relationship, and put him muchly in her power. It would be amusing to dominate him, and order him about. She could imagine him hurrying to serve her, in this way or that. Yes, it would be amusing.

Her name would be "Constantina." Not the best choice, perhaps, for it was more of a free woman's name than a slave's name, but she wanted something stately and impressive. A more typical slave name would have been, say, Lana or Lita, or, say, a more familiar Earth-girl name, such as Jane, Audrey, or Cecily. Earth-girl names commonly serve as slave names on Gor. That is perhaps because Goreans think of Earth girls as being of slave stock, of superb slave stock. Indeed, some Goreans look for them in the markets, and it is said they are seldom disappointed. And the name of White, whom she easily recruited, would be "Pertinax."

Miss Wentworth paced back and forth in the hut, angrily.

Later, she was occasionally less certain of the wisdom of her choice in recruiting White, for he was much larger and stronger than she, was, in his way, strikingly good looking, and, annoyingly, was as swift, if not more so, than she, in learning Gorean and certain ways of Gor. Certainly the dolt could not be more intelligent than she! She would have found that intolerable. Accordingly, any evidence of his intellectual superiority she discounted. He was, of course, a man of Earth, and so there was little to fear. Sometimes she felt distinctly uneasy when she was near him, as a female, particularly when she was in her costume, that of a slave. Once, in a fearful dream, as I would learn, she had dreamed he had stripped her publicly in the company offices while others looked on, bemused, or unconcerned. Then he had thrown her to his feet, kicked her, and put a collar on her, and had then put her to his pleasure, while the others continued to look on, and later politely applauded. She recalled going to her belly, crawling to his shoes, and, head down, frightened, kissing them.

After that dream she was very surly, and bitter, toward him.

If she suspected he might be regarding her, perhaps the arch of her chin, the curve of a calf, the turn of an ankle, she would berate him savagely.

She took much pleasure in ordering him about.

Pertinax, or White, if you prefer, understood little of this, and merely, as a man of Earth, redoubled his efforts to please his demanding employer.

By now, some five days after being met in one of the reserves of Port Kar, the yellow signs which we had originally followed east from the coast would have disappeared. Had one followed them, and not been met, it would have been supposed that the likely destination of our trek would have laid still to the east. If one had then elected to continue in this direction, one would then have merely penetrated deeper and deeper, fruitlessly, and possibly dangerously, into the forests. The most direct route from the hut of Pertinax to the camp would have been, as nearly as I could determine, lacking maps and coordinates, either south by southeast, or, more likely, southeast.

The indirection, or circuitry, of our route had been a matter, I supposed, of security. Whatever projects might be afoot in the forests, they were, it seemed, a matter of great secrecy.

I had had a sense of where, in any event, approximately, we might be heading, probably to the Alexandra, some pasangs upriver, but how many pasangs I had no idea, fewer if the direct route was, say, south by southeast, more if it would have been southeast.

This surmise, however, as noted, proved to be incorrect, at least with respect to our destination being the Alexandra, or, perhaps better, it was not so much incorrect as premature.

I became more confident, day by day, that the Alexandra would figure in these matters.

"Is my tea ready?" asked Miss Wentworth.

"Nearly, Mistress," said Cecily, who was tending the small pot on its rack, over a tiny fire, it in a small hole, a shallow hole, scooped out in the dirt floor of the hut.

"You are slow," said Miss Wentworth.

"Forgive me, Mistress," said Cecily.

"Take off your clothes," said Miss Wentworth.

"What?" said Cecily.

"Completely," said Miss Wentworth.

"'Mistress'," I suggested.

"Mistress?" said Cecily.

"Now," said Miss Wentworth.

"Must you humiliate her?" asked Pertinax.

"Certainly," snapped Miss Wentworth. "She is no more than a slave. They exist to be degraded and humiliated."

Whereas a slave may be degraded or humiliated, or beaten, or chained, or such, at the merest caprice of the master, it is seldom done. There would be no point to it, particularly in the case of a girl who is trying to please. The slave, like any animal, is to be governed with understanding, sympathy, and intelligence. Too, the Gorean master is usually quite fond of his slave, though I suppose few would be likely to admit this. But, fond of her or not, discipline is not to be compromised. Discipline must be firm, strict, and unyielding. She is, after all, a slave. She is to be held under an exact, uncompromised, unswerving discipline. She expects that, and is not disappointed.

The least infraction, she knows, may be punished with the switch or lash.

That is doubtless why there are so few infractions.

The slave thrives under discipline; it comforts her, and orders and regulates her life; she is content; she is mastered; she rejoices in the discipline to which she is subject. She would not have it any other way.

The greatest kindness a man can show a slave is to put her to his feet.

Cecily cast me a frantic, plaintive look.

I think she hated Miss Wentworth, and Miss Wentworth, surely, was not her mistress. Cecily's relationship to her, of course, was radically shifted, following the unwelcome revelation that her blond, blue-eyed rival in beauty, so to speak, was not like herself a slave, but a free woman.

"Do it," I said, gently.

Tears in her eyes, Cecily slipped from her tunic.

"Serve me," said Miss Wentworth.

"Yes, Mistress," said Cecily.

"No," I said to Cecily. "Serve me."

"Yes, Master," said Cecily, gratefully.

The word of the master, of course, takes precedence over the word of a free person who is not the slave's master or mistress.

"What of me?" snapped Miss Wentworth.

"Serve yourself," I said.

"Pertinax!" she snapped.

Pertinax then hurried forward, to fill another cup, which he then, promptly, delivered to Miss Wentworth.

The slave girl, incidentally, and I suppose this is obvious, does not serve a beverage to a free woman in the manner she would serve a male, and certainly not in the way she would serve her master. For example, in paga serving, as in a paga tavern, the serving is done in such as way as, in effect, to entice and seduce the male. In such a situation the girl is trying to interest and excite the male and, at the very least, is petitioning his attention, presumably with the alcove in mind. The use of the girl comes with the price of the drink, and thus which girl is summoned to the table, or which, approaching the table, is accepted, has an import which might not be obvious to the stranger to such establishments. To be sure, many fellows are out for little more than a drink. They enter, they drink, talk, and leave. The customer's option need not be exercised. Even if one does not conduct one's waitress, so to speak, to an alcove, it is pleasant, in any event, to be served by a beautiful woman, collared, perhaps belled, in a bit of diaphanous silk, if that.

As noted, then, the slave does not serve the free woman in the manner in which she is likely to serve a male, particularly her master. She would be savagely beaten, if not slain, should she be so ignorant or foolish as to do so. To the free woman the slave girl is, at best, a despicable convenience. She is loathed, probably because of her interest to men. The cruelty of the free woman to the slave is legendary. It is quite different from the usual relationship between a male master and his slave. Gorean slave girls dread free women. It is their fervent hope that they may be purchased by an attractive male, and, ideally, be his only slave.

Sometimes, of course, as an act of cruelty, a free woman, for her amusement, before company, consisting of other free women, will order a terrified slave to offer her drink as she might a male, and then, when she does so, she will be denounced. "What are you doing, you wanton slut? How dare you! Do you think I am a gross, lustful beast! I am a noble free woman, you miserable, disgusting, salacious hussy, you abject, collared she-tarsk! I am insulted! You will pay for that! Bring me the whip!" "Yes, Mistress," weeps the slave, and hurries to fetch the whip which, to the amusement of the free woman and her guests, will be used on her.

The camp seemed to be, more than anything, a lumber camp, for logging was in process in the vicinity, and one, not unoften, heard the striking of axes, the crash of falling trees. These logs were trimmed, sawn, harnessed, and dragged by grunting, hissing draft tharlarion to staging areas where, skinned of bark, and piled, they awaited hoisting by weights and pulleys onto wagons, which were then drawn by tharlarion down a narrow, muddy road, soon disappearing amongst the trees. Interestingly, this road did not seem to lead west, toward the coast. Rather it seemed to lead southeast. As several of the logs bore the badges of Port Kar, at least some of them must have been taken from reserves, one supposed, illicitly.

I did hear, upon occasion, away in the forest, the scream of a tarn.

The camp was not palisaded, but its perimeters, for those expected to remain in the camp, not the work crews, were clear, a set of wands encircling the camp, rather like those which marked the reserves, but these wands bore no ribbons, with legends.

I had, in wandering about, intended, for my interest, to cross the border of the wands, to scout the area, but I had been warned back by a prowling larl, which was, as nearly as I could determine, although it was not collared, a guard beast. I understood then why the camp, despite the richness of timber about, was not palisaded, at least not in the sense of being encircled by a close-set wall of sharpened palings. It did, of course, in a sense, have its palisade. Such beasts were its palisade.

I held the cup of tea, and looked upon Cecily, who knelt before me. She knelt in the position of the tower slave, not that of the pleasure slave, as there was a free woman present. Cecily looked at me, shyly, and smiled. I, too, smiled. Well she knew that any beautiful woman on her knees, stripped and collared, is pleasant to look upon, in whatever position she kneels.

The position of the Tower Slave is respectful, and demure. Further, she is usually well tunicked, or even robed. To be sure, her collar must always be visible. It would not do to confuse her with a free woman. The position of the pleasure slave, of course, is also respectful, but it is also provocative, and inviting. It must leave no doubt in the observer's mind as to what sort of slave she is. The palms of her hands are usually down on her thighs, and her head up, but, if she is petitioning caresses, as is not uncommon, the palms are usually up, the backs of the hands on the thighs. The palms of a woman's hands, as is well known, are unusually sensitive, as might be noted, for example, if one were, lightly, with the tip of a finger, to trace the form of a "Kef" on them. The palms, then, so offered to the master, with their exposed, sweet, sensitive cupping, the backs of the hands down on the thighs, as though bound to them, as though not permitted to leave them without permission, present a sign not difficult to read. Too, at the same time, the girl's head is usually lowered. This makes clear her humility and need, and how much she is at the mercy of the master, for the least touch. Variations, of course, occur. Sometimes, perhaps in markets, the girl will kneel with her wrists crossed behind her, as though bound, or will have her hands clasped behind the back of her head, or the back of her neck. This lifts the breasts, nicely.

"Oh," said Miss Wentworth, impatiently, "have the filthy little tart, the disgusting trollop, put her clothes on!"

"She is neither a tart, nor a trollop," I said. "She is a slave. That is less than both."

The former Miss Virginia Cecily Jean Pym smiled. She was far, now, from her antecedents, from Mayfair, from Oxford.

She was now naught but a Gorean slave girl, on a world on which men knew what to do with such as she.

I did not, incidentally, despite Miss Wentworth's command, or behest, give Cecily permission to reclothe herself. Without that permission she would remain naked.

Cecily was quite attractive.

And this is not surprising.

Is not a woman most attractive when she is naked, in a slave collar?

"Slut, then!" said Miss Wentworth.

"Every good slave," I said, "should be a slut at her master's feet."

"Disgusting!" said Miss Wentworth.

"Not at all," I said.

"Is that what men want, sluts?" said Miss Wentworth.

"Far more than that," I said, "a slave. Every man wants a slave, a helpless, vulnerable, ardent, needful slave."

"White," she said, "does not!"

"I am Pertinax," said Pertinax.

"What?" said Miss Wentworth.

"There is no ship," he said.

"There will be a ship!" she cried. "I shall demand it!"

"I am Pertinax," he said.

"You are mad!" she said. "That is over!"

"No," he said, quietly. "It has just begun."

"Pertinax," she said, angrily, "is a man of Earth. He is civilized!"

"High civilizations," I said, "have invariably held slaves."

"He is a gentleman!" she said. "He would not want a slave."

"Gentlemen," I said, "have often held slaves."

"Reassure him, Pertinax," she snapped. "Tell him that no true man would want a slave!"

I thought it interesting, how words could be twisted about, and used as levers, as cudgels, as whips, and such.

"I am not sure of that," he said. "Perhaps it is otherwise. Perhaps it is rather that any man who does not want a slave is not a true man."

"Certainly men desire slaves," I said to Miss Wentworth. "I think that is clear. Beyond that the dispute seems to me verbal. I suppose one could define the true tarn as one that does not fly, the true larl as one that does not hunt, and so on, but this does not seem helpful in understanding the world. Putting aside cultural and historical considerations, as somehow irrelevant, surprisingly so, or illegitimate, astonishingly so, one might ponder whether or not biology is relevant to the matter, for example the radical sexual dimorphism of the human species, genetic predispositions, the pervasive relationships in nature of dominance and submission, and so on."

"I am a free woman!" said Miss Wentworth.

I was not clear as to the pertinence of her claim, which was uttered almost hysterically.

"There is also," I said, "the test of life consequences. For example, what are the effects of one modality of life as opposed to another? Suppose one way of life reduces vitality, produces unhappiness, boredom, even misery, and anomie, a sense of meaninglessness, and another modality of life increases vitality, enhances life, produces happiness, charges one with energy, gives meaningfulness to one's existence, and so on. Which is to be preferred?"

"I am a free woman!" she cried.

I was not disputing that. I wondered at her outburst.

She was still, of course, in her tunic.

Perhaps that was what motivated her outburst. Perhaps she wanted to utter something which might seem to belie her appearance, an appearance which doubtless made her uneasy, or somehow troubled her. Certainly Pertinax and I had no difficulty in accepting that she was a free woman. It did not seem, then, that she should be trying to convince us of that. Who then was she trying to convince? Pertinax naturally, from his background, I supposed, the antecedents of our situation, and so on, would think of her as a free woman. And I, too, thought of her as a free woman, particularly in view of her awkwardness, clumsiness, stiffness, and such, to say nothing of her manifest psychological and emotional problems. The contrast with Cecily was obvious. Cecily, now, not only accepted her sex, but rejoiced in it. At a man's feet, owned, and mastered, she had found herself.

She had wanted to end her confusions and conflicts, and had discovered the sweetness and wholeness of a total surrender to the male, her master.

She kissed his feet and became herself.

"I am a free woman," said Miss Wentworth, "a free woman, a free woman!"

"Of course," I said.

"I wonder," said Pertinax, thoughtfully.

Pertinax's remark surprised me. I had not expected it.

"What?" cried Miss Wentworth.

"In the offices, amongst the desks," said he, "did I not imagine you often not in your svelte business wear, and high heels, so chic and yet so provocative, so arrogantly, insolently, calculatedly, deliberately provocative, but rather barefoot on the carpeting, naked and collared?"

"You beast, White!" she screamed.

"You will address me as Pertinax," he said.

"I do not understand," she said.

"There is no ship," he said. "Much has changed."

"There will be a ship!" she cried. "Nothing has changed!"

"I have changed," he said.

I had the thought, now, that Pertinax might leave a hut, to look after a trussed property, even were a sleen in the vicinity.

And certainly a property, helplessly trussed, lying outside in the darkness, might fervently hope that he might do so.

"I trust," said Miss Wentworth to Pertinax, "you are not toying with contemplating the possible meaning of your bestial strength, that you are not tempted to acknowledge your desires."

Pertinax regarded her, angrily.

How fortunate she was that he was not Gorean!

"Your strength and desires must be ignored," said Miss Wentworth. "It is best if you can convince yourself that they do not exist. Struggle desperately to do that. If that is not possible, you must put them to the side. One must choose sorrow and righteous grief over opportunity and gratification."

Yes, very fortunate.

"Why?" asked Pertinax.

"Because you are of Earth!" she said.

"Perhaps an Earth which has too long ignored certain truths," he said, "an Earth in sorry need of recollection, of reformation."

"You are a cultural artifact," she said, "engineered to conform to imposed standards, as much as an envelope or motor."

"No," he said, "I am a man."

"A cultural construct!" she said. "A manufactured product, designed to cohere with a complex set of systematically interrelated roles."

"Surely," I said, "a test of cultural value should have some relevance to the happiness and fulfillment of human beings."

"No," she said.

"To what then?" I asked.

"To the culture itself," she said, "its prolongation."

"I see," I said.

A culture did seem to have its own dynamics, its own life, a life, a biography, to which the welfare or happiness of its components might be only indirectly related, if at all. A plant was organic, and the health of the plant assured the health of its components. A culture, on the other hand, though it might crumble and lapse into obsolescence, was commonly not organic, but mechanistic, and the functioning of the machine required not the happiness, health, or welfare of its parts, but only that they functioned appropriately, contributing to the pointless longevity of the machine itself.

"Is there no such thing as nature?" I asked. "Is there only misery, prisons, guns, and hatred?"

"Nature does not exist," she said.

"You cannot be serious," I said.

"It does not exist in any important sense," she said.

"If not," I said, "why must it be so fiercely contested, so strenuously fought against?"

"It is inimical to civilization," she said.

"Only to unnatural civilizations," I said.

"All civilizations are unnatural," she said.

"Not necessarily," I said. "There is no reason why a civilization cannot be an expression of nature, rather than her enemy, in its way an enhancement of nature, a celebration of nature."

"There are no such civilizations!" she said.

"There have been several," I said.

"None now!" she cried.

"I know of at least one," I said.

"No!" she said. "No, no, no!"

"What are you afraid of?" I asked.

"I am not afraid!" she cried. She pulled down, desperately, at the hem of her tunic, with both hands. "Do not look at me so!" she cried to Pertinax.

"There is no ship," said Pertinax.

I think Pertinax had begun to sense how a woman might be viewed, particularly one in such a tunic.

Women were not men.

They were quite different.

"Do not look at me so!" she said to Pertinax. "Are you some boor, or brute? Have you not been educated?"

"I was not educated," said Pertinax. "I was trained, indoctrinated. Perhaps only now has my education begun."

"Beast!" she cried.

"What of the test of life consequences?" I asked.

"I do not understand!" she wept.

"Does the mastery not fill a man with power," I asked, "with zest, with vitality, with a sense of reality and identity, with a sense of fittingness, with a sense of being himself, with a sense at last of being a part of nature rather than a dislocated, lost, wandering fragment shorn from her?"

"Why have we not been brought before Lord Nishida!" she cried.

"The mastery fulfills a man," I said. "What man is complete until he has at his feet a slave?"

"A slave! Oh, yes, a slave!" laughed Miss Wentworth, scornfully.

Then she turned to Cecily.

"Slave!" she said.

"Mistress?" said Cecily.

"You are a slave, are you not?" asked Miss Wentworth.

"Yes, Mistress," said Cecily, frightened.

Surely Miss Wentworth could see that her fair throat was enclosed in the circlet of bondage.

"Worthless, degraded, meaningless, naked slave!" said Miss Wentworth.

"Yes, Mistress," whispered Cecily.

"You, slave," cried Miss Wentworth scornfully to Cecily, "are you happy as a slave, do you want to be a slave, are you fulfilled as a slave?"

"It does not matter, Mistress," said Cecily, "whether or not I am happy to be a slave, whether or not I want to be a slave, whether or not I am fulfilled as a slave. I am a slave."

"Answer me, slut," cried Miss Wentworth. "And speak the truth!"

"I must speak the truth, Mistress," said Cecily. "I am a slave."

"That is true," I said to Miss Wentworth. "The slave must speak the truth. She is not a free woman."

"Yes, Mistress," said Cecily. "I am happy to be a slave. I want to be a slave. I am fulfilled to be a slave! It is what I have always been, and knew myself to be, and now the collar is on me! I am a slave, and should be a slave. It is what I am, what I want to be, and what I should be!"

"Disgusting, disgusting, disgusting!" screamed Miss Wentworth.

I did not understand her concern. If some women were slaves, and wished to be slaves, and loved being owned, and wanted to be at the feet of masters, why should she object? What was it to her?

"Have I come at an inopportune time?" inquired Tajima.

"No," I said.

He had entered in his quiet, polite way, unobtrusively.

"Lord Nishida," said Tajima, "regrets the delay, but he was awaiting an envoy, one from exalted personages."

I supposed that would be some Gorean. Perhaps it would be Sullius Maximus, pretending, again, to be an agent of Priest-Kings. I had little doubt that the true agent had been disposed of, doubtless long ago, probably cast to the nine-gilled sharks of Thassa. They often follow in the wake of a ship, to retrieve garbage.

"There!" said Miss Wentworth. "At last! Now we will receive our pay, be conducted to the coast, board ship, and, soon, brought first to an appropriate base, find ourselves again on Earth."

"Your slave is very pretty," said Tajima, noting Cecily.

He viewed her as what she was, a lovely animal, perhaps even a prize animal.

"Thank you," I said.

Masters are often pleased when their beasts are commended. Such commendation, you see, reflects credit on him. In such a way he is complimented on his taste in women, in slaves.

"You may finish my tea," I told the slave, handing her the cup, with its residue, "and then you may clothe yourself."

"Yes, Master," she said. "Thank you, Master."

She put her head down to drink. She held the cup with two hands, as a Gorean cup is commonly held.

"Do white women make pleasing slaves?" asked Tajima.

"Yes," I said.

"That is well," he said.

"I cannot see Lord Nishida like this," said Miss Wentworth, indicating her brief tunic, little now but a rag, given our journey through the forest. "Bring me something suitable!"

"I have," said Tajima, who held, over his left forearm, what appeared to be, arranged in several narrow folds, a sheet of rep cloth.

"Give it to me," said Miss Wentworth, putting out her hand.

"Outside," said Tajima, "there are three tubs, filled with hot water, in which you may soak, and enjoy yourselves. It will be very pleasant, and there are, at hand, smooth scrapers of sandalwood, scents, oils, and towels."

"Outside?" said Miss Wentworth.

"She is not used to public bathing," I said.

"Interesting," said Tajima. "We shall have one of the tubs brought within the hut."

"No," said Miss Wentworth.

"No?" asked Tajima.

"I insist on being brought immediately to Lord Nishida," said Miss Wentworth.

"You do not wish to bathe?" asked Tajima, surprised.

"No," she said. "Bring us to Lord Nishida immediately."

"We shall proceed immediately then," said Tajima.

"No, no," said Miss Wentworth, suddenly. "I must dress!"

"Perhaps we might have the honor of greeting Lord Nishida," I said, "and Miss Wentworth might then follow, shortly."

"A most suitable suggestion," said Tajima. "The yellow-haired one may then, if she wishes, dress in privacy."

"I certainly so wish," she said.

He handed the rep-cloth sheet to Miss Wentworth, who seized it from him.

"I will send two men to conduct you to the audience," said Tajima to Miss Wentworth.

"I will wait outside, and accompany her," said Pertinax.

"As you wish," said Tajima. "Also, as I recall, it is you who are to present Miss Wentworth to Lord Nishida."

"I can present myself, I assure you," said Miss Wentworth.

"It is not customary," said Tajima.

I then accompanied Tajima from the hut, as did Pertinax, save that he waited discreetly outside, until Miss Wentworth would be ready to attend the audience.

Cecily, now tunicked, heeled me, as was proper.

As I left the hut, I paused, to glance at the three tubs. I would have been pleased to have had the bath. To be sure, I would keep my weapons at the side of the tub. If any approached too closely, I would arm myself. More than one warrior has been slain in the bath.

Outside, at the three aforementioned tubs, Pertinax and I found, waiting, two lovely young women. They might have been of Ar, or Venna, or Telnus, from almost anywhere.

"These would have bathed you," said Tajima.

"I see," I said.

Both women looked down, frightened.

Perhaps they were new to their collars.

Both were naked.

"You may look upon them as you wish," said Tajima. "These are not contract women, trained, refined entertainers, or such. They are simple, coarse slaves, no different from those with which you are familiar. You may note that their necks are encircled with collars, and may be confident that the collars are closed, and locked. Too, if you care to examine their left thighs, you will note, just under the hip, a brand."

I examined the brands. Both wore the cursive kef, the most common Gorean slave brand.

"They were both free women of Ar, even of high station," said Tajima. "Several such have come recently into our hands."

"Ar is troubled, of late," I said.

"I have heard that," said Tajima.

"I am surprised," I said. "I thought such women might not be cultural for you."

I had some sense of the milieu from which the "strange men" might have sprung. I did not doubt but what ancestors of theirs, from hundreds of years ago, or perhaps thousands, might have been brought to Gor by Priest-Kings on the Voyages of Acquisition, as had representatives, or, perhaps better, specimens, of a number of other backgrounds and cultures. The Garden of Gor, so to speak, both botanically and zoologically, had seemingly been stocked with care, at least at one time, apparently for interests both scientific and aesthetic.

Most Goreans, on the other hand, were, I was sure, completely unfamiliar with the "strange men."

To be sure, much of Gor is *terra incognita*.

But what did it bode, or signify, I wondered, that some such men might now be here, in the northern forests, engaged in some project, which appeared to be both mysterious and secret?

And I had been debouched on the northern coast, at specific coordinates, supposedly by the order of Priest-Kings, though Kurii, too, obviously, had been apprised of those coordinates.

What might be, I wondered, the interest of Priest-Kings, or Kurii, in this area, at this time?

"We are a formal, traditional people," said Tajima. "The old ways are important to us. But we are also an intelligent, adaptive people, and are always ready and eager to adopt useful devices, pleasant customs, and such."

"I understand," I said.

"Also, of course, it is not unusual for women to come into our keeping as a result of sale, of raiding, of war, and such."

"Still, I am surprised," I said. "I thought such identificatory and custodial details, brands and collars, and such, might not be cultural for you."

"We have had them for centuries," said Tajima. "It may be, I do not know, that they were not original with us, but one does, does one not, mark animals?"

"Certainly," I said.

"Thus, we may very well have come up with them independently, but, if not, we are happy to learn from others. Those of the high cities are so elegant and efficient in these matters that it would do us great honor to recognize, if we did, the perfections which they have developed in their handling of women."

"Of slaves," I said.

"Of course," he said.

It was true. Over centuries the Goreans had developed the handling of female slaves into a fine art.

That is something an Earth woman might remember, if she is brought to Gor as a slave.

"There were three tubs," I said, "two slaves."

"One slave to bathe you," said Tajima, one to bathe Pertinax."

"We could bathe ourselves," I said.

"Assuredly," said Tajima, "but is it not pleasant to be bathed by a naked slave?"

"Yes," I said.

"The small pleasures of life," said Tajima, "are not to be scorned."

"True," I said.

"Besides," said Tajima, "the act is beneficial for the women, as well. It helps them to understand that they are women, and that, as women, although they are women, they may prove to be of some value, however humble."

"What of Miss Wentworth?" I asked.

"Miss Wentworth, as she is a female, may bathe herself."

"There were only three tubs," I said.

"Your slave," said Tajima, "would use your tub, after you had finished."

"I think you speak English," I said.

I remembered this from the reserve.

"I learned it far away," he said.

"On Earth?" I said.

"Yes," he said.

"Have you come recently from Earth?"

"Yes," he said.

At that moment I heard the roar of a larl.

"Do not be dismayed," said Tajima, "it is from the pavilion of Lord Nishida."

"It sounds close," I said.

"It is," said Tajima. "There is the pavilion."

Chapter Ten

In Which Is Recounted a Portion of What Occurred in the Pavilion of Lord Nishida

"Greetings, Tarl Cabot, tarnsman," said Lord Nishida. "Welcome to Tarncamp."

"Greetings," said I, and bowed, politely, which salutation was graciously acknowledged by Lord Nishida, with an inclination of the head.

Lord Nishida was garbed in white robes. He sat cross-legged, within his pavilion, on a low, flat platform of lacquered wood, some twelve feet square. Beside him, one on each side, lay two swords, one short, one long, each with a large, slightly curved hilt, wrapped in silk, and a curved blade. The longer of the two swords was not unlike that carried by Tajima, thrust in his belt, edge uppermost. Lord Nishida's countenance was refined, even delicate, but refined and delicate in the way a light, carefully edged weapon is refined and delicate, as, for example, the shorter of the two blades beside him.

"I trust that your journey hither was pleasant, and uneventful," said Lord Nishida.

"Yes," I said.

It would have been considerably less pleasant for the girls, of course, as they had been bound, and hooded, and led on leashes, for much of the journey.

"I trust, as well, that your quarters, though regrettably primitive, a consequence of the rude and transitory nature of our camp, are satisfactory."

"Thoroughly satisfactory," I said.

"I am pleased to hear that," said Lord Nishida.

"You have made the acquaintance, of course," he added, "of our trusted and loyal servitor, Tajima."

"Yes," I said.

"I trust his service was satisfactory."

"Eminently so," I said.

Tajima was standing behind me, to my right.

"He is in training," said Lord Nishida.

"I am sure he will do well," I said.

"We will see," said Lord Nishida. "He has much to learn."

"We are grateful," said Lord Nishida, "that you deigned to accept our invitation to Tarncamp."

"It was my pleasure," I said.

I had heard a tarn in the vicinity, but I had seen none in the camp, either taking flight or alighting.

Lord Nishida smiled, slightly.

"And had it not been my pleasure?" I asked.

His eyes briefly clouded. "That would have been most regrettable," he said.

A fellow sitting beside him, seated as he was, cross-legged, on his right hand, remained impassive.

The fellow was not of the "strange men."

He had short-cropped blond hair, and squarish, heavy features. He wore an informal, brown robe, which betokened no caste in particular. He was, I took it, the envoy whose arrival Lord Nishida had been awaiting. I supposed him an agent of Kurii, one who might pose as an agent of Priest-Kings. He was not, however, Sullius Maximus.

At the edges of the lacquered platform, one on each side, crouched two larls. Behind Lord Nishida, at the back of the platform, stood six of the "strange men," each armed with a glaive, the blade of which, socketed in its stout pole, was some two-and-a-half feet in length, and curved. It was presumably an infantry weapon. It could be used for either thrusting or slashing. It would not be thrown. Whereas I would not have anticipated difficulty in getting behind one such weapon, it would be exceedingly dangerous if there were two such weapons, as an aggressor would be likely to be vulnerable to the blow of the second weapon. As the glaive is used most effectively forward or to the soldier's left, if the wielder is right-handed, one would try to keep to the wielder's right. Behind Lord Nishida, to his left, stood what I took to be two women of the "strange men," each lovely, each fully clothed, neither veiled, unlike most Gorean free women, particularly of wealth or high caste, in what I supposed, on Earth, would be spoken of as kimonos. I shall, in any event, use that word for such garments, henceforth. Too, interestingly, the garment worn by Lord Nishida, as it is called by the same word in Gorean, *korti,* I will refer to as a kimono, as well. The woman's kimono is rather different from that of the man. The man's kimono is informal, elegant, and loose, and allows much freedom of movement. The woman's kimono seems narrower and, particularly from the waist down, much more constrictive. The women would walk with short, graceful steps, which gave them an unusual, distinctive gait. The robes of the Gorean free woman, while layered and cumbersome, have much greater play at the hem. The kimono, incidentally, is not allowed to the collar-girls of the "strange men." This is not surprising, of course, as they are animals.

I wondered if they were examples of the "contract women" of which Tajima had spoken. In any event both were on the platform with Lord Nishida, which suggested status, though in a subordinate position. It seemed clear that neither was, so to speak, a Ubara, who would have shared a throne with a Ubar, if not his power. Neither, too, seemed a "display woman," a "trophy woman," or such. In the high cities "display slaves" are not uncommon. For example, a rich man's palanquin, borne by slaves, may be followed by a single or double coffle of display slaves, uniformly tunicked, back-braceleted and neck-chained. They are a display of wealth. Similarly, slaves might be displayed about the foot of a Ubar's throne, stripped and chained. These are commonly former high women taken in war. For example, the daughters of a Ubar defeated in battle, now the slaves of the conqueror, may be so displayed, as trophies attesting to the victor's might and skill.

"You have a lovely slave," said Lord Nishida.

Cecily had heeled me into the pavilion. After entering with me, she had gone, as was proper, to first obeisance position, beside me, a bit back and to my left. In first obeisance position, often assumed by a slave in the presence of a free man, she kneels with her head to the ground, and the palms of her hands down on the ground on either side of her head. The usual second obeisance position has the slave go to her belly, her hands on either side of her head.

"Thank you," I said.

"Please allow her to kneel up," said Lord Nishida.

"Kneel up," I told Cecily.

She then knelt up, her back straight, her head up, her hands on her thighs. As was appropriate in the circumstances, she kept her knees modestly together.

"Excellent, excellent," said Lord Nishida. "How pretty they are."

I glanced to the two women of the "strange men" on the lacquered platform. They were looking upon Cecily, but I saw no sign of envy, hostility, or jealously. This was quite different from the way in which a Gorean free woman would look upon a slave girl. They see the slave girl as a vulnerable, but hated rival, with whom, for the interest of men, they could not begin to compete. These women, however, seemed to view Cecily more as one might have a lovely pet, doubtless of great interest to men but not really constituting a threat to themselves, and their position. I would later learn that these were, indeed, "contract women," who, as girls, were often sold to pleasure houses, most often by their parents. Sometimes, too, they would sell themselves to such a house, to be trained in arts of pleasure, for example, music, dancing, singing, conversation, and such. As their contracts could be bought and sold they were, in effect, slaves, but they were not thought of as such. For example, they occupied an understood, accepted, and generally respected niche in their society. They were not tunicked, not branded, not collared, and so on. They were not "collar-girls." Indeed, they regarded themselves, without arrogance, and with much justification, as far superior to collar-girls. They were, in their view, in a different category altogether. The collar-girl was an animal who might be put to the straw in a stable, and would not even be permitted within the refined precincts of the pleasure house. The collar-girl was ignorant of the simplest things, even the proper serving of tea, the careful, delicate, symbolic arrangements of flowers, and such. She would be of little interest to a gentleman, save for her performance of lengthy, servile labors, and her squirmings, gaspings, moanings, thrashings, and beggings, perhaps back-braceleted, in his arms. Certainly the contract women knew the attractions of simple collar-girls for males, but they did not regard them as rivals. When, wearied of a world's concerns, he wished to spend a leisurely, elegant evening, gratifying his various cultivated senses, physical, intellectual, and aesthetic, his choice would not be the collar-girl, but the women trained to comfort and delight him in traditional and cultural manners. Interestingly, though I suppose there must be exceptions to this generalization, the women of the "strange men" seem generally reconciled to the fact, and will even expect, that their males will seek gratifications beyond the walls of their own domiciles. Nothing culturally heinous seems to be associated with this matter. As many companionships are arranged between families, with considerations not of love, or even of attraction, paramount, but of wealth, prestige, status, and such, and the young people often being scarcely considered in the matter, this is, I suppose, understandable. The female companion's complacency in this matter, or her understanding, or her tolerance, is, one gathers, quite different from what would be expected in the case of, say, a Gorean free companion, who, commonly, would find these arrangements outrageous and insufferable. For example, she would not be likely, resignedly, without question, to pay a bill arriving at her domicile from a pleasure house, pertaining to a pleasant evening spent there by her companion. In the light of these considerations, to the extent they might apply, then, it should be clear why the "contract women" would not be likely to concern themselves overly much with collar-girls. First, they regard the collar-girls as far inferior to themselves, and thus scarcely in the category of rivals, and, secondly, they share the general view, as I understand it, of the women of the "strange men," namely that they have little or no hold over a male, and he may be expected to pick flowers, so to speak, where he pleases. If, however, a contract woman might find herself in love with a client, she, being quite human, and utterly helpless in her contractual status, might, understandably, resent his interest in, say, another contract woman, or, even, as absurd as it might seem, a collar-girl.

In any event, neither of the women, whom I took to be contract women, took much interest in Cecily, or gave her much attention. To be sure, they doubtless recognized that she was attractive, and might, accordingly, be of interest, even considerable interest, to men, but what would that, really, have to do with them? She was different. She was nothing. She was a collar-girl.

Lord Nishida turned to the fellow sitting beside him, to his right. "Two met our friend, Tarl Cabot, as planned, and brought him to the reserve, where contact took place between him and Tajima," he said.

"Yes," said the fellow with short-cropped blond hair.

"These two," said Lord Nishida, "were selected suitably, as specified?" said Lord Nishida.

"One was selected with great care, following diligent inquiry, and exacting research, from amongst several, from over two hundred," said the blond fellow, "according to your various specifications."

"You made the selection yourself?" said Lord Nishida.

"I would trust it to no other," said the fellow.

"The appropriate background, the appropriate characteristics, egotism, ambition, greed, a lack of scrupulosity, and such?"

"Yes," said the blond fellow.

"And are my senses likely to be pleased?" inquired Lord Nishida.

"I think you will be pleased," he said. "Indeed, two businessmen in our service concurred in my judgment."

"Excellent," said Lord Nishida.

"The other did not much matter," said the blond fellow.

"True," said Lord Nishida. "Tajima," said Lord Nishida, quietly.

"Yes," said Tajima.

"The other's purpose was served, surely, when the reserve was reached," said Lord Nishida. "Yet I understand he is in the camp. Why did you not kill him?"

"I was reluctant to stain my blade with inferior blood, that of a weakling," said Tajima. "I would have left him behind, for animals, but Tarl Cabot, tarnsman, our guest, desired that he be permitted to accompany us."

"I see," said Lord Nishida. "You did right, then, to bring him to the camp."

Tajima bowed his head, slightly, acknowledging this judgment of Lord Nishida.

"He may be disposed of later," said Lord Nishida.

"I am sure," I said, "he may prove of service."

"There is no place in this camp," said Lord Nishida, "for cowards or weaklings."

"He may be neither," I said.

"Summon him forth," said Lord Nishida. "Put a sword in his hand, and put him against our servitor, Tajima."

"He is less than unskilled," I said. "He knows nothing of the sword."

"Summon him," said Lord Nishida.

"I protest," I said.

"Summon him," said Lord Nishida, not unkindly.

His attitude gave me pause.

In moments Pertinax was conducted within the pavilion. He had apparently been in the vicinity, which led me to believe that Miss Wentworth, too, must now be nearby, though perhaps not yet permitted within the pavilion.

One of the long, curved swords, with the large hilt, was placed in the hands of Pertinax, at which he looked, apprehensively. A colored cord dangled from the hilt, which terminated in a tufted blue tassel. Tajima then backed away from him, and, smoothly, drew forth his own weapon, which he gripped with two hands, and assumed what, for such a weapon, was apparently an on-guard position. The position seemed formal, and quite stylized, but there was no mistaking the readiness, or menace, of his attitude.

"You will fight," said Lord Nishida. "One of you is to die. Prepare to fight."

Pertinax cast me a look of bewilderment, and misery.

But he did not turn about, and run.

I was proud of him. Too, I did not think he would have made it to the exit of the pavilion.

Four fellows now stood there, two armed with glaives, two with swords.

Tajima moved toward Pertinax, and, twice, feinted toward him.

Pertinax lifted the blade, weakly, and then, putting down his head, in defeat, lowered it.

"You will now kill him," said Lord Nishida to Tajima.

I recalled Tajima was in training.

Tajima turned away from Pertinax, and faced Lord Nishida. "Lord," said he, "set me rather the slaughter of a tethered verr."

Tajima had his back to Pertinax.

But, from my training, I knew his every sense was alert, on a knife's edge of cold fire.

I trusted that Pertinax would not act.

Tajima seemed wholly at ease, even disgusted, certainly indolent. There was insult emblazoned in his very posture.

I trusted that Pertinax would not act.

In a moment it became clear to me that Pertinax would not seize his apparent opportunity.

I smiled to myself, and, suddenly, almost inaudibly, I moved my foot, quickly, in the dirt.

Instantly Tajima had whirled about, his sword ready to fend a blow.

His action was so quick that I, familiar with the reflexes of warriors, which often spell the difference between life and death, must admire it, and Pertinax, startled, gasped, his blade still haplessly lowered.

"He may be permitted to live," said Lord Nishida, "for the time."

One of the guards relieved Pertinax of the weapon.

"Well done!" I said to Pertinax.

"I did nothing," he said.

"That is why you are still alive," I said.

I turned to Lord Nishida.

"My thanks, great lord," I said.

He inclined his head, a little.

Tajima returned his sword to his belt.

Pertinax stepped back, shaken.

"If I may," I said to Lord Nishida, "I would now like to speak of matters of importance."

There was much I wanted clarified.

What was going on here? Why had I been brought here? What was I to do here? What was expected of me? It seemingly had something to do with my being a tarnsman, but, beyond that, I understood very little, little or nothing.

"Yes," said Lord Nishida, "we must speak of matters of importance, and soon, but, first, we should attend to a matter which is not important."

I stepped back.

Lord Nishida then looked to the blond fellow with short-cropped hair, he in the nondescript brown tunic, who had had little to say, but had been muchly attentive to all that had transpired. In his seemingly slumberous stolidity he reminded me a bit of the inert larls who crouched at the edges of the platform. I trusted they had been well fed.

"I think you will be pleased," said the blond fellow.

Lord Nishida then looked to Tajima.

"We thought it might be appropriate," he said, "if one agent, Mr. Gregory White, introduced his superior and colleague, Miss Margaret Wentworth."

"'Gre-gor-e-white' and 'Mar-gar-et-went-worth'," said Lord Nishida. "Barbarian names are so difficult." Then he said, "Please proceed."

Tajima bowed politely, and then motioned for Pertinax to follow him, and went toward the threshold of the pavilion. Shortly thereafter, a small figure, completely covered, from head to foot, wholly concealed in a large sheet of white rep-cloth, was conducted forward, a guard on each side of it, Pertinax a little before it, on its left, and Tajima in the background.

This group stood, then, before the platform, or dais.

Lord Nishida leaned forward.

The small figure, as noted, was covered, from head to foot, in the rep-cloth sheet.

I supposed this must be Miss Wentworth, from the slightness of the figure and the rep-cloth sheet, but I would have expected Miss Wentworth to be quite urgent and vocal, now that she had been permitted within the pavilion. Perhaps it was not she.

From the size of the figure and hints of the sheet it seemed clear that the figure within the sheet was that of a female, and, quite possibly, one who might stimulate spirited bidding.

I could see where the sheet was bunched, before her body, where she held it about her with two small fists.

I could see the small figure was barefoot.

It must be Miss Wentworth, but her silence was surprising.

I wondered that she did not speak.

Perhaps she was unaware that she was now within the pavilion, and standing before the dais of Lord Nishida.

Miss Wentworth had been muchly dismayed with her tunic, and particularly so after I had altered it more to a male's satisfaction. She regarded the simple, graceful garment, it seems, as not only unconscionably brief, but despicably insulting. Too, I think she suspected its likely effect upon males, and this caused her considerable uneasiness.

A male, seeing her in such a garment, would doubtless suppose she was exactly what she appeared to be, a slave.

And who knew what consequences might then ensue?

It might not be amiss to insert a parenthetical remark here.

Whereas a Gorean free woman, used to extensive robing and veiling, reduced to bondage, and tunicked, not only face-stripped, now forbidden veiling, but revealingly clad, might almost die of shame to be seen so displayed, a girl of Earth is far less likely to have the same emotional response to brief or revealing clothing. She is, for example, familiar with miniskirts, sun suits, beachwear, and such. Indeed, the typical Gorean slave tunic is a great deal more modest than much of what might be routinely encountered at poolside in various resorts, hotels, spas, and so on. The acceptability of such garmentures to the Earth female is commonly taken by the Gorean, who tends to be a bit prudish in such matters, save where slaves are concerned, as evidence of the suitability of Earth females for the collar. Any Gorean female who appeared so, publicly, would be taken as "courting the collar." Indeed, the state might take her in hand, and brand and sell her. Needless to say, as well, the nature of much of Earth lingerie confirms this view of the Earth female in Gorean eyes. Consider the brevity and softness of such garments. Are they not, then, secret slaves, slaves awaiting their masters? So Earth girls brought to Gor must largely learn the shame and degradation of the tunic, which, however, is not too difficult to grasp when, shortly, they see the contrast between their garmenture and that of the free woman, and understand how they are viewed. Then they may learn to weep in shame at their exposure. This, of course, is a temporary phase, for, soon, the slave, whether a barbarian fetched hither for the block, or a Gorean free woman reduced to bondage, discovers how special, different, and wonderful she has now become, that she is now a mere slave. They come to understand that they are now desired, as never before. They come to see free women as dangerous, but pathetically unhappy, repressed creatures. They fear free women, but, in their way, pity them for they cannot know the ecstasies, fulfillments, and joys of the slave. They come to a new understanding of their bodies, and are at peace with them, perhaps for the first time in their lives, and rejoice in them, and come to love them, and come to see them as delicious and lovely contrasts to the sternness and power, the rudeness and brutishness, of the male bodies, to which they will be forced to submit. They come to understand the magnificent complementarity of nature, and their lovely role in this complementarity. They would not now be other than they are, for they have finally come to understand the glorious preciousness of themselves, even though they may sell for no more than a handful of copper tarsks. The slave now knows that she is beautiful and desired. Accordingly, she soon walks happily, and beautifully, walks as a desirable female, and the most desirable of all females, the female slave, something for which men will pay. She now wears the tunic, or camisk, well, shamelessly, no longer dismayed that her beauty is brazenly displayed, but is now well pleased that it should be so. "Let me be seen, Masters. Look upon me! This is what you have collared!" The beautiful female body is no longer something which is to be hidden, as though it were a blemish or sore, something of which one is supposed to be ashamed, rather than something of which one is to be accepting, and pleased. So the slave now rejoices in her beauty, and, in her female vanity, relishes the fact that it must now, by the will of men, but as she wishes, too, be displayed for their pleasure. And so, slave-clad, she appears in public. The slaves of a city are amongst its most beautiful sights. Behold them in the streets and markets! How exciting and beautiful they are! And does the slave's beauty, shamelessly flaunted before the master, not tempt him to its taking! How it torments him, and drives him wild, and the briefly clad, sinuous she-sleen are well aware of what they are doing. Well they know the power that lurks in an ankle, or the turn of a head. Do masters not sometimes bind and lash their slaves for their insolence and pride, until, at his feet, they offer him their beauty's placation, piteously reminding him that it is his to do with as he wishes. And do they not even smile, or laugh, under the lash, until, say, the third or fourth stroke, well reassured of their effect upon him.

And I suspected then that she, Miss Wentworth, had gratefully disdonned the tunic and had welcomed the sheet as a transitory salvation, pending the providing of a suitable garmenture. Her concern to appear before Lord Nishida as soon as possible and demand her immediate return to Earth, before an additional and possibly greater delay might take place, had doubtless determined her to avail herself of any expedient at hand, and the sheet, if nothing else, was voluminous and, were the light not behind it, opaque. In any event, as nearly as I could tell, from the appearance of things, there was nothing beneath the sheet but Miss Wentworth herself.

To be sure, she would be in a collar.

I had seen to that.

On the other hand, perhaps it was not Miss Wentworth. The figure did seem very quiet. I supposed that that would be unusual for Miss Wentworth, not only because of her dispositions and personality, but because of her acute concern to make known her demands.

In any event, this mystery, if it were a mystery, was to be soon dispelled.

Lord Nishida made a tiny motion with his right hand, and Tajima put his hands, gently, to that portion of the sheet which was wrapped about the head and face of the bundled figure.

As soon as she felt his hands at the sheet a series of urgent but unintelligible noises emanated from within the cloth.

I knew then at least one explanation for the small figure's silence.

A slave may be simply warned to silence, and she will then

remain silent until permitted to speak. A free woman, on the other hand, or a woman who believes herself to be free, may require something further.

Tajima then, carefully, lifted the sheet away from the figure's head, and it was, indeed, Miss Wentworth, who shook her head, angrily, as though to free her head even the more swiftly from the folds of the sheet.

She looked about, then, suddenly, wildly, taking in the scene about her.

She uttered a tiny noise of fear, and her legs gave out beneath her, but she was steadied by the two guards who held her in place, by the upper arms, beneath the sheet. Her fear, understandably enough, was a reaction to the sight of the two larls, one on each side of the platform. She had perhaps never seen a larl before, and even if she were familiar with these large carnivores, finding oneself in their vicinity, without viewing them through thick bars or ascertaining that they were, say, tethered on stout chains, would be enough to unnerve a heart more experienced and stouter than hers. In any event, I had certainly shared a similar apprehension upon my entrance into the pavilion. The fact that the beasts seemed somnolent and that they seemed to provoke little concern amongst the others in the pavilion had, of course, considerably, if not entirely, assuaged my apprehensions. The larl, of course, is never fully tamed. Like the tarn, it has a wild blood. Too, if one makes a sudden movement in its vicinity, for example, a paw may, as by a reflex, lash out and a hand may be half torn from a wrist, or an arm may be shredded.

Miss Wentworth, desperately, clutched the sheet about her.

Then she straightened her body.

She now understood the two larls to be harmless. She was mistaken in this conjecture, but it was a rational conjecture considering that the two beasts were quiet, crouched in place, and that their presence seemed to be accepted without question by the others present. She might have been less confident had she known more about larls. Pretty obviously the two beasts were domestic larls, probably raised from cubhood, and trained to respond to certain commands. On the other hand, as noted earlier, no larl is ever fully tamed. A thousand generations of stalking and killing lay concealed, lay in wait, in every corpuscle of those pelted, passive giants.

More tiny, inarticulate sounds emanated from Miss Wentworth.

Her eyes were a confusion between anger and chagrin.

Her mouth was widely opened, as it must be, to accommodate the ball, which was fastened in place by straps buckled behind the back of her neck.

It is a very embarrassing and humiliating gag, particularly for a proud woman. She does look absurd, or silly, with her mouth so widely opened, the ball fastened in place. The common Gorean gag, whether associated with a hood or not, consists of wadding, or packing, and binding. It muffles sound quite effectively, and is commonly used if one, say, might wish to transport a bound capture between sleeping guards, conceal a back-braceleted woman in a wagon making its way through a city's gate, or such. The prisoner of such a device can make only tiny, miserable sounds. The usual code in such matters, if the prisoner is interrogated, is one sound for "Yes," and two for "No." The gag fixed on Miss Wentworth, in contrast, allows a good deal of noise, and would not do for the usual considerations of security. It does, however, share one virtue with the common gag, of course, which is that it makes articulate speech impossible. When a woman cannot speak she commonly feels frustrated and helpless. The blindfold, or hood, in its way, has a similar effect. One effect of the ball arrangement which is not shared with the common gag is that of making the woman appear ridiculous, her mouth widely opened, the ball in place. This attacks the vanity of the woman, with the consequence that she often becomes quite docile, hoping to be soon relieved of this indignity. Afterwards, a simple frown, or brief word, may be enough to silence her, perfectly. She does not wish to be again subjected to the humiliation of the ball and strap. She has then learned she may not speak, if men do not wish it. In passing, a bit gag might be mentioned. These may be fastened in place, or be as simple as a stick held between the teeth, which the woman is forbidden to drop. Both the ball gag and the bit gag are safer than the common gag, as they permit breathing through the mouth. A prisoner should never be left untended if fastened in a common gag. For example, if certain forms of distress occur, such as regurgitation, the gag should be torn free instantly. A captive is not to be lost, but brought safely to your chains.

The ball in Miss Wentworth's lovely, but widely distended mouth was blue, and the straps which held it in place, buckled behind the back of her neck, were yellow. These are the colors of the slavers.

Miss Wentworth was then silent, absolutely, unwilling to further embarrass herself.

She threw a piteous look at Lord Nishida, one less then of anger than of supplication.

Surely he must understand her plight, and take pity on her.

She was now learning, too, I supposed, what it was to be in the power of men. She continued to clutch the sheet about her, tightly. The two guards held her, still, by the upper arms.

There was a bruise on the left side of her face, and I noted some discoloration, dirt, I supposed, on the sheet.

This soiling was in the vicinity of her knees.

A small gesture from Lord Nishida, a lifted finger, indicated that the embarrassing impediment to her speech might be removed.

She looked angrily at one of the guards, he to her right, and with, too, a look of vindictive triumph.

I supposed it must have been he who had seen to her inconvenience and discomfiture.

Tajima, carefully, unbuckled the gag and handed it to the guard on Miss Wentworth's left, who slipped it in his pouch.

It was doubtless he who had supplied the device to his colleague.

"Lord Nishida!" she cried.

"Please," said Tajima, "do not speak yet. You have not been presented."

"I can present myself!" she cried, angrily, clutching the sheet even more closely about her. The two contract women observed her, with interest. They were unfamiliar, I supposed, with this tone of voice being used by a woman to a man.

But Lord Nishida smiled, and shook his head a tiny bit,

negatively, and lifted his hand a little, in a benevolent, cautionary gesture.

"Then present me!" said Miss Wentworth, in fury.

"One moment," said Tajima.

He then reached to the hair of Miss Wentworth.

"What are you doing?" she said, angrily.

"Please," said Tajima, politely.

He then rearranged the hair of Miss Wentworth, first lifting it to the sides that its length and sheen might be noted, and then he put it carefully behind her back, spreading it nicely, evenly, behind the sheet.

Lord Nishida nodded. I gathered he was pleased.

I noted the interest, too, of the two contract women on the dais behind Lord Nishida, and to his left. I supposed they had seen few examples of such hair, given their presumed backgrounds, long, glossy, silken yellow hair, or blond hair.

Tajima stepped back, and seemed satisfied with his work.

Miss Wentworth seemed to smolder and fume with fury.

Tajima then turned to Pertinax.

"Mr. White," he said, politely, "please do us the honor of presenting Miss Wentworth to Lord Nishida."

"Do it, you fool," snapped Miss Wentworth.

"Lord Nishida," said Pertinax, "this is Miss Margaret Wentworth."

Lord Nishida inclined his head, slightly, graciously, acknowledging her presence.

"I have been kept waiting," said Miss Wentworth. "Why?"

"Deplorably, certain minor details of business were to be attended to," said Lord Nishida, "before we were prepared to entertain your august presence."

"The delay," she said, "is rude, and inexcusable. I discover that a brutish warrior, a half-naked, meaningless slave, and my employee, White, are all here before me. I have priority over each of these. No business could conceivably be more important than mine."

"And what is your business?" asked Lord Nishida.

"First," said Miss Wentworth, "not only was I kept outside, kept waiting, but I was subjected to violence!"

"Yes?" said Lord Nishida.

"I demanded entrance, and was denied it, by this brute to my right," she said, indicating one of the two guards who flanked her. "I was warned to silence, but would not be denied. I was struck! Struck!"

I now understood the bruise on her left cheek. I supposed she had been cuffed, struck with the open hand. One does not strike a woman as one might a man.

"I could not believe that one had dared to lay a hand on me," she said. "When I expressed my indignation, and warned him that I would see to his punishment, the hideous, degrading device you saw but moments ago was forced into my mouth and fastened in place, and then I was put to my knees, to my knees, though a free woman, and must then wait outside, unable to speak, and kneeling, until brought within."

"Most regrettable," said Lord Nishida.

That she had been knelt would account for the soiling of the sheet, in the vicinity of her knees.

Given the personality, antecedents, and presuppositions of Miss Wentworth I could understand something of her frustration and outrage.

She had brought much of this, if not all of it, on herself, of course.

An obedient slave, of course, would almost never be struck. There would be no point to it. Similarly, if she were knelt, and, say, hooded, she would think little of it, for she is slave, and knows it will be done with her as the master pleases.

"Then," she said, "when put to my feet and ready to be brought within, my head was covered in the sheet, completely, so I could not see my way!"

"That is common," said Lord Nishida, "when one such as you is to be presented before a *daimyo*."

"What?" said Miss Wentworth.

"A lord," said Tajima.

"One such as I?" she said.

"Yes," said Tajima.

This was not unlike a practice in the court of some Ubars, when a certain form of gift, or tribute, is being presented.

I would later learn that *daimyo*, or "great names," were vassals to a *shogun*, a high lord, usually a military governor, with an army at his disposal. A *shogun* was nominally subject to an emperor, but the emperor's role was largely ceremonial, and the true power, as is commonly the case, lies with those who are the masters of men and weapons.

"I denounce this brute to my right," said Miss Wentworth. "He struck me, he denied me speech, by means of the humiliating object fastened in my mouth, and he put me to my knees before him. I, on my knees, before a male! I demand his punishment. He is to be slain, or flogged to the bone!"

"What is your business, that of which you spoke?" asked Lord Nishida.

"Is it not obvious?" inquired Miss Wentworth.

"Please speak," said Lord Nishida.

"You have heard of the world, Earth, I presume," said Miss Wentworth.

"Yes," said Lord Nishida.

"I was approached by an agent on Earth, one doubtless in your employ," she said, "and engaged, for a stipulated compensation, to pursue certain projects on this world on your behalf, in particular making contact with a Tarl Cabot and seeing to it that he was delivered to an agent of yours in a timber reserve of a city called Port Kar. To abet this project it was meet that I disguise myself, which I did, adopting the guise of a Gorean slave girl, even to allowing myself to be seen in the insulting, disgusting garmenture of such sleek, meaningless, lascivious, groveling little beasts. To complete the disguise I would require a subordinate to play the role of a master, and for that purpose I had no difficulty in recruiting a suitable male weakling, a minor employee in the very firm in which I worked, a fool, one of several, hopelessly besotted with my beauty from afar, who would take orders from me, docilely and unquestioningly."

"Mr. White?" said Lord Nishida.

"Yes," said Miss Wentworth. "And now I come to my demands."

"But, please," said Lord Nishida. "You were approached by no agent of mine."

"I do not understand," she said.

"Can you make tea?" he inquired. "Properly?"

"No," she said, puzzled.

"Can you arrange flowers," he asked. "Properly?"

"No," she said.

"Can you play a stringed musical instrument, a lyre, a lute, a samisen?"

"No," she said.

I saw the two contract women exchange amused glances. One giggled, slightly, she on the right, as one faced them. This displeased Tajima, but the girl did not seem disconcerted by his disapproval.

Lord Nishida did not see fit to acknowledge the contract woman's indiscretion.

The woman's name was Sumomo, and Tajima, I would later learn, was interested in her contract, which he could not afford.

"Perhaps you can dance," said Lord Nishida.

"No," she said.

Lord Nishida would surely not have in mind dances which might be indigenous to his own culture. Miss Wentworth could not be expected to have such skills. They would be quite foreign to her.

He must have in mind then, I supposed, Gorean slave dance.

To be sure, she would doubtless know nothing of that, as well.

The forms of dance of the women of the "strange men" would, I supposed, be lovely and would be backgrounded by a rich cultural tradition, but I also supposed they would be quite different from Gorean slave dance.

Whereas Gorean slave dance can be as subtle as the opening of the petals of a flower it is commonly richly, luxuriantly, unmistakably, outspokenly, unapologetically, brazenly erotic. It is hard for a woman to be more beautiful than in slave dance, where the slave, barefoot in sand, in a swirl of diaphanous silk, bangled, belled, and collared, dances before masters.

A skilled dancer brings high prices. I had once owned one, Sandra, whom I had sold long ago to a dealer in such wares, for a golden tarn disk.

Many masters require that their slaves learn at least the rudiments of such dance.

One supposes that the motivation of this is clear.

"Are you skilled," asked Lord Nishida, "in the art of conversation?"

"No," said Miss Wentworth, "and I do not understand the purport of these bizarre questions."

"What then are you good for?" asked Lord Nishida.

"I do not understand," she said. "I have fulfilled my part of the bargain, and I now demand my compensation, and to be conducted to some point, from which I may be promptly returned to Earth, to New York City. Please secure the moneys as soon as possible, or arrange for their delivery on Earth, as I intend to waste no more time here."

"It will be seen to," said Lord Nishida, "that your time is not wasted."

"Good!" she said.

"But I fear it is not within my power," he said, "to see to it that you are returned to your world."

"I was promised!" she said. "Your agent, or some agent, arranged this whole matter! I do not understand what is going on."

It was not difficult to tell that Miss Wentworth was now not only puzzled, but frightened. She had, as she had pointed out, fulfilled her part of a bargain, be it one of unscrupulous betrayal, and now she found herself in an alien environment, in which little or nothing of the arrangements into which she had entered seemed to be known.

She turned about. "White, White," she exclaimed, "what is going on?"

"There is no ship," said Pertinax.

"No, no!" she cried. "There is a ship!"

"No," said Pertinax.

"Perhaps I can explain," said a voice.

"You?" she said, questioningly. Then she cried out, "You!"

He who had spoken was the fellow on the platform at the right hand of Lord Nishida, he in the informal, brown robe, seemingly indicative of no caste in particular, he of the short-cropped blond hair, and heavy features, he whom I took to be an agent of Kurii.

"Joy! Joy!" cried Miss Wentworth suddenly, in wild relief, now certain it was he whom she thought. "There! He will tell you! He will tell you!" she cried to Lord Nishida. "Now things are all right! Now, all will be explained!"

"You have met before?" said Lord Nishida.

"Certainly!" she cried. "It is he, Mr. Stevens! He was my contact! It was he with whom I entered into agreement! I received an advance payment of several thousand dollars from him! Mr. Stevens, explain all to these fools!"

"You know him?" said Lord Nishida.

"Certainly!" she said. "He is Thaddeus Stevens, of Stevens and Associates."

"I am Thrasilicus," said the man. "As you were disguised on Gor so I was disguised on Earth. There is no firm 'Stevens and Associates.'"

I did not think that it was really surprising that Miss Wentworth had not immediately recognized Thrasilicus. She had probably met him only once or twice before, probably months ago, in very different circumstances, and in very different garb. Here he would seem much different, in a different garmenture, in a different environment. Too, he had been rather in the background, and her attention had been much fixed on Lord Nishida, who occupied the center forefront of the platform. Too, Miss Wentworth had been distracted by her various concerns and the perhaps intimidating unfamiliarity of this milieu. Too, his appearance might have been somewhat different on Earth. For example, he would presumably have attempted to duplicate the diffident, half-apologetic body language of the man of Earth, and the subdued discourse of the typical, reduced male of Earth, culturally engineered to betray his natural power and manhood.

"Explain who I am to these fools!" said Miss Wentworth. "Get me out of here!"

"You have had little difficulty in the past," said Thrasilicus, "in having your way with men."

"So?" she said.

"And men strove to please you," he said.

"Yes?" she said.

"Perhaps now," he said, "men will have their way with you, and you will strive to please them."

"I do not understand," she said. "Explain things to these fools, and get me out of here!"

Thrasilicus then turned to Lord Nishida. "Miss Wentworth,"

he said, "was an employee in a large business establishment of a sort with which you would be unfamiliar, and one of which I doubt that you would approve. Her office was to solicit funds from male clients to be invested in other enterprises, for which she spoke, through the auspices of the business establishment she represented."

"In this endeavor she was successful?" asked Lord Nishida, with interest.

"Very much so," said Thrasilicus. "Men would do much to please her, to win a smile, a glance of gratitude, to avoid a frown, a tear, a trembling lip. She is a highly intelligent, sophisticated, beautiful woman, and she used her sex brilliantly. Few men realized how blatantly they were being manipulated. Some others understood her game only too well, and played the game with her, she not understanding how the player was being played. She supposed them as much the victims of her charm and beauty as their simpler brethren. In any event, she brought large amounts of coin to her employers, and accordingly soon stood high, in arrogance, in her company, was welcomed into her establishment's chambers of power, and so on. Colleagues of mine, for purposes which you can guess, scout attractive females. Indeed, there are many women of Earth who, unbeknownst to themselves, are even now being scouted."

"What are you saying!" cried Miss Wentworth.

"Please," said Lord Nishida, gently cautioning Miss Wentworth to silence.

"These colleagues," continued Thrasilicus, "when they are convinced of the potential value of a given woman, enter her on an acquisition list."

"I do not understand!" said Miss Wentworth.

"I myself," said Thrasilicus, "was the first to note Miss Wentworth, at a business luncheon, in which she was rather obviously cultivating potential clients. For a woman of Earth she was unusually attractive, and I thought something might be done with her. I was there, of course, as Stevens, of Stevens and Associates. She introduced herself, engaged in conversation, even light-hearted banter, and subtly attempted to suggest, from the very first, that she found me physically attractive. I pretended to take this seriously, and she grew bolder, even touching my hand, and then drawing back, as though in embarrassment, or confusion, as though in fear she had gone too far. I think she knew her work well. Naturally I encouraged her to believe that Stevens and Associates might have considerable investment capital in hand, and that we were looking to put it to use, pending the location of a suitable firm to handle this matter. By the end of the luncheon, after which we lingered for drinks, I had learned a great deal of Miss Wentworth, how she operated, clients she had obtained for her firm, and so on. Interestingly, two of these clients were associates of mine. In any event, quite soon, almost immediately, and long before our conversation was concluded and I had placed the business card of Miss Wentworth in my wallet, she had been found, unbeknownst to herself, an apt candidate for a Gorean slave block. Indeed, I myself, that very afternoon, convinced of the matter, with no hesitation, entered her, by my own hand, on an acquisition list. The matter was then settled. All that remained was to determine a suitable time for her harvesting. I thought some fellow would have an amusing time teaching her her collar."

"Collar?" said Miss Wentworth.

"But we concern ourselves, of course," said Thrasilicus, "not only with acquisition lists, but want lists, as well, and a new customer, whom we were muchly concerned to please, for various reasons, had specified a particular form of merchandise. We examined the acquisition lists, and a large number of potential candidates for that list, more than two hundred, as I believe. And, all in all, after considering these women, those listed, and those under consideration for listing, it seemed to me, personally, and to others, as well, that Miss Wentworth was a splendid choice. To be sure, I admit the possibility that some aspects of her personality, and a certain personal annoyance with her, from when she had tried to manipulate me, might have had some influence on my choice. I hope so. Although the final choice was mine, I thought it judicious to subject it to the consideration of two of my associates, prominent in business in New York City, aware of my concerns and interests in certain matters, and muchly aware through personal experience, as they were clients of hers, of Miss Wentworth's personality, techniques, practices, and activities. These were two, of course, of presumably several, who understood quite well what she was trying to do, and, for their amusement, or in their contempt, had let her think that they had been taken in, so to speak, that they were, as many others, the unwitting dupes of her charm and beauty. They were also aware, of course, that my primaries often make use of such women. In any event, they concurred with my judgment, and so the matter was settled, over drinks, and the clinking of glasses, in a dimly lit bar in Manhattan, that is, a drinking place in an area on the planet Earth. Miss Wentworth would strike two targets with one arrow, so to speak, a transitory purpose of interest to my primaries in the north and the satisfaction of an order from a new and valued client, currently in the same area."

"Excellent," said Lord Nishida.

"All that remained then," said Thrasilicus, "was to waft the fantasy of wealth before the greedy, unscrupulous, shapely Miss Wentworth. She rushed to it as a vulo to sa-tarna."

"Good," said Lord Nishida.

I gathered that Miss Wentworth was exactly what Lord Nishida had had in mind.

"I do not understand any of this," said Miss Wentworth.

"You are worthless," said Thrasilicus.

"I do not understand any of this!" she cried. "You hired me! We had an agreement! You paid me! You gave me a retainer, a token retainer, as you said, of one hundred thousand dollars!"

"That money was never deposited," he said.

"I saw papers, certifications," she said.

"Of course," he said.

"I do not understand!" she said.

"I do not think it is so hard to understand," said Thrasilicus.

"Who were these business men you spoke of!" demanded Miss Wentworth.

"Two known to me," said Thrasilicus.

"That you fabricated," she said. "There were none such! All fawned upon me. There were none I did not dazzle, and charm! All sought my favor, my smile. I was popular!"

"I do not doubt your popularity," said Thrasilicus. "There were probably none who did not consider, from time to time, how you might appear, naked, and bound at their feet."

"No!" she said. "They were gentlemen!"

"A gentleman," said Thrasilicus, "not unoften contains a man."

"A woman," she said, "is entitled to use her charms, to tease, to appear to offer, when there is no offer, and such."

"Perhaps a certain sort of woman," said Thrasilicus.

"I was successful," she said. "I won many investments, much largesse, considerable capital, for my firm!"

"True," said Thrasilicus. "And your practice always wore the veil of mutual interest, of the earnest exploitation of timely opportunities, of the utmost business efficiency, of the highest standards of commercial professionalism, but, underneath, was concealed an agenda of unilateral advantage, for your firm and yourself, an end you shamelessly pursued by attempting to appeal to, and twist, the needs of men, with a thousand smiles, the suggestion of promises, the scattering of various seductive hints."

"I was successful," she said. "I fooled them all!"

"Several of your clients, as I understand it," said Thrasilicus, "lost a great deal of money."

"That is not my concern," she said. "They were dupes, gullible fools, all of them!"

"It is interesting," said Thrasilicus. "You seem to believe that none of these men understood your techniques and stratagems, that none of them understood what you were doing, and how you were doing it."

"None did!" she said.

"Some did, surely," said Thrasilicus, "and doubtless several others, as well. Not all men are naive, not all are silly fools."

"None did," she insisted.

"Some understood you only too well," said Thrasilicus. "While pretending to succumb to your rather labored wiles, they found your meretricious trickeries transparent, and secretly regarded you with amusement, even contempt."

"No!" she said. "And, if I might ask, who were these two alleged businessmen to whom you referred earlier?"

"You may ask," he said. "But that is all."

"Who were they!" she demanded.

"Curiosity," he said, "is not becoming in one such as you."

"One such as I?" she said, puzzled.

"If you persist in this matter," said Tajima, "it may be necessary to once again restrict your speech."

Miss Wentworth regarded him, angrily, but said nothing.

She was unwilling, it seemed, as many women, to undergo again the shameful indignity of the ball and strap, which had given her a proof that on this world a woman might not always be permitted to speak how and when she wished.

I think she had then begun to suspect deeper meanings of her sex than she had been aware of on Earth.

"I have heard much of your sort," said Lord Nishida to Miss Wentworth. "I have long looked forward to meeting one of you."

"Of my sort?" she said. "One of me?"

"Yes," he said.

Then Lord Nishida addressed Tajima. "Please draw down the sheet to her shoulders."

Miss Wentworth struggled, but was held in place by the two guards. Tajima held the sheet in place.

"You wear a slave collar," said Lord Nishida, concernedly.

"It was part of my disguise!" she cried. "I am a free woman!"

"It is very attractive," said Lord Nishida. "Remove it."

"I cannot!" she cried, angrily.

"You cannot?" asked Lord Nishida.

"No," she cried. "I had the key, I could have removed it, but that brute, that monster, Tarl Cabot, he whom we brought here, for you, as agreed, took the key from me, and cast it into the sea!"

"I see," said Lord Nishida.

Slave collars, of course, are not made to be removed by the slave.

"Get the hateful thing off my neck!" she cried.

Cecily looked up at her, startled. Cecily loved her collar. Had she been capable of owning property, it would have been her proudest possession. Actually, of course, it, like herself, belonged to the master. She had a security, and an identity, in the collar. In its way it defined her, and governed her behavior, how she should act, how and when she might speak, what she might do, and not do, and so on. She wanted to be owned, and loved being owned. She loved belonging to a man, as his helpless, vulnerable, utter property. How free she was then, kneeling at his feet, and how right, and perfect! Too, it betokened that she was a woman of value, that she had worth, that she could be bought and sold. Too, not every woman was collared. The collar attested to her desirability as a female. It said, in its way, "Here is a female who has been found of interest to men." And, from the woman's point of view, it said, in a sense, "See me. Look upon me. I have been found worth collaring." It was, in its way, thus, a badge of excellence, a certification of quality.

Lord Nishida looked to one of his subordinates, near the entrance to the pavilion. "Bring suitable tools," he said.

"Good!" said Miss Wentworth.

The fellow was gone, in a moment.

Miss Wentworth cast me a look of triumph.

She then regarded Thrasilicus. "There has been a misunderstanding here, Mr. Stevens," she said. "That is obvious. Now, in the light of the sympathetic understanding and thoughtful consideration of our mutual friend, the noble Lord Nishida, to whom I take it you are subordinate, we may shortly renegotiate our concerns. There remain matters such as my compensation, which should now, incidentally, be considerably increased, given my inconvenience and embarrassment, my return to Earth, and such."

"Actually, Miss Wentworth," said Thrasilicus, "Lord Nishida and I are, in a way, allies, and neither of us is subordinate to the other."

"I take it, however," she said, "that Lord Nishida's wishes would weigh heavily with you."

"Certainly," he said.

She then turned to Lord Nishida. "I will need a wardrobe," she said. "It need not be clothing of Earth, expensive, well-tailored, tasteful, elegant, fashionable, chic, and such, such as I was accustomed to on Earth, for I well understand that such might be difficult to obtain here, but, you understand, it should be concealing, ample, and decorous, perhaps robes of concealment, such as might be favored by free women of Gor. Veiling, too, given certain aspects of the relevant culture, would not be inappropriate."

Lord Nishida smiled.

At this point the fellow who had left the pavilion a bit ago returned and, with him, was a burly fellow, not of the "strange men," carrying tools, who was, if not of the caste of metal workers, one at least, it seemed, who was familiar with certain aspects of their craft.

In a few moments Miss Wentworth's slender, aristocratic, fair throat was freed of the light, attractive collar.

She straightened her body, and shook her head, and her hair swirled about her shoulders. She did it well, and it was fetching. It was doubtless intended to have its effect on Lord Nishida. I could understand how certain men might rush to please such a woman. "Thank you," she said to Lord Nishida.

"Now," said Lord Nishida to Tajima, "let us see her."

Miss Wentworth regarded Lord Nishida, startled, disbelievingly.

Tajima lifted a finger, and each guard, of those flanking Miss Wentworth, and who had held her, generally, respectively, by the upper arms, now each took a wrist, and, a moment later, an upper arm.

"What are you doing!" cried Miss Wentworth. "No, no!"

She fought to cling to the sheet, to hold it together, before her, but her strength was nothing to that of the two men, and her fingers were pried from the sheet, and her arms were separated, and drawn to the sides. She had her head down, and was bent over, and was struggling wildly, frantically, as she could.

"Please, please," protested Tajima. "This is to be done gracefully."

"Stop! Stop!" cried Miss Wentworth, squirming in the grasp of the guards.

It was certainly not done gracefully. When a female gift, or prize, is to be revealed to a master, a merchant, a captain, a Ubar, or such, the gift, or prize, as shy as she might be, is commonly revealed formally, gracefully, even ceremoniously.

Then the guards held apart her arms, each with a grasp with one hand on her wrist, and a grasp with the other on her arm, above the elbow. They held her in such a way that her arms were slightly behind her, and this pressed her forward, accentuating her figure, toward Lord Nishida.

Her eyes were startled.

A look of utter dismay bespoke itself on her troubled features.

The Earth woman was well displayed, and Lord Nishida scrutinized her closely, and, seemingly, though he gave little overt expression of this, approvingly.

It was my surmise that his senses were pleased, well pleased.

"What are you doing!" she cried, aghast.

"I am appraising my new slave," said Lord Nishida.

"I am not a slave!" she cried. "I am a free woman!"

"Not at all," said Thrasilicus. "You have been unwittingly a slave for months, even for some weeks when you were still engaging in your petty, deceitful games on behalf of your firm, plying your wiles and charms, seemingly so innocently, to wheedle and coax wealth from clients, pathetically dazzled males as you saw it, men whom, given your own words, recently spoken, you obviously held in contempt. You were a slave from the time your name was first entered on the acquisition lists."

"No," she cried, "no!"

"I entered it myself," said Thrasilicus, "and, as noted, on the very afternoon of the aforementioned business luncheon, following which, you may recall, you attempted to entice me to join your list of clients, that line of naive fellows begging for your attention, those eager to please you, to render homage to your charm and beauty, ready to exchange capital, often not their own, for one of your smiles. My interest in you, and I trust you find this flattering, was immediate. Indeed, as soon as you approached my table, so innocently, so charmingly, like a sleek, predatory little animal, I considered that you would look less well sitting at my table in your carefully chosen chic business ensemble than you would kneeling beside it, on the carpet, head down, naked, in a collar. And after a few moments of conversation I decided I would enter you on an acquisition list, for subsequent harvesting at our convenience. I did so, and, as noted, in the moment your name appeared on that list you were no longer a free woman, but a slave."

"No!" she cried.

"Lament not," he said. "Given your nature, character, dispositions, actions, and such, it is appropriate that you be enslaved. Bondage is right for one such as you. One such as you should be a slave. One such as you deserves bondage. For one such as you, bondage is not only a suitable fate, but one superbly fitting and apt."

"Lord Nishida!" she cried. "Let this cruel jest proceed no further. I am naked, and men may look upon me!"

"Of course," said Lord Nishida, "you are a slave."

"You freed me of a collar!" she insisted.

"Only that it may be replaced with another," he said. "Mine."

"I am willing to pretend to be a slave!" she cried. "Let me reassume my disguise. I am exposed! I will willingly wear again even that shameful tunic, though it be but a humiliating badge of degradation!"

"You are a slave, stupid slut," said Thrasilicus.

"No, no!" she cried. She struggled vainly in the grip of the two guards.

Tajima had retrieved the sheet and had now refolded it, and held it over his arm.

"See how fair-skinned is my new slave," said Lord Nishida, over his shoulder, to the two contract women.

Both giggled.

The contract woman on the left, as one looked toward the dais, said, "Does she not smell, Lord Nishida?"

"She will have to be scrubbed," said Lord Nishida.

"Please, please," begged she who had once been Miss Wentworth, "give me the tunic!"

"Do you beg it?" asked Lord Nishida.

"Yes, yes!" she said.

"That shameful tunic, which is but a humiliating badge of degradation?" he asked.

"Yes," she cried, "yes, please!"

"One must strive to become worthy of a tunic," said Lord Nishida. Then he said to the two fellows who had the blond, distraught slave in custody. "See that she is cleaned, thoroughly, and then see to her branding and collaring. Let the brand be the Kef."

That was the most common slave brand on Gor. Most female slaves bore it. It is commonly sited on the left thigh, just under the hip, perhaps because most masters are right-handed. Similarly the disrobing loop of certain tunics is at the left shoulder, presumably for the same reason.

"White! Gregory! Gregory!" cried she who had once been Margaret Wentworth.

"I am now 'Gregory'?" he said.

"Yes, Gregory, Gregory! Please, Gregory, explain to them that a terrible mistake is taking place."

"I was never Gregory before," he said.

"Help me, Gregory!" she wept.

"Why?" he asked.

"I will let you hold me in your arms!" she said. "I will let you kiss me! I know you always wanted to do that! Help me! Help me!"

"You think to bargain with a free man, slave?" inquired Lord Nishida. "Get on your knees, and lick and kiss his feet, begging forgiveness."

The guards released the slave, and she knelt, terrified, before Pertinax, and put down her head and began to lick and kiss his feet. "I am sorry," she said. "Forgive me, Gregory."

"I am Pertinax," he said.

"Yes, yes," she said. "You are Pertinax. Please, Pertinax, forgive me."

"A slave," I said, "does not use the name of the master to the master. All free men are to be addressed as 'Master', all free women as 'Mistress'."

The slave looked up at me, in misery, her eyes bright with tears, and put her head down, again, to the feet of Pertinax. "Forgive me, Master," she said.

"More," said Pertinax, sternly.

And the former Miss Wentworth again, softly, frightened, addressed her fair lips and small, soft tongue tenderly, for several moments, to the feet of a free man.

I thought I saw a small movement of sudden comprehension, of profound understanding, pass through the slave's body.

Undoubtedly this was the first time she had ever knelt thusly before a man, let alone addressed herself in such a manner to his placation.

Outside the guard had apparently put her to her knees before him, as a matter of convenience or discipline, but this, obviously, was quite different.

She looked well at his feet, as a slave, but, then, do not women look well at the feet of men, as slaves?

"Please, forgive me, Master," she whispered.

"I do," said Pertinax, kindly.

She looked up. "Help me," she begged.

"I fear I can do nothing," said Pertinax.

"Please tell them I am not a slave," she begged.

"I gather," said Pertinax, "that you are a slave, or will soon be one."

Kneeling, she put her head in her hands, and wept.

"Take her away," said Lord Nishida.

One of the guards reached down, and jerked her to her feet by the upper left arm.

She turned wildly to me. "Save me!" she cried. "Do something! Fight for me! Rescue me!"

It interested me that the former Miss Wentworth, in this milieu, if in no other, suddenly understood the dependence of women upon men. Men might, if they wished, do with women as they wished. This simple, obvious fact had not been so clear on her former world, though it was a fact there, as well as here. That world was one in which women stood commonly within the shelters of civilized proprieties, within the fences of society, encircled by innumerable customs and laws, with their diverse enforcements and sanctions. In such a situation women take much for granted, not even understanding that it is being taken for granted.

"I fear, Lord Nishida," said Tajima to Lord Nishida, "the woman is unutterably stupid."

"No," said Thrasilicus, "she is not stupid. She is merely ignorant. At present, it is true, I fear, that she knows little of the collar, and nothing of the furs."

"She must learn, quickly," said Lord Nishida.

"The whip will teach her, and quickly," said Tajima, with, oddly, a glance at Sumomo, the contract woman who was on the right, as one would look to the dais. She was, indeed, a lovely young thing.

She sneered at Tajima. I gathered he had low status, for the women of the "strange men" are taught much respect to males. Even an older sister must bow first to a younger brother.

"Tarl Cabot, tarnsman," said Lord Nishida, "what do you think of my new slave?"

I shrugged. There seemed little to say.

"I see," said Lord Nishida. "Would you like her?"

The slave looked at Lord Nishida with disbelief. In that moment I think she first understood herself as property, which might be handed about, exchanged, bought and sold, and so on.

Cecily looked up, too, distressed. She knew herself as property, as well. She loved being property, and knowing herself property, but I did not think she was eager to be bestowed or vended. She loved being a possession, but, rather clearly, if I am not mistaken, she wished to remain the possession of a particular master, wished to remain my possession. Her distress, I think, had to do with the apprehension, this now again made clear to her, that she might without a second thought be given or sold to another. The slave, totally, is property, at the mercy of the master. Too, she may have feared that I might accept Lord Nishida's offer, and then she would no longer be my only slave. Most slaves desire, fervently, to be a man's only slave. That she might become, in such a situation, "first girl," over the formerly insolent "Constantina" would be small consolation for sharing the attentions of a master with a rival. Some masters, of course, as it can be afforded, have more than one slave, that each may try to outdo the other, to please him the more. My own feeling is that it is best to have one slave, so that she will strive to be so loving, so pleasing, so hot, so needful, that the master will feel no desire for another. A master may have many slaves, of course, a merchant, say, may have dozens, a Ubar hundreds, and so on, but the slave, in her needful femininity, commonly wants to be the single property of a master, whom she need not share with another.

"My thanks, great lord," I said, "but I am content with she who kneels to my left."

Lord Nishida nodded.

His offer, in honor, had to be genuine, but I am confident he did not expect it to be accepted.

"Your name is Pertinax?" said Lord Nishida to Pertinax.

"Yes," said Pertinax.

"Would you like this slave?" he asked.

"No," said Pertinax.

The slave regarded him, with incredulity. "You always wanted me!" she exclaimed.

"I did not know you then," he said. "Here I have learned, for the first time, your true nature and character, who you are, and what you have done."

"Accept me! Take me! Own me!" she begged.

"No," said Pertinax.

"Please!" she said. "Own me!"

"You would be owned," he said, "but you would not think yourself owned. But sometime, I am sure, you will understand, in your heart and belly, that you are owned, truly owned."

"Save me from this fate!" she wept.

"Your lips and tongue felt well on my feet," he said.

"Keep me," she said. "Own me!"

"No," he said.

"I do not understand," she wept.

"You are worthless," he said. "You are petty, radically petty, to the core."

She stood there, in the grip of the guard, naked, forlorn, shaken, stunned.

Again, I thought the offer of Lord Nishida was genuine, but, again, I was confident he did not expect it to be accepted. He was, I gathered, a shrewd judge of men. I did not find this surprising, from my estimation of his position, and apparent acuity. Indeed, I suspected that these formal overtures on his part were largely intended to express his contempt for the slave. Some men, of course, find it pleasant to embond a woman they hold in contempt, and then treat her accordingly. And, when the slave fires have been ignited in her belly, and she is the helpless prisoner of her needs, it amuses them to have her at their feet, prostrate, piteous, begging for their least touch.

"I trust, Lord Nishida," said Thrasilicus, "the slave pleases your senses."

"She pleases my senses," said Lord Nishida, "but I am not sure she pleases my heart."

"In bondage," I said, "a woman is often muchly transformed."

This was true. Bondage, in which the woman learns her womanhood, effects in a woman not only a sexual but a moral and personal redemption. In the collar, and in submission, she learns service, fulfillment, wholeness, and love. In the collar, and in her complete and categorical submission to the master, sexually, emotionally, and personally, she becomes herself, and happy.

"If Lord Nishida is not pleased," said Thrasilicus, "we may search out another."

"And this one," said Tajima, who had had, from the beginning, as I understood it, reservations pertaining to the former Miss Wentworth, "as she would be unworthy meat for larls or sleen, may be bound and cast into the garbage pit for the delectation of swarming urts."

There seemed a general assent to this, amongst those present.

They took her to be poor slave stuff.

I myself, however, did not think she would look poorly on a block, if well exhibited.

"We shall see," said Lord Nishida. Then he addressed the two guards who had had the former Miss Wentworth in custody. "After her branding and collaring," he said, "shave her head, and send her to the stables, and see that she learns she is a slave."

"Yes, great lord," they said, and exited the pavilion, the former Miss Wentworth, whimpering, but afraid to speak, held by the upper left arm, in the grip of one of them.

"Regrettable," said Lord Nishida.

"Another may be procured," said Thrasilicus, concerned. "You may return her to me. I would not mind having her under my whip."

"Your choice," said Lord Nishida, "was excellent."

Thrasilicus seemed surprised.

"If she learns her collar well," said Lord Nishida, "another may find her pleasing."

"I had thought you wanted her for yourself," said Thrasilicus.

"No," said Lord Nishida. "Her yellow hair, blue eyes, and fair skin will be rare at home. She may figure amongst a variety of gifts, for another."

"For whom?" asked Thrasilicus.

"For the *shogun*, of course," said Lord Nishida.

Lord Nishida then looked at me. "Now," he said, "we may address ourselves to matters of importance."

Chapter Eleven

Cecily and I Look In on the Former Miss Wentworth

A few days after her interview with Lord Nishida in his pavilion, curious, I decided to look in on the former Miss Wentworth, and so, after an inquiry or two, I made my way, heeled by Cecily, to one of the large stables in which draft tharlarion were housed, those which aided in the logging, and drew the wagons down the narrow path between the trees, to some destination, to the southeast. The stable was a long, large building, with a towering roof, to contain the longer-necked tharlarion. It would house several beasts, but I supposed, at this time of day, most, if not all, of the tharlarion would be about the camp, or active on the road to the southeast, hauling logs, or returning. By nightfall, as these things go, before the beasts returned, the stable should be cleaned, fresh straw strewn about, deeply, and the feed and water troughs filled. I chose the late afternoon for my visit, supposing the time one opportune to encounter the former Miss Wentworth alone. Late in the afternoon many of the "strange men" enjoy a pleasant soak in a warm tub. I trusted that the stable grooms might be enjoying this homely indulgence. Several collar-girls, such as those who had been former free women of Ar, were humbly, attentively, silently, here and there, bathing the men. I did not think that the former Miss Wentworth would be engaged in this activity, as it is regarded as a great privilege for a collar-girl to be permitted to bathe a master. Indeed, it is one of the lovely services in which a contract woman, naked beside her client in the pool, was expected to excel.

I found the former Miss Wentworth toward the back of the stable, on the right, as one would face the large double gate which gave access to the structure. She was facing the back of the stable. I watched her for a time. She was on her knees, moving about, leaning forward, a small, pathetic figure. She would reach down and, again and again, with her small, lovely hands, quite bare, her bare arms stained to the elbows, scrape together tharlarion dung. When a suitable heap had been formed, she would lift it, again with her bare hands, and place it on a low flat cart, which she drew beside her.

She was naked, not yet permitted a tunic, and was filthy, and doubtless stank.

She had not yet been permitted even a slave strip.

The common slave strip is a single, narrow, dangling piece of cloth anchored in binding fiber, double-looped about the waist of the slave. It is usually tied snugly, to accentuate the figure of the slave. It is fastened with a slip knot that it may easily, with a tug, be undone. The binding fiber, of course, is long enough to bind the slave, hand and foot, or, if one desires, to serve as a leash, the slave strip then usually folded and placed between the slave's teeth, which she dare not drop. Sometimes the binding fiber, in its double loop, is looser, that it may ride low on the hips. The point of this is to exhibit the navel of the slave, which, in Gorean, is known as "the slave belly." The Gorean free woman, as I understand it, who often mates while gowned, commonly refuses to reveal her "slave belly" to her companion, because of the shame of it. What if he should become excited, tear off her gown, and put her to use with the same audacity, aggression, exhilaration, and exultation with which he might use a vulnerable, meaningless animal, say, a chain-slut or paga girl?

I watched the former Miss Wentworth for a time, she unaware of my presence.

They were teaching her what it was to be a slave.

Yet I feared she had not even, as yet, begun to learn.

I considered her.

How far she was now from the seats of commercial power,

far from the treasure houses of wealth, far from paneled board rooms, long corridors, marshaled desks, and bright offices.

This was a world other than that to which she had been accustomed, and which she had thought to leave behind only for a life of wealth and leisure.

I continued to regard her.

I saw there was a collar on her neck. The lock was in the back, as is common. It was doubtless that of Lord Nishida.

I had no doubt she had no access to its key.

Now, doubtless as never before, she knew what it was to be in a slave collar.

"Saru," I called.

She threw herself to her belly in the straw, facing away from me, and covered her head with her hands. "Please, please do not whip me!" she begged.

The slave had been given the name 'Saru'.

The saru is found variously on Gor, but usually in tropical areas. For example, it is common in the jungles of the Ua. Also, I had learned from Tajima, it is found, here and there, in the home, so to speak, of the "strange men." The saru is a small, usually arboreal animal. It is usually regarded with amusement, or contempt. It figures in children's stories as a cute, curious, mischievous little beast, but also one that is stupid, vain, and ignorant. Although the saru, as far as I can tell, is not a monkey zoologically, it surely occupies a similar ecological niche, and resembles the monkey in its diet, habits, groupings, and such. It is tailless. I think it would not be amiss to think of the saru as a Gorean monkey. In any event Tajima, when he put the slave before him on her knees, in the stable, to be named, told her, in English, that there be no mistaking the matter, and she clearly understand what was being done to her, what 'Saru' meant, its connotations, and such. She was, in effect, he told her, going to be named "Monkey." "Yes Master," she whispered. The slave, of course, is named by masters. She has nothing to say as to what she will be named, no more than a sleen or kaiila. Names may be changed, from time to time. Some names, like 'Saru', are belittling names, or contempt names. Other names may be fit for low slaves, others for prized slaves, and so on. Names may be used to punish or commend, to humiliate or delight, and so on. Earth-girl names, which may be put on any slave, regardless of her world of origin, are commonly used for low slaves. 'Cecily', the name of my slave, had once been one of her free-woman names. Now, of course, it was not the same name, for I had given it to her as a slave name. The slave understands, of course, that she has no name, not in a legal sense, and that the name she is given is a name bestowed on her by a master, and removable by a master. Even the name which appears on formal slave papers is a slave name.

"You are no longer Miss Margaret Wentworth," Tajima explained to her. "As soon as you were entered on an acquisition list, months ago, you were only a nameless slave."

"Yes, Master," she said, kneeling before him.

"I have explained to you the meaning of 'Saru'," he said. "You have understood?"

"Yes, Master," she said.

"I am now going to name you," he said.

"Yes, Master," she whispered.

"You are Saru," he said. "Rejoice that you are no longer a nameless slave."

"Yes, Master," she said, frightened.

"You may thank me," he said.

"Thank you, Master," she said.

"What is your name?" he asked.

"'Saru', Master," she said.

"Who are you?"

"I am Saru," she said, "Master."

He then turned about, and left her, and she collapsed to the straw of the stable, wracked with sobs.

She shuddered in the straw, naked. "Please do not whip me!" she begged.

"It is I, Tarl Cabot," I said. "Do not be afraid. I have not come to whip you."

She rose to all fours, and turned about, and regarded me, in the gloom of the stable, almost half-uncomprehendingly.

Cecily stood, behind me, to my left.

"Do not be afraid," I said. Then I snapped my fingers, and pointed to the floor, before me, and she crawled to that place, on all fours, and looked at me.

Her head had been shaved.

I thus inferred that the gifting of her, amongst other gifts, to a *shogun* by Lord Nishida, which I understood to be his intent, would not be imminent, but perhaps months away.

Surely she was in no condition to be presented, now, to anyone, even a herder of tarsks, a lowly shearer of the bounding hurt.

But her bondage journey had begun. By the time she had learned her collar, and her skin would again sparkle, and her hair would be again a glory, and her eyes would no longer reflect terror but rather the eagerness of a surrendered slave, hoping to be found pleasing by her master, she would be worthy, I was sure, of having the vestiture of a silken presentation sheet removed before a *shogun*, or even a Ubar.

"Master?" she asked, her head lifted to me.

"Slave?" I said.

"Has Master Pertinax inquired after me?" she asked.

"No," I said. "Why do you ask?"

She put down her head, "Nothing, Master," she said.

"Perhaps," I said, "it is his whip you would like to feel?"

Among slaves, a common way for one slave to inquire of another her owner is to ask, "Who whips you?"

To be sure, the slave may never have been whipped. She is, of course, subject to the whip of the master, for she is a slave. Sometimes a slave may be bound and whipped, to remind her that she is a slave. After this, she is under no illusions as to her condition. She now knows well what she is; she is slave, only slave.

The slave was silent, but trembled.

"As a slave, of course," I said, "you are unworthy of any free man."

"Yes, Master," she said. Then she looked to Cecily. "She is standing," she said.

"Of course," I said. "You are a slave. If you were a free person, she would be on her knees."

She looked at Cecily. "I am sorry," she said, "that I was cruel to you."

"It is nothing," said Cecily.

Saru looked up from all fours, her knees and hands in the straw. "May I kneel, Master," she asked.

"Yes," I said.

She had not asked for permission to stand. She knew herself in the presence of a free man.

I wondered if Thrasilicus was looking into a different slave for Lord Nishida. Perhaps a better slave would be sought.

"Back straight, head up," I told her.

"Yes, Master," she said.

"Knees," I said.

"Before her?" asked Saru, in misery. Cecily was standing.

"Before me," I said.

"Yes, Master," she said.

"Wider," I said.

"Yes, Master," she said.

"I see you are collared," I said.

"Yes, Master," she said.

"And you have been branded?" I asked.

"Yes, Master," she said.

I crouched beside her. "It is an excellent mark," I said. It was, as I had expected, the common Kef.

"I am told so," she said. "I am now well marked. There will be no confusing me now with a free woman."

"Nor should there be," I said.

"No, Master," she said.

"You look well, kneeling, with your knees spread," I said.

"Thank you, Master," she whispered.

"A slave is pleased, if she is found pleasing," I said.

"I am pleased if I am found pleasing," she said.

"Understand it," I said.

"Yes, Master," she said.

A tear coursed down her cheek.

She would soon, I was sure, as a slave, aside from fear, take great pleasure in being found pleasing, and be genuinely grateful for having been found so, and, if not, there was always the leather.

How desperate, I thought, are slaves, once they understand their condition, to be found pleasing. Surely the switch, the lash, are unpleasant. Saru was new to her bondage, but, thanks to the grooms, she was already well aware of the consequences of failing, in any particular, to be pleasing to free men.

But most desirably the slave should eventually desire to be found pleasing, should strive to be so, for the joy of being found pleasing by her master, and not from dread of the boot or leather.

"To whom do you belong?" I asked.

"To Lord Nishida," she said.

I had supposed that that would be the case. On the other hand, if a different slave were being sought, with her coloring, and such, it was quite possible that she might have been given to another.

I examined the collar. "I cannot read the collar," I said. I supposed it was in Gorean, but it was not in a common Gorean script. I had encountered something similar, long ago, in the Tahari, where Gorean was written in a quite different script, a flowing, beautiful script common in the Tahari.

"It was shown to me," she said, "but I, too, could not read it."

"Can you read Gorean?" I asked.

"It was not thought necessary that I learn it," she said.

"Many Earth-girl slaves are kept illiterate in Gorean," I said. "Why should a slave be taught to read?"

"I was not a slave!" she said.

"In the view of some, it seems, you were," I said. "But, in any event, illiteracy would seem a suitable aspect of your disguise."

"And I understand," she said, bitterly, "they had a collar in mind for me, even from the beginning."

"Certainly," I said.

"Yes, certainly," she wept.

"I assume your collar was read to you," I said.

"Yes," she said.

"What does it say?" I asked.

"'I am the property of Nishida of Nara'," she said.

This was doubtless Lord Nishida.

"What is Nara?" I asked.

"I do not know," she said.

On the common Gorean collar it might be a city, a district, even a cylinder. On her collar, for all I knew, it might be a place, a port, a caste, a family, a clan, or something else. I did not know what. I would later learn it was a citadel, a lofty fortress castle.

"Were you given slave wine?" I asked. I recalled she had had "the wine of the noble free woman."

She closed her eyes and, involuntarily, shuddered with misery. Then she looked at me, shaken. "My hands were tied behind my back," she said, "and then I was knelt and my head yanked back by the hair, and held in place, and the spout forced between my teeth, and my nostrils pinched shut, and it was poured into me, and I must imbibe the beverage or suffocate. It was most bitter, most foul. And then, unable to disgorge the brew, even later, for the tying of my hands, I must endure to have my head shaved."

"The shaving of the head was doubtless to help you understand better your bondage," I said, "but, too, it is perhaps not entirely regrettable considering the applications to which you have been put. Your hair was very beautiful, as well you knew, in your vanity, and it would have been a sorry thing for it to have been fouled in the ordure of tharlarion."

"I protested my work, and as they would have me attend to it," she said, "and my face was forced down, into the dung of tharlarion. I protested no more."

Whereas, as suggested earlier, the effects of slave wine and "the wine of the noble free woman" are identical, the common ingredient being sip root, there is a considerable difference in the two drinks. Slave wine makes no attempt to conceal the bitterness of ground, raw sip root, whereas "the wine of the noble free woman" is flavored, spiced, and sweetened in such a way that it offers no offense to the delicate and more refined sensibility of the free woman. A slave, of course, as any domestic animal, is to be bred only if and when, and how, the master wishes. A releaser, interestingly, deliciously palatable, is administered to the slave prior to her mating. In the mating, which is supervised by masters, she will be crossed with a male slave. Both slaves will be hooded, and are forbidden to speak, that neither will later, should they meet, know the other.

"As I recall," I said, "on the beach, several days ago, you informed me that you were, at that time, a virgin."

"Yes," she said, looking down.

"Why?" I asked.

"I hated men," she said. "I despised them. I could not bear the thought of one of them doing that to me. How vulgar it would be, and how helpless I would be! I would be in their arms no better than a slave."

"Are you still a virgin?" I asked.

Saru cast a swift, distressed glance at Cecily, who was standing behind me, a bit to my left.

"Must I speak?" she asked,

"Yes," I said.

"No," she said, looking down to the straw, "I am no longer a virgin."

"Lord Nishida opened you," I said.

She looked up.

"'Opened'?" she said.

"Yes, to have you more ready, for the pleasure of men," I said.

"No," she said. "It was not he who opened me."

"I am surprised," I said.

"After the pavilion," she said, "he had no more interest in harvesting the virginity of one such as I than of harvesting that of a she-tarsk. I was hooded, and given to grooms."

"Are you different now?" I asked.

"They use me as they wish," she said.

"Are you different now?" I asked.

"But not so much as before," she whispered. "Now, often, they make me wait."

"Doubtless at Lord Nishida's command," I suggested.

"Perhaps," she said. "I do not know."

"I see you are different now," I said.

"Yes," she said, "I am different now."

"They have put squirmings in your belly," I said.

"Yes," she said, lowering her eyes. "They have put squirmings in my belly."

"I see," I said.

She looked up, agonized. "Can you not understand me?" she cried. "I can no longer help myself!"

"Nor should you," I said. "You are becoming vital. You are coming to a state of health scarcely suspected by a free woman. You are being redeemed as a female."

"I find myself, again and again, in heat, like a she-tarsk!" she cried.

"As a slave," I suggested.

"Yes," she said, "as a slave!"

"Excellent," I said. "To be sure, there are often miseries in such things."

"For the first time in my life," she said, "I now want the touch of men! Nay! I must have the touch of men! I now need, desperately, helplessly, piteously need, the touch of men!"

"Of course," I said, "you are a woman."

"I was a woman before!" she said.

"Yes," I said, "but not a slave."

"No," she said, "not a slave."

"You have work to do," I said. "Tharlarion will soon be returning to the stable."

"Yes," she said.

"Where are you housed?" I asked.

"In the corner, over there," she said, pointing toward the back of the stable, to the right, as we faced the back of the stable. "At night I am chained there, by the neck, to a ring on the floor. I have two pans there, one for water, one for gruel. I must feed as a she-tarsk, head down, my mouth to the food and water, forbidden the use of my hands."

"That is not all that unusual," I said, "with a girl who is first being taught that she is at the total mercy of men, one who is beginning to learn her collar."

"Yes, Master," she said.

"There is a bucket, surely, for your wastes," I said.

"I must use the dung cart," she said.

"I see," I said.

"Why has Master Pertinax not come to see me?" she asked.

"I do not know," I said. "Would you like to see him?"

"As I am now?" she said.

"How else?" I said.

"I am collared!" she wept.

"You were collared before," I reminded her.

"But now I am truly collared," she said. "I am a slave."

"You think of Pertinax?" I said.

"Yes," she whispered.

"Doubtless you are distressed, should he see you as you are now, but, I think, still, you would like to see him."

"Yes," she whispered.

"Perhaps you think he would sympathize with you, would be horrified at the fate which is now yours?" I said.

"I do not know," she said.

"I suspect," I said, "he would think it a fate you have earned, and one which you richly deserve."

"I do not know," she said.

"Perhaps you recall," I said, "kneeling before him, and ministering with your lips and tongue to his feet?"

"Yes, Master," she whispered.

In the performance of even so simple an act, a woman, to her uneasiness and astonishment, so before a male, can sense herself in her proper place in nature, and can sense herself becoming irremediably aroused.

"May I speak, Master?" asked Cecily.

"Yes," I said.

"I could speak to Master Pertinax," said Cecily, to the slave. "I could ask him to visit you."

"I am no longer a free woman," she said. "He could no longer respect me."

"True," I said, "nor should he, but he might find you of interest."

"Of interest!" she exclaimed.

"Yes," I said, "as a slave."

"I dream of myself at his feet," she said. "I dream of myself naked in his arms!"

"In a collar?" I asked.

"Yes," she said, "in a collar!"

"I could ask him to see you, when the grooms are out," said Cecily.

"Tell him to bring a switch," I said.

I was reasonably sure that Saru, whatever might be the momentums and the future of the journey on which she was embarked, would try to turn Pertinax to her will, perhaps even to the foolishness of attempting an escape.

She had not yet learned that there is no escape for the Gorean slave girl.

To be sure, I suspected that she now thought of Pertinax rather differently than she had in the earlier phases of their relationship, being now much aware, in the manner a slave will find herself aware, and must be aware, that he was a man.

I would be curious to know, if he saw fit to call on her, if she would immediately, in his presence, go to first obeisance position.

If she did not, I trusted he would use the switch on her, liberally.

"I do not know if you would now recognize Pertinax," I said.

"Master?" she asked.

"He is different now," I said. "He helps with the logging. He uses the ax, mightily. He is becoming bronzed. His muscles harden. Were he now to take you in his arms you would know yourself helpless, and held."

"And would I know myself slave?" she asked.

"You would be slave, and would know yourself slave," I said.

She regarded me, frightened.

"Would you like for me to invite Master Pertinax to visit you?" asked Cecily.

"Yes," said the slave. "Please! Please!"

"You would like to see him, I gather," I said.

"Yes!" she said.

"Do you beg?" I asked.

"'Beg'?" she said.

"Yes," I said.

"Yes," she said, "I beg it."

"As a slave?" I asked.

"Yes," she said.

"Who begs?" I asked.

"Saru begs," she said.

"Humbly?" I asked.

"Yes," she said.

"As the slave she is?" I asked.

"Yes," she said.

"With lowered head?"

"Yes," she said, putting her head down. "Please tell Master Pertinax that Saru, the slave, as the slave she is, with lowered head, begs Master Pertinax to see her, humbly begs it."

"Cecily," I said, "you may inform Pertinax of the petition of a stable girl."

"Yes, Master," said Cecily, happily.

I heard, outside, the bellowing of a tharlarion.

"We shall withdraw," I said.

"May I kiss your feet, Master?" said Saru.

"No," I said. "You are filthy."

"Yes, Master," she whispered.

I then left the stable, followed by Cecily.

"Do you think, Master," asked Cecily, "that Master Pertinax will attend on the slave?"

"I suspect so," I said, "and I trust he brings his switch."

"Yes, Master," said Cecily, delighted. "Whence now we?"

"There is a warm pool in the forest, nearby, within the wands," I said. "Several use it, the "strange men," and others. It was shown to me by Tajima, for he often visits its vicinity, though for what reason other than the water I know not. You may bathe me there, and freshen yourself, as well, and then we might, in a shallow place, splash a little."

"Yes, Master!" she laughed.

"We will later," I said, "return to the hut and you will then cook for me."

"Yes, Master," she said.

"And after your work," I said, "we will devote the evening to blanket sport."

"I trust I will be found pleasing on the blanket," she said.

"If you are not," I said, "you will be lashed."

"Yes, Master," she said.

"I am thinking of buying a slave for Pertinax," I said. "There was a brunette on the chain of a fellow named Torgus, whom I met on the beach. She seemed ready for a master."

She was a former high woman of Ar, who, with several others, all embonded, and their hair shortened, had been taken from Ar, when the rising had occurred in the city. Had they been caught in the city they would have doubtless been impaled, or worse, as profiteers, traitresses, collaborators, and such.

"I think, Master," she said, "Master Pertinax might prefer another slave."

"Another slave," I said, "might be otherwise owned."

"True," she said.

"One slave is as good as another," I said.

"I doubt that," she said.

"It is true," I said, "that some sell for more than others."

"Would you sell me?" she asked.

"What am I offered?" I asked.

"I shall endeavor to be so good on the blanket," she said, "that you would have no desire to sell me!"

"You do fit well in my arms," I said, "and you do have a luscious cubic content, and you moan and squirm well."

"I cannot help such things, Master," she said.

"Nor should you," I said.

"No, Master," she said. "Master."

"Yes?" I said.

"Tomorrow," she said, "may I seek out Master Pertinax, and inform him of the petition of a stable slave?"

Pertinax was currently housed in one of the barracks occupied by the loggers.

"You will wait three days," I said.

"Master!" she protested.

"Three days," I said.

"Yes, Master," she said.

"Give her some days to fear," I said, "that you have forgotten, or were forbidden to contact Pertinax, or that he, informed of the petition, chose to ignore it. Let her ponder such possibilities, and others."

"But she will be tormented, will be in misery," said Cecily.

"Yes," I said.

"Is it not time we bathed?" I asked.

"Yes," she said. "The stable was terrible."

"Commonly," I said, "the bondage of the stable is not miserable, or dreadful, as the stable girls have proper tools for their work, and such. To be sure, it is common for them to have their heads shaved, or their hair cropped, for reasons of sanitation. There are many worse slaveries on Gor. To be sure, undeniably, it is a low slavery, and slaves, in the ways of females, will do much, as they can, to obtain for themselves a lighter and more pleasant bondage."

"Surely you do not blame us," she said.

"Of course not," I said.

"I hope to be found pleasing on the blanket," she said.

"I am sure you will be," I said.

"I do not wish to be lashed," she said.

"I am sure you will not be," I said.

"And afterwards, what is to be done with me, Master?" she inquired.

"You will be chained for the night," I said, "at my feet."

"Yes, Master," she said.

Chapter Twelve

The Plaza of Training

"You have trainers?" I asked Tajima.

"Several," he said, "who brought the tarns from Thentis, some from elsewhere."

Thentis was famed for her tarn flocks.

"I am not a tarn trainer," I told him.

We were walking within a path, leading from the logging camp deeper into the forest. The path was lined with wands, on each side, and the guard larls, which were occasionally seen, would not intrude within the wands.

"No," said Tajima, "you are a rider, and a warrior."

"My role here, I am given to understand, is to form and discipline a tarn cavalry," I said.

At that moment, from afar off, perhaps two hundred to two hundred and fifty yards to our right and ahead, there was a terrible roar, surely of a larl, followed, a moment later, by a harrowing scream.

Tajima seized my arm. "No!" he said. "Do not depart from the wands!"

"Help is needed!" I said, pulling away.

"No," said Tajima. "It is no longer needed. The kill has taken place. Do not disturb a larl when it is feeding."

"Someone was beyond the wands," I said.

"Now, and again," said Tajima, "some will flee the camp."

The roar of the larl commonly startles and freezes the prey. Then the larl is upon it.

"The camp, I gather, is not to be fled?"

"No," said Tajima, "it is not permitted."

"Why do men flee the camp?" I asked.

"They are afraid," said Tajima. "They do not wish to die, and then they flee, and then they die."

"There are secrets here, too," I said, "and men might flee, to make them known, to sell them."

"That, too," said Tajima.

"A perilous endeavor," I remarked.

"True," said Tajima.

Those brought to Tarncamp were, I had gathered from Pertinax, mercenaries, bandits, brigands, thieves, murderers, wanderers, low men, cast-off men, men lost from Home Stones, and such. Many, I understood, had come from the occupational forces now expelled from Ar. The word of such men might be as the rustle of the wind amidst leech plants. Their loyalties would on the whole be to their own hides and purses. They would on the whole be as much for hire as the Assassins, save that the Assassin, once the dagger has been painted on his forehead, signaling he is hunting, is loyal to a fee.

"Why do you and your people wish a tarn cavalry?" I asked.

"For purposes of war, of course," said Tajima.

"On continental Gor?" I inquired.

"Elsewhere," said Tajima.

This made sense to me, as whatever might be afoot in the forest would not be likely to be of sufficient size and potency to effect much success against Gorean cities with their own tarn forces, which might number in the hundreds and, as of old, in Ar, in their thousands. Similarly it seemed that formidable island ubarates such as Tyros and Cos would have little to fear from, say, a squadron of bandit tarnsmen. And would one not require the means to reach those sovereignties, which lay hundreds of pasangs to the west? The tarn is a land bird, and will not fly beyond the sight of land. And even if the tarn could do that, no tarn could make that flight, but would fall exhausted into the sea. They are not sea birds which can rest on the wind, aloft for Ahn, wings spread, not moving, and, if they wished, descend, and rest on the sea itself.

"Where?" I asked.

"Elsewhere," said Tajima, politely.

"Your forces," I said to Tajima, "seem to have means. Why do you not hire a tarn cavalry from another city, say, Treve, in the Voltai?"

"Such a cavalry," said Tajima, "would be theirs, not ours. Also, how could such a hiring be concealed?"

"I understand you have lost men," I said.

"We have lost twenty-two men," he said, "to the talons and beaks of tarns, some of them trainers."

"Then you are dealing with wild tarns," I said. Such losses would not be expected with the training of domestic tarns.

"Yes," said Tajima, "but from the vicinity of Thentis, from the mountains of Thentis. Any purchase of a considerable number of tarns from the cots would surely attract attention."

"Doubtless," I said.

Wild tarns are common in the mountains of Thentis.

"Four of my people," said Tajima, "fled back from the tarns, and two found they could not approach them."

"That is understandable," I said.

"But not acceptable," said Tajima. "But each has regained his honor."

"I do not see how honor is involved in this sort of thing," I said, "courage perhaps, but how honor?"

"For us, honor is involved," said Tajima. "But do not fear, for they have regained their honor."

"How?" I asked.

"By the knife," he said.

We then heard the scream of a tarn, from a hundred or so yards before us.

"We are near the place of training," said Tajima.

"I would now speak, if I might," I had said in the pavilion.

"Surely," had said Lord Nishida.

"I am grateful, great lord," said I, "for your hospitality. But I understand little of what is going on here. I have been brought to you at what must be considerable time and expense. Agents, or operatives, have colluded in my presence here. I would like to know what I am to do, how it is that I might serve you."

"You are here," said the blond fellow to me, "as I suppose you know, in the service of Priest-Kings, the gods of Gor. We will speak their will, and you will obey."

"You are then," I said, "the agent of Priest-Kings?"

"Yes," he said.

"Indeed," I said, "you must be the agent of Priest-Kings. How could it be otherwise, for I was disembarked on the northern coast according to the exact coordinates of Priest-Kings, secret coordinates doubtless, was there met by two agents, doubtless also in the service of Priest-Kings, though that apparently unknown to them, was conducted to a reserve of Port Kar, and was there contacted by Tajima, servitor to Lord Nishida, and brought hither."

"Certainly," said Thrasilicus.

Lord Nishida seemed to smile, slightly.

I doubted that either Thrasilicus or Lord Nishida believed me to suppose they truly labored for Priest-Kings, but it did not seem judicious to them, obviously, to express doubt as to my convictions in this matter, nor did it seem judicious to me to challenge their claim, or, perhaps better, that of Thrasilicus, for Lord Nishida had never proclaimed that thesis, nor, as far as I could tell, did he care what I might believe in this matter.

Both would presumably be aware that the coordinates had been supplied to Kurii on the Steel World, formerly that of "Agamemnon," later that of "Arcesilaus," by Priest-Kings, and that, accordingly, some Kurii, at least, perhaps unauthorized Kurii, despite the supposed confidentiality of the matter, might have had access to them. Expressions, incidentally, such as "Agamemnon" and "Arcesilaus" are used for convenience, as the actual names, being in Kur, cannot be rendered in the phonemes of either English or Gorean. The two names given were used by humans on the Steel World in question to refer to the individuals involved. I have retained the usage.

I gathered it did not make a great deal of difference to either Thrasilicus or Lord Nishida whether I took them, in fact, to be laboring in the cause of Priest-Kings or not.

Too, why should they believe, in the first place, that I would wish to labor on behalf of Priest-Kings?

Surely I had not been treated well by Priest-Kings.

But if it did not matter to them, what I believed in this matter, why would it not matter to them?

I recalled that the former Miss Wentworth had said that there was a hold over me, which had something to do with a woman. This had not, however, been made clear to me, nor would it be, I supposed, unless I proved hesitant or uncooperative. The hold, I was sure, had naught to do with the slave, Cecily, who would be discounted, first as she was a slave, and, secondly, they presumably would not have known that I would bring her to Gor, in her collar, heeling me. I did know that Priest-Kings had wished me debouched on the beach at the designated coordinates, and so they would have had something in mind for me, but what I did not know. Perhaps I could discern it, if only indirectly, if I continued to accommodate myself to the wishes of Thrasilicus and Lord Nishida. Thrasilicus, in my view, clearly, was laboring on behalf of Kurii. He was obviously associated with certain Gorean slavers who had access to the shores of Earth. The ships of such slavers were furnished currently, or originally, as the case might be, by the Steel Worlds, as the sophisticated technologies involved would be far beyond that of Gorean humans, and, currently, at least, beyond those of Earth, who were not even subjected to the weapon and technology laws of Priest-Kings, concerned to protect themselves and their world from the ignorance, cunning, and rapacity of what they regarded, with considerable justification, as an inferior species. Freedom, obviously, is not an absolute value, as only fools could believe. Freedom for what is an obvious consideration. Children should not be permitted to romp on the high bridges. Tharlarion should not be permitted to trample cultivated fields. Slaves should not be permitted to wear the garments of a free woman, and so on. Ships from the Steel Worlds might be crewed by either humans or Kurii, but, I supposed, seldom would the crews be mixed. Kurii tend to be powerful, short-tempered, dangerous beasts. I personally would not care to share confined spaces with them for days at a time. I supposed much of the business of Kurii on both Gor and Earth would be conducted, for obvious reasons, by their humans. An obvious inducement, or partial inducement, to certain Goreans, for example to certain members of the caste of slavers, for their assistance, in a variety of tasks, would be something all males understand, women. On Gor, women, that is, slaves, are negotiable items of value, a currency of sorts. Indeed, on Gor a salary may be paid in women. Sometimes a fellow's wages may be two slaves, or three. The women of Earth, unlike Gorean women, who tend to be zealously protected, are largely undefended and easily obtained. They are much like wild fruit which may be picked as one pleases, for personal use, for marketing, and such. Accordingly, access to the women of Earth, slave fruit, ripe for harvesting, is a not negligible emolument for Goreans, whose views of women tend to be less romantic than sexual and utilitarian. Indeed, one of the surprises to many Earth women brought to Gor for the sales cages of slavers is to learn that on this world they are not viewed through clouds of misrepresentation and nonsense but, radically and profoundly, as what they are, basically and fundamentally, females. Too, if they are slaves, they will learn that such a thing as males exist, males in a rather different sense from that to which they were accustomed on Earth, and that they will be owned by these males, very different sorts of males, who will be their masters, as much or more so as if they were, say, pigs or dogs. Interestingly, it seems that not every ship which plies the slave routes between Earth and Gor is in the service of Kurii. A goodly number, it seems, perhaps the majority of them, are now independent, doing their own scouting, maintaining their own acquisition lists, and so on. These commonly, it seems, sustain their own bases, on Earth or Gor. I had no doubt, however, that Thrasilicus was closely associated with Kurii.

A normal Gorean slaver, for example, commonly harvests his slave fruit, brings it to Gor, brands and collars it, pens it, gives it some training, that it not be slain the first night off the platform, and then sells it. He would not be involved in the complex arrangements which had surrounded the arrival of Miss Wentworth on Gor, her application to a particular deceit, and so on. Clearly she had been recruited as an agent of Kurii, even if she had not the least idea what Kurii might be. Then, when she had finished her task, and was no longer of use, she could be disposed of, in one way or another, usually, one supposed, in the markets. It was not surprising that female Kur agents were almost always quite beautiful. One intended to sell them later, and beautiful women tend to bring higher prices. Also, most Goreans, and Kurii, too, for that matter, despite their willingness to utilize such creatures, disapprove of liars, hypocrites, traitors, and such. Thus the fate to which the former Miss Wentworth was consigned was one intended for her from the very beginning. Sometimes such an agent, after her branding and collaring, is given to the male agent with whom she may have been associated. Usually, she is just sold in a market, commonly a low market where her sale is not likely to attract much attention. Miss Wentworth was intended, it seems, to answer to an item on a want list.

"And how may I be of service to you?" I had then inquired of Lord Nishida, in the pavilion.

"I understand you have commanded, in the far south," said Lord Nishida.

"In the land of the Wagon Peoples, long ago," I said, "I was honored to command a thousand, kaiila riders of the Tuchuks."

"You are familiar, then," said Lord Nishida, "with the tactics of a cavalry, its movements, its applications, and such."

"Light cavalry," I said. I had never commanded the massed, thundering, earth-shaking charges of war tharlarion.

"Excellent," said Lord Nishida.

The riders of the Tuchuks were subtle clouds of war, almost impossible to close with, dangerous archers, with the short, horn bow, fit for clearing the saddle, to left or right. A thousand arrows could be loosed in an instant, like death rain, on a foe, and then the riders were gone. And then, again, the storm of death might appear on another horizon, tiny dots on the horizon, and then, in moments, be upon one again. And when the Tuchuk did close it was the quiva in flight, and the light, black temwood lance, thrusting and drawing back, and thrusting again, often against a foe on foot, fleeing, being ridden down.

The Tuchuk, all in all, was a subtle and dangerous foe. His tactics tended to be executed swiftly, and precisely. They might have been better known, had more survived to spread their fame. Even his flight might well be a ruse, for one of his favorite tactics was the backward flighted arrow, loosed from the platform of the smooth-gaited kaiila. Tuchuk war was characterized by deception and cunning. It was also ruthless.

"You did command on the 25th of Se'Kara," said Lord Nishida.

"Yes," I said.

However, I thought, what was done that day was surely unlike the clash of cavalries in the sky.

"You have an opponent in mind?" I asked.

"You understand, do you not," he asked, "the drums, the synchronization, the ascents and descents, the circlings, the wheelings, to left and right?"

"You do not need me, great lord," I said, "surely a thousand tarnsmen might serve you as well, or better."

"But you understand such things?" asked Lord Nishida.

"Yes," I said.

"Excellent," he said.

"Perhaps others might serve as well," said Thrasilicus, "a possibility which I lack the expertise to dispute, but the Priest-Kings have chosen you."

"Someone it seems," I said, "has chosen me."

"Priest-Kings," said Thrasilicus.

"Why?" I asked.

"Is that not lost in the wisdom of the Sardar?" asked Thrasilicus.

"Doubtless," I said.

"Who would not wish these things to be in the hands of Bosk of Port Kar," said Lord Nishida.

"I would suppose many," I said. "And perhaps Priest-Kings."

"The Priest-Kings," said Thrasilicus, "command you to take Lord Nishida as your captain, to follow his instructions, and in all ways possible to abet his projects."

"I understand," I said.

Surely Kurii were well aware of my ambivalence toward Priest-Kings. With the new dynasty in the Nest had they not turned against me? Had I not been imprisoned in the holding capsule on the Prison Moon, in such a manner as to torture me, and jeopardize my honor?

Might I not, then, of my own will, so treated, have turned from the Sardar to the Steel Worlds?

"Our loyal servitor, Tajima," said Lord Nishida, "will explain much to you, and will often attend upon you."

I gathered the interview was then concluded, and I turned and left the pavilion, followed by Tajima.

Outside the pavilion I had turned to Tajima. "You are to spy on me?" I had asked.

"I fear so," he had said, "Tarl Cabot, tarnsman."

Tajima and I emerged from the path which led to a great plaza cleared in the forest.

About the edges of this area, which was better than a hundred yards in width, there were several structures. Most of these were rudely timbered, and most were windowless. Some, on the other hand, had an open wall, facing the area. Two seemed to be shops, with an open wall, one for metal workers, the other for leather workers. Some of these structures, it seemed, served as storehouses, for supplies and tack, such as saddles and harnessing, and others as shelters, for trainers and craftsmen, and doubtless, too, for those whom one might think of, in a way, as recruits. There was a larger building, too, which had a plank floor and an open wall. This, I would learn, was a *dojo*, or training hall. To one side there was a tank for water and there were several racks from which hung meat, probably tabuk, forest tarsk, and forest bosk. The greater forest tarsk, unlike the common tarsk, can be quite large. When I first came to Gor I saw a tapestry depicting the tarn hunting of such beasts, and, from the sizes involved, I had thought the tapestry to be based on some fantasy or myth. Only later did I discover that there were beasts of such a size. The common tarsk, on the other hand, is much smaller. When a slave, or even a free woman, is disparaged as a "she-tarsk," the smaller animal, the common tarsk, is invariably in mind. Otherwise the metaphor would be unintelligible. Indeed, many Goreans have never seen the forest tarsk, and many do not know of its existence. The forest bosk tends to be territorial, and, as I have already suggested, it can be quite dangerous. Most interestingly to me were the cots in the area, of which there were several. These cots were mostly improvised, walled with rope nets strung between trees, and, too, large, heavy poles, doubtless from local trees, trimmed of bark and branches. Rope netting is used rather than wire to protect the birds. Tarn wire, for example, sometimes used to "roof a city," to defend it from tarn attack, is almost invisible, and can easily cut the wing from a descending bird. A lighter form of wire is called "slave wire," and it, too, is dangerous. A slave attempting to escape through such wire is likely to be found suspended within it, piteously begging for help, half cut to pieces. Two of the cots were large and conical. Their framing, formed of light metal tubing, fitted together, was not untypical of a form of cot found in open camps. I supposed it derived from Thentis, and might have been brought to the coast by wagon, and then north by ship, as doubtless was the case with many forms of supplies.

"There are many tarns here," I said.

"There are more than a hundred and fifty now," I was told, "and more are due to be delivered."

"Who are the tarnsmen?" I asked.

"Some are tarnsmen," he said, "but many of your people, and mine, must learn the tarn."

Training was going on in the open area.

Between two sets of poles were slung ropes and a saddle, and in each saddle was a fellow who was being flung from side to side, and dropped, and lifted, and spun about, by others, and even, by ropes, on each side, being whirled about a vertical axis. Shortly both had been pitched into the sand some ten feet below. Their place was then taken by others. The two who had fallen were placed on a narrow plank, to the side, and forced to walk its length, while being screamed at, and execrated, from both sides. If one fell from the plank, in dizziness, he was struck with switches.

"The proper tarn saddle," I said, "has a safety strap. There is no way one can lose the saddle if it is fastened."

"True," said Tajima. "But what if the safety strap is cut in battle?"

"One then seizes, as one can, if one is in danger of falling," I said, "one of the saddle rings."

"Yes," said Tajima, "but he who just fell, it seems, missed the ring."

"True," I smiled.

"So let him improve his skills," said Tajima.

"True," I smiled. It was better to learn this while threatened with a ten-foot fall to the sand rather than a thousand-foot plunge to the ground."

I saw another fellow, one of the people of Tajima, fall from the plank, and then submit, unprotestingly, to being shouted at and beaten.

"I was not trained like this," I told Tajima.

"It was not necessary," said Tajima. "Such training would have dishonored you."

"How is that?" I asked.

"In your veins," he said, "flowed the blood of warriors, of tarnsmen."

"I do not understand," I said.

"No one," he said, "teaches the tarn to fly, the kaiila to run."

Elsewhere in the open area, which was, it seems, a training plaza, some tarns were out, some with wings bound, others, farther along in their training, hobbled, a heavy log chained to a taloned foot, and, in each case, held in ropes, so that if the tarn charged one trainer, it could be restrained by three or four others. The ropes were choke ropes.

"I see no tarn goads," I said.

"No," said Tajima. "The mechanism might malfunction, the charge might fail. A discipline wand may be used, or even a branch, with a blow to the cheek or beak. Too, the strike of the goad, with its shower of sparks, might attract attention at night."

In another area I saw a fellow mounted on a bird, the bird prevented from flying, hobbled, as were several others in the area. Its beak was strapped shut, so it could not turn and seize the rider. When it flung its head about, it was struck a terrible blow on the side of the head. Another fellow, further along, had the harnessing in place, with the rings and straps, by which he moved the head of the bird, back, or down, or to the sides.

"I note no slave girls here," I said. "I thought they might be used, to content the men, to cook, to fill the tank with water, such things."

"In the vicinity of tarns," said Tajima, "it is best for women to be hooded and bound."

"Doubtless on the whole," I said. It was true that most women were terrified of tarns, and with good reason, particularly the more imaginative, intelligent women, well aware of the danger of the bird and their own slightness, weakness, and vulnerability. Indeed the only experience many women had with tarns was to be slung naked as one of a pair, one on each side, fastened to a saddle ring, or to be, if a single quarry, hauled aloft by a tarnsman's braided, leather rope and then, their clothing cut from them, to be put on their back across the saddle, before their captor, their wrists crossed and bound to one ring, their ankles crossed and bound to another, their first writhing then, and crying out, to take place on the saddle, under the idle caresses of their captor, on the long flight back to his city or camp. It was less terrifying, of course, to be bound in a tarn basket, slung beneath a tarn, usually a draft tarn. "Some slaves work in the cots, in the cities," I said. "They grow accustomed to tarns."

"They are rather like stable sluts?" asked Tajima.

"Yes," I said. I thought of the former Miss Wentworth. She was now, technically, a stable slut.

"The men," said Tajima, "are brought food by tharlarion wagon, and, if they wish, they may visit the cook houses in the main camp."

"Some relief is provided, I trust," I said, "for the ferocity of other hungers, as well."

"For slave hunger, of course," said Tajima. "In the slave houses there are mats aligned, a row on each side, and each mat has its ring and chain, and slave. As the house is dark one carries a taper within, and picks out a slave. When one enters one is given a switch, which may be used, if one is not pleased, the switch being surrendered upon one's exit."

I supposed that some of the slaves brought in by Torgus and his fellows, whom I had encountered on the beach, former free women of Ar, might, if not yet disposed of to private masters, be found on the mats of the slave house. Far were such now, surely, traitresses, profiteers, and collaborators, from their jewels and palanquins, from their delicate viands and sweet wines, from their balcony gardens and lofty tower apartments. Muchly had their lives changed, and doubtless that of many others, as well, following the rising in Ar. So let their necks be closely and well encircled in slave steel, and let them lie in the darkness, waiting to be illuminated by a taper, thence to their knees and the kissing of feet, and beggings to be found pleasing.

My attention was then drawn to an area of the training plaza where a fellow was standing quietly before a hobbled tarn. Its beak was unbound. It lifted its unhobbled taloned foot as though to rake the fellow from head to foot. It opened and closed its large, razor like beak. In a tarn strike on a tabuk the animal's back is usually broken by the strike, and then the beak, like a shearing engine, slashes through the back of the neck. The fellow had no disciplinary wand, no branch, no club in his grasp. He was defenseless if the bird were to attack. I would not have wished to be placed in that position. The tarn screamed hideously, menacingly. Then it made a hissing sound. That sound is intended to intimidate. It is not uncommon in intraspecific aggression. At that sound the smaller bird, or younger bird, or less aggressive bird, usually backs away. That response has presumably been selected for. Had it not been presumably there would be commonly but one male in a flock. The male which retreats one day, of course, may not retreat another day, and then a fight to the death, or to the disabling of the defeated, is likely to take place. Eventually the younger bird will grow stronger and fiercer and the older bird weaker and less fierce, and, sooner or later, a new Ubar, over the body of its torn, quivering foe, will scream its conquest, and its claiming of the flock.

But the fellow menaced by the tarn did not move.

"He will be a tarnsman," I said.

"I think so," said Tajima.

Then the fellow put his hand out, on the bird's beak, which touch the bird, as though puzzled, suffered without protest. It is hard not to show fear in the presence of the tarn, but it is extremely dangerous to do so, for the tarn, as many animals, can sense fear, and this stimulates its aggression. The fellow, of course, was not another bird, or a tabuk, or verr, but a different life form, the human, which is not an unknown form of prey for a tarn, but it is certainly not its customary prey. Too, the tarn commonly attacks from the air. It is not unknown for tabuk to graze in its presence, if it has alighted. The fellow then embraced, as he could, its large head. The bird's eyes gleamed, brightly, wickedly, but it did not pull away. The fellow then began to groom the bird, smoothing its feathers. The tarn raised its crested head to the sky, and then lowered its head, again, for the pleasure of the fellow's touch. I could not hear, but I supposed the fellow was speaking to it, soothingly. Human speech, even a soft crooning, can settle a restless tarn. The girls who tend tarn cots sometimes, in the evening, after the feeding, sing to their charges. It is sometimes hard to know when the tarn is asleep as it, as many birds, sleeps with its eyes open. To be sure, interestingly, it apparently does not see then, although the eye is open. It seems to be something like a window through which no one at the time is looking. Occasionally in its sleep the tarn moves uneasily, and tosses its head, and a taloned foot will move, sometimes marking the floor of the cot. One supposes that the bird is dreaming, doubtless of flight, perhaps of the hunt. Some human beings, incidentally, occasionally sleep with their eyes open. This tends to be somewhat unnerving, for an observer. To be sure, sleepwalkers sleep with their eyes open, as well, but, clearly, they are seeing at the time, given their avoidance of obstacles, and such.

"I wanted you to see the training area, and the tarns," said Tajima. "There is little for you to do now, though you are welcome, as you wish, and whenever you wish, to visit this area. The training will continue. Also, we are awaiting the arrival of more leather for saddles and harnessing. Once we have a hundred or more men who have flighted a tarn and lived, we will begin a more disciplined endeavor, and will try to form riders, with such skills as they will then have, into prides, which you may then form into a cavalry."

The expression 'pride', in this context, was a metaphor, of sorts, taken from the usual grouping of larls, such a group being commonly called a pride. The term is Gorean, but, like a great many terms in Gorean, not surprisingly, given the voyages of acquisition, it is taken from another language, in this case, English.

"I am anxious to begin work," I said. I had considered, for a long time, possible innovations in the tactics of tarn attack, and the armament of riders. Too long, in my view, had the common tarnsman been too much of a mounted foot soldier, too long had he been the passenger of the mount, rather than a component in a single, unified weapon. An analogy, though quite imperfect, might have been the early transition from cavalry as a supportive arm, used to reconnoiter, harass, and ride down stragglers, to a central arm, a shock arm, of stirruped lancers fit to strike, split and disrupt serried ranks. The latter role on Gor, of course, belonged to war tharlarion. But I thought much might be done with tarn cavalries. For example, it seemed to me that much might be learned from the almost evanescent appearing and disappearing of Tuchuk cavalry. Too, the usual missile weapon of the tarnsman, as the longbow, or peasant bow, was impractical, was the crossbow, but it was difficult to reload from the saddle, and its rate of fire, accordingly, was slow. Usually one quarrel would be discharged, and then the crossbowman was well advised to withdraw from action until it was possible to ratchet back the cable for another load, or, if a foot stirrup was used, which was quicker, but gave less power, to haul it back with two hands, get it over the catch, and then, with an additional operation, set another missile in the guide. In either case, the rate of fire was, in my view, prohibitedly slow.

"I am pleased," said Tajima. "So, too, I am sure, will be Lord Nishida."

"I must speak to him soon," I said, "for there is much to be done."

"What of the riders?" asked Tajima.

"We do not know, now, who will be the riders," I said, "who will survive the training."

"True," said Tajima. "And I fear the larls will have much hunting to do."

"When the riders are well asaddle," I said, "I will speak to them, but not before."

"So it will be," said Tajima.

I was then prepared to leave the plaza, but, in turning about, I saw a sight which, to me, if not to Tajima, and his people, seemed exceedingly odd.

"What is going on there?" I asked.

"One is preparing to recover his honor," said Tajima.

On a small platform, in a white kimono, one of Tajima's people, which I will now refer to as the Pani, as that is their word for themselves, knelt. His head was bowed, and before him, on the platform, was a curved wooden sheath, which contained, doubtless, a knife. Near the fellow, also clad in a rather formal kimono, white, stood a fellow with an unsheathed sword, of the longer sort.

"Do not intrude," said Tajima.

"What is the fellow with the sword doing?" I asked.

"It is sometimes difficult to perform the act," said Tajima. "If it cannot be well completed the swordsman will assist. There is no loss of honor in that."

"Stop!" I called.

"Do not interfere!" cried Tajima, whose suave placidity was for once not at his disposal.

I thrust Tajima back and strode to the figure on the platform, who had now loosened his robe and drawn forth a small dagger from the sheath.

The man with the sword stood to one side, two hands on the hilt of the weapon. He regarded me. He did not seem resentful, outraged, or such. Rather, he seemed puzzled. He had not expected this intrusion, nor had the fellow on the platform.

The fellow on the platform gripped the knife. I thought blood had drained from his hand. He looked up, not fully comprehending this disruption. He had already, I understood, given himself to the knife, and all that remained now was to finish the deed.

"Allow him dignity!" begged Tajima.

"I will not allow this," I said.

"Who are you to stop it?" asked Tajima, once again in command of his emotions. The Pani are an extremely emotional, passionate race, as I would learn, and the calmness of their exterior demeanor, their frequently seeming impassibility, even seeming apathy, was less of a disposition than an achievement.

Civility is not an adornment, but a necessity. Is the beast not always at one's elbow? Behind the facade of a painted screen a larl may lurk. Every chain can snap, every rope break. Savagery lies close to the precincts of civilization. The borderland between them is narrow and easily traversed. Courtesy, or politeness, you see, must not always be understood as a lack, a debility, or insufficiency. One must not recklessly part curtains.

Behind them might be found things you would just as soon not see. He who writes poetry and sips tea, and waits expectantly for a flower to blossom, may, in a frenzy, on the field of battle, take head after head.

In any event, it is unwise to take mountains for granted. They may conceal volcanoes.

"I am commander, I am captain," I told Tajima.

"This man is a coward," said Tajima.

"No," I said, "he is not."

It seemed to me that the act he contemplated was sufficient evidence of that.

"He fled from a tarn," said Tajima.

"He will not do so again," I said.

"Do not interfere," said Tajima. "You can make no difference. He will simply complete the act later, when you are not present."

"No, he will not," I said.

"Why not?" asked Tajima, genuinely interested.

"Because I forbid it," I said. "I will have no more of this amongst men who will dare the tarn."

"It is our way," said Tajima.

"Who is captain?" I asked.

"You, Tarl Cabot, tarnsman," said Tajima.

"It is not my way," I said.

"You are captain," said Tajima, quietly.

"I will not lose men in this fashion," I said.

"It is better to lose such men," said Tajima.

"If you want to die," I said to the kneeling figure on the platform, "do so under the talons of the tarn."

"It is wrong for you to interfere in this, Tarl Cabot, tarnsman," said Tajima. "One must recover honor."

"One recovers honor in life," I said, "not in death. If he lives, he may begin again, and gain honor."

"That is not our way," said Tajima.

"But it is a way," I said.

"Doubtless," said Tajima.

"And it is my way," I said.

"Yes," said Tajima. "It is your way."

"And I am captain," I said.

"Yes," said Tajima. "You are captain."

"Return to your training," I told the fellow kneeling on the platform. "You are late."

"Yes, Captain San," he said.

Stumbling, shaken, he made his way toward the barracks.

"I will see that your views on this matter are conveyed to all," said Tajima.

I then bowed to the fellow with the sword. "Thank you for your attendance," I said to him, "but your honorable assistance is no longer required."

He returned my bow, sheathed the sword, and left.

"This pertains only to your command, you understand," said Tajima.

"At least now," I said, "you have something interesting to report to Lord Nishida."

"That is true," smiled Tajima.

Chapter Thirteen

I Seek Information in the Slave House

It was night.

I entered the slave house and received a lighted taper and a switch.

Others, similarly accoutered, were in the slave house, as well, perhaps seven or eight. The house was more than a hundred feet long, and built of thick logs, with a roof of branches and thatch. The structure was some twenty feet in width, and windowless. Its ceiling was some eight feet from the flooring. On each side there were aligned some twenty-five to thirty mats. These mats were some three to four inches in thickness, and something like a yard wide. They were sewn of heavy, striped canvas, and stuffed with straw. When I had entered I heard tiny sounds in the darkness, whimperings, small noises of fear, here and there the movement of a body on the straw-filled mat, the rustle of a chain.

I was interested in a particular slave.

I moved slowly down the aisle, lifting the taper first to the left, and then the right.

Each slave was chained by the neck, to a ring anchored in the floor, to the left of her mat, as she would look toward the aisle. Each had some four feet of chain.

As I lifted the taper one slave, kneeling, head down, crouched down, and tried to cover herself.

Surely she knew that was not permitted.

I did not strike her.

Another lay on her side and drew up her legs, and, bent at the waist, held her arms, too, tightly, frightened, about her.

That, too, was not permitted.

Nor did I strike her.

Both were dismayed, and terrified. I gathered they had not been long on the mats.

Torgus, the mercenary leader whom I had met on the beach earlier, had rented some of these, former high women of Ar, to the house.

I had ascertained those he had sold, either to the loggers, or craftsmen, or suppliers, or trainers, and such, or to the Pani themselves, and she whom I sought was not amongst those.

Accordingly I sought her here.

Several of the mats were empty, but I conjectured there might be some sixty or so girls in the house.

I lifted the taper again.

A girl, illuminated, but much in shadows, too, shrank back, half kneeling, half lying.

"Do not be afraid," I told her, and went on.

Surely several of these were new to the mats, unfamiliar with being illuminated in the darkness by tapers, fearful of the chain on their necks, wary of the switches of masters, women who knew themselves no longer free but did not yet fully understand what it was to be a slave, an understanding which would be soon and perfectly achieved.

She whom I sought, and had considered buying for Pertinax, was she whom I had noted on the chain of Torgus, on the beach, kneeling with others, neck-chained, in the surf and sand, she who had seemed most ready or needful, she whom I thought would be the first to plead for a man's touch. Sometimes a woman's igniting ensues as soon as she feels a collar put on her neck, one she cannot remove. Other times it may be a thing as simple as stripping her and binding her wrists behind her body. Sometimes it may be as simple as finding herself slave-naked, on her knees, before a man. Sometimes it may be when she first licks and kisses the feet of a man, when she feels the weight of a chain on her body, and so on. These things in themselves, interestingly, are often no more than keys which open a door which has long imprisoned a distressed and yearning slave. She has in her heart desired to be taken, owned, and mastered. She has never been more free than when most his.

I lifted the taper again, and one of the slaves scrambled, frightened, to her knees, and put her head to the mat, assuming first obeisance position. Her hair seemed sweaty. There were welts on her back.

Her response was in the vicinity of what was expected of her, but was not what it should have been.

When the slave is illuminated, she is to display herself as provocatively as possible. This can vary from girl to girl. Many are the suitable posings of the female slave. Indeed when a woman is put through slave paces, whether leashed or not, what is this but an exhibition, a detailed and sometimes tormentingly lovely display of property? If the fellow with the taper lingers, or seems interested, she then goes to first obeisance position, and begs to be found pleasing. Interestingly there was no coin box on the necks of the slaves, as would be the case with "coin girls" in some cities, usually port cities, or coin dishes beside the mat, as in great camps, and such, in which coins might be left by clients or patrons. Indeed, I had not even given a tarsk bit at the entrance. These slaves were furnished as a perquisite of the camp, to content the men who might not have their own slave or slaves. The rent money given to Torgus for his girls then, as with others, was furnished by the Pani, rather as they might have underwritten other forms of expense, clothing, bedding, housing, tools, weapons, food, ka-la-na, paga, kal-da, and such.

I continued on my way.

She whom I sought, I had learned, upon inquiries, was the former Lady Portia Lia Serisia of Sun Gate Towers, an exclusive district, near Ar's Street of Coins, where were found most of the banking houses of the city. The name of the enclave was derived from the Sun Gate, one of Ar's major gates, though it was better than two pasangs from the gate itself, the gate's name being derived from the fact that it was regularly opened at sunrise and closed at sunset. Many of the larger merchant enclaves were found near the walls, within which were several warehouses. This is convenient for the receipt of goods coming into the city, and for those being sent from the city. Caravans are usually formed outside the walls. Goods from these warehouses, of course, are often later distributed for retailing throughout the city. The Lady Serisia, as we may say for short, was a scion of the Serisii, one of Ar's older banking families. It was predominantly wiped out in the rising, it seems, for its collaboration with the occupational forces, its extending of credit to them, to meet its payrolls, when the funds for these failed somehow to reach the city, its purchases of great quantities of loot, including women, for later retailing elsewhere, its arranging for the confiscation of rival house's assets, and so on. For a time it had become the wealthiest and most powerful house in Ar, but then had come the rising. The Lady Serisia, I suspected, might be the last surviving member of the house. Proscription lists tend to be exacting, and Gorean justice, which tends to be expeditious and efficient, tends to pursue such matters with diligence. I did not doubt but what many a profiteer, traitor, and such, burdened impaling stakes within Ahn of the rising. Free women take part in the commercial life of Gorean polities as men do, owning and managing businesses, lending coin, negotiating loans, organizing caravans, investing capital, conservatively, or risking it variously, in real estate, voyages, commodities, and such, in translating goods about to find the most favorable markets at a given time, and so on. To be sure, much of this is done through male agents, as, in theory, such concerns are regarded as beneath the dignity and attention of a free woman. She is supposedly, in her dignity and nobility, above such crass concerns. That she exists, in the glory of her freedom, that she is so different from the shameful female slave, that she adds luster to the city and its Home Stone, is enough; that she be dedicated to refined and tasteful pursuits, such as attendance at the theater, at song dramas, poetry readings, and such, is deemed sufficient. In essence, the free woman, aside from being regarded as a priceless treasure, so different from the slave who, as a beast, may be purchased for a given amount of coin, is considered an ornament to the city, an adornment to her polity. But many grow wealthy and powerful, and others fail, and so on.

I lifted the taper again, now to the left, as I made my way down the aisle, and the woman, actually now a girl, as she was a slave, put her hand before her eyes, shielding her eyes.

It was she.

There was a rustle of chain as she sought first obeisance position.

"Kneel up," I told her.

She did so. I do not think she recognized me, at first.

"Have you not been taught the way of the mat, girl?" I asked.

"Master?" she said.

"Do you not understand the meaning of the mat and chain?" I asked. "Interest me."

"I do not know how," she whispered. "Is my body, before you, a male, not enough?"

I smiled. How like a stupid free woman was she still! Did the free woman not think there was nothing more to attracting a man than that she be a woman? To be sure, the hint of a bosom, the suggestion of the sweet width of hips, within the robes of concealment, was indeed attractive, and even free women understood this quite well, for not all slaves were in collars. Similarly a tone of voice, a turning of the head, perhaps provocatively, the hurried readjustment of a veil, it having somehow become inadvertently disarranged, could turn the knife in a fellow's belly. Yes, I thought, I suppose she is right, in a way. That a woman is a woman can be a thousand times more than enough, so to speak. Had not nature, in her indifferent judgments, brought these complementarities together? Suppose there were somehow ten thousand randomnesses. Amongst these some would be more likely to result in the replication of genes than others. Is the swiftest of the tabuk not most likely to escape the sleen or larl? How is it that the vision of the tarn can discern the movement of even an urt at a thousand feet? The shark who detects the trace of blood in remote water, will he not be the first to feed? Will not the moth who detects the odor of its female four pasangs away through the warm, night air be the first to flutter to her side? The beast which, somehow, sees fit to defend its young, is likely to have young which will survive it. Amongst all adventitious assortments some embody the future, not all. Yes, I thought, I suppose it is enough for the female to be a female. Something in that luscious configuration will trigger a genetic response selected for over millennia. From the point of view of rationality one shape is presumably little different from another. What is to choose from between the circle and triangle, but blood and time are attuned to a different geometry.

And, of course, the slave, as the others at their mats, was bared to the vision of free men. How different they are from us, I thought, and was therein well pleased. It also occurred to me that women go to great lengths, almost always, unless subglandular, moronic, insane, culturally suppressed, or somehow ideologically perverted, to dress themselves attractively. For example, the robes of concealment, prescribed for, and almost universally accepted by, Gorean free women, certainly of the higher castes, were not uniform, drab garmentures imposed on them by, say, an oppressive society which regarded women as inferior, unclean, and morally dangerous, but, in their abundance, in their layers and veilings, in their arrangements and drapings, were tasteful and attractive, and, above all, surely, bright and colorful. One may not see that much of a woman in the robes of concealment but there is no doubt that there is one in there somewhere, and there is no missing that. Yes, a woman can be quite attractive in the robes of concealment, and there is no doubt of that. Once again we note that not all slaves are collared. To be sure, the robes of concealment are, in their way, a tease, a provocation. Surely the women are not unaware of that. Perhaps that is one reason that men so relish the removal of such garments and the placing of their occupants in the more revealing and delightful garmentures of slaves. "You will tease no more. I will now look upon you as I wish, for you are now no longer yours, but are now ours, the property of men. Rejoice, the games are over. You are beautiful. Know yourself exhibited, and owned."

But the girls on the mats, of course, were not even accorded a slave strip. They were mat slaves, and bared suitably.

Was her body not enough?

In a sense, one supposed, surely, but, so far beyond that, so far indeed, were the fluidities and graces, the appetitions, the performances, the subtleties, the movements, the needs, the readinesses, the petitions, of the female slave!

"In one sense," I said, "your body is enough, and more than enough, but, in another sense, and one more important than that of brief, mindless couplings, that body is no more than a beginning, something needed, but something not enough in itself, something far from enough in itself."

"But, why, Master?" she asked.

"Because you are no longer a free woman," I said. "Because you are now a slave."

"I do not understand," she whispered.

"Because you are now a thousand times more female than before," I said.

"Master?" she said.

"Because you are now a slave," I said.

"Have pity on me!" she wept.

"Display yourself," I said, "girl."

"I do not know how!" she said.

"It is instinctual in you," I said. "It is in your blood. You are a female."

"Do not so humiliate me!" she begged.

"Begin," said I, "slave."

"Yes," she wept, "I am a slave!"

"Now," I said.

"Yes, Master," she wept.

"Ah," I said, "I see you have thought of these things before, perhaps in your dreams, perhaps in the secrecy of your boudoir, perhaps in your imaginings, perhaps in putting the loop of a strap about your left wrist, and, suddenly, dramatically, drawing it tight."

She sobbed.

"Excellent," I said. "It is a shapely limb, is it not? Would it not look well in an ankle shackle?"

"Have mercy!" she begged.

"You are well aware, are you not, of the weight of the chain on your collar, of the sound of its links, and how you are fastened to the floor ring, naked, before a male?"

"Master!" she protested.

"Continue," I said.

"Must I?" she said.

"Now," I said.

"I was free," she said. "You are making me behave as a slave!"

"And how are you behaving?" I asked.

"As a slave!" she said. "I am behaving as a slave!"

"Is it not appropriate?" I asked.

"Yes, Master," she said.

"Why?" I asked.

"Because I am a slave!" she said.

She collapsed to the mat, sobbing.

"Kneel up," I said to her, kindly. "You did well."

She then knelt before me.

"Keep your knees together," I advised her. I was, after all, only human. I then put the switch before her, and she leaned forward and, timidly, licked and kissed the supple leather implement.

She looked up. "Have me," she whispered. "Please."

There was a small stand, near the mat, in which a taper might be held.

"As a free woman?" I asked.

"No, Master," she said, "as what I am, a slave."

I gathered she had often thought of what it might be, to be a slave in the arms of a master.

"You are," I said, "the former Lady Portia Lia Serisia of Sun Gate Towers."

She regarded me, terrified.

"Do not deny it," I said. "I know it is true."

"Do not kill me!" she begged.

"That is not my intention," I said.

"You are of Ar?" she asked.

"No," I said.

"You want me, for a bounty," she said.

I supposed there were bounties on certain citizens of Ar, who had managed to escape the wrath of vengeful crowds, the pursuits of licensed and unlicensed capture squads.

"No," I said. "And, as far as I know, there is no bounty on you."

"I saw my name on a proscription list, posted on the public boards," she said.

"I do not doubt it," I said.

"They want me, to kill me," she said.

"Perhaps in the heat of the moment," I said. "But I would suppose, after a time, that their sense of vengeance would be more than satisfied if they found you wore a collar in the north. Indeed, I have learned from others that various women of your sort were merely publicly flogged and collared, some then to become state slaves, most to be sold out of the city, to be distributed with contempt amongst inferior markets."

"Does the proscription list not mean death?" she asked.

"Strictly," I said, "it means apprehension, but it is true, that it is commonly a warrant for death, certainly for males, and often for women, free women."

"They wanted our blood," she said.

"At the time, in the rage of the crowd, I do not doubt it," I said. "But, now, you might rather be brought before a praetor, for the iron and the collar."

"Is that true?" she said.

"I do not know," I said. "We could always take you there, and see."

"No," she said. "No!"

I smiled.

"I am not what I was," she said. "The Kef has been fixed in my thigh, the steel is on my neck."

"It is true," I said. "You are not what you were."

"I was not high amongst the Serisii," she said. "I did not enter into their business. I was a lowly daughter, pampered and spoiled, given to a life of luxury and indolence! I had no control over the affairs of the house!"

"But you bore the name," I said.

"Yes," she said. "I bore the name."

"But no longer," I said.

"No," she said, "no longer." This was true. There was no longer a Lady Portia Lia Serisia of Sun Gate Towers. She was gone. There was now, not even really in her place, only an animal, a lovely animal. As far as I knew Torgus had not even, as yet, seen fit to give her a name. She then regarded me, frightened. "You know me," she said, "or who I was. What do you want of me? If you do not want my blood, or to bind me, and trade me for a bounty, what do you want? Why have you sought me out?"

"No woman in a collar," I said, "should be curious as to why a man might seek her out."

"No, no," she said. "You want more."

"Perhaps I wish to buy you for a friend," I suggested. I had, indeed, toyed with the idea of buying her for Pertinax. She was quite attractive. Might she not look well chained to his cot in the barracks? A strong man needs a slave, and is never content with less. Pertinax could certainly do worse than having his collar on one such as this.

She looked at me, frightened. I think it had not really occurred to her, other than as an abstract possibility, that she might be simply purchased and given to someone.

"Buy me?" she said, weakly.

"Yes, like a kaiila or tarsk," I said.

"And then I would belong to another?"

"Of course," I said.

"No," she said. "There is something else, and I am frightened." She looked up, blinking against the light of the taper. "What is it?" she asked.

"I want to speak to you," I said. "I will question you. I want information."

"I know nothing," she said. "I am naked. I am on a chain. I am a slave."

"The Serisii were high in Ar," I said, "close to the throne. You, and others, sought escape from the city. Plans must have been laid against such eventualities as the rising. You must have heard one thing or another."

"Master?" she said.

"What of Seremides?" I asked. "He was powerful in Ar, a deputy, so to speak, of Myron, the *polemarkos*."

"Surely he was apprehended and impaled," she said.

"I have not heard so," I said. A capture and impalement of such consequence would surely have been noted, and broadcast, I thought, throughout a dozen cities and a hundred camps.

The slave was silent.

"You have heard nothing?" I said.

"Nothing," she said.

Too, I thought his capture would be a coup of considerable dimension, and one whose fame would be soon registered on the public boards of a dozen cities, whispered about a thousand campfires, even as far north as the forests, but, here, too, I had, as yet, heard nothing.

"Were you," I asked, "as a scion of the Serisii, a confidante of the Ubara?"

"Surely not, Master," she said. "But, as of the Serisii, whose fortunes were closely intertwined with those of Cos and Tyros, I, and others, were often entertained in the Central Cylinder."

"What was the nature of these entertainments?" I inquired.

"They were not unusual," she said, "for the occupation. There were exquisite feasts from the largesse of Ar. While some in the streets hunted urts to live, we enjoyed the most delicate of a hundred viands, the richness of a hundred rare wines. The foremost poets of the city sang their works for us. The preeminent musicians, of those who remained within the walls, played for us. Theatricals were staged. Acrobats and jugglers were engaged. Former free women of Ar, collared, but decorously attired, served the tables. Sometimes slaves were brought in, to dance for us, though probably, in particular, for the men, officers of Tyros and Cos, mercenary captains, bankers, such as the Serisii, high merchants, well-known traders, and such. One slave, a very beautiful slave, who had been given to Myron, the *polemarkos,* was brought forth several times, and forced to dance before the men, bejeweled, bangled and necklaced, but otherwise naked, under whips. Her name was Claudia."

"Once Claudia Tentia Hinrabia," I said, "the last of the Hinrabians." Claudius Tentius Hinrabius had been an administrator of Ar, later deposed. He who acceded to the rule of Ar had been Cernus, in effect, a usurper."

"Yes," said the slave.

Talena had held Claudia as a rival to her own considerable beauty, which was alleged to be unsurpassed on all Gor. These sorts of claims, of course, were absurd, as there was no dearth of beauty on Gor. The markets were filled with it. Who is to say that this very beautiful woman is more or less beautiful than this other? To be sure, both Talena and Claudia, in their different ways, were very beautiful women. I suspected the hostility of Talena toward Claudia was as much motivated by considerations of politics as of vanity. Claudia had been the daughter of a former administrator of Ar; and Talena was merely the disowned daughter of the great Ubar, Marlenus, whose whereabouts had then been unknown. Her position had been bestowed upon her by foreign enemies, who had found it expedient to have a puppet on the throne of Ar. Indeed, Claudia's claim to stand high in Ar was far sounder than that of Talena herself, who had been disgraced, and sequestered shamefully, in effect imprisoned, in the Central Cylinder, while Marlenus carried on the business of the state, prior to his hunting trip to the Voltai, in which it had been feared he had perished.

"Once," said the slave, "Claudia, at the conclusion of her dance, seized up a goblet of wine and dashed it upon the Ubara. We feared the slave would be instantly slain, and she was flung to the floor, under a dozen blades, and it was only the hand of her master, Myron, the *polemarkos,* interposed, which saved her. The Ubara was outraged and screamed and screamed and struck and kicked the slave repeatedly, and pressed and stamped upon her with her tiny jeweled slippers. And finally the slave, sobbing, and groveling, trembling and shuddering, bruised, miserable, her pride broken, her spirit vanquished, well informed now that whatever she might once have been, she was now no more than a slave, wholly submitted, and helpless, crawled to the feet of the Ubara, kissing them, as a slave, begging mercy, and forgiveness. She was spared, I think to please the *polemarkos*. It was said that after that Claudia became a true slave to her master. She was never again, of course, permitted by the *polemarkos* to dance at the entertainments in the Central Cylinder. She was used, often, however, it was said, to dance in the headquarters and garrison camp outside the walls, for Myron and his high officers. He was, it was said, much envied for his slave."

"Speak to me of the Ubara," I said.

"She was very beautiful," said the slave, "as I am sure she well knew, and as we might easily discern, for in privacy we might all dine unveiled, it not being unseemly."

"Of course," I said.

Veiling was common amongst free women in public. In private. veiling would be an encumbrance. Few women would veil themselves in their own household, unless in the presence of strangers. In public dining the woman might feed herself discreetly, delicately, beneath the veil. Some lower-caste women, on the street, will literally drink through the veil.

"Speak further," I said.

"It is interesting," said the slave. "For a long time the Ubara was as a Ubara, informal or stately as the occasion demanded, a ruler, or a host, witty and charming, or cold and demanding. At one moment she would warm one with a smile and in the next moment chill one with a frown. Within limits, Ar was hers. She was an exceedingly proud woman, and was confident, sure of her place and of herself. It was well to struggle to please her. A word from her could demote an officer of Ar, a phrase exile a councilor, or break or banish a merchant, and another could reduce another woman, even one of high station, to the collar. She was charming, vain, secure, and arrogant. Muchly did she relish her power, such as it was. Limited as it might be in great things, it was formidable in that which did not concern the occupation. Men and women strove to please her. She was muchly feared. But then, strangely, a change came over the Ubara. An entertainment had been planned, but it was canceled, presumably because the Ubara was indisposed. But, after that, she was different. Entertainments became fewer, and then ceased. The Ubara seemed distracted, even fearful. She would not leave the Central Cylinder. We understood, even in her private chambers, which were locked and guarded, she would keep candles ablaze during the hours of darkness. She became frightened of food and drink, lest, perhaps, it might be drugged, or poisoned. Frightened slave girls, former free women of Ar, were used as tasters. It was as though she were hunted. It was as though she feared somehow, as absurd as it might seem, she being so secure, and being Ubara, that she might feel the capture rope upon her any instant, like a common or private woman, and be carried away into what fate she knew not, perhaps even one as frightful as the collar itself. Imagine she, a Ubara, in a collar! What state would be powerful enough, clever enough, bold enough, to seize a Ubara? What Ubar mighty enough to have her naked, in chains, at the foot of his throne! It was strange, incomprehensible, the change that had come over her. Then, later, of course, the rising took place."

"What then," I asked, "was the fate of the Ubara?"

"I do not know," said the slave. "The rising came suddenly, and there was terror in the streets for many. I and some others were taken in hand by mercenaries and, stripped, and self-pronounced as slaves, and neck-roped, were used by them as a ruse to approach the walls, they pretending to be citizens of Ar conducting us to impaling stakes. At the wall they managed to fight their way free to the outer country, and join Cosians in retreat. Our hair was shortened, that we not appear free women to flighted tarnsmen, and we were soon chained by the neck, and conducted from camp to camp, until we reached the vicinity of Brundisium, from which port, subsequently, we, cargoed, were shipped by sea to the north, where we made landfall."

"Do you recognize me?" I asked.

"It is dark, Master," she said. "The light is tiny, and poor. There are shadows. Do I know you?"

"Not really," I said. "But we have met. I met your party on the beach."

"You are he?" she said.

"Yes," I said.

"I thought perhaps," she said. "But I dared not speak."

"You impressed me," I said, "as a slut well collared."

"Master!" she protested.

"Just now," I said, "you displayed yourself well."

She put down her head. "Yes," she said, "I am a slut well collared."

"Talena," said I, "must somehow have escaped."

"Perhaps," she said, "but it seems impossible. The Central Cylinder was surrounded even before the bars sounded the rising."

"I have heard no word," I said, "of the capture, the torture, or impalement of the Ubara."

"No," agreed the slave.

I was sure the Central Cylinder would have been examined with care, each chamber, even to measurements of the thickness of walls, and such, being considered.

"She must have escaped," I said.

"Perhaps the crowds found her, tore her to pieces, and fed the scraps to sleen," she said.

"By tarnflight, from the Central Cylinder," I suggested.

"Perhaps, Master," she said.

To be sure, this was highly unlikely, for a careful watch would have been kept. As this would be a most obvious possibility, a most likely route for escape, it would have been guarded against with zealous care.

"If she escaped, Master," said the slave, "I think it unlikely she will long remain at large."

I nodded. Her conjecture seemed to me plausible.

"I heard the masters speaking," she said, "in the camps. A price of ten thousand tarn disks, of double weight, has been placed on the Ubara's head."

I nodded, again. I had heard that, too, from Torgus, on the beach. Every bounty hunter on Gor, professional or amateur, would seek the Ubara. Too, it was unlikely that she would be long shielded from discovery, given the price on her head, and the hostility with which she was so generally regarded. Her vanity, her arrogance, the insolence with which she had abused power, her betrayal of her Home Stone, and such, militated against her concealment. Perhaps, as Torgus had suggested, she had already been captured, and her captors were negotiating for an even higher remuneration.

"You have been helpful," I told the slave.

"You are not going to take me back to Ar?"

"No," I said. "Such things are behind you."

I turned to go.

"Master," she called, softly.

I turned back.

"What are slave fires?" she asked.

"Put your knees apart," I told her.

She gasped, but obeyed.

She seemed pathetic, in the darkness, kneeling on the small, striped straw mat, her skin so white, illuminated in the light of the taper.

The light reflected from the chain, dangling from her neck.

"Can you not sense what slave fires might be?" I asked.

"Yes," she whispered, "I think so."

"Fear them," I said. "Resist them mightily. For once they burn in your belly, you can never again be truly free. You will always be a man's slave."

"I am not permitted to resist them," she said, "for I am a slave."

"That is true," I granted her.

"Master," she whispered.

"Yes?" I said.

"I can sense what they can be," she said. "I do not want to resist them."

"They will change you," I said, "forever."

"I want to be changed," she whispered.

"Put your knees together, and go to first obeisance position," I told her.

With a rustle of chain, she obeyed.

"You are a mat girl," I told her. "You may now beg as one."

"Master?" she said.

"You may kiss the free man's feet, and beg to be found pleasing," I said.

I then felt her lips at my feet.

"You may both kiss, and lick, lovingly, deferentially," I said. "It is a great honor for a slave girl to do this, for he is a free man, and she is a mere slave."

This was true, for some masters will not permit a slave to perform this simple act, even when she begs for the privilege. From the point of view of a free woman this act may seem humiliating, and perhaps it is, for a free woman, but, for the slave, it is a beautiful act of submission, even of love, in which she testifies to her joy in bondage, and expresses, humbly, and symbolically, her gratitude to her master, that he has consented to have her, one such as she, only a slave, in his collar.

Many free women cannot even begin to understand the love of a slave for her master, but it may be the deepest and most profound love possible between a human female and a human male. Indeed, in the view of many, it is exactly that, the deepest and most profound love possible between the human female and the human male, that of slave for master, and of master for slave.

What else can so fulfill the natures of both?

She knelt at my feet, her head down, her neck in the chain. There was a rustle of chain as she trembled, understanding where she was and what she was doing, and then she, again, bent to her task.

"What are you?" I inquired.

"A slave," she whispered, "a mat girl."

I considered her hair. It had not been well shortened. It was ragged, and uneven.

"It is enough," I said. "Keep your head down."

She was quite beautiful. That had been clear when she had knelt at the beach, the cold surf coming and going, washing up, now and again, about her thighs, feet, and calves. She was beautiful now, too, in the flickering light of the taper.

"You may beg," I said.

"I beg to be found pleasing, Master," she whispered.

Torgus and his fellows, in my opinion, had shown her, and her chain sisters, too little respect. They had regarded the chain as raw, poor stuff, as largely worthless slut merchandise, little better than free women. Could they not see the females as what they might become? Washed, combed, brushed, trained a bit, silked or tunicked, their slave fires ignited, taught to fear the whip, they might prove exemplary merchandise. I wondered again if Pertinax might like her. He had never owned a slave. How then could he know what it was to be a whole man?

"You may kneel up," I told her.

"Master?" she said.

"You are beautiful, and you did well," I said. "It is my hope that you will be permitted to live."

"Surely you are not leaving," she said.

"Yes," I said.

"But you sought me out!" she said.

"Yes," I said.

"Did you not want my body?" she asked.

I smiled. How much like a foolish free woman was she still, who so often so little understood men. The Gorean master possesses the whole slave, and the slave understands she is wholly possessed. He will have everything out of her, her feelings and thoughts, her imaginings, her hopes, her dreams, her fears, everything, and, if necessary, he will have this out of her by the whip. And soon the slave desires, too, desperately, to convey the wholeness of her to the master. She knows her beauty is to be placed at his feet, his to do with as he pleases, but she learns that he will have, too, if it pleases him, as it may or may not, spilled at his feet like her tresses, the treasures of her inner life. It is a miserable slave who is kept as a mere body.

Much, of course, depends on the master and the slave.

Bondages are plentiful, and various.

A slave may be kept in contempt, as nothing. She may grovel in fear at her master's presence. She may crawl to him, not knowing if she is to be struck or not.

She may be a delight to him, and be much as a companion, but at a mere word be naked before him, on her belly.

There are the slaves of great houses, those ornamenting pleasure gardens, those chained behind palanquins for display, those sold to brothels and taverns, those of the fields, and mines, and laundries and mills, those of the stables and barracks, and inns, those belonging to regiments, to shipping lines, to caravan masters, and so on. Many and various are the countries of bondage.

The master may have many slaves, but the slave may, by law, have but one master, even if it be the state, or some corporate entity.

Most slaves desire a private master, and they hope to be his only slave.

The most personal and intimate relationship possible between a man and a woman, is that she is his slave. What greater intimacy can there be between a man and a woman than that the woman is wholly his, that she is literally owned, that she is his possession, his slave?

"Your body is well worth wanting," I said, "but if it were not animated, not living, not whole with feelings, emotions, and thoughts, it would not be worth wanting. It would be only meat, not slave."

"All of me is wanted?" she asked.

"Yes," I said, "and do not forget, it is the whole of you which is in the collar."

"In my heart and mind," she said, "I want to yield!"

"Of course," I said, "all of you is in the collar."

"But you are leaving?" she said.

"Yes," I said, turning away.

"Wait!" she begged.

I turned, again, lifting the taper, to face her. Tears had coursed her cheeks.

"Why did you come here?" she asked.

"To question you," I said, "as a former high woman of Ar, of an important house, one who might know aught of the Ubara."

"But, why, Master?" she asked. "What is the Ubara, and her fate, to you?"

"Curiosity," I said, "is not becoming in a *kajira*."

"Do not go!" she wept.

I paused.

She put the chain over her left shoulder, behind her.

Tears were in her eyes, her lips trembled. "I beg to be found pleasing," she said.

"Do you have a name?" I asked.

"No," she said.

I put the taper in the stand near the mat.

Chapter Fourteen

Tajima and I Hold Converse

"You are quick," said Tajima, lowering the wooden blade in the *dojo.*

"So, too, are you," I said.

Several of the Pani sat about, cross-legged, at the interior wall of the open-walled, wooden-floored structure. It was, as might be recalled, at the far edge of the plaza of training.

Tajima and I bowed to one another, and then sat, side by side, cross-legged, toward the back wall.

Eight of the Pani then rose from their places and four of them, unarmed, faced the other four, similarly unarmed. They then bowed to one another, warily squared off and, shortly, engaged. Another of the Pani, an umpire or referee, or, better, I suppose, an adjudicator, began to observe and supervise the practice. He occasionally commented, even scolded. In this engagement no mortal blows were to be dealt, of course, and when a stroke which would have spelled death or disablement was held up short, the adjudicator pronounced his verdict, and one of the fellows would politely withdraw from the contest, in effect having been ruled dead or, one supposes, disabled. One-on-one combat can be stylized amongst the Pani, and may proceed rather formally, for all its sudden swiftness and violence, alternating with an almost unnatural stillness, reminiscent of a larl or panther, intent, immobile, subtly quivering, before its attack. Interestingly, although four were engaged on a side, when one was removed from the contest, his opponent did not then join with his fellows to overwhelm the survivors, but stood back. In effect, then, one had what seemed to amount to four one-on-one contests. In actual warfare, I trusted this civility would not be respected. Courtesy is one thing, but courtesy at the expense of victory seemed to me a dubious tactical election. Finally one fellow held the floor from one team, so to speak, and he was faced by three of the other group. He defeated two and was defeated by the third. The eight fellows then stood, exchanged bows, and resumed their places.

"May we speak?" I asked Tajima.

"Not now," said Tajima, softly.

A large number of contests, of various sorts, took place in the *dojo*, most with weapons of wood. These were surrogates for several weapons, in particular the short sword, or companion sword, and the long sword. Some glaives without blades were used. An interesting variation on these surrogate weapons was supple poles, long, light, peeled, whiplike branches which might flash about, scarcely visible. These, I gathered, were less surrogate weapons than training devices, to quicken reflexes, and enhance skills. Occasionally steel was used, but, again, of course, the strokes were held up short. Sometimes one surrogate weapon was put against a different surrogate weapon. Sometimes an unarmed individual was to engage an individual armed, say, with a sheathed dagger. Understandably, a reasonable amount of care was taken in the *dojo* to reduce injury and, certainly, to prevent death, the holding of strokes, and such, but, nonetheless, bloodshed was not infrequent, and broken limbs, wrists, and arms, were not unknown. These injuries seemed to be accepted with equanimity, save where it was suspected that intent was involved. The Pani seemed to feel in such a case that something was out of balance, however slightly, and an adjustment was in order. A disharmony was in need of correction. In such case one slash reddening a wooden blade might be used to pay for another.

"Now?" I asked Tajima.

"No," said Tajima.

The exercises and contests within the *dojo* were obviously intended to provide serious and detailed martial training, and I am sure they had great value in this regard. Why should they not? Indeed, had I not, long ago, in Ko-ro-ba, the Towers of the

Morning, engaged in similar exercises, though commonly with actual weapons? But one can do only so much in such training, of course, whether with wood or steel. It is one thing to face a fellow with a wooden sword, say, who will hold his stroke, or try to do so, and quite another to face a fellow armed with finely edged steel who has every intention of killing you. In the latter case every corpuscle comes alive, and the whole business is commonly done within a flash or two of steel. There is no training, as it is said, which can compare with the *dojo* of blood.

Two days ago I had spoken to Lord Nishida, again in his pavilion, and he had been receptive to my recommendations, and I had, accordingly, sought out certain craftsmen in the camp, leather workers and metal workers, and certain suppliers, who might, over the next months, secure certain goods, formed to my specifications.

With respect to weaponry the Gorean warrior is commonly trained in the blade, shield, and spear. The blade is commonly the *gladius*, which is quick, light, and double-edged, suitable for both the thrust and the slash. It is an excellent infantry weapon. On tarnback, naturally, there is little call for it. Similarly, the saber, which might be used with some efficacy from, say, horseback is of little use from either kaiilaback or tarnback. The kaiila, a lofty, silken beast, stands too high at the shoulder to warrant a saber. The Tuchuks, for example, use the temwood lance, which is long, light, tough, and supple. It has no difficulty in engaging an opponent on foot. The Tuchuks also use the quiva, or saddle knife, which is balanced for throwing. I thought we might substitute for the quiva the Anangan dart, a weighted, metal dart, some eighteen inches in length, which is flung overhand and, because of its fins, requires less skill than the quiva. It would be, I supposed, primarily an auxiliary weapon, to which recourse might be had in special circumstances, those, for example, in which, on the ground, one might employ the quiva. Such circumstances, those in which the quiva might be used, would commonly be in the swirl of close combat, where even the bow might be impractical. The typical Gorean shield is heavy, large and round, of layered leather bound with metal stripping. It may shield a soldier but it cannot, even given its size, protect a tarn. More practical on the whole, I thought, everything considered, would be the metal buckler, smaller and easily managed, with one hand, rather than an entire arm. It could turn a spear thrust, whereas a thrust or thrown spear would be likely to anchor itself in the common shield. Indeed, a common infantry tactic is to disable the opponent's shield by penetrating it with one's spear. This, in effect, renders the shield not only ineffective but a liability, as the attack then proceeds with the *gladius*. The buckler I had in mind was not only easily manageable but would have two additional features of interest. First, it might be easily slung at the saddle, freeing the tarnsman's hands, for a purpose which will soon be obvious, the use of the bow, and, second, as in some arena bucklers, it would have a bladelike edge, thus allowing it to be used to cut at an opponent's body, ideally the throat. I did not expect there would be much call for this latter feature unless the tarnsman was on foot, but sometimes tarnsmen do lock in combat, even on tarnback, as the birds, spinning about, buffeting one another, screaming and twisting about, do grapple in the sky. The buckler, too, though with less efficacy than the larger shield, would provide some defense against flighted quarrels, at least for the most vulnerable areas of the body, those most frequently targeted. Lastly, its lightness, compared to the usual infantry shield, would to some extent, if only one rather negligible, increase the speed and maneuverability of the tarn.

Given the size of the tarn, the beating of its wings, and such, there is no simple way to protect it from arrow fire, either aerial fire or fire from the ground. When I had first come to Gor war tarns had often been lightly armored and the beak and talons sheathed with steel. The armor, light as it was, encumbered and slowed the bird, considerably decreasing not only its speed but its maneuverability. It also, in its alien aspects, tended to make the bird harder to manage. Lastly the enhancement of the beak and talons proved of little merit for two reasons. First, in most tarnflight, the beak and talons do not come into play, and, second, when they do come into play they are formidable weapons in themselves, as in, say, tearing at the eyes and vitals of an enemy bird, far above the ground. Evolution, on whatever world might be that of the tarn's origin, had armed it well. Whatever world that was, I suspected, it had been a high-gravity world, one with a deep gravity well, for the strength of the tarn was considerable, far beyond what one would normally expect of an avian creature of a more typical world, such as Earth or Gor. I have always referred to the tarn as a bird, and will continue to do so, for it is surely that, at least in a sense, given its ecological place, its feathering, its wings, and such, but, zoologically, one supposes, it is something rather different from what are normally taken as birds, either on Earth or Gor, or, perhaps better, one should say it is an unusual bird. Its massive size and wing spread may not be its only remarkable features. It does nest and reproduce itself oviparously. Indeed, I would soon learn numerous items of unusual value were stored in the warmth of certain of the sheds at the plaza of training.

The average Gorean spear is some seven feet in length, with a socketed bronze blade some fourteen to eighteen inches in length. It is a formidable weapon on the ground, but, on tarnback, in resisting an aerial tarn attack, I thought that the light, slender temwood lance, favored by the Tuchuks, would be more formidable, being quicker, with its lightness, and longer, as well, giving the advantage of a greater reach. Too, it was also more secure, given the wrist strap. Obviously, to lose a lance from kaiilaback is a serious matter. One cannot not well, in the midst of battle, dismount and retrieve it. And, of course, if one is aflight, a lost lance is highly unlikely to be recovered.

It might be recalled that the usual missile weapon, if one were carried, of the tarnsman was the crossbow, either of the ratchet or stirrup variety. The mighty peasant bow, because of its size, obviously, could not be well used from the saddle. Too, the rate of fire of both these weapons was lamentably slow, particularly that of the ratchet variety, which not only limited the number of missiles which could be launched in a given period of time, but placed the archer, did he not withdraw, in the interval between firing and reloading, in considerable jeopardy. Too, of course, the archer might be pursued and brought down in the interval. The obvious recourse then would seem to be something like the Tuchuk saddle bow, which could easily clear the saddle to left and right, and could even be used, the rider turning in the saddle, to backward flight arrows. The saddle bow lacked the power of the peasant bow but it was practical from the saddle, and could match the rate of fire of the larger weapon.

Metal workers could fashion Anangan darts.

I set them to such work.

I also dealt with leather workers at the plaza of training. What I needed from them were adjustable stirrups. In long flights one might use the common stirrups, for one's ease of riding. On the other hand, if one were to use the bow, it was better for the stirrups to be shortened, so one could easily rise in the stirrups, if one wished, for firing over the head of the bird, over its wings, and so on. Tuchuks regularly use shortened stirrups, but my fellows were not Tuchuks, not trained for years to the saddle. Indeed, it is not uncommon for a Tuchuk to be tied in the saddle as soon as he can sit up, even before he can walk.

I also ordered the production of weighted nets. Nets are familiar on Gor. There are, for example, war nets, so to speak, such as the nets of the "fishermen" in the arena, who are armed with net and trident, and capture nets, such as are used by hunters for small animals and by slavers for women. Such a net, well cast, I hoped, might entangle an enemy tarn or its rider in the sky, interfering with the bird's flight or the rider's capacity to engage. They might also be used, I supposed, from a low-flying tarn in support of ground forces.

To bring some of these things together then, I envisioned the tarnsman not so much as a mounted infantryman, so to speak, either a spearman or a crossbowman, than as something different, a new form of warrior, a component, so to speak, in a unified weapon system, that of man and tarn.

Lord Nishida had declined to inform me of the likely applications of this projected tarn cavalry, so I had designed it for more than reconnaissance and attack from the air on ground targets. I designed it also for aerial combat, tarnsman to tarnsman, tarn to tarn.

Interestingly, that Lord Nishida had declined to inform me of the projected applications of this arm convinced me that, though nothing was said to this effect, one must be prepared for both forms of war.

That these men of the Pani, such as Lord Nishida and Tajima, and their fellows, so unusual to continental Gor, or even the western islands, should be here, whether in Brundisium to the south, or here in the northern forests, was to me, at the time, inexplicable. In this matter I suspected the hand of Priest-Kings, or Kurii. To be sure, here in Tarncamp I had counted no more than some two hundred to two hundred and fifty of the Pani. In Tarncamp and, I suspected, elsewhere, say at the end of the mysterious road to the southeast, there were far more Goreans, of a familiar sort, than Pani. I had gathered from Pertinax that hundreds had beached in the north, following, say, the rising in Ar, and, clearly, there were not that many in Tarncamp itself, though, as mentioned, there were several in Tarncamp, and they would, if counted, have considerably outnumbered the Pani in the area.

In summary, the tarnsman, as I envisioned him, would be primarily an archer, and his bird would carry a large number of arrows, far more than might be carried in the common quiver. The temwood lance and Anangan darts would be at hand for close combat, should that arise. For defense, primarily, a light buckler might defend against the spear, and, possibly, some arrow fire. One could assess the probable arrival of the quarrel from the reaction of the archer, the stock pounding back against his shoulder, and the distance involved. Its knifelike, circular edge might also, in some situations, enable it to function not only as a defensive weapon, but one of offense, as well. I was not sure of the practicality of the net in aerial combat but its use in handicapping opponents and snaring prey was well established on the ground. And the usual kit of the tarnsman would include such items, of course, as binding fiber and slave bracelets, for in Gorean warfare the taking of female slaves is common. Indeed, the Gorean woman is well aware that outside the compass of her Home Stone, outside a certain circuit of civility, beyond comfortable environs in which her loftiness, nobility, and preciousness are unquestioned, she is likely to be viewed not so much as an esteemed fellow citizen and an untouchable, lovely adornment to a grateful polity than as booty, quarry, prey, and prize, an item to be seized, branded, and collared, and then kept or sold, as a master might please.

"We will need two hundred bows, at least, saddle bows, thousands of arrows," I had informed Lord Nishida.

"They will be supplied," he had said, quietly.

"There will be other things needed, as well," I had said.

"You will receive them," he had said.

The audience had then been concluded.

Outside the *dojo* I spoke to Tajima.

"Your training," I said, "extends well beyond the *dojo*."

He did not respond.

"I have noted, upon occasion," I said, "that you have frequented the area of the warm pool, where some bathe, far from the tubs."

His taciturnity could sometimes be annoying.

"Too, I have seen some others frequent that area, and I do not think for the warmth of the waters."

We continued on, toward the hut I occupied with Cecily.

"I have seen some carrying food," I said.

"Oh?" said Tajima.

"As I suspect you yourself do, as well, sometimes," I said.

"Is it not I who am to spy on you?" asked Tajima.

"Surely," I said, "you do not object to a reciprocity in such matters."

"That would be churlish of me," he admitted. "How may I be of service to you, Tarl Cabot, tarnsman?" he asked.

"In the forest," I said, "though doubtless within the wands, there is further training, a teacher, a master, for some particular few, amongst whom I would suppose yourself."

"You are perceptive," he said.

"To be sure," I said, "perhaps you are merely sneaking off for a secret rendezvous with the lovely Sumomo."

"You have noted my interest in her," observed Tajima.

"Your expression betrays little," I said, "but the pupils of your eyes much."

"It is hard to control such things," said Tajima. "The movements of contract women are closely supervised. Collar-girls have much more freedom, as would domestic sleen or scavenging tarsks. Besides, she scorns me."

"Perhaps she has a pretty body," I said, "which would look well in a collar."

"She is a contract woman," said Tajima.

"Surely, wherever you come from, which I suspect is faraway, you have collar-girls."

"Yes," he said.

"And I suppose they are not all light-skinned or dark-skinned."

"No," said Tajima, "but they are not of the Pani."

"How is that?" I asked.

"Because as soon as they are collared, they are no longer of the Pani, but only slave beasts."

"I see," I said.

"There are many such slave beasts," he said. "War is frequent amongst the Pani."

"And would not Sumomo," I asked, "look pretty as such a slave beast?"

"Perhaps," he said. "I cannot afford her contract."

"What if you could?" I asked.

"An interesting thought," he said.

"And she would then be yours to do with as you wished, would she not?" I asked.

"There are expectations, customs, and such," he said, "but, yes, she would then be mine to do with as I wished."

"Absolutely?" I asked.

"Yes," he said. "Absolutely."

"And do you not think she might look pretty as a slave beast?"

"Yes," said Tajima, "I would think so."

"With whom do you train in the forest?" I asked.

"Nodachi," he said.

"He is not a two-name person?" I asked.

"That is not his name," said Tajima. "His name is secret. He conceals it. He is called 'Nodachi'. That is merely a name for a battle sword, one to be used in the field."

"I understand little of this," I said.

"He is *ronen*," said Tajima. "A fellow of the waves, as it is said, one with no home, one carried by the current, one with no master, no captain. There are many such."

"A mercenary?" I suggested.

"Ah, Tarl Cabot, tarnsman," said Tajima, "how little you know of these things."

"Doubtless," I said.

"Loyalty," said Tajima, "is required of the warrior. His lord must be dead, or imprisoned. Or it may be he was betrayed by his lord, or that his lord proved unworthy of his devotion. It is lonely to be of the *ronen*. One remembers. One does not forget. Over the ice a cloud drifts. The bird clings to the cold branch. It cries its pain in the night."

I said nothing more, but, after a time, we arrived.

"Your weapons, your skills, your talents, Tarl Cabot, tarnsman," said Tajima, "are not ours."

"I would like to meet with he with whom you train," I said, "but not to learn his weapons."

"There are more than weapons," said Tajima. "There is the thought, the way."

"I would seek his help," I said, "not for me but for my friend, Pertinax. He is not allowed in the *dojo*."

"He is a weakling," said Tajima.

"He has grown strong," I said.

"Not all strength," said Tajima, "is of the body."

"Some is," I said, "and, I assure you, as you are slight, and he is large and strong, he could break you in two."

"Only if I permitted it," said Tajima. "The tusks of the forest tarsk, too, could tear me in two, and I could be rent by the horns of the forest bosk, but, like the wind, I do not intend to put myself beneath their tusks or horns."

"But such beasts are dangerous," I said.

"Not to the wind," he said.

"Beware," I said, "that the wind is not caught in a box, and the lid snapped shut."

"The wind," smiled Tajima, "does not enter boxes with lids."

"Pertinax is different now from what you remember," I said.

"I could kill him, easily," said Tajima.

"Now," I said.

"Yes," said Tajima, "now."

"I would that you brought Pertinax to the school of Nodachi, and inquire if he might accept him," I said.

"So that his skills might one day equal or exceed mine?" asked Tajima.

"Certainly," I said.

"I do not think that would happen," said Tajima.

"Quite possibly not," I said.

"You ask much, Tarl Cabot, tarnsman," said he.

"There must be balance, harmony," I said, "and so I offer something in return."

"Sumomo?" he asked.

"Not at all," I said. "She is a mere female, and belongs in a collar. I offer you something of far greater value."

"What?" he asked.

"The tarn," I said. "You will be taught the tarn."

"I am afraid of tarns," he said.

"So are we all," I said.

"Fear is not acceptable," said Tajima.

"Fear is acceptable," I said. "Cowardice is not."

"I will speak to Nodachi," he said.

Chapter Fifteen

I Have Purchased a Slave for Pertinax; I Learn Something of the Lessons of Pertinax

"He is a barbarian, Master!" cried the slave, distressed.

"So, too, am I," I told her. "Get on your knees, put your head to his feet!"

She went to her knees before Pertinax, her head to the floor of the hut. Her small hands were high behind her, as she knelt, her small wrists closely encircled in slave bracelets. The leash, on which I had led her naked from the slave house to the hut, looped up, to my hand.

She was, of course, the former Lady Portia Lia Serisia of Sun Gate Towers, of Ar, of the house of the Serisii, now vanished.

"Whip her," I suggested, tossing Pertinax a whip, "so that she understand she is your slave."

"My slave?" he said.

Pertinax, having become a student in the school of Nodachi, for some weeks now, no longer assisted in the logging, but, at my request, had become resident with Cecily and myself, occupying with us the hut which had originally been put at our disposal by Lord Nishida.

"Yes," I said. "I bought her for you, from Torgus, from the slave house."

"For me?" he said.

"Yes," I said. "Do not be concerned. She did not cost much."

Indeed, I had had her for a handful of copper tarsks, to be sure, not tarsk-bits, but tarsks.

"I was Portia," said the slave, "Lady Portia Lia Serisia of Sun Gate Towers, of Ar, of the Serisii!"

I gave her a slight kick, in the side, and she put down her head again, quickly.

"She has much to learn," I said. "She just now spoke without permission. Perhaps you wish to punish her for that."

"She was important?" said Pertinax.

"I was entertained many times in the Central Cylinder itself!" said the slave, her face judiciously to the floor. "I was known personally to the Ubara. I shared her table. I drank her wine! I conversed with her!"

"Actually," I said, "she was really never more than a pampered, spoiled brat, the young, meaningless, but surely shapely, offspring of a wealthy family."

"Master!" she protested.

"But now," I said, "she has no more than her slave worth, and that is very little."

"He is a barbarian, Master!" said the slave.

"I suggest you use the whip on her," I said, "that she may learn that bondage to a barbarian, just as that to a more civilized fellow, may be quite meaningful, and sometimes distinctly unpleasant. Indeed, she has much to learn, and there is no reason why she should not begin to learn it at the feet of a barbarian. That may prove quite instructive to her."

"She is very pretty, Master," said Cecily. "You did buy her for Master Pertinax, did you not?"

"Yes," I said.

"Good," she said.

The kneeling slave cast a quick look at Cecily.

"Where did you find her?" asked Cecily.

"I first noted her on the beach," I said, "at the time of the landing of the ship bearing Torgus, and several others. She was one of a chain of slaves."

"But more recently?" inquired Cecily.

"In the slave house," I said.

"I suspected as much," said Cecily.

"Do you object?" I asked.

"I do not like it," she said, "but I may not object. I am a slave."

"I trust you are in no danger of forgetting it," I said.

"No, Master," she said. "I am in no danger of forgetting it. And certainly not now. I suppose you put her to your pleasure."

"Yes," I said.

"Was she any good?"

The new slave looked up at me, suddenly, startled, indignant, embarrassed, angry. "Please!" she begged.

Cecily, incidentally, in the sense she had in mind, was quite good, even exquisitely, helplessly precious. A touch could ignite her, and she had grown in her bondage, and, clearly, was still growing. Indeed, there is no end to such things, as the horizons of the collar are forever beckoning, and are endless. Too, Cecily and I had been matched to one another, as tormentingly attracted lovers, by the wisdom, cruelty, and science of Priest-Kings. Indeed, she had originally been intended, as a free woman, unbeknownst to herself, to tempt and torture me from my codes, to play a role in my humiliation and downfall. I could not have indefinitely resisted the taking of her, despite the fact that she was at that time free. The intervention of Kurii, in a raid on the Prison Moon, where we were captive, prevented this situation from reaching its inevitable denouement. Later, after having been appropriately thigh-marked on the Steel World, she had come into my collar.

"Yes," I said.

"Master!" she wept.

Whereas such questions would be highly impertinent, and, indeed, improper, asked of a free woman, they are appropriately asked of a slave. A slave, unlike a free woman, is expected to be good for something, to have her utilities.

"I trust," I said to Pertinax, "you do not mind that she is red silk, that she is not white silk."

"I do not understand," he said.

"Virgin slaves," I said, "are very rare."

"Oh," he said, "I see."

"At least," I said, "she does not have her ears pierced."

"At least," he agreed, puzzled.

Commonly, on Gor, it is only the lowest of slaves who have their ears pierced. On Gor pierced ears are regarded by many as a mark of shame and degradation exceeding even the brand. Slave brands are familiar, and taken for granted. They are routine in the marking of a slave. The piercing of ears is not. The brand, too, is covered by the common tunic, whereas the piercing of ears is exposed to all, to the contempt of free women and the interest and stimulation of men. This is cultural, of course, and Earth girls whose ears are pierced , something they have generally thought little of, are often startled when they are brought to Gor, to learn how this tiny thing, to which they have usually attached little importance, at least consciously or explicitly, can provoke unusual interest and lust in males. Certainly the mounting of earrings in a slave's ears can adorn her nicely. But, too, the puncturing of the softness of the lobes by the rigid bars anchoring the adornments has its symbolic bespeakments. Naturally it is the master who selects the adornments. Some slavers, noting that pierced-ear girls sell well, have the slaves' ears, whether they be in origin of Earth or Gor, subjected to this simple, homely operation. Initially this is likely to produce a great deal of dismay and stress in Gorean girls. This passes, however, when they discover how much more exciting these things make them. Indeed, some girls are so thrilled with these enhancements to their meaning as a slave and their beauty as a slave that they wear them before men almost insolently, or brazenly, or defiantly, or tauntingly. "Yes, here I am. I am owned. I am a slave. What are you going to do with me?" She relates to free women, of course, quite differently, and there, kneeling before them, will commonly attempt to convey to them a sense of her own self-acknowledged worthlessness, as a pierced-ear girl. In this fashion, thus seeming to accept and share the view of the free woman as to her abysmal degradation, she is less likely to be switched. It is well known that free women often have troubled dreams, inexplicable, unaccountable, frightening dreams, that they dream of themselves, to their embarrassment upon awakening, as having been shamefully branded and collared. One supposes they might, too, sometimes, dream of themselves not only as branded and collared, but as pierced-ear girls, as well. Goreans, incidentally, accept nose rings without any particular ado. Indeed, amongst the Wagon Peoples, where veiling is unknown, such rings are common even with free women.

"At any rate," I said, "she is yours."

"Mine?" said Pertinax, uncertainly.

"Yes," I said.

"What would I do with a slave?" asked Pertinax.

The slave looked up at him, startled.

Did he truly not know what to do with a slave?

"You, Cecily," I said, "will be first girl."

"She, too, is a barbarian!" said the slave. "I can tell."

"Life is hard," I informed the slave.

I had every confidence in Cecily, that she would be a kind, understanding, tactful, fair first girl, that she would share the work, would not mistreat her subordinate and inferior, and so on. I was less certain that she would maintain an appropriate discipline. One has to introduce a hierarchy amongst female slaves, backed by the power of the master. Otherwise one commonly invites chaos into the house, the kitchen, the gardens, the kennel area, and so on.

"Consider her," I said to Pertinax. "Put your head down," I said to the slave. She quickly, again, put her head down. "Look upon the sleek, vulnerable little she-beast," I said to Pertinax. "I give her to you, as your animal. Scrutinize her slave curves. She is raw, and young, but surely she has collar promise. Consider her waiting on you, hand and foot. Consider her licking and kissing your feet. Consider her, squirming, moaning, and begging, in the furs. Am I to suppose that you, truly, would not know what to do with a slave?"

"Perhaps, Master," said Cecily, "he would prefer another slave."

"No!" said Pertinax, suddenly. He then lowered his eyes, embarrassed.

"Another slave," I reminded Cecily, "is otherwise owned."

"I do not know what you are talking about," said Pertinax.

"Have you visited Saru in the stables?" I asked.

"No!" he said, quickly.

"You might enjoy seeing her as a naked, collared stable slut," I said.

"Surely not," he said.

"I am sure some of the fellows she knew on Earth would," I said.

"Perhaps," he said.

"And perhaps you, too, would," I said.

"Perhaps," he said.

"She is there to be seen," I said.

"I understand," he said.

"From what I understand," I said, "that slavery, that of a stable slut, is an appropriate, excellent slavery for her."

"Undoubtedly," he said.

"Certainly she makes a pretty little slave," I said.

"Doubtless," he said, reddening.

"You did, I take it, after three days," I said to Cecily, "inform Pertinax of the petition of the slave Saru, that he might call upon her?"

"Yes, Master," she said. "But I do not think he did so. And you forbade me to inform the slave of aught of this."

"Did you make clear the earnestness of the slave's petition?" I inquired.

"Yes, Master," said Cecily, "and I begged him that he might consent to accede to her supplication."

"You are a kindly slave," I said to Cecily, "to feel the misery of another slave, and beg for her."

She put down her head.

"But he declined to do so?"

"Yes, Master."

"Surely," I said to Pertinax, "on Earth, in your offices, or wherever, you must have considered the former Miss Wentworth as naked, in a collar, or on your leash, or roped at your feet, or such."

"I did not allow myself such thoughts," he said.

"But you had them, did you not?" I asked.

"Yes!" he said, angrily.

"Good," I said. "Then you were vital, and in lively, delightful, robust health."

"She is worthless, and I hate her," he said.

"She is not worthless, really," I said. "She is now a slave, and would be worth something, even if only a few copper tarsks. Only when she was a free woman, busy with being priceless," I said, "was she worthless."

"I hate her," he said, angrily.

I found his vehemence interesting.

"May I speak, Master?" asked Cecily.

"Surely," I said.

"Master Pertinax," said she, "the slave Saru plaintively calls herself to your attention. You are her only link with her former life. You must understand how important this is to her, how precious it is to her. What else has she, on this perilous world, seemingly so harsh and strange, to cling to? Who else understands her, and whence she has come, and what has been done to her? Who else is there with whom she might speak, with whom else might she hope to share her thoughts, or fears?"

"She may speak with the tharlarion," said Pertinax.

Cecily was then silent.

"She is cunning, she is clever," said Pertinax. "A tear, a trembling lip, a pathetic, stammered sound and I would again be hers."

"Then you do not truly understand that she is now a slave," I said.

"She did not treat me well, or others," he said, irritably.

"Have pity on her," begged Cecily. "She is now only a helpless, frightened slave! She is much at the mercy of any free person! Do you not feel for her?"

I am beginning to understand manhood," said Pertinax. "I will not now surrender it."

"A slave, well handled, well mastered," I said, "does not produce the surrender of manhood, but assures its triumph."

"And at the feet of a master," said Cecily, softly, "the slave finds herself."

"I hate her!" cried Pertinax.

"She wants to be in your arms," said Cecily.

"Absurd," said Pertinax.

"The slave fires have been set and ignited in her belly," I said. "She now needs men, as a slave needs men. But it is you whom she wishes to serve."

"Serve?" he laughed.

"Yes," I said.

"She wants to be in your arms, Master," said Cecily.

"Oh, yes," he laughed, "anything to escape the stable, the collar! For that what sacrifice would she not make? Even that of becoming what she hitherto most despised, a wife, or companion!"

"No, Master," said Cecily. "She wants to be otherwise in your arms, not as wife or companion, but as slave."

"Absurd," said Pertinax.

"Do not forget," I said, "that slave fires have been kindled in her sweet, vulnerable belly. Once that is done, what can a woman be but a slave?"

"I suspect," said Cecily, "she often fantasized about you as her master."

"Impossible," said Pertinax.

"Why else," I asked, "would she, of all others, have chosen you to accompany her to Gor, to complete her role on Gor, that of seeming to be her master?"

"She brought me with her to have a manipulable weakling," he said, "one to despise, one to do her bidding, unquestioningly."

"I do not doubt she thought that," I said. "But deep within a woman's belly flow mysterious currents, floods she is unable to control, forces and truths which mock and deny, and stir, the uneasy films and surfaces with which she labors to identify herself."

"She is humanly worthless," said Pertinax, "even if not economically so, whatever coin she might sell for, whatever price might take her off a slave block, whether a silver tarsk or a copper shaving. She is despicable. I hate her."

"Yet," I said, "as is not unoften the case, you want her."

"I?"

"Yes," I said. "You desire her."

"No!" he said.

"You would like to own her, and have her naked at your feet."

"No, no!" he cried.

"In any event," I said, "the matter is moot, as she belongs not to you, but to Lord Nishida."

Pertinax turned away, to face the wall of the hut.

"In the meantime," I said, "we have a pretty little slut here."

Pertinax turned back, angrily, to survey the kneeling slave.

Her head was down. She was on my leash. Her tiny wrists were braceleted behind her.

"She is Gorean, of course," I said.

"I do not want her," said Pertinax.

The slave gasped.

What man would not want one such as she, if only to trade or sell her to another?

One of the things a Gorean father often does, if his finances permit, is to buy a young female slave for his son. The son, of course, is familiar with slaves, and, as part of his education, has been taught their management, discipline, binding, and such. Pertinax, of course, lacked these advantages, those of culture, background, and practice.

I thought, however, that giving Pertinax a slave would be not only a thoughtful gift for him, for what is a nicer gift for a fellow than to buy him a lovely slave, but that it would help him to learn the ways of Gor, and, too, in its way, help him become a man.

Too, it should help him learn how he might best relate to, handle, and treat, should he someday wish it, some other slave, say, the former Miss Margaret Wentworth.

His task and challenge, of course, difficult as it might be, would be to make certain she was kept as a full and perfect slave, despite their previous lives and background. Only in this way could they both achieve their very different human perfections. Men and women are not the same. I had little doubt but what she would use every trick, every subtlety and wile, every cleverness, every asset of beauty and wit available to her, to reduce him again to the pathetic level of a typical male of Earth, something at her disposal, and that he would be muchly challenged to resist such artifices, and bring her to his feet, she then fully apprised, to her relief, that such games were over, and she was truly slave.

"You are fortunate I am not of the Pani," I said. "To refuse such a gift might injure one's pride, and would certainly generate bad blood. It might even be taken as an insult, that you found the gift beneath you, or unworthy of you. To refuse such a gift might injure one's pride, and it is not wise to injure the pride of one of the Pani, as they are a well-intentioned, sincere folk, and take such things very seriously."

"I accept her," said Pertinax.

The slave, head down, trembled, accepted. She now knew her master. It was Pertinax.

"There are welts on her back," said Pertinax.

"From switches, in the house of slaves," I said.

"Did you beat her?" he asked.

"No," I said. "I had no reason to do so."

The infliction of gratuitous pain would be incomprehensible to most Goreans. It would be pointless, and stupid. One expects such things only in a pathological society where the natural relationships between the sexes are denied, confused, or nonexistent. That a slave desires to please, and attempts to please, is usually more than enough to keep the whip on its peg. Should she fail to please, of course, she will expect the whip to come off its peg. And that, I suppose, is why it almost always remains on its peg.

"If you do not want her, of course," I said, "there may be a price on her head as a former free woman of Ar, a bounty, and if that is the case you could always turn her in for a good bit of coin."

"Please, no, Master!" cried the slave suddenly, alarmed, and flung herself to her belly to the feet of Pertinax, sobbing, and covering them with kisses. Her wrists, behind her, jerked against the bracelets, and I noted how her small fingers moved, pathetically, helplessly. "Please, no, Master!" she wept. "I will try to be good! I will try to please you, wholly, in all ways, my Master!"

"Surely you like a woman there," I said to Pertinax, "at your feet."

"It is not displeasing," he said.

Doubtless he recalled how the startled, terrified Miss Wentworth had once been at his feet, though somewhat differently, in the pavilion of Lord Nishida.

Needless to say, it is pleasant for a fellow to have a woman at his feet.

Then he said to the slave, "Kneel up, keep your head up, that I may see your face. No, you may kneel with your knees closed."

"Yes, Master," she said. "Thank you, Master."

I hoped he would have the common sense to be strong with her. The slave wants strength in a master. Too, she responds to it, in obedience, and sexuality.

She turned in the leash collar and smiled at me. She then clenched her knees even more closely together, victoriously.

I expected that when he became more accustomed to the mastery, and more excited, and so on, he would better see the slave as an object, a possession, from which great pleasure might be derived.

Then I expected he would see to it that her knees would be spread appropriately, nicely.

"You will need a name for her," I said.

"My name," she said, "is Lady Portia Lia Serisia of Sun Gate Towers."

"'Was'," I reminded her.

"Was," she said. "But surely I might suggest a suitable name."

"Certainly," said Pertinax.

"'Lady Portia Lia Serisia of Sun Gate Towers'," she suggested.

"That should draw in bounty hunters," I said, "like zarlit flies to honey, urts to cheese, sharks to blood."

"True," she said, quickly. "Perhaps then something like 'Lady Philomela of the Amaniani'?"

"I doubt that the Amaniani," I said, "to whom I doubt that you are related, would appreciate the borrowing of their name, particularly by a slave."

"Perhaps," she agreed. "But my aristocratic origin should surely be suggested."

"Not at all," I said. "You are no longer an aristocrat, but are now only a vendible, curvaceous, little she-beast."

"What of 'Lady'?" she asked.

"It might do for a domestic she-sleen," I said, "but not for a slave. As you know, 'Lady' applies only to free females, not slaves."

"What of 'Philomela'?" she asked.

"Too fine for a slave," I said. "It is better as a free woman's name."

"We do need a name for her," said Pertinax.

"Not really," I said, "but it would be useful to have one, say, to summon her, order her about, and such."

"I do not know what to call her," said Pertinax.

"In any event, it is your decision," I said.

"True," he said, regarding the slave.

"Why do you not call her 'Margaret'?" I said.

"No!" he said. "No!"

"Pick, then," I smiled, "another name."

"You bought her," he said. "You name her."

"Very well," I said. "I think that 'Jane' is a lovely name for a female slave."

"No!" cried the slave. "That is a barbarian name! I am Gorean! I once had an Earth girl, a serving slave, by that name! Men wanted her. I often had to switch her, for she would sometimes dare to look at them! How she wanted to be in their arms, as a slave! In spite of being my slave, a lady's slave, a lady's serving slave, she was no better than a needful tart! Disgusting! Despicable! She was an insult to me! I later arranged that she be sold to a kaiila drover, and she was muchly pleased, so I whipped her well and lengthily before I had her delivered to him."

"'Jane' is a lovely name," I said.

"Do not belittle me!" she begged. "Do not shame me! Do not so demean me! It is a slave name, fit only for a barbarian brought here for the markets! Men will see me as a low slave! They will see me as no more than switch meat!"

"I am now going to name you," I said.

"No!" she wept. She cast a wild look at Pertinax. "Please, no, Master!" she wept.

"Be silent," said Pertinax. I gathered that he was not overly pleased with the slave's view of certain names. Too, he probably agreed with me that 'Jane' was a lovely name. I had never understood why its simplicity and beauty, on Earth, was not more widely recognized. I could understand that the name on Gor, being a barbarian name, was associated with *kajirae*. But men on Gor certainly had no objection to the name because it, as most female Earth names, suggested a barbarian slave, and barbarian slaves, though not selling as well in some markets as Gorean slaves, particularly those once of high caste, tended to be prized by many masters. The general reputation of the barbarian slave was that of a chattel who would soon prove to be hot, devoted, and dutiful. Indeed, given the sexual desert from which most Earth slaves were extracted, and the mechanistic social ecology of that world, which alienated both men and women from their depth natures, Gor came to many as a welcome revelation. On Gor, many found a human and sexual redemption, a rescue and a salvation. Typically, *kajirae* from Earth adapted quickly, and gratefully, to their collars. In them they enjoyed a medley of fulfillments and gratifications which might have been not only denied to them on Earth, mindlessly execrated, and such, but might even have been incomprehensible to them on Earth. To be sure, Gorean women, too, soon learned their womanhood at the feet of masters.

Women, after all, are women.

"Look at me," I said. "I am now going to name you."

"Yes, Master," she said. Her eyes were bright with protest, and tears.

"You are Jane," I said. "Rejoice that you are no longer a nameless slave."

"Yes, Master," she said.

"What is your name?" I asked.

"'Jane', Master," she said.

"Who are you?"

"I am Jane," she said, "Master."

"Perhaps we should now think of supper," I said to Cecily.

"She is clothed," observed Jane.

"To some extent," I agreed. A slave tunic leaves little to one's imagination.

Jane looked to Pertinax. "Master," she said, "will surely see that his slave is attired."

"Certainly," said Pertinax.

"Decorously, as befits a former free woman of Ar," she said, and then she added, with a glance at the brief tunic of Cecily, "and not as a barbarian."

Cecily said nothing. She had been a slave long enough to appreciate, and relish, and take delight in, the freedom of the tunic. Too, it thrilled her, in her vanity, well aware of her considerable beauty, to be shamelessly exhibited for the delectation of men. She knew herself to be an excellent specimen of the most desirable of all human females, the female slave.

The slave is not ashamed of her beauty, but proud of it.

Let the free woman be concerned with her veils, and fear that an ankle might be glimpsed beneath layered robes.

The slave loves men, and wishes to be found pleasing.

"It is true," I said, "that it would be wise to see that the slave is attired, for there are strong men in the camp."

A subtle tremor betrayed the slave's apprehension.

"Do not fear, Jane," said Cecily. "After supper I will go to the supply shed and obtain some cloth."

"I will come along," I said.

"Master?" said Cecily.

"I have been wondering," I said to her, "how you would look in a camisk."

"A Turian camisk?" she asked.

"No," I said, "the common camisk."

"Never!" cried Jane.

"Once you have seen your girl in a common camisk," I said to Pertinax, "I suspect that you will not permit her to kneel with her knees together."

"Oh?" he said, interested.

His Jane was a shapely brat.

"Too, I will look into a collar," I said to Pertinax. "I did not have one prepared, as I did not know how you might want it engraved."

"What would you suggest?" he asked, again evincing some interest. I took this as a good sign.

"Something like 'I am Jane. I am the property of Pertinax of Tarncamp'."

"Excellent," he said.

"I do not need to be collared, Master," said the slave. "I am branded. None will mistake me for a free woman."

"No," he said. "Nor will any be in doubt as to who owns you. You will be collared."

She looked at him, angrily.

He still retained the whip I had tossed to him when I had first brought the slave into the hut.

"Do you wish to be displeasing?" he asked.

He shook out the blades of the whip. It was a simple five-stranded slave whip, designed for use on female slaves, designed to punish, and well, but not mark.

"No, Master," she said, hastily.

"Perhaps you should beg to be collared," I said.

"Please, Master," she said, "collar me."

"Who begs?" I inquired.

"Jane," she said, "Jane, the slave of Pertinax of Tarncamp, begs to be collared."

"It will be done," said Pertinax.

She sobbed.

"You may thank your master," I told her.

"Thank you, Master," she said. "Jane, your slave, thanks you for having her collared, for permitting her to wear your collar, for deigning to grant her the honor of wearing your collar."

"To his feet," I said.

The slave then went to the feet of Pertinax.

When I thought she had performed sufficiently I freed her of the bracelets and leash.

She knelt then, naked, but free of bonds, at our feet. She put her arms about herself, and trembled.

I then reminded Cecily that we might think of supper.

"Come, Jane," said Cecily. "I will find you something to wrap about your body. We must gather wood. We must make supper. We have work to do."

Soon the girls had exited the hut.

"Pertinax," said I, "how do your lessons proceed?"

He had been studying for some weeks now with the warrior in the forest, a master of the sword, who was known as Nodachi. I had never seen this person. The arrangements had been made through the thoughtful offices of Tajima. I had given Tajima one of the rubies I had retained from the Steel World, that Nodachi might be compensated for his services, but Tajima had returned the stone to me. Food might be brought to the swordsman that he might live, but he was unwilling to set a price on his instruction. "One does not sell life and death," he had informed Tajima. "No price is to be set on such things."

"I do not know," said Pertinax.

"How is that?" I asked.

"How can one see what cannot be seen?" he asked.

"What do you think is meant by that?" I asked.

"It is poetry, is it not?" he asked.

"I suspect," I said, "it is a poetry which speaks of differences, say that between the living and the dead. One, I suppose, must sense things, infer things, expect things."

Sometimes one understands things without understanding how one understands them.

How does one know that one man who smiles is a friend and another is an enemy? Perhaps one sees what cannot be seen.

"Much makes sense to me," said Pertinax, "the nature of the ground, the position of the sun, day and night, the season of the year, but much seems mysticism."

"There are probably mysticisms and mysticisms," I said. "Some, I suspect, speak of the world."

"One should not die with a weapon undrawn," said Pertinax.

"Do not be taken by surprise," I suggested.

"One should pay attention to little things," said Pertinax.

"They can be important," I said.

"From one thing learn ten thousand things," he said.

"Things lead to one another," I suggested. "They are bound together."

"One who has faced death at the point of a sword has an elevated understanding," said Pertinax.

"I think that is true," I said. "At least one is different, and one has a better sense of life. For such a one the world is then other than it was."

"Step by step walk the thousand-mile road," he said.

"Be patient," I suggested. "Do not give up. Excellence is not easily achieved."

"Are there such things in the codes?" asked Pertinax.

"There are many things in the codes," I said, "similar, and different. Much of this, I think, is wisdom, doubtless deriving from one teacher or another, in one place or another, perhaps over centuries."

"There are many things," said Pertinax, "many, many things."

"Few will understand them all," I said. "Be humble, learn what you can."

"The spirit of fire is fierce," smiled Pertinax, "whether it is large or small, and the spirit is like fire, and can be large or small."

"Master Nodachi, I suspect," I said, "has a large spirit, and, unseen, it burns fiercely."

"I am learning swords," he said.

"And what is the purpose of the sword?" I asked.

"It is to kill," he said.

"Yes," I said.

There was something much like that in the codes. The purpose of the sword is not to fence, not to match blades, and not to exhibit skill, nor is its purpose to reach the enemy, nor even to cut him. Its purpose is to kill him.

He shuddered.

"Are you strong enough for that?" I asked.

"I do not know," he said.

Some who excelled in the *dojo* were the first to fall in the field.

"Seek to learn more," I said.

"If I would live?" he asked.

"Yes," I said.

Chapter Sixteen

The Exercise; What Followed the Exercise

"One-strap!" I called, and Ichiro, who was behind and on my right, blew the blast on the war horn, and two hundred tarns, with riders, ascended, as one, the forest far below, Tarncamp a clearing below in the forest.

There are six strap positions on the common tarn harness. On the tarn's collar there are six rings, to which straps are attached, which straps ascend to the saddle, which, too, has six rings, corresponding to the collar rings. The six saddle rings are arranged on a vertical ring. The one-ring is at the top of the main saddle ring, and the four-ring is at the bottom. The two-ring and three-ring are on the right side of the main saddle ring, and the four-ring and five-ring are on the left side of the main saddle ring. Given the correspondences, drawing on the one-strap exerts pressure at the bottom of the tarn's throat, to which pressure it responds by ascent, and drawing on the four-ring exerts pressure on the ring at the back of the tarn's neck, to which pressure it responds by descent. Similarly, it may wheel to the high right and the low right, and to the high left and low left, by drawing on the appropriate straps. If one wishes a lateral motion to the right one draws on both the two and three straps at the same time, and if one wishes a lateral motion to the left one draws on the four and five straps simultaneously. Similar adjustments may be made by drawing on the one and two straps, on the three and four straps, and so on, about the ring. A simple knot in each strap prevents it from slipping back through one of the saddle rings.

"Three-strap," I called, and Ichiro blew the signal, and the flock turned downward and to the right.

"Rings free!" I called to Ichiro, and he blew the appropriate blast, and the flock leveled out in its flight, and continued on the path on which it had been set.

Of great assistance in such matters is the natural flocking behavior of tarns, which consists of three genetically coded behaviors, two of which deal with spatiality and one with velocity. A tarn flock will tend to cohere, to stay together, and it will also maintain a bird-to-bird distance. These spatial habituations are then linked with a tendency to match velocity. In this fashion a flock of birds, even in the wild, will engage effortlessly in what appear to be astonishingly swift and complex maneuvers.

"Five-strap!" I called. "Rings free!" The horn gave forth this command, and the flock descended to the left and leveled in its flight.

I personally preferred solitary tarnflight, and I supposed most tarnsmen would, as there is a wild sense of freedom on tarnback, sometimes almost of exaltation, as one seems one with the bird. One is muchly alive. One becomes almost another form of life, one with the bird, and one with the wind, the clouds, and sky. I suspect this is something which is missed in most mechanistic flight, but was probably hinted at, or suggested, by the small, responsive, single-engine aircraft which were used, say, in the first quarter of the twentieth century on Earth.

To my left was Tajima.

He was armed, as the others, with the small bow, and broad quivers on each side of the saddle. Too, mounted there, were six Anangan darts, three on each side. In the side-slung saddle boot, on the right, horizontal with the flight, was the black, temwood lance. On the left, at hand, was the small, edged buckler, suitable for turning a spear thrust. Behind the saddle, folded, was the weighted net.

I communicated with Ichiro by hand signals as well as voice, and I indicated that we were now to return to Tarncamp, and that bows were to be freed. This was conveyed by notes to our tarnsmen. Dozens of targets had been set up in the training area. On the ground, in extensive training, I had practiced the men with their weapons, the arrow, the dart, the lance, the edged buckler, the net.

I thought we were now no more than an Ehn or two from Tarncamp.

The cavalry was not, of course, a simple flock, or pride. The two hundred riders might be thought of, I suppose, as the cavalry, or group, to take an analogy. The group then was divided into, say, two "centuries," of one hundred riders each, each century into five squadrons, so to speak, of twenty riders each, each squadron into, say, two flights, of ten riders each, and each flight into two "prides," of five riders each. There were in short, then, in the group as a whole, two centuries, ten squadrons, twenty flights, and forty prides. As is often the case there is no really satisfactory correspondences between certain Gorean terms and English. I have, on the whole, taken roughly equivalent expressions. One might think, if one wishes, of the cavalry, then the hundreds, then the twenties, then the tens, and then the fives. In any event these arrangements allowed for considerable differentiation and flexibility, in attack, in reconnaissance, in foraging, and so on. I was captain, or high captain, and each subdivision had its clearly understood leader, down to the smallest units, which I have referred to, for convenience, as "prides." Groups of tarnsmen are often referred to as prides, so, in a sense, any of the divisions, including the cavalry as a whole, might be accounted a "pride." For convenience, as noted, I have referred to the smallest units by that designation. One might mention, in passing, that all the groupings had either appellations or numbers. This facilitates planning, distribution of supplies, the clear and expeditious issuance of orders, and so on. Also, this tends to produce a sense of unit, and pride in unit, which is good for responsibility, camaraderie, mutual support, and morale. Along these lines, as well, the larger divisions had their own banners or standards. These devices may be used for a variety of purposes, identification of location, often important in the confusion of battle, signaling charges, retreats, maneuvers, rallying scattered troops, and so on. Too, after a time they tend to acquire something of the charisma or potency often associated with certain images, or symbolic devices, such as flags. Needless to say, various insignia were developed, too, to mark ranks and units. Also important was what was, in effect, a uniform. This tends to effect cohesion, solidarity, self-image, and so on. It also has its role to play, particularly in tumult, in distinguishing one's fellows from the enemy. Also, it can intimidate a less organized, less disciplined enemy. They have the sense that something unified, purposeful, and dangerous is coming against them. I had chosen gray, as being difficult to discern in poor light. In flight this would make little difference, but if my men were to function on the ground, in, say, commando activity, or such, I thought it might be helpful. A braver, more pronounced color might have been better for parade purposes, but I had not designed the cavalry for parades. Cos, incidentally, is usually identified by blue, and Ar's infantry, at least, by red. Scarves are often used in Gorean warfare, particularly by mercenaries, because uniforms are by no means universal. One advantage of the scarf, it seems, is that it might be removed, or changed, depending on the fortunes of war. One expects the mercenary to fight for coin, not a Home Stone. To be sure, some mercenaries will die for a given commander. Some command such loyalty, such as Dietrich of Tarnburg, Pietro Vachi, Raymond Rive-de-Bois, and certain others.

I gave the signal for putting arrows to the string, and drew my tarn up, over the cavalry, to better observe the outcome of the exercise.

Lord Nishida, I had been informed, too, on the ground, would be on hand to observe the results of the exercise.

I trusted that he would be pleased.

I had gathered from several executions, outside my own command, that the Pani tended not to be tolerant of failure.

Too, there were rumors there were spies in the camp.

Certainly the recruitments of the Pani here and there, the several landings on the northern beaches, the numbers of men involved, the securing and importing of supplies, would be difficult to conceal.

Much tenseness roved Tarncamp.

Far below, and to the front, I could see an observation platform set up at one end of the plaza of training. Some individuals were there, and among them, I supposed, would be Lord Nishida. A figure in white was toward the center of the group, and I supposed that must be he.

The war horn's blast burst out from beneath me and I saw the cavalry, in its diving, wedgelike, suddenly widening, formation, to allow for a broad front of arrow fire, rank behind rank, deploy.

I suppose, to many, certain things might seem dreadful, the blast of the war horn, the thunder of tarn drums, the soaring descent to the attack, the scream of the tarn, the music of the bowstring, blood's lyre, with its song of death, but, too, to some, there is little which so speaks of life as these musics of intent, of risk, and peril, little else which seems to speak so avidly and preciously of life.

Whereas I have spoken of two hundred tarns and riders, and this seems to me acceptable, it must be understood that, like any military unit, it might, from time to time, be above or below its official strength. Similarly, I have not included in the two hundred myself, certain subofficers, adjuncts, liaison personnel, and so on. Also, of great importance, but not included in the figure of two hundred, would be various forces on the ground, responsible for support, such as metal and leather workers, fletchers, tarnkeepers, suppliers of various sorts, and so on.

I pulled the tarn up, further, and then, briefly, held it almost stationary in the air, drawing back on all the straps simultaneously, the bird then hovering, wings beating fiercely.

The first wave loosed its missiles, and would then circle, to renew its attack, in turn. The attack was a simple one, a continual frontal assault, with each wave attacking thrice.

Needless to say, one of the great advantages of tarn attack is that one can get behind parapets, and such, and rake from the inside of fortifications, as well as from the outside. This possibility is neutralized in some fortifications by roofing the parapets, but this, of course, exposes the roofing to fire arrows, fire bombs, and such. In such a case the defenders will usually protect the roofing with wet hides, or slates. Similar considerations pertain to an attack on vessels. Tarn attack is often effective against ground troops, as they mass in formation, might march in columns, might be exposed in open camps, be discommoded in traversing marshy ground, be struck while fording bodies of water, and so on. Tarn attack is also useful in discouraging foraging by an enemy on the march. The harassments of tarn attack can do much to fatigue and alarm ground troops. Such troops should possess their own tarnsmen, to clear the skies as they can. Spies are often resorted to in Gorean warfare. But one of the most effective and inaccessible of spies is the distant, reconnoitering tarnsman. One might also note, in passing, the rapidity of communication by tarn, the timely reporting of developments, the swift conveyance of messages, and such. Supplies, too, in tarn basket, may be transported by tarn, usually by draft tarns, a breed of the tarn which is bred less for speed and agility than strength and stamina. Too, obviously, small numbers of raiders or infiltrators may be conveyed by tarn, and disembarked behind enemy lines or within enemy walls. For this purpose tarn baskets are sometimes used, but, if the journey is short, the tarn, even a common tarn, may carry a number of warriors, clinging to a knotted rope, some seven or so, to their destination. This tactic is not uncommon.

One of the major innovations I had introduced was to condition the birds to associate ring cries with ring tensions. For example, I would occasionally have the men cry out, say, "one-strap" at the same time as drawing on the one strap. After a certain number of repetitions this cry alone would induce the bird to respond as though the one-strap had been drawn. I thought this might prove of value. This was not necessary to facilitate archery, incidentally, freeing the hands for the bow, as some might suppose, as the kaiila of the Tuchuks, or the tarns of my men, once set on a course, pursue it. For example, although some Tuchuks retain the reins in the bow-gripping hand, many others have their hands fully free when using the bow, and only have recourse to the reins when they wish to alter the course of the kaiila. This functions the same way on tarnback, whether one is utilizing the straight bow or the crossbow. If the kaiila or tarn does swerve, which does happen, this is compensated for by the archer's adjustment in his aim. If the kaiila's track or the bird's flight tends to be erratic, for example, in the midst of shouts and confusion, in which it is tested, it will be rejected for purposes of war. One desires, in so far as possible, a steady, reliable platform from which to launch one's missiles. In this respect, obviously, the smooth flight of the tarn, particularly in its soaring, wings-spread approach, is far superior to the gallop of the racing kaiila.

I had neglected to avail myself of Lord Nishida's suggestion for tarn-to-tarn archery practice, in which bound prisoners, aflight on leashed tarns, would serve as targets. I had substituted, instead, flighted targets, small, wooden disks, slung on ropes, carried beneath carrier tarns. If my archers could judge, lead, and strike such targets, smaller than a man's body, I had little doubt they could manage the more likely targets. Too, there is a great difference between executing helpless prisoners and facing an unencumbered foe who has every intention of killing you. If one is familiar only with the sham of combat one might well panic in a different situation, when no charade is involved. Too, I was hoping to train warriors, not butchers.

"Yes, yes!" I whispered. "Fire, fire!"

There would be three sweeps of each of the flighted ranks.

An attack of this sort might be prolonged indefinitely, but I had ordered only three sweeps. I thought this would be adequate for the archers to accustom themselves to the attack, its speed and slope, and make any adjustments necessary. I would expect the third sweep of each rank to be more successful than the first or second, certainly more so than the first. This was the first time I had had the cavalry strike publicly, while under official observation, at ground targets in formation. Each rider, as indicated, had two broad quivers at his disposal, in each of which was a hundred arrows. The common quiver of the great bow, familiar to the peasants, would contain between twenty and thirty arrows. A crossbowman would commonly carry even fewer bolts or quarrels. Let us suppose that a crossbowman on tarnback had twenty bolts, and, drawing and cocking the cable, and extracting the bolt, and placing it in the guide, and aiming, could fire one every twenty Ihn. He could thus fire twenty bolts in 400 Ihn, or ten Ehn. On the other hand, with the short bow one could fire an arrow every five Ihn. Thus, in 400 Ihn, or ten Ehn, he could fire 80 arrows. Thus, the fellow with the short bow could fire four times as many arrows in a given period of time as the crossbowman. Further, given the quantity of arrows housed in the two broad quivers, whereas the ammunition of the crossbowman would be exhausted in ten Ehn, the ammunition of the other fellow, he with the short bow, even at the increased rate of fire, would last twenty-five Ehn. Thus the bowman could fire four times to the crossbowman's once, and continue to fire for two and a half times as long. These figures are approximations, assuming averages, and typical marksmen. On the other hand, the differentials in fire power, with respect to rate of fire, and duration of fire, clearly and considerably favor the fellow with the short bow, at least until an enemy would adopt similar measures. In calculating these ratios I have supposed the crossbowman to be equipped with the stirrup bow, which may be reloaded and fired much more rapidly than the crank-and-ratchet bow. The range and striking power of the stirrup bow somewhat exceeds that of the short bow, and the range of the crank-and-ratchet variety exceeds that of the stirrup bow. On the other hand, given the usual proximity to targets in both cases, the rate and duration of fire of the short bow supplies it, in this sort of warfare, as it would in Tuchuk warfare, with a clear advantage. This is not to disparage certain advantages of the crossbow. For example, as with a rifle, it requires less skill to use it effectively than does the long, or short, bow. This is important if one is working with large groups of recruits from various backgrounds who may have been lured into service with inducement fees, or, not that infrequently, impressed into service. Similarly, the crossbow can remain ready to fire, for Ahn at a time. It is thus useful in door-to-door fighting, in stalking, in ambush, and so on. It is the weapon *par excellence* of the caste of Assassins.

The second sweep had now been concluded.

Rank after rank of the third sweep struck.

The rapidity with which these attacks may be mounted and concluded is impressive.

My attention was much focused on the flights, and the prides. The third sweep was now well in progress.

Below, targets bristled with arrows.

"Well done, fellows," I thought. "Continue!"

But I must remind them, I thought, that posts and targets do not shoot back.

The final ranks had now entered into their long, sloping

dive. More complex formations and attacks would have to be planned, I thought. Aerial maneuvers, too, I thought, perhaps with tipped, blunted arrows, might be useful. Too, they must be taught to fight and strike in pairs, or more, never to engage, if possible, on equal terms. One should avoid the application of force, if possible, except against lesser force, and, ideally, much lesser force. An enemy consistently divided and attacked piecemeal is an enemy doomed to defeat. General engagements are sometimes unavoidable, and too often unavoidable, but their outcome is too often, as Goreans might say, a matter not of kaissa, but of the casting of dice. A change of wind, a rising of dust, a prolonged battle, in which the angle of the sun changes, the loss of a commander, the loss of a standard, an unexpected, unpredictable wave of alarm in the ranks, an unfounded rumor of entrapment, the failure of a wing to hold, the hesitation or confusion of reserves, the tardiness of reinforcements, almost anything, may lead to disorder, and thence to the breaking of ranks, and thence to rout, and thence to massacre. Too, despite who holds the field, who decorates the trophy tree at the day's end, a general engagement is often lost, in effect, by both sides. Two such victories may destroy an army, and ruin a state. Wars are often lost in wholes, and won in bits and pieces. Victory is often less the fruit of valor than of information, patience, calculation, and cunning.

The third wave had now discharged its missiles and was wheeling about, when cries came from below, which drifted up to me. I had wheeled the tarn about, to alight at the end of the training plaza, to which, by prearrangement, the cavalry had returned, when I wheeled him about again, puzzled at the confusion below. On the observation platform there was much milling about, shouting, cries. At the same time I saw one of my fellows, from the final flight of the third wave, I thought, still in flight, and moving south. A figure, in white, below, on the platform, was being supported by two of the infantrymen, or *Ashigaru*, as the Pani spoke of them. Instantly I realized what must have happened. I cried out in rage that I was not a lone tarnsman, that I might immediately set out in pursuit of the fugitive. As captain I could not do so. I must remain with the cavalry. My men were in formation below, not having been dismissed. They, too, were in a state of apprehension, if not of consternation, as something, clearly, was amiss in the vicinity of the observation platform. None broke ranks. Some twenty percent were Pani, and their discipline was as iron and they steadied the mercenaries about them. In a moment I dispatched Tajima and Pertinax, whom I had had train with Tajima, to pursue the fugitive, whom they had not even seen. I doubted they could overtake him. His name I would learn later. I also put Ichiro, my signalman, whose ritual suicide I had forbidden weeks ago, into the air, fearing that more might be on the wing than a single fugitive. I then placed Torgus in command of the cavalry, with orders to remain on alert, and designated Lysander, a mercenary, once of Market of Semris, to second him. Torgus commanded the first century, and Lysander the second. I had first encountered Lysander on the beach with Torgus, and his other men. It was he whom I had thought bore himself as one once of the Warriors. This proved correct, and he was, as well, a tarnsman, who had turned mercenary. I did not think it meet to inquire into his past. In such cases there is not unoften a killing, and sometimes a woman, most often a slave, sometimes a seductive, manipulative, conniving slave who would, for her perceived advantage, or sense of power, set masters against one another. There is a saying that a man conquers with the sword, the slave with a kiss. As Lysander had been subordinate to Torgus in his mercenary troop, I thought it best to keep him second here. As the leader of a century, of course, he was equivalent. In dealing with men an able commander must be sensitive, as well as he can, to the possible consequences of his decisions and appointments, consequences which may affect the efficiency of his force, and to what might be thought of as the realities of the heart, such things as perceptions of propriety, possibly surmised slights, perceived unwarranted preferments, questions of honor, and the almost inevitable conflicts amongst vanities. These things do not dictate command, but they influence it. The paramount question is always the maximum efficiency, either in the long run or short run, depending on the situation, of the unit's military effectiveness. Decisions which are made on any other basis not only favor the ends of enemies, but constitute treason.

Ichiro was now high overhead.

I dismounted, and ran across the plaza of training, toward the observation platform.

In a moment I was at the foot of the platform.

The figure who had been in white, a white of dignity, and a color that stood out amongst the others on the platform, was lying on the platform, his head in the arms of one of the *Ashigaru*. An arrow was lodged in his shoulder, and the white kimono was spotted there with blood. The missile, of course, as it closes its own wound, does not produce blood in the same way that a wound opened by a knife, or blade or some sort, would. The blood flows when the missile is withdrawn. One of the Pani, a wound dresser, crouched over the fallen figure.

What an admirable target would have been the white kimono on the observation platform!

To be sure, it would have been a difficult target from tarnback, with the short bow, for one of my men, given the distance. It would have been a much more likely target for a stationary archer, armed with the peasant bow. But even then it would not have been a sure kill, across much of the plaza of training.

I heard a cry of misery from the platform, and the wound dresser stood up, the bloodied arrow in his grasp, held with two hands.

There would now be a great deal of blood, which must be stanched.

It was even now on the platform.

I could not well see the features of the fallen figure, for the men crowding about.

They would allow the wound to bleed, briefly, to wash it out.

In a few moments one of the fellows about was pressing the kimono down to the wound.

"He will live," said the wound dresser. "Bring a panel. Place him upon it. Take him to the barracks."

"I do not understand," I said to a fellow beside me. "Should Lord Nishida not be taken to his pavilion?"

"Lord Nishida, of course," said the fellow, "would be taken to his pavilion."

"I do not understand," I said.

"It is not Lord Nishida," said the man.

I looked about. To one side I saw Lord Nishida. He was dressed much as others, who had been on the platform.

"Tal, Tarl Cabot, tarnsman," said Lord Nishida.

"Lord Nishida!" I said.

"The exercise," he said, "seemed to go well, though my eye is not practiced in such matters. What is your view?"

"The men are raw, but eager," I said. "But they are growing in discipline, and skill."

"Excellent," he said.

"I thought you were struck," I said.

"He who fled will think so, too," he said.

"I set two aflight on his track," I said.

"Not a twenty?" he asked.

"Those two would be sufficient," I said.

"Excellent," he said.

"Tajima and Pertinax," I said.

"Pertinax?" he asked.

"Yes," I said. "He is becoming a man."

"Excellent," said Lord Nishida. "We will need men."

I did not inquire further into his remark, but I took it that by men, he meant something beyond mere males, that he meant men.

"But I do not think they will overtake him," I said.

"Let us hope not," he said. "For I should like others to believe his mission was successful."

"I see," I said.

"It is important, of course, that the assailant believes himself to be earnestly pursued."

"I understand," I said.

"I have many spies, in many places," said Lord Nishida.

"One must have maps, one must have eyes," I said.

The importance of intelligence cannot be overestimated. It is a quiet business, without drums and trumpets, less apparent to the eye than wagons, bellowing tharlarion, the dust of marching columns, trains of cordaged artillery drawn through mud, and such, but I think it not less essential.

Information is essential to war.

The intellect of battle must guide its brawn.

How much of war is mind, how futile without it is its muscle!

It had not been Lord Nishida on the platform, in the white kimono.

Is not deception another name for war?

There are men, and cities, which gold can buy. Thus it is noted in the "Diaries," usually attributed to Carl Commenius of Argentum. Similar sayings are not unknown. "The sharpest of swords has an edge of gold." "More gates answer to a key of gold than one of iron." "What can be purchased with gold need not be bought with blood." And so on.

There are always jealousies, resentments, hatreds, and factions in cities, and the clever will exploit them to his own advantage.

Much will be sacrificed by many for position and power.

How often are Home Stones betrayed!

I thought of Ar.

Lord Nishida, I did not doubt, was well aware of the nature of men. I wondered if he were well aware of my nature, perhaps more so than I. One stands close to one's self. How can the eye see itself, and even in water, or burnished plates, or bright mirrors, it sees but an image of itself, and who knows what lies behind it?

"Tarnsmen," said Lord Nishida, "have been recruited from better than two dozen cities."

"I do not understand," I said.

"If the commander of an army had fallen," said Lord Nishida, "would that not be an ideal time to attack?"

"Surely," I said, and shuddered.

At that moment, from high above, I heard the war horn of Ichiro, signaling the alarm, and then the signal to mount.

In the distance, far off, coming from the south, it seemed a cloud had formed, obscure, uncertain, at first, and then swift and dark, and then, in a moment or two, it seemed the cloud might be a flight of insects, a dark swarm, a plague of predators.

I did not wait, but raced toward the cavalry. Torgus and Lysander had already marshaled it, and the first birds, in line, were already climbing.

Two tarns, returning, those of Tajima and Pertinax, ahead of the swarm, streaked overhead, and then turned, to take their place in the ascending formation.

Again and again Ichiro sounded the alarm.

I seized the mounting ladder of my tarn, hastened to the saddle, strung the ladder, fastened the safety strap, and yanked back on the one-strap, and, in a moment, the field of the training plaza, with its numerous, riddled targets, was falling away, beneath me.

Behind me the men of Tarncamp sought weapons and took cover.

Many of the slaves would be lashed indoors. If there were time many would be chained to rings, to await, as the lovely beasts they were, as might tarsks or kaiila, other tethered domestic animals, the outcome of the doings of men.

They were properties, and, as women generally, would belong to the victors.

What more desirable as booty than beauty?

Men will kill to possess and collar it.

Too, if one wishes, it sells well.

I looked to the south.

I had never seen so large a tarn cavalry as now approached Tarncamp.

Then I was aflight and to the head of our formation, and issued orders, and the first and second centuries wheeled away, each to flank one side of the coming swarm. It would not be met head on, but, in moments, after it had plowed past, like a torrent between banks, it would be afflicted from the sides, and then, the centuries dividing, now into flights, from behind and above, as well. In the meantime let the rushing swarm spend its bolts and quarrels on the roofs of sheds and barracks.

As Tuchuk cavalry we would close as little as possible.

Our tarns carried less weight, this increasing agility and speed, and we might thus choose our moments of engagement, to strike when, and as, and where, we wished, and to withdraw as we might please, with little fear of being overtaken.

A hundred maneuvers we had planned and practiced on the field of the sky, feints and encirclements, and sallies and lures, massings and dividings, but these maneuvers were untested in battle, and our men were for the most part new to the saddle.

The alarm bars were ringing.

Chapter Seventeen

The Battle

I had no doubt that the cavalries ranked against us, which would intend to confront us and engage in the traditional modalities of Gor's aerial warfare, consisted of veteran tarnsmen. The heavy shields and mighty spears borne by them would alone far outweigh the armament and accouterments of my men. Too, the tarns of some were encumbered by armor, and the beak and talons were still shod with steel, turning their mounts into little more than massive, lumbering aerial tanks. Their missile weapons were the short quarrels and the stout, metal bolts of the stirrup and crank-and-ratchet crossbows. I knew the armament and tactics of such forces well, having been trained in them, and I had designed my forces, following the Tuchuk model, to deal with massive infantry and earth-shaking tharlarion charges, now adapted to flight, to deal with them. The infantrymen of the sky would be effective, I conjectured, only against forces similarly equipped, and trained. Indeed, the common Gorean warrior tended to hold the bow, even the peasant bow, in contempt, as weapons unworthy of the hand of a warrior, whose proper weapons were the shield, spear, and sword. His reliance on the crossbow was more a concession to the difficulty of closure in the sky than a respect for its military potential. His preference was to bring the combatant birds together, to the point at which, across the saddle, his spear might come into play. Seldom, even, did he have a spear strap, to better secure the weapon. His thinking here was that such a strap might wrench him in the saddle, possibly breaking his back, if the weapon became anchored in a shield or body. The temwood lance, on the other hand, light, lengthy, and supple, handled more easily than the heavier weapon, and had a farther reach. Too, the narrowness of its blade, in the Tuchuk fashion, unlike the broader blade of the common war spear, was designed to minimize the danger of its anchoring in either a shield or body. To be sure, the major value of the lance, as I saw it, would be in fencing away enemy birds, or, in a low, swooping flight, attacking ground troops or tharlarion riders. A tarnsman's usual close-to-the-ground flight was used to rope fleeing females, thence to be hauled helplessly to the saddle. A similar approach may be used on the high bridges or against unsuspecting loungers or sunbathers on the roofs of high cylinders. The capture of females of the enemy is a popular sport with tarnsmen, in which tallies are kept, and many a collared, tunicked beauty in a given city has, at one time or another, felt the suddenly encircling capture rope tighten mercilessly upon her.

Such women, it might be mentioned, in passing, once enslaved, are irremediably slaves. They are rejected as free females not only by their former compatriots, with whom they once shared a Home Stone, but by their families, as well. Once collared, as the saying is, always a slave. Even if such a woman is recaptured by fellows of her former city she will be brought back to her former city as only another slave, and will be held there as a slave, and a low slave. To be sure, she is likely to be soon sold out of the city, as her very existence in that city is regarded as an embarrassment, and a reminder of the dishonor she has brought to her fellow citizens, her Home Stone, her caste, her clan, and family. Once collared her life has changed; once collared, her old life is superseded, even obliterated; it is beyond recall. It is gone. The ties have been cut. She is now no more than property, and knows herself as such, and she then, in all her plaintive helplessness, hopelessness, and needs, in her astonished, newly liberated, vulnerable femininity, seeks her proper place, at a man's feet. Perhaps then, for the first time in her life, she has a purpose, and an identity; her anomie and ennui are gone; she is now meaningful. She now, perhaps for the first time in her life lives, truly lives, though now as no more than a benighted slave, lives as she must, and now desires to live, as a slave, for her master.

It is no wonder that they are kept slaves.

What else is to be done with them?

They are good now for nothing else.

They have been spoiled for freedom.

And what man does not want one at his feet?

Lord Nishida had informed me that these tarnsmen had been recruited in more than two dozen cities. Although the numbers were prodigious, considered merely as military units, these riders, I supposed, would be less a cavalry than a conglomerate or horde. They would be, I supposed, little used to riding together, and would presumably lack familiar, common signals and maneuvers. They would expect, in numbers, if in nothing else, to overwhelm and destroy a smaller force. I would learn later that our foes of the afternoon numbered better than two thousand, to our two hundred. To be sure, more important than simple numbers was firepower, and our two hundred possessed the firepower of a group much larger, if the larger group was armed in the usual manner. Too, the size of the group is unimportant if it cannot make contact with the enemy. And the size can be a handicap from the point of view of movement and supply. Smaller groups, obviously, with a given quantity of supplies, can be kept much longer in the field. A larger group may well defeat a smaller group but it cannot do so if the smaller, more agile group refuses to engage to its disadvantage. All I could see at the time were hundreds of tarnsmen, some so closely clustered that the birds, unable to keep their spacings, literally, here and there, buffeted into one another. Our centuries had swept to the sides and allowed the enemy to proceed to its destination, which was Tarncamp. As hundreds of birds alighted in the plaza of training, tarnsmen dismounted, to fire the camp. On the ground, of course, the tarnsman was a common infantryman, and I had no doubt their incursion, despite their superiority in numbers, would be fiercely met by the *Ashigaru* of the Pani and several of our mercenaries. The Pani, I was sure, would be loyal to their lord, their *daimyo*, Lord Nishida, for that seemed to be their way, and a cornered mercenary, one with no hope of a higher fee or escape, much like the cornered seventy-pound canal urt of Port Kar, is a most desperate and dangerous foe. The mercenary who fights for his life is more to be feared, surely, than one who fights merely for his pay. The larls, of course, prowled, still, beyond the wands. Some of our foes would learn that, to their dismay. I do not doubt that the invading force, for the moment seemingly unopposed, would suppose our smaller cavalry had judiciously forsaken the field, even as, unbeknownst to the central body of the invaders, dozens of our tarnsmen, darting to and fro, were shredding its margins. If a tarnsman were so maddened, or unwary, as to pursue a given foe, two others from behind, to the sides, would close upon him. When groups of enemy tarnsmen, in their rear, or at the sides, would flight after our fellows, our fellows would simply flight away, and leave them behind, separated from their group, and thus, soon, spread out, to be exposed to the crossfire of tens and twenties who seemed to appear from nowhere. Many fled back to the group where the birds milled, confused, and arrows, then, like sleet, unmet, fell amongst them. And in the meantime the prime body of the invaders had dismounted, most in the plaza of training, confident that the camp was theirs, naively unaware of the blood in the sky. But then tens and twenties from each of the centuries fell upon them, as they might upon unsuspecting, exposed verr. Hundreds of the enemy must have already alit in the plaza of training and set about their work, but even now others, newly arrived, startled, looking upward, saw birds diving, soaring in, and, in moments, were in the midst of sheets of arrows. He who defended himself from one side with the shield could not simultaneously protect his back. Too, many fell victims to the backward-flighted arrow, in which I had trained my men. The enemy, to his relief, would often assume the danger past as the bird passed, only to be struck from behind by the backward flighted arrow, a device familiar to the Tuchuk. Interestingly, most of the invaders did not even realize the dangers they faced. I saw one dragging a slave girl by the hair toward his tarn. He did not reach it. Two buildings were aflame. The *dojo* was fired. I saw, too, flames consuming the stately pavilion of Lord Nishida. As the birds milled above, crowded and screaming, hemmed in by our fellows, their riders, wise now to the dangers of breaking formation, but much aware now, too, of hundreds of arrows fired into their mass of birds and men, which constituted a large, almost stationary target in the sky, knew themselves, to their terror, at the mercy of our soaring fellows. Indeed, men tried to bring their birds into the center of the flock, to protect themselves from arrows, and the interior positions were then fought for, as the enemy competed with one another, and wounded and lacerated one another, to command this cover. And unto this mass, from above, were hurled dozens of weighted nets, which tangled the birds, and riders, and dozens, half crippled, unable to fly, fell brokenly toward the earth, and some riders freed themselves of the safety straps and tried to leap to the saddle rings of other birds, and some failed to grasp them, and fell screaming to the earth. Others fell with the tarns to earth, the nets half cut to pieces. I saw another net fall gracefully, like a broad, circular, open veil, on a bird starting to climb from the plaza, and the bird fluttered back to the earth, screaming, protesting, rolling in the dust, the rider caught in the safety straps, and then the helmeted head was twisted about, and the body was inert, a raglike, meaningless object in the saddle. I saw one of our fellows, I think Tajima, take a mounting tarnsman, climbing to the saddle, with the temwood lance. The tarnsman was carried a dozen yards before he slipped from the lance, to the stirred dust below. Others of my fellows were soaring downward, lance in hand, hunting targets. Above, in the sky, suddenly, the gigantic, tumbling, fighting knot of birds and men broke, like a burst of alarmed jards, startled in their feeding, and hundreds fled. I saw tens and twenties, and prides, streaking after them. I turned away, for what ensued would be slaughter. A moment later, a cry to the side arrested my attention and I saw Torgus, grinning, gesturing with his lance to the south. His bannerman with his lance-mounted pennon was within yards of him. I feared for a moment reserves might be entering the field. But presumably such a cavalry as we engaged, massive, overconfident, and clumsy, would not think in terms of reserves, certainly not for turning the tides of battle. What would be the purpose when its enemy was understood to be overwhelmingly overmatched? How many tharlarion would it take to press to the earth a single, scampering field urt? And, clearly, Torgus had seemed pleased. I wheeled about, my gaze following the direction of his lance. Our fleeing foes had now broken apart into a rout of single flights. Their rallying would now seem out of the question. This maneuver, though I doubt it was centrally calculated or dictated, I thought wise of them. In this fashion many would escape, as their numbers still considerably exceeded those of their pursuers, and, if a pursuer successfully brought down one, two or more others would escape. But I did not regret that many of our foes might thusly escape. We held the sky, the high battle was at an end, our men, our training, our tactics, had been vindicated. There is little pleasure for the warrior in pursuing broken, terrified men, defeated and almost defenseless, though he can recognize the military value in doing so, following up the victory. It is good to consolidate a victory, to prevent regroupings and rallies, to further dispirit a foe, and such, and, obviously, any fellow one brings down today need not be met tomorrow. He whom you do not kill now may kill you later. But I thought that few of them would return. They would not be eager to return to Tarncamp. Too, one finds executions, so to speak, distasteful. "Victory!" cried Torgus, grinning. "Victory!"

"War!" I cried, and gestured downward, toward the plaza of training. The sky was ours, the ground was not.

With a laugh Torgus then, with a declination of his lance, followed by that of his bannerman, followed by the twenty, in its four prides, in its ranks, that twenty which was his personal guard, swooped downward to join the fray below.

Oddly, some of the invaders about the camp seemed unaware of the catastrophies that had overcome so many of their fellows.

This sort of thing, however, is not unknown in combat. Often one thinks a battle is won because one is successful in one's own narrow corridor, on one's own plot of ground, while a few hectares away it has been overwhelmingly lost. It is often difficult to know what is happening anywhere but where one is at the moment. A skirmish can be won and a battle lost, and a battle can be won while a war is lost. The weathers of war are not only difficult to predict, but are often, and sometimes for days, difficult to ascertain. The tale of the past is often told only in the future.

Looking downward I saw a swooping, riderless tarn seize a fellow in its talons and beat its way upward. Commonly the tarn strike breaks the back of the verr or tabuk, and then it begins to feed, while the animal is still alive. Sometimes it seizes the animal, carries it to a height, and then releases it, and then descends to feed. To one side I heard a long, wailing cry and saw a fellow dropped from some two or three hundred feet to the ground below, the riderless tarn, reverted without its rider, then descending to feed. Elsewhere another riderless tarn was pinning a fellow to the earth with one taloned foot, and striking at him with its beak. Then it had an arm loose and the ground about, to thrashing and screaming, was muddied with blood. Some of our tarns, most perhaps, had been captured in the wild. Lord Nishida, in his attempts to conceal his project, or to at least reduce a cognition of its extent, had wished to avoid any unusually large purchase of domestic tarns. There were many free now, however, on the plaza of training. Some of my men, dismounted, apparently oblivious of the fact that elsewhere fighting might still be raging, were gathering them in.

Chapter Eighteen

Fighting Continues; We Report to Lord Nishida; The Stable

I brought the tarn down, to the field of training, followed by Tajima and Pertinax, and Ichiro, my first, or lead, signalman.

Shortly afterward Torgus, with his bannerman and guard, alit, and Lysander, too, with his bannerman and first twenty.

My major officers were then with me.

We had perhaps a century of men either on the ground or in the air, in the vicinity. Several were doubtless still in pursuit of fugitives.

"We are victorious!" cried Torgus, pleased, dismounted, holding the reins of his tarn.

"Swords still cross," I informed him, looking about.

Smoke rolled upward from the housing area, from beyond the narrow track which led to the Plaza of Training.

"Let them come to us!" laughed Torgus, sweeping an arm back, indicating the crowded plaza.

Tarns screamed. Dust swirled, raised by war and the beating wings of tarns, the gigantic, monstrous saddle birds of Gor. Here and there my fellows were still at their work. Enemies spun about, encircled, fenced by lances, thence to be pierced by arrows. I saw an Anangan dart lodge itself in a fellow's throat, who tried to pull it free, and, blood bursting from the neck, he sprawled into the dust, the vessel of the artery exposed, as it had caught behind the point of the dart, which point is broad, and barbed. In two or three places men fought, interestingly, with blades. I saw one fellow's spine severed as he tried to mount the saddle ladder of an unguarded tarn. There was shouting. Some tarns were being led away by my men, to be secured in our cots.

"They will," said Tajima.

As the tarns of the dismounted enemy were on the plaza of training, and we now held that ground, they had no access to the tarns without challenging us. Some were now coming down the track which led from the housing area to the training area, burdened with loot, some leading bound, leashed, female slaves. Muchly were they then dismayed to realize the training area was occupied. Several understood their peril and abandoned their loot, and slaves, and, drawing their weapons, hurried toward the waiting birds. Here, however, my men, now well outnumbering their foe, withdrew before them, if on foot, only to circle them, suddenly, like pack sleen, and fire arrows into backs or sides, whatever area might be clear of the shield. Some had recourse to the lances, to fend them back, while others used their bows or Anangan darts. It was much like the tactics of the air, but employed upon the ground. Engage, if possible, only when it is to your advantage, I had cautioned them. When charged they melted away only to reform again in a circle of death, where the turning warrior, confused and frightened, could defend himself on only one side. Few of our fellows could have stood up singly to such an enemy but, like harrying pack sleen, could easily deal severally with him. Too, some of our fellows, still on tarnback, their tarns on the ground, used their arrows to advantage. If approached, they merely pulled on the one-strap and hovered in the air, to fire further. Some other strikes were made from the air with the temwood lances.

"Cowards! Cowards!" cried one of the warriors, turning about, wildly. But then he fell, pierced by a dozen arrows.

He who would throw himself into the jaws of a larl may not be a coward, but he is surely a fool.

Some of the enemy then turned about, to flee back to the shelter of the trees and, momentarily, the housing area. Few reached the track, even backing away. Others fled into the forest, beyond the wands. I heard the roar of larls, and screams, from north of the track.

I would keep men on the field, for I was not sure of the number of enemies that might be left in the area.

There were many bodies about, the debris of war, distributed in accord with a fray's whims. Few were in our gray.

The foe, it seemed, had not fared well, neither in the sky nor, as far as I could determine, on the ground.

"There are no prisoners?" I asked a fellow, one of the Pani.

"No," he said.

I thought no more of this at the time.

I called to my side Tajima and Pertinax, and some dozen or so mercenaries, who well knew the sword.

"I suspect there is work to be done," I said.

"I think so," said Tajima.

"You are learning the blade," I said to Pertinax. "Are you ready to use it?"

"Yes," he said.

"Truly?" I asked, regarding him closely.

"I think so," he said.

"Bucklers and blades," I said to the mercenaries.

I secured my own buckler from the saddle.

"You, too, buckler and blade," I said to Tajima and Pertinax. It is true the blade may be used for both offense and defense, but I would not trust it against a flighted quarrel.

"Nodachi," said Tajima, "could deflect a quarrel with the blade of even a companion sword."

"And do you possess his skills?" I asked.

"No," said Tajima.

"Fetch your buckler," I said to him.

"Yes, Tarl Cabot, tarnsman," he said.

The edged buckler, of course, as in the arena, is an offensive weapon, as well as a defensive one.

I put Torgus in command.

"We will report to Lord Nishida," I said to Tajima.

"It is well," he said.

At that moment, running toward us, then stopping short, was one of the enemy.

"Please, Tarl Cabot, tarnsman," said Tajima, politely, "may I have him?"

"Yes," I said. And then I said to Pertinax, "observe."

It was done very quickly.

"Do not do swords with Tajima," I said to Pertinax.

"He despises me," said Pertinax.

"No," I said, "for as of this afternoon you have ridden together."

"We are rivals," said Pertinax.

"Are you interested in Sumomo?" I asked.

"Who is Sumomo?" he asked.

"You are not rivals," I assured him.

"My skills increase," said Pertinax.

"Good," I said. "See that they are employed properly."

I then, with some dozen or so men, mercenaries, together with Tajima and Pertinax, addressed myself to the path which led to the housing area. We had not been on the track for more than a handful of Ihn, however, moving rapidly but circumspectly, lest crossbowmen be about, when we heard shouts before us, and we saw some dozen or so of the Pani *Ashigaru*, with their glaives, approaching.

"It seems we will not need our blades," said Tajima.

"Resistance is at an end," said one of my fellows.

"The camp is clear," said another.

"Do not be certain of that," I said. I conjectured that enclaves of war might linger. More dangerous would be foes who were unseen, who, frenzied, and terrified, might be here and there, in hiding.

Then we had come to the housing area.

"I would see if Sumomo is alive," said Tajima.

"You are dismissed," I informed my pantherine associate, and he bowed, briefly, and hurried away, toward the area of Lord Nishida's still-burning pavilion.

I anticipated no resistance in the open areas.

I saw some Pani about. Some had heads fastened at their belt.

I saw no prisoners.

I heard a scream from within one of the huts about the periphery.

"Should we not concern ourselves with Cecily and Jane?" asked Pertinax.

"You mean Saru, do you not?" I asked.

"With slaves," said Pertinax.

"War is first," I told him.

"Duty?" he said.

"Certainly," I said. "But do not fear for them. Female slaves are not slain, no more than verr or kaiila."

"They are animals?" said Pertinax.

"Yes," I said, "and the sooner you learn that then you will relate to them the more appropriately."

"As animals?"

"Of course," I said, "as the lovely animals they are."

"Speaking, feeling animals?" he said.

"Yes," I said, "the best sort."

"What if they were free?" he asked.

"Then they would be priceless," I said.

"Then one might concern oneself?" he asked.

"Eventually," I said.

"But war, duty, is first," he said.

"Certainly," I said. "But remember that even the free woman is only a woman."

"I see," he said.

"Do not fear," I said. "Only the insane would kill a woman. There are better things to do with a woman than kill her."

"What?" he asked.

"Capture, collar, and master her," I said.

"I see," he said.

"In the collar," I said, "they learn they are women."

"And what is a woman?" he asked.

"A slave," I said, "though not all are in collars."

"All women are slaves?" he said.

"Yes," I said, "though not all are in collars."

I thought of a high woman, one who was, or had been, the daughter of a Ubar. I recalled her from the Plaza of Tarns, in conquered Ar, where she, a traitress, had been installed as a puppet Ubara. I had watched her consign woman after woman as booty to the victors, though under the guise of an allegedly reparational bondage, an act of justice, to compensate for the faults and crimes of her city, in this carefully selecting out, amongst others, her critics or enemies, such as the beautiful Claudia Tentia Hinrabia, the daughter of a former administrator of Ar. How imperiously she had reveled in that modicum of power accorded to her by the occupational forces of Tyros and Cos!

To one side a group of Pani were considering a hut. The door had been shut, and, I supposed, blocked from the inside.

In the midst of the Pani before the hut was a figure who wore a large, masklike helmet, whose features could not be discerned. Most of the Pani helmets, on the other hand, were open, though winged, that is, were rimmed to the sides and back, with something like a descending metal brim. They, like Gorean warriors, wore no visible body armor, as this defensive device was contrary to the rulings of Priest-Kings. I have never understood, perfectly, why this was so, but there are two major theories, which I might mention. The first theory would seem to presuppose a historical origin, though perhaps one rather idiosyncratic. In ancient times, on Earth, surely in the Homeric era, at least, it seems the defensive accouterments of the warrior often consisted of a helmet and shield, and the offensive accouterments of a sword and spear. Body armor was rare, and doubtless expensive, and, it seems, many warriors, even by preference, went into battle nude, save for helmet and shield. One gathers this from ancient sculpture, if from no other source. The most likely explanation for this, if it is true, as it seems to be, would presumably be to lighten and free the body to the greatest extent possible for great exertion and quick movement. Even much later Gauls encountered by Caesar's legions, at least occasionally, seem to have gone into battle with little but a golden neck band, these being prized as loot by victorious legionnaires. One supposes that some warriors might have supposed, as well, that their foes might have been intimidated by their scorn for body armor, or perhaps they regarded, interestingly, body armor as effeminate or unworthy a courageous warrior, who should not fear wounding or death. Perhaps even vanity or preening entered into such matters. It is hard to know. In any event, body armor, in time, became rather general in warfare on Earth. Its use declined with the widely spread utilization of gunpowder, particularly as its quality improved, and advances were made in connection with its packaging and delivery, cartridges, rifled barrels, and such. For example, in two major wars on Earth in the Twentieth Century, body armor was generally unknown, with the exception of the helmet. Later, with new developments in metallurgy, moving toward lightness and strength, it became, once more, rather general, at least where it might be affordable. There are often "arms races," so to speak, in such matters, in which an improvement in offense spurs an improvement in defense, and so on. In any event, the historical explanation, for what it is worth, is that Priest-Kings arranged their laws in such matters based on indulgently codifying what they took to be current human practices in such matters. Few Gorean warriors, incidentally, go into battle nude, but male nudity is not as uncommon on Gor as it is on Earth. For example, it is not unknown for Gorean laborers, if engaged in heavy work on hot days, and so on, to work nude. Most people do not think much about this, one way or another. The human body, on Gor, is not regarded as shameful. Even Gorean women of high caste, who are commonly robed and veiled in public, do not regard bodies as shameful. That would be absurd for a Gorean. They do, however, usually, regard their bodies as special and provocative, and exquisitely private, and certainly not for public viewing. The Gorean free woman then does not think of her body as something to be hidden for reasons of shame but as something to be hidden for reasons of propriety. As is well known the usual Gorean free woman is more concerned with the concealment of her facial features than her body. Her face is much more revealing of herself than her body. It might be noted, in passing, that the face of the female slave must be bared publicly. This is a difference between her and the free woman. Anyone may look upon the face of a female slave with impunity, as much as upon a verr or kaiila. She is, of course, enslaved, an animal. Also, she is usually garbed briefly and provocatively. This is, I suppose, not only to distinguish her, and dramatically, from the free woman, with whom she must not be confused, but because she is usually owned by men, and men enjoy seeing the beauty of women. Also, it is difficult to conceal weapons in a slave tunic. Indeed, the slave herself is scarcely concealed.

The second major theory proposed to explain the ban of Priest-Kings on body armor is that the Priest-Kings, in their benign concern for human beings, one of the diverse life forms with which they stocked the planet, thought the banning of body armor would reduce injury and conflict, that it would lead humans to abandon war as too dangerous and perilous of pursuit by a rational organism. If this is the case, it seemed they may have overestimated the rationality of the human species, or underestimated the lengths to which it might go to acquire land, wealth, women, and other valuables. A variant on this theory, though one less benign, or misguided, is that the regulation from the Sardar was intended to help keep the numbers of human beings on the planet in check, that it functioned, in a sense, as a populational control device. They might have been less inclined to use other devices, say, disease, because of the danger of a mutation which might affect the denizens of the Sardar, sooner or later, as well. To be sure, other theories might be proposed, too, for example that warfare conducted under such conditions might tend to improve the species, selecting for, say, intelligence, quickness, agility, and so on. It might be noted that on the planet Earth war would seem to be counterproductive along these lines, as, on the whole, the healthy and robust do the fighting and the sickly, weak, and frail remain behind to replicate their genes.

Whatever the truth may be in these matters the Priest-Kings, as is their wont, did not explain the rationale for their rulings. They do enforce them, however, mercilessly, with the Flame Death. Perhaps the rulings on body armor were not even particularly rationally motivated, at all; perhaps they were the result of a random notion or an idiosyncratic whim on the part of one or more Priest-Kings. Whatever the case may be the rulings, as in the case of certain forbidden developments or innovations in weaponry and communication, and such, are in place.

You may recall that I had heard a scream issuing from one of the huts. I now saw one of the Pani emerging from the hut, carrying a head.

These heads were clearly trophies of a sort. For example, a warrior might win favor from his *daimyo* or *shogun* by garnering heads, this understood as a proof of prowess in war. In such a way one might earn promotion, land, gifts, preferments, and such. I would also later learn that these heads, particularly if one of a celebrated foe, might be treasured, and kept indefinitely, the hair being carefully combed and dressed, the head being perfumed, the teeth painted black, and so on. The blackness of teeth was apparently regarded as cosmetically appealing. Indeed, certain beauties of the Pani, I would learn, blackened their teeth to enhance their charms. To be sure, neither of the contract women of Lord Nishida, one of whom was Sumomo, who was apparently of interest to Tajima, and the other of whom was Hana, as I later discovered, I was pleased to note, had adopted this practice.

He in the helmet mask turned toward me, and I saw that the mask, in design and color, was garish. Too, it was horned. The entire effect was that of a hideous face, as of some frightful creature, or monster of sorts, surely not even a human face.

"That is Nodachi," I speculated. Pertinax was at my side, and would presumably be familiar with that individual. I myself had never seen this mysterious and, it seemed, almost legendary, figure.

"No," said Pertinax.

Although the gaze of the figure was upon me, it gave no sign of recognition.

"Bow," whispered Pertinax.

"Of course," I thought to myself. There are understandings in such things. I am not even of the Pani. I understand very little of this. Pertinax may be more informed than I, having profited from the tutelage of Nodachi. It did seem to me that the fellow in the helmet mask, as it was the only contrivance of its sort in view, might be important. I am not of the Pani, I reminded myself. I will be expected to bow first. There is a complex order in such matters.

And so I bowed, and lifted my sword, in a warrior's salute.

This business on my part was accepted, it seemed, for the individual returned my bow, though less deeply, and then turned away.

I did note that his sword, the long sword, with its beautifully curved blade, and its tasseled hilt, suitable for a two-handed grasp, was bloodied.

I took him to be a high officer, of which there were several in camp. From the mask, the stature, the carriage, the nature of his garments, the tone of the skin, I took him to be Pani.

I looked about, wondering on the whereabouts of Lord Nishida.

Even as I did so, to my right, his pavilion collapsed, crashing downward in a sudden flurry of sparks and smoke, then settling into a mass of flaming planks, timbers, and panels.

I regretted the loss of the pavilion.

It had been a small, but a beautiful, and exotic, building, and might have been more suitably situated not in a rude camp, but, withdrawn, in a sheltered garden.

I trusted Lord Nishida had escaped the firing of his pavilion. I supposed he would not have been personally sought, as the archer who had attacked him may well have reported him slain. Lord Nishida had impressed me as being politically astute, and coldly subtle, but also as constituting an epitome of a civilized gentleman, at least relative to his own background, or lights. Certainly I recalled his interest, manifested in his interviewing of the former Miss Margaret Wentworth, in the delicacies of flower arrangements, tea ceremonials, and such. Such a sensitive and delicate gentleman, and particularly one so important, I hoped, at the first sign of trouble, would have been hurried to a location of safety, and a guard set about him to protect his person. One such as he was not to be risked. I did assume him safe. If he had come to harm I had little doubt that that would have been broadcast in the camp, and a new leader made known.

The Pani made no effort to save the pavilion. It was lost. It burned lower now. The smoke filled the air.

To one side I saw two women in their kimonos, with their small steps, being ushered forward by one of the *Ashigaru*. I supposed they had been concealed somewhere. I took them to be Sumomo and Hana. They were being brought into the open, I supposed, for their security. We controlled this area. Buildings might be especially dangerous. Fugitives might take shelter within them, turning them into small fortresses. One would not wish them to be seized as hostages, though I did not think the Pani would be excessively concerned with them, as they might be replaced, I supposed, with others. On the other hand, I was sure they would be taken as of greater value than, say, a common collar girl.

I caught sight of Tajima, now, again, in the clearing. He approached Sumomo. She turned away. Though she was a female, and he a male, and though she was a contract woman, and he free, she had not bowed to him.

I understood this to be an insult of some sort, and I noted that Tajima's body, briefly, stiffened with rage. He then remained standing, where he was, where he had been rebuffed, looking after Sumomo, who was now with Hana, facing away from him, several feet from him, not far from the smoldering embers of Lord Nishida's collapsed, blackened pavilion.

"I fear the contract woman," I said, "did not treat Tajima well."

"She has nothing to fear," said Pertinax.

"She may have more to fear than she understands," I said.

"I do not understand," said Pertinax.

"It is nothing," I said.

"Her contract is held by Lord Nishida," said Pertinax.

"Contracts may change hands, be purchased, and such," I said.

"Doubtless," said Pertinax.

"Why should she treat Tajima badly?" I asked.

"Doubtless for the same reason that the Lady Portia Lia Serisia of Sun Gate Towers would, if she dared, not treat Pertinax well," said Pertinax.

"You are referring, incorrectly, I take it," I said, "to a meaningless slave, your Jane, in her collar, who must now obey, fetch, and serve, unquestioningly."

"Yes," he said, "to my slave, Jane."

"Your insolent slave," I said.

"Yes," he said.

"No slave is insolent," I said, "whom you do not permit to be insolent."

"Perhaps," he said.

"That lovely brat still has to learn her collar," I said.

"Perhaps," he said.

"Do not fear to use the switch, or whip," I said. "The slave learns quickly to respond to its discipline, to its swift, informative, lashing sting, its sudden monitory caress on her soft, smooth skin."

"Perhaps," he said.

"Certainly," I said. "The next time your Jane's behavior, in any way, whether verbal, physical, or attitudinal, asks for such a stroke, or even seems that it might ask for such a stroke, see that she receives it. You will learn shortly thereafter that her behavior will then seldom ask for such a stroke, or even seem to ask for such a stroke."

"She will learn to fear, and will then attempt to avoid, the stoke," he said.

"Certainly," I said.

"A switch in time saves nine?" he smiled.

"You could put it that way," I said. "The sooner she kneels before you and sees you as her master, the better for the both of you."

"She as slave, I as master," he said.

"Yes," I said. "How can she be slave, if you are not master?"

"I fear I lack the courage, the strength, to be a master," he said.

"Then sell her to another," I said, "who will treat her as she deserves, and, in her heart, desires to be treated."

He was silent, angry.

What man, after all, does not, in his deepest heart, want to own a woman? What could begin to compare with such a property?

Perhaps, I thought, he has dreamed of another woman, a different slave, his, helpless at his feet?

Would he have the courage, the will, the determination, the kindness, the compassion, I wondered, to put her at his feet, keep her there without the least compromise, and fulfill her?

"Why should Sumomo not respect Tajima?" I asked. "Or Jane Pertinax?"

"Perhaps because we are weak," said Pertinax.

"I do not think so," I said.

"Perhaps," said Pertinax, "because neither of us speak Gorean natively, perhaps because neither of us was born to this world. We are seen as different, as barbarians."

"I, too," I said, "would be such a barbarian."

"No," he said, "you are Gorean."

"Tajima," I said, "is now of Gor."

"I do not think Sumomo understands that," said Pertinax.

"A dangerous misunderstanding," I said.

"Perhaps," he said.

"Pertinax," I said, "may one day, too, be of Gor."

"It is not easy to be of Gor," said Pertinax.

"At one time, long ago," I said, "none were of Gor."

"Now, many?"

"Of course," I said.

"Is it good to be of Gor?" asked Pertinax.

"That question can be asked only by one who does not know Gor," I said.

"I do not understand," said Pertinax.

"Is it good to be alive?" I asked.

"Yes," said Pertinax.

"Then you sense Gor," I said. "Once one has known Gor, one is alive. Once one has known Gor, one never goes back."

"Tajima is now approaching," said Pertinax.

"Yes," I said. Sumomo, I noted, perhaps alerted by Hana, had turned about, to watch Tajima withdraw. She seemed amused. Tajima did not look back at her. My pantherine associate did not seem pleased. Although his face was a careful study in composure, there was a tightness about the jaw, a rigidity, that bespoke a rage and shame he was too proud to display. He had been genuinely concerned with the safety and welfare of the contract woman, Sumomo. His concern had seemingly been scorned, perhaps even mocked. Certainly, from the looks of it, he had been treated badly, very badly. I suspected he now viewed the contract woman differently, doubtless now as less worthy of his concern, which he would now recognize had been seriously misplaced. Had we been elsewhere on Gor and she branded and naked in a slave cage I did not doubt but what he would bid on her, and soon, doubtless regardless of the cost, would have her on his chain. She might then look forward to a perfect and exquisite bondage at his feet, one from which he would see to it that he derived much satisfaction. To be sure, there was little prospect of this, as Sumomo's contract was held by Lord Nishida. And doubtless the proud Sumomo was only too well aware of this fact. Within the fortress of etiquette and custom she doubtless supposed herself to repose secure. I supposed it would take some time for Tajima to nurse his wounds. And the deepest of wounds, we note, do not always bleed. Too, the Pani have long memories.

Tajima had now joined us.

"You saw?" asked Tajima.

"Sumomo belongs in a collar," I said.

"She is Pani," said Tajima.

"Doubtless some women of the Pani are in collars," I said.

"Yes," he said, "primarily women of enemy houses. Taken, they may be reduced to collar girls."

"Enemy houses?" I asked.

But Tajima was silent.

I suspected, but did not remark it, that Sumomo's treatment of Tajima might have obscure motivations, motivations more subtle and deeper than a mere scorn for one she might despise as having been extracted from an alien world. I suspected she was fighting irresistibilities within herself, longings to feel his switch, curiosities as to what it might be to kneel naked before him and press her lips upon his bared feet, what it might be to writhe in his arms, helpless, and owned, as only a woman may be owned, owned to the tiniest tremor of her subdued and surrendered heart, to the last obedient cell of her mastered body.

I did not speak these things, of course, to Tajima.

We turned our attention to the door of the closed, presumably blockaded hut.

Several of the Pani with the masked figure had now ranged themselves on either side of the door of the hut.

I did see, briefly, a frightened face within, in the small, open window, to one side of the door.

The figure in the hideous mask-helmet, with the bloodied sword, gave a sign and several *Ashigaru* fetched brands from the fallen, now-smoking pavilion, and hurled them to the dried branches with which the hut was roofed.

I would have thought it well to have warned the walled-in, dangerous, doubtless panic-stricken prisoners of the hut of the intention of the besiegers, that they might consider the wisdom of surrender, but they were extended no such cordiality.

"No," said Tajima, now at my side, as I moved to approach the hut.

"They will be burned alive," said Pertinax, with horror.

The roof took the fire almost instantly, raging like tinder.

"Let Lord Nishida be notified," I urged, "that he may intervene."

"That is Lord Nishida," said Tajima, indicating the figure in the fearsome mask with the bloodied sword.

"It cannot be," I said.

"It is," said Tajima.

"But his sword is bloodied," I protested.

"Lord Nishida is a great warrior," said Tajima.

"He fights, he, sword to sword?" I asked.

"Certainly," said Tajima. "It is our way. Who would follow another?"

"Take prisoners!" I said.

"We do not require prisoners," said Tajima.

In common Gorean warfare it is not unknown for prisoners to be taken. They may be interrogated, worked, sold, and such. Too, occasionally, if important, and of station, they may be ransomed. The Pani, it seemed, might take prisoners but seldom did so. Sometimes prisoners were tortured, and crucified, presumably primarily as examples to terrify enemies, reduce the temptation to sedition, and such. A common form of Gorean execution is impalement. The Pani regarded this as barbarous, but looked lightly on crucifixion. Such things apparently vary culturally. Perhaps one reason the Pani are not prone to making prisoners is that it is thought that the prisoner might be expected, if honorable, to end his own life, to erase his shame at having fallen into the hands of the enemy, and thus, if this is so, he might as well be spared this indignity by being granted an earlier surcease. Also, if heads are prized, and important with respect to advancement, and such, this militates against taking prisoners. An interesting exception to this sort of thing is that a prisoner, or one on the verge of capture, may be accorded the right to accept a new *daimyo* or *shogun*. Once he does this he is then honor bound to serve the new leader, as he did the old, and, it seems, he may be depended on to do so. He is not a mercenary, but he is a loyal follower, whomsoever he follows. The prime reason for not taking prisoners, or not making it that much of a common practice, if this should be truly so, is probably that the male prisoner is dangerous. He is feared, and perhaps wisely. Thus it seems supposed that he might be well done away with. Similarly, as in several periods in the Middle Ages on Earth, prisoners were done away with, there being no satisfactory provisions for their incarceration, particularly in the field, no prisoner cages, or such.

Screams emanated from the burning hut.

"Take prisoners!" I cried.

"Subside, Tarl Cabot, tarnsman," said Tajima. "They would have killed us. We will kill them."

The door was suddenly flung open, from the inside.

A fellow, clothes aflame, shielding his eyes, stumbled from the hut and was cut down, from each side.

Smoke billowed from the hut. The walls were afire.

Another fellow, coughing, burst into the open, and ran two or three paces, and was cut down. Another followed him, and was similarly dealt with.

I think the fellows in the hut were blinded with the smoke, and burned. Two more emerged, to be cut down.

I looked within the hut, and the roof fell in, turning the enclosure into a furnace. I saw two or more dark shapes like shadows, silhouetted in the flames. Two more rushed from the hut, and died. One or two remained inside, and fell in the midst of the flaming branches, unable, I supposed, to reach the door. There was screaming for a few Ihn, and then it was quiet, save for the crackling of the flames.

The figure in the hideous, horned, masklike helmet removed it, and faced me. "You have come to report?" he inquired.

"The sky is ours," I informed Lord Nishida.

"Some will have escaped," he speculated.

"Yes," I said. "They fled. They separated. They were many. We were few. We could not kill them all."

"Unfortunate," said Lord Nishida. "Our plans must now be advanced."

I did not understand this.

Others approached, and Lord Nishida politely received their reports, as well. The camp was clear, it seemed, save for one or two huts, which would be soon attended to.

Lord Nishida turned to me. "We are pleased, Tarl Cabot, tarnsman," he said.

I bowed, acknowledging this compliment.

"Now," smiled Lord Nishida, "it seems a feast, a victory feast, would be in order, when things are done, and matters cleared, of course, a feast in, say, a day or two, after the day's work. Is it not the Gorean way?"

"Perhaps," I said, "if a watch is kept, and sufficient men are armed and at hand, to prevent unpleasant surprises, and such."

Most such feasts, of course, take place within a holding within the environing walls of a city, perhaps one over which the tarn wire still sways in the wind, not in the open, not in a camp.

"It is unfortunate," he said, "that we have not captured suitable numbers of the enemy's free women, that they might serve such a feast naked."

"Yes," I said.

"That is the Gorean way, is it not?" he asked.

"Yes," I said, "but I suspect that it is also a way not unknown to the Pani."

He smiled.

"It seems, Lord," I said, "we are short of such serving maids."

It is common to have the women of the enemy serve such a feast naked. It is one of the pleasures of victory. The women may either be collared prior to their service or not. It is usually thought best to save their collaring for later. That they should serve such a feast while still free is thought to shame them excellently, and to teach them that even the glorious free women of the defeated are worthy only to be the naked servitors, and later slaves, of the victorious.

"I trust the slaves are well, and in hand," I said.

"Yes," said Lord Nishida. "Doubtless you are concerned with your pretty Cecily."

"She is well curved," I said.

"Even now," said Lord Nishida, "she is within a ring, her small hands upon the rope."

This was a reference to the "rope circle." In the "rope circle," a single rope is tied about a group of slaves, either kneeling or standing, at their belly. The hands of each slave must then grasp the rope and may not, until permitted, release the rope. This holds a group of slaves together, nicely.

"How fares the blond-haired, blue-eyed slave whom I believe is now named 'Saru'?" asked Lord Nishida of me.

"The stable slut?" I said.

"Yes," he said.

"I have not seen her in weeks," I said.

"Doubtless the honorable Pertinax, tarnsman, has more recent news," said Lord Nishida.

I recalled that Lord Nishida had had plans for the former Miss Margaret Wentworth.

"No, Lord," said Pertinax, "I have not seen her since the pavilion, when you remanded her to the tharlarion stable."

"That seems strange to me," said Lord Nishida.

Pertinax shrugged.

"My fellow, Pertinax, I fear," I said to Lord Nishida, "fears to look upon her."

"'Fears'?" inquired Lord Nishida.

Pertinax reddened.

"Much of him," I said, "remains of Earth. He fears, I think, that he would succumb to her charms, that she would manipulate and dominate him, that she would easily bend him to her will, that she would make of him much what she once made of him, her slave."

"The slave of a slave?" smiled Lord Nishida.

"Yes," I said.

"Surely, Pertinax," said Lord Nishida, "you know her neck is in a collar."

Pertinax nodded.

"Even so," I said, "the beauty of a woman, a tear in her eye, the trembling of a lip, such things, are formidable weapons."

"Until she is suitably mastered," said Lord Nishida.

"True," I said.

"Perhaps she should be whipped," said Lord Nishida. "The whip is useful in convincing a woman she is a slave. Perhaps if she were weeping, and squirming, and begging for mercy, under a whip, she would no longer be in doubt as to what she was."

"I think she is in no doubt as to her bondage," I said. "I am sure the grooms in the stable have seen to that. The fear is that she might not know herself a slave before Pertinax, that she might attempt to use the subtle wiles of Earth, guilt, and such, to work her will in a hundred ways upon him."

"And perhaps the honorable Pertinax fears she might prove successful in such endeavors?"

"I think so," I said.

"Then he is weak," said Lord Nishida.

"He fought well today," I said.

"One who is strong in one way may be weak in another," said Lord Nishida.

"True," I said.

How many men are conquered by a look cast over a shoulder, by a smile! Some men are drunk on kaissa, others on power, others on kanda, others on paga. I recalled a warrior, on a Steel World, who, in misery and futility, once risked ruin, harkening to the siren lure of a swirling, golden beverage.

"Be a master," I said to Pertinax.

He looked down.

"No woman can find herself," I said, "until she finds herself at the feet of a master."

Pertinax regarded me.

"And the slave, Saru," I said, "is no different."

"By now, the hair of the slave should be grown out a bit," said Lord Nishida. "Had I realized that our plans must be advanced, I would have had it cropped, and not shaved."

I knew nothing of his plans.

I did know he had anticipated giving Saru to an important individual, a *shogun*. I had no doubt that cleaned up, and trained, whip trained, and otherwise, that she would be likely to make a lovely gift. Her coloring and such would be, I gathered, unusual amongst the Pani, and her slave fires, as I had determined, had already been nicely ignited.

She was now a slave.

She needed men.

Without them she would be in torment.

I hoped that Pertinax, from his absurd conditioning on Earth, would not scorn her for her vitality, and needs. Her belly was now hot, and alive, even piteously so. Rather, let him accept her now as what she was, and now only was, a slave. A Gorean male, of course, is not surprised by female needs. He may not expect such things in a free woman, but he does expect such things in a slave. The repressed free woman, struggling against her own sexual nature, often in misery, may scorn the slave, whom she envies, for her needs, but the master, naturally, does not. He accepts them. They are exactly what he expects in a given form of merchandise, a property girl, a collar slut, a luscious, needful, obedient, owned female, a slave.

"Do you think," asked Lord Nishida, "that the slave, Saru, is ready to leave the stable?"

"I am sure of it," I said. "I am confident she will be eager to leave the stable, and will strive desperately, in all ways, to avoid being returned to it."

"Good," said Lord Nishida. "I will have her prepared. Perhaps she may serve at the feast, scrubbed clean and naked." He turned to Pertinax. "Would you like that?" he asked.

Pertinax looked down, reddening.

"How of Earth he is," commented Lord Nishida.

I shrugged.

"You will be present, of course," he said.

"I would be honored," I said.

"Your colleagues may accompany you," said Lord Nishida.

"We are honored," I assured him.

"There will be many tables," said Lord Nishida.

"The men will be pleased," I said.

"Guards must be posted," he said.

"Of course," I said.

"Unfortunately," said Lord Nishida, "our friends did not bring free women with them."

"No," I said.

Sometimes overconfident forces do bring free women with them, camp followers, courtesans, and such, and, even, not unoften, highly placed free women, to companion high officers, preside over victory feasts, have the first chance to bid amongst the women of the enemy for serving slaves, and such. Indeed, some accompany such campaigns as an escape from boredom, if nothing else, apparently in search of thrills and adventures. If unable to observe actions from remote, secure, and convenient heights, by means of the glasses of the Builders, they remain behind, in their silken tents, awaiting the announcements of victory, in the keeping of camp guards. Sometimes, of course, things do not go well, and they must forsake their heights, now being swept by the enemy, and flee downward, in terror, scattering to the grassy valleys, running before mounted foes intent on collecting them. About them they hear the squeals of kaiila, the shouting of men, the shrieks of their sisters, the sudden pounding of paws in the grass behind them, and then the bright sound of a flighted, swirling, belled capture net. And later those in the camp rejoice, seeing the dust approaching, which they take for the rapid, joyful return of their forces, triumphant. But the camp guards have reconnoitered, and have hurriedly departed, that their swords may be saved for the defense of their Home Stone. And then the women discover the camp is surrounded, and invaded, and then tents are afire, and then men are about, rude strangers, laughing and shouting. Coffers are being forced open, and precious vessels, and handfuls of coins and jewelry, are being seized; silken hangings are draped on brawny arms; amphorae are unearthed; the odor of paga pervades the camp, and common warriors, perhaps for the first time, taste rare ka-la-na, guzzling it like kal-da. The women, then, of whatever station, whether low-born or high, whether of high caste or low, together with camp slaves, are herded to the center of the blackened, smoldering camp, where all must, at a word, disrobe themselves, both bond and free, to be assessed, as though in a field market. One woman speaks imperiously to a slave, as is her wont, and, to her astonishment, and pain, is slapped. And then, later, the free women, who thought to feast this night in a conquered city, are led in coffle, naked, hastened by whips, through alien gates.

"How then will the feast be served?" inquired Tajima.

"By women," said Lord Nishida. "What else are they good for?"

"Pleasure," I suggested.

"Yes," said Lord Nishida, "that, too, is a purpose of women."

"By slaves, of course," I said.

"Alas, yes," said Lord Nishida. "We must make do with slaves. To be sure, we might free them all, have them serve, as free women, and then recollar them."

"I think slaves will do," I said.

"Yes," said Lord Nishida. "Why should a slave be granted even a moment of freedom?"

I include, in passing, for those who might find it of interest, the following brief, ritual dialogue, in the form of a simple question and answer, which, in certain cities, is not unusual between a master and his slave.

"What are you for?"

"To serve you, and give you pleasure, Master."

This exchange usually takes place in the morning, when the girl first kneels before the master.

In a sense, it begins her day. Too, of course, it may be required at any time, say before meals, before serving wine, before bedding her, putting her to use, and so on.

I supposed Tajima had been interested in whether or not Sumomo might serve at such a feast.

She would not.

She was a contract woman, and above such vulgar applications.

Then, far off, several hundred yards away, we heard the bellowing of tharlarion.

The men of Lord Nishida had been methodically examining each structure in both the housing area and those surrounding the Plaza of Training.

"It seems urts have been discovered in the stable," said Tajima.

"They are trying to cover their flight by stampeding tharlarion!" said Pertinax.

From where we stood we could see the lumbering bulks of crowded tharlarion, buffeting one another, moving from the stable. We saw *Ashigaru* in the vicinity with glaives. Another figure or two, also, was seen, mixed in with the tharlarion. One, I thought, fell, and was trampled.

"Margaret! Margaret!" cried Pertinax, wildly, and, turning about, ran toward the stable.

"With your permission?" I asked Lord Nishida.

"Certainly," he said.

Tajima and I then, following Pertinax, hurried toward the stable. We were followed by some mercenaries, and glaive-bearing *Ashigaru*.

Chapter Nineteen

At the Stable

"Wait!" I called to Pertinax, who would have rushed headlong into the confines of the stable.

He drew up short, sword drawn.

"Do not frame yourself in the threshold," I said.

Lord Nishida had remained in the centrality of Tarncamp, directing officers and men. He spoke directly to Pani. He communicated with mercenaries through their officers.

There was much dust about, like gray clouds, settling slowly, from the movements of the tharlarion.

The stable had its strong, distinctive odor.

Men coughed.

Pertinax wiped his eyes.

Darkness would fall within the Ahn.

There were grooms about, and one of the Pani, a subaltern, set them to recover, as they could, frightened, confused tharlarion. *Ashigaru* accompanied them, lest fugitives be encountered. Some had surely escaped. To be sure, I was confident the last thing such fugitives would desire would be to encounter Lord Nishida's *Ashigaru*. They would be more likely to dare the forests, and hungering beasts. Few, I suspected, would find their way back to their Home Stones, if Home Stones they had. Fortunately the gigantic draft beasts, disoriented, snorting and lumbering, had not been loosed amongst buildings, or much of the camp, where it was intact, might have been reduced to shambles. I had no doubt hundreds of the wands would now be uprooted. I trusted this would not result in an eventual, casual intrusion of larls into formerly secure areas. A small building of wood, as were most of the camp structures, would not fare well against the bulk and momentum of a distressed, uncontrolled, rapidly moving tharlarion. Indeed, the beast might scarcely notice the obstacle, almost ignoring it, thrusting through it as it might through brush or picketing. The inertia of a tharlarion is formidable. It cannot be turned and halted with the same ease as might, say, a kaiila, or horse, which may be instantly turned or halted, pulled up short, and so on. When the tharlarion has its own head it is difficult to control. Consider the difficulties of trying to communicate with, or control, a boulder tumbling down a mountainside. Draft tharlarion, of which variety these were, are normally driven slowly, and with care. War tharlarion, often larger than draft tharlarion, can be, and are, used in charges. There is little defense against them if encountered on unprepared, level ground. Open formations will try to let them pass, and attack them from behind. Closed formations seek uneven ground, use ditches, diagonally anchored, sharpened stakes, and such. If they become slowed, or are milling, they can be attacked by special troops, with broad-bladed axes, designed to disable or sever a leg. I have never much favored tharlarion in combat, as, if they are confused, or wounded, they become uncontrollable, and are as likely to turn about and plunge into their own troops as those of the enemy, thereby, indiscriminately, wherever they trod or roll, whether amongst friends or foes, spreading disorder and death. Some kaiila, incidentally, become hard to handle in the presence of tharlarion, if they are unfamiliar with them. The issue of more than one battle had turned on this seeming oddity. For this reason, the Tuchuks, and others of the Wagon Peoples, and, I suppose, others, accustom their kaiila to the sight and smell of tharlarion. In the case of the Wagon Peoples, these are usually taken from raided caravans.

Tajima looked at me.

"Not yet," I said.

"Very well, Tarl Cabot, tarnsman," he said.

The enemy which stampeded the tharlarion would have realized the value, if danger, of such a cover. I recognized their cunning, and understood their desperation. It was an excellent strategy. I could think of only one better, and it would have required the execution of the first.

"Do not enter the stable," I warned Pertinax.

"What of Miss Wentworth?" he demanded.

"Saru!" I snapped. "The needful slave."

"'Needful'?" he said.

"Yes," I said, irritably. He did not realize what had been done to the female, how she was now different, how she was now a slave.

"Surely it is safe," said Pertinax. "The enemy has fled!"

"No," I said.

"How so?" said he.

"Some flee," I said. "One might suppose all have fled. Some remain, clever ones, in hiding, their presence unsuspected, to escape in the darkness."

"Why do you think this?" asked Pertinax.

"Put yourself in the place of the most astute, the shrewdest, of your enemies," I said. "What might you do, if you were they? Too, Saru is presumably within the stable, and, I am confident, alive, as she is a slave. One would no more kill her than any other domestic animal. But she has not called out to us. I infer she is being kept silent. If this is the case, one or more enemies are within."

"I think that is true," said a quiet, even voice, behind me. I knew the voice was Pani, but I could not place it.

I heard men gasp, and sensed them drawing back.

This was, I took it, a reverenced personage, one of whom lesser men stood in awe.

Who could this be?

I turned about.

I then saw before me one of the Pani, but one such as I had not seen before. Had a larl by some incantation taken the form of a man, I thought it might be such a man. He was not large, but I felt a largeness somehow within him. Although of the Pani his visage was bearded, thinly, roughly, uncut, save perhaps by the sword, and his hair was long, and unkempt. His clothing was soiled, and uncared for. He was barefoot. In his belt, blades uppermost, were the two swords, the companion sword and the longer blade. There was blood on his loose, short-armed robe.

Some of it was spattered, and, in other places, he had apparently drawn his blades against the cloth, to clean the blade. I was startled to look upon him, for he seemed so different from the other Pani. He might, I supposed, be a hermit, or a recluse, one who lived by himself, with his thoughts. Perhaps he was a madman. That seemed to me possible, but then it seemed to me, rather, that there was a solidity about him, and a finely tempered, perhaps dangerous, rationality about him. I thought surely he was an unusual man, and one of perhaps a ferocious singleness of interest and purpose. I would learn later, however, that he carved wood, and composed small poems on bark. I had the sense he was without companion or slave, and by choice. Perhaps such might have distracted him from some more remote purpose, or goal, or ideal. He seemed to me a man driven, like a thing of nature, but from what or to what I did not know.

"Master," said Tajima, bowing deeply, which greeting was politely returned.

"Master," said Pertinax, putting down his head.

"It is he," said one of the *Ashigaru.*

"He has come from the forest," said another.

"He came to the sound of striking steel," said another.

"He took seven heads," whispered a man.

I bowed then, for I knew in whose presence I stood.

"I am Nodachi," he said.

"I know," I said.

"It will be dark soon," said one of the *Ashigaru.*

"May I speak to the men?" I inquired of Nodachi.

Whereas he held no office to my knowledge, nor any instituted authority, as far as I knew, I felt the inquiry, the question, was appropriate.

I sensed that those others in the vicinity, too, felt a deference, a respect, a recognition, a salute, a propriety of some such sort was in order.

His consent or approval seemed important to me, somehow, and to the others.

Some men are not officers, or *daimyos,* or *shoguns,* but are such that officers, *daimyos, shoguns,* or such, in their presence, would not hesitate to be the first to bow.

I sensed the awe in which this man was held, an awe to which I, not even of the Pani, was acutely sensitive. It seemed an awe as palpable as an atmosphere. Doubtless this was in part due to many things, perhaps to his unusual, imposing, even wretched, appearance, and in part to his reputation, an understanding of who this was, and what he had done, and what he could do, and perhaps, in part, too, to that sense of being in the presence of one who lives alone, undeviating and undistracted, one who is absorbed in, and centered upon, a quest, one not altogether clear to other men, a journey as much within as without. Some men are alone, essentially solitary, their lives given over unswervingly to an ideal, or dream, the search for a fact, the discovery of a cause, or planet, the unraveling of a mystery, the creation of a perfect poem. I thought of Andreas of Tor, and his longing for a song that might be sung for a thousand years, of Tersites, of Port Kar, and his plans for a mighty ship, finer than all others. This man was such a man, I suspected, a seeker, a traveler on uncharted, even invisible, roads, roads thusly undiscerned by others. The perfection he sought, I gathered, was a simple one, one sought by many, and found by few, one which I, even of the Warriors, and others of my brethren in arms, would find harrowing, and almost incomprehensible, and to which we surely dared not aspire, a perfection of heart, eye, mind, and body, to undergo a lifetime of meditation, sacrifice, and discipline, to understand and become one with, as it was said, the soul of the sword.

He was Nodachi.

"I am near the camp, but I am not of the camp," he said. "I am one who is outside."

I thought he was, indeed, in many ways, one who was outside.

I gathered from his remark that he eschewed an engagement in our work, that he chose not to concern himself with it.

This was his decision.

I bowed.

"Master," said Tajima, bowing.

"Master," said Pertinax, bowing.

These deferences were accepted by the strange figure who then turned about, and withdrew.

"It was Nodachi," said a man.

"I have only now seen him, but I knew him," said another.

"Who would not know him?" asked another.

"He is more than a man," said one of the *Ashigaru*.

"He would deny that," said another.

"I think he is less than a man," said another. "He is part of a man."

"Men are various," said another. "He is one thing a man can be."

"A single, terrible thing," said another.

"Within him resides a demon," said another.

"And a holiness," said another.

"Or an evil," said another.

"He is a monster," said another.

"He is the blade's brother," whispered another.

"He listens to the sword," said another. "It speaks to him."

"The sharpness of his blade, unmoving in the water, can divide a floating blossom," said a man.

I had seen that sort of thing, and did not doubt it.

It was not unusual for silk to fall, parted, from a shaken blade.

"His stroke can descend like lightning, cutting in two a grain of sa-tarna placed on the forehead of a man, without creasing the skin," said another.

This was possible, I supposed, but I would not have cared to be the fellow involved in the demonstration.

"One stroke can cut through seven bodies," claimed another.

If we were talking of the bodies of men this was unlikely. The force required would surpass the violence of a hurricane.

"He can strike out in eight directions at once," claimed another.

Some of these things seemed to me obviously impossible, and were clearly the fruits of imagination, and myth, but it is common to suppose that at the foot of legends, in the lost soil of the remote past, there is a seed from which such legends sprang, and I had little doubt, in any event, that the mysterious fellow who had just appeared, and then departed, was both unusual and remarkable.

He himself, I was sure, was not the source of such conjectures. Indeed, I suspected they were legends founded on another individual altogether, legends to which he found himself, however reluctantly and unwillingly, an heir. Such legends tend to blossom and enlarge long after their alleged source has vanished, and is no longer about to contradict them. Humans are so fond of wonders that it seems almost churlish to call them into question. To be sure, such legends, in their way, betray and belittle he whose origin they might have been. Hercules and Perseus, and so on, if they existed, were doubtless remarkable enough in themselves, and might have found the wonders attributed to them embarrassing, at the least. Nodachi, I was sure, was a dedicated, great, and charismatic teacher and swordsman, in his own right, and did not require, and doubtless would not appreciate, the mantles of myth, woven for others, and misplaced upon him, mantles which might be cast upon him by smaller men, needful of marvels.

"Why did he come here?" asked one of the *Ashigaru*, uncertainly.

"We do not know," said a man.

"He took seven heads," said another.

He left them at the feet of Lord Nishida," said another.

"Now he is gone," said another.

I could see the trees through which he had disappeared. I wondered what his relationship, if any, might be to Lord Nishida, and his mysterious project. If he had put the seven heads before Lord Nishida, that suggested that Lord Nishida was his *daimyo*. To be sure, it seemed he had asked nothing of Lord Nishida. Was the presentation rather, then, in the nature of an assertion, a token, or even a defiance, or insult? Nodachi was clearly Pani, and yet seemed other than the Pani. He must be here for some reason, in the forest, I supposed, but for what reason?

I would learn more of Nodachi later.

I recalled that Lord Nishida, after the attack, had said that his plans would be advanced.

Nodachi, I did not doubt, figured in these plans.

"It is growing dark," said one of the *Ashigaru*. "Shall we enter the stable?"

I had little interest in risking men, and I had no way of knowing how many foes, if, indeed, any foes, were concealed in the stable. Too, I wished, to the extent possible, to protect Saru, assuming she was within. I doubted that she would be in danger, as she was a slave, any more than a verr or kaiila, but it is hard to anticipate the actions of frightened, desperate men. The situation would have been much different, of course, if she were a free woman. A free woman would constitute an excellent hostage. To be sure slaves, too, have their value. For example, they can be sold.

"No," I said, loudly enough to be heard within the stable. "No one is within. We will return to the main camp."

The men about looked at me, puzzled, and disappointed, some angrily, or reproachfully, but I waved them back, away from the stable. "No," I said to Pertinax, who seemed on the brink of rushing through the threshold.

I did not suppose that any foe within would be so simple as to suppose we thought the stable empty, as no search had been made. I did hope that they would be cognizant of the dangers we would face in seeking them out, either in darkness or in the light of lamps or torches. Torches, in particular, would not be practical as a single torch, fallen into the straw, would result in the loss of the stable, and its housing for several tharlarion. A similar danger, of course, but one considerably less, would attend the use of lamps, whose flames were small, and whose effects might be more easily smothered or stamped out. To be sure, the lamps would cast less light, and the dangers, accordingly, to those who entered would be the greater. What I did hope was that the foes within, if any were there, would suppose that the attending commander, in this case myself, preferred discretion to a hazardous intrusion into darkness.

Once withdrawn I stationed my men about the stable, encircling it fully, lest any makeshift exit be attempted. I set archers in place, particularly in the vicinity of the entrance, and, in support, *Ashigaru*.

I put some men to the gathering of firewood.

I also sent several men to the training area, to storage sheds which were adjacent to several of the improvised tarn cots. I expected them to return within the Ahn.

Meanwhile darkness was almost upon us.

"I am going into the stable," said Pertinax.

"Remain where you are," I said.

"Miss Wentworth may be in danger," he said.

"Saru," I said, "a slave, in effect 'Monkey'."

"She may be in danger," he said.

"She may be dead," I said.

He regarded me, agonized.

"But it is unlikely," I said, "as she is a meaningless beast."

"I must know!" he said.

"You would risk your life for her?" I asked.

"Yes," he said.

"She must never know that," I said. "She must think you despise her."

"I do despise her," he said. "But I desire her, as well."

"She belongs to Lord Nishida," I reminded him.

"I know," he said.

It is interesting, I thought. The slave is nothing, no more than a purchasable beast, a mere animal to be ordered about, who must obey instantly and unquestioningly, and yet men will die for them. How is it that one would risk one's life for a soft, sleek, curvaceous little beast, one at whose least indiscretion, lapse, or failure to please one would put unhesitantly to the whip. And the slave was not even his own.

"Wait," I said.

"How long?" he asked.

"Perhaps until morning," I said. "There will then be sufficient light, even within the stable."

"If any are within," he said, "they will attempt to flee before morning."

"I think so," I said. "That is my hope."

"Your hope?"

"Certainly," I said. "They are almost certain to be seriously outnumbered. Would you wait until morning?"

"No," he said.

"Men have returned from the tarn cots," said Tajima.

"Good," I said. "Let them follow their instructions."

Tajima nodded, and disappeared into the gloom, darkness now about.

In a few Ehn I gave a signal and, one by one, so that they would be immediately visible within the stable I had the lighting of six fires begun, lit at intervals of twenty Ihn, these fires to ring the threshold of the stable.

Such fires could be fed and tended until morning.

Shortly, even before the third fire was burning, there was movement within the stable as I had hoped and several foes, concealed within, realizing their danger, and the greater danger of morning, rushed outward, to slip away before the entire area might be illuminated.

At that point the roll of netting, some six feet in width, cut from the cordage used for the repair of the improvised tarn cots, was lifted upright from the ground and formed a wall impeding the fugitives.

In a moment the *Ashigaru* were upon them.

Heads were extracted from the cordage and tied to belts.

"They are dead, all of them," said Pertinax.

"Some, less swift, some less valorous, some more fearful, some less frightened, some more circumspect, some more clever, may remain within," I said.

Tajima joined Pertinax and myself.

"You took no heads," I observed.

"I am Pani," said Tajima, in English, "but not every custom of my people appeals to me."

"In the Barrens," I said, "they take scalps."

"The Barrens?" he said.

The Barrens were east of the Thentis Mountains.

"Great, central plains," I said.

"That does not appeal to me either," said Tajima, again in English. "One knows what one has done. That is sufficient."

"Nodachi?" I said.

"Yes," he said. "Nodachi."

"It is a cultural thing," I said.

"Doubtless," said Tajima. "But culture should serve one, not be served by one."

"I see," I said.

"Vanity is pleasant," said Tajima, "but it is dangerous, as well. While seeking and gathering trophies, while grasping at evanescent glories, while posing and preening, one may die."

"Nodachi?" I asked.

"Tajima," he smiled.

It was one of the few times I had seen him smile.

"Surely the fruits of victory are desirable," I said.

"Victory is the fruit of victory," said Tajima.

"Tajima?" I asked.

"No," he said, smiling, "Nodachi."

"Men desire fruits of victory other than victory herself," I said. "They desire land, power, gold, ships, villas, cities, women, other valuables."

"Not Nodachi," said Tajima.

"Nodachi is not as other men," I said.

"No," said Tajima, "he is not as other men."

"He must desire something," I said.

"Perhaps," said Tajima.

"What?" I asked.

"The recovery of honor," said Tajima. "Why else do you think he is here, with Lord Nishida?"

I was then silent, sensing that this matter might best be left unaddressed.

"What do we do now?" asked Pertinax. He had remained with me, and had not participated at the slaughter within the nets.

"We keep the fires lit," I said. "We arrange watches. Arrows are to remain at the string. And we wait until morning."

"What if any remain within and sue for quarter?" asked Pertinax.

"There is no quarter," said Tajima. "It is the law of Lord Nishida."

"I have heard nothing from within, of Miss Wentworth," said Pertinax, and then he corrected himself, "of the slave, Saru."

"She may be dead," I said.

"I would know," he said.

"In the morning we will know," I said.

"I would know now," he said, angrily.

"Remain where you are," I said.

"And if I do not?" he asked.

"Then I will have you killed," I said.

"I hate you," he said.

"I accept that," I said. "It is a familiar hazard of command." I then turned to Tajima. "Tajima," I said, "set watches, and see that most of the men at any given time are at rest. In the morning they must be fresh. Food must be brought before dawn."

"Yes, Tarl Cabot, tarnsman," said Tajima.

"What will you do now?" asked Pertinax.

"Sleep," I said.

"You can sleep?"

"Yes," I said. "And I recommend that you do the same."

"I think I shall stay awake for a bit," he said.

I turned to two of my fellows at hand, mercenaries. I indicated Pertinax. "Bind him," I said, "hand and foot."

Pertinax struggled, but was subdued, and soon trussed. He struggled, futilely, and glared at me.

"I do not really want to have you killed," I said.

"But you would?" he said.

"Yes," I said. "It is a matter of orders, of maintaining discipline."

"I see," he said.

"Get some sleep," I advised him.

He struggled, fiercely.

"Do not bother," I said. "You have been bound by Goreans. You are now as helpless as a trussed vulo, or, should we say, a bound slave girl, a nicely tethered *kajira*."

"Tarsk," he cried, "tarsk!"

"Good," I said. "You are becoming more Gorean by the day."

His struggles subsided. He would wait, helplessly. He had been bound by Goreans.

I lay down and thought of the hundreds, nay thousands, of slave girls I had seen on Gor, many of them deliciously helpless, fully at a man's mercy, roped, braceleted, chained, collared, and such. How incredibly beautiful, I thought, are women. It is no wonder men desire to own them. Indeed, what male would not desire to own one? What could give a man more delight and pleasure than the owning of a lovely, well-mastered slave?

How beautiful they are, I thought, that most exquisite form of domestic animal. And how abundant they are on Gor! I had seen them tunicked in the cities, laboring in the fields, and so on. I had seen them in markets, awaiting their sale, and during their sale; I had seen them trekked in coffle, transported in slave wagons, reclining in cages, looking out at men who might buy them; I had seen them hurrying in the streets, bargaining with vendors, busy on the quays, laughing, and teasing, and running about; I had seen them kneeling, laundering at the public troughs; I had seen them chained to the side in matches, even kaissa matches, waiting to be awarded to victors; I had seen them belled in paga taverns, serving their master's customers; I had seen them, serving quietly, demurely, in their masters' houses; I had seen them dancing in the firelight, in camps, to the rhythms of the czehar, the kalika, the flute, and tabor.

Yes, I thought, what could give a man more delight and pleasure than the owning of a lovely, well-mastered slave.

It is said that there is only one thing more miserable than a master without a slave, and that is a slave without a master.

I hoped that Saru was still alive.

Then I slept.

Chapter Twenty

What Occurred Within the Stable; A Tarn Is Requested

It was near dawn.

Some bread was handed to me.

I had taken the report of the last watch, and no one had exited the stable. The six fires had been tended during the night, and the net had been raised and anchored to posts. The fires would shortly, with the coming of light, be extinguished.

"Free him," I said to a nearby mercenary, indicating Pertinax.

"Did you sleep?" I inquired.

"There was little else to do," he said.

"I see you are in good humor," I said.

"I was a fool last night," he said. "Forgive me."

"It is nothing," I said. "If any remain within I feared you would die in the darkness, or, if there was a lamp, constitute a target which would be difficult to miss at the range."

"I am grateful," he said.

"Rub your wrists and ankles," I said. "Exercise your limbs, move about. Then eat, but not much."

"You are going to enter the stable," he said.

"We will enter together," I said.

"I, too," said Tajima. His blade was already in his hand.

"Of course," I said.

"This is not the work for a commander," said Tajima.

"Lord Nishida, and some others," I said, "are commanders, ones less dispensable."

"The cavalry," said Tajima.

"The substance of my work there is done," I said, "the organization, the training. You, Torgus, Lysander, and others, could command her."

"You forged the weapon," said Tajima.

"Others may now wield it," I said.

"Why will you enter the stable?" asked Tajima.

"Curiosity," I said.

"He intends to protect us," said Pertinax.

"No," I said. "I am seeking someone."

"One who wears our gray?" said Tajima.

"Yes," I said.

"The mercenary, Licinius Lysias of Turmus," said Tajima.

"Yes," I said.

It was he, it had been determined, who had fired upon he whom he thought was Lord Nishida during the exercises of the preceding morning, and had then fled, to soon return, guiding the horde with which we had done contest, in the sky, on the ground. It had been easy to determine this, first from startled witnesses to his perfidy, and a later call of the roll, to confirm the matter, lest the witnesses were confused, mistaking one uniform for another in the haste, the commotion, and turmoil of the moment. Too, indisputably, later in the afternoon, he had been noted amongst enemies in the camp, leading a party, firing structures, and such. He had worn a yellow armband to insure his safety from his own cohorts, an armband later removed, in an attempt to blend in with our men, an attempt unsuccessful as he had been well noted in the fighting. He had then, it seemed, with several others, taken refuge in the stable, doubtless first urging others to loose tharlarion and attempt to escape in the confusion, an attempt in which he had apparently declined to participate, preferring to remain concealed, planning to make away in the darkness. His name had been brought to me the preceding evening. It was not certain, however, that he was within the stable. If he was, I wished to meet him. Lord Nishida had assured me that there were spies in the camp. Licinius Lysias of Turmus had obviously been one of them. Others doubtless remained.

"I do not urge this," said Tajima, "but would it not be wise to enter the stable in force?"

"It would be better to first reconnoiter," I said.

"Surely you are not concerned with a slave?" said Tajima, puzzled.

"She has some value," I said, "an unusual coloring, and such. Too, recall that Lord Nishida intends her for a *shogun*."

Tajima nodded. If a general melee was in store, involving close fighting with several men, taking and giving ground, even a frightened, bounding kaiila might suffer, terrified in the rush of men, the shouts, the movement of blades, the fending of strokes, the thrust of spears, the slashing of glaives, the flight of arrows.

"No," said Pertinax, smiling. "You do not wish to risk losing your man."

"Ah!" said Tajima.

I think he was reassured then that Saru was, appropriately, not of importance, or at least of no particular importance. She was, after all, only a slave. She was not of the Pani, nor a contract woman. She was, when all was said and done, only another collar girl. Too, she could always be replaced with a slave of similar appearance, perhaps one even more beautiful. I did not think he would have viewed the matter in the same light had the girl been, say, Sumomo. To be sure, Sumomo was of the Pani, and had the status of a contract woman. She was not a collar-girl.

"Are you ready to kill?" I asked Pertinax.

"I think so," he said.

"It would be better to be sure of it," I said.

"—I am ready," he said.

"Let us enter," I said.

There was a musty odor in the stable, and the strong smell of tharlarion dung. The light was acceptable.

"Bucklers," I cautioned Tajima and Pertinax.

We crouched down, bucklers forward, to cover as much of our bodies as was practical, and surely the chest and throat. Helmeted, we looked over the edge of the bucklers.

I had positioned myself on the right. There was no particular need for this in the situation, but it was a natural thing to do, almost without thinking. In the Gorean phalanx the field commander leads the right wing, which tends to drift to the right, this resulting from the natural tendency of each man to take advantage of the protection of the shield of the man on his right, as well as his own shield. Accordingly, the right wing of the phalanx tends to outflank the left wing of its foe, while the foe's right wing tends to outflank his left. In this way the phalanxes tend to turn in the field, rather like a wheel of war. Some commanders, well aware of this dynamic, increase the depth of their left wings, a tactic which often leads to victory. The typical Gorean commander, perhaps unwisely, does not "lead" from a position of safety, from interior lines, so to speak, but leads from the front. He himself will be where steel meets steel. In this sense, I suppose he is less a general, and more a warrior. Wisely or not, this seems to be the typical Gorean way. Men, of course, are then ready to die for him, for he is with them, and one of them.

There was a sudden flash, almost invisible, and a shriek of gouged metal and a brightness of sparks and Pertinax, who was in the center, was spun half about, and almost lost the buckler, but then again had it in place.

"Ai!" he said.

"A quarrel," I said.

Taken frontally the quarrel strikes like an iron fist. It might have gone more than half way through the layering of a leather shield. It could not penetrate the buckler, which was of metal.

Pertinax, clearly, had not anticipated the force of the missile.

"There!" he cried. "I see him! He will have to reload. I can have him before he can set the quarrel."

"No," I said. "Stop!"

He looked at me, wildly. The opportunity seemed golden to him. It was not.

"There will be others, to the side," I said.

Had Pertinax rushed forward he would have been exposed to side fire, and, if he entered far enough into the stable, might have been hit in the back.

Trained crossbowmen, in such a situation, do not volley their fire. They will keep one or more bows ready, waiting.

We heard a woman scream.

"Margaret!" cried Pertinax.

There was then the sound of a blow, and we heard her whimpering.

"Tarsk!" screamed Pertinax.

"Draw back," I said. I had ascertained what I had intended. There were five foes in the stable, two to each side, a bit back, and one at the center and rear. Three had bows, one on each side, and the one toward the back. I supposed them short of quarrels but could make no determination on this point.

The fellow toward the back of the stable, who had fired the quarrel, was Licinius Lysias, he of Turmus.

This pleased me.

"She is alive!" said Pertinax.

"You put her at great risk," I said to Pertinax. "You showed concern. Thus they will see her as important. Thus they will see her as a possible hostage, a tool with which to bargain."

"What does it matter," said Tajima. "She is only a slave."

"It matters to Pertinax," I said.

"He is a weakling, and fool," said Tajima, angrily.

"Suppose it had been Sumomo," I said.

"I would have evinced no sign of concern," said Tajima, "and thus she would have been safer than otherwise."

"Pertinax," I said, "does not yet have your resourcefulness, and cunning."

"Perhaps one day," said Tajima.

"Perhaps," I said.

"Yes," said Pertinax. "I am a fool."

"No," I said. "One who makes mistakes is not a fool. Only one who fails to learn from his mistakes."

"But the beast struck her," he said.

"Do not concern yourself," I said. "She is only a slave."

"Perhaps—in a sense," he said.

"In every sense," I said, "categorically, and absolutely." I gathered that Pertinax had no sense of what it was to be a Gorean slave, the absoluteness and wholeness of it, which the former Miss Wentworth now was, and had no inkling of the transformations which had taken place in her, the unfoldings, the revelations, the self-discoveries, the new understandings, the admissions, the confessions in the light of which she could no longer be what she had been. I supposed he would choose to project upon her an image of what he thought she should be, and, indeed, perhaps she, too, would struggle to deny her newly discovered deepest self, and conceal it behind a facade prescribed by an ugly and unnatural culture. Perhaps she would think it in her best interests to do so. Perhaps she would pretend to be what she thought he wanted her to be, to please him, to the grief of both. Perhaps, even more foolishly, she would attempt to conceal from him what she was, and use his sympathy or compassion to manipulate him, to bend him to her will. That is an extremely dangerous thing for a slave girl to do. Perhaps, in order to more successfully exploit him, she would attempt to enlist the social engineering to which he had been subjected on Earth, attempting to instill guilt in him, attempting to make him feel ashamed of the pleasure with which he, as a man, might now regard her, as a slave. Surely such might seem an attractive female stratagem to a naive, conniving slave, particularly to one of Earth origin, to whom such a device might seem plausible. But what if he should only look upon her with perception, and scorn, and laugh? What if he would feel no guilt, no shame, but would see her in triumph as she should be, a female at his feet, in her place in nature, in a collar?

Cultures seldom conform to the needs and desires of human beings, but will have the needs and desires of human beings conform to them. They are, in a sense, as the bed of Procrustes, to which the human being is to be fitted, at whatever cost to his life or limbs, to his health or happiness.

"You must learn to strike her yourself," I said.

"How could I do that?" asked Pertinax.

"It is easy," I assured him. "Treat her as what she is, and only is, a slave."

"Shall we now enter in force?" asked Tajima.

"No," I said. "Be to the side."

I then went to the side of the threshold, taking cover near the threshold. "Licinius," I called, "Licinius Lysias, spy and traitor, he of Turmus!"

"I am no traitor," I heard. "I am loyal to my fee!"

"I would have with you a conversation of steel," I called.

"I know you," he called. "I am not mad!"

"Come forth, disarmed," I called, "and I will let you depart in peace."

"A clever ruse," smiled Tajima, "worthy of Lord Nishida himself."

"You think me mad!" laughed Licinius, from within. The voice had a ring, from the walls of the stable.

"Warriors within," I called, "other than Licinius Lysias, he of Turmus. Seize him, he of Turmus, and bring him forth, bound, and you may depart in peace."

"He is lying! It is a trick!" screamed Licinius.

"Do not move," I said to Tajima and Pertinax. Both had their blades drawn, were ready to spring within.

"Back! Back!" cried Licinius.

As I had hoped, his cohorts, mercenaries, as well, would be more willing to act on my offer than Licinius himself. What had they to lose, in their situation, and they might have much to gain.

There was a sudden vibration of a bow cable within and I heard a man scream with pain.

"Back, away, away, sleen!" screamed Licinius. There was then the clash of blades, briefly, fiercely, and I entered the stable, rushing within, followed closely by Tajima and Pertinax.

It took only a moment to see that Licinius Lysias was well worth his fee, which had doubtless been considerable.

I wondered from what purse it had been drawn.

I, and Pertinax and Tajima, halted our advance, abruptly.

A body lay to our left, a quarrel's fins protruding from its chest, and, toward the back of the stable, three other bodies lay, one still squirming. Licinius Lysias, like a wild beast, was half crouched down, regarding us, balefully. His sword was in his right hand and his left hand was tight on the right arm of a blond slave, now yanked to her knees. Hitherto she had been lying on her belly in the straw, her head turned to the side, in *bara,* her wrists crossed behind her, with her ankles crossed, as well. It is a common holding, and helplessness, position for a slave. In it, of course, she is positioned perfectly for a swift and secure binding.

Licinius drew the girl rudely before him, and his blade was at her throat.

Pertinax cried out in protest.

Licinius smiled. "Approach no more closely," he said.

I looked at the four fellows about, one struck by the quarrel, and three in the straw, the one now no longer moving.

"You are skilled," I said. "I do not see that you needed have feared a discourse with steel."

"Another step forward," said Licinius, "and she dies."

The girl whimpered, piteously, held well, helplessly, in place.

"She is only a slave," I pointed out.

"Apparently she is a punished high slave," said Licinius. "In any market she might bring two silver tarsks."

"She is not trained," I said.

"She has value," said Licinius.

"Certainly," I said, "perhaps as much as a silver tarsk."

"I think more," said Licinius.

It was true, of course, that she had some value to Lord Nishida, so much that he was even considering her as a possible gift for a *shogun*. Beyond this, of course, I knew that she was of some interest to Pertinax, at least as an attractive collar slut. Too, to any man, she would have some value as a property, as would any beautiful slave.

"Release her," I said, "and I will let you depart in peace."

"I do not believe you," he said.

"If you draw your blade across her throat," I pointed out, "you are a dead man."

"Put down your blades," said he, "or she is a dead slave."

"Very well," I said. I thrust my blade down, into the floor. Pertinax did so, as well, angrily. Tajima then did so, as well. In this fashion the hilts were within grasping distance.

"Step back," said Licinius.

We did so.

"She is pretty, is she not?" asked Licinius.

"Some might find her of interest," I said.

"I will need a tarn," he said, "a swift tarn, and none are to follow. And I will need binding fiber for the slave."

"You will take her with you?" I asked.

"Certainly," he said. "If I am followed, or intercepted, she dies."

"What will you then do with her?" I asked.

"What does one do with a slave?" he laughed.

Pertinax cried out, in anger.

"Of course," I said.

"Then I may sell her to the first merchant I meet," he said.

"You will not keep her?" I asked.

"Her coloring, and hair," he said, "suggests that she is cold."

This differs, of course, from woman to woman. Whereas there is a general conjecture that brunettes are the hottest and most helpless of gasping, moaning, begging slaves in a master's arms, I suspect this is because most slaves, simply, like most women, are brunettes. Blondes, on the other hand, suitably collared and properly mastered, I had discovered were as helpless, and as pathetically, defenselessly needful, and as whimperingly, uncontrollably, supplicatingly passionate, as their darker-haired sisters.

Women, their natures discovered, their natures revealed, are the properties of men.

Licinius pressed the razor's edge of his blade against the girl's throat. "Are you cold, my dear?" he inquired.

"No," she whimpered. "No!"

"No?" he said.

She cast a wild glance at Pertinax, and trembled.

"No," she said, "*—Master*!"

"Slave!" cried Pertinax, in fury.

"The tarn," said Licinius. "Quickly!"

"Very well," I said. "Remain here. I will see to the arrangements."

I then turned about, and left the stable, followed by Pertinax and Tajima.

Chapter Twenty-One

Licinius Lysias Takes His Departure from Tarncamp

"On your back, slave," said Licinius, "over the saddle, wrists and ankles crossed."

From the commanded distance, one of several yards, we watched Licinius fasten the slave over the forward capture leather of the saddle, tethering her crossed wrists to the saddle ring to his left, and then her crossed ankles to the saddle ring to his right.

Shortly she was secured in place.

I gathered that she was not the first capture he had helplessed in such a manner.

Pertinax was distraught.

Yet, too, his eyes glistened.

Perhaps he sensed what it might be to have a woman so before him, a tethered prize, supine, across his saddle. How far then seemed the former Miss Wentworth from the corridors of power, from the cabs of Manhattan, from the large, wood-paneled offices of the investment firm. Perhaps he wondered what it might be, were she his, and the binding fiber his own.

But I feared he did not understand that she was now a slave.

"I wish you well!" called Licinius, and drew on the one-strap.

"Lord Nishida will not be pleased," said Tajima, gloomily.

We watched the tarn ascend, and streak away, to the southeast.

"He escapes," said Pertinax, angrily.

"No," I said.

"No?" asked Pertinax.

"No," I said. "The tarn will return."

"I do not understand," said Tajima.

"You will see," I said.

Chapter Twenty-Two

Licinius Lysias Has Returned to Tarncamp; I Choose to Deal with Licinius Lysias in a Certain Manner; Saru Is to Be Taken from the Stable; I Return to My Hut, Followed Later by Pertinax

Growling, enraged, struggling, now awakened, Licinius Lysias, he of Turmus, fought the straps which held him, hand and foot, at our feet.

The slave, lying to the side, had not yet awakened.

"Licinius," I said, "had not eaten nor drunk in several Ahn. There was no food, no water, in the stable. He would be hungry. Worse, he would languish in thirst. Frightened, in his haste to put many pasangs between himself and the camp, he would hesitate to bring the tarn down. Too, he would suspect himself pursued. He would remain in the saddle at least until darkness."

"The bota at the saddle," said Tajima.

"Fresh, cool water," I said.

"And Tassa powder," said Tajima. "I have heard of it."

Tassa powder is a harmless, tasteless, swift-acting drug. It is commonly used in the taking of women. It might be introduced into the parties of maidens, into the private, candle-lit suppers of high-born beauties, into the beverages of inns or vendors. Commonly the women are innocent, guilty only of their unusual attractiveness, which will bring them to the slave block. To be sure, a woman might be less innocent, and might partake of, say, wine, with a stranger, one on whom she hopes to employ her wiles to her profit, one from whom she might hope to win some favor or advantage; perhaps she regales him with some contrived tale of hardship or woe, designed to elicit coins; perhaps she merely delights in tormenting a fellow, teasing and taunting him, leading him on to dazzling expectations and hopes which she has no intention of satisfying. She exercises her presumed beauty, seductive and mysterious within her robes and veils, to gratify her vanity, or even her dislike of males, such oafish, vile brutes. There are many ways, obviously, in which a woman can torture a male. In any event, it is not altogether unknown for such a woman to awaken later, helpless, gagged and bound, hand and foot, in a slave sack, being transported from her city. One interesting case involved a woman's intention to arrange for the capture and enslavement of a hated rival, but it was she instead who found herself stripped and chained, and was delivered to the rival as her serving slave. From a cage, naked, branded, her throat enclosed in her rival's collar, she was permitted to watch the ceremony of her rival's companionship with the male she had sought. Present, too, at the celebration, was he whom she had sought to enlist on her behalf, a friend unbeknownst to her from the childhood of the male companion. Drawn from the cage, she served her rival's feast, and, later, knelt before her, nostrils pinched shut, and head held back, was forced to imbibe not the festival wine, but bitter "slave wine," that she might, before her rival, be readied for slave usage, before being sent to the kitchen.

Similar reflections, one supposes, obtain in the cases of many women of Earth, luscious slave fruit harvested by Gorean slavers. It is not their fault that their intelligence is high, their features sensitive and exquisite, their figures shapely. Too, I suspect that the choices of slavers are not always clear to those lacking their training and skills. One supposes more is involved in such things than the turn of a hip, the rounding of a calf, or forearm, the slimness of an ankle, the slenderness of a throat, such things. Is it a way of speaking, an expression, a hesitation, a gesture, a turning of the head, a shyness, a glance, a subtle, revealing, furtive unwillingness to make eye contact when a certain word is spoken, what? There are a hundred subtle cues, readable by the experienced and skilled. Some can read the needful slave in a woman when the woman herself fears to recognize it, and, in any event, dares not reveal it. In any event, much diversity occurs in the markets, and a multitude of choices are available to buyers. Perhaps, on the whole, the women have little more in common than the fact that they are lovely, and will be sold.

To be sure, it is clearly not the case that every woman brought from Earth to the sawdust of the Gorean slave block is so innocent, guilty of no more, say, than her intelligence and beauty. Doubtless many women, both of Earth and of Gor, have been inserted on one acquisition list or another for no reason other than the fact that it has pleased some fellow that it should be so. Perhaps some behavior, or attitude, a rudeness, a glance, a hasty word, an insolence, or such, displeased a fellow, and it was decided then that the fair creature will pay for her indiscretion, the matter made clear to her while she is awaiting her first sale.

I had no doubt, for example, that it had pleased Thrasilicus to bring the former Miss Margaret Wentworth into a Gorean collar.

She had been, in my opinion, an excellent choice.

Given the number of Gorean mercenaries in the camp I had not doubted that Tassa powder would be available in the camp, and it had been. I had then had it introduced into the bota, where its presence could not be detected.

It was toward dark, and a fire burned nearby.

"How did you know the tarn would return?" asked Pertinax.

"When the rider lost consciousness, it was no longer controlled," I said. "It would then, having no guidance, return to its cot, perhaps even hastening, that it might not miss the evening feeding."

It had arrived, interestingly, some Ehn before the evening's distribution of meat.

We had then recovered Licinius and the slave, both unconscious.

The effect of Tassa powder is not felt for a time, but when it takes effect, it does so swiftly. Presumably Licinius would not have a weapon at the ready swiftly enough to slash the girl's throat. Even more likely, he would not think to do so. Goreans frown on gratuitous injury to a slave, as they would to any other animal. Too, if he had had time to think, which seemed unlikely, the last thing he would wish to risk would be falling into the hands of vengeful captors. He had lost. He would abide by the consequences.

"Licinius was kept in the saddle by the safety strap," said Pertinax.

"Of course," I said.

"And the slave was quite safe," said Tajima.

"Yes," I said, "secured in utter helplessness, as befits one such as she, merely a soft, smooth, shapely beast, nicely tethered, a bound *kajira*."

"She, too, was unconscious," said Tajima.

"I thought she would be," I said. "It did not really matter, of course, but I supposed he would give her of the water. Why should he not? Would she not be thirsty, as well? Are animals not watered?"

"Yes," said Tajima.

"Too," I said, "there was plenty. Also, water rounds the belly of a slave nicely, and freshens her appearance."

"True," said Tajima.

It was common, of course, to water women before their sale.

"How you think of her, how you speak of her!" protested Pertinax.

"She is a slave," I said. "And the sooner you learn to so think of her, and so speak of her, the better."

"Never!" said Pertinax.

"Did you not note," asked Tajima, "how she denied being cold, and addressed Licinius Lysias as 'Master'?"

"She was frightened," said Pertinax.

"Surely, even in fear, truth may be spoken," I said. And, I thought, though I did not bring this to the attention of Pertinax, a slave who is frightened is often afraid not to speak the truth. The Master may know the truth, and be examining her. Too, whereas a free woman may lie as profoundly and frequently as she wishes, a slave girl is forbidden to lie. A free woman may lie with impunity; a slave girl does not have this privilege. The slave girl fears to lie. Lying is not acceptable in a *kajira*. Punishments are terrible. She is not a free woman.

"Would you prefer," inquired Tajima, "that the slave was frigid?"

"Surely such things are a matter of private concern," said Pertinax.

"Not in a slave," I said. "In a slave they are quite public, like eye color and hair color. They affect her price."

"You would wish her to be frigid?" asked Tajima, politely.

"She is not a free woman," I reminded Pertinax.

"—I suppose it is better for her to be frigid," said Pertinax, "in order that she may remain her own woman, retain her self-respect and self-esteem, her dignity."

"The slave," I said, "is not her own woman. She is her master's woman. Too, whereas she may well think well of herself, rejoice in herself, celebrate herself, love herself, as well as the master, for how can one love another if one does not love oneself, and so on, she is not likely to have self-respect and self-esteem in the senses that I think you understand such things. She is, after all, an animal. And certainly she is not permitted dignity. She is a beautiful animal, and whereas she has far more attractions than, say, a she-tarsk, she has no more dignity than a she-tarsk."

"I see," said Pertinax.

"The slave is not a free woman," said Tajima. "She is to be hot, helplessly so. She must juice upon command. A touch readies her. At a snapping of the fingers, she must hasten to assume whatever attitudes or positions you wish. Indeed, she may assume them hoping that her master will see fit to caress her. Usually she conveys her desires by kneeling and nuzzling, and making tiny noises and whimpering, and kissing the feet and legs of the master, looking to him, lips parted, hoping for attention, such things. There are many variations. Slaves are very inventive, and very clever. Too, I assure you, my dear Pertinax, it is pleasant to have one in one's arms, squirming, and writhing, and gasping, and moaning, and crying out, and weeping, and begging, and yielding."

"They are not free women," I reiterated.

"Such things," said Pertinax, "are for low women, not for such as Miss Wentworth."

I smiled to myself. Pertinax did not know, as Cecily and I knew, that the stable grooms had well ignited, as it had amused them, and doubtless in accord with the instructions of Lord Nishida, slave fires in the belly of the former Miss Wentworth, at that time a stable slave at their disposal. Any woman in whose belly burn slave fires is a slave, and henceforth and thereafter can be but a slave. Ropes, straps, and chains were not the only bonds to which the former Miss Wentworth was now subject. A free woman might, of course, look upon the former Miss Wentworth and, in virtue of the brevity of a tunic, perhaps, or a brand, or a collar, easily see her as slave, but they might sense, too, to their jealous fury, that something less visible and far more profound was involved, that she now, supplicatingly and irremediably, belonged to men. In her belly, smoldering, ready to spring into flames, seldom far from the surface, was the heat of a slave, and of this, perhaps, a brand on her thigh, a collar on her neck, might be understood as little more than institutional tokens hinting at the possibility of a far deeper bondage.

No wonder they hated slaves with such vehemence.

How could they, free women, hope to compete in interest with a slave? A slave, of course, came with no companion dowry, no land, no wealth, no social or mercantile connections, but men, nonetheless, somehow, enjoyed having them at their feet.

"Perhaps," said Tajima.

"Certainly," said Pertinax, irritably.

"She is stirring," I noted. The effect of Tassa powder, on a smaller body, given identities of quantities, and such, is more lasting than on a larger body. Licinius had regained consciousness, in his bonds, something like a half of an Ahn past. Too, of course, I did not know the size of the draught accorded to the slave. She would not have been freed to drink, of course, but, tethered, supine, would have had the spike of the bota thrust between her teeth.

Licinius again fought his bonds.

He was well swathed with straps.

"Lord Nishida will have him crucified," said Tajima.

"For the sake of the Priest-Kings," said Licinius, addressing me, "use the sword, swiftly."

"I fear that is not practical," said Tajima, "for you are a spy, and traitor."

"No traitor!" he said.

"You wear the cavalry's gray, and betrayed it," said Tajima.

"I am in another's fee," he said.

"Whose?" I asked.

"I do not know," he said. "I was approached in Turmus."

"You may be tortured before you are crucified," said Tajima. "Perhaps that will to some extent refresh your memory."

"He would either die, or lie, to stop the pain," I said. "Too, I doubt he knows from what purse his gain was taken."

"I do not know," said Licinius.

"I believe him," I said. "Those who bought his services would be discreet in such a matter. A spy, he might be apprehended, and tortured. He can not reveal what he does not know."

"Use the sword, before they come for me," begged Licinius. "We are not of the Pani. It is a small favor to ask. Did I not attempt to escape? Slay me, and then loosen and discard the straps. None will know."

"I fear several would know," I said.

Licinius groaned.

"One is tied on the cross, closely," said Tajima. "It is hard to move. Thus, in even a short time there arises from within the constricted muscles a great deal of pain, even agony. Too, one languishes for two or three days, until one dies of the pain, or of dehydration. Sometimes one is given some fluid, that the agony may be prolonged."

"The sword! The sword!" begged Licinius.

"Impalement would be a Gorean way," I said to Tajima.

"That is barbarous," said Tajima.

"True," I said.

"Too, it would be too quick," said Tajima.

"It can last a long time," I said.

"Interesting," said Tajima.

"Yes," I said.

"The sword!" said Licinius.

"I have sent for *Ashigaru*," said Tajima. "They will take the prisoner in charge, and, too, will conduct Saru to the central camp."

The girl, freed of bonds, naked, in Lord Nishida's collar, lying nearby, the stains of the stable still on her, turned to her side, uneasily, and whimpered.

She was recovering from the effects of the Tassa powder.

I had noted some activity on her part a few Ehn ago.

One normally recovers slowly from the effects of Tassa powder, at least for a few minutes, and then one might, after a time, suddenly comprehending, awaken suddenly, hysterically, struggling, screaming, if one is not gagged. It is not uncommon for them to awaken in a stout, canvas slave sack, in which they can barely squirm, or bound hand and foot, say, on a carpet in an empty tent, or chained to a ring in the darkness. Such awakenings, too, may characterize Earth girls brought to Gor for the markets, as they are commonly sedated in tiered slave capsules for the journey from Earth to Gor. Many are even unaware of their journey, having perhaps been sedated in their own beds and then transported to Gor unconscious, only to awaken later in the pens, sometimes to the stroke of a slaver's lash.

Saru now had her hands under her, and lifted her body a little, and looked up at me.

"You are back now," I said. "You are near the stable, in the camp."

She looked at Licinius near her, bound. I do not know if she understood what, even in general, had happened. Presumably she would have thought Licinius had been intercepted, or overtaken. Then she went to her belly, her head turned toward us. I did not know if she were capable of kneeling now, as she might be unsteady from the effects of the drug.

"The water in the bota was drugged," I said. "The tarn returned."

"Are you all right?" asked Pertinax.

"Show no concern," I snapped. "Do you not know what she is?"

Saru regarded me, frightened. She averted her eyes. I sensed she knew what she was, even if Pertinax, in his naivety, did not.

"*Nadu*!" said Tajima, sharply.

The girl struggled to *nadu*, kneeling back on her heels, her head up, her back straight, the palms of her hands down on her thighs. She did not make eye contact with any of the free men, but kept her gaze forward.

It is a beautiful position.

"Split your knees," said Tajima.

"No!" said Pertinax.

"Now!" said Tajima.

The girl spread her knees.

"Wider!" said Tajima. She was, after all, a collar-girl.

The former Miss Wentworth complied, quickly, docilely, with Tajima's command. She had learned obedience to men, slave obedience, in the stable, at the hands of the grooms.

"Please!" protested Pertinax.

"Stay as you are," cautioned Tajima.

The slave remained in the adjusted *nadu*, as directed. It was a common form of *nadu*, one almost invariably expected of a particular sort of slave, the pleasure slave.

I had the sense she very much wanted to look to Pertinax, for whatever reason, perhaps to see how he might view her, as she was, as she had been positioned, but she did not dare to do so. In any event, she knew she was before him, in *nadu*.

"Whose prisoner am I?" asked Licinius.

"You are the prisoner of Lord Nishida," said Tajima.

"No," I said, "you are my prisoner."

"Captain?" asked Tajima.

"My prisoner," I said.

"*Ashigaru* will soon be here," said Tajima.

"Saru, I understand," I said, "is finished in the stable. *Ashigaru* will call for her, see that she is cleaned up, and conduct her to Lord Nishida."

"Yes," said Tajima.

"You have learned the lessons of the stable, I trust," I said to the slave.

"Yes, Master," she whispered.

"Do you wish to be returned to the stable?"

"No, Master!" she said softly, quickly.

"You will learn to wear tunics, and silks, and bangles," I said. "You will be taught to kneel and move. You may be perfumed and painted. You will be taught to please men. You will learn something of slave dance, and of the kisses of slaves. You will learn the use of your fingers, your hair, and tongue."

"Yes, Master," she said, shuddering.

"If you do poorly," I said, "you will be slain."

"Yes, Master," she whispered.

"The wholeness of your life," I said, "and your meaning, the fullness of it, all of it, and the very reason for your existence, and the only reason for your existence, is now to be a pleasure object for masters. You are an animal, and a property, only that, nothing more. Do you understand?"

"Yes, Master."

"You will now exist for, and only for, the service and pleasure of men. Do you understand?"

"Yes, Master," she said.

"Do you understand why?" I asked.

"Yes, Master," she said.

"Why?" I asked.

"Because I am a slave, Master," she said.

I turned to the prisoner. "Licinius Lysias," said I.

"Please, the sword!" he begged.

"You did not slay the slave," I said.

"I would have," he said, "had you not supplied my needs."

"Of course," I said, "but you did not do so."

"Is she so important?" asked Licinius.

"Not at all," I said, "but she is pretty, is she not?"

"Yes," he said.

"We are pleased to recover the goods," I said, regarding the slave.

"Perhaps then," said Licinius, hopefully, "the sword?"

"It must take great courage to spy here, in such a camp," I said.

"I was well paid," he said.

"I think you are very brave," I said.

"I wagered, I lost," he said.

"I think," I said, "you are an excellent swordsman." I recalled the fellows in the stable, his own cohorts, whom I had set to secure him, one struck by a quarrel, but three felled by steel. The skills involved in such a display are rare. It is difficult for even a fine swordsman to defend himself against even two assailants, for one need only engage, setting the target, so to speak, and the other strike. I would not, comfortably, have set Tajima against him, who was skilled, as I had determined in the *dojo.* And I certainly would not, at his present level of training, have allowed him to engage Pertinax, certainly not singly.

"I would not have cared to conduct the dialogue in steel with Bosk of Port Kar," he said.

It seemed he knew me.

I did not acknowledge this.

Tajima looked at me, puzzled. He had heard me referred to as Bosk of Port Kar, in the pavilion of Lord Nishida, but he knew me, primarily, surely, as Tarl Cabot, a tarnsman. I gathered he knew little or nothing of Bosk of Port Kar, or of the port itself.

"I accorded you an opportunity," I said, "to come forth from the stable, disarmed, and depart in peace."

"Surely it was a ruse," he said.

"But you did not come forth," I said.

"It seems the slave has value, after all," he smiled.

"Every pretty slave has value," I said. "This one might be worth as much as a silver tarsk."

A tremor coursed the body of the slave. A man was conjecturing what might be her sales price, what might bring her into the hands of anyone, anyone whomsoever, who possessed the requisite coin or coins.

"Two," suggested Licinius.

There are few things which so convince a woman that she is a slave, as to hear her value candidly discussed, in terms of prices, markets, and such. She then has a better sense of what she is worth, as what she is, as a collar property, to masters. A free woman, of course, is priceless, and thus, in a sense, without value. A slave, on the other hand, is not priceless, and thus has an actual value, a particular value, usually what men will pay for her. Slave girls, in their vanity, for they, as other women, are vain creatures, often compete on the slave block, each trying to bring a price higher than the others. Also, of course, there is a supposition that the higher the price the wealthier the master, and thus, hopefully, the easier and more comfortable will be the girl's bondage. On the other hand, it is not unoften the case that the girl so purchased will find herself expected to do the work of, and supply the pleasure of, several slaves. It is not unusual, too, when a slave is introduced into a house, no matter what her purchase price may have been, that she will be bound and whipped, this to let her know that in that house she is truly a slave, and no more than a slave. Often, interestingly, the plainer girls purchased by the less well-fixed masters enjoy a bondage which, though strict and absolutely uncompromising, as is the Gorean way, might be the envy of many slaves who went for higher prices. The slave is grateful for the master, and the master is grateful for the slave. The relationship of female slave and male master, though one established, sanctioned, and enforced by law, is founded obviously on one common in nature, that of, so to speak, the conquered, possessed female and the conquering, possessing male. Indeed, legal bondage is an institutionalization of, and an enhancement of, a natural relationship, the male who, in a very real sense, owns, and the female who, in a very real sense, is owned, as much as a bow or spear. The rightfulness and naturalness of the relationship, so sanctioned by nature, and a thousand generations of selection, often leads to love. It is not unknown, accordingly, for a master and slave to discover, one day, and often sooner than later, that they are in love, that they are now love master and love slave. Let him beware now that he does not become easy with his girl. Indeed, she does not wish that, for her love for him is that of a slave.

"Surely you were not serious, Tarl Cabot, tarnsman," said Tajima. "This man would have slain Lord Nishida, he fled, he brought foes to our camp, he is a spy, he fought against us!"

"You would have permitted me to depart?" said Licinius.

"Yes," I said.

"Surely not!" exclaimed Tajima.

"If so," said Licinius, "I beg the sword, its quickness, its mercy!"

"No," said Tajima.

"Will the knife do?" I asked Licinius.

"Surely!" he cried, gratefully.

"Never!" said Tajima. "What are you doing?" he said.

I had slashed away the straps binding the ankles of Licinius, and he struggled to his feet.

"Into the trees," I instructed him, indicating the direction.

Gratefully he turned, stumbling toward the woods.

"Wait for the *Ashigaru,*" said Tajima.

"I dislike ugly deaths," I said to him.

"Tajima's hand was on the hilt of his gently curved sword.

"Would you draw against me?" I asked.

"No," said Tajima. He removed his hand from the hilt of the sword.

I knew he did not fear to do so, even though he were newer to the roads of war than I. I was pleased he was unwilling to do so. How mighty, I thought, are the bonds of friendship. How sturdy stands, too, the banner of honor, even in the tempest, even on trembling ground.

"I must report this to Lord Nishida," said Tajima.

"I know," I said.

"Make it last," said Tajima. "Let it be a thousand cuts. Perhaps Lord Nishida will be satisfied."

"It is I who must be satisfied," I said.

"He is your prisoner," granted Tajima.

I then, the knife still in hand, followed Licinius into the darkness of the woods. He had not run, but was waiting for me.

"Thank you, Warrior," he said. "Be swift, if you would."

"You are unarmed," I informed him. "You are far from villages, even huts. And you know not their locations, or your directions. There are larls in the woods but, hopefully, they are now well fed, and sleeping. You are without weapons and supplies. Many are the dangers in the forest. I do not expect you to survive."

"What are you doing?" he asked, wonderingly.

"I am cutting you free," I said.

"Free?" he whispered.

"Others will think you slain in the woods," I said. "By the time they search for a body, you should be well away."

He moved his arms, and rubbed his wrists.

"You would have let me depart in peace?" he said. "Truly?"

"Yes," I said.

"Why?" he asked.

"I gave you my word," I said.

"I do not understand," he said.

"It is called honor," I said. "Now, begone, quickly!"

"I will survive," he said.

"Perhaps," I said.

He then turned and disappeared into the darkness, between the trees.

In a few moments I had returned to Tajima, Pertinax, and the slave.

"Tarl Cabot, tarnsman," said Tajima, "your knife is not bloody."

"It seems not," I said, and sheathed it.

"Perhaps you broke his back or neck, or strangled him," said Tajima.

"Perhaps," I said.

"I will send *Ashigaru* to recover the body," he said.

"Have them wait until morning," I said.

"Lord Nishida will not be pleased," said Tajima.

"Have them wait until morning," I said.

"Very well, Tarl Cabot, tarnsman," said Tajima.

I then turned to the slave, who was still kneeling, slimly erect, hands down on thighs, head up, in *nadu*. She had not been given permission to break position.

"You were spared," I said to her. "You could have had your throat cut, and been thrust from the saddle to the forests below, shortly after the flight had begun, as soon as it became clear there was no obvious pursuit. You were extra weight for the tarn to carry and would thus reduce its speed and shorten its range."

"Yes, Master," she said, not daring to look at me.

"But you were spared."

"Yes, Master," she said.

"Though only a slave," I said.

"Yes, Master."

I did not tell her that now, too, another had been spared.

"You must clearly understand," I said, "that you needed not have been spared."

She gasped, in sudden terror.

"No," I said, "slave."

"Yes, Master," she whispered.

Her situation, of course, had been unusual, for, after the first few moments of her flight, she would have been little more than a hampering burden to the fugitive, and yet he had not disposed of her. She was fortunate. Licinius Lysias had spared her. I had spared him.

Normally, of course, as an animal, and booty, the female slave on Gor has little or nothing to fear as power arrangements and assortments are determined at the points of weapons. She will only have a new rope on her neck, be whip-herded with others on an unfamiliar road, toward an unfamiliar destination, and market, will only find herself in a new cage, pen, or kennel, will have on her neck a new collar, and such things. Indeed, when a city falls, amidst its burning and sacking, free women will often strip and collar themselves, to escape the sword. When it is later discovered they are not branded, they are often severely whipped, but the blood lust, by then, is commonly dissipated, and they are spared. To be sure, they will soon be put under the iron, have transition collars hammered about their necks, and put with other female slaves who will doubtless have their vengeance upon them, switching them and using them as their own serving slaves, as though they might be the slaves of slaves. How eager then the new female slaves, former free women, will be, to be sold, and put their lips to the feet of a male master.

I stepped away from the slave.

"I am thinking of Cecily," I said to Pertinax.

"Tarl Cabot, tarnsman, is heated, and aroused," said Tajima.

I nodded. That is not unusual, of course, after battle. It is common then, when the blood has been shed, when the weapons are quiet, when one lifts one's head and surveys the field, and realizes one is alive, to think of the softness of women, eagerly, even angrily and aggressively. Are they not the prizes of battle? Are they not flesh loot? Are they not, so to speak, lovely morsels, to be seized, to be aligned, to be examined, to be selected forthwith, to satisfy the appetites of masters? After the suppers' desserts, surely then the slaves who served it. When one has survived it is natural to think of pleasures and playthings. There is a Gorean saying that the female slave is the warrior's prize, and toy. The needs of males are many and they have their various assuagements, for hunger food, for thirst drink, for pleasure the slave.

I felt it well to remove myself from the proximity of Saru.

She was attractive, and a slave, and I was no more than what I was, a male in the vicinity of a woman who perhaps did not even understand the impact and lure of what she was, a female slave, an impact and lure so much more powerful than that of a mere free woman, indeed, a slave who might not, as yet, even understand fully the meaning of the collar on her neck.

It could, of course, be soon taught to her.

No, I thought, I must leave.

I had little doubt that Cecily would be still within the rope circle, though perhaps now asleep, with some others. Most, presumably, would have been taken from the rope by now. As mentioned, when the slaves are awake, they must be within the circle, grasping the rope. Later, to be sure, Ahn afterward, if not extracted from the circle, the same rope is usually looped and knotted about the slave's waist. The effect then is rather like a circle which contains a number of smaller circles, each of which encircles the waist of a slave.

I looked about.

A tharlarion snorted nearby.

Beast by beast, over the past Ahn, several of the stampeded tharlarion, now slowed or milling, even grazing, many hemmed in by trees, and snared by brush, had been gathered in. I doubted that more than seven or eight were still missing. Tharlarion are not sleen, panthers, or larls. They leave an easy trail to follow. I did not doubt but what they would be eventually found and returned to the stable, perhaps, with some luck, by noon of the next day.

I looked about.

There was little to do now, here, by the stable.

I was thinking of Cecily. A woman in a collar is very easy to think of. Indeed, it is hard not to think of them, as they are beautiful, and slaves. How lovely to return to one's domicile and be greeted by an eager, ready slave, who kneels, and looks up, happily, into one's eyes, and then, humbly, lowers her head, before her master. Perhaps she lifts her small wrists to you, hoping that you will bind, or bracelet, them. Slaves wish to be in the power of their masters, and know themselves within the power of their masters. Soon, with your permission she is in your arms, her lips to yours.

There was to be a feast tomorrow, after the day's work, as Lord Nishida had suggested. It would probably take place toward evening, even after dusk. After that, the next morning, I had gathered the camp would be abandoned. The plans of

Lord Nishida, it seemed, given the discovery of the camp, were to be advanced.

What might be involved in these plans was not clear to me, but I was confident they involved, ultimately, no local objective.

Given the rough, narrow road leading from the camp, cut from the forest itself, muddy, unpaved, deeply rutted, the wagon loads of timber and planking transported almost daily upon it, its direction and such, to the southeast, I conjectured that it would lead to a waterway. There was no large town within hundreds of pasangs. The waterway would drain to Thassa.

Pertinax had spoken, long ago, of the Alexandra.

Pani were unusual in known Gor.

The waterway would provide access to Thassa.

We saw some torches, down the road, approaching, from the central camp.

"*Ashigaru,*" said Tajima.

"They will be coming for Licinius and you, Saru," I said. "They will not find Licinius, and will be dissuaded to search for his body until tomorrow, given the darkness, and such. On the other hand they will find you."

"Yes, Master," she said.

"Do not call men 'Master'," said Pertinax, angrily.

"I must," she said, "Master. I am a slave and must address all free men as 'Master', and all free women as 'Mistress'."

I was glad Saru understood this. To be sure, I suppose she had encountered few free women since Earth. She may have encountered some on Gor, of course, earlier, when she had thought herself to be masquerading as a slave, before arriving in the northern forests. I supposed, then, she might have, perhaps to her amusement, used the term "Mistress" to some free women, enjoying the supposed pretense. I gathered she had done this well. Had she not she would probably have been leaned against a wall, the palms of her hands on the wall, and had her calves switched. At the time, of course, as she had been entered earlier on an acquisition list, she had actually been a slave, unbeknownst to herself. Had she realized that, it might have given a very different cast to her docility. Indeed, she would have been a slave, though not yet a collected slave, weeks, or more, before her transition to Gor. Thus, technically, in that time she should have been exhibiting deference to the free, addressing free men as "Master," free women as "Mistress," and so on. She could not be blamed for this lapse, of course, as she was at that time unaware she was a slave.

I supposed that Mr. Gregory White, now by choice Pertinax, who long ago in the offices, aisles, and corridors of the investment firm might have furtively, yearningly, stolen glimpses of she whom he had taken at the time to be the ambitious, sophisticated, insolent, out-of-reach Miss Margaret Wentworth, so far above him, might have viewed her differently, rather differently, had he realized at the time that she was in actuality no more than a female slave.

And so a slave, how that had been concealed!

And so she, in all her smugness, pretensions, pettiness, and vanity, had gone about, from day to day, conducting herself as usual, taking her cabs, dining in her restaurants, cultivating her potential clients, and such, thinking herself a free woman, not knowing herself only a slave, that she should be fittingly on her knees, head to the floor, before them. Did she not know the slave rope, invisible, was already upon her? It required only that it, at the convenience of masters, be tightened. Had White known this, might he not have conjectured seizing her from behind, holding her helplessly before him, and whispering in her startled ear, "Slave."

And so her slavery had been concealed, even from herself.

How many women, I wondered, even aside from acquisition lists, and such, are slaves, and do not know they are slaves.

Or do they know themselves slaves, lacking only a master?

How, I thought, might a civilization distort and pervert truth! How it can veil nature and conceal reality! How it can demean one thing and bedeck another, how it can in so many ways flee the serious, mighty, and worthy, and embrace the insignificant, the pathetic, the absurd, and ignoble.

How it can lie, say, about men, and about women.

They are not the same.

She had, as far as I knew, encountered no free women since coming to the northern forests. Few free women frequent the forest. The forest is dangerous, and the men in the vicinity, hungering for slaves, would soon have them in collars.

"Let her do so," I said to Pertinax. "She must."

He looked at her, irritably. She was small before him, slight, lovely, desirable, and, deliciously obvious, as she was in *nadu,* a female.

"Very well," said Pertinax, angrily. But he then addressed himself to the slave, angrily. "But do not so address me," he said.

Saru nearly lost position.

Clearly she was uncertain, confused, frightened.

"She must," I said. "You are a free man. She would be terrified not to do so."

"She is a slave," said Tajima. "Understand that. Be kind."

"Slave," I said. "Look up, now, meet the eyes of Master Pertinax, good, and now address him as 'Master'."

Her eyes met those of Pertinax. "Master," she said.

I thought that would be a moment that neither of them would forget.

Pertinax turned away, abruptly, angrily. "Very well," he said.

The former Miss Wentworth, toward whom he entertained such mixed and ambivalent feelings, and intense feelings, kneeling before him in *nadu,* knees split, back straight, had lifted her head to his, and, tears in her eyes, with trembling lip, as the slave she was, addressed him, appropriately, as "Master."

I sensed this was one of the most thrilling, disturbing moments in his life, and I sensed that it was one of the most meaningful, and thrilling, moments in her life.

What man does not wish to be addressed as "Master" by a beautiful slave, and particularly by one he wishes he owned, one for whom he languishes? And what woman, kneeling before a man whose slave she wishes to be, does not long to call him "Master"?

I saw he was unwilling to see her as what she was now, a slave.

"Break position," he said.

She went to all fours, looking up at him.

"Why did you have her break position?" I asked, innocently.

"She makes me uneasy, like that," he said.

"I understand," I said. In *nadu,* as the back is straight, the shoulders are back, and this accentuates the delights of the bosom. The widening of the knees suggests the vulnerability of the slave and displays the softness of the open, exposed thighs. The placement of the palms down on the thighs, apart and down, to the sides, suggests that they will be held as they are, and thus are not permitted to fend or thwart a caress. The kneeling position itself is symbolic of submission. The head's being up displays the beauty of the master's property, the beauty of the features, the slenderness of the neck, and such, and, too, of course, in this attitude, the badge of his ownership, her collar, is well exhibited. To be sure, this can differ from master to master. Some prefer the slave's head to be submissively lowered. The slave's eyes may or may not be permitted to meet the master's eyes without permission. This differs from master to master.

It will doubtless be recalled that Saru's head had been shaved before she was consigned to the grooms in the stable, to assume the duties of a stable slut. That had been several weeks ago and there was now a blondish scrub of hair on her head. I hoped her master, Lord Nishida, would now permit her hair to grow. To be sure, the decision was his.

"Would you like to have a tunic, Saru," I asked, "or perhaps a camisk, or a *ta-teera*?"

"Oh, yes, Master," she said. "Yes, yes, yes!"

"I think it may be permitted," I said.

"I hope so, Master!" she said.

It is interesting, I thought. Though a slave, technically, is not permitted modesty, few slaves are not eager for the merest shred of clothing, at least in public. In private, they may be limited to their collars. Clothing, of course, is at the discretion of the master. Sometimes a slave must perform well, even to be granted a string and slave strip. Many slaves, for example, in the morning, must have the master's permission before dressing. "Master, may I clothe myself?" Such things help the girl keep in mind that she is a slave. To be sure, few slaves are likely to forget that. Occasionally they may be whipped to remind them, and they may even, themselves, sometimes request the whip, that they be reassured of their master's attention, and the reality of their bondage.

As there were no free women in the camp, captured from the enemy, and such, I supposed the slaves would be permitted clothing, such as it might be, while serving the feast.

Lord Nishida, I surmised, had been amusing himself at the expense of Pertinax, when he had suggested that Saru might serve nude. There seemed little point now in denying her garmenture, as she had, by now, presumably, been properly instructed as to the nonacceptability of her former attitudes and behaviors, now that she had learned the lessons of the stable, now that she had begun to understand what it was to have a collar on her neck. Her *kajira* journey had been well begun. If he did have her serve nude, I conjectured it would be merely in order, for his amusement or his information, to observe Pertinax. Would Pertinax avoid looking upon her? Would he look upon her, and, if so, how, obliquely or openly, and, if openly, with disapproval or with, say, the unfeigned interest and delight of a Gorean master? Masters think nothing of nudity in slaves. They are familiar with it. For example, that is how women are sold. They may, however, revel in it, as in admiration of the lines of any fine animal, and, of course, they are likely, given the commonality of species and their maleness, to find it potently arousing, and sometimes irresistibly so. In any event, the matter was up to Lord Nishida. I expected him to have Saru serve clothed. She might, of course, at as little as an expression or gesture, have to reveal her beauty.

"You would like some clothing?" I asked.

"Yes, Master, yes!" she said, fervently.

I smiled to myself.

Usually the clothing permitted to slaves was such as was fit for slaves. Usually there was not much to it, and it was designed to leave few of the slave's charms to conjecture. The slave did not realize, it seemed, that in many slave garments the slave might seem more naked, given its judicious suggestions and such, than if she were literally stripped. Some new slaves must be whipped from the house, to embark upon an errand, so terrified they are at the scantiness of the garmenture in which they have been placed. Certainly it is a change from the stiff, heavy, ornate, cumbersome robes of concealment, and the multitudinous hoods and veils, of the high cities.

I wondered what Saru would look like in armlets and anklets, in bangles, belled and necklaced, perhaps in a swirl of diaphanous, scarlet dancing silk.

I was sure she might please the senses of a man, perhaps even those of a *shogun*.

I suspected that it was for such a purpose, ultimately, that she had been brought to Gor.

The *Ashigaru* approaching from the central camp were now closer.

Saru, on her hands ands knees before Pertinax, cast a glance toward the approaching torches. I sensed she was desperate, and had no idea when she might, again, if ever, have a moment with him. I recalled how she had wanted him to call upon her in the stable, and recalled that he had not chosen to do so. I was sure that she, now well knowing herself a slave, wanted to nestle, collared, subdued, submitted, obedient, in his arms. I suspected she had dreamed of him, even long ago, on Earth. She had selected him, as I recalled, to accompany her to Gor. Too, I had no doubt he had found her excruciatingly attractive, even on Earth, even as a free woman. It was not difficult then to conjecture that he would now find her a thousand times more attractive, and in a thousand ways, now that she was a female slave.

"What are you doing!" he cried, in anger.

Saru was on her belly before him, her hands on his ankles, her lips pressed to his feet, weeping, covering them with piteous kisses.

Pertinax drew back, in fury.

She lifted her head to him. "I want you as my master!" she sobbed. "Be my master!"

"You do not know what you are saying!" he exclaimed. "What is wrong with you? You are of Earth! You are a woman of Earth! Where is your pride, your dignity! Be ashamed of yourself. Shame! Shame! Get up! Get up! You make me sick! You are disgusting! Disgusting!"

She put her head down to the dirt, crying.

"She is not a free woman," I said to Pertinax. "Do not address her as such."

"Can you not accept her femininity," asked Tajima, "her needs, her womanhood, her helplessness, her defenselessness, her desire to submit?"

"Do not impose your values upon her," I said. "Do you want

her to lie? She is a woman. Why can you not accept her for what she is, not what you feel she should be? Are you only interested in women who have adopted, who have yielded to, who have succumbed to, the masculine values prescribed for them by an odious, inhuman, unnatural, self-alienating culture?"

Pertinax regarded me angrily.

"She is not a man, even if you demand it of her," I said. "Let her be what she is, a woman, and a slave."

"Let him alone," said Tajima. "He understands nothing of these things. Let him belittle and shame her, humiliate and scorn her, if it pleases him. Is it not amusing, an exercise in power, though one somewhat cruel? Let him see to it that she is distraught, confused, uncertain, and miserable. She is only a slave, after all. Is this not a pleasant, gratifying torture to which he may subject her? Let him strive to deny her to herself, if he wishes. Let him demand such a denial of her. Let him disrupt and divide her. Let him torture her, as he will. Let him attempt to estrange her from her deepest being and needs, if it pleases him. He is, after all, Master, and she is merely slave. Let him strive then, by tearing and torture, to remake her, in an alien image, in his own image, to force her to discard and surrender herself, and hide herself behind a wall on which he would prefer to look."

I supposed that the former Miss Wentworth, for years on Earth, had longed for what she felt was missing in her life, for the precious, incredible womanhood which she had only recently found, on Gor, and she was now, it seemed, to be shamed and punished for discovering on an alien world what had eluded her for so long on her native sphere.

"She is scum," said Pertinax.

"Yes, Master," wept the slave, at his feet.

"Slut! Slut!" he said.

"Yes, Master," she wept.

"But surely," I said, "you find this slut, this bit of scum, of some interest. I suspect you would not mind owning it."

"'Owning'!" cried Pertinax.

"Precisely," I said, "owning."

"She is worthless," he exclaimed.

"She was worthless on Earth," I said. "She is not worthless

in a collar. She would go for a price, perhaps better than a silver tarsk."

"Worthless!" he insisted.

"Doubtless worthless as a female slave is worthless," I said, "but some men find them of interest."

"Worthless!" he sobbed.

"But pretty," I said.

"Yes," he said, angrily.

"And on Gor," I said, "you can buy such things."

"I think you want her, my dear Pertinax," said Tajima, "and as what she is, and should be, a slave."

"Is that not what you have always wanted," I asked, "from the first moment you laid eyes on her, her as a slave?"

"I think your desire was so fierce," said Tajima.

"Was it not?" I asked.

"She belongs to Lord Nishida," he said, angrily.

"Yes," said Tajima, "and she was selected with care, in compliance with a very special order, one requisitioning a particular sort of slave, one worthy of a being a suitable gift for a *shogun*."

"More is involved in these matters," I said to Pertinax, "than intelligence, a lovely figure, a particular coloring of hair and eyes, and such."

"What?" asked Pertinax, uneasily.

"Dispositions, needs, and latencies," I said. "Slavers are alert to such things."

"I do not understand," said Pertinax.

"They can read the language of the body and eyes, and voice," I said, "in general, and in given contexts, and situations, sometimes even contrived stimulus situations."

"I do not understand," he said.

"Perhaps the woman hears the word 'slave' or 'collar' spoken in her vicinity, seemingly innocently, seemingly inadvertently, it having supposedly nothing to do with her. But someone notes her subtlest response, the slightest alertness, or fear, or hesitation, or such. Perhaps a *kajira* on Earth, owned by a slaver, briefly, so briefly, by design, arranges a scarf or such and, for an instant, the other woman glimpses a collar. What is her reaction? Is it such as to suggest that she, too, belongs in a collar and, perhaps in her fantasies, has had one about her neck, snapped shut, locked? Perhaps the *kajira* sees the woman's awareness, and smiles shyly, even apologetically, before adjusting the scarf, and hurrying away, leaving the woman standing there, astonished, unsteady. Is the glance of the *kajira,* radiant in her bondage, a hint, or an encouragement, or reassurance? Perhaps she hopes that the other woman, whom she instantly likes, will be found suitable, will qualify for the chains of a slave. Does that glance not say to the woman, however briefly, "I am happy. Are you my sister?" A slaver, of course, perhaps from over a newspaper, or one standing nearby, perhaps on a subway, clinging to a support, or one apparently merely waiting in a corridor or doorway, notes the woman's reaction. Does it say, in effect, "I, too, belong in a collar. I wish I knew such a man, a man such as you know, lovely sister, one strong enough to put me in a collar. I am a woman. I belong in a collar. I want one!" Too, of course, there are such obvious things as the natural feminine grace of the woman, the width of her love cradle, the betraying movements of her body within her garmenture, the noted movements of her thighs, and such."

"The *Ashigaru* are here," said Tajima.

"Wait, a moment," I said to them.

"It is dark," said Tajima to the officer with the men. "In the morning you may search for the body of a scoundrel, in the forest, nearby."

They would not be likely, of course, to find it.

The officer looked to the prostrate slave.

"Wait, a bit," I said.

Saru struggled to her knees, before Pertinax.

"I have failed to please you," she said.

He looked down on her, angrily. "Are you a slave, truly?" he asked.

I smiled to myself. There was clearly no question about the legalities of the matter. His question, I gathered, went far beyond legalities.

"Yes, Master," she said, not looking up at him.

"Truly?" he asked.

"Yes, Master," she said. "A slave may not lie."

"I find you disgusting," he said.

"Yes, Master," she said. "Thank you, Master."

"You are covered with dirt," he said, "and sweat dampens and streaks the dirt. Tears stain your cheeks. Your body is soiled and foul. You stink."

"She smells of the stable," I said.

"I no longer respect you," he said to her.

"I do not want to be respected," she whispered. "I am a slave. I am not to be respected, no more than a tarsk. But I do want to be owned, and mastered."

"You will be," said Tajima.

I gestured to the officer of the *Ashigaru.*

He approached the slave and indicated that she should stand. He then said, very sharply, "*Lesha*!"

Instantly the girl turned away from him, lifted her head, turned it to the left, and placed her small wrists, crossed, behind her back.

Pertinax uttered an angry sound.

In a moment the girl's wrists were thonged together, tightly, behind her back. A leash was then snapped about her neck, and she was led from the fire, toward the road, toward the central camp.

Pertinax went to the wall of the stable, and, in fury, sobbing, struck it with his fists. There would be dried blood there in the morning.

I then bid goodnight to Tajima and returned toward the central camp, and the hut I shared with Pertinax. Near the hut I removed Cecily, who was asleep, from the rope circle, and carried her, gently, to the hut. I did not awaken her. I put her on a slave mat, at my side. Her tunic had slipped up, about her waist, and I drew it down a bit, and smoothed it. She was an incredibly beautiful slave. She had originally been selected by Priest-Kings to tempt me to the subversion of my honor, and had been, accordingly, with all their wisdom and expertise, chosen with exquisite care to attain that end. She had been chosen to appeal to me in ways of which I had not even dreamed, and, by a parity of design, her own needs and desires had been taken into consideration, and mercilessly exploited, as well, and unscrupulously so, in that she had been selected as one who by her own nature would find herself similarly attracted, and, indeed, helplessly so, and, indeed, as might be a slave before her master. In short, by the devious machinations of Priest-Kings, to forward their own dark purposes, we had been matched to one another, superbly, and helplessly. The plan of Priest-Kings would have succeeded, sooner or later, I was sure, had it not been for the intervention of Kurii, in a raid on Gor's Prison Moon. She was, of course, in the beginning, when we first became acquainted, in our imprisonment, a free woman. Had she not been, my honor would have not been the least in jeopardy. She was English, as I, and was a student at an Oxford College, as I had once been. She was unusually intelligent, and extraordinarily beautiful. She had been spoiled, and she derived from a wealthy mercantile background with pretensions, mistaken pretensions it seemed, to an aristocratic origin. To be sure, a lovely ancestress of hers had apparently been selected out from the fields in the Fifteenth Century to be a stirrup mistress to a knight, but the resultant, oblique line, as it turned out, was without spurs. This fact, however, seems to have been regarded as negligible to the line in question. It was not important, it seems, that a snapping of fingers might have once brought the lips of a low-born lass to a knight's boot. In any event, she had been haughty, arrogant, supercilious, refined, and insolent. She had despised men, though on some level had found them fascinating and troubling, and had enjoyed leading them on and tormenting them with her wit and beauty. Too, however, she had had strong slave urges, something of which the Priest-Kings undoubtedly took note. Later, on the Steel World to which the raiding Kurii took us, I brought her into my collar.

I regarded her, but would not awaken her.

Her intelligence was high. Her features and figure were delightful. Her slave needs were overpowering. The slave fires were always ready to spring into flame in her belly. In a fair market I thought she might go for two tarsks or more. Under a man's touch she was helpless. I was pleased to own her.

She was tired. I would not put her to use.

Pertinax had not yet returned to the hut.

I had little doubt he was wandering about, angrily, trying to sort out a variety of thoughts and feelings, most of which were doubtless troubling. I trusted he would remember to retrieve his Jane, the former Lady Portia Lia Serisia of Sun Gate Towers, near the Street of Coins in Ar, from the rope circle. I did not think she would be pleased with his lateness.

I dropped off to sleep, but later, I am not sure how much later, but it was not yet light, Pertinax returned to the hut, his Jane following him. She was modestly tunicked. To be sure, her neck was in his collar. I wondered if I should have purchased her for him.

I gave no indication that I was awake.

She seemed in a foul mood and Pertinax, of course, given the events of the day, and particularly of the evening, was possibly even less benignly disposed.

"Where were you?" she asked. "What kept you? I spent Ahn in the rope circle! My hands were raw from standing and clutching the rope, under the eyes of the *Ashigaru*. Too, they dared to look at my legs and ankles! How could they help themselves? You have them bared, you brute! Then we were knelt and we must still cling to the rope! Ahn later our waists were encircled, and we were permitted to recline! Only then we were given gruel and water! I was the last to be freed! The very last! The *Ashigaru* had even left! Why were you so late! You are never again to keep me waiting in such a fashion!"

"Were you given permission to speak?" he inquired. There was a quiet menace in his tone, and I hoped that the slave was aware of that.

"What?" she said, uncertainly.

He leaped to her and seized her collar, and, by it, with two hands, he held her.

She regarded him, frightened. Never before had he behaved in such a fashion.

He lifted the collar, as he held it, with both hands, and it was tight under her chin, and then she was lifted rudely, stretched, standing, before him. She was then straight before him. She could not get her feet fully on the ground, but, at best, her toes. It was clear she was frightened, and quite uncomfortable. In this fashion a girl may be reminded that she wears a collar, a slave collar.

"Master?" she whispered.

He then removed his hands from the collar, and she stood before him, uncertain, frightened, and docile.

He then put his left hand in her hair, tightly, and, measuring her, carefully, deliberately, cuffed her once, and then again, once with the front of his hand, and then once with the back of his hand. Her head snapped back, and forth. Her eyes were confused, and frightened.

He then turned her about, and tied her hands together behind her back. He then turned her about, again, so that she faced him.

"Master?" she asked.

"Oh!" she gasped, turned and twisted by the force of it, and her tunic had been torn from her.

He then threw her to her knees before him, fetched a whip, and thrust it to her lips.

Instantly, terrified, she pressed her lips to it, kissing it, desperately, fervently, placatingly.

He then cast the whip aside, dragged her on her knees by the hair to a slave mat, and threw her back upon it, supine.

She looked at him, in awe, frightened. "Master!" she exclaimed.

I smiled, for I knew then that she knew she had a master.

He then put her to his pleasure.

Later, toward morning, her hands still bound behind her, she began to thrash, and beg.

I decided that it had not been a mistake to purchase her for him.

Women, I recalled, were the prize of the warrior, and his toy.

"That lovely brat still has to learn her collar," I had said. She had known herself in a collar, of course, but perhaps she had not realized that the collar of Pertinax in which she had found herself was a true collar, a slave collar.

I heard her whimpering and moaning.

She now knew.

She was lovely.

She was no longer a brat.

She was now a slave.

There might be some consequences for Pertinax, I supposed, given the events of the night. I supposed he might find himself, now and again, perhaps sometimes inconveniently, importuned by a needful slave. But then one can always thrust them away, or cuff them from one's thigh.

One does what one wishes, for they are only slaves.

In any event, Pertinax had now sensed what it might be, to be a woman's master.

I had no doubt, despite what he might say, despite possibly even hysterical asseverations to the contrary, that he wanted Saru, and wanted her as what she was, and should be, a slave.

It was light when Cecily, beside me, awakened.

I felt her lips, soft, and tender, on my body.

Pertinax and Jane were asleep, Jane still bound.

"Very well," I whispered to Cecily.

Chapter Twenty-Three

The Feast; Some Leave the Feast Early

"Serve him," I called to Saru, indicating Pertinax.

She was some yards away, amongst the tables, clutching her vessel of ka-la-na.

She sparkled, having been fiercely scrubbed by reluctant slaves. She had been immersed, entirely, more than once, in a hot tub, and thrice oiled, and strigiled, and toweled. Her body, in effect, had been scoured, and her brush of blond hair, I was pleased to note, had not, in the zeal of the slaves, been pulled from her head. It was still wet. She was clothed, in a brief, pressed, white tunic. Her legs were lovely. I congratulated Thrasilicus on his selection, his choice, his taste.

The former Miss Margaret Wentworth, now Saru, was a beautiful animal, exquisitely featured and figured. She would look well on a chain, at the foot of a master's couch. I thought she had the makings of an excellent slave. Even now I thought she could please the senses of a *shogun*, and, properly trained, might be a suitable gift for one. Too, of course, given her coloring, of skin, hair, and eyes, she would make an unusual gift, perhaps one of great value. I supposed one such as a *shogun* would suffer no dearth of collar-girls, say, women purchased in one market or another or captured from alien houses, but I supposed she would be rare, if not unique, amongst his female possessions. I speculated that she might be in some danger if she were felt as a threat by the other girls, for the attention, and favor, of the master, but this sort of thing is not unusual in the slave quarters. The slave's best defense against discrimination and abuse, of course, is to endeavor to be so prized by the master that her sister slaves fear to attack her, steal her food, and such. A mere hint dropped by a preferred slave may bring a rival to the whipping ring, something the rival is not likely to soon forget. The favorite, incidentally, is not likely to be "first girl," that slave placed in charge of the others in the house, but she may nonetheless exercise considerable power, and candidates for "first girl" are likely to cultivate her favor. Much depends, of course, on her remaining the preferred slave. If a new slave should usurp her place at the master's slave ring, her life may become a misery, particularly if she is not popular with her sister slaves, is perceived as having abused her power, and so on.

Saru shook her head, pathetically, frightened.

I saw she was reluctant to approach Pertinax, which was not surprising, given certain occurrences of the preceding evening, near the stable. She was well aware of the reproach with which he now viewed her. He had done his best to make her feel shamed, inferior, and worthless. And I feared he had succeeded in this endeavor, given the lingering effects of her Earth conditioning, a conditioning in virtue of which she remained poignantly vulnerable to such assaults. How strange it is, I thought, that one should feel ashamed at being what one is, and wants to be, rather than at being what one is not, and does not wish to be. It is interesting, I thought, that there are individuals who wish to impose their values, and even their miseries, insecurities, and fears, on others. As they are constrained, fearful, and unhappy, they would have others share the suffering, bigotry, and poverty on which they congratulate themselves, as though it was some badge of honor to be narrow, intolerant, stunted, and stupid. Pertinax, it seems, had an image, an image of his own, of what Saru should be, what she should believe, how she should feel, and such. He wanted her not to be herself but to conform to some image which, really, in the full analysis, was not so much his own as one which he had been taught should be his own, one formed blindly by happenstance in a society which was, in effect, in many ways, an unfortunate, monstrous, inhumane accident. Interestingly, though he had hurt Saru deeply, one had the sense he was fighting more with himself than a slave. The knives of his hate were turned as much inward as outward.

It might be noted, in passing, that it is quite unusual, and almost unknown, for a Gorean master to hurt a slave as Pertinax had injured Saru. A slave is seldom subjected to cruelty so subtle and insidious, a cruelty which would seek to deny her to herself, which would seek to impose falsehood and pretense upon her, punishing her not only for what she cannot help but for that which is most precious in her, what makes her most herself. Let the slave be what she is, in all her beauty, radiance, warmth, devotion, love, and service. Why demand that she lacerate herself on the nails of lies? How merciful, quick, and how easily done with, is a cuffing or the stroke of a switch. How dreadful, comparatively, is the administration of acids and poisons which, seeping and unseen, corrode from within, which would feed mercilessly on the heart itself.

Interestingly of course, though I was not sure how much aware of this was Pertinax, he was muchly drawn to the slave, and as a slave. He must have had some sense of this, else his hostility, his cruelty, would seem without motivation or explanation. It was almost a madness, almost as though a larl might, in the presence of food, his natural provender, fitted to his appetite by a thousand generations of hunting, seizure, and feeding, torment himself, and refuse himself not only the food he wanted, for which his hunger raged, but without which he could not live.

I was sure Pertinax wanted Saru, and as a Gorean master wants a woman, wholly, and uncompromisingly.

I suspected he had often, even on Earth, speculated on what she might look like at his feet, naked and bound, in his power.

Doubtless he, too, had considered her, even on Earth, in a collar, his collar.

What man can truly, deeply, desire a woman, wholly, fully, without contemplating her in his collar?

Too, I recalled the preceding night.

Pertinax had tasted slave.

And what man, having tasted slave, will be content with less?

I viewed Saru.

As mentioned, she was a bit away, some yards away, amongst the tables. She had her two hands on the vessel of ka-la-na. It is commonly so held.

Again I indicated Pertinax.

She, piteously, supplicatingly, shook her head, begging for mercy.

She would receive none.

I gestured that she should approach, and serve Pertinax.

She did so.

She knelt before the small table, before Pertinax. Her head was down. She did not dare to meet his eyes. "Wine, Master?" she asked.

"No," he snarled. "Away!"

She withdrew gracefully, gratefully, still facing the table, and then turned away. "Wine!" called a fellow. "Yes, Master," she said, and hurried to him, to kneel and fill his extended goblet.

Jane and Cecily were elsewhere, in service.

The tables had been set in the open air, and the area was lit with the glow of torches.

Four or five hundred men were at the tables.

The slaves were clothed, most tunicked, or camisked. One wore the Turian camisk, rare in the north, and two were in cleverly contrived *ta-teeras,* a form of garment which some think of as "slave rags."

Whereas some slaves, indeed, say scullery slaves, garbage slaves, or such, may be clothed, if at all, in no more than a tiny rag, in any shred of cloth, perhaps one soiled from the soot and grease of the kitchen, to conceal their nudity, the subtler *ta-teera* is carefully tied or sewn. It is carefully wrought, artfully designed, to accomplish two objectives, first, to seem to convey the thought that the slave is a low slave, and one of little value, one worthy of no more than brief, demeaning rags, though she may in actuality be a prized, high slave, and, secondly, to well exhibit the charms of the slave, such things accomplished by the brevity and openness of the garment, as by, say, a short, uneven hem, ragged at the edges, a slit hem, showing a flash of thigh, as though inadvertently, and by, say, a rent here, a gap there, and so on. I noted the eyes of several men on the *ta-teera*-clad slaves, a master's inspection, a Gorean male's inspection, of which the slaves pretended to be oblivious. I had little doubt both girls would well be put to use at the feast's end, probably somewhere in the neighborhood of dawn.

There was plenty of tabuk and tarsk, and the slaves brought it to the men on steaming platters. Wine was plentiful, and paga, too, and slaves hurried about, with vessels, and botas, to refill goblets. Hot bread with honey was on the table, on wooden trenchers.

I sat near Lord Nishida, and he had offered me a sip of a different fermented beverage, one I had once tasted on Earth, though not of so fine a quality. It was warm, in its small bowl. "It is *sake*," I was informed. I nodded. There are rice fields on Gor, in the vicinity of Bazi, famed for its teas, but rice is not as familiar on Gor as the grain, sa-tarna. And Pani, as far as I knew, were not found in Bazi, or its environs. To be sure I supposed the rice might be Bazi rice, but I was not sure of that, not at all sure of it.

"Good," I said.

Lord Nishida smiled. He had said nothing of the matter of Licinius, but I was sure he was well aware of what had happened, or might have happened. His *Ashigaru*, of course, had failed to find the body in the forest.

I doubted that Lord Nishida had given orders that I was to be slain after the feast, for he had shown me something surprising earlier in the day, in a tour of some of the remoter storage sheds, near the training fields.

It seemed he still had use for me, or might have use for me.

I did not know.

"Eggs," I had said, finally, "hundreds." I had seen them nestled in their straw-lined boxes.

Obviously they had been the eggs of tarns.

"They will not hatch," I said. "They are without females, they lack incubators."

"Incubators?" he asked.

"Devices, heated," I said, "to hatch eggs."

"Touch one," he suggested.

I reached into one of the boxes, and placed my hand on the egg.

"It is warm," I said.

"It is a matter of fluids," he said. "There are two, one to keep the egg viable, another, later, to induce hatching."

"I see," I said.

The matter, I gathered, was in effect a chemical incubation. I supposed we owed this development to the Builders or Physicians. I supposed the Builders, some of whom concerned themselves with industrial and agricultural chemistry, might have been paid to inquire into such matters. The Physicians, I thought, would have regarded such research as beneath the dignity of their caste.

The feast was well underway.

I caught sight of Cecily, four tables away. She had a vessel of paga, on its strap, over her small shoulder.

Pertinax's Jane bore a large wooden plate of roast suls. More than once it had been replenished at the kitchen area, the suls withdrawn from the ashes of several "long fires." When a great deal of food is involved, particularly in the open, or in large halls, as in Torvaldsland, the fires are almost always narrow, and long, as this increases the amount of food which can be simultaneously prepared, and allows easy access to it, from both sides of the fire. Such a fire, too, it might be noted, given its length, distributes heat over a wide area. This can be important in heating a large structure, such as a hall.

I watched Saru, across the tables.

Pertinax, as suggested, had done his best to make her feel ashamed, inferior, and worthless.

Too, he had, it seemed, succeeded in this matter.

The last thing a typical slave feels in her bondage is shame. Typically, after a time, she finds she is freer in her bondage than she ever was as a free woman, freer not only in her movements, in the lightness and looseness of her garmenture, but freer emotionally and sexually. She finds herself owned, but liberated, in the collar. She must obey instantly and unquestioningly, but she delights to do so. She is thrilled and fulfilled to be owned. She knows that, in a sense, she is superior to all other women. She has been adjudged worthy of a collar. The collar, in itself, is a badge of her desirability and beauty. Her desirability and beauty are such that men will be contented with nothing less than owning her. Thus, rather than being ashamed of her bondage, the typical slave finds in it a source of reassurance and pride. Too, the slave finds herself fulfilled in her womanhood, responding emotionally and sexually to a dominant male who will have everything of her, and more, and what woman does not wish to have no choice but to yield all to such a man? Who would wish to relate to a lesser male? All women dream of masters. Some find them. Too, it might be noted that the female slave on Gor is a familiar and important part of Gorean society. Their identity and place are clearly defined and established. And who other than jealous, envious free women does not relish the sight of lovely slaves? Would you not like to buy one? Two powerful forces are thus conjoined to assure the perpetuation of female bondage on Gor, the society's unqualified acceptance and approval of the institution, it is pleased with its female slaves, and will have them, and the effects on the slave. In bondage, she finds her fulfillment, a fulfillment society not only has no interest in denying to her, but supports and favors. It is no wonder so many slaves revel in their collars. They are as they wish to be, at last, and how they wish to be is not only accepted, but approved. Indeed, society not only approves of her bondage but it will marshal all its considerable resources and forces to guarantee that her bondage, whether she wishes it or not, will remain inflexible and inescapable, that the collar, so to speak, will remain securely locked on her lovely neck. In all these matters, she is choiceless, and she knows herself so. The chain is real, and, whether she is pleased or not, it is on her.

It is an independent question, of course, as to whether or not the slave is inferior, or worthless, and such.

There is obviously a sense in which the slave is inferior. She is, after all, a slave.

Chasms separate her from the free woman, and so on.

On the other hand, as we have suggested, far from feeling inferior, the slave is likely to feel, as a woman, far superior to her free sister. For example, to refer to a free woman as "slave beautiful" is a considerable compliment. It means she is beautiful enough to be a slave, beautiful enough to be of interest to men, beautiful enough to be publicly exhibited and sold, beautiful enough to be collared. Too, apart from considerations of economic or social advancement, and such, clearly men prefer slaves. Who would want a free woman if one could have a naked, vulnerable, defenseless, adoring slave at one's feet? Few, if any, free women know the crawling, fetching of a whip in the teeth, the licking of confining slave bracelets, the writhing beneath a slave ring, the kisses of the slave, and such.

Similarly, although slaves are often castigated as being "worthless," and such, even high slaves, who might sell for gold, it is quite obvious that slaves are not worthless, and not simply because they, as other goods, have a monetary value, nor simply because they are beautiful, as a fine animal is beautiful, nor simply because of the servile labors they will perform, cooking, sewing, cleaning, laundering, polishing boots, and such, but because of the manifold and profound delights which attend their ownership, delights with which masters are pleasantly cognizant. If slaves were truly worthless, they would not be fed, sheltered, guided, guarded, instructed, nurtured, prized, and such, to which attention and care they respond gratefully, as the animals they are. Who would not wish such a lovely beast at one's slave ring? No, they are not worthless.

I was sorry that Pertinax had been so cruel to the girl, Saru.

It was no wonder she wished to avoid him.

To be sure, I sensed she could not help but soften and oil in his presence. I had little doubt that, even in his hatred of her, she would desire to kneel before him, her head bowed in a slave's submission.

She was no longer a free woman.

Why could he not now accept her as what she was, a slave?

I regarded her.

She was a female.

She had been brought to Gor.

She had begun to learn Gor.

She was lovely, collared and tunicked, and serving men.

I had little doubt she wished to be owned by Pertinax, but she was not owned by him. She belonged to another. I had little doubt she wished the hands of Pertinax on her slave's body, and not as the timid, reluctant hands of a typical man of Earth, but commandingly, imperiously, and possessively, as the hands of a master on the body of a slave. But she was not his.

Courses followed courses.

Men grew more riotous, more drunk.

At one table, I noted, however, they seemed sober. Five sat there, partaking of food, though meagerly, but waving away slaves, who would ply them with wine or paga. There is some reason, I thought, which might explain such an anomaly.

Is it not difference which takes one's attention, amongst snow sleen a darker fur, amongst the odor of penned verr, the suggestion, ever so slight, a whisper in the night, of the larl's scent?

I might have called this to the attention of Lord Nishida but he had withdrawn from the tables. I suspected that he found the raucous boisterings of the evening less than agreeable to his refined taste. The typical Gorean male, particularly of what the high castes think of as the lower castes, tends to be direct, open, uninhibited, unrestrained, high-spirited, exuberant, and emotional. He is quick to take umbrage, quick to fight, quick to forgive, quick to forget.

It is said that in the kingdom of the blind the one-eyed man is king. So, too, it might be said that in the kingdom of the addled and staggering, he is king who is sober, swift, and purposeful.

I waved aside a slave, who approached me with paga.

Judging by the moons it was near the twentieth Ahn.

A slave fled past, to laughter, between the torches, into the night, her *ta-teera* gone, pursued by two unsteady brutes.

Another slave was between the tables, gasping, squirming.

I turned to Pertinax. "Perhaps it is time for your Jane to hasten to the hut," I said.

He put down his goblet, looked about, briefly, and nodded.

His Jane, you see, was a personal slave, one privately owned. She was not a camp slave intended to be generally available, at least under certain conditions at certain times. Fellows are usually respectful of one another's property rights, this as a matter of simple civility, if nothing else, but sometimes, when they are drunk enough, passion may encourage them to put their principles in the cabinet of tomorrow, so to speak. In any event, they may not stop to make inquiries, read collars, and so on. Indeed, they may be in no condition to read collars. Certainly I did not wish Pertinax to be challenged for her, nor feel he had to pull her from the arms of another, which might be rather like trying to take meat from a feeding sleen.

Pertinax stood up, not too solidly, and motioned to his Jane, who instantly surrendered her trencher of suls to another girl, and hurried to him, to kneel and put her head down, softly, her forehead to his sandals. I was pleased to note her alacrity and deference. I thought she now understood whose collar was on her neck. This she had well learned the preceding evening. This lesson a girl can learn in a single night, perhaps even within an Ahn or two of her purchase. I saw her draw back a little and kiss his feet, tenderly. Then she kissed them suddenly, more fervently. I smiled. The slave was aroused. I saw her tremble with desire. How far she was now from the Serisii, and the Street of Coins. A world lies between the naive thigh and the marked thigh, between the unencircled neck and the neck in its collar.

Pertinax spoke to the slave, and she sprang to her feet, her head lowered. He gestured that she should precede him. He, too, it seemed, would return to the hut. The girl was, after all, of slave interest.

I glanced to the five fellows who, unnoticed by most, it seemed, had remained at the table, not drinking.

One stood up, and looked about.

I recalled that those of the dark caste, the caste of Assassins, were often sober fellows, often denying themselves much of what most prized as giving meaning to life. Theirs was a narrow, dark life. Few held slaves. Some, before the hunt, would use a woman, briefly, ruthlessly, unfeelingly, leaving her shuddering, crumpled, and broken, sobbing, at their feet, before honing the selected blade, one of six, before painting the dagger on their forehead, that crowds might part uneasily before them, that taverns might fall silent, that children might flee, that men might bolt their doors. For whom is the dagger painted? Seldom did those of the dark caste drink ka-la-na or paga. The eye must be sharp, the senses acute, the hand steady. The hunt must be cold, passionless, rational, deliberate, relentless. Seldom did they recreate themselves with the bodies of slaves. Muchly they stayed to themselves. Each seemed to dwell in the cave of his own intent, as though in a cell, a cell in a large, dark, walled household, from whose gates he might emerge, a grayness at dawn, an enigma at noon, a darkness in the darkness of the night. I thought them less than human, more than human, perhaps, best, other than human. I wondered if they had feelings. Even the venomous ost had feelings. Were they beasts? But beasts had feelings. It was said they were immune, like knives, to compassion. Surely there was no place for such things in the gloom and solemnity of their pursuits. Might one not more profitably implore a stone for mercy? In their dark, narrow world what light was there? Did they live with hate, or even without hate, as in a winter without even cold? Did they know pleasure? I did not know. They lived for the kill. Perhaps they took pleasure in that. I did not know. They were of the dark caste, of the Assassins. I recalled one I had met, long ago, on the height of the Central Cylinder in Ar, Pa-Kur, master of the Assassins. He had leapt from the height of the Cylinder and the body, it seemed, had been lost amongst the crowds below. It had, in any event, never been recovered. Doubtless it had been torn to pieces by the crowd. He was gone. Gor was safer without him. Men had feared even his shadow.

A second one of the fellows had now stood up.

They did not wear the Assassin's black. I did not think the dagger was borne on their foreheads. They were unhelmeted. Had the dagger been in evidence men, even drunk, would have drawn away from them, regarded them, clutched at their weapons, however clumsily.

My fears were doubtless groundless.

Perhaps they had been assigned the third watch.

That must be it.

Commonly, the slave heels the master, usually behind him on his left, as his sword arm is usually the right arm. In this way her presence is not obtrusive, and is unlikely to either distract or encumber him. Also, in this way, he is usually between the slave and other males, possible danger, and such, that she, unarmed and half naked, may be shielded. This also tends to protect her from free women. Too, of course, the position is one of subordination, and is thus fitting for a slave, and domestic animal. For example, a domestic sleen is also likely to heel the master, and also on the left. A free woman, of course, either walks next to a free male, or, in some cities, precedes him, as a mark of her status. This practice also, of course, tends to distinguish her from the slave, a distinction which is of enormous importance in Gorean society. The free woman is a person; the slave is an animal.

Pertinax, however, would have his Jane precede him. I think she well understood that. Masters sometimes like walking behind their briefly tunicked slaves, for the pleasure this affords them. Sometimes the slave's hands are bound before her body, and fastened closely to her belly by a loop of binding fiber. When the slave precedes the master, of course, she is well aware of the effect that she may be having on him, and she, from her point of view, cannot read his expressions, be certain of his closeness, or of what he will do. This can make her uneasy.

"Do not look back," said Pertinax.

"Yes, Master," said Jane.

If she disobeyed, I did not doubt but what Pertinax would use the switch or whip on her.

If the slave disobeys, of course, she has only herself to blame for the consequences of any such disobedience. As a result, the slave seldom disobeys, and is seldom switched or whipped.

All five fellows were now on their feet.

They had not been drinking.

"Wait," I said to Pertinax.

I then caught the eye of Cecily, and summoned her. She gave her bota of paga to another slave, and hurried to me, where she knelt before me, put her head down, kissed my feet, and then knelt up, looking at me, waiting to see what would be required of her.

The five fellows were now filing from the feasting area. One of them paused at the edge of the torches, and looked back. Our eyes met. He then, with the others, disappeared into the darkness.

"Master?" asked Cecily.

"Pertinax," I said, "returns to the hut. Accompany him."

"Surely Master returns, as well?" she said, puzzled.

"No," I said.

"What is wrong?" said Pertinax.

"I am frightened," said Cecily, suddenly.

I loosened the sword in my sheath.

The Pani had largely placed their long swords in racks near the edge of the feasting area, but none who bore them had surrendered the companion sword. That blade is to remain at hand. A similar practice I would learn often obtains in houses and barracks amongst the Pani, a practice in which the long sword is often set to one side, stored or racked, in a hall or vestibule, but the companion sword is kept at one's side, even near the sleeping mats and blocks. To be sure, if danger is felt to be imminent, both weapons are likely to be kept in the vicinity of the warrior.

I saw Saru was to one side.

She was muchly aware of how Pertinax had placed Jane before him. I suspected that she wished it was she who had been so positioned before him, in that position of slave display.

Tears ran down her cheeks.

"Ka-la-na!" called a fellow, and she turned about, and hurried to him, to kneel before him, and replenish his cup.

"Let me come with you," said Pertinax.

"No," I said, "get the slaves to the hut. I intend to join you."

"Something is wrong," he said.

"It is early for the third watch, is it not?" I asked.

"Yes," he said.

"Come with us, Master!" said Cecily.

"Go," I said to Pertinax. I then indicated Cecily, angrily. I feared there might be little time. "Take this slave with you," I said, "and chain her to one of the hut rings, closely, hand and foot."

"Master!" protested Cecily.

"Do you wish to be ordered to beg on your belly to be switched when I return to the hut?" I asked.

"No, Master!" she said, quickly.

"Go!" I urged Pertinax.

"Move!" said Pertinax to Jane and she hurried amongst the tables, to leave the feasting area. Pertinax followed her, and Cecily, looking back once, frightened, hurried after them. Their exit attracted little attention.

I then moved swiftly from the feasting area.

The five fellows who had left the feasting area had taken their way into the darkness. They had moved purposefully. I had met the eyes of one. He had realized himself seen. There had been no mistaking that. Were they waiting for me in the darkness, it was most likely they would be interposing themselves between me and the center of the camp. Their waiting would cost them time, and gain me time. I would take a roundabout way, and rapidly, to what I supposed to be their destination, which then I might reach before them.

I thought of Licinius, and the attempt he had made on the life of Lord Nishida.

It seemed unlikely the enemy, whomsoever, or whatsoever, it might be, would have placed its entire wager on a single arrow fired from tarnback, would have placed the outcome of a large and bold enterprise on a single cast of the marked stones.

Chapter Twenty-Four

In the Tent of Lord Nishida

Two *Ashigaru* crossed their glaives, barring my passage.

Another warrior, one of the Pani, unsheathed his long sword, which he gripped with two hands.

The temporary quarters of Lord Nishida was a double tent, pitched not far from the ashes of his pavilion.

Four more *Ashigaru* appeared, as though from nowhere.

"I must speak with Lord Nishida!" I said. "Is he well? Is he within? There is danger. I bring a warning."

"Disarm yourself," said the fellow with the long sword, and I slipped the shoulder scabbard, letting it fall to the ground.

I did not know if Lord Nishida, given his cunning and warcraft, would be within the *daimyo*'s tent or not, but it was surely the obvious place to bring my suspicions.

"I would speak with Lord Nishida!" I said.

"He is at ease," said the fellow with the long sword, whom I took to be the captain of the guard.

"The canvas of a tent may be rent," I said. "Call him! Disturb him! Is he alive, even now?"

The two A*shigaru* who barred my way tightened their grip on the glaives.

"Inform him he is in danger!"

"He is in no danger, now," said the officer, "for you have been deterred."

"I?" I said.

"You have come here, uninvited, in the midst of darkness, hastily, armed," he said.

"An attempt on his life is imminent, I fear," I said.

"No longer," said the officer. "Bind him."

I felt ropes looped about me, pinning my arms to my side.

"I have come to warn you!" I said. "I come on no dark errand!"

Then I was bound.

"Release me!" I said. "I tell you Lord Nishida is in danger!"

"No longer," said the officer.

"Is that you, Tarl Cabot, tarnsman?" came a voice from inside the double tent, calling out, pleasantly.

"It is he!" I cried, gratefully. "Lord Nishida! He is safe!"

"Now," said the officer, with satisfaction.

"Yes, now!" I said. "But perhaps not in a moment! Be vigilant!"

"Please enter," called Lord Nishida.

I was thrust stumbling past the first tent wall. Within, between the two walls, there were several more *Ashigaru,* far more than were outside.

I was then pushed through the inner entrance, and found myself within the large, inner tent.

The inner room of the double tent was lit by tharlarion-oil lamps, and I found Lord Nishida sitting cross-legged, at his ease, behind a small table, with a small cup in hand. On each side of the table, somewhat behind the table, were two contract women, demurely and tastefully kneeling, in their kimonos, Hana and Sumomo. More to my surprise were five fellows, not of the Pani, who, cross-legged, sat about, in attendance. These were the same fellows whom I had suspected at the feast, whom I had hoped to precede to the tent of the *daimyo.*

"May I present," said Lord Nishida, "five retainers, who, though barbarians, like yourself, are loyal retainers, trusted servitors. Quintus, Telarion, Fabius, Lykourgos, and Tyrtaios."

I nodded.

"You are known, of course, to them," said Lord Nishida.

"I came to warn you," I said. "I took them to have dark intents. I watched them at the feast. I feared an attempt on your life."

"It was intended you should suspect them," said Lord Nishida.

"I see," I said.

"You have passed our small test admirably."

"How is that?" I inquired.

"You have the wariness, the alertness, of the warrior," said

Lord Nishida, "as I had thought you would. Moreover, for whatever reason, for honor, for gain, or adventure, or to see things out, or whatever, you have proved, or seem to have proved, your willingness, and your intent, to protect my life. I find that gratifying."

"Seemed to have proved?" I asked.

"Yes," he said. "For you arrived rather late. Quintus and his fellows arrived well before you. Perhaps you intended to arrive a bit late, after the deed had been done."

I shrugged in the ropes. "I thought they realized my suspicions," I said, "and would wait to silence me, caught in the pursuit, and then return to their objective. I circled about, to arrive here first, supposing them to be waiting for me."

"Also," said Lord Nishida, "it would be a bit foolhardy to overtake them in a direct route to the tent, would it not?"

"I suppose so," I said.

"Your Pertinax would probably have sped here directly, and died," said Lord Nishida.

"I do not know," I said. "Perhaps."

"Quintus?" asked Lord Nishida.

"I made certain," said Quintus, "almost face to face, across the tables, that Cabot knew his suspicions detected."

"Good," said Lord Nishida. "That alone would guarantee he would not rush directly toward the tent, for he might be met by five blades in the darkness, and be surely thus delayed, if not killed."

"It might also," said Quintus, "have saved one or two of us."

"True," said Lord Nishida. "Tarl Cabot, tarnsman," said he, "was it not clumsy of you to allow your suspicions to be detected."

"Doubtless," I said.

The exchange of glances had been almost inadvertent. I now realized it had been manipulated by the fellow called Quintus. Still, it is surely difficult to be looking at someone and not, if the person looks back, be seen as looking. Perhaps a subtler individual might have managed something. I could still feel the paga. I also felt like a fool.

"I think," said Lord Nishida, "all things considered, we have tested your alertness, your cleverness, and your benevolent dispositions concerning my person, whatever might have been their motivations. I accept your loyalty, at least as of this moment."

"I think your captain of the guard," I said, squirming a bit in the ropes, "thought I intended an attempt on your life, perhaps under the ruse of entering your presence to warn you of danger."

"He is to be commended for his caution," smiled Lord Nishida.

"Doubtless," I said.

"You could have struck at me many times, if you had wished," said Lord Nishida. "To be sure, you would doubtless then have been promptly slain, assuming you were that fortunate. And surely it would seem an oddity for a fellow to rush loudly and openly on a well-guarded tent in the middle of the night on an assassin's errand."

"I would think so," I said.

"Noble friends," said Lord Nishida to the five fellows with us in the tent, "you have done well. I am pleased. You may retire. Sleep well."

At this point Quintus, Telarion, Fabius, Lykourgos, and Tyrtaios rose to their feet, made their farewells, and left the tent.

"Ito!" called Lord Nishida.

The captain of the guard then entered, followed by two *Ashigaru*. One carried my scabbard, the blade housed lightly within.

I think the captain of the guard was still suspicious of me. In moments, however, I was freed of the confining loops with which I had been securely pinioned, and had again, on my shoulder, the weapon. Sometimes one feels uneasy without it. The captain of the guard was then, with his accompanying fellows, dismissed. Too, with a gesture, Lord Nishida released the two contract women and they, rising to their feet, with small steps, took their exit from the tent.

"Stay a bit, Tarl Cabot, tarnsman," said Lord Nishida, and I sat down, cross-legged, across from him, across the small table, and watched him pour himself, and then me, a tiny cup of *sake*.

"Do you like it?" asked Lord Nishida.

"Yes," I said.

"What do you think of me?" asked Lord Nishida.

"I think you are a remarkable man," I said, "a gifted leader, highly intelligent, subtle, wise, and cunning."

"Do you trust me?" he asked.

"No," I said.

"Good," he said.

He lifted the small cup to his lips, and regarded me over the white, porcelain brim.

"Do you know why I brought you to the tent this evening?" he asked.

"I was not brought," I said. "I thought you in danger. I hurried hither, hoping to warn you, perhaps to save your life."

"No," he said. "You were brought."

"Lord Nishida is subtle," I said.

He sipped the *sake,* and then placed the cup on the lacquered table between us.

"It was not a test of awareness, or loyalty, or such," he said. "Concerning such matters I do not hold you in doubt, or no more than any other."

"I am flattered," I said.

"The five servitors, whom you met," he said, "were given to understand that it was such a test."

"They were used," I said.

"Thusly were they assured of my trust, that such a task was accorded to them."

"Now," I said, "they are off their guard."

"It is my hope that that is so," smiled Lord Nishida.

"That is why I was brought here," I asked, "that they might feel themselves secure in your confidence?"

He smiled.

"Why is this important?" I asked.

"Do you know them?" he asked.

"No," I said.

"You must have seen them about the camp," he said.

"Perhaps," I said. "They are not of the cavalry."

"Recall them," he said.

"Quintus, and Fabius," I said, "perhaps of Ar, or Venna, Telarion, possibly of Ar, Lykourgos and Tyrtaios, perhaps of the island ubarates."

"Those may not be their true names," said Lord Nishida.

I nodded. Many Goreans, particularly those limited to the First Knowledge, have "use names" to conceal their real names, for fear the real names might somehow be used against them, perhaps in spells. Too, it should be noted that the names given were not unusual on Gor. I had known others who bore those names, particularly Quintus and Fabius. Those names are common in Ar. The names might have been altered, too, of course, simply to obtain the convenience of an alias.

"I wanted you to meet them," he said.

"Yes?" I said.

"At least one is a spy," said Lord Nishida.

"Which?" I asked.

"I do not know," said Lord Nishida. "What do you think I should do?"

"I do not know," I said.

"I could kill them all," he said.

"Some would do that," I said.

"Would you?"

"I do not think so," I said. "I would probably dismiss them, send them away, on some pretext or other."

"Might that not arouse their suspicion?" he asked.

"Perhaps not, if it were subtly done," I said, "perhaps mixing them with others, but it would doubtless prompt the spy or spies to act."

"Or the assassin to strike?"

"Yes," I said.

"I will proceed differently, with patience," said Lord Nishida. "A detected spy may be of value. A spy regarded as undiscovered is not a spy to be replaced. Too, it is a spy who may be used to convey misinformation, lies, deceits, false plans, and such, to an enemy."

"Lord Nishida is indeed subtle," I said.

"I am troubled by one thing," said Lord Nishida.

"What is that?" I asked.

"One," he said, "is of the dark caste."

"The Assassins," I said.

"I fear so," smiled Lord Nishida.

"Then," I said, "dismiss them all, and the sooner, the better."

"I think not," he said.

"Do not sup with an ost," I said.

"Many do, and know it not," said Lord Nishida. "I have the advantage of them, for I know that in one of five places before me, at my own table, tiny, curled in one of five cups, there lurks an ost."

"Beware you do not lift that cup," I said.

"One must lift the cup," he said. "Else the ost will know its presence is suspected."

"I do not like it," I said.

"The ost listens, is attentive, and patient," smiled Lord Nishida. "It will not strike until it is ready."

"It may be ready now," I said.

"I do not think so," said Lord Nishida. "Remember the five. You may have to kill one, or more."

"I see," I said.

"Have you ever crossed swords with an Assassin?"

"Once," I said, "long ago."

"And you survived," smiled Lord Nishida. "You must be skilled."

"They are men, like any other," I said.

"Not like any other," said Lord Nishida.

"True," I said. "Not like any other."

"Finish your *sake,*" suggested Lord Nishida.

I threw it down, which brought a slight tremor of surprise, and distaste, or, perhaps better, disappointment, to the fine features of the *daimyo,* for *sake* is not to be so drunk. Perhaps kal-da or paga, but not *sake.*

"You are a refined, civilized individual, one of taste," I said. "Perhaps you do not realize the risks with which you bedeck your environs."

"Nor you yours," responded Lord Nishida, quietly.

"I see," I said.

"*Sake* is to be sipped," said Lord Nishida.

"I do not know why I was brought to the forests," I said, "or who saw to my bringing, but I have formed your cavalry, for whatever purpose it might serve, and others, Torgus, Lysander, Tajima, Ichiro, might now command it. My work here, I take it, is done."

"You have forged a sword, and are not curious as to its purpose?" asked Lord Nishida.

"One wonders," I said.

"I assure you, it has one," said Lord Nishida.

"Not here?"

"No, not here."

"Far away?"

"Quite far."

"I would be curious to see a far shore," I said.

"I thought so," he said.

I recalled the wands, and the larls. "Too," I said, "I think few would choose to withdraw from your service."

"It would be an unwise choice," said Lord Nishida.

In the shadows I sensed that Kurii might lurk. But, too, it might be Priest-Kings.

"I do not serve beasts," I said.

"Or Priest-Kings?" he asked.

"Nor Priest-Kings," I said.

"We all serve beasts," he said. "What are we, or others?"

"Whom do you serve?" I asked.

"My *shogun,*" he said.

"And he is a beast?"

"Surely."

"And you?"

"Of course."

"And I?"

"Of course."

The tapestries of existence are darkly woven. What hand, or paw, I wondered, jerks tight the knots of destiny.

But might not the blade of will, no matter how foolishly, lash out at the cords, and slash them, though the fabric itself be disfigured?

Or is the slashing, the weeping, and grief, the anger, the fear, the resentment, only another element in the design?

No, I thought, no.

"It is the third watch," I said. "I shall make some rounds, and see that all is well."

"Splendid," said Lord Nishida.

"You have given me much to think about," I said.

"That was my intention," said Lord Nishida.

I rose to my feet, bowed, and turned away.

"Tarl Cabot, tarnsman," said Lord Nishida.

"Yes?" I said.

"*Sake,*" he said, "is to be sipped."

"I shall remember," I said.

I then left the double tent.

Chapter Twenty-Five

A Lantern Will Fail to Convey Its Signal in Due Course; I Am Invited to an Interview

Outside the tent I stopped, and lifted my head, and looked up, into the night, to the stars.

They are very bright in the Gorean night.

Many on Earth, I supposed, had never seen stars so.

I took some deep breaths, that I might be steadied.

I wanted to clear my head, of the lingering whispers of paga, and the fumes of confusion and fear.

I touched the shoulder strap of the scabbard. I was fond of leather, steel, the cry of the tarn, the softness of slaves. Such things were comprehensible to me. I did not care for what had occurred in the tent of Lord Nishida. I did not care for the ambiguities of men, the opacities of motivation, the secret springs which governed the engines of diplomacy and policy. I did not care for the veils with which reality so frequently chose to clothe herself, nor for the thousand mirrors, with their ten thousand reflections and images, each claiming that the truth is here, the ten thousand reflections and images, mirages, betraying belief and hope.

I began to make my way through the camp, having no destination clearly in mind.

It was the third watch.

I had spoken of rounds to Lord Nishida. One post or another might be passed. I wanted time to think.

The night was warm.

"How goes the night?" I asked a fellow.

"Well, Commander," he said.

I was not pleased with what had occurred in the tent of Lord Nishida. I had been manipulated, easily, expertly. I supposed it was well that I had learned what I had, but truth can draw blood. Many men, I supposed, were better off without it. Lord Nishida was brilliant, and cunning. I did not dare to suppose that I understood him. Some men move others with words, as others move the pieces on the red and yellow board of kaissa. I thought Lord Nishida such a man. I did not know if he spoke truth to me, or if he spoke to me merely what he wished me to take for truth. I wondered if others understood him. He must, in his own heart, I thought, have been much alone. Perhaps he wished it that way. I did not know. Seldom are the burdens of command easily borne, particularly if one is possessed of a conscience. Many in power, I suspected, did not labor under that handicap. I suspected Lord Nishida, for better or for worse, did not. I suspected that he would pursue a project without reservation or hesitation. I thought him purposeful, and probably unscrupulous, and perhaps cruel. If one did labor so, handicapped with a conscience, I suspected it likely that others, not so slowed, not so burdened, would be before him, be first to seize the scepter, sit upon the throne, and place about their necks the medallion of the Ubar. I wondered if Lord Nishida was truly loyal to his *shogun*, and, if so, I wondered if his *shogun* was such as to deserve such loyalty, or might he, rather, in his way, regard lightly the feudal pledges which would bind a lord and vassal. Did Lord Nishida covet the *shogunate*? Is not power the drug of all drugs, the most dangerous of all, transcending the trivialities, the banalities, of chemistry, to which even the most professedly humble and self-effacing might be irremediably addicted? But perhaps he was loyal. There are such men, men to whom the treasure of their word, once given, however foolishly, commands the single irrepudiable allegiance. What of his own status? Was it secure? Perhaps there were others who aspired to the pavilion of the *daimyo*. Did not Lord Nishida himself, as *daimyos* and *shoguns*, as Ubars, and tyrants, and kings and princes, sit uneasily beneath the sword of Damocles? Men were men, I thought, whether of Ar, or Cos, or Schendi, or of the Pani.

I touched the shoulder strap of the scabbard, again, for reassurance. It was tangible. So many realities were not.

Animals are innocent, I thought. They kill, and feed. Men smile, and soothe, and praise, and then kill, and feed.

Is it honor and the codes, I wondered, which separate us from animals, or, rather, is it they which bring us closer to the innocence of the animals.

"How goes the night?" I asked.

"Well, Commander," I was assured.

There were apparently spies in the camp, and perhaps an assassin. If Lord Nishida was correct at least one of the five men I had met in his tent was a spy, and one was an assassin. If one were an assassin then Lord Nishida was, indeed, so to speak, living with an ost. To be sure, if the assassin were also a spy, or the spy, to be sure a role unusual for one of that caste, I supposed that Lord Nishida was in no immediate danger, for the spy would wish to gather information, and would be unlikely to make his strike, until his reports were complete, or no longer required.

Sometimes free women, collared and branded as slaves, were recruited for purposes of espionage. Is not the beautiful woman, curled at one's feet, avid to learn the secrets of a house, petulant and pouting if denied, ideally suited to gather the flowers of intelligence? Is it not a natural, and simple, and innocent thing to purchase one of their smiles, at so small a cost as an expression, an unimportant, dropped word, which must, in any case, be meaningless to them? Some did not realize that as soon as they were branded and collared they were truly slaves, and others, doubtless, expected to be freed. They would not be freed, of course, none of them, for their slavery was intended by their employers from the beginning. Is it not a fit recompense for their treachery? Let them stay then in their collars, and, bound at a punishment ring, absorb the lessons of the whip, informing them as to the reality of their condition and the nature of their future. Sometimes, too, amusingly, one of these women, intended for a given house, finds that house outbid, and finds herself wagoned away to another house, perhaps out of the city. Her lamentations and protests, too, soon cease beneath the whip. She learns, too, she is then a true slave, and discovers she is perhaps a thousand pasangs from the house of her intended destination. To her horror, she soon realizes, too, that her recruiters will not attempt to reclaim her, for that might draw attention to themselves and their intentions. She then learns the collar is truly on her, that collar so closely encircling her lovely neck, and so securely, so nicely, locked. She, too, is now a slave. And another woman may easily be obtained to replace her, one with whose placement the employers will hope to have better success. A true slave will never betray her master, for she understands the terrible gravity of such a thing, and her absolute vulnerability. Too, she is now at his feet, and is his slave, and knows herself his slave, and hopes only to please him. To be sure, she might be seized and tortured, and would then speak all she knows. One does not blame her for that, nor any human being, if the torture is exquisitely done. So slaves are kept in ignorance. They cannot reveal what they do not know. Too, it is theirs to serve and please, not to be apprised of the designs and doings of men. Curiosity, it is said, is not becoming in a *kajira*. The collar is often a woman's greatest safeguard. Slaves are commonly spared, even in the sacking of a city. But so, too, of course, are verr, tarsks, kaiila, and such.

In the distance the feast was still in progress. I heard strains of a song, an anthem of Cos. Interesting, I thought, how mercenaries, outlaws, renegades, even those who have betrayed and repudiated their Home Stones, remember such things.

I was passed by some fellows returning to their quarters, some leading leashed slaves, their hands tied behind their backs. Others passed, too, with slaves in custody, but differently, the slaves bent over, in leading position, their heads at the hips of free men, held there by the hair, these slaves' hands fastened, too, behind their backs.

I did not doubt but what these fellows would derive much pleasure from the slaves.

Obviously one of the principal utilities of the female slave is the enormous pleasure which one will see to it that he obtains from her.

How marvelous is the property female!

I passed a post.

"How goes the night?" I inquired.

"Well, commander," I was told.

At least one of the five was a spy, it seemed, and, perhaps, too, of the dark caste.

I wondered from what source Lord Nishida derived his information. He, too, doubtless had spies. I wondered if he thought me a spy. I wondered if one or more of the five were a spy, or one an assassin, truly, or if I had been told that merely to produce some effect in me. If so, what effect? How would he know that one or more of the five was a spy, or that, amongst the five, there might be an assassin? Might this be conjecture on his part? Might it not even be the result of some aberration, or paranoia? But I did not think Lord Nishida insane. He seemed one of the most coldly sane individuals I had ever met. In a way he reminded me of Pa-Kur, once master of the Assassins, save that Pa-Kur was not such as to be distracted by flowers, by poetry, the servings of tea, by *sake*, by the delights of delicate women under contract. Pa-Kur had sought power, single-mindedly, at the blade's edge. For this he had forsworn vanities, or was it, rather, he would sacrifice all for what might prove to be the most evanescent, elusive, and alluring of all vanities, the vanity of vanities, power?

I encountered another sentry.

The night it seemed, was going well.

I thought of the assassins of the medieval Middle East. The caste of assassins was quite different. They were not dupes, fools, madmen, too stupid to understand how they had been manipulated by others, young men drunk with the wine of death, who think they will somehow thrive in the cities of dust. Against such mindless puppets, such naive fools, such lunatics, manipulated by those who send them forth, sitting safe in their mountain fastness, safe in their lair of prevarication and deceit, it is difficult to defend oneself. But the Gorean Assassin, he of the Black Caste, is not a naive, twisted, deluded, managed beast serving the purposes of others, but a professional killer. He wishes to kill and vanish, to live, to kill again. Otherwise he is no more than a clumsy oaf, a failure, having accomplished no more than might have a desperate, simple, misguided fool. If he himself dies, he has botched his work, he has failed, he has shamed his caste.

"Hold!" said a voice, at the edge of the camp, where the track begins, which leads to the plaza of training.

I stopped, and held my hands away from my body, and blinked a little against the light of the lifted, now-unshuttered dark lantern. There were three there. There might be others, in the shadows, with bows.

"How goes the night?" I asked.

"Commander," said a voice.

"Well," said another, "it goes well."

I lowered my arms.

"I would proceed no further, Commander," said one, "until light."

"My thanks," I said. "I shall free the blade."

"Two might accompany you," said one of them, "one with a lantern."

I slipped the blade free from the sheath. The shoulder belt, if over one's shoulder, may be instantly discarded. This may prove an important wisdom in a perilous situation. A scabbard, hooked to a buckled waist belt, or slung across the body, might be seized in combat, discommoding its wearer, perhaps pulling him off balance, or into the blade of a waiting knife. But the belt on the shoulder is easily shed. If one is in a territory thought safe, of course, the scabbard belt is not unoften slung across the body, looped from the right shoulder to the left hip, if the swordsman is right-handed, and, naturally enough, looped from the left shoulder to the right hip, if the swordsman is left-handed. Both modalities facilitate the swift, across-the-body draw. This arrangement provides a convenient, secure carry.

"Remain at your post," I said.

"Enemies, Commander," said one, "may linger."

I thought this possible, but unlikely.

Few, I thought, would care to linger in our precincts, risking discovery by *Ashigaru*.

Would they not now, scattered, defeated, haggard, desperate, frightened, half-starved, have sought flight?

Too, they might well fear larls.

Certainly some of these large, dreaded, clawed, fanged, fearsome beasts occasionally roared within the forests. These were, doubtless, given the latitude, the larls of Lord Nishida, which might well still be in the vicinity, frequenting their former haunts, making their rounds as though the encirclements of wands was still in place.

"Take a lantern," pressed one.

"Shuttered, it is a burden," I said. "Unshuttered, it illuminates a target."

"Take a buckler," said another.

"Darkness," I said, "serves well as shield."

There is a saying among warriors that he who attacks a shadow plays with death.

"We have caught the scent of a sleen," warned another, who was Pani.

Such beasts were in the forest.

"Then you have little to fear," I said. "The sleen to fear is the one of whose presence you are unaware."

The sleen, as most predators, whether panthers, larls, or such, will stalk in such a manner as to approach the prey from downwind, from the direction toward which the wind is blowing. In this manner the scent of the prey is borne to them, and their own scent is carried backward, away from the prey. To such animals scent not only detects prey, but can be informative as to its distance, movements, numbers, and sex. Some predators, interestingly, will favor male prey over female prey, particularly in times of estrus. The favoring of male prey, it is conjectured, tends statistically, over time, to increase the number of prey animals. To be sure, risks are involved, as the male animal is usually wary, alert, aggressive, large, and armed, so to speak, wickedly horned, sharply hoofed, and such.

I wondered if something similar might not be the case with humans. Is it not the female who is most commonly seized and coffled, who may, in time, breed sons for her master? To be sure, it is the female who is desirable, and the male who is dangerous, the female who longs for and is fulfilled in her bondage, and the male who longs for, and is fulfilled by, the female at his feet. And so for the female the collar, and for the male the whip.

"These two will accompany you," said the command sentry.

"No," I said.

"I insist," he said.

"Why?" I asked.

"It is dangerous," he said.

"I will take those two," I said, indicating two others.

"As you wish," he said.

"You will all remain at your post," I said.

He seemed puzzled.

"All," I said.

Perhaps I had spent too long with Lord Nishida. That two had been singled out, without consultation, to accompany me, suggested that I might be set upon in the darkness. The readiness of the command sentry to furnish two others without demur, however, reassured me that his offer had been solicitously motivated. It seemed unlikely that an entire guard group would have been recruited to set upon me in the darkness. If that were the case, why would they wait? Too, who would know I would make the rounds at the third watch?

The command sentry stepped back. "Yes, Commander," he said.

I then turned about, and addressed myself to the track leading to the training area. I did not, of course, resheathe my blade.

It was not impossible that enemies, one or more, concealed, terrified, hungry, miserable, might be in the vicinity.

I would encounter the guard group at the far end of the track, and then, a bit later, after circling the training area, the field, cots, and sheds, retrace my steps.

I had my memories of such places, and of the sky above them, from which blood had rained.

From time to time I stopped, and crouched down, and listened.

I heard only the noises of the forest.

Once I did catch the scent of a sleen.

I was then again afoot.

In the morning, the camp, Tarncamp, I had been given to understand, would be moved. This transition would include, as well, I supposed, at least some of the structures of the training and storage area. Lord Nishida's plans, I had been informed, had been advanced. The attack had made it clear his project, whatever it might be, despite his efforts at secrecy, displayed in diverse precautions and the studied remoteness of the camp, lay in jeopardy. Our victory would doubtless gain some time, but one did not know how much. Lord Nishida might, as other commanders, gamble, for such things are inevitable in war, but, as most other commanders, as well, I did not think he would do so without necessity.

In the morning things would be much changed.

I considered leaving the service of Lord Nishida.

With a spear I did not greatly fear larls. With a keen blade, and the great bow, I did not much fear men.

The warrior is trained to live off the land.

I remembered the wands.

One did not lightly leave the service of Lord Nishida.

On the other hand, I did not think I would much care to be any who might follow me.

Yet I was curious to see a far shore, if it might be reached. I did not suppose that the world ended a bit beyond the waters of Tyros and Cos, or beyond the Farther Islands, even far beyond them, that at some point, some brink, Thassa plunged a thousand pasangs downward, like a planetary waterfall, only to be lifted by fiery Tor-tu-Gor, Light Upon the Home Stone, the common star of Earth and Gor, as might be a drop of evaporating rain, thence to be bestowed in the east, in tens of thousands of storms, to flow then, again, in time, into the mighty Vosk, the sinuous Cartius, the tropical Ua, and a hundred other rivers, to continue its great cycle. This theory, espoused by many privy only to the First Knowledge, was dismissed by mariners, for it would require a constant current to the west which did not exist. Another theory held that the world did, indeed, end at some horizon, for in a finite world there could be no infinite number of horizons, but maintained that at the final horizon, or final shore, as in a lake, Thassa would find her final limit. But, interestingly, Thassa herself, in one such theory, constituted this limit, at that point being hardened, or frozen, a part of her, like a wall, holding back the rest. And beyond this limit there was nothing. A similar theory maintained that Thassa was restricted within her bounds by a great wall of stone, constructed eons ago by Priest-Kings. And beyond this wall, again, there was nothing. Most mariners, however, believed that the world was spherical, surmising this from a plenitude of considerations, that one first discerns the masts of approaching ships, that

Gor's shadow, round, is occasionally cast on a moon, that not all stars are visible at all latitudes, as would be the case if the world were a plane, and so on. To be sure, they often thought the lower surface of the sphere, below embedded Thassa, likely to be uninhabitable. Would not creatures fall from the world if they ventured too far thence? Too, if they could somehow cling to the surface, and move about in such precincts, fugitives or madmen, adventurers or explorers, perhaps by means of ropes or nailed sandals, would not such a life be uncomfortable and dangerous, precariously inverted as they must be? No, such depths must be uninhabited. On the other hand, Goreans with access to the Second Knowledge, recognized the sphericity of Gor, the viability of the antipodes, the action of gravity, and such.

A mystery did remain, of course, to the west, even for those admitted to the Second Knowledge, usually those of the higher castes.

The mystery was a simple one.

What lay to the west?

And, I fear, associated with this mystery, there was another. Why did ships not return from that area?

There were, of course, the Pani.

How came they to known Gor?

What were the projects of Lord Nishida?

Secrets had been breached. War was afoot.

I still did not know what might lie in the dark background of these strange matters, whether the meshes about us had been woven in the Sardar or on one or another of the distant Steel Worlds.

Perhaps I would remain in the service of Lord Nishida, at least for a time. Is a far shore not always tempting? Who does not wish to cross a new river, to venture upon untrodden grass, to see a new sky, to glimpse a hitherto undetected horizon?

And are there not an infinite number of horizons, after all.

Who would have it otherwise?

Through the trees, looking up, I saw the unshuttered lantern of an aflight tarnsman.

I was reassured, for the lantern shone green in the night.

It was a guard, making his rounds.

The lantern may be either shuttered or unshuttered. Shuttered, the light cannot be seen. Unshuttered the lamp casts its light. The guard lantern was so constructed that the color of the light it casts may be changed at will, by means of hinged, glass panels, red and green. In this way the color of the light may be easily, quickly, changed at will. Commonly the lantern is shuttered, that the guard's presence may be less easily detected. When he returns to the vicinity of the training area he unshutters the lantern, showing green if there is nothing to report, and red, if something has been detected. The light alternates between red and green to indicate an ambivalence in the rounds. This will mean that one or more tarnsmen, waiting below, mounts saddled, will join him to take his report, or to assist him in making further determinations. In this fashion, in a matter of moments, a ten or more may be flighted, and perhaps a century alerted. If the light is an uninterrupted red cavalries are mounted. During daylight hours the signals were conveyed by banners, detectible at better than a pasang by the glasses of the Builders.

Then I was again still, absolutely still.

"Bosk, Bosk of Port Kar," said a voice, in the darkness.

I must have detected the presence, for I had stopped. I did not recognize the voice.

"Bosk of Port Kar," said the voice, again.

I did not respond.

Who would know I was here? I must have been followed. I did not know if the owner of that voice had passed the posts, accepted, or had avoided them. That might make a considerable difference.

In any event, one does not respond, and reveal one's position. Every sense was alert. I would have supposed that the owner of the voice might have moved, following his first words, but the voice had come again from the same quarter.

This suggested the absence of hostility, or simplicity.

I supposed there might be more than one.

One to mark the target, the second to strike, from behind.

"Very well," said the voice, from the same quarter. "I will speak. I speak on behalf of a high personage. Go to the cots, take tarn, ride south for two Ehn. You will see a lantern, a rider. He would speak with you."

I did not respond.

I sensed then that the owner of that voice had backed away, turned, and hastened into the forest.

I waited for several Ehn, and then, warily, blade ready, continued to pursue the track toward the training area.

In a few moments I encountered the guards at the far end of the track, and was then in the training area. I heard an occasional tarn but there seemed little amiss, or irregular.

A lantern burned here and there.

I would seek out Tajima, who had not attended the feast, perhaps because of the absence of Sumomo, and other contract women, or perhaps because of the presence of female slaves. He might not trust himself with them. This is quite understandable. It is hard to resist them. But then they are clothed, if clothed, in such a way as to make it hard to resist them. Too, they are trained in such a manner, even as to the femininity and grace of their movements, as to be difficult to resist. The female slave, naked or half naked, collared, utterly vulnerable, is the most helpless, needful, and, however inadvertently, or unwillingly, the most seductive of women. Too, she exists for the pleasure of men, understands this, surrenders to it, wholly, and humbly, and takes great pleasure in it. She loves to serve, to obey, and please. It is what she wants to do. It is her life. And, too, when the slave fires, long ago ignited, and then never far from the surface, begin again to flame in her fair belly, as under the cruel and shameful imperatives of biology they frequently must, earning her the contempt of free women, her seductiveness is then, soon, far less than a matter of inadvertence, or reluctance. See her glance, the trembling of a lip, the faltering of a word, the pleading of the eye. A glance, a touch, can ignite her. Few things are more seductive than a beautiful woman squirming on her belly before you, miserable in her need, her lips pressed fervently to your feet, begging for your caress. I wondered if he ever thought of the delicate, arrogant Sumomo so. I supposed so. Why not? He was a man. I thought she might make a lovely collar-girl, a lovely, *mere* collar-girl.

I expected to find Tajima in the barrack assigned to the guards, whose dispatch and returns he would log, but instead I encountered him crossing the training area, toward the track which led to the main camp area. With him were some five *Ashigaru*, two of whom bore lanterns.

"Tarl Cabot, tarnsman!" he said.

"What is wrong?" I said.

"I was going to send a runner for you," he said.

"What is wrong?" I asked.

"The night," said he, "is amiss."

The *Ashigaru* with him exchanged glances.

"How is this?" I asked.

"Look to the sky," he said, looking up, and pointing, toward the south.

"I see nothing," I said.

"That is what is to be seen," he said.

"The guard?" I said.

"There is no guard," he said.

"He is due?" I said.

"Four Ehn past," said Tajima.

"Saddle a tarn," I said.

"It is waiting," said Tajima. "Too, a ten is armed, and asaddle."

"I go alone," I said.

"No, Tarl Cabot, tarnsman," he said.

"This," I said, "I fear, has to do with me."

"How can that be?" asked Tajima.

"I do not know," I said.

"The tarn is waiting," said Tajima.

Chapter Twenty-Six

What Occurred in an Interview

The night was cloudy.

I was aloft.

The tarn pierced the wind. Vapor, foglike, swept past. I felt moisture, a spattering of rain.

On the ground it had been warm. But here, aflight, there was the sharp, cutting, rushing of wind. My tunic whipped about me. Commonly the tarnsman jackets himself in leather, but I was as I had been, as I had come from the feast. I was unhelmeted. It was cold.

I was responding to a summons.

I did not think my life was in jeopardy. I could have been set upon in the darkness, but had not been.

Might this be some new thread in the obscure tapestry which Lord Nishida, or others, were weaving?

A ten would soon be aflight, to search for the overdue guard, whose failure to return when expected had concerned Tajima.

Thusly had I instructed the guard.

But I wanted, first, my lead.

I had little doubt the absence of the guard had something to do with the voice in the darkness.

The sky was to be clear, and any rendezvous was to be unnoted.

It had been a man's voice, of course. Few women, slave or free, are about in the Gorean darkness, and certainly not in the forests, or outside a city's walls. Those familiar with the Gorean culture will find nothing anomalous in this. Women, even free women, are regarded as trophies, and prizes. They make such lovely slaves. Sometimes a girl will flee a projected, unwanted companionship but these flights are seldom successful, and the fair fugitives are likely to find themselves soon caged and collared. Sometimes they are returned to their city where they are given, now as a naked slave, to he from whose companionship they had fled.

For a slave girl herself, a chain daughter, there is no escape, given her garmenture, the collar, the brand, and the entire culture, which is arrayed to remand her into the authority of the free. At best she might come into the keeping of a new master, and then, as a caught runaway, be subjected to a far more heinous, confining, and terrifying bondage than that from which she had fled. And at worst she might be torn to pieces by pursuing sleen or be hamstrung, to spend the rest of her life pulling herself about by her hands, being whipped, and living on garbage, and serving as an object lesson for other slaves. A first attempt at escape is usually punished only by a severe whipping. After all, not every girl, early in her collaring, can be expected to understand the impossibility of escape. The more intelligent the girl, of course, the more clearly this is understood. Soon all understand the collar is on them, that they are in it, and that it is locked. For the Gorean slave girl there is no escape.

Let us briefly consider the matter of the fugitive from the unwanted companionship, who is returned to her former suitor, now as a slave.

The perquisites he might have sought via her companioning, resources, connections, and such, are then no longer available, but the girl herself is his, to do with as he pleases. As the projected social and economic losses he may have sustained by her flight will presumably far outweigh her value on a sales platform one may appreciate his likely disappointment, if not actual disgruntlement, consequent upon her untoward and unacceptable behavior. Accordingly he may not, at least immediately, put her into the markets, but might keep her for himself, for perhaps months, to derive from her skin, so to speak, an ample compensatory retribution of servitude and pleasure, prior to having her led to a convenient market, hooded, braceleted, and leashed. Indeed, she who was in her view once too fine for his couch may later plead, her lips to his sandals, with all her heart, to be kept at his slave ring.

The decision, of course, is his.

There are masters, of course, and there are slaves, and much depends on the individuals, but, always, the masters are masters and the slaves are slave.

It was fall.

Below me I could see the lanterns of the training area.

I thought the missing guard most likely safe. If someone wanted something of me, it would be unwise to do more than divert, delay, or waylay a guard.

Commonly the price of a death is another death, or more.

The guard might, of course, have been acting under the command of Lord Nishida, or another officer.

Somewhere he might be waiting to resume his rounds.

But I did not think Lord Nishida was involved in this. He could have spoken to me in his tent. There must be another, or others.

I took the tarn then south, abruptly, and tried to count the Ihn, compounding them into Ehn. Soon, much at my own level, some four hundred yards above the trees, I saw what I had anticipated, the brief unshuttering of a lantern. The color, of course, was green. If it were noted, it might even be mistaken for that of a guard. I supposed there would also be a possible display of red. Our signals, particularly such simple ones, might well be understood by means of espionage, but, on the other hand, the colors were in general accord with the color codes familiar in many cities. For example, red tended to be associated with blood, with warriors, with danger, and green with physicians, health, safety, and such.

In some situations, guards might be ranged for several pasangs beyond a camp, a fortress or city, at serial intervals. In this fashion signals could be relayed from post to post, rather in the nature of beacons on the Vosk. By means of such beacons, fire by night, smoke by day, an alarm, or signal, or message, could be conveyed a thousand pasangs in a matter of Ehn. This arrangement, however, is commonly practical only where danger is perceived to threaten from a given direction, or a small number of directions. When the guards are not stationary but aflight in concentric circles, some with a much greater radius than others, the timing and synchronization of signals, even with chronometers, is likely to be sporadic. In such a situation it is very difficult to guard against intrusions, particularly by single intruders. Accordingly, about Tarncamp, we commonly posted a single sentry for the sky, with his circular pattern, but several for the ground.

The lantern flashed green again, and then again went dark.

I wiped some rain from my eyes.

There was a single tarn, a single tarnsman. I loosened the buckler at the saddle. In moments I had drawn up beside him and, in moments, we flew parallel to one another, some yards apart, as though describing the circumference of a great circle. I kept him to my left, where I might interpose the buckler against a flighted missile, but, it seemed, he was unarmed.

"I am prepared to buy her," he called.

I did not understand this eccentric modality of address.

"A guard is missing," I said. "Where is he?"

"I do not know," said the man.

"Then I do not parley," I said, and made to draw away.

"He is safe," called the man, angrily, as though this was of no moment, given weightier concerns.

"Return him, unharmed," I said.

"I did not arrange this to discuss the welfare of a minion," said the man, in fury.

"Then," I said, "permit me to wish you well."

"Hold!" he cried. "He is below, somewhere in the forest. A physician's pellet was concealed in the tarn's meat, before flight, the coating dissolving in some twenty Ehn. The bird is downed, sluggish, drugged. Both mount and rider, I assure you, are unharmed. Both, before morning, will return to your camp."

"Guards are to be soon aflight, searching," I said.

"Then we have little time," he said.

I supposed the downed rider would have the signal lantern, and might make his presence known to searchers. Too, if the fellow aflight with me spoke the truth, they might both, mount and rider, before morning, return to the cots.

"You are, of course," said he, "Bosk, of Port Kar, or Tarl Cabot, once of Ko-ro-ba?"

"One supposes so," I said. "Was it not he who was invited to this interview?" I had, too, long ago, been known as Tarl of Bristol. Indeed, I had learned that songs were sung of him, of him and of a siege, long ago, of Ar. Many, today, wise and sophisticated, supposed that personage merely a creature of myth and legend. In a sense, I supposed they were right. He seemed now, to me, more an image than a man. I, at least, was no hero, no creature of fame. How often I had been weak, frail, and troubled. How often I had been confused, and frightened. How often I had been ignoble, drunken, cruel, petty, and unworthy. How often had I fallen short of my codes! How striking are the enlargements of time! And one supposes, as well, that there must be a thousand heroes, ten thousand heroes, better men, nobler men, who have no songs. But they are there in history, a part of her, and without them she would be different, and poorer. Perhaps the singers might compose a new song, a song for those who have no songs.

"I speak with Tarl Cabot," he said.

"You speak with Tarl Cabot," I said. "I gather you are a high personage."

"Once high," he said, "and one who is again to ascend."

"Who spoke to me in the forest?" I asked.

"Do not concern yourself," he said.

"Was it he who drugged the tarn?" I inquired.

"Surely," he said, "and then waited for you, in the darkness."

"How would one know I would follow the path to the training area?" I asked.

"Had you not," he said, "another means would have brought you to the cots, a dropped word, a message, anything."

"The pellet would act," I said, "within the period of the guard's rounds, and ground the mount for an Ahn or more."

"At least three Ahn," he said.

"Which would give your man more than ample time to encounter me," I said.

"It was somewhat narrower than that," he said, "for you must be aflight between the guard's failure to complete a round and the dispatch of a party of inquiry."

"When the sky would be clear," I said.

"Yes," he said.

"It seems you have made two errors," I said.

"How is that?" he asked.

"First," I said, "there would be few who would have had access to the tarn during the evening."

"True," he said.

"Then your man," I said, "will be one of few."

"Certainly," he said. "What was the second error?"

"He spoke to me," I said.

"So?" he asked.

"I will recognize his voice," I said.

"No," he said. "He is dead."

"You are thorough," I said.

"One must be," he said.

"Of course," I said.

"Let us parley," he suggested.

"Speak," I said.

"How much do you want for her?" he asked.

"She is not for sale," I said. Had not Cecily and I been fitted to one another, selected for one another, matched to one another, by the shrewd wisdom or insidious machinations of calculating Priest-Kings, to serve their purposes, not ours, to be mutually irresistible? She had been selected to bring about my downfall, to so tempt me that my honor might be not only jeopardized but irremediably lost. As a free woman she had been placed with me in a containment capsule on the Prison Moon, in such a proximity and under such circumstances that no man might indefinitely resist the toils of nature in which men and women, helpless captives, had been enmeshed even before small hominids had grown wicked enough and bold enough to challenge larger beasts for defensible lairs. As a free woman she could not be touched, given the codes, but it was as though steaming, juicy, roasted meat had been put before a starving larl, one forbidden to so much as touch his tongue to its heat, to its temptation. But Kurii had intervened. Later, appropriately collared, nicely become slave, a fate perfect for her, and one richly deserved, she became mine. No longer did scruples and codes, of whatever world, divide us. She was then slave, mine, as much as a cup, a belt, a sandal. I wondered sometimes if the Priest-Kings, who think in terms of generations, and even millennia, had selected us for one another, or had bred us for one another. Certainly it sometimes seemed to me that I had been bred to stand over her, as master, and she to kneel before me, as slave. To be sure, it made little difference. She was on her knees, I stood. I wondered if the Priest-Kings had miscalculated. She had been designed to be torment and temptation to me, and to bring about the loss of my honor, my destruction as a man and warrior. To be sure, she was still torment and temptation to me, as any slave girl to a master, but now I owned her, and, as I wished, she was at my feet, and bidding.

Is it not pleasant to have a woman so?

"Every woman is for sale," he said, angrily.

"She is not," I said.

"I will offer you five thousand tarns of gold," he said, "of double weight."

"You are mad," I said. Such wealth, if any man might possess it, might purchase a fleet, a city. Cecily, adjudging her in the light of markets, and seasons, with which I was familiar, if put on the block, despite her intelligence, beauty, and passion, would not be likely to bring more than two silver tarsks. She was exquisite goods, but the markets were filled with such. Earth males, sometimes brought to Gor, tended to be startled and amazed at the abundance and beauty of female slaves on Gor. This plenitude of attractive, available merchandise is not, of course, unusual for a slave-holding culture, and the collar, too, is not easily come by. On the whole, it is only the loveliest who ascend the block. Even women who sell as pot girls and kettle-and-mat girls are often well worth looking at twice, and bidding on. Too, of course, the female slaves are trained, and taught their collars, and, most often, have had their slave fires ignited. This puts them much at a master's mercy. Accordingly, their abundance and affordability, and nature, comes often as a welcome surprise to the new male immigrant, so to speak, on Gor. Sometimes he discovers a girl he knew on Earth, one perhaps hitherto far from accessible to him, who is now a Gorean slave girl, whom he then buys for his own. Indeed, sometimes, as I understand it, a young recruit for slavers, and such, may suggest that one or more girls he knew on Earth be brought to Gor, for his slave ring.

"Then six thousand!" he cried, in fury.

"Surely you are mad," I said.

"How mad?" said he. "Consider the danger to yourself, the difficulty of the business. It is unlikely you could manage it yourself. Surely you should be satisfied with six thousand tarns."

"Speak further," I said.

"She is a liability to you," he said. "Worth nothing, unexchanged. Dangerous to keep. Others will seek her out, and kill for her, for the gold."

"I do not understand," I said.

"I am no fool!" he cried.

I watched his hands, assuring myself he kept them on the reins. The shuttered lantern he had slung at his saddle, on the right. I gathered that he was right-handed. Most Goreans are. As nearly as I could determine he was unarmed. In this way I was flattered. Few Goreans would place themselves in proximity to a stranger, if they were unarmed. That he did so suggested forcibly to me that he was relying on a warrior's honor, for a warrior will seldom attack an unarmed adversary. It is disapproved of in the codes. In this way he showed respect for my caste, and, simultaneously, if I observed the codes, as he apparently expected would be the case, he assured his own security.

"If this interview is to be prolonged," I said, "I advise you to speak quickly, and clearly. Tarnsmen may be aflight even now."

"Do you think I do not know why you are here, concealed in the northern forests?" he asked.

The rain, which had been light, stopped. The light of the yellow moon, high to my right, broke through some clouds. I could see the sheen on the wings of the tarn, the streaking on its beak.

Tarns, as other birds, do not much care to flight in the rain. Whereas the feathering tends to shed water, it is only a matter of time before the penetrant fluid soaks through the layerings and impedes the flight. For maximum efficiency the feathers must be dry and the sky clear and dry. In the wingbeat in the rain, after a sudden clearing, the rain water is flashed into the sky, sometimes taking the light in an instant's rainbow, vanishing almost instantly to be replaced with another, and another. More than one battle was lost when an infantry took advantage of heavy rainfall to attack a foe, a foe temporarily deprived of the support of its tarn cavalry.

"Tell me," I said.

"How did you manage it?" he asked. "Many are curious. The darkness in the midst of day. We held her, to make use of her, to use her as a counter, if necessary, in bargaining for our lives, our tarns ready, the crowds crying out below, the rebels climbing upward, on the height of the Central Cylinder."

"The Central Cylinder!" I said.

"Certainly," he said, angrily.

"Then she was gone, her ropes and all, from our very side, and the cloud swept away, and there was then a light, moving away, a blinding light, like a second Tor-tu-Gor, a light on which we could not gaze. No longer had we anything with which to bargain. We took flight. Many died. The tarns of the avengers were disconcerted and confused by the light. Some of us, thus, in the confusion, made it over the walls, northward."

"I know you!" I cried. "From the Plaza of Tarns, from Ar! From the occupation!"

"You cannot," he said. "I am a humble tarnsman, Anbar, of Ar."

"You are Seremides," I said, "master of the Taurentians, the palace guard, conspirator, high traitor, with Talena, and others, to the Home Stone of Ar."

"I am pursued," he said. "I would again stand high in Ar, or elsewhere. There is an amnesty for any who bring forth for punishment the false Ubara, Talena, once daughter of Marlenus of Ar, now again Ubar."

"The usurpation then is done," I said. "I have heard this, from others."

"There is a considerable reward for the return of Talena to Ar," he said.

"Ten thousand tarns of gold, of double weight," I said. "That is considerably more than six thousand."

"You cannot bring her to Ar," he said. "Hundreds would intercept you, and kill you, and take her from you, for the gold."

"But you would not?" I said.

"No," he said, "my oath upon it!"

"The oath," I said, "of one who betrayed his Home Stone."

"I am willing to give you six thousand tarns of gold," he said, "in good faith, and I believe I can bring her, with a hundred men, to some point of negotiation. You cannot."

"There is a cavalry here," I said.

"It is not yours," he said.

"I do not have the false Ubara," I said.

"You must!" he cried.

"I do not," I said.

"You speak falsely!" he cried.

"Do you truly think I can create darkness in the midst of day, that I can seize a woman and fly off with her, in a blazing light?"

This sort of thing, of course, spoke to me of no ordinary matters, even of deception and smoke, such as might have been contrived by mountebanks skilled in illusions. It spoke to me rather of Priest-Kings, or Kurii. The smoke would conceal the abduction, simply enough, and the blazing light would be a shielding, concealing, bewildering, dazzling illumination emitted from a departing vessel. Neither Priest-Kings nor Kurii cared much to advertise their devices. Large metal objects provoke curiosity and inquiry. Mystery and terror do not. They tend to close off curiosity and inquiry. Such concealments and stratagems have familiar social uses.

"You are in league with those who can," he said. "I have the Second Knowledge. It is not unknown to me that not all ships cleave seas, the fluid roads, but that some, like tarns, sail over mountains, are fleet amongst the clouds, spread their sails not upon the liquid fields, but in the sky, that they dare to venture upon the wind roads themselves."

"I know nothing of the abduction," I said.

"You must," he said. "She is your slave."

I was silent.

"The matter became public knowledge shortly after the rising of the people, the return of Marlenus," he said. "Two magistrates furnished the details, Tolnar, of the second Octavii, and Venlisius, by adoption, a scion of the Toratti. The former Ubara had been embonded in accord with the couching law of Marlenus of Ar, any free woman who couches with, or prepares to couch with, a male slave, becomes herself a slave, and the property of the male slave's master. She was preparing to couch with Milo, a slave, and actor, when apprehended, and, it seems, you were at that time, by some stratagem or subterfuge, the master of the slave, Milo, and so became the master of the former free woman, Talena of Ar. The whole thing was very cleverly done, it seems. Considering the nature of the case, papers were carefully prepared, and measurements and prints taken, that there be no mistake about the legality of the proceeding, nor any possible problem later in the exact identification of the slave. Interestingly you did not hurry her surreptitiously from the city, as one might have supposed you would have done, but left her in the Metellan district, where she had been embonded, to be discovered, that she might then, though now a slave, continue her tenure upon the throne of Ar, as her fellow conspirators would have it, as the puppet of the forces of Cos and Tyros, under the governance of Myron, the *polemarkos* of Temos. We did not discover that she had been embonded until the testimonies of Tolnar and Venlisius had become public. When it became clear that Marlenus had indeed returned, he recognized by some meaningless female slave in the city, and that the rising would be successful, we took our way to the height of the Central Cylinder, from which point we hoped to either escape or negotiate our way to freedom, turning the former Ubara over to authorities, alive, for the tortures intended for her. Given the situation and what we had discovered of her, we had removed from her the raiment of the Ubara, put her in the rag of a slave, roped her, and had her at our feet, on her knees, head down, as befits a slave."

"And then you lost her," I said.

"Yes," he said.

"Interesting," I said.

"Where is she?" inquired Seremides.

"I do not know," I said.

The rain then began again.

"In Ar," said Seremides, "you would be slain."

"Why is that?" I asked.

"You did not turn over Talena, once the daughter of Marlenus of Ar, to the resistance, to the Delta Brigade, when she was in your power," he said, "but returned her to power, thus abetting the usurpation."

"I see," I said.

"You cannot return to Ar," he said. "Too, secondly, you have her, and have not immediately returned her to the justice of Ar, and are thus in defiance of the edict of Marlenus, Ubar of Glorious Ar, willfully concealing a fugitive, a traitress."

"I see," I said.

"Where is she?" asked Seremides.

"I have no idea where she is," I said.

"Seven thousand tarns of gold, double weight!" snapped Seremides.

"No," I said.

"No woman is worth that much," said Seremides.

"Honor is worth much more," I said.

"Surrender her," said Seremides.

"I do not know her whereabouts," I said.

"You are her master!" cried Seremides. "That is clear from the records, from the testimony of Tolnar and Venlisius!"

"I was her master," I said. "It has been a long time. By now she may have fallen to another. Lapses have occurred. Who knows what collar is now on her neck. She may be a camp slave, a paga girl, a field slave, a caged brothel slut. Others may now have as much claim on her as I." Possession, particularly after a lengthy interval, is often regarded as decisive, by praetors, archons, magistrates, scribes of the law, and such. What is of most importance to the law is not so much that a particular individual owns a slave as that she is owned by someone, that she is absolutely and perfectly owned. It is the same with a kaiila, a verr, a tarsk, and such.

"Speak!" cried Seremides.

It was true that the lovely Talena, given what had occurred in the Metellan district, was now no more than another slave, one perhaps more beautiful than most, but doubtless less beautiful than many others, but I was not at all sure that she was still mine. To be sure, there was another sense in which the lovely Talena was not merely another slave. The slave that was now she was wanted by the high justice of Ar, and might bring a bounty price of ten thousand golden tarn disks, tarn disks of Ar, and of double weight.

"Where is she!" cried Seremides.

"I have no idea," I said.

The rain began to fall more heavily.

The tarn screamed in protest. I thought it well to bring it to shelter.

"There are lanterns," I said, gesturing past Seremides, to the left. We could see some three or four lanterns, perhaps four hundred yards away, over the dark trees.

"Liar!" cried Seremides. "You have had your chance! We shall find her!"

I lifted the buckler free, swiftly, and interposed it between my body and the flash of steel which, with a spitting of sparks, caromed off the edged, wet, curved surface, disappearing in the night, over the neck of the tarn, to my right. At the same time Seremides, with a curse, pulled his tarn away and fled. I did not pursue him. I drew the tarn northward. I would return to the cots.

"Tarl Cabot, tarnsman!" cried Tajima. Ichiro was behind him, with a lantern. With them were several riders, a ten, with its officer.

"I am well!" I called. "Return to camp!"

"The guard has not returned!" said Tajima.

"He will return by morning," I said. "To camp!"

"What has occurred, Tarl Cabot, tarnsman?" called Tajima.

"Strange matters," I said, "of which I understand little."

I loosened the guide straps and the tarn extended its head, snapped its mighty wings, spraying water back, and sped toward the shelter of the cots.

I was followed by the others.

Seremides, I had learned, had one or more men in the camp. He believed Talena was somewhere alive. He apparently thought me privy to her whereabouts, which was mistaken. Either Priest-Kings or Kurii must have taken Talena from her captors on the height of the Central Cylinder. The false Ubara, the puppet Ubara, it seemed, had fallen. The robes of the Ubara had been exchanged for a rag, that of a slave, according to the decision of free men. The chasm on Gor between the free woman and the slave girl is momentous and unbridgeable, the difference between a person and a property, between an honored, awesome personage, the exalted possessor of a Home Stone, and an animal, a beast, a mere beast, a form of stock purchasable in a market. What, then, in view of such a chasm, would be the distance between a Ubara and a slave, even a lovely slave? Talena was no longer of use to Cos or Tyros, or conspirators and traitors. Her primary use now, if any, was that of an item of goods which, given an unusual political situation, might be exchanged for ten thousand tarns of gold, of double weight. I did not know her whereabouts.

I wondered who did.

In any event, it was no concern of mine.

Chapter Twenty-Seven

Tarncamp Is Abandoned

Doubtless the smoke could be seen for pasangs. As the huts and sheds, the warehouses and bath houses, and cook houses, dormitories and arsenals, and the *dojo*, collapsed in flaming timbers and planks, hundreds of men, in columns, following wagons, drawn by tharlarion, took the mysterious well-rutted road which had led eastward, southeastward, from Tarncamp and the training area. By evening the debris of these areas would cool into blackened wood and warm, gray ash, and these residues of the conflagration, extinguished, would be scattered about, broken up, and dragged by designated work gangs into the forest. In two or three years I supposed the forest would reclaim these hitherto cleared areas, and there would remain few records and clues as to what had taken place here, where timber had been harvested and men trained for wars whose projected venues were unknown, and possibly remote. In any event, Tarncamp and its plaza of training were being abandoned.

"Do you not march?" asked a fellow, a pack on his shoulder, slung over the haft of a spear.

"Later," I informed him.

"You are not aflight," he said.

"No," I said.

The tarns, from the plaza of training, had been early aflight, their squadrons led by Tajima.

"Are you out of favor?" he asked.

"Perhaps," I said.

"Put yourself on your sword," he said. "It will be quicker."

"Join your unit," I advised him.

I did not know if Lord Nishida had further need for me or not. In any event, Pertinax and I had been invited to accompany him, with his guard, and the invitations of *daimyos,* however politely extended, are not to be ignored. I did not doubt that Tajima had reported to Lord Nishida my flight of the preceding late evening, and my seeming encounter with an unidentified tarnsman, an encounter I had refused to explain to him. I did not begrudge the conveyance of this sort of intelligence to Lord Nishida, nor did I resent Tajima being the modality of its conveyance. He owed that duty to his *daimyo,* as I might owe similar duties to captains in whose commands I might serve, or to those codes which did so much to define and clarify my caste, the scarlet caste, that of the warriors.

"Look," said Pertinax, pointing.

"I see," I said.

In one of the wagons trundling past were several contract women, among them Sumomo and Hana, both of whom were under contract, as I understood it, to Lord Nishida.

Neither woman signified that she recognized us.

This is not unusual, in public, with such women.

I wondered what each might look like, slave clad.

But then I recalled they were contract women.

I speculated that Tajima would not have minded having the lovely, haughty Sumomo at his feet, not as a contract woman, of course, but as something far less, and far more desirable.

Then the wagon had disappeared amongst the trees.

I was sure Lord Nishida did not trust me, but I did not feel slighted by any suspicions he might harbor. In his place I would doubtless have entertained a similar wariness. He did not know me, I was not of the Pani, I had not turned a failed assassin, Licinius, over to him for the expected justice of prolonged torture, and there was the matter of yesterday night, when I had mysteriously left the camp and had apparently engaged in a clandestine rendezvous with a stranger. I doubted that, under similar circumstances, I would have trusted myself.

He must have need of me, I thought. I doubted the Pani were indulgent with respect to redundant personnel, hangers-on, parasites, passive burdens. But this is not unlike Goreans, as a whole. They see no point to sheltering and sustaining those who can work and do not do so. They are commonly sold to quarry gangs, harbor dredgers, laborers in the *latifundia,* the great farms, and such. Sometimes they are simply put outside the walls, naked, for beasts, human or otherwise. Even brigands have no use for them, unless it be to sell them, or use them as feed for sleen. But there are few such cases, for it is part of the Gorean *ethos* that one, if able, should work. And the capacity for work is determined by physicians, neither by politics nor rhetorics. Perhaps if the caste and council democracies, so to speak, had taken a different turn such individuals might have constituted a constituency, so to speak, exploitable by the unscrupulous, but the several forms of democracy, of aristocracies, of oligarchies, of tyrannies, and such, amongst which power tended to be divided, had not taken such a turn. Theft is rare on Gor, and so, too, is ambition masked as compassion.

A cage wagon rolled past, in which, turning and twisting about one another, agitated, were several larls. These were the beasts, primarily, who had patrolled outside the wands. They were trained from cubhood, to respond to secret commands. Accordingly, one who knew these commands might command them, venture beyond the wands, and so on. *Ashigaru* prowled the edges of the road, lest any of Lord Nishida's minions, primarily mercenaries, be tempted to avail themselves of an unobstructed highway to another prince, one with perhaps a deeper purse.

Some smoke hung in the air, from the burning.

More wagons took their way past, and more men, afoot, with packs.

I had in the past noted certain tharlarion, their comings and goings. From the departure of one to its return I had counted, on the average, six days. I took it then that whatever destination might lie at the end of the road to the east was some three or so days distant, on foot. Most of the camp would, of course, move on foot. I supposed those on tarnback might complete their journey in a few Ahn.

I conjectured that I knew the mysterious destination. Had it not been hinted at, even long ago, by Pertinax? But I did not anticipate what I would encounter there.

"Look," said Pertinax, approvingly, for he was becoming male, and Gorean, "—slaves."

"Yes," I said.

The lead girl, on a slack, coarse tether, fashioned of Gorean hemp, was fastened by the neck to a ring on the back of a wagon. She followed it, on her tether, some seven or eight feet behind. The others followed her in line, all on the same rope. The ends of the tether were only at the ring, before the first girl, and behind the neck of the last girl. In this way, when the rope is knotted about the neck of each girl, save for the first and last girl, there being no free end, there is no access, save perhaps by a knife, or such, to a means of undoing the knot. The small wrists, too, of each girl were corded together behind their backs. They walked well, maintaining the lovely, erect, graceful posture of the female slave, rather like that of a dancer, which was by now second nature to them. Free women may be slovenly, and shuffle, or slouch or slump to their heart's content, but such luxuries are not permitted to the collar girl, for she is owned by men. They also kept their heads up, and their eyes forward. Girls in coffle are often forbidden to look about, but are to keep their line, their head position, and so on. Too, they are often forbidden speech in coffle. Here and there, as another such wagon passed, it, too, with its coffle of beauties, I noted a switch-bearing *Ashigaru* in attendance, doubtless lest one of the slaves be tempted to look about, or be so foolish as to attempt to communicate, or even whisper, to another of the "beads on the slaver's necklace." The girls following the wagons were barefoot, and tunicked. Slave girls are often conveyed in slave wagons, their ankles chained about a central bar locked in place and aligned with the long axis of the wagon, but these were afoot. Most commonly in coffle, however, though not in this march, the girls have their hands free but, naked, are chained together by the neck. Too, they are permitted, within reason, to look about, to converse, and such. In the common coffle there is usually much freedom, particularly when being conducted between cities. They are normally naked, to save on laundering, to prevent the soiling of garmenture, and such. These slaves, however, as noted, were tunicked. I speculated that this was permitted not so much for their sake, for they were slaves, as to reduce the temptation which they might otherwise present to the hundreds of males in the march. On this point I wondered if that psychological stratagem, if such it was, was well founded, as there are few sights as sexually provocative as the sight of a lovely, young female in a slave tunic.

I watched another coffle pass by.

Women are so beautiful!

It is no wonder men make them slaves.

"Thank you for abiding," said Lord Nishida.

I bowed.

"It will be easier," he observed, "when we are beyond the smoke."

"Yes," I said.

He was with a guard of some twenty *Ashigaru*, with officers. The captain of his guard, Ito, was prominent among these men. I found I did not much approve of Ito, and this assessment, I fear, was darkly reciprocated.

As I could, I examined the countenance of Lord Nishida, but it appeared benign and pleasant. I detected nothing indicative of displeasure in that bland facade which might indifferently mask either approbation or menace. Perhaps, I thought, I might read the heart of the *daimyo* more easily in the countenance of his captain than in his own. I had no doubt, as noted, that Lord Nishida knew of last night's flighted interview over the forest with some unrecognized tarnsman. Perhaps he suspected me of having had the tarn of the guard drugged, which guard had, incidentally, as Seremides had assured me, returned unharmed to camp.

"Would you like to speak with me?" I asked.

"It is always a pleasure to speak with you," said Lord Nishida. "Of what would you like to speak?"

"Of nothing," I said.

"The smoke is unpleasant," said Lord Nishida. "Let us address ourselves to the road."

We fell in then with a company of *Ashigaru*, their glaives shouldered.

It did not surprise me that Lord Nishida accompanied his men on foot. The wagons were for supplies, for contract women, for the ill and lame, and such, if there were any. Commanders, unless wounded, incapacitated, or such, are not goods or freight, so to speak. Had there been kaiila he would doubtless have ridden, but there were no kaiila. Too, though some *daimyos* might have had recourse to sedan chairs, palanquins, or such, Lord Nishida, whom I had seen as a warrior, and one of some formidableness, would eschew such.

I wondered if he knew the location of the former Ubara of Ar, Talena, once the daughter of Marlenus, Ubar of Ubars.

Surely she could have been taken as she had been taken, from the very height of the Central Cylinder, if Seremides' account was at all correct, only by means of either Kurii or Priest-Kings.

I considered putting the question to him, directly, but did not do so. It is unwise to move in kaissa when the board is obscure, when the number of pieces, their nature, and their positions are uncertain.

Only a fool would move then and risk a Ubar, or a Ubara.

I heard the snap of a switch and a girl's sudden cry of pain. The switch of one of the attending *Ashigaru*, I gathered, had found its mark, administering a stinging rebuke for some slave's indiscretion.

Earlier this morning *Ashigaru* had gathered in the slaves. Part of the camp was even then burning. One could smell the smoke, and sense the heat. Following the summons and the concomitant instructions, Pertinax and I had tunicked Cecily and Jane and tied their wrists behind their backs. If masters can strip slaves at their pleasure why can they not dress them, as well? One may either face the slave or have them face away from one. One then has them raise their arms, and one can slip the tunic over them, perhaps jerking it down and tight, so that they will well understand that the garment is a slave garment, and is put upon them by a male. As is well known the garmenture of a slave, if any is permitted, is at the discretion of the master. Interestingly, this is extremely meaningful to a woman, and is profoundly sexually stimulatory to them. We had then tied their hands behind their backs and prepared to turn them over to the nearby *Ashigaru*. Also profoundly sexually stimulatory to the female is the hands-behind-the-back tie. This increases their sense of vulnerability and helplessness, which, in turn, given the pervasive natural ratios of dominance and submission, and the female's understanding of herself, that she is a slave, stimulates, enhances, and intensifies their slave reflexes, nicely readying them for their conquest and use. So I took Cecily in my arms and felt her squirming gratefully against me, her moist lips eagerly seeking mine. Pertinax similarly took his Jane in hand, and, bending her backward in his arms, ruled her lips with a master's kiss. We then thrust them stumbling to the waiting *Ashigaru* who took the hair of each in a separate hand and, bending them over at the waist, conducted them both in a common leading position to some point of collection.

"Would you not, rather," I had asked Pertinax, "it had been Saru?"

"Jane is excellent collar meat," he said.

"I am sure of it," I said. "But would you not rather it had been Saru?" I was pleased, incidentally, as suggested earlier, that he now seemed to grasp the nature of women, and their proper place in an advanced civilization. Many men of Earth had not.

"Saru is a slut," he said.

"Yes," I said, "but such make excellent slaves."

"She is different," he said. "She is from Earth."

I saw then that he wished, or seemed to wish, to see the females native to Gor in one way, and those native to Earth in another way, those of Gor as natural slaves, fit for the collar, ideally to be embonded, and those of Earth not, despite their absolute identity as human females. Did he truly think the women of Earth, I wondered, were different from, or superior to, the women of Gor? That seemed to me absurd. They made slaves every bit as good as the women of Gor. Certainly slavers thought so, and so, too, did buyers in hundreds of markets. Were this not so they would not be brought to the slave platforms of Gor. Indeed, some Goreans preferred them. In any event, the Earth-girl slave, having been starved of her sex on Earth, taught by a pathological, adversarial culture to fear, belittle, resent, and suspect it, discovers on Gor to her astonishment and elation that her sex is here not only of interest, but of inestimable importance and value. She will even be bought and sold as a female. Too, on Gor, she is likely to find herself the property of a dominant male, by whom she will find herself wholly mastered, as only a slave can be mastered, and handled and desired, and possessed, with a raw, animal passion for which her old world has failed to prepare her. And so, bidden with as little as a snapping of fingers, she quickly kneels and presses her soft lips to his whip, and rejoices, and is alive. I doubted Pertinax would have his rather disparaging comparison of the Gorean woman and the woman of Earth, in terms of dignity and such, had he ever met a Gorean free woman, particularly of high caste, compared to whom the free woman of Earth, less free than merely not yet collared, would be thought of at best as little more than a possible serving slave, perhaps one who might serve as a serving slave to her serving slaves. Could he not bring himself to understand that women were women, that the Gorean woman and the woman of Earth were both females, that neither was, nor should be, an imitation man, that they were quite different from men. To men they were complementary, neither, given those whims of nature which had been selected for and validated in the arena of possibilities, confirmed in caves and justified in villas, mansions, and palaces, ratified over millennia, identical nor antithetical. Should the women of Earth, then, any more than the Gorean woman, be denied her womanhood, her most profound needs and desires, the right of the natural woman, in her heart desiring to be mastered and possessed, the right to be owned, and fulfilled, the right, so to speak, to be collared? Must they comply with alien requirements, forever manifest facades and images imposed upon them from without? Too, did he not understand that his precious Saru was now, as a simple matter of fact, no longer a petty, haughty scion of fluorescently lit corridors and paneled offices, but was now a slave, merely that, nothing more, as much so as had she been such in Assyria, in Babylon, in Rome, or Damascus, and that her slave fires had been ignited? Interesting, I thought, that he thought little of, and would understand, accept, and welcome slave needs and slave passions in his Jane, recognizing their propriety, perfection, and naturalness, but was unwilling to understand, accept, or approve of them in Lord Nishida's Saru. Did he not understand that Saru was as much a slave, and every bit as appropriately, naturally, and fittingly so, as his Jane? The collar was on her neck as rightly, as ideally, and perfectly, as it was on his Jane. Indeed, whip-exhibited on a sales platform she might have brought a few tarsk-bits more.

She was a slave. Could he not understand that?

"She is not different," I said. "She is a woman." Indeed, as noted, Saru's slave fires had been ignited, and she was now their helpless, pleading prisoner, as much as any other slave, whether of Gor or Earth, in whom this lovely, irreversible development had occurred.

Once a woman's slave fires have been ignited she can no longer be but a slave. She then needs the collar.

Without it she is in torment, and lost.

With it, she is whole.

"She is worthless," he said.

"She is pretty," I said.

"She is the property of Lord Nishida," he said.

"True," I said.

"Let us go to the center of camp," had said Pertinax. "We are to join the guard of Lord Nishida, as I understand it."

"Yes," I had said.

We then left the hut which, shortly thereafter, was set afire.

Chapter Twenty-Eight

In the Forest, Its Miseries; A Talena; I Am Attacked; A Sleen Is in the Vicinity

It was now the third day on the forest road.

The rain which had intruded itself lightly, intermittently, then more heavily, briefly, for some Ehn, when I had been aflight, responding to what had turned out to be the summons of Seremides, had been little more than a harbinger of storms which had begun in earnest some two days later.

The track was muddy, and we were surely far behind schedule, for wagons, on the already deeply rutted road, became frequently mired. Often they required a twenty of men, and levers, to free them, and then, an Ahn later, one must again strive to unfasten them from the deep pools and clutching mud. Finally some tharlarion were unharnessed from a given wagon and added to the team of another wagon, simply to free the wagon. One had then, again, of course, to take the time to put them once more in their proper traces. Often, too, the wagons must be unloaded, freed, and then again loaded. Sometimes trees were felled to widen the road, to avoid the miring. Twice the road was washed out and a bridge of felled, roped trees must span it, a bridge that would sometimes break and be swept away, given the current and the weight to which it was subjected. I doubted that we would reach our destination for another two or three days, due to the impediments we faced.

The weather had been hitherto unusually warm for the season, even given the moderations in temperature, and the warmth, associated at this latitude with the current of

Torvald, but now a chill snapped in the air. My calculations, corroborated by those of Torgus and Lysander, placed us in the fourth day of the Eighth Passage Hand, the five days preceding the ninth month, on the last day of the passage hand of which occurs the winter solstice, the Gorean new year beginning when the world begins its own, on the vernal equinox, which follows the last day of the waiting hand, which follows the passage hand of the twelfth month. Most Gorean months are numbered, and not named, rather as October would have been the eighth month, November the ninth month, December the tenth month, and so on, of the Julian calendar. On the other hand, some months are named in given cities, for example, the third month is called Camerius in Ar, Selnar in Ko-ro-ba, and so on. Generally the four named months are associated with the solstices and the equinoxes. For example, the fourth month, that following the third passage hand and the summer solstice, is En'var or En'var-Lar-Torvis, the First Standing of the Sun; the seventh month, following the sixth passage hand and the autumnal equinox is Se'Kara or Se'Kara-Lar-Torvis, The Second Turning of the Sun; the tenth month, following the ninth passage hand and the winter solstice is Se'Var or Se'Var-Lar-Torvis, the Second Standing of the Sun; and the first month, following the twelfth passage hand and the waiting hand, culminating in the vernal equinox, is En'Kara or En'Kara-Lar-Torvis, the First Turning of the Sun. The passage hands and the waiting hand are five days each. A Gorean month consists of five five-day weeks. The Gorean year, as that of its sister world, Earth, is approximately 365 days in length. Every few years, as necessitated, an additional day is inserted into the calendar, at the end of the waiting hand, but, as the Gorean year is apparently somewhat shorter than the Earth year, and as its orbit seems to vary somewhat, from time to time, presumably due to the adjustments of Priest-Kings, the insertion year varies somewhat. The calculations in these matters are due to the devices and measurements of Scribes. Two important fairs take place in the vicinity of the Sardar Mountains, in the spring and fall, that of En'Kara in the spring, and Se'Kara in the fall.

I heard the snap of a whip and a cry of pain.

One of the slaves had fallen into the mud.

Had she been careless, or was it something that could not have been helped, something for which she was utterly blameless?

But such discriminations, one supposes, are too subtle for the whip.

"Please do not strike me again, Master!" I heard.

But there was then another stroke of the whip, and another cry of pain.

The trek was not pleasant for the slaves. Such treks seldom are.

Their hands had been unbound though the ropes stayed on their necks. In this way it was easier for them to keep their balance in the mire.

Yet the reprimanded slave had fallen.

Doubtless she had been careless.

For the most part they followed the wagons to which they were neck-fastened.

Men, too, slipped, and fell, and cursed.

The girls were cold, and rain was falling.

Several, standing to the side, waiting, wept and shivered.

The rope which fastened them together was wet, cold, and stiff. They held their arms about themselves and shuddered, barefoot, in their tiny, clinging, soaked tunics.

How miserable, I thought, they must be.

But, too, it was clear they were well-figured. One could scarcely fail, under the circumstances, even in their helplessness and misery, to notice the excellence of their slave curves.

But it is for such reasons, and others, that such as they are brought into the collar. Men will have it so.

Several slaves, a few yards ahead, were thrusting against the back of a wagon, lending their small strength to the effort to free it. Some had their slight shoulders to the two rear wheels. Some others were trying to turn the wheel by means of the spokes. Rain was falling, cold and pelting, almost blinding. Their hair was clotted with mud and their tunics were filthy. Mud covered their legs to the thighs.

"Mercy, Masters!" cried one, on her knees in the mud, lifting her hand piteously, and her outcry, unacceptable and importunate, was answered with a stroke of the switch.

She regained her feet and, joining her coffled sisters, pressed, weeping, with the palms of her small hands against the rude back of the wagon.

"Hold," I said, moving forward.

I put my back under the wagon, facing backward, and, straightening a little, managed to lift it from the mud, and thrust it forward a foot or two. "Ai!" said a mercenary, nearby. "Master!" breathed one of the slaves. Others stepped back, and stood in awe, in the mud, on their neck-rope. I withdrew from the wagon, and stepped back, away, to the side of the road. Many men could have done what I had done. Leverage is important in such matters. One lifts mostly with the legs, the back little more than a lever. At least I had not slipped. I moved away. I did not think my contribution had made much difference. I did not doubt but what the wheel would soon again be arrested.

I walked down the line of wagons, toward the head of the march, some two or three hundred yards. The march itself must have been a pasang or more in length.

It was toward evening, and the light, in the rain, and within the looming trees, was poor.

The rain continued to fall, but it had lessened from some Ehn before.

Several of the wagons had a coffle of slaves.

Some of them, lips trembling, looked piteously upon me as I passed. Could the march not stop? Could they not rest?

Did they think I was in charge of the march? I was not.

I had no doubt they were weary, even exhausted, and that, from their unaccustomed efforts at the wagons, their small bodies must be unsteady, and tremble and ache. It was no wonder that so many had fallen.

"Forward!" cried men, and the wagons moved again, creaking, and many of the slaves, the cold, muddy water to their thighs, whimpered, and again, wading, staggered forward, obedient to the tether which bound them.

At dawn the march had begun, as much on Gor begins with the first light. And it was now late. And there was the rain and cold.

I changed my position.

The water here was only ankle deep.

Once again the rain began to fall heavily. A wind swept

the forest, with a rushing noise, whipping wet, overhanging branches, tearing away leaves, shedding and spattering more and more water onto the pools in the road.

Another coffle passed, fastened to the back of its wagon.

This coffle was much as the others.

The hair of the girls, sopped, and bedraggled, spread about their faces and shoulders. Their tiny tunics were drenched. And not one tunic was without its stains and soiling. Some were open at the back, cut apart, and reddishly stained, where the whip had fallen. One could see the track of rivulets of water on their necks and shoulders, and note the progress of its tiny, coursing, chill streams elsewhere on their bodies, on their arms, and muddied thighs and calves. Their scanty, revealing garmenture, suitable for slaves, was chilled and soaked, the cold, pelting water easily penetrating the light, porous cloth, not only from without but from within, as well, as water ran from their bodies. Some of the girls clutched the tunic about their neck, tightly, to keep water from slipping within the garment. Some of the girls, staggering, clung even, with both hands, desperately, to the stiff, wet, cold neck-ropes, perhaps that they might be steadied in the march, or perhaps merely that they might have something, anything, to cling to, even be it the bond which fastened them, directly or indirectly, to the back of a wagon, the very bond which in its way left them in no doubt that they were women, and slaves. Muchly were their eyes filled with anguish and fear, and muchly did they shiver and tremble. Could one not read in their countenances a mute plea for pity? They did not dare speak for fear of being struck. "Please, Master, please!" begged their eyes.

Was mercy not to be shown to them?

Was it not understood that they were females, and slaves?

I continued on my way.

I wondered how many of them, as free women, might have teased men, or led them on, or sported with them.

Such days, if they had been, were now behind them. They were now slaves, and the properties of men.

An unharnessed tharlarion was led by, his might to be applied to some wagon forward.

A whip master, too, passed by.

One is not to intrude oneself, incidentally, between a whip master and his duty.

Although one should show no concern for slaves, I felt sorry for them. They are, of course, to be understood as, and treated as, the animals they are, that goes without saying, but this does not mean that one should not be concerned for their health, comfort, and safety. After all, it is appropriate to care for one's animals. One should be concerned with the health, comfort, and safety of all one's stock, of whatever sort, even that which is well-curved and two-legged. To be sure, a typical husbandman is likely to be more concerned for the welfare of his kaiila than his female slaves, but then the kaiila is a far more valuable animal. But it is obvious that an animal which is well cared for is likely to provide a much better service and last longer than one which is ill fed, frightened, and abused. Slaves, like other animals, respond well to kindness, provided it occurs within a context of a never-compromised, iron discipline.

Somewhere a tharlarion bellowed.

It was probably hungry.

I hoped we would soon halt for the night. Tenting would be set up for the men, the Pani, the craftsmen, the teamsters, mercenaries, and others. Small fires, fueled with sheltered, dried kindling, collected earlier and brought hither, in the wagons, could be set under the roofing of canvas shelters, permitting some cooking. Certainly I would appreciate a cup of steaming kal-da, and later an opportunity to take refuge under a tarpaulin in the back of one of the wagons. The slaves were slept under the wagons. Bedded, they were kept on their neck-ropes, but their hands were retied, behind them, lest any be so foolish as to try to address themselves to the knots at the ends of the coffle rope. Their ankles were not bound, lest men, late at night, might be inconvenienced in the darkness.

I suspected the terminus of our journey would be the Alexandra.

As it was we were nearly in the ninth month.

A time was approaching in which the temperamental vagaries of restless Thassa would predictably begin. Goreans seldom brave her churning, often towering, violent green waves between the winter solstice and the spring equinox.

That is the season of bitter cold in the northern latitudes, and of high winds and storms. In such a season Gorean mariners refrain from taunting mighty Thassa. Their ships remain in port, and, in Torvaldsland, even the slim, open dragons of the Torvaldslanders, as resilient and supple as they are, remain in the sheds. Let Thassa close her roads then as she will. Let her have then her season of privacy, of isolation and ferocity, of storms and terror. In such moments she wills to be alone. Do not then venture upon her. Leave her to her moods, and her dark, swelling frenzies. Later the sun will ascend, the air will warm, and the waves subside. Then fit and rig your vessels; then roll your dragons to the shore. No, the winter is not a time to venture forth on Thassa. It is a time rather for the taverns and halls, for fires and brew, for paga and kaissa, for brawls and slaves, and the waiting for En'Kara, when, one's resources likely having been depleted, one will seek out captains and merchants, and seek perchance a new bench, a new oar.

Pertinax and I had, from time to time, sought out Cecily and Jane who, as their embonded sisters, were tunicked and coffled. We had assured ourselves thusly that they were well, or, at least, no more miserable than the others. As at Tarncamp, we had no free women with us, and no male slaves. We did have, obviously, as at Tarncamp, several female slaves. Females make excellent slaves. Had it not been for the female slaves I do not think the discipline at Tarncamp, particularly with the mercenaries present, could have been maintained. Gorean males expect to have access to female slaves, rather as the right of a free male. They expect them to be in attendance, to be provided, rather as they might expect, on some venture or another, food and lodging to be provided. Strong men do not care to do without women in collars. This, for example, is something well known to any paga slave.

With a great bellowing, calling out, and a creaking of wagons, the long line of our march came to a halt.

It was here, on the road, we would stay for the night.

I was looking forward to meat and kal-da.

Later, after supper, and a cup of hot kal-da, this doing much to restore my spirits and reconcile me to the day's travails, rather than immediately retiring to a damp tarpaulin and the hard, chill, soaked boards of a wagon, a respite to which I had earlier looked forward, I took it upon myself to make the rounds of the march. This could be done in less than an Ahn. Too, whereas a tarpaulin and a wagon bed may be preferable to the mud beneath a wagon it is, in itself, as you might suppose, no prize lodging either. It is certainly inferior to the furs and a well-curved slave chained at one's feet, against whom one may warm one's feet. Here and there a lantern hung on a wagon, and I could make my way about without much difficulty. Occasionally, in passing a wagon, I would hear a gasping and moaning, and a rolling and thrashing in the mud where, it seemed, some fellow, presumably a mercenary, had pulled a slave from under a wagon, to the end of her tether, and was in the midst of reminding her of her bondage. I did not interfere in such matters, nor was I expected to do so. These were matters internal to the camp and not within the province of myself, or guards.

"How goes the night?" I asked a fellow.

"Well, Commander," he said.

I passed an enclosed, windowed, sutlers' wagon. It was one of several recently allotted, given the weather, to the contract women. They would ride, of course, in any case, and not go afoot, as the collar-girls. Even so I did not doubt but what they had been jostled well about, and sorely discomfited by the lurchings and tiltings of their conveyances. I could imagine them within, amongst rattling pans, shifting vessels, and boxes, bracing themselves against walls, or clinging to supports. I supposed they would have, even so, some rude discolorations which might be laid to the account of the journey. Lord Nishida, interestingly, marched with his troops, braving the cold and mud, and slept in his pavilion tent. I did not know what might be typically the case with one of his rank amongst the Pani, but, if he were typical, they chose to share the hardships of their men. To be sure, he occasionally removed his mud-caked garments, bathed, donned a kimono, and honored his contract women with his presence.

I accepted the greeting of a guard, and continued on my way.

I have chosen, incidentally, in this narrative, as you have perhaps noted, to omit any explicit account of signs and countersigns. I am supposing the rationale for this is sufficiently obvious. Although such devices are frequently changed, some are used more than once. Also, certain recognition devices are portions of a secret tradition within Pani clans, the members of which may be separated by thousands of pasangs, and these are either permanent, or relatively so.

Pertinax, I suspected, was with his Jane. The former free brat of Ar, now nicely collared, thrashed well.

It is easy to caress a slave into submission, a submission in which she is yours, pleading and piteous, helplessly begging for the least continuation of your touch.

Too, it is pleasant to have a slave so.

Are they not lovely in their collars?

Pertinax had avoided Saru.

It seemed he had not forgiven her for having become a helpless slave, now in obvious, plaintive need, as other slaves, of the caresses of men.

As his Jane was a Gorean female he had no reservations about accepting her slave nature. I thought this somewhat arrogant on his part. It was also, in its way, quite amusing. His Jane had been a Gorean free woman, with all that that entailed, and thus, on Gor, until her collaring, she would have been regarded as immeasurably superior to a mere barbarian female, an Earth female, such as the former Miss Margaret Wentworth, who would have been regarded as far beneath her as a pig beneath a princess. Goreans tend to view the women of Earth as natural slave stock. Do they not commonly bear their faces? Are their shapely calves and ankles not visible in public? Consider the frequent scandal of their garmentures, beach, and summer wear, the shortness of skirts, and such. Consider, too, the provocative nature of their secret undergarments. Do they not say, "Strip me, and find a slave!"? Some even dare to color their lips, or eyelids, a liberty on Gor permitted only to slaves, and sometimes forced upon them. Too, consider that many Earth females, of their own free will, have their ears pierced, an act which on Gor is likely to be inflicted only on the lowest of slaves. Many of the new slaves brought to Gor from Earth, who are, naturally, not yet familiar with Gorean, are startled, in their sale, while they are being exhibited, to understand that the bidding on them has suddenly become much more heated. The reason is often simple. Most likely, the auctioneer has just called it to the attention of the bidders, at a moment he deems propitious, that she is a "pierced-ear girl." In any event, from the Gorean point of view, chasms separate the free woman of Earth, in so far as she has not yet been legally embonded, from the dignity, nobility, and glory of the Gorean free woman. The Gorean free woman, for example, is not only not a meaningless barbarian, but she has a Home Stone. What Pertinax's Jane and Lord Nishida's Saru had in common, of course, was that they were both human females, and thus, from a common Gorean point of view, at least amongst Gorean males, they were both, and should be, natural slaves. Many Goreans believe that all women are slaves, only that some are in collars and some are not. Certainly Pertinax's Jane was now a slave, only a slave. And I suspect that anyone, with the possible exception of Pertinax, could see that not only was Saru a slave, but that she had the makings of a superb slave. Or was it that Pertinax saw this only too clearly, but, for some reason, was reluctant to accept it? I really found it hard to believe he did not want her at his feet, in his collar. And, too, it seemed clear that that was the dream, and hope, of the girl. In her heart, it seemed, she wanted to be his slave, and knew herself his slave.

The collar well liberates a woman's deepest and most feminine nature, the desire to wholly and helplessly serve and love, to be fully pleasing, in all ways, to her master.

Women long for masters, as men for slaves.

Saru, interestingly, was the only collar-girl in the march who was not afoot but wagoned. She was back-braceleted and shackled, and put on blankets, that she not be bruised, and was occasionally covered with a tarpaulin to protect her from the rains. This was obvious evidence of her specialness. It would not do, of course, for her to share a wagon with contract women, but, on the other hand, as she was intended for a *shogun*, one would certainly not wish to risk her either in the mud and cold of the march, put her at the mercy of impatient whip-masters, who might mark her back, or place her in possible jeopardy from the attacks of men or beasts along the way. This special attention accorded to Saru, of course, earned her the resentment, even the hatred, of many of her sister slaves, behind the wagons. "She is not more beautiful than I," doubtless thought many of them, and doubtless correctly. But, her eye and hair coloring was unusual. Occasionally, as the opportunity afforded itself, she was spat upon by other slaves. Saru herself, I did not doubt, did not relish her privileges, and would have much preferred to be on a neck rope struggling with the others, but it was not permitted. I did talk to Lord Nishida once about her, commenting on the rationale for her special treatment, that doubtless being to protect her from the miseries and ardors of the march. "But, too," had said Lord Nishida, "we wish her to fear her fellow slaves." "Why is that?" I had asked. "That," said Lord Nishida, "she will see men as her only protectors, her only defense, and will thus be the more anxious to be fully pleasing to them." The lovely Saru wore one other bond than I have mentioned, other than, of course, the common bond of all Gorean slave girls, their brands and collars, and that was a chain on her neck, which fastened her to a ring set in the wagon bed. This was intended to make her theft less practicable. Are not valuable objects often chained down? Indeed, many a female slave, at night, is chained to her master's slave ring. In this fashion, they are not only nicely secured but are conveniently at hand should the master desire them in the night.

I passed two more sets of guards.

A bit later I stopped suddenly, back from a lantern.

Two guards were there.

We exchanged glances.

"Yes," said one of the guards, "they are in the forests."

"Have you seen one?" I asked.

Taking light, even that of a lantern, the membrane behind the eyes can suddenly flash like molten copper, an anomaly in the darkness. It is the same with panthers and larls.

"No," said one of the guards.

"If you have taken its scent," I said, "it is not on your track."

When the fur is wet the scent is even more obtrusive. It might be fifty yards or more, back in the trees.

"No," said one of the guards.

It is well known that the undetected sleen is he to be most feared.

"Observe the night," I said.

"Yes, Commander," said the guards.

I continued on my way.

I recalled that the scent of a sleen had also been detected back in the vicinity of Tarncamp, on the road between the central camp and the training and storage area. Vigilance is certainly to be recommended, but, on the whole, the human is not the common prey of sleen.

I had the edged buckler with me, brought from the wagon after I had supped. I made my rounds in what, from the point of view of an Earth chronometer, not a Gorean chronometer, would be a clockwise fashion. In this way the buckler, on my left, was always between myself and the darkness. Too, one did not linger in the light of lanterns. I thought the forests empty of men, but one did not know, and I had been assured that there were spies in the camp of Lord Nishida. Someone, too, in league with Seremides, must have slain the fellow who had drugged the tarn, and accosted me in the vicinity of Tarncamp.

Surely it was not impossible that a metal-finned quarrel might rest on its guide, patient in the darkness.

I thought of the fellows encountered in the tent of Lord Nishida, at Tarncamp, Quintus, Telarion, Fabius, Lykourgos, and Tyrtaios. One or more, I had gathered, were spies, and one was possibly of the dark caste, the Assassins.

Some leaders would have had all five killed, innocent and guilty alike, to guarantee the elimination of the guilty. Lord Nishida, however, had not done so. His motivations in this matter, I suspected, were primarily political. The spy is, after all, a conduit to the enemy.

I thought of Seremides, and the strange conversation we had shared, on tarnback, in the darkness, partly in the rain.

"Master!" I heard, a soft, pleading voice, from my right, in the darkness, from the ground, from beneath a wagon.

I stopped.

"Please, please, Master!" said the voice.

Gorean men are not unfamiliar with that sound. They know it from their own slaves.

"Please, Master," said the voice.

The voice bore within it the easily recognized, unmistakable note of the needful slave, a sound soft, tiny, uttered as though by one who might fear to be whipped, half a whimper.

"You may speak, girl," I said, authorizing her to speak.

She squirmed a bit from beneath the wagon, until arrested by the neck tether. Her hands were tied behind her back.

"He aroused me, and left me helpless," she said.

This is a cruel thing to do to a slave, of course.

"What did you do," I asked, "to be so punished?"

"I did nothing!" she said. "He did this for his hatred, for his amusement. I was of Cos, and he of Ar! So he brought me to this point and left me! Have mercy on me!"

"You are no longer of Cos," I said. "You are only a slave."

"Yes, Master," she wept.

"Only a slave," I said.

"Yes, Master, yes, Master!" she wept.

There are many warring polities on Gor, and there is often a deep-seated hatred amongst them. After all, do not enemies threaten one another's cities, goods, fields, and resources, their walls, and Home Stones? Some vendettas and rivalries have continued for generations. Too, wars on Gor are fought not only for adventure and sport, but for gain, as well. An enemy's trading posts may be looted, his mines seized, his crops harvested. Wars may be fought for arable land, for markets, for high ground, for defensible passes, for routes, for access to the sea, for olive groves and stands of timber, for orchards and vineyards, for precious metals, cloths, and jewels, for kaiila, tarsks, verr, many things. Indeed, a warrior's pay is commonly the loot he can acquire. Too, we might note that amongst the most prized and sought-after fruits of war are the females of the enemy. They are valuable loot and bring good prices in the markets. Too, one may wish to keep them. One of the greatest pleasures of a Gorean warrior is to have a woman of the enemy as his slave. And often, she in his power, and as he is teaching her her collar, he may have it, however foolishly, that she stands proxy for her city and he may, however absurdly, vent upon her all the contempt and spleen he feels for a hated foe. Does she not then, chained in her cage at night, try fruitlessly to tear the collar from her throat? Then, in the morning, after sobbing herself to a fitful sleep, she is ordered forth from her cage again, naked, on all fours, in her shackles, to be again abused and set once more to arduous, exhausting, seemingly endless, humiliating labors, to be once more subjected to a misplaced vengeance, a vengeance now as meaningless, as inappropriate, and as out of place, now that she is a slave, as would be the gratuitous abuse of an innocent, helpless, tethered verr. One supposes the master's victimization of his property will eventually subside, one certainly hopes so, when he no longer sees her as a scion of, and in terms of, hated foes, but comes to understand that she is no longer a proud, exalted free woman of the enemy toward whom a sword may be legitimately directed, but is now no more than a collar-beast he owns, a sleek, lovely collar-beast fully in his power, one who depends upon him, totally, and one who hopes to be found pleasing. She knows, of course, that Home Stones are now behind her, forever. She is collared. Too, she now has what she has always desired, a master, and she hopes to please him, to warrant a caress, and to one day win his love. As a former free woman certainly the extraordinary pleasure she gives her master and the extraordinary pleasure, psychological and physical, she derives from his mastery has come as a revelation, a welcome and astonishing joy which she as a free woman had only suspected in fearful, secret moments. Already it seems she is a love slave.

"Please, Master," she begged. "Complete his work! I beg it!"

"What is your name?" I asked.

"Talena," she said.

"No," I said, suddenly. "You are not Talena!"

"It is the name I have been given," she said, frightened. "If it does not please you, name me as you will."

I fetched a nearby lantern, and held it over the supine slave, who half closed her eyes against the light.

"You are not Talena," I said.

"I was of Cos," she said. "They gave me a name of the mainland, of Ar."

"As masters may," I said.

"Yes, Master," she said.

This was not surprising. Had she been of Ar and taken to Cos it was likely she would have been given a Cosian name. The same animal on Earth, say a dog, would be likely to receive one name in Britain, another in France, another in Italy, and so on.

"'Talena'," I said, "is the name of one who was Ubara of Ar."

"A false Ubara!" she said. "That is known even in Cos."

My hand tightened menacingly on the ring by means of which the lantern was suspended.

"Do not strike me!" she pleaded.

"Yes," I said, drawing back, wearily, "she was a false Ubara."

"There are many Talenas," she said.

"Yes," I said. 'Talena' was a not unfamiliar name on Gor, at least on the mainland. To be sure, it would be an unusual name for a slave. There was at least one other Talena, of course, who was a slave. I recalled the Metellan district. I had not changed her name on the embondment papers, but had permitted her to retain the name 'Talena', though then, of course, not as a free name but as a slave name, put upon her by the will of her master. Now, I supposed, she would, if somewhere collared, have yet a different name.

"I do not like the name 'Talena' for you," I said. "It is too fine a name for a slave."

"Forgive me, Master," she said.

"When you have a private master," I said, "should you be so fortunate, beg him for a different name. Masters are commonly indulgent in such matters."

"I will!" she said.

Slave names are often short, and convenient, such as 'Lita', 'Lana', 'Dina', and such. Earth-girl names, it might be noted, are commonly accounted slave names on Gor, and may be put upon Gorean girls as well as slaves harvested from the fields of Earth. For example, 'Jane', on Gor, would be clearly understood as a slave name. There are many names on Gor, of course, both masculine and feminine, which are frequently encountered, as is the case on Earth. My own first name, 'Tarl', for example, was quite common in Torvaldsland.

I placed my hand on her right knee.

"Yes, Master," she said. "Please, Master!"

I was annoyed at my reaction to being apprised of the slave's name. Her voice had not been that of Talena. And I had even fetched the lantern to look upon her. She had not been Talena, of course, not *the* Talena.

Again I recalled the conversation with Seremides, in the darkness above the forest.

I gathered that the Ubara had not yet been brought before the throne of a Ubar's justice.

Strange, I thought, that so mighty a bounty, ten thousand tarn disks, of gold, of double weight, had not yet been claimed.

What value might she have to someone, or something, which might exceed such a sum?

Did a captor wait for even so incredible a sum to be increased? Were negotiations now in progress? Perhaps a captor was amused to have the former Ubara at his slave ring for a time, before, say, tiring of her, and then delivering her to the justice of Ar. I could well imagine the slave, in such a situation, striving mightily to please whoever, or whatever, might be her master of the moment, to postpone as long as possible the day of her return to Ar.

"Please, Master," whispered the slave.

I rose from her side and returned the lantern to its place.

I heard her sob behind me.

I returned to her side.

"Master?" she whispered, disbelievingly.

She had thought, I supposed, that I had abandoned her.

"Are you still in heat, girl?" I inquired.

One would seldom use so vulgar an expression, I supposed, in the case of a free woman, but it is often used in the case of animals, which makes it acceptable in the case of a slave, as she is an animal, a lovely form of domestic animal.

"Yes," she said.

It is not unusual for a slave girl to approach her master, kneel before him, kiss his feet, straighten up, and inform him that she is in heat, openly, clearly, frankly, honestly, and innocently. The slave is not ashamed of her sexual needs, no more than it would occur to the free woman to be ashamed of her needs for, say, food and water. "Master's girl is in heat," she might say. "She begs for his caress."

I lightly touched the interior of her right thigh.

"Yes," she said. "A touch will free me, the least touch!"

I bent gently to her and, to her astonishment, put my tongue to her heat.

In an instant I had to place my right hand over her mouth, tightly, that her cries might not disturb the camp. It was hard to hold her in place, even with my right hand over her mouth, and my left hand grasping her arm, above the elbow. She thrashed wildly, gratefully, kicking mud about, half rising up, and twisting from side to side, and then lay back, and still. I became, only a bit later, aware that she was kissing and licking at the palm of my right hand, desperately, gratefully. I drew it away a bit and she still sought it with her kisses, on the side of the hand, on the back, and fingers, and wrist.

"Thank you, Master," she whispered. "Thank you, Master!"

"You are not a Talena," I informed her. "You are a Lita."

"Lita, Master?" she said.

"You are a camp slave, are you not?" I asked.

"Yes, Master," she said.

"You have been renamed 'Lita'," I said. "If any object, have them bring their complaint to me."

"And who is Master?" she asked.

"Tarl Cabot," I said.

"He who is captain, commander, of the cavalry?" she said.

"Yes," I said.

"Then I am Lita," she said.

I then stood up and brushed away some mud, and wiped my hands on my tunic. I gathered in the edged buckler.

"Master!" called another girl.

"Please, Master," called another.

"No," I said, and continued on my rounds.

I had not realized that others had been aware of my presence.

I supposed we were bound for the Alexandra.

If there were ships there, they could not make voyage, of course, until the spring.

Yet, from the time of the attack on the camp, Lord Nishida had made it clear to me that his plans, whatever they might be, must be advanced. It seemed he would, at least, change camps. That must be all. He surely could not be mad enough to contemplate braving Thassa unseasonably, between the winter solstice and the spring equinox.

My interlude with the needful slave, a girl once of Cos, who had been named 'Talena', now 'Lita', put me naturally in mind of the former Ubara, and her possible fates.

I recalled that, long ago, Miss Margaret Wentworth, before she became the slave, Saru, had spoken of a hold over me, by means of a woman. This had made little sense to me at the time.

I thought now, however, from my rendezvous with Seremides, once of the Taurentians, the woman would be Talena.

But how could someone or something think they had a hold over me, in virtue of one such as she, a false Ubara, now deposed, last seen bound on the height of the Central Cylinder in Ar, kneeling at the feet of men, fearing apprehension, fittingly placed in the rag of a slave?

How could anyone, or anything, think that?

But, if so, how grievously then had someone, or something, whether human, Kur, or Priest-King miscalculated!

What now would Talena be to me?

I did not want her.

I would not now buy her, even as a pot girl for my kitchens in Port Kar.

She had been beautiful, but, too, she had been proud, ambitious, selfish, vain, and cruel. Had I not understood that, long ago? Had I not then understood that she belonged, if at all, only under the whip? I recalled how badly she had treated me and how with such delight and venom she had scorned me in the holding of Samos of Port Kar, when I had been confined to the chair of an invalid, thought perhaps never to walk again, imprisoned there by the lingering effects of a poison contrived by Sullius Maximus, a renegade captain of Port Kar, then in the fee of Chenbar, the Sea Sleen, Ubar of Tyros. Later, at the first opportunity, escaping her sequestration in the Central Cylinder of Ar where she, disowned by her father, had been confined in dishonor, having begged to be purchased, a slave's act, in the northern forests, she had betrayed her Home Stone, conspiring with the forces of Cos and Tyros to bring down, belittle, and subdue her own city, mighty Ar, to achieve a meretricious ascent to a Ubara's throne, to reign there as a puppet, her strings in the keeping of enemies and invaders. But then her father had somehow returned, it seemed from the Voltai, and the insurrection had subsequently occurred, casting forth, violently and bloodily, the occupying forces and restoring the rightful governance of the city.

I smiled to myself.

How fitting that I had had her trapped and embonded in the Metellan district, then arranging that she should be returned to the throne of Ar, though knowing herself, so secretly, as then a slave. How she must have lived in terror, fearing that this secret might be revealed, which was then indisputable and certifiable. What hubris that a slave should dare to don the garments of a free woman, let alone take a place on a Ubara's throne! Would not each tiny particle of her flesh, one after another, have been publicly removed over weeks, or months, on a needle's point?

I had seen to it that she was enslaved, in her own city, making use of a couching law of Marlenus himself, Ubar of Ubars.

It had been easily and perfectly done. I trusted that she, to her rage, consternation, and chagrin, in all her utter helplessness, that of a female in the hands of men, had realized that.

How pleasant it is to enslave a woman.

How better can one degrade them? But how strange it is that they so thrive in their degradation. Do they not understand what has been done to them, or do they understand it only too well? How is it that they kiss your feet in gratitude, leap instantly to do your bidding, kiss their fingertips and touch them to their collars, buck and squirm in your arms, gasping and writhing in grateful, uncontrollable, orgasmic ecstasy, kneel, heads bowed, before you. How radiant and joyful they are in their collars! Are they not born to thongs? Is it so strange that they find their joy and fulfillment at a man's feet, or is it merely to be expected, given a genetic heritage of the surrenders of love, without which a woman cannot be whole?

Who is the man who truly loves a woman, he who denies reality or he who recognizes it, and embraces it, he who betrays her and panders to propagandas, or he who consents to answer the cries of her heart?

So Talena was now a slave, no different from any other slave, save for the bounty on her head.

Excellent, I thought, save for the bounty.

I did not think I would buy her even for a pot girl. And surely many were the slaves more beautiful than she!

She had thought herself the most beautiful woman on all Gor.

How absurd that was!

She had never been ranged naked in a coffle, standing, legs widely spread, hands clasped behind the back of her head, for assessment.

Yes, she was beautiful, but there were thousands more beautiful than she. Had she not once been the daughter of a Ubar, what might she have brought? Perhaps three silver tarsks? Much would depend on the market, and the season. Spring is a good time for selling slaves.

If then some thought to have a hold over me in virtue of a slut named Talena, doubtless even now somewhere in a collar and a slave's rag, if that, they were muchly, and profoundly, mistaken!

I wondered where she might be.

In any event, it was no concern of mine.

There was suddenly a rush from my left, and something emerged from the darkness, from the trees, and I knelt down, on my right knee, heard the scrape of a blade on the metal, and, almost simultaneously, rose up, swinging the edged buckler up, violently, to the left, and it met resistance, and there was an ugly gurgling cry, and something stumbled back, and fell, away from the buckler. I crouched down, alert. At the same time, from within the trees, I heard a screaming, and a shaking and a tearing, as though an arm might be being torn from its shoulder. Within moments lanterns were rushing toward me, and men, and guards. "Call Lord Nishida!" I heard.

In the light of the lanterns I looked down on the shape at my feet. The edged buckler had caught it under the chin, and taken the head half from the body. From the trees there was a hideous wailing and four Pani, glaives ready, slipped amongst the trees. In moments they drew forth from the darkness, dragging it, a sobbing, mauled figure, the left arm missing. It was trying to stanch the flooding stream bursting from its body with its free hand, and then it was thrown to the mud amongst us, several mercenaries and Pani now having hurried forward.

I watched the living figure twitch before us. Then I thought perhaps it felt no pain, its body perhaps then flooded with endorphins. Its eyes were wide with shock. Blood ran freely between the fingers of its right hand.

"Stanch his wound," I said.

The fellow's hand was pulled away and cloth was thrust into the hole in his body.

"Where is the arm?" asked a man.

Two Pani, with lanterns, entered the forest.

I became aware of Lord Nishida, now standing at my side. "What is going on?" he asked.

"I know not," I said.

"Give me a lantern," said Lord Nishida, and was handed a lantern. He bent down, to examine the two fellows before us. And then he stood up.

The two Pani who had just entered the forest returned. One carried a crossbow.

"The assassin's weapon," said Lord Nishida.

"A weapon commonly employed by assassins," I granted him.

"We could not find the arm," said one of the Pani, he without the crossbow. "It was a sleen attack," said the other. "The beast must have carried it away, into the trees, to feed."

"We caught the scent of a sleen in the vicinity earlier," said a mercenary, one of the guards.

"Apparently the bowman did not," said a fellow.

"Nor would he," I said.

"Double the guard," said Lord Nishida.

"Behold," said one of the Pani, indicating with the shaft of his long glaive the figure brought recently to the road. "This man is dead."

"He bled to death," said a mercenary.

"Unfortunate," said Lord Nishida. "We might have learned much from him."

A man drew the wadded, blood-soaked cloth from the inert body.

"Well, Tarl Cabot, tarnsman," said Lord Nishida, "we have solved one of our problems."

"How is that?" I asked.

"We have discovered our assassin," said Lord Nishida. "This

man, whose head is still muchly in his helmet, is Lykourgos, and this other, he with the crossbow, is Quintus, so one or the other, perhaps both, are of the Assassins."

"Both may have attempted the work of the assassin," I said, "but neither, I fear, are of the Assassins."

"How so?" asked Lord Nishida, interested.

"This man," I said, indicating he who had been caught beneath the chin by the edged buckler, "rushed clumsily from the darkness. He lacked the skill one would expect from a professional at dark work, and the other, he with the crossbow, did not risk a miss, preferring to leave the strike to the knife of his confederate, he himself then serving muchly as support, either for a second strike, or, more likely, to disconcert any who might too quickly approach, to cover the retreat of his companion. The professional assassin, I would suppose, would have trusted to his own quarrel, and not waited. Too, the professional assassin will usually choose to work alone, depending on himself, no others."

"Interesting," said Lord Nishida.

Although I said nothing, it seemed to me that we had now limited the suspicions of Lord Nishida, expressed to me earlier in Tarncamp, in his tent after I had left the feast, if they were warranted, that they had now been narrowed to Fabius, Telarion, and Tyrtaios

"But why, then," asked Lord Nishida, "would these men attack you?"

"I think," I said, "this has to do with a personal matter, which I would prefer to keep to myself."

"As you wish," said Lord Nishida.

Doubtless he supposed this had something to do with the seemingly inveterate and irascible tensions and tempers of barbarians. I myself supposed the attack was founded on my failure to satisfy Seremides in our interview of some nights ago. I had not furnished him with information as to the whereabouts of Talena, former Ubara of Ar, so was now useless to him, and he had revealed to me his identity and his interests in her pursuit, both matters he doubtless preferred to be kept unknown. He must have had a way of contacting his minions at Tarncamp or in the march, but I suspected he had had no more than two with us. If that were the case, I had nothing to concern myself with at present from that quarter. I hoped not. Similarly, if there were spies or assassins in the camp, it seemed to me that their target of primary interest, once it was decided to strike, would be not me but Lord Nishida.

"May I have a lantern?" I asked one of the Pani, and, given this artifact, I moved back, between the trees. Two or three men accompanied me, and, too, so did Lord Nishida.

It was easy to discover where Quintus had been attacked, from the dislodgment of the leaves, the rupture of the earth, the sight and smell of blood. There was no doubt the attack had been by a sleen, as there were sleen tracks about. One could see where the sleen had made its leap, from the deeper indentations in the soil, and the absence of prints between that point and the point where the prey was struck. It was several feet. The sleen must have been large, and powerful. The slight wind moving the branches would have been toward the sleen. This was what I would have expected.

"Sleen do not normally attack humans, do they?" asked Lord Nishida.

"Not usually," I said.

"You are sure those are sleen tracks?" he asked.

"Yes," I said. "Do you notice anything unusual about the tracks?"

"No," he said.

"The sleen was lame," I said.

"Interesting," said Lord Nishida.

Chapter Twenty-Nine

We Emerge from the Forest

I heard the cries of joy from forward, and knew the scouts, if not others, had now emerged from the forest, and beheld, in the morning sun, sparkling below in the valley, the winding Alexandra.

Men rushed forward.

Slaves crowded, as they could, to the sides of the wagons, on their tethers, striving to understand the commotion.

Saru, in her wagon, precariously in her shackles, stood up, trying to peer ahead.

I heard more shouts now, and was sure the first wagons had emerged from the forest.

I saw Sumomo and Hana, shading their eyes, emerge from the portal on their closed wagon and, standing on its small porch, strain to see what might be the cause of the ebullition.

Tharlarion, down the long line, lifted their heads, distended their nostrils, and bellowed. They could smell the water, perhaps the verdant grazing near the river.

Pertinax was with me.

Knowing that we should reach the Alexandra in the late morning we had freed Cecily and Jane.

"Master!" cried Cecily, elated.

"Heel us," I snapped.

Dutifully the girls fell in behind us, on our left.

No matter how indulgent or permissive one is with slaves, they must never be permitted to forget they are slaves. If necessary, they may be whipped, to remind them. Indeed, some masters feel that a slave should be occasionally whipped, if only to help them keep in mind that they are slaves. To be sure, given Gorean discipline, a slave is seldom likely to be in any doubt about the matter. Certain prosaic regularities contribute to this purpose, that the slave will commonly kneel upon entering the master's presence, that she may speak only when having the master's permission to do so, that she must often kneel and kiss the whip or switch in the morning, that she may not clothe herself without his permission, that she may not take food before the master, that she may not leave the domicile without his permission, and she must give an account of her intentions before leaving and an account of her activities upon returning, and so on. Many such things remind her of her bondage. Too, one must not forget what occurs at her master's slave ring.

"I will relish a bathing in the river," said Pertinax.

"I did not know barbarians were fastidious," I remarked.

I feared all on the march, with the exception of the contract women and Saru were the much the worse for the past few days.

"May we bathe, Master?" asked Cecily.

"You will be better off to seek oils and a heated tub," I said. "The river will be cold."

Too, I thought the slaves should soon be better garmented, for in spite of the late summer, so to speak, it was now fall, and the weather, with the season, must soon chill.

The march had certainly been cold enough and miserable enough, even for the men.

"Tarl Cabot, tarnsman!" called Tajima, hurrying beside the wagons, toward us. He, with the cavalry, had come ahead, days ago.

We bowed to one another. He was uncomfortable, I had gathered, with the clasping of hands, even the mariner's grip, wrist to wrist. Much varies from culture to culture.

But, clearly, he was pleased to see me, and I him.

He looked at Pertinax.

"Say 'Tal'," I said to Pertinax.

"Tal," said Pertinax.

"Tal," said Tajima, pleasantly. There is an order to such things, and Tajima, correctly or incorrectly, regarded himself as senior to Pertinax, who was a mere barbarian. That he had addressed me first, rather than I him, was appropriate, given that I was his captain, so to speak, with respect to the cavalry. I occasionally erred in these rituals, but these lapses tended to be accepted with good grace, being attributed to my innocent lack of couth, and that no affront was intended. Amongst those who know what they are doing in such waters things can become subtly tense. I sometimes sensed that social duels were in progress which were simply beyond my comprehension.

"Look," whispered Pertinax.

Both he and Tajima bowed as Nodachi passed, going forward.

"I did not know he was with the march," I said. Certainly I had not seen him.

"He was not with the march, but behind it," said Tajima. "He followed the march, to protect its rear."

"I see," I said.

"You are all very filthy," said Tajima.

Cecily and Jane lowered their heads. The female slave is expected to keep herself neat, well-groomed, clean, combed, brushed, and so forth. She is, after all, not a free woman. Too, she is usually expected to keep herself at her "block measurements," namely the measurements she was sold at. Accordingly, regimens of diet and exercise may be forced upon her. Again, she is a slave, not a free woman. Much may be concealed beneath the "Robes of Concealment," but a slave tunic conceals almost nothing.

"How is Sumomo?" asked Tajima.

"I think you will find her clean and dry, and nasty, as usual," I said.

"Excellent," said Tajima.

"How excellent?" I asked.

"I can continue to think of her as fit for the collar."

"I see," I said.

"But come along," he said. "See the river camp."

"We will spend the winter there," I said.

"No," said Tajima.

"I do not understand," I said.

"Come along," he said.

We moved toward the head of the column, it now arrested,

as most of the drovers, and others, had abandoned the wagons to hurry forward, to see at last before them a vista, and not the gloomy, enclosing walls of a seemingly endless corridor of trees.

"What is it, Master? What is it?" called a slave to a passing guard, but then she cried out in fear, turned her back, crouched down, and covered her head with her hands and arms, and was struck several times with his switch.

"Curiosity," said the guard, "is not becoming in a *kajira*."

"Yes, Master," she wept. "Forgive me, Master!"

It is well known hat *kajirae* are amongst the most curious of beasts. How eager they are to be informed, to be brought up to date, to learn the latest! They will beg, wheedle, scratch, and scramble for the tiniest particle of news. The girl who knows something the others do not is as a Ubara in the slave quarters. How she is pressed! How all hang upon her superior, sly glances, her least, carefully rationed word!

How pleasant it is sometimes to frustrate them, and see them pout and squirm in ignorance, tears in their eyes. In this way, too, of course, they may be reminded that they are no more than slaves.

We came then, at last, to an opening in the trees, and stood upon a rise, from which a road led gently downward through the valley toward the river.

There were more than four or five hundred men there, come forward from the column.

I could see Lord Nishida and his guard making their way down toward the river. Some from the shore, and the structures there, were climbing to meet them.

The sky was very blue, and cloudless.

In it, being exercised, were several tarns.

The river, broad and apparently navigable, lay some pasang or so in the distance.

"That is the Alexandra," I said.

"Yes," said Tajima.

Its width could not begin to approximate that of the Vosk, in much of Vosk's length, but it was wide, wide enough, some hundred yards or so in width.

"It is very beautiful," said Cecily.

She, I fear, had not yet accustomed herself to the beauties of a natural world, but still thought in terms of another world, a grayer world, a more tragic world, a world in which, incredibly, pollutants and poisons were routinely discharged into the atmosphere, into the very air its creatures, large and small, innocent and guilty alike, must breathe. But it was true, I supposed, the vista was indeed beautiful.

"Quarters have been prepared for you, near the shore, near the cots," said Tajima.

Orders were being given, behind us, by various wagon masters, and drovers, Pani, mercenaries, and all, began to withdraw to the wagons. In a few Ehn the tharlarion would again grunt and bellow, and the wagons would again trundle forward, and now downward.

"What is that large building, that structure near the shore?" I asked.

It seemed large enough to house an *insula*. It must have been seven or eight stories high.

"Beyond that," said Tajima, "though you cannot see them, are several galleys."

"But what is the large structure?" I asked.

"You do not know?" inquired Tajima.

"No," I said.

"That," said Tajima, "is the ship of Tersites."

Chapter Thirty

I Speak with Aëtius

I felt small, standing on the shore, beside that towering, mighty body, that massive structure, held in its building frame, sloping down to the water.

"There is much to be done," said Aëtius, once of the arsenal at Port Kar, apprentice to the mad, half-blind shipwright, Tersites, once of the same city, now an embittered expatriate. "The rudder has not been hung at the sternpost."

"A single rudder?" I asked.

"Yes," he said.

The common Gorean galley has two side-rudders, each with its helmsman.

"The masts have yet to be added," said Aëtius. "There will be six, two aft, two amidships, and two forward. They will be square-rigged, with four spars to the aft and amidship's masts, and three to the forward masts."

The usual Gorean ship has a single mast, which is lateen-rigged. In a fighting ship this mast is lowered before battle. Usually the Gorean ship carries three or more sails, to be fastened, as needed, to the long, sloping yard, depending on wind conditions. The smallest sail is the "storm sail."

"The masts are fixed, permanent?" I asked.

"Yes," he said.

The lateen-rigged galley can sail closer to the wind, but, for a given length of yard, it exposes less surface to the wind. The square sails, reefed according to conditions, are all-weather sails, permanent sails. The masts need not be lowered to accommodate changings of sails. Square-rigged vessels are not unknown on Gor. The dragons of Torvaldsland, for example, are square-rigged. Too, they have a single rudder, the "steering board," which is located on the right side of the vessel, as one faces forward. On Earth vessels of centuries ago the "steering board" on the right side, as one faces forward, apparently gave rise to the expression "starboard." The "port side," or left side of the vessel, facing forward, at least on Gor, and perhaps on Earth, may have received its name from keeping harbor buoys to one's left as the port is entered. This custom regulates harbor traffic, before a berth is reached. Leaving the port, of course, as one is reversing direction, the same line of buoys is once again on the left. This may be a mariner's tradition brought from Earth. I do not know. Road traffic on Gor, naturally, keeps to the left. In this fashion, one's weapon hand, if one is right-handed, faces the passing stranger. In Gorean, as in many languages, the same word serves for an enemy and a stranger. To be sure, not all strangers are enemies, and not all enemies, perhaps unfortunately, are strangers. I noted that the ship was carvel-built, with fitted planking, as opposed to being clinker-built, or with overlapping planking. The dragons of Torvaldsland are clinker-built. In this respect they ship more water, but they are more elastic in rough seas, and thus less likely to break apart.

"As you will note, in the frame," said Aëtius, "the keel is unusually deep."

"The ship is large," I said.

"Even so," he said.

This information made me somewhat apprehensive, for it suggested that the designer of the ship was planning it not for swiftness and maneuverability, common features of a Gorean galley, even the so-called "round ships," but for stability in serious weather. Most Gorean ships put into port, or beach, frequently, even daily, being light enough to be drawn onto the beach. Many Gorean pilots are reluctant to venture beyond the sight of land, and open-sea voyages of more than a few days are rare, except in Torvaldsland. A ship of this stability and size, of course, might remain at sea indefinitely. I had the sense that this vessel had been designed with an unusual voyage in mind.

"Such a vessel," I said, "might sail even beyond Cos and Tyros."

"Perhaps," he said.

"Beyond even the Farther Islands," I said.

"Perhaps," he said, looking away.

"There are no shearing blades, at least as yet," I said. Such blades are designed to shear away a galley's oars, thus crippling her, and preparing her for a ramming, usually amidships, which is a blow of considerable force, easily sufficient to rupture and flood the prey vessel, and occasionally sufficient to snap her in two. One of the dangers of ramming is the possibility of fixing one's ram in the victim and inadvertently sharing her fate. The structure of the ram is designed, naturally, to minimize this eventuality, and to facilitate its withdrawal by back-oaring. Indeed, some rams are fitted with a flaring collar that determines the quantity of penetration into the target. Still the pressures are such that the ram, even so, is occasionally, dangerously, anchored in the victim. Some captains reduce the ramming speed at the last moment to minimize this form of engagement. It is not necessary for the ram to shatter the opposing vessel to guarantee its destruction. If the enemy ship takes in more water than she can expel the ram has done its work. Shearing blades, incidentally, had been an invention of Tersites, many years ago. They had soon become common on all long ships, even those of Cos and Tyros.

"The ship is too massive for them to be effective," he said.

I did not doubt that. The usual galley could easily avoid such devices.

"There is no ram, as yet," I observed.

"One is not needed," he said.

"I suppose not," I said. I supposed that any vessel so slow or unwary as to come beneath the bow of this leviathan would be shattered like kindling, crushed like a cache of vulo eggs beneath the tread of a tharlarion. Tersites, incidentally, had recommended that the rams of galleys make their strike above the waterline rather than below it. Some shipwrights had acted on this recommendation and others not. The advantage of having the ram above the waterline is that it increases the speed of the ship, particularly if the ram has a flared collar. If the strike is made at or near the waterline the ram's effectiveness is little compromised, given the rise and fall of the sea.

"How can the ship defend itself?" I asked.

"Variously," said Aëtius. "To begin with, it is difficult to attack, given its size. The height of the bulwarks, as in round ships, discourages boarding. Here we have an extreme instance of that. Consider the difficulty of scaling the walls of a city, particularly if the city were at sea. And the timbers, particularly at the bow, and in the vicinity of the waterline, are layered horizontally, and interlaid with sheets of metal, to a depth of five feet. Similarly the ship, when fitted, will be equipped with the usual implements of offense, catapults and such. Too, it will have a crew of a thousand or more."

"So many?" I said.

"We will have here," said Aëtius, "a fortress, a floating city, with hundreds of defenders, swordsmen, spearmen, archers, and such, who will have the advantage of height."

"It will move only under sail, I take it," I said.

"That is its design," he said. "It is not a galley."

"The size, the weight," I said.

"Of course," he said.

I saw no thole ports, near the waterline, even for the great oars, with grips, those used on some round ships, five men to an oar.

"And you yourself, as I understand you to be Bosk, of Port Kar," he said, "have armed the ship most devastatingly."

"I do not understand," I said.

"Was it not you, on the 25th of Se'Kara," he asked, "who first used tarns at sea?"

"It was a gamble," I said.

"The stones were cast well," said Aëtius.

"As it turned out," I said.

The tarn is a land bird and will not fly beyond the sight of land. What I had done was to house tarns below decks until we were far from land. Then, in battle, I had released them with riders, primarily to cast vessels of fire upon the ships of Cos and Tyros. Fortunately for us the tarns responded to their straps as though over land. They may have taken the ships below as land, as islands, so to speak, or, perhaps, it was a mere matter that we had not triggered or engaged the bird's reluctance to forsake the sight of land. I supposed this disposition had been selected for in the course of the beast's evolution. Tarns which were disposed to leave the sight of land might have perished in the sea, and thus failed to replicate their genes. Tarns which, for whatever reason, or random gift of genes, were reluctant to leave the sight of land might nest, and reproduce.

"The size of the vessel," said my informant, "is such as to house tarns, their tarnsmen, their tarnsters, their gear, their provender, and such. They may be exercised regularly at sea, and then return to their vessels. Ports for their entry and exit are built into the hull."

"It is very different from what I am familiar with," I said.

"There are here, as well," said Aëtius, "six common galleys. They might prove of use, and are such as may be housed in the great ship."

"Within the great ship?" I said.

"Precisely," said Aëtius.

"Are you sure about the single rudder?" I asked. That there was to be a single rudder was clear not only from the claim of Aëtius, but from the massive socketing, at the stern.

"One is enough," said Aëtius. "The design is effective."

"I see," I said. It did seem to me that in a vessel of this size a double rudder might be impractical, and difficult to mount. Too, in a vessel of this size one would not, in any case, look for a delicate responsiveness to the helm, or helms. This was not a long ship, or a dragon of Torvaldsland.

"In a calm sea," said Aëtius, "there need be only a single helmsman."

"I see," I said. One helmsman, of course, can observe, and communicate with, a second helmsman, some yards across the helmdeck. On the other hand, even a single helmsman would not be likely to be alone. There would presumably be a watch in place.

"Where is Tersites?" I asked.

I remembered having seen him long ago, from the Council of Captains, which, at that time, was subordinate to the Five

Ubars, competitive captains in the port. Later the council itself had become sovereign. He had tried to bring several of his proposals, dreams, and ideas, before the council, but they had been deemed too radical, even absurd, and had provoked much derision. This lonely genius, or madman, had become a laughing stock. Certainly he had been badly treated. He had tried later to carry his ideas even to the enemies of Port Kar, Cos and Tyros, but had met with no better success in these island ubarates. He had returned destitute to Port Kar, and had fed off garbage in the canals, and, on a pittance provided for him by the shipwrights, despised and derided, had begun to frequent the taverns of the city. He had then disappeared from Port Kar, and his fate had become unknown, at least to most. It was rumored he was somewhere in the vicinity of the northern forests. I had now begun to suspect that someone, or something, sometime, somewhere, had paused to listen, and carefully, thoughtfully, to the ravings of the demented shipwright, and that that someone, or something, had had plenteous resources at its disposal. Repudiated in Port Kar, mocked in Cos and Tyros, humiliated, outraged, and hating, mad, half-blind Tersites, here on the banks of the Alexandra, was selling the fruits of his genius to a buyer whose identity I doubted he knew. Who cares from what purse the gold to realize dreams may be drawn?

"Where is Tersites?" I asked, again.

"I do not know," said Aëtius, "perhaps on board."

"I did not see him coming to greet Lord Nishida," I said.

"We have had nasty weather here," said Aëtius. "You must have encountered it in the forest."

"We did," I said.

"Given a few days," said Aëtius, "the ship will be ready. The galleys are seaworthy now."

I supposed the galleys had come from the south, and had been brought upstream, under oars, or towed, perhaps by tharlarion on shore, where the current might be difficult.

"Have you see Tersites of late?" I inquired.

"No," he said.

"I would like to see him," I said.

"I am sure you will," said Aëtius.

"When?" I asked.

"The weather has now changed," said Aëtius. "This is better for the carpentry."

"Doubtless," I said.

"The tarns can be exercised now," he said.

"I am glad to hear it," I said.

"What do you think of her?" asked Aëtius, gesturing to the incredible structure looming over us.

"It is not a ship," I said. "It is an *insula,* a fortress, a city of wood."

"Do not look for the lines of a long ship," said Aëtius. "She is not intended to be such."

"It is a country, an island of wood," I said.

"No," said Aëtius. "She is a ship."

"She is not made for the shelter of coasts," I said.

"No," agreed Aëtius.

I considered the mighty structure. How different it was from the common ships of Gor. It was not built for speed, and its low bulwarks and lowered masts, for concealment. It was not made for approaching, difficult to detect, low on the horizon, for the raid and swift departure. It was not made to come and go, severally, frequently, to beach at night, and embark at dawn. This vessel might venture far, might spend months at sea, with no sight of land. This, I feared, was no common vessel, and intended no common voyage.

"When you get to know her," said Aëtius, "you will see her might, her power, the beauty of her lines."

"Perhaps," I said.

"And soon," he said, "she will be ready, and will depart."

"Soon ready, perhaps," I said. "But not to soon depart."

"Yes," he said, "to soon depart."

"Not soon, surely," I said.

"No, soon," said he.

"It will soon be winter," I said.

"I know," he said.

I was apprehensive.

"How many men were brought from Tarncamp?" asked Aëtius.

"I do not know," I said, "perhaps eighteen hundred, perhaps nineteen hundred."

"That is more than we will need," he said.
"Then release them, with pay," I said.
"Do not be foolish," he said.
"You will not pay them?" I asked.
"They will have to be killed," he said.
"I think not," I said.
"Do not fear," he said, "tarnsmen, tarnsters, and such are precious. They are safe. And Lord Nishida will not consent to the decimation of his men. Therefore it is mercenaries, preferably those less skilled, who will have to be thinned."
"No," I said.
"Most are renegades, outlaws, sword hirelings, killers," he said.
"No matter," I said.
"Berths are limited," he said.
"I have fought with these men," I said. "They are sword brothers."
"Do not fear," he said. "All this will be done of their own free will. Gold will set them upon one another. They are such. Too, in this way the most skilled will survive."
"Who is first in this camp?" I asked.
"The *daimyo,* Lord Okimoto," said Aëtius.
"I would see him," I said.
"You shall, you shall," I was assured.
At that moment we heard the roar of caged larls, as, down from the forest, came the cage wagons housing Lord Nishida's pets, of which there were some ten, as I had counted, two from the pavilion, and some eight, who had prowled the wands. The larl, as noted, is not native to the northern forests.
"There are several decks on the ship," Aëtius was explaining to me, outlining, in general, their housings, functions, stores, and such, but I was not listening.
"What is wrong?" he inquired.
"I would see the *daimyo,* Lord Okimoto," I said.
"You shall," said Aëtius.
"Now," I said.
Aëtius turned then away from the great frame, in which rested the ship of Tersites, like a mountain of fitted wood, a shaped, swelling geometry of tiered planking, and summoned

three or four fellows to him, large, burly fellows, artisans I supposed, perhaps dock workers. He indicated me. "Seize and bind him," he said.

Chapter Thirty-One

I Hear of the Selections

"We anticipated your reluctance, Tarl Cabot, tarnsman," said Lord Nishida. "But you must try to understand."

"Some things," I said, "are not to be understood."

"Do not judge where you do not yet understand," he said.

"I understand what I am asked to understand," I said, "but I choose not to understand."

"You refuse?" asked Lord Nishida.

"Yes," I said.

"Of course," he said. "The codes."

We sat across from one another, cross-legged, the small, low table between us.

"I expected it," said Lord Nishida.

"You must intervene," I said.

"Lord Okimoto is cousin to the *shogun*," said Lord Nishida.

My bonds had been removed, but I had been kept in confinement, in a shed near the river.

"Pertinax, even Tajima, and Ichiro, and others, have objected," said Lord Nishida.

I was silent.

"They have been reprimanded," said Lord Nishida.

"Tortured, crucified?" I asked.

"Certainly not," said Lord Nishida. "They are of value, even Pertinax. His skills increase. They will not be involved in the selections."

"What of Nodachi, swordsman?" I asked.

"He is outside," said Lord Nishida. "He is not involved."

"I see," I said.

"Too," said Lord Nishida, "who could stand against him?"

"True," I said.

"The selections will take place tomorrow," said Lord Nishida.

"I will not participate," I said.

"You will not be expected to participate," said Lord Nishida. "You, and others, are outside the selections."

"These men have fought for you," I said.

"They are mercenaries," said Lord Nishida, "and the dregs of such, chosen for skill and venality, brought from a hundred cities, from the ruins and rubble of Ar, from the alleys of Besnit and Harfax, from the wharves of Brundisium and Schendi, men without Home Stones, thieves, outlaws, murderers, outcasts, *ronen,* men carried by the currents, men whose word is worthless, men of no lords, save a stater or tarn disk of gold."

"They have fought for you," I said.

"No one needs fight who does not wish it," said Lord Nishida. "The matter is simple, pairs will be matched, and a golden tarn disk to the survivor, and a berth on the great ship."

"Perhaps, with a tarn disk of gold in his purse, a fellow may decline such a berth."

"That would be unfortunate," said Lord Nishida.

"How many do you expect to die?" I asked.

"Some five hundred," said Lord Nishida.

"What if some choose not to fight?" I asked.

"They are mercenaries," said Lord Nishida. "They will cut their brother's throat for a silver tarsk, so why not that of a stranger for a disk of gold?"

"And who," I asked, "will preside over this slaughter?"

"Lord Okimoto, of course," said Lord Nishida.

"He is a greater name, a greater *daimyo,* than you, I take it," I said.

"He is cousin to the *shogun,*" said Lord Nishida.

"Dissuade him from this madness!" I urged.

"The selections," said Lord Nishida, rising, "take place tomorrow."

Chapter Thirty-Two

The Selections

The sun was bright at the beach.

One could hear the cry of birds, the lapping of the Alexandra at the sand, and about the pilings of river wharves.

I was not bound, but was in theory in the keeping of two of Lord Okimoto's *Ashigaru*. I had little doubt that I might have eluded them easily, would not two swift, unexpected blows have sufficed, but there were others about, many others. Lord Okimoto himself sat cross-legged, on a woven mat, on the platform behind me. At his right hand sat Lord Nishida. Pertinax, Tajima, Ichiro, and some others stood with me. All were unarmed, as I was. There were many *Ashigaru* and officers about, both of the commands of Lord Nishida, many of whom I recognized, and many others, I took it, of Lord Okimoto.

Matters had been explained by crier to hundreds of mercenaries. Many others, drovers, tarnsters, skilled artisans, and such, were not permitted on the beach. My men, of the cavalry, were not in evidence either. The place of killing was the beach, a corridor between the soft flow of the Alexandra and the platform, on which were found Lords Nishida and Okimoto, with its fronting and flanking, extended mass of armed observers, almost wholly Pani. Some mercenaries, I supposed, who did not die on the beach, would be forced back, wading, fighting, into the river, to die there and be washed downstream.

A blast was blown, this on a large conch trumpet.

This trumpet is called a *horagai*. It is sometimes used in

Pani warfare as a battle horn, a signaling device to regulate the movements of troops. I had trained the cavalry, it might be recalled, to respond to the notes of such a device, a war horn. These, however, in the usual Gorean fashion, were formed of metal.

In response to this signal a long column of men, in rows of ten, mercenaries, armed and accoutered, came about the platform, made its way to the beach, spread itself along the water's edge, in five rows of pairs, and then turned, so that these rows of pairs, of which there was a large number, faced the platform.

Between the mercenaries and the platform, some yards between the first row of mercenaries and the platform, there was a table of sorts, formed of planks mounted on two trestles. On this table, by two men, there was placed a small, apparently quite heavy, iron-bound coffer. A fellow of the Pani opened the lid, let it fall back, and, with two hands, lifted tarn disks above the coffer, better than a foot or so, and then opened his hands and let them spill back into the container. He did this several times. The sun caught the falling, showering metal, again and again, and it was as a rainfall of gold. One could easily hear the weight of the falling metal, even yards away. I had little doubt that there was not one fellow there at the river's edge who might not kill for even one of those prizes. There were many markets in which even one of those coins might purchase a tarn, five kaiila, ten lovely slaves. Many Goreans had never touched such a coin, let alone owned one.

"They are ready, Lord," said Lord Nishida to Lord Okimoto.

Lord Okimoto was shorter than Lord Nishida, and, on the platform, seemed immobile, almost somnolent, like a sack of sand. He was very stocky, even obese. He wore a yellow kimono, with a reddish belt. He carried the companion sword, with tasseled hilt, in the belt, blade uppermost. He had a rolled knot of hair at the back of his head, as did Lord Nishida. In this I gathered they shared some status, or station. Lord Okimoto had small, narrow eyes, and they squinted out, from between rolls of fat. Lord Nishida was straight, lean like a blade, imperturbable. When one looked upon him one had the sense of a quiet, coiled spring, or, perhaps better, that of a clever, cunning, coiled, watchful ost. Yet I somehow did not discount Lord Okimoto, or see him as negligible or ineffectual. One might despise his exterior, thinking it pathetic, swollen, and sluggish, that it housed no more than something fat, sly, and ugly, something complacent with power, something which might idly toy with cruelty, but, at the same time, one sensed that somewhere within that mound of flesh something wise and dangerous prowled, as might a larl, impatient, curious, waiting in its lair, not yet emerged to address itself to its hunt, and its fang work.

I would not dismiss Lord Okimoto.

He was, after all, a *daimyo* of the Pani. Doubtless some might have come to such a position by inheritance, but few, I supposed, would be likely to long retain its prestige, and its apparent harrowing might, coveted by others, by such means. Though many who receive gifts prove too weak to keep them, I did not think Lord Okimoto was of their number.

One of the Pani, of the entourage of Lord Okimoto, advanced before the platform and addressed the assembled, massed pairs, reiterating the terms of the contest, that each pair would do battle to the death, and the survivor would receive a tarn disk of gold.

So simply, I thought, does Lord Nishida, and Lord Okimoto, select amongst skills, and divest themselves of superfluous minions.

In any event, no one, I was sure, was to be permitted to return to the lower latitudes.

I recalled the wands, and the larls.

Lord Okimoto, without turning his head, said something to Lord Nishida, which I could not hear, and Lord Nishida lifted his hand slightly, signaling the fellow of the Pani, who was serving as herald.

"Begin!" called the herald.

Aëtius was standing near me.

No man moved.

"Fight!" cried the herald. "Begin! Fight! The gold, the gold!"

Then a thousand blades were drawn forth, as though with a single flash of sound, from a thousand sheaths. The hair on the back of my neck rose.

"Fight!" called the herald.

Then each of the thousand, in their ranks, their back to the river, faced the platform.

"Good!" I said, aloud.

Aëtius smiled.

Hundreds of Pani stirred, looked to the platform, uneasy. Glaives, the long-shafted, curved-bladed *naginata,* were grasped.

From behind the platform, Pani archers rushed forth, standing between the platform and the mercenaries. Arrows were set to the strings of the Pani longbow, arrows which are released at the bow's lower third, muchly different from the release point of either the peasant or saddle bow.

"They do not fight!" called the herald, in consternation.

I thrust my two Pani attendants to one side and went to stand before the platform, facing the seated Lord Okimoto. Lord Nishida rose to his feet. I became aware then, suddenly, that Tajima, Pertinax, Ichiro, and others, stood with me.

"They will not fight!" complained the herald to the platform.

Pani, both wielders of the glaive and graspers of the bow, looked to the platform.

"No," I said to Lord Okimoto, "they will not fight. They are sword brothers."

"They are mercenaries," cried the herald.

"And sword brothers," I said.

Lord Okimoto said something to Lord Nishida, which I could not hear, and then, slowly, ponderously, assisted by servitors, he rose to his feet and retired from the platform.

"What did he say?" I asked Lord Nishida, who had remained on the platform, standing.

"He said," said Lord Nishida, "'these are the men I would have with me.'"

"I do not understand," I said.

"It has been a test, Tarl Cabot, tarnsman," he said. "Many men will kill for gold, selling their sword to one for a silver tarsk, to a higher bidder for two, and so on. Of such men we have no need. We have need of men who will place steel before gold, honor before advancement, whose service, once pledged, is inalterable, men whose loyalty is not for sale, men who cannot be divided, and cannot be bought. Many men can, you see, but these are not amongst them. They are the sort of men we need. Our cause deserves them."

"What is your cause?" I inquired.

"You will learn," he said. Then he spoke to the herald, "Give each a tarn disk of gold, and dismiss them."

"There are a thousand tarn disks in the coffer?" I said.

"Of course," said Lord Nishida. "We did not know what the outcome would be."

"We hoped," said Aëtius, "that it would be thus."

"What if they had fought?" I asked Lord Nishida.

"Then," said Lord Nishida, "regrettably five hundred would be dead."

"And what of the survivors?" I asked.

"Each," he said, "would have been given his golden tarn disk, as promised, and then each," and here he indicated the glaivesmen and archers about, "would have been killed."

"I see," I said. "And what of the limited number of berths on the great ship?"

Lord Nishida smiled. "There is much room," he said. "Of such men we could use an additional thousand."

I watched the mercenaries filing past the coffer, each receiving his coin.

Chapter Thirty-Three

I Hold Converse with Lord Nishida

"Your plans, I understand it," I said to Lord Nishida, "have been advanced."

"Necessarily," he said, "for our project is no longer secret. The attack at Tarncamp, repulsed, has made that clear. Foes will come again, in much greater strength."

"Who is the foe?" I asked.

"One of great wealth and power," he said.

"I do not understand," I said.

Did these things have to do with Priest-Kings or Kurii, each of which faction was skilled in utilizing humans as their instrumentalities?

I wondered what kaissa was being played, and who were the gamesmen. I did have some sense of the pieces.

"This is a skirmish," said Lord Nishida. "The war is elsewhere."

"Where?" I asked.

"I trust," he said, "you will learn."

"Perhaps," I said, "I might be now enlightened."

"I think not, at present," he said.

"I think," I said, "I have served sufficiently."

"Alas," said he, "we cannot permit our friends, now so informed, to withdraw from our service."

"Do you think you can stop me?" I asked.

"Yes," he said, "but I would greatly regret having to do so."

"What is your war," I asked. "Where is it to be fought?"

"The war," he said, "is far away, and its nature you may learn."

"It has to do with a far shore?" I said.

"Yes," he said. "I see that you are interested."

"I choose my wars with care," I said.

"One does not always have that option," said Lord Nishida.

"Allegiances, dynasties?" I asked.

"Perhaps," he said.

"Men such as you," I said to Lord Nishida, "are rare in what we sometimes think of as 'known Gor'."

"So?" he said.

"How came you here?" I asked.

Surely they had not come to these shores by such a ship or ships. How, then, had they come? And why, then, could they not return as they had come?

A cloud seemed to move in the narrow eyes of Lord Nishida.

I suddenly realized, with a start, that he might know as little of this as I.

"I think," said Lord Nishida, "that a wager is involved, or perhaps a contest of sorts, amongst spirits, powerful beings."

"How so?" I said.

"There were battles, several," said Lord Nishida. "Losses were heavy. Lands were lost. The camps were crowded with the wounded and starving. Our forces were divided. We were pushed to the shore. Our world reeled."

"You are here," I said.

"A straight-eyed, raving man, a barbarian, such as yourself, was washed upon our shore, while we awaited our doom. He spoke of a world we did not know, of strange ships, and great birds."

"Tersites?" I asked.

"Yes," he said.

"You were on Cos, or Tyros, or one of the Farther Islands?" I said.

"No," he said. "No."

How, I wondered, might the mad, half-blind shipwright, Tersites, have found himself on a remote shore.

He had been brought there.

"How is it that you speak Gorean?" I asked.

"Strange men, dour men with shaven heads and white robes, appeared amongst our ancestors, mysteriously so, long ago, very long ago, claiming to speak for the gods."

"Initiates," I said.

I supposed some might have been placed amongst the Pani by Priest-Kings. Apparently the Priest-Kings wanted there to be at least one commonly spoken language on Gor, by means of which they could communicate with at least a majority of Gorean human beings. Perhaps they thought that that would lead to harmony, peace, and understanding. It had not. Amongst themselves the Priest-Kings communicated by scent. On the rare occasions when they dealt with human beings directly, translators were utilized.

"We must learn their language or be destroyed," said Lord Nishida. "Some recalcitrants and zealots were consumed by fire, streaming from the sky."

That would be the Flame Death. It was commonly used for enforcing the technology laws, and, doubtless, could serve other purposes, as well.

"So Gorean was learned?" I said.

"Who disputes the will of the gods?" asked Lord Nishida.

"Who, indeed?" I said.

"Other things were brought, as well," said Lord Nishida, "recipes, seeds, serums, and such."

Normally such gifts would be received through cultural diffusion, through trade, and such. I gathered that this was impractical in the case of the Pani.

"But these strange men," said Lord Nishida, "attempted to rule us."

"I see," I said.

"They were crucified," said Lord Nishida.

"There were no retaliations from the sky?" I said.

"No," said Lord Nishida.

Their purposes served, it seems the Priest-Kings had no further need of their missionaries, so to speak.

"What of Tersites, and your fate?" I pressed.

"It was the night before the final battle," said Lord Nishida, "when we were to be swept into the sea."

"Yes?" I said.

"A great darkness came suddenly over the moons, watch fires mysteriously ceased to burn, guards struggled to remain awake at their posts, we fought, crying out, and beating on drums, and blowing trumpets, to rouse ourselves, to stay awake, but we were overcome, and in Ehn we lay down to die."

"What happened?" I asked.

"We awakened in many places, on the shores of what you have spoken of as 'known Gor', though, I assure you, it was not known to us. I myself awakened in the vicinity of what I learned was Brundisium."

"I know it," I said. It was a major port. Indeed, it had been used as the port of entry for the invasion forces of Cos and Tyros, bound for Ar.

"We encountered, and were dealt with," said Lord Nishida, "by many Goreans, prepared to welcome and direct us. Too, these barbarians had at their disposal considerable wealth, abetting that which had been sent with us from our home, not only from our camp, but apparently from elsewhere, as well, perhaps even from the stores of our enemies. In any event, when our foes attacked in the morning they would find an empty camp, picked clean as though by centuries of looters. Doubtless they were much displeased, at the loss of gain, and perhaps the mysterious loss of much of their own wealth, as well. Their anger would not be lightly dissipated."

Lord Nishida shuddered, and I did not inquire the cause of his concern. It had to do, doubtless, with those left behind, not in the camp, not at the edge of the sea, but others, for whom they had fought, perhaps hundreds of vulnerable thousands of others, townsmen, retainers, peasants and such, in undefended districts, then perhaps at the undisputed mercy of some disappointed, vindictive foe.

"I understand little of this," I said.

"I fear," said Lord Nishida, "it is a game, which we are to resolve on another's board."

"I do not understand," I said.

"The gods wager," he said. "Doubtless they have their sport, their interest in which drop of water will be first to reach a sill, which insect will be the first to cross a line."

My blood seemed for a moment to turn cold.

I then began to suspect that it was not in the toils of Priest-Kings that we labored, or in those of Kurii, to achieve their ends. It was our own game, in its way, but one on which more powerful beings, Priest-Kings or Kurii, in a moment of recreation, or perhaps truce, had seen fit to wager.

"This is madness," I said. "It cannot be."

"Much has been prepared," said Lord Nishida, quietly.

"The attack," I said.

"Must not each god have a side," he asked, "a favored outcome?"

Surely, I thought, the foes of Lord Nishida and Lord Okimoto will have their resources and allies, as well.

A wager?

Perhaps.

Yet, too, surely each party would have darker, more remote thoughts in mind.

"I see now," I said, "why your plans were to be advanced."

"Of course," said Lord Nishida.

"But the other side has already won," I said.

"How so?" asked Lord Nishida, interested.

"You intended to winter here, until spring, did you not?" I asked.

"Yes," he said.

"You are trapped," I said.

"How so?" he inquired.

"Your project is no longer secret," I said. "One attack was beaten away, but there will be, I gather, others, in greater force, most likely, I would suppose, on foot through the forests, muchly inaccessible to tarn attack, and you will be unable to escape."

"I have not been quite candid with you, Tarl Cabot, tarnsman," said Lord Nishida.

"This revelation does not take me by surprise," I said.

"Such a force," said Lord Nishida, "is already on the march."

"You are undone," I said.

"How so?" he asked.

"You will be trapped in your winter camp, the river will freeze."

"When the enemy arrives," said Lord Nishida, "he will find only ashes."

"Abandon the camp and ships," I said, "and flee, saving what you can, in a thousand directions."

"No," he said.

"You cannot stay here," I said.

"That is true," he said.

"Flee," I said.

"No," he said.

"What will you do?" I asked.

"Soon," said Lord Nishida, "the ship will sail."

"The time of year is wrong," I said.

"Soon," said Lord Nishida.

"You cannot be intending to descend the Alexandra," I said.

"To Thassa," said he.

"Winter is coming," I said.

"That is why we must not loiter," said Lord Nishida. "Any day ice may form in the river. Already, upstream, in tributaries, some hundred pasangs north, plate ice has been detected."

This discovery would have been made by tarn scouts.

"You cannot be serious about taking the ship to sea," I said.

"We have no choice," said Lord Nishida.

"The ship cannot sail," I said.

"Tersites believes it can withstand the winter sea," he said.

"Tersites is not a captain, not a mariner, he is a shipwright, and he is mad," I said.

"I do not doubt his madness," said Lord Nishida, "but, too, I do not doubt his genius. It is his ship, and his design."

"Beware of Thassa," I said. "She is not your ally, not your friend."

"We cannot remain here," said Lord Nishida.

"Winter looms," I warned.

"Ice has already been seen in the north," he said.

"Thassa," I said, "will tear the sails from your ship, snap her masts, break her keel, crush her sides, lift her a hundred feet, two hundred feet, into the air, and then drop her like a broken toy, plunging to the waves below. One does not go upon Thassa in the winter. It is madness."

"Soon," he said, "she will sail."

Chapter Thirty-Four

In the Shed, Which Is Our Quarters

"She is a slave," I told Pertinax. "Put her to your pleasure."

"No," said Pertinax.

Saru knelt before us, in the half light of the shed we had been assigned for our quarters.

"Spread your knees more widely, girl," I told her.

"Yes, Master," she said.

"More," I said.

"Yes, Master," she said.

"Use her," I told Pertinax.

"No," he said.

"It is all right with Lord Nishida," I assured him.

"No," he said.

"Speak," I said to the slave.

"The slave," she whispered, "is eager to serve master."

How different she was from when on Earth, in her tailored garments, heels, silk stockings and such.

"No," said Pertinax.

"Consider the collar on her neck," I said to Pertinax. "It is lovely, is it not?"

"Yes," he said.

"And it is locked," I said.

"Of course," he said.

"Consider her in the rep-cloth tunic," I said. "It is a slave garment. It conceals little. Surely you find her attractive."

"Of course," he said, angrily.

"The hair is still too short," I said. "But some women are sold with less."

"If you say so," he said.

"Surely that does not give you pause," I said.

"No," he said.

"Use her," I urged.

Angrily Pertinax turned about and left the shed, the door closing more fiercely behind him than I thought necessary.

I smiled.

"He does not want me, Master," she whispered.

"On the contrary," I said, "he wants you mightily, with the ferocity of Gorean desire, wants you crushed, subdued, helpless, begging, at his feet."

"That cannot be, Master," she said.

"He wants you in a way that he dares not admit to himself," I said, "wants you in a way that he feels he must not permit himself to want you, wants you that much, wants you wholly, without a particle of reservation or hesitation."

"But there is only one way in which a man can so want a woman," she said.

"Yes," I said.

"He cannot so want me," she whispered.

"His passion, his desire, his ardor, are such," I said.

"Surely not," she whispered.

"He sees you at his feet," I said, "scarlet and braceleted, illuminated in the flame of his lust."

"It cannot be," she said.

"He wants to own you," I said, "like a dog, own you as a dog is owned."

"I am less than a dog," she said. "I am a slave."

"Precisely," I said.

"He wants me so much?"

"Yes," I said.

The slave is the master's possession, wholly and perfectly, vulnerable and defenseless, his to do with as he wishes.

"It is thus," she said, "that I have dreamed of being wanted, it is thus that I want to be wanted."

I was silent.

There were tears in her eyes.

"What woman would be satisfied," she asked, "to be less desired? What woman would be satisfied, truly, to be more weakly, more feebly desired?"

"I suppose it depends on the woman," I said.

Surely many were content with tepidities.

Perhaps they knew of nothing more.

"Some of us want more," she said, "want to be so wanted that we will find ourselves collared, want to be so desired, so lusted for, that he will be satisfied with nothing less than having his collar on us, with putting it on our necks and locking it there."

"You wish to be so lusted for?" I asked.

"Yes," she said, "—to the collar."

"Then you would be owned," I said.

"Yes," she said.

"You would belong," I said.

"Yes," she said, "—to our masters."

I noted that she, in her intentness, her earnestness, and tears, had permitted her knees to close, but I did not effect anything critical.

"I did not bring you here," I said, "to torment Pertinax."

"Master?" she asked.

"Long ago," I said, "when you naively thought you were a free female, and that the name Margaret Wentworth was still yours, you spoke to me of various things, amongst them that you understood someone or something had, or would have, a hold over me in some way, by means of a woman."

"Yes, Master," she said.

"That was not clear at the time, I gather," I said, "but it seems reasonably clear now that the agency involved must be the Pani, say, Lord Nishida, or Lord Okimoto, or those in whose behalf they labor."

"I would think so, Master," she said.

"You did not know the woman in question at that time," I said.

"Nor do I now, Master," she said.

"You have heard nothing more, or such?" I asked.

"No, Master," she said.

"The woman, I believe," I said, "is Talena, once daughter of Marlenus of Ar, Talena, recently deposed as Ubara in Ar."

"I know little of these things, Master," she said, "but surely that seems unlikely."

"Why?" I asked.

"The importance of the Ubara," she said, "the height and grandeur of her place, your modest status, if I may remark it, Master, that we have heard nothing of the Ubara, that we are here, in a remote location, far from the cylinder cities, the ports, the caravan routes, the trading places, somewhere in the northern forests."

I nodded.

I had not thought the outcome of this gentle interrogation would prove other than it had.

She knew nothing, of course, of my conversation with Seremides, formerly of the palace guard, the Taurentians.

"What are you about this morning?" I asked.

"I must scrub the floor of the quarters of the contract women," she said.

"You may leave," I said.

"Thank you, Master," she said, rose lightly to her feet, backed away a step or two, and then turned, and left the room.

She was beginning to move well, I noted. Lord Nishida had made arrangements for her training. There were several trained pleasure slaves in the camp. The former free women of Ar in the camp sought a similar tutelage though they must pay for it, by parting with portions of their rations, relieving the pleasure slaves of various chores, and such. Slaves are to be pleasing. Free women need not be pleasing, and, commonly, are not so, as it is beneath their dignity to be pleasing, and to be pleasing is to be too much like a slave. The slave, of course, if not pleasing, is likely to be well whipped. On the other hand, something in every woman, presumably the slave, desires to please, and to be found pleasing by, men. This desire to be found pleasing by men, of course, is not only liberated in the slave, but required of them. This naturalness in a woman, and her desire to please the opposite sex, thus, is not only permitted and encouraged in the slave, but incumbent upon her. Some women require a lashing before they feel genuinely entitled to accede to what they really want to do, using the strokes, one supposes, as an excuse to gratify their vanity, that they have no choice now, poor things, but to do what they would wish to do anyway. But there is something to that, of course, because they really do not have a choice, which, interestingly, is the way they want it. Soon, of course, freed in the collar, at the feet of a master, they are eagerly disposed to be found, and are striving to be found, as pleasing as possible. Thus, they soon realize they are concerned to give the master exquisite pleasure, and, with the joy of the slave, are doing so. And, it sometimes comes as a surprise to them that, in the grasp of the master, whether they wish it or not, they will endure, and submit to, ecstasies they never realized possible as a free woman, ecstasies often prolonged for Ahn. But then masters like to see their slaves so, so helpless, so pleading, so gasping, so moaning and writhing, so beyond themselves, so much at their mercy.

Saru, as far as I knew, had not been seen by Lord Okimoto. Lord Nishida, it seemed, had not see fit to present her before the greater *daimyo*. I wondered if this might be an oversight or an inadvertence. Perhaps she was of insufficient interest or importance. Still, she was very beautiful, and, in the collar, was becoming ever more beautiful. I supposed that a *shogun* would relish such a gift, from whomsoever's hands it might be received.

I feared that the Pani did indeed intend to descend the Alexandra, before she froze.

This seemed to me a madness, but the only alternative seemed to be to abandon the camp, and scatter, seeking individual refuges and safety, thus surrendering the efforts of the past months and forswearing whatever projects might have brought the Pani to known Gor. This second alternative, the dictate of reason, however, I knew would not be accepted by the Pani. To them, I suspected, the two alternatives were otherwise, either to descend the Alexandra, or to put themselves to the knife.

This had to do with honor, either a travesty of her, I suspected, or, as they would see it, with she herself.

I made no pretense to understanding the Pani.

I was reluctant to take either Cecily or Jane down the Alexandra, but I did not think Lords Nishida and Okimoto, who were unwilling to accept the resignations of men, but would rather put them to the sword, would be more willing to accept the defections of slaves. I had put the matter to Lord Nishida and he had reminded me that it would be difficult for a naked woman to survive the winter in the forests, particularly if neck-chained in a coffle, shackled and back-braceleted. "Too," he said, "we will be taking other animals along, and the men will need their pleasures."

Cecily and Jane, at the moment, with two sacks, had been set to gathering berries. When they returned they must put their heads back, open their mouths and extend their tongues. If there was any evidence of their having tasted a berry, either on their tongue or breath, they would be beaten. The berries were for the masters. Some could always be fed by hand to the slaves later, as they knelt at hand, naked, hands clasped behind their backs, or thrown before them to the floor, which they might then delicately retrieve, heads down, on all fours, without the use of their hands.

I had refrained hitherto from directly confronting either Lord Nishida or Lord Okimoto with the matter of the supposed hold over me, in virtue of some woman. Indeed, perhaps there was no such woman, and this menace or threat was a hoax, no more than an instrument of tactical efficacy, relying on my supplying in my own imagination some particular woman, with whose welfare I might be supposed to be concerned.

Now I would put the question to either Lord Nishida, or, if necessary, to Lord Okimoto.

If they wanted to retain my sword, at least as a willing instrument in their armory, then I would have an assuagement to my provoked curiosity.

With this resolution in mind I exited the shed which had been assigned for my quarters, quarters I shared, as before, with Pertinax, a free man, and two female slaves.

Chapter Thirty-Five

What Occurred in the Pavilion of Lord Okimoto

"Though you are a barbarian," said Lord Nishida, "you are honored."

"I am sensitive to the honor," I said.

My sword had been kept at the entrance to the wooden pavilion, which was the largest building in the camp.

Lord Nishida and I were now in the vestibule of this building.

"It is sometimes difficult to understand Lord Okimoto," said Lord Nishida. "It has to do with a knife wound sustained in war."

"I understand," I said.

"I will try to be of assistance," said Lord Nishida.

"Thank you," I said.

"And I may speak more than he."

"I understand," I said.

"You will stand," he said, "unless permitted to sit."

"I understand," I said.

I was then ushered into the presence of the large, inert shape of Lord Okimoto. He was resplendent, broad and leaden, now in a scarlet kimono, with a yellow *obi,* or belt. In this belt was the companion sword, blade uppermost. He sat cross-legged. There were four contract women in attendance, of unusual beauty, who withdrew, unobtrusively, as I entered. On each side of Lord Okimoto, somewhat behind, arms crossed, stood a guard.

"This is Tarl Cabot, tarnsman, commander of the tarn cavalry, victor at the battle of Tarncamp, of whom I have spoken," said Lord Nishida.

Lord Okimoto nodded.

"May I speak?" I inquired.

Again Lord Okimoto nodded.

"The victor at Tarncamp," I said, "was Tarncamp's commander, your colleague, Lord Nishida. It was my honor to command his cavalry."

Lord Okimoto smiled.

I thought he said something, for his lips moved.

"You may sit," said Lord Nishida.

"Thank you," I said. I gathered that this was meaningful.

"I have explained to Lord Okimoto," said Lord Nishida, "your reservations pertaining to descending the Alexandra, the lateness of the season, the impending cold, the force of winter, the perils of the sea at this time."

"He understands all this," I said.

"Completely," said Lord Nishida.

"You have then reconsidered your plans?" I asked.

Lord Okimoto smiled, a small smile, almost lost in the bloated mass of that vast countenance. It seemed he had small eyes. His raiment, of silk, stretched over that large body, was elegant.

"I see you have not reconsidered," I said.

"No," said Lord Nishida. "It is not practical."

"Enemies, I gather, approach," I said.

"Yes," said Lord Nishida.

"They will move first to the mouth of the Alexandra," I said, "to cut you off, and then proceed upriver."

"That is our surmise," said Lord Nishida.

That was certainly what I would have done.

"How close are they?" I asked.

"Perhaps you know," smiled Lord Nishida.

"How would I know?" I asked.

"They are too close," said Lord Nishida. "And they hasten their marches."

"How many days?" I asked.

"Some," said Lord Nishida.

"Break camp, and flee," I urged.

"It is not our way," said Lord Nishida.

"Your defeat is assured," I said, "either by sword or sea."

"Yet few," said Lord Nishida, "have ventured to depart."

"They do not understand their situation," I said.

"Perhaps," said Lord Nishida.

"What of those few," I asked, "who, as you put it, 'ventured to depart'?"

"Desertion is not acceptable," said Lord Nishida.

"I see," I said.

Outside I heard the wind. It was coming from the north.

"There is still time," I said, "to break camp, to withdraw."

"Do you understand us, Tarl Cabot, tarnsman?" asked Lord Nishida.

"I do not think so," I said.

"How do you see us?" he asked.

"As implacable, relentless, cruel, single-minded, uncompromising, merciless," I said.

"And so, too," said Lord Nishida, "is the enemy. It is a war, knife to knife, a war without quarter."

"Not here?" I said.

"No, not here," he said.

"Flee," I said.

"It is not our way," he said.

"It is a war you have already lost," I said.

"We did not have tarns," he said.

"I think you are mad," I said.

"We are going back," he said.

"I did not request this audience," I said, "to apprise you of the hopeless nature of your situation, for that is something of which you are doubtless aware, perhaps more so than I, nor to impress upon you the advisabilities of desperate strategies, nor to urge even the simplest and most modest wisdoms of sanity, such as escaping while you may, for I am cognizant of your determination here and I have no hope of swaying you to adopt a wiser or more rational course, but I have come here for another purpose altogether."

"We are pleased," said Lord Nishida.

Lord Okimoto looked up.

"Speak," said Lord Nishida.

"I heard, long ago," I said, "from a female slave, though she did not then, amusingly, know herself slave, that there was to be a hold over me of some sort, in virtue of a woman—in virtue of which I must abet your projects."

"Interesting," said Lord Nishida.

"It seemed so to me," I said.

"How seriously would you take this," asked Lord Nishida, "considering its source, as it was emitted from the doubtless lovely lips of a mere female slave?"

"I do not know," I said.

"I see," said Lord Nishida.

"How seriously," I asked, "should it be taken?"

The wind was rising, outside.

"I fear," said Lord Nishida, "very seriously."

"What hold is this," I asked, "and who is the woman?"

He looked to Lord Okimoto, and Lord Okimoto inclined his head, authorizing, it seemed, Lord Nishida to proceed.

"We hoped you would not hear of this," said Lord Nishida.

"I do not understand," I said.

How could this leverage be applied to me if I knew nothing of it?

"There is much here which you do not understand," said Lord Nishida, "but much which we, too, I fear, do not understand. We have heard, as well, however obliquely, of the matter of which you speak, and doubtless, ultimately, from the same source."

I noted he did not mention the slave, Saru, nor had I done so.

Lord Okimoto, I gathered, did not know of the existence of Saru, and of her possible value, as a gift to a *shogun*. Then, again, I suspected there was likely to be little in the camp of which he would be ignorant. As Lord Nishida I supposed he would have his tentacles, his informants.

"First," said Lord Nishida, "this is not a matter of our doing, this business of a 'hold', and of a woman; secondly, we do not know who might be the woman in question; thirdly, it is our surmise that the hold over you is one in virtue of which you are not to serve us, but betray us."

"You profess no such hold over me?" I said.

"Your blade," he said, "was put freely, voluntarily, at our disposal."

"Who, then?" I asked.

"The enemy," he said. "The slave, misled by a spy, probably in the south, was no more than a dupe, an unwitting conduit. It was her role, it seems, merely to inform you of a menace, one she would take, naturally enough, as emanating from us, things to be made clear to you later."

"What do they want from me?" I asked.

"Treachery," said Lord Nishida.

"Their choice, then," I said, "is a poor one."

"Let us hope so," said Lord Nishida. "But men have killed their own brothers for a city, a ship, for gold, a woman."

"True," I said.

"You released an attempted assassin, Licinius Lysias of Turmus," said Lord Nishida.

"I disapprove of ugly deaths," I said.

"He was recovered, by *Ashigaru*, in the forest," he said.

"I am sorry to hear it," I said.

"In deference to your sensibilities," he said, "he has been spared, for chains, and the bench of a galley."

"Good," I said.

"Many would prefer crucifixion," he said.

"Perhaps," I said. Certainly it was sooner finished.

"With whom did you secretly rendezvous at night, by tarn, in the vicinity of Tarncamp?" asked Lord Nishida.

"It is a private matter," I said.

"Do you think we should trust you?" asked Lord Nishida. "Would you, in our place?"

"No," I said.

"Now," said Lord Nishida, "it seems clear that others bid for your service, and would lure you from us."

"I know little of that," I said.

"Treachery is punishable by death," said Lord Nishida.

"I am not surprised," I said.

I was wondering if I would leave the pavilion of Lord Okimoto alive.

"Without you," said Lord Nishida, "the cavalry might mutiny."

"I doubt it," I said.

"What do you know of this alleged matter of a hold, and a woman?" asked Lord Nishida.

"I know as little, or less, than you," I said.

"Opacity is troubling," said Lord Nishida.

"It is also part of life," I said.

"Who knows," asked Lord Nishida, "if the petals of a flower will open, and, if so, when, and which first?"

"Who, indeed," I said. I did not care for this sort of talk on the part of the Pani.

"Our patience is not inexhaustible, Tarl Cabot, tarnsman," said Lord Nishida.

"Who is the woman?" I asked.

"Tell us," said Lord Nishida.

"I do not know," I said. "Do you not know?"

"No," he said.

"Have you no sense, no hint, of who the woman is?" I asked.

"Perhaps you may," he said.

"I?" I said.

Lord Okimoto then clapped his hands, sharply, and one of his contract women, with small steps, her head bowed, ushered herself gracefully into the presence of the *daimyo.*

"This is Hisui, in service to Lord Okimoto," said Lord Nishida.

The lovely creature, a comb in her hair, wore a muchly figured kimono, and a single piece of jewelry, which fell upon her breast.

"Hisui," said Lord Nishida, "wears a bauble, which is meaningless to us, but may be meaningful to you."

"May I?" I inquired, and Hisui lowered her head, and I lifted the pendant, in the palm of my left hand, on its light, golden chain.

"We gather," said Lord Nishida, "it is a token of some sort. It was intended for you. We learned this from its carrier, but little else, before he died, far too soon, unfortunately, lifted and dropped, again and again, onto the sharpened sticks."

I released the pendant, and it fell again upon the bosom of its bearer.

I turned and faced Lords Nishida and Okimoto.

"You are going back, to the 'far shore'?" I asked.

"Yes," said Lord Nishida.

"I will go with you," I said.

"Of course," said Lord Nishida.

I then turned, and left.

The pendant had been the medallion of the Ubara of Ar.

Chapter Thirty-Six

The Pyre

Soon, I supposed, the eyes of the great ship would be painted.

She was to ply the Alexandra.

Should she reach Thassa, the sea, I supposed, would be gifted with wine and salt, and oil would be poured into the waters, that they might be soothed in her path. Such things are traditional.

Six days ago a great pyre had been lit on the beach, and I had stood beside it, with Aëtius, and dozens of others, amongst them carpenters, sawyers, oar makers, and sail makers.

We stood yards back. The flames burned fiercely. Though it was night, one could scarcely look upon them. One could see them reflected redly on the countenances of the stolid, or grieving, men gathered about. Tears streamed from the eyes of some of them, hardened men, yet weeping. Pani, too, were with us, and a number of mariners, and mercenaries. The wrapped form in the canvas, sail canvas, was consumed in a torrent of flame.

It was odd, I thought, that the pyre had been lit at night. Such things are usually done in the afternoon.

"He would have liked to have seen the eyes painted," said a man.

I supposed that this was true.

But Tersites, I knew, was a strange man.

"It was not to be," said another.

"I would have liked to have seen him," I said to Aëtius.

Aëtius did not look at me. "He was not well," he said.

"What," I asked, "was the cause of his death?"

"His health was poor, and for a long time failing," said Aëtius.

I recalled him from years ago, at the Council of Captains. It was hard to think of that small, twisted, wiry, energetic body, the unlikely frame of so mighty and unusual a mind, belabored and weakened, succumbing to the ravages of illness. I had sought out the physicians, those of the green caste, in camp. None had been summoned. Four had been refused admittance to his presence.

"There will never be another such as he," said Aëtius.

"Doubtless," I said.

Aëtius regarded me, narrowly, and then looked away.

We waited until the flames had muchly subsided, and then returned to our quarters.

The next morning, at dawn, I returned to the remains of the pyre, the blackened wood, the mounds of ash.

I was not surprised to find that Aëtius had done the same.

"What are you doing here?" he asked, not pleasantly.

"Sometimes," I said, brushing through the ash with the side of my foot, "there is a bone or two."

"Go away," said Aëtius.

"I see you have found some," I said. He carried, in his left hand, a small sack.

"Come no closer," said Aëtius.

I took his left hand at the wrist, and pulled the sack toward me.

"Away!" said Aëtius. "Stop!"

With my right hand I emptied the bones into the ash. I bent down, as Aëtius stood by, helpless. I sorted through the bones. I lifted one or two of them up, to show them to Aëtius.

"Now you know," he said.

"Yes," I said.

"You suspected," he said.

"Yes," I said.

I then stood up.

He bent down, angrily, to gather the bones together, which he hastily returned to the sack.

I had little doubt but what they would be quickly disposed of, probably buried in the forest, without a marker.

"Your secret," I said, "is safe with me."

"It was thought necessary," he said, not looking up.

"Why, by whom?" I asked.

"I do not know," he said.

"Where is Tersites?" I asked.

"I do not know," he said. "I do what I am told."

"Clearly he is alive," I said.

"I think so," he said.

I had suspected some form of subterfuge, or hoax, from the apparent absence or inaccessibility of Tersites, from my inquiries amongst those of the green caste, and from the igniting of the vast pyre after dark.

Perhaps he had been in fear of his life.

Doubtless he would now be safe, for a time.

I then turned away.

The bones were tarsk bones.

Chapter Thirty-Seven

The Ship Is to Sail

Strangely, this unsettling me, and many others, the eyes of the great ship had not been painted.

Yet it seemed she was to ply the Alexandra, and, if all went well, reach Thassa.

Should she reach Thassa, the sea, I trusted, would be gifted with wine and salt, and oil would be poured into the waters, that they might be soothed in her path.

I would prefer that these things had been done before she would sail.

I was uneasy.

I knew little of many things.

Tersites, I knew, was a strange man.

Orders must have been given.

Aëtius, I was sure, would respect such orders, had they been delivered to him by his master, and mentor, lame, brilliant, twisted, half-mad Tersites.

I knew little of many things.

I did know that Tersites was a strange man.

Ice had crusted about the cold shore. Pieces, some large, were seen in the river, from upstream.

I drew my cloak more closely about me.

The slaves were now warmly garmented, though not, of course, as might have been free women. The robes of concealment in winter are much like those of gentler weathers, save for darker colors, more absorptive of, and retentive of, heat, heavier materials, some additional layering, and such. In the case of the slave a short, long-sleeved jacket, coming high on the hips, its length resembling that of a slave tunic, is worn over an undershirt. They are also put in trousers, belted with binding fiber. Whereas in the case of the free woman her legs are concealed within her enclosing garmenture, in the case of the slave, even in the winter, it is clear, however warmly they may be clothed, that she has legs, and that this is to be obvious to the scrutiny of men. The wrappings of the legs and calves is wool, over which leather is wrapped. The last garment is a warm, hooded cloak, which may be held closely about the body. Her face is commonly bared, except in severe weather, and, in any case, there is no mistaking her status, given her garmenture. Too, there were no free women in camp. Incidentally, there is a superstition amongst many Gorean mariners that it is bad luck to have a free woman aboard. The foundation of the superstition, I suppose, is not difficult to discern, even if the woman, in such a situation, resists to the best of her ability the manifestations of the lovely temptations natural to her sex. If the meat is not to be eaten, it is a mistake to put it before larls. They may fight amongst themselves, and such. Perhaps larls should not be carnivorous, and should never be hungry, but they are carnivorous, and do get hungry. If there are any objections here, they are best taken up not with larls, but with nature, the disposition to replicate genes, and such, without which there would be no meat and no larls. This superstition, incidentally, does not apply to slave girls, for they are such that, even if one does not get one's hands on them, one knows they are such that, as the properties of men, they are at least in theory available, and this, interestingly, is often enough to content the male. Too, one may always look at them, tease them, flirt with them, slap them on the fundament, order them about, get them to their knees before you, as you wish, be addressed by them as "Master," and so on. There are many ways to enjoy a woman without putting her to your pleasure. That is, after all, for her master.

Their collars, of course, even in the winter, are kept on the slaves. They remain collared. They are slaves.

I had heard nothing more of the approach of enemy forces, but I entertained no doubt as to their imminence and reality.

Even now they might be in the vicinity of the Alexandra.

The blows of great hammers were striking away the chocks that held the ship of Tersites in place, on the great sloping frame.

Hundreds of men were gathered on the beach, and slaves, too.

A signal was conveyed by a banner from the stern castle of the great ship, and the hammers struck again.

There was a cry from the crowd.

There was a thundering roll of wood and the mighty body of the ship of Tersites slid toward the river.

It debouched into the Alexandra.

There was a cheer from the crowd.

Then she turned slowly to starboard, downriver, prow westward.

Water slid from her bow, swelling, washed her sides, closed about her huge rudder, and left its flecked, gentle wake.

Many were the cries of pleasure.

She rode well.

She was stately, majestic, surely no lightness like that of a Vosk gull, given her bulk, but as serene and mighty, and as unchallenged here, as might be some vast lake or river tharlarion in its own domain, some ponderous thing, unable and awkward on land perhaps, but, in the water, oddly graceful, and dangerous, a serene monster, at home in the element in which it was Ubar.

I considered carefully the temporary markings on her bow. Unladen, and without her nest of galleys, the river should come to the first mark. It was so. They had calculated well.

Few, I supposed, understood why shipwrights seized one another, cried out, and threw their brimless caps into the air.

An extra tenth of a pasang had been allotted for the turn, in building her wharfage downstream. Given the absence of empirical precedents it had not been clear how responsive she would be to the helm. But she needed not half the length. To be sure, she had not yet nested her galleys, taken on her crew, her supplies, all that she might care to contain. In the vicinity of the camp, as she was under construction, the river had been deepened, to accommodate her keel near shore. Soundings had been taken, months ago, before construction had begun, to determine that the Alexandra would be navigable, as charts claimed, to Thassa herself. To be sure, in many places she must seek the center of the river. Elsewhere she would feel her way by multiple soundings, sometimes between bars, called upward from small boats preceding her. Such things can change, even overnight. Her galleys, of course, were shallow-drafted long ships and could maneuver in water in which a man might stand upright.

In some fifteen Ehn she was alongside her long, readied wharf. Dozens of ropes had been cast down from her starboard side, to be bound about heavy, deeply anchored mooring cleats.

I trusted that she would not move with the current, and drag the cleats free of the wood, or draw the wharf itself, splintering, from its pilings.

I became aware that Lord Nishida was at my side.

"She is huge," said Lord Nishida.

"Yes," I said.

"Do you think she is sufficiently secured?" he asked.

"On a few moorings, no," I said, "on many, yes. The helm, too, will be tied, to lead her back to shore, should she be tempted to stray."

"I know little about these things," said Lord Nishida.

"Many," I said, "know little about these things. We are here in new countries."

"What do you think of her?" he asked.

"I do not know," I said.

"She will be fitted and rigged in two days," said Lord Nishida.

"So soon?" I said.

"Necessarily," he said.

"I see," I said. So close then was the foe.

"It is unfortunate," said Lord Nishida, "that Tersites did not live to see this day."

"Yes," I said.

Lord Nishida then smiled, and withdrew.

Chapter Thirty-Eight

The Destruction of the River Camp; Unexpected Cargo Is Boarded; The Ship Begins Her Journey

"Nodachi is on board," said Tajima, in answer to my question.

It was early morning.

A sturdy, planked ramp led upward from the wharf. All night men and slaves, by the light of torches, carrying burdens, had come and gone on this ramp, which led to a large now-opened port in the hull, far below the higher bulwarks. Within this opening many men, some once of the scribes, sorted through these mountains of material and assigned its disposition, in virtue of preconceived arrangements, to various decks and holds.

"It is cold," said Tajima.

"It will be far more bitter on Thassa," I said.

I was uneasy noting the quantities of stores brought aboard. It reminded me of the preparations of a city knowing its besiegement was imminent. Months might be spent at sea, never viewing land, on such largesse. Great quantities of water were also brought aboard, this despite the common expedient, on round ships, of adding to one's stores by capturing rain in extended volumes of sail canvas, thence conducting it to on-ship reservoirs. Commonly of course, the long ships replenish water from their many landfalls, which may be as frequent as every evening. Crates of larmas were brought on board, these to add important elements to a diet which, otherwise, in a long voyage, might lead to diseases of deficiency. The larma does not grow naturally in Torvaldsland, but certain hard fruits do, which, happily, will serve a similar purpose. One might suppose that food might be obtained from the sea itself but that source cannot be relied on. Most edible fish frequent banks, shallow banks, which are commonly near shores, where they are plentiful, not the open sea, where there is little for them to feed on. The nine-gilled Gorean shark will sometimes trail a ship, for garbage, but that is not a source to be relied on either. The shark, being a hunter, is likely to frequent prey areas, the banks, and the shallower waters. Too, sharks are less plentiful in colder, northern waters, than in warmer, southern waters. There would be few sharks, if any, for example, in the vicinity of the Alexandra. The waters are too cold. I had seen many bales of cloth brought aboard, and assorted boxes of various descriptions. I supposed there would be silver and gold, but I was not sure of the value, if any, of these commodities should our voyage succeed in reaching its projected terminus, wherever that might be. There were naval stores, too, lumber, tars, resins, and such, in abundance, and additional canvas. Sometimes sails are shredded in high winds, even carried away, with snapped masts. Much oil was brought aboard, not so much for the ship's lamps, but for a substance with which to fill clay vessels, with wire handles, of which there were hundreds. These would constitute fire bombs which might be flung from tarnback or launched from catapults. These would be devastating at sea, as on the 25th of Se'Kara, and perhaps effective against tents and wooden buildings, but I feared they would not seriously discommode an infantry. The shield roof in an infantry is usually proof enough against even the arrows and missiles of tarn attack, but the tarn attack is commonly coordinated with an infantry advance. Clearly the shield cannot be used simultaneously to defend one both from the air and the ground. Catapult stones, too, were brought aboard, in hundreds, and "heavy arrows," almost spears, which might be sped either singly, as from *ballistae*, or, from a *springal*, in showers, their flight propelled by a single fierce blow, that from a horizontal spring-driven board. Luxury items, as well, were in evidence, or what I supposed were luxury items at least, from amongst what was discernible, rich furs, rolled silks, wines and pagas, pans of jewelry, bracelets, anklets, armlets, bangles, necklaces, and such. One girl had carried, on her head, balancing it there with two hands, a bale of what I took to be diaphanous dancing silks. I had little doubt the slaves would later be hurrying about, lightly, serving, in the pleasure cabins on the ship. The men might pick and choose then from amongst what one might think of as on-board paga taverns.

The paga girl, or paga slave, is a well-known form of slave to Gorean free males. Indeed, many a slave, with an envied private master, had begun her bondage, fresh from the block, in the taverns, no more than another belled slave, summonable to the whips and chains of an alcove, her use accompanying, if one wished, the price of the drink she brings to the table. And, too, of course, many men first found their personal slave in so unlikely a place, little suspecting that the collared beauty, kneeling, head down at the table, serving their paga, one of others, might somehow come to seem special to them. Idly, perhaps as little more than a matter of course, she is ordered, as might be any other, to an alcove. But in the alcove, fastened in her chains, she seems to him interestingly, surprisingly, different from many others. He tests her body and discovers, to his interest, that her responses to his touch are extraordinary, and piteous. With what hope she looks at him and presses her lips to his whip. There seems something special in her responsiveness. He fears she might become of interest to him, and so, finished with her, he spurns her, thrusting her aside with his foot, leaving her behind him, in her chains, unable to follow, in tears. But he finds it difficult to forget her, her startled eyes, the leaping of her body. He recalls the slight sound of her silk, almost inaudible, as she knelt by the table, and how it fell about her, with its diaphanous mockery of concealment, as she preceded him obediently to the alcove. He recalls, in the alcove, how, writhing, she grasped the chain above her wrist rings, how she lifted her body and implored him not to desist in his touch, and, later, the wild jangle of the bells on her ankle as, ungovernedly in his power, she kicked wildly. He patronizes the tavern again, perhaps, and again, and finds she hurries to kneel before him, and take his order. When he dares, he sends her again to the alcove, and perhaps confirms what he had most feared, that she is not merely another slave to him, but that she is muchly different, and that they may have been selected for one another by nature, he as master, she as slave. So, eventually he buys her. She costs him more than he would care to admit to his fellows, but he will make it up, many times over, out of her lovely hide. And it is not such a fearful thing, he later learns, really, to have at his feet one for whom he would die, a love slave, and one who knew him, from his first touch, as her long longed-for love master. And so in the mysterious ways of nature the match is made. One must, of course, be particularly strict with a love slave, severe in her discipline, and such, not hesitating to put her to the whip for her least laxity or failure to fully please, but she would have it no other way, for he is her master.

I had stopped one girl at the foot of the ramp, my finger to her shoulder, who was carrying a number of garments. She stood very straight, and kept her head up, and looked straight ahead. "Slave tunics," I said. "Yes, Master," she said. "Proceed," I said. "Yes, Master," she said. "Thank you, Master." I had seen other girls, similarly burdened. These were surely more tunics than were required for our girls. I had similarly examined the burdens, shallow boxes, of two or three fellows, as well, as they would ascend the ramp. These boxes, to my interest, contained an abundance of custodial hardware, coffle chains, siriks, slave bracelets, ankle rings, and such. It was light chaining, such as is used for the chaining of women. I saw more than one fellow ascend the ramp with, strung on a spear, over his shoulder, a large number of dangling slave collars, with their keys wired to them. The collars were sturdy, but light, and comfortable, such as are put on women. Another fellow carried a number of irons, of the sort which are used to brand animals. From these observations I supposed that Lords Nishida and Okimoto might have in mind a disposition for the women of the enemy or, at least, those who pleased their senses. The women of the enemy, of course, become the property of the victors. I noted, incidentally, no such arrangements, heavy chaining or such, prepared for male prisoners. The war, as I recalled from a remark of Lord Nishida in the pavilion of Lord Okimoto, was to the knife, without quarter.

Torgus, Ichiro, Lysander, and others, would be with the

cavalry. The birds would be brought aboard later, in some four days, joining us near the mouth of the Alexandra.

On the other side of the ship, larger ports had been opened now, and, on ramps sloping up from the water, the six galleys were being drawn on board, and were being rolled to berths in a lower hold. Similar boarding ports were on the starboard side, which was now near the wharf, lying against its cushions of rolled leather, these to prevent damage to either ship or wharf. In this way, galleys might be nested from either side of the great ship.

Tajima, who was standing beside me, suddenly stepped back, and bowed. I, too, bowed. Lord Okimoto himself was boarding, being borne in a sedan chair by eight Pani, which chair was followed by an entourage of contract women and guards.

After this, Aëtius, who seemed to be the fellow in charge of supervising matters, began to marshal and board, in long lines, both Pani and others.

"Four days," said Tajima. He would be with the cavalry.

"That is our estimate," I said.

"I understand," said Tajima.

Much depended on the current, and whether or not the descent of the Alexandra would be without incident. The downriver journey had been sounded with care, but a river is not a bridge, a street, a reliable road of stone, layered in blocks, like a sunken wall, feet into the earth, like the Viktel Aria, leading to Ar, built for millennia. The river is less reliable. Its twists and turns might differ from week to week, even day to day. Floods can extend her shores, and rearrange her depths and course. Droughts can dry and parch her. It is hard to know, to predict, the whims, vagaries, and moods, the surfeits and famines, of a river.

The estimate of four days was from the time it had taken two small boats to reach Thassa.

"Be certain," I said, "to board the tarns before we are beyond the sight of land."

"I understand," he said.

I did not think that Lord Nishida would care to delay his voyage at the mouth of the Alexandra, nor be forced to return.

The tarns had been familiarized, over the past few days,

with departing from, and returning to, the quarters prepared for them. Three areas were involved, each on its own deck. The first area was on the first deck below the open deck, and the second and third areas were on the next lower decks. Three ramps were involved, one leading from the third lower deck to the second lower deck, one from the second lower deck to the first lower deck, and one from the first lower deck to the top deck, or open deck, once a great hatch had been rolled back.

Three men passed, lifting their hands in salute, which salute I returned. These were Telarion, Fabius, and Tyrtaios, whom I had met in the tent of Lord Nishida at Tarncamp, the night of the feast. At least one, I had gathered from Lord Nishida, was a spy, and one amongst them, the same or another, was of the Assassins. These three, I had noted, had been present at the pyre a few nights past, which pyre had supposedly been that of the shipwright, Tersites.

"I would you were with the cavalry," said Tajima.

"Perhaps we will ply the wind road later, together, at sea," I said.

"Lord Nishida does not trust you," he said.

"I know," I said.

Tajima was to command the cavalry in my absence.

As we were speaking, numerous Pani, and mercenaries, were ascending the ramp, boarding.

I could already see smoke to the east.

"They have begun to burn the camp," I said.

"I must return to the cavalry," said Tajima.

"I wish you well," I said.

"I, too, wish you well, Tarl Cabot, tarnsman," he said. He then turned about, and withdrew.

I watched men ascending the ramp, boarding.

"Pertinax," I said, for he had approached. With him were Cecily and his Jane, both protected against the cold. Both were fetching, even jacketed and cloaked as they were. It is interesting how attractive slaves are, even when bundled. Perhaps that is because one knows they are slaves, and not free women. One can then, so to speak, unbundle them. One is well aware of what lies beneath that bundling, a slave, in her collar.

"Tal," said he.

"Tal," said I.

To be sure, not even free women are immune from the speculations of virile males. Do they not sometimes understand the eyes of men are upon them, *speculatively*. One would suppose so. One wonders if they suspect, within all those layerings, scarves, hoods, and veils, what the men are thinking. Would they be uneasy if they knew how they were viewed by strong men, would they tremble, would they be afraid, or would they redden and glow, as though helpless at a master's feet? Surely they must understand those looks. They must be aware that men are conjecturing their lineaments, curiously, even idly, appraisingly, wondering if, under all that paraphernalia, all those wrappings, there might be something worth putting to its knees, worth collaring, and owning. Are the men conjecturing what they might look like, on a chain, being exhibited to buyers, naked, as women are sold, and such, perhaps groveling on the furs in an alcove, hoping to be found pleasing, perhaps even tunicked, barefoot, being sent to a market, running along, lightly, collared, on their errands.

The great majority of women on Gor are, of course, free women, of many diverse castes. On the other hand, female slavery is common. One sees them in the streets, in the markets, in the fields, and so on. Few slaves, statistically, are obtained from the slave farms. Most were originally free women, obtained by capture, in raids, by abduction, in war, and such.

As noted earlier the women of the enemy become the property of the victor. They are booty, as much as vessels, cloths, metals, kaiila, and such. To be sure, they are a particularly desirable form of booty, and men enjoy having it about, as slaves. Most slaves are purchased, of course, in the markets, where their captors put them up for sale. The sales-platform girls are supplemented, to some extent, by captures brought from Earth, but those captures, though quite numerous, abstractly considered, constitute only a small fraction of Gorean female slaves, perhaps one in two or three hundred. They do tend to be popular in the markets, however, perhaps in part due to their charms as barbarians but, too, I suspect, due to their responsiveness to Gorean males, men of a sort for whom their former civilizations and cultures have but ill prepared them. Never had they thought to be at the feet of such men, slaves, to what are to them uncompromising and magnificent beasts. They are, of course, merely the natural male, who is a master by nature.

It seemed clear, from materials brought on board, shackles, collars, and such, that Lords Nishida and Okimoto might have in mind, were their projects successful, the acquisition of large numbers of women, who might then be distributed, or sold. This is a way, of course, familiar on Gor, of financing further campaigns, further actions, and such.

Consider such women, now the property of victors.

Their rich raiment and status will be exchanged for the tunic of a slave, if that, and a collar. No longer do they possess goods but are now themselves goods. And let these goods then kneel and press their soft lips to the boots of conquerors, gratefully, thankful for their lives, spared now, at least for a time. And let them tremble, as well, realizing they are now no longer their own, but belong to masters, in whose grasp they will discover what it is to be a slave. The tiring, complex games of the free woman are now behind them. It is now theirs to serve and please, or die. Surely in their dreams they have considered this sort of thing, and now they discover, on their knees, it has become their reality. And what might it be, they might wonder, which has won them this incredible, welcome reprieve, temporary as it might be, from the ax or torch? Could it be that it is their sex and beauty, their exquisite features and lovely slave curves, to which they may have hitherto given little thought, save for occasionally regarding them in the mirror, perhaps wondering what they might be worth on a sales platform, those and, of course, the lust of men, to which they owe their lives? Perhaps. Had they been hitherto curious, perhaps idly so, as to what they might sell for in an open market, what price they might bring an owner who vends them, with others? They may now learn. Had they considered, hitherto, what it might be to be in the arms of a master? They will now learn.

"Thank you for bringing her," I said to Pertinax, indicating Cecily.

He nodded. We had arranged it so, for I had come early to the wharf, to observe more of the lading.

I spoke of Cecily as having been brought, for she was a slave.

In this sense, she had not accompanied Pertinax, but had been brought by him, as might have been, say, a dog. The same held for his Jane, of course.

Last night, leaving the slaves chained in the shed, we had boarded our gear.

Pertinax, no more than I, by the instructions of Lord Nishida, was to be with the cavalry. In its way, this was flattering. It indicated that Lord Nishida now regarded Pertinax as someone with whom to reckon. Too, of course, Pertinax and I shared quarters, could speak a language unfamiliar to most of the Pani, and so on. Pertinax, then, probably primarily because of his relationship with me, was now conceived of as deserving suspicion.

I supposed this was a compliment, in its way.

On the other hand, it was one which I, at least, would have been just as pleased to be without.

I wondered if he realized that his life must now be in greater danger.

If Lord Nishida decided to do away with me, I would suppose that Pertinax would be included in the instructions.

On the wharf, their progress arrested, Cecily and Jane knelt, as was appropriate for slaves in the presence of free persons. It would have been the same had a free woman been present.

Such things might seem unimportant or inconsequential to those unfamiliar with cultural protocol, but they are not. They are quite important and quite consequential. Such things, perhaps seemingly small to an outsider, are rich with significance. They, in their beauty and appropriateness, make perfectly clear relationships and conditions which are momentous. The *kajira* realizes very clearly why she is on her knees. She is a slave. Such a posture and attitude is quite meaningful to the collar-wearer. What may be more difficult for the outsider to grasp is that she regards this posture and attitude as appropriate for her. She feels comfortable and secure on her knees. As a slave, she knows she belongs on her knees. But, too, mastered, she wants to kneel, and loves doing so.

"When do we board?" inquired Pertinax.

"Soon," I said.

I was waiting for Lord Nishida. Lord Okimoto had already boarded.

"Have the slaves been boarded yet?" he asked.

"Saru was put on board last night," I said.

"Oh?" he said.

"About the twentieth Ahn," I said. "She is doubtless within somewhere, nicely chained, probably by the neck."

"My question was general," he said. "I have no interest in the slut, Saru."

"That is surprising," I said. "Most men would find her of interest."

"She is a slut," he snarled.

"Yes," I said, "and the best sort, a helpless, needful slut, who is a collared slave."

"I despise her," he said.

"She wants to be at your feet," I said.

"I would kick her away," he said.

"And she would crawl back, to kiss the boot which kicked her," I said.

"She is contemptible," he said.

"Not at all," I said. "She is a needful slave."

"Contemptible!" he said.

"Not at all," I said. "There is nothing contemptible in a slave's plaintive, desperate need. Most men find such needs unobjectionable, even pleasant."

"She is worthless, utterly despicable," he said.

"Strange then," I said, "that she would be thought fit for a *shogun*."

"As a slave!" he said.

"Of course," I said. "As what else?"

"I find her of not the least interest," he said.

"Even on Earth," I said, "you wanted her naked, in your collar."

"No!" he said. "No!"

"And you want her now," I said.

"No!" he said.

"At your feet, yours, helpless, in your collar, your slave," I said.

"No!" he cried.

"No?" I said.

"Her hair is too short," he said, angrily.

"I grant you that," I said.

Jane, kneeling near him, took this opportunity to brush back her hood, and arrange her hair more evenly, more attractively, over her shoulders.

Saru had been put on board at night, singly, several Ahn before Lord Okimoto, this morning, had been borne up the ramp.

I wondered if he knew of her existence.

She would doubtless make a lovely gift for a *shogun*. Perhaps Lord Nishida might purchase high favor by means of such a gift, a favor which might possibly exceed even that of a *shogun's* cousin.

But Lord Okimoto, I was sure, was no fool.

Lord Nishida might be putting himself at some risk. To be sure, he had a large number of men, swordsmen, glaivesmen, archers, and others, at his disposal. Such cohorts tend to reduce risks, at least in battle. They afford, however, little shelter from the flighted quarrel, the knife cast from the darkness. I had taken it as a foregone conclusion that the unknown assassin of whom Lord Nishida was wary was in the fee of an understood foe, but I supposed that that need not be true. Not all enemies, I recalled, are strangers. In Gorean the saying would literally translate as not all strangers are strangers.

"My question was innocent, and general," said Pertinax. "Have the slaves been boarded yet?"

"Look behind you, to the east," I said.

"Ah," said Pertinax.

The majority of public slaves, or, perhaps better, the slaves without private masters, camp slaves, kitchen slaves, laundry slaves, girls selected for trading and selling, girls from the slave house, and such, would be soon conducted on board. I could see the column forming now, east of the wharf, on the beach. Private slaves were taken on board, for the most part, with their masters.

Most of the men, artisans, storesmen, smiths, tarnsters, Pani, mercenaries, and others, marshaled and hastened by Aëtius, had now boarded.

Almost every female slave desires a private master, and, too, hopes to be his only slave.

The slaves to the east would be bound and coffled.

I had seen coffles, and sometimes more than one such linkage, after the fall of cities, which contained fifteen hundred to two thousand women. Needless to say this considerably depresses the market, and it is, accordingly, often the case that these coffles must be broken up and widely dispersed, or marched far afield, sometimes better than a thousand pasangs, to more favorable markets. Sometimes too, the women are kept off the market, sometimes for months, while their owners wait, hoping for better prices. During such times they are exercised and trained, which increases their value. Slavers often buy such women in lots, for pittances, on speculation. Considerations of these sorts, of course, as a matter of economics, appertain to any sort of goods, the value of which is likely to fluctuate according to the condition of the market.

"They are nearly ready," I said to Pertinax.

"I see," he said.

The column of camp slaves, and others, had now been formed. Pani were now tying their hands behind their backs, and putting them on a long rope, which was strung from neck to neck. It was thus they would ascend the ramp. They did not know to what they were being taken but neither, too, did other animals already boarded, tarsk and verr.

I heard the sound of chains, heavy chains, strike the ascending ramp, dragging upon it, and looked about. Licinius Lysias of Turmus, who had made the attempt on the life of Lord Nishida during the training exercise, laden with chaining, was being prodded up the ramp by the butt of a Pani glaive. Perhaps unwisely, I had spared him at Tarncamp, that he might have some chance for life. This had doubtless been regarded by Lord Nishida as a woeful indiscretion, if not an act of outright treason. On what grounds, comprehensible to one such as he, might a would-be assassin be freed? Had I been in league with him? I suspected that one of less stature in the camp, one who, say, was not the commander of the cavalry, might have fared rather poorly following such an act. Certainly it gave Lord Nishida excellent grounds for regarding my services with considerable circumspection. And later I had participated in a mysterious interview, on tarnback, over the forest, the nature of which I had been reluctant to disclose. It was not surprising,

I supposed, that I was not this morning with the cavalry. In any event, Lord Nishida had sent numerous Pani forth to track and return Licinius to custody. They had discovered him some pasangs from Tarncamp, where, for four or five days, frightened, haggard and starving, he had apparently wandered in circles. He had soon been brought back, back-shackled, on a neck chain. Perhaps I had done Licinius no great favor, considering he seemed ill equipped with forest craft, was seemingly unable to live off the land, hold a direction, elude pursuit, and such. He was presumably less a warrior than a mercenary, and less a mercenary than a brigand. I knew he had sword skills but they would do him little good when, weakened, scarcely able to stand, he would find himself ringed by glaives. Licinius, partway up the ramp, saw me. He stopped for an instant, but did not attempt to address me or communicate in any way. Then he was struck by the butt of the glaive, and thrust rudely upward. Had I turned him over to Lord Nishida he would doubtless have been tortured. The Pani, I gathered, had methods likely to encourage volubility in their informants. Subsequently he was to have been crucified. Now, supposedly in deference to me, he had been spared crucifixion. I did not know if he had been tortured or not. If so, and if Lord Nishida had cared to do away with me, it would have been easy enough for him to extract incriminating testimony from a harried body which would beg to babble whatever might be wished, if only the pain would cease, or the welcomed knife plunged mercifully to the heart. But I had seen nothing in the glance of Licinius which had suggested shame or pleaded for pity and understanding. Accordingly I gathered he had not yet, at any rate, been forced to utter fabrications under duress. I had gathered he was to be chained to a bench, presumably in one of the galleys. Most oarsmen, of course, would be free. Round ships, incidentally, commonly made use of slaves, fastened to the benches, but the long ships, ships of war, commonly relied on free oarsmen, for reasons which, I suppose, are obvious. Many consecutive shifts at the oars, as free oarsmen exchanged positions, would doubtless be imposed on the wearied, aching body of Licinius Lysias of Turmus. I dismissed him from my mind. I had given him, perhaps unwisely, given his treachery and crime, an opportunity for escape and freedom, an opportunity which, as it turned out, he had been unable to turn to his advantage. He was no longer my concern. He was now the prisoner of Lord Nishida. I did not know what his present life might be. Lord Nishida had informed me that many would have preferred crucifixion.

The camp slaves, and others, were now boarding.

Last night hundreds of tarn eggs had been brought aboard, to be nestled in padded containers below decks. These were being chemically incubated, to keep the egg viable. Later, responsive to a second chemical, which might not be administered for months, hatching was to occur. Clearly Lord Nishida's plans involved tarns beyond those of the present cavalry.

The wind was bitter now, at the river's edge.

Whistles came from the stern castle of the great ship.

The structures of the camp were now much aflame, and the flames were whipped by the wind.

I could see the mighty, towering frame, which had held the ship of Tersites, was now, too, afire.

"I do not like the direction of the wind," said Pertinax.

"No," I said.

The men who had fired the camp, and some stragglers, were now hurrying down the wharf, to board.

"Is Lord Nishida aboard?" asked Pertinax.

"I do not think so," I said.

"What of his contract women?" asked Pertinax.

"I do not know," I said.

Again we heard the whistles from the stern castle.

"Should we not board?" asked Pertinax.

"Shortly," I said.

"The wharf itself may soon be afire," said Pertinax.

"Yes," I said.

I could see some mariners, far above, at the railing of the stern castle, reading the flames and their progress.

"The ship may be in danger," he said.

"Eventually," I said, "not now."

To be sure, I expected that mooring ropes would be soon cast off, and the great ship, obedient to rudder and current, would edge into the river.

Aëtius, I was sure, was anxious to depart.

"Perhaps we should board," said Pertinax.

"I would be curious to see the last to board," I said.

"Where is Lord Nishida?" asked Pertinax.

"He may be dead," I said.

"You jest," he said, uneasily.

"I think it unlikely," I said. I did not, of course, rule it out. There might be, I thought, frictions or dissensions amongst the Pani. Surely they were human, and not unaware of the attractions of power. Perhaps Lord Nishida had served his purpose, supplying lumber to the shipwrights at the Alexandra camp, arranging for the formation and training of a tarn cavalry, and such. Perhaps he was no longer required by Lord Okimoto, who was, it seemed, a cousin to the *shogun*, some *shogun*.

"They are going to raise the ramp," said Pertinax.

"Not yet, surely," I said.

The great frame in which the ship of Tersites had been formed was now muchly ablaze. A timber collapsed with a crash.

"I fear for the wharf," said Pertinax. "The ship must cast off."

In the river some ice drifted downstream.

I estimated that there must be some twenty-five hundred to three thousand men on board.

Many lined the rails, far above.

Enormous quantities of foodstuffs had been brought on board. This had caused me considerable uneasiness. So might a city have been supplied, anticipating its beleaguering. And who might the foe be, if not the sea? How long was this voyage to be? Such stores would suffice to carry one beyond Cos and Tyros, and beyond these, the farthest of the western islands. But I feared they might be but little used. I feared, rather, given the coming of winter and its season of storms, that the walls of this city, so to speak, would be shortly breached, that they would be unable to resist the raging blows of green Thassa, the blows of her towering, mountainous hammers, that the city must soon fall, succumbing to the implacable, voluminous ingression of cold waters. One does not venture upon Thassa in this season.

"You do intend to board, do you not?" asked Pertinax.

"Certainly," I said.

"The fire encroaches," said Pertinax, uneasily.

"There is time," I said.

"Look," said Pertinax, "across the river."

We could see a longboat putting away from the shore, on the opposite bank.

"Enemies?" asked Pertinax.

"Unlikely," I said.

"The camp is on the northern bank," said Pertinax. "The boat departs from the southern shore."

"Something, then," I said, "was housed there."

"What?" he said.

"I do not know," I said.

We saw the oars dipping, water falling from the blades.

There were numerous small cabins for officers on the great ship. Pertinax and I each had our cabin. Doubtless much ampler quarters were provided for Lords Nishida and Okimoto, and those ranking high amongst the Pani, probably in the stern castle. I did not object to the tiny quarters. In a sense they were a luxury, inside, sheltered from the weather. In many Gorean ships, shallow-drafted galleys, with which I was familiar, and on which I had sailed, there was not much in the way of cabins at all, though there might be a hold in which one might place stores, chain slaves, and such. Officers and crew often slept on the deck, under the stars, or at the side of the ship, on land, if it were beached at night. The holds were not pleasant. Slaves often petitioned, most piteously, to be permitted on deck, though it be but to be chained to a stanchion, or caged.

To an outsider, one unfamiliar with such things, I suppose that our cabins would have seemed miserably tiny and cramped, but space is usually precious on a ship, even a large ship. And to me, if not to Pertinax, as I suggested, it was something of a luxury to have a cabin, at all. I was well pleased. There was a single berth in the low-ceilinged cabin, on the left, as one entered. This berth was built into the wall. Beneath the berth, also built into the wall, was a locker, which was the primary storage facility. Across from the berth was a cabinet for small articles. The only furniture, so to speak, in the cabin was a small bench, some three feet in length. There were also, here and there, hooks in the ceiling, from which paraphernalia might be suspended. A small, glass-enclosed tharlarion-oil lamp was hung from the ceiling, at the center of the cabin. It could not be removed from its chain. Fire at sea, particularly in wooden ships, is a hazard which must be taken with the utmost seriousness. Most welcome was a tiny port, some four inches in diameter, with its hinged window, opposite the door. By means of this aperture, one could look outside, and, the port opened, ventilate the cabin. Closed, the window was proof against cold and high seas. From a distance, given their tininess, these ports, if noticed at all, would seem little more than dots in the hull. The door was small and narrow, and would swing inward from the adjacent companionway. In this way, if opened, it would not obstruct the companionway. I could not stand fully upright in the cabin, but one does not intend to spend much time there. Both Cecily and Jane could stand upright in the cabin, with room to spare. I hoped they understood the luxury of their quarters. It was far superior to the pens, kennels, cages, chaining rings, and such, which were the lot of several of their collar-sisters. To be sure, even such accommodations were likely to be far superior to those afforded on typical slave ships, in which the slaves were often supine and tiered, chained, wrists over head, ankles together, on pallets of slatted wood, enclosed by mesh, to keep away the urts. All the hair on their bodies is removed, to reduce the infestation of parasites. The chaining arrangement, incidentally, is not only to keep the girls from tearing the mesh, which might allow the entry of urts into the space, but, also, to keep them from lacerating their own bodies, tearing at them to relieve the misery consequent upon the depredations of parasites, usually ship lice. Racks of these tiers stretch substantially from wall to wall in the hold, with only a tiny walk space between and about them. A panel in each space opens, by means of which a crust of bread may be placed in the mouth of each slave. Similarly, they are watered, by means of a bota or hose.

The approaching boat was now midriver.

It had eight oarsmen, and a fellow at the tiller, and another at the bow. Its cargo, between the gunwales, was covered by a tarpaulin.

I looked to Cecily and Jane, kneeling on the planks, beside us.

"You know your cabins?" I asked.

"Yes, Master," said each.

Two days ago we had taken them on board, to show them our cabins, and, in general, familiarize them with the ship. In this tour we had tied their hands behind their backs and then tied them together by the neck. From a custodial point of view this was unnecessary, of course, but such things are seldom done for custodial purposes. Where is a slave to run? Indeed, when a slave is chained, if we are interested in custodial matters, it is commonly done not so much to confine her, though she is confined, and perfectly, and knows it, but to prevent her theft, for she is property. It is no great challenge for a male to subdue and carry off an untended slave. The two most common reasons for binding slaves, which is very frequently done, are, first, mnemonic, and, second, stimulatory. Binding, thonging, chaining, and such, makes it exceedingly clear to them that they are such that such things may be done to them, that they are subject to such things, that that is what they are, slaves. When the girl is helpless, and knows herself such, there can be little doubt about what she is, that she is a slave. Thus they are frequently bound, caged, and such. Secondly, bonds, in virtue of reinforcing the slave's sense of her lesser strength, her vulnerability, and helplessness, are sexually stimulatory. They know themselves then objects vulnerable to, and readied for, sexual predation. This is related to the radical sexual dimorphism of the human species, the obvious complementarity of the sexes, and the dominance/submission ratios pervasive in nature. That the slave is helpless, then, not only accentuates the acuteness and viability of these natural responses, but intensifies them, exponentially. Surely Pertinax and I had had ample proof of this matter when we returned that afternoon to our quarters. The slave is likely to very well understand what is done to her, and why, but this avails her naught. She is still helpless, and a slave. Too, if her slave fires have been kindled, as is likely to be the case, she desires and needs the pleasures of her bondage. It is not unusual for her, left in her bonds, to beg for sexual relief.

Too, it might be noted, as a passing, prosaic observation, that when a woman's hands are tied together behind her back she is likely to get into little trouble. It would not do, for example, on such a tour, to have them fussing about, rearranging objects, straightening things, folding things, picking up things, handling things, noting textures, and such. Having them on a neck bond, too, of course, keeps them together. Thus they are not likely to wander off, become separated, and find themselves lost in the labyrinthine companionways of the great ship.

"Cecily," I said.

"Master?" said the English girl, formerly a student at an Oxford College, the name of which, as mine, shall not be noted.

I regarded her, I standing, she kneeling.

She was a lovely slave.

She looked up at me, to attend my words.

We had been selected for one another by Priest-Kings, to be irresistible to one another. Her shallow, empty, pretentious life on Earth had changed overnight, so to speak, she retiring one evening, smug in her beauty, indulged and practiced in the pleasures of despising, attracting, and tormenting men, and awakening, to her astonishment and terror, unclothed, pressing her small hands against the thick, stout, transparent walls of a containment capsule on the Prison Moon, one of the three moons of Gor. This capsule she found occupied by two others, myself, and a beautiful, young, human female from a Steel World, a Kur pet, who was unspeeched. The English girl had been placed in the capsule to bring about my downfall. Who could long resist her? And should she fail in this there was the Kur pet, in her way a primitive human animal, as innocent and sexual as a cat in heat. In one way or another, then, my honor was to have been lost, as, sooner or later, given the imperatives of nature and the provocations to which I was exposed, I must be unable to resist, as I must feast upon one or both of these delicacies, putting one or both of them, again and again, to my pleasure. Neither, you see, was a slave, at least legally. Both were free, at least legally. And therein lay the difficulty. I have little doubt but what, sooner or later, I would have taken the proud, vain, selfish English girl in my arms, and she would learn what it would be to be used by a Gorean warrior, and as might be a mere slave. This denouement did not materialize, however, because, as recounted earlier, Kurii raided the Prison Moon and freed me, a raid which had had me, interestingly, as its very object. During the raid the English girl, hoping to avoid death, had declared herself slave. She intuitively understood that as a free woman she was worthless, save perhaps as food to the beasts, but might, as a slave, have whatever worth a slave might have. Intuitively she sensed she might have that value, some value, however minimal, as a female slave. But the cry, too, had seemed to come from her heart, as an outburst from the depths of her heart, releasing a tension that might have been pent-up for years, a cry of enormous relief, a cry that seemed to suggest she had at last cast aside a dreadful, encumbering falsity, that at last a great weight, an immense burden of fear and denial, had been cast from her. As many women, if not all, she had recognized from puberty onward that there were two sexes, quite different, and devastatingly complementary to one another, and that she had, from whatever source, slave needs. She was well aware of these needs, for years, in many ways, from dreams from which she awakened suddenly, discovering she was not truly in chains, that her lips were not truly pressed to a master's whip, from persistent fantasies from which she tried to flee, but to which, in fascination and fear, she must constantly return. How often she dreamed of herself, and fantasized herself, helpless in the power of dominant males, as no more than their possession, their prize, and plaything, their slave. Hating the tepidity, the ineffectuality, the weakness of the males she knew she took out on them her spite and disappointment, torturing them as only her beauty made possible. She did not hate men, truly, but only males who refused to be men, who would not see to it that she was put to their feet. But how soon, after her declaration on the Prison moon, she had tried to unsay her confession! But the words once spoken are irrevocable, for the speaker is then a slave. She was later branded and owned by male cohorts of the Kurii. Torn between her lingering pretenses of freedom and her slave needs, she had been found insufficiently pleasing by her masters, and was to be cast to eels in a pool in a Pleasure Cylinder, associated with a Steel World. She had begged my collar. I consented to the piteous pleas of the slave, and would honor her with my collar, which I then locked on her neck. That night, chained in an alcove, at my mercy, she was taught, finally and well, what it is to be a slave. A natural slave, she had become a legal slave; then, a legal slave, she had become a true slave.

"Cecily," said I.

"Master?" she said.

"Go to the cabin," I said, "remove your clothing, completely, and lie in the berth, and wait for me."

"Yes, Master," she said, and leapt up, hurrying to the ramp.

"Cecily," I called.

"Yes, Master?" she said.

"And first lay out the whip," I said.

"Yes, Master!" she said, and was then up the ramp.

I had no intention of using the whip on her, but this small ritual has its effect on the slave, reminding her she is a slave, and readying her and loosening her for use. Sometimes, in the use of a slave, one might ask, "Do you see the whip?" "Yes, Master," she might say, "it is on its peg." "Do you wish it to remain there?" she might be asked. "Yes, Master," she responds, with fervency. "Are you being sufficiently responsive?" he might ask. "It is my hope that I might be found pleasing," she says. "Excellent," might say the master. "Yes, Master," she might exclaim. "Yes, Master! Yes, Master!" Then perhaps her mouth needs be covered, with the flat of one's hand, that her cries may not be obtrusive. To be sure, it is often pleasant to hear her cry out, weep, gasp, and moan, she in your arms, beside herself in helpless, uncontrollable ecstasy.

"Jane," said Pertinax, "go to my cabin and lay out the whip, and then wait for me, naked, in the berth."

"Yes, Master!" said his Jane, happily, and hurried after Cecily.

It is not unusual for a master to have his slave await him, naked, in the furs. The wait, and her nudity, well impresses upon her that she is a slave. Too, when he arrives, she is heated, needful, and ready for him.

And if the whip is at hand, so much the better.

"Would you not enjoy having Saru in your berth, naked, waiting for you?" I asked.

"—Yes," he said.

"Good," I said.

"She is a slave," he said.

"Do not forget it," I said.

"No," he said.

"And could you use the whip on her?" I asked.

"Yes," he said.

"Excellent," I said. "Unfortunately she belongs to Lord Nishida."

"I am well aware of that," he said.

"Do you think she would make a nice gift for a *shogun*?" I asked.

"I do not know," he said. "Perhaps."

"Perhaps you would like to receive her as a gift," I said.

"She is from Earth," he said.

"Some of the loveliest gifts come from Earth," I said.

The boat which had come from the other side of the river had now drawn up on the beach, below the wharf.

"There is some cargo there," I said, "covered with a tarpaulin."

The great frame in which the ship of Tersites had been formed suddenly collapsed in a shambles of burning timber.

"I fear for the wharf," said Pertinax.

I nodded. Indeed, the far end of the wharf was beginning to burn. Some Pani were there.

"Look," said Pertinax, pointing to the right, to the end of the wharf farthest from us, away from the flames, that nearest the bow of the great ship.

"Good!" I said. It was the retinue of Lord Nishida. With him were his guard, several officers, and two contract women, who were doubtless Sumomo and Hana.

I was much relieved to see Lord Nishida. I had feared the worst.

"Let us meet him," I said. "We will now board."

I pulled my cloak more about me.

I now expected to hear once more the whistles from the stern castle, which would now be the final signal, or warning, that prior to casting off.

Behind the stern of the ship, some fifty yards back, the wharf was now clearly afire. Pertinax's apprehensions had now some justification. Certainly the ship must soon cast off.

Wind whipped my cloak about me, wind from the east.

I could see its passage on the river, in raising swells. I saw a log from upriver turning in the current.

Followed by Pertinax I made my way to the other side of the ramp.

"Greetings," said I to Lord Nishida.

"Greetings," said he, "Tarl Cabot, tarnsman."

"Did you expect me to be here?" I asked.

"Certainly," he said, politely. "You are curious, you wish to accompany the cavalry, you find it difficult to resist the unknown, you are unwilling to step aside from the path to adventure, a trait with which we of the Pani are not unfamiliar, and you are interested in a far shore."

"True," I said.

"Had I not been sure of this," he said, "I would have had you killed."

"I see," I said.

We then approached the ramp.

Men stood by, with ropes and weights, on pulleys, to draw the ramp within, after which the port would be drawn up, similarly moved, and closed.

"Winter," I said, "is not yet afoot, and yet there is ice in the river."

"True," said Lord Nishida.

"Your contract women," I said, "are cold."

Certainly Sumomo and Hana, even though warmly wrapped, seemed miserable, in the background.

"They prefer a milder climate," said Lord Nishida.

"At least you will not be wintering by the river," I said.

"I do not much care for this clime, in this season," he said.

"Nor perhaps will you much care for Thassa in this season," I said.

"I had thought," he said, "that you would now be aboard."

"I was waiting for you," I said.

"I see," he said.

I gathered he was not pleased.

"Lord Okimoto is already on board," I said.

"Excellent," he said.

"Shall we board?" I asked.

The eastern third of the wharf was now afire.

Above, mariners, at the rails, were marking the blaze.

Lord Nishida indicated to his retinue that they should proceed up the ramp. Certainly Sumomo and Hana hurried aboard. Ito paused, but was waved ahead by Lord Nishida.

Lord Nishida and I, and Pertinax, then stood alone on the right side of the ramp, which was approximately amidships.

I looked back to the beach, and noted that the tarpaulin had been thrown aside. Huddled, kneeling, crouched down, crowded between the gunwales, were a number of pathetic figures. These were the cargo which had been brought to the beach from the opposite side of the river. The fellow who had been in the bow yanked on a chain leash and the first of the figures was yanked its feet, and drawn rudely over the gunwales, and it fell, helpless, and miserable, on the sand. The other figures were lifted over the gunwales, and knelt, brutally, in a line, on the sand. The first figure then, which had fallen into the wet, cold sand, and still lay there, prone, frightened, afraid to move, by its upper arm, the right, was pulled to her knees, and knelt as well. The figures were then aligned, kneeling. They were fastened together, coffled, by the neck, with chain. Their hands were behind their backs, doubtless fastened together there. Interestingly, each was hooded, the entire head covered in the hood, a slave hood. In such a device its prisoner is disoriented, and helpless, dependent for movement and direction on its custodian.

"Shall we board?" said Lord Nishida.

"Presently," I said.

The coffle was then ordered to its feet, and it struggled to stand, barefoot, on the cold beach.

A command was barked, and there was a snap of the whip, and the coffle, the left foot of each figure first moving, began to move, approaching, paralleling the beach side of the wharf, several yards of which were now ablaze.

"Tarl Cabot, tarnsman?" inquired Lord Nishida, politely.

"Presently," I said.

At various points along the wharf there were steps leading to its surface from the shore.

"Draw back a bit, Tarl Cabot, tarnsman," said Lord Nishida.

We withdrew some yards from the ramp.

"Steps," we heard, uttered by the fellow who had the leash on the first figure.

There was a cry of pain as the first figure on the chain was drawn against the steps, and stumbled, and was then jerked to its feet.

As the cry of pain had been audible the hoods must not be gag hoods, hoods furnished with internal straps and packing. Such hoods are sometimes used in the abduction of free women, in order that they may be unable to call attention to their plight, perhaps while being transported through the streets and beyond the gates of their city, doubtless often within yards of guardsmen. I supposed, however, that the figures would have been forbidden speech. That is commonly forbidden to the hood's occupant.

"Steps," cried the man, "did you not hear me call 'Steps'?"

But the figures, of course, could not see the steps, nor know their height nor width, nor number. They were confused, and helpless. The whip fell amongst them. They could not use their hands, either to break their fall or to assist in maintaining their balance. I think that in that clumsy, agonizing ascent, there was not one who did not fall, and more than once, upon the steps, thence to struggle frantically to regain its feet, only sometimes, drawn unexpectedly, off balance, by the chain again, to fall yet again, and some were unable to regain their feet, and were half dragged upward, on their knees. One, unable to find its feet, was drawn upward, on its side, thrusting, scrambling, with its feet. At last some, mercifully, were lifted and carried upward by oarsmen, and set on their feet, on the wharf.

"Clumsy fools!" cried the fellow who had been in the bow. "Two blows for each!"

These were administered, the figures bent over, and cringing, each receiving its two prescribed lashes.

"It seems these are being treated with unusual cruelty," I said to Lord Nishida.

"They are slaves," he said.

"Why were they kept across the river?" I asked.

"Some are superb," he said. "We did not wish the men to fight over them."

The slaves were now being aligned again, at the foot of the ramp.

The fire on the wharf was roaring, some seventy yards to the east, only several yards away, now, from the stern of the great ship.

A spark stung my cheek.

"These slaves," I said, "appear to be held in a splendidly effective custody."

"That is not unusual, is it not?" he asked.

"No," I said. "Not really." Still, for the latitude, the menace of the forest, and such, I was surprised at the precautions, the hoods, and a coffle not of rope, but of iron collars and chain. One would suppose that they might have been slaves in a city, or women of some value or importance.

Too, as their hands were doubtless fastened behind their backs, given the other arrangements, I supposed their hands would be fastened behind them not with thongs, cord, or rope, but metal, that their small wrists would be enclosed snugly in linked, steel circlets, in slave bracelets, designed to be put on women.

Some of the slaves wept, and cried out with pain, recoiling in their tethering, stung by sparks from the fire.

The fellow who had been in the bow looked back at the fire and then drew on the chain leash, and the first girl, whimpering, was drawn forward, she followed then by the others.

The ramp, with its slope, would be easily negotiated by the coffle.

The first girl was now on the ramp.

I saw that my conjecture as to the girls' wrist fastenings was correct. The hands of each were pinioned behind them in steel, in slave bracelets, and, I noted, in close-linked slave bracelets.

Before the first girl reached the top of the ramp, her progress was arrested, by a whip held to her bosom.

The girls were then all on the ramp, standing.

They began to shiver and tremble, but were not allowed to proceed.

"Why have they been stopped?" I asked Lord Nishida.

"My instructions," he said.

"It is bitterly cold by the river," I said. "Why are they naked?"

"That they may better learn they are slaves," he said.

I gathered then that these were new slaves. Once a girl has been a slave for a time, she has well learned she is a slave.

"What do you think of them?" asked Lord Nishida.

"You had better get them inside," I said. "You do not wish to lose them from exposure."

"What do you think of them?" he asked, again.

"It is hard to tell," I said, "as they are hooded."

"Of course," said Lord Nishida.

"Their figures are superb," I said.

"They are not Pani," said Lord Nishida, "but all are comely."

"Collar-girls?" I said.

"Perfectly so," he said.

I considered the girls. One could not determine their features, of course, for the hoods, but their figures, their slave curves, were fully worthy of a Gorean block. Not one of the slaves, I was sure, was more than five feet six inches in height. Each was slender enough, but not in the Earth sense. Each, rather, had the exciting body of the genetically honed slave of men, the typical body of the natural human female, deliciously seizable, and lusciously curved, curves selected for, turned on the lathe of masculine lust, for centuries, the sort of female body hunted, sought, prized, enslaved, and sold for millennia. The typical Gorean male is a natural male, ambitious, possessive, energetic, powerful, a master. It is no wonder then that his taste, as is evidenced in his buyings and huntings, runs to the natural female, she whom nature has appointed to him as his proper slave.

"You do not think Gorean males would be disappointed in them?" I said.

"Certainly not," he said, "nor Pani."

"Excellent," I said. "Now perhaps you might put the stock inside."

"Do you notice, Tarl Cabot, tarnsman," he asked, "anything of particular interest about the second to the last slave on the coffle?"

"No," I said. "She does have one of the better figures."

Lord Nishida gestured to the coffle master, and he drew his whip away from the bosom of the first girl. He then said, "Proceed," and the coffle ascended the ramp and disappeared inside the great ship.

"Do not fear, Tarl Cabot, tarnsman," he said. "They will be warmly bedded within. There will be an abundance of straw in each stall, within which each will be chained by the neck."

I nodded.

I suspected then that Saru had probably been similarly quartered.

I wondered why Lord Nishida had asked me about the second girl from the end of the coffle. She had had one of the better figures. Too, interestingly, there had been something familiar about her slave flanks.

"The fire approaches," said Pertinax. "Let us board."

The third whistle, insistently, almost frantically, sounded from the stern castle.

Pertinax and I followed Lord Nishida aboard. Behind us came some other fellows, some Pani, some oarsmen, and such. Several docksmen freed the great ship from its moorings and, as the ropes were drawn upward, leaped to the ramp, and assisted in drawing it inboard. Shortly thereafter, the large side port was raised and closed. Aboard, the port closed, I sensed the ship begin to move.

I recollected the slave brought to my attention by Lord Nishida. There had seemed something familiar about her slave flanks.

Then I dismissed the thoughts of the slave from my mind. She was only another slave.

I made my way upward, from deck to deck, emerged onto the open deck, and went aft, to the stern castle.

The wharf behind us was raging with fire.

The ship was safe.

She, caught in the slow current, had begun her journey down the Alexandra.

I watched for a time from the stern castle, seeing the beauty of the river, and the forests slipping behind, to each side, and then I made my way to my cabin, where Cecily would be waiting.

Gorean men have what they want from women.

Chapter Thirty-Nine

A Report Is Received; Enemies Are Discussed

Tajima brought the tarn down, expertly, to the stem castle of the ship, and leapt from the saddle.

He cast the guide straps to a tarnster, who then conducted the bird, with its stately gait, toward the large descent way to the in-ship cots.

Tajima, sent to reconnoiter, had been awaited by Lord Nishida. I was present.

"Speak," said Lord Nishida.

"They are waiting for us," said Tajima.

"What of the sky?" I asked.

"The skies are clear," said Tajima. "Ten would have opposed us, five were killed, and five fled. It seems they have learned little."

I gathered that few tarnsmen cared to meet with the cavalry after the battle of Tarncamp. I suspected we had crippled, or reduced, the intelligence of the enemy. Their tarn scouts had been routinely dealt with, removed from the sky or driven toward the coast, pasangs before our passage. Doubtless some had reconnoitered by night. I wondered if their reports would be believed at the coast. Some may have been in the forest, along the shore, but, on foot, in our passage downriver, in its steadiness, we would have been likely to have outdistanced them. Some small boats had been attacked and driven back to the river bank. Doubtless we carried our spies on board, but they were likely to be of little value to an enemy with whom they could not communicate.

"What may we expect to encounter?" inquired lord Nishida.

We had been three days on the Alexandra, mainly carried downstream by the current. Small boats, oared, had occasionally preceded us, to confirm soundings. Oddly, I was not clear as to the identity of the ship's master. It was alleged to be Aëtius, who was often seen on the stern castle, but I was uneasy in this matter, as I knew him, rather, as of the shipwrights. To be sure, there was no reason why a shipwright might not possess the seacraft, the judgment and wisdom of a high mariner, but it would be an unusual combination. We did have aboard several mariners, who had had service in round ships. The six nested galleys had their oarsmen and captains, but these captains, presumably, though familiar with the sea, would not be familiar with the problems and requirements of a ship such as that of Tersites. There was no Gorean precedent for the mastery of such a ship. Lords Nishida and Okimoto, of course, were highest amongst us, but neither, surely, was fit to command a vessel of this size, might, and design. Perhaps Aëtius was in command. It was not impossible.

"I think," said Tajima, "they do not realize our nature. They have linked small boats across the mouth of the Alexandra, and prepared others, with ladders and grappling irons, suitable for dealing with round ships. On the banks they have set catapults."

"Beware," I said, "of great stones, and flaming pitch."

"Do you feel, Tajima," said Lord Nishida, "that the cavalry may deal with such weaponry?"

"Yes," he said.

"At what strength do you put their forces?" asked Lord Nishida.

"They are like the sands of the shore," said Tajima. "Their tents are spread for pasangs. I do not doubt but what they have ten thousand men."

"Surely we have no intention of engaging them," I said.

"Certainly not," said Lord Nishida.

"Are there galleys off shore?" I inquired.

"Dozens," said Tajima. "They dot the sea."

"Do you think, Tarl Cabot, tarnsman," said Lord Nishida, "they will dispute our passage."

"Not successfully," I said.

"Good," said Lord Nishida.

"I do not think, Lord Nishida," I said, "that you realize your most dangerous and fearsome enemy, that which you should most fear."

"And what is that?" he asked.

"Thassa," said I.

"Ah, Tarl Cabot, tarnsman," he said, "I think it is you who do not understand the most dangerous and fearsome enemy."

"And what is that?" I asked.

"That which lies at the conclusion of our voyage," he said.

Chapter Forty

That Which Occurred at the Mouth of the Alexandra; The Ship of Tersites Has Entered Upon Thassa; The Salute

There was much shrieking and splintering of wood far below, on both sides, as the ship of Tersites, undeterred, made her way to gleaming Thassa. A dozen small boats, unable to escape, many fastened together, were crushed in the passage of the mighty bow of the great ship, and she brushed others aside, dozens, brushed them aside as the limb of a stately, insouciant larl might sweep leaves from its path, scarcely noticing this consequence of its passage. Many of the small ships drew away, their crews awed, white-faced. Never had they seen so mighty a ship as that of Tersites. Other ships, with bolder governors, many with ladders and irons, clung to her flanks, clustered about her, like insects, but their ladders were unavailing, foolish against this behemoth's sides, and what arm had the strength to cast an iron so high that it might engage the railings towering above? Many of the ships struck into one another, stove one another in, and others were swamped in the swells attending the passage of the great ship. The waters on both sides were filled with debris and struggling men. On both banks there were marshaled infantries, ranks upon ranks, prepared to do war. Many in the farther ranks broke ranks, to press forward, to witness so unaccountable a sight, as though a city might be afloat. Hundreds of men waded into the river, wondering, some pressed by those behind them. The passage of the great ship had not been arrested. There would be no boarding, no escaping of hundreds of men from a grounded, caught, foundering, sinking, burning ship, men to be cut down as they tried to elude the small boats and clamber to shore. And so the infantries stood to the side, on each bank, many men to their waist in the river, astonished, wondering, in the cold water. And I think none then expected to raise their shields, to put their blades and spears that day to battle. Hundreds of tents spread along the beach, perhaps for pasangs, on each side. Our tarnsmen, launched from the ship, attended not to them. We owned the sky. The infantry was not attacked, as the shield roof is easily raised. Massed infantry has little to fear from tarn attack unless, as suggested, it be combined with an attack on foot, with similar forces. Isolated infantrymen fare less well against tarn attack, as the tarnsmen can pick and choose their targets, with relative impunity. Too, it is difficult to defend oneself from low-flying tarns, attacking in concert, from two or three sides at once. The shield, whatever its attitude, can protect from but a single bearing. The attentions of our tarnsmen had been divided between the artillery, the *ballistae,* the mangonels, the catapults, the *springals,* on the shore, armed with their missiles and fire, and several galleys offshore. The enemy artillery, where it was not burning, had been deserted. It had been death to man those engines. Bodies, bristling with arrows, lay about them. Most such devices, given their height, or the angle of their fire, could not be well defended from above. Too, roofing, where practical, if not sheathed in metal or coated in wet hides, would succumb to the canisters of pitch and fire, lit and cast by our tarnsmen. Too, a pasang from the beach we could see two galleys aflame, and others had withdrawn from our path. And so it was that at the mouth of the Alexandra, mighty, its passage now uncontested, as tarns returned to the ship, one by one, canvas fell from the yards, took the wind, and the ship of Tersites, her wings spread, set her prow westward.

There was shouting from the shore, as we passed, of hundreds, perhaps thousands, of men, and a drumming, rhythmic, that carried over the cold, green waters of gleaming Thassa.

I joined Lord Nishida, and Aëtius, at the stern castle.

"We are free of the river," I said.

"It is treacherous, a liquid snake," said Aëtius.

"It is a beautiful river," I said, "and one of the few this far north navigable by a vessel this deeply keeled." Most Gorean galleys could negotiate water as shallow as five to seven feet Gorean. The round ship would need only a few feet more.

"A snake," said Aëtius.

To him, concerned with reaching the sea, bringing his great charge to gleaming Thassa, it had been a menace, a liquid valley, which might contain unseen, submerged mountains of rock, which might tear the bottom from a passing ship. At best it was a twisting, dangerous road.

I looked at the sky. "Perhaps," I said, "in a day or two you would wish yourself again on the river."

Surely he could see the lowering sky, the movement of the water ahead. Might not any captain discern such signs, and be wary?

We looked back, at the shore, some two hundred yards astern.

The shouting and drumming continued, but was now little more than a rumble in the distance.

"What are they doing, those soldiers?" asked Lord Nishida, looking back.

There was shouting, and the clashing of blades, and the pounding of spear metal on metal-rimmed shields.

"Master," said Cecily, who had approached.

I indicated that she might stand beside me, at the stern rail.

"Thank you, Master!" she said, and hurried forward.

Normally the slave remains behind the master, commonly on the left, as she would in heeling him. The free woman, of course, either walks beside the free man, or precedes him. The slave walks behind, for she is a slave. She heels on the left, by custom, as most men are right-handed, and their weapon arm is not to be encumbered. On the other hand, these arrangements are not without value to the slave. In walking behind him, for example, she is protected, sheltered from danger by the wall of his arm and steel. On savage, untamed, perilous Gor, you see, women are vulnerable, and in need of the protection of men. Even free women, whatever their denials or resentments may be, are well aware of this. It is only within the walls formed by the blades of men that their nobilities and privileges, their precious vanities and pretensions, can exist. Otherwise they would be in collars, at the feet of masters. This is the same, incidentally, in all cultures, though in several of them the matter is obscured, and almost invisible. Some women take for granted a boon granted to them by men, unaware of the favor shown to them. Any culture, if it wished, could enslave its women.

And have not several, in effect, done so?

I permitted Cecily to stand beside me.

I did not begrudge her this privilege. I could always cuff her back, behind me, should I wish.

The slave, commonly, is to be unobtrusive, and deferent. In the presence of free persons she will commonly kneel, and keep her head down. When she speaks to free persons, if given permission to speak, her voice is to be suitable to her condition, modest, soft, and respectful, that of a slave. Too, she is to speak clearly and with excellent diction. She is not a free woman. Therefore, there must be no slurring of speech, or mumbling. Masters will not have it.

One of the common requirements for a Gorean female slave might surprise those who are unfamiliar with such things. Aside from her beauty and passion, the Gorean female slave is commonly quite intelligent. I wonder if that is surprising. One hopes not. Few men, if any, are satisfied with a mere body. They wish a body it is a delight to own and master, a richly minded body, and it is probably for this reason that, for the most part, only highly intelligent women are brought into the collar. The average slave, accordingly, is likely to be intellectually superior to the average free woman. Indeed, I have sometimes wondered if that is one of the reasons, doubtless only one of several, why the free woman so hates the slave. She suspects, in fury then, on some level, at least, that the frightened, half-naked creature kneeling before her, collared, cringing, hoping not to be struck, is quite possibly her intellectual superior. Naturally this surmise does not please her. The switch may then strike. In any event, highly intelligent women make the best slaves. They are much more aware of their sex, and its needs, and desires, than shallower women, more ready to listen to the whispers of their heart than simpler women, and have prepared themselves for years, it seems, in their dreams and fantasies, to kneel and kiss the feet of masters. Aside from the pleasures of owning and mastering such a woman, for it is a joy to possess one, a property so intellectually stimulating, one profits from an apparent genetic linkage, doubtless selected for over millennia, from the caves and markets onward, between intelligence and sexual responsiveness. There is a correlation between her intelligence and her slave needs, between her intelligence and her helplessness, between her intelligence and her soon-to-be-discovered, uncontrollable, spasmodic helplessness beneath a master's touch. It is easy to ignite the slave fires in the belly of an intelligent woman. She is vulnerable, and remarkably helpless under your touch. She will then beg. She then belongs to men, and knows it.

So dominate her, wholly, in every way, and own her.

And relish her, all of her, every bit of her, her mind and her body, her sensitivity, her vulnerability, her feelings, her thoughts and emotions, her high intelligence.

Who would want less in a possession?

Are not such things of value in any animal?

But be certain to keep her on her knees.

She knows she belongs there.

It is what she needs and wants.

So much then for her intelligence, and such.

Whatever the nature or quality of such things, they are now, with her, merely more of your possessions.

It is the whole slave, you see, which is owned.

The richer the slave in properties, intellectual and otherwise, the more profit and pleasure in owning her.

And such things, of course, will surely improve her price.

Much, of course, goes beyond her gratitude and helplessness in a master's hands, hot and begging. That is only a part of her life, though surely a part which informs, signals, and makes clear the nature of the whole. While polishing boots how can she forget the sound of the chains, which were fastened to her shackles, the feel of the slave bracelets or thongs which fastened her hands behind her back, or to a ring over and behind her head, her writhing in bonds? The life of the slave girl is a whole and total life. The radiation of her servitude and sexuality permeates her entire existence, even to the smallest, homeliest task she performs, the polishing of boots, the baking of bread, the cleaning of her master's domicile, the laundering of her master's tunic. She is attentive, and serves well; she is devoted; she is dutiful; she is sensitive to the master's moods and behaves accordingly; sometimes he wants her to speak, and sometimes not; sometimes he wants her naked, licking at his thigh, and sometimes not; always it is the master's will which determines matters; her obedience, of course, is to be unquestioning and instant, for she is a slave; and, as she is highly intelligent, she is muchly concerned, as she should be, to be found pleasing, wholly pleasing. It is hers to please, and his to be pleased. She lives to please. A frown or a sharp word may bring tears to her eyes. She may fear such much more than the stroke of a switch, or whip, to which she, as a slave, is subject. Such women converse well from their knees. Who would want a stupid slave? And so one seeks the finest, the most beautiful, the most needful, the most intelligent for one's collar. Behold such, stripped, and put up for sale! See her turned, extolled, exhibited! Would you not bid on such goods? Who would wish to take anything less off the block? Who would wish to own anything less? Surely you would not wish to have anything less in your collar? So bid well. See if you cannot bring her into your collar. Consider her at your feet, collared, yours. Would it not be pleasant to have her there, or one similar? Too, it is they, such slaves, who know what it is to be owned, and they will labor mightily, fearing to be deprived of their most profound fulfillments, to be found worth keeping. "I will improve, Master! Please do not sell me, Master!" They long to be, abject and overwhelmed, conquered and surrendered, subdued and submitted, wholly, at the feet of a dominant male. At his feet they are fulfilled. They know it is where they belong. Their dreams, their heart, has told them so. It is where they want to be. The master is, for such a woman, so needful a woman, her dream come true. With tears in her eyes she kisses the chains that bind her. Kneeling, gratefully, she presses her lips to her master's whip, held before her, and licks and kisses it, at length, tenderly, not daring to touch it with her hands, this symbol of his sovereignty over her. Humbly she kneels before him and kisses his boots, rejoicing to be permitted even so simple a privilege. At suppers, she usually serves in silence, particularly if a free woman is present.

When not serving she will usually kneel in the background, at hand, ready, particularly if a free woman is present, lest she be summoned. For she is not free; she is slave. When alone with the master, of course, much may be expected of her. She knows what it is to fetch his sandals in her teeth, to dance naked, pleadingly, before him, to sustain his caresses, perhaps roped or chained, thus unable to resist even should she desire to do so, to strive to please him in the furs, and with perfection, and as the lowly, abject slave she is, such things.

Her bondage is her life.

In her servitude she finds fulfillments and joys scarcely conceivable by the free woman, fulfillments and joys unutterably beyond those of the free woman.

She is in a collar.

She is a man's slave.

She is happy.

We were now some four hundred yards from shore. The shouting and drumming continued, but little of it now reached us.

"I would be answered," said Lord Nishida.

There had been shouting, the clashing of blades, the pounding of spear metal on metal-rimmed shields. The sound of a trumpet now carried across the cold water.

As Pertinax had now joined us, I turned to him. "What do you think is going on, on the beach?" I said.

"How would I know?" he asked.

"I think you can guess," I said. I was interested to see how far Pertinax had come from Earth, not in miles, but in heart, in blood.

"In its way," he said, "it seems celebratory."

"It is," I said.

"I do not understand," said Lord Nishida.

"It is a salute," I said. "They are saluting you. You are praised, and honored. They acclaim your power, your bravery, your success."

"But they are our enemies," said Lord Nishida.

"Surely such things exist amongst the Pani, as well," I said.

"Yes," he said, "but I had not expected to find them here."

"It is important that those who would kill one another respect one another," I said. "One would not wish to kill an unworthy foe, one whom one did not respect. There is efficiency in that, and it may be practical, or necessary, but little glory. It is more like the crushing of lice, the extermination of urts. Many Gorean warriors, in private matters, will not cross swords with a foe they do not respect."

"Interesting," said Lord Nishida.

"It is a strange thing," said Pertinax, "but I think I understand it."

"You are becoming Gorean," I said.

"That is my hope," he said. His Jane was with him, and she knelt at his thigh.

"Doubtless," I said, "some on the beach have the glass of the Builders. Let us then raise our hands. Let us acknowledge the salute."

Lord Nishida, I, and Pertinax, standing at the rail of the stern castle, lifted our hands.

On the shores of the river, to the left and right, we saw hundreds, perhaps thousands of spears raised.

I then turned away from the rail.

"What do you think of the sky?" I asked Aëtius.

He looked for a time. Then he said, "We have our course."

"Master," called Cecily, from the rail.

I joined her at the rail.

"Look," she said, "there is something there, in the water."

It was hard to make out, at the distance. It was behind, on the starboard side, away from the wake of the ship.

"What is it?" asked Cecily.

"I am not sure," I said. "I think it is a sea sleen."

I then made my way forward, heeled by Cecily.

Chapter Forty-One

We Are Pursued; This Is Noted by Two Mariners

This was the beginning of our third day at sea.

Two mariners were at the starboard rail, amidships, leaning out, looking back.

I joined them, noticed nothing, and then looked out, across the water, squarely abeam.

The sea was calm. Tor-tu-Gor was low behind us, on the horizon, in our wake. It was a winter sky, though we had not yet come to the Ninth Passage Hand, following which is the winter solstice. Toward the tenth Ahn, the Gorean noon, after we had emerged from the Alexandra earlier, in the morning, some three days ago, at, say, the fifth Ahn, the ship had changed course, radically. I gathered that Aëtius had reconsidered the sky, or that someone to whom he might report had done so. About the sixteenth Ahn, the storm was well to the north. This could be seen from the darkness over the water. Had we kept the former course we would have been in the vicinity of the storm, if not embroiled within it. To be sure it might have been no more than a robust squall. Perhaps, in its passing, it would have lasted for little more than a quarter of an Ahn. Perhaps a galley might have weathered it, without even sheeting itself with canvas. Still, it is hard to know about such things. One does not know what the sky portends, only that it portends. I myself, particularly with an untried ship, would not have challenged it. And so, too, had ruled whoever might be the master of the ship of Tersites. To be sure, many storms cover the sea for hundreds of square pasangs and one can no more avoid them than the sea herself. Too, some storms last several days. One strives to weather such storms, and sometimes one must flee before them. In a galley one would normally take down the mast and yard, that they not be lost in the wind, or, if necessary, rig the smallest of her sails, the storm sail, get the storm astern and run before her, as might a tabuk attempting to elude a pursuing larl. I had confirmed with the helmsman the following morning that we had returned to our former course. It would take us south of Cos, north of Tyros.

As noted, this was the morning of our third day at sea.

"It is falling behind," said one of the mariners.

"It has been with us since the Alexandra," said the other.

"It weakens," said the first.

"It is foundering," said the second.

"It is drowning," said the first.

How odd, I thought, that a sea sleen would be with us from the Alexandra.

Perhaps they frequented these waters. Still we were far from shore, and the sea sleen, as other forms of predatory sea life, tends to range the fishing banks, so to speak, shallower waters closer to shore where sea plants can get sunlight, these plants then forming the basis of a rich marine ecology.

But we were now far from shore.

Too, sea sleen commonly swam in packs. They were seldom alone.

"How could a sea sleen drown?" I asked.

"That beast is mad," said the first fellow.

"That is not a sea sleen," said the second mariner, turning about. "That is a land animal. See the width of the head, the jaws."

The sea sleen is an unusual animal, presumably related somehow to the varieties of land sleen. Its body is much narrower, and the head is narrow and knifelike. The six powerful appendages attached to that long, narrow body are flippered, not clawed. It is not fully clear whether the sea sleen is a marine adaptation of the sleen or a similar but independently evolved animal. Its body is snakelike, and it approaches its prey silently, gliding, usually from the rear right or left, and propels itself, when making its strike, by the sudden lashing of its tail. It is the fastest creature in the sea. Its greatest moment of danger is at its birth, for the mother's casting of the offspring and blood into the water stimulates the investigation of predators, in particular that of the nine-gilled Gorean shark. At such times several male sea sleen will ring the mother and infant, protecting them. The narrow snout of the sea sleen, driven into the shark at great speed, can destroy the capacity of gills to extract oxygen from the water, and crush cartilage. The razorlike teeth aligned in two rows within the narrow, triangular jaws, too, some eighteen inches in length, can seize, shake, and tear the head from many varieties of shark. The mother, within the ring, has only a few Ehn within which she must bring the infant to the surface, for its first breath.

"It is not a sea sleen?" I said.

"No," said the first mariner.

"It is exhausted," said the other.

"It is an amazing beast," said the first mariner. "It has been with us since the Alexandra. It swims all night, in the darkness, following us, somehow keeping up with us, and we with a fair wind. It must have incredible strength."

"Which now fails," said the other.

"As it must," said the first.

"And so it dies," said the other.

"It has followed the ship?" I said.

"Yes, Commander," said the first of the two mariners.

"But why, why?" I asked.

"It is mad," said the first.

"In any event, it drowns," said the second mariner. "We must now be about our duties."

"Ho!" I cried, suddenly, frightened, to the officer of the watch, and climbed the steps past the helm deck, to the stern castle.

"Commander?" he said.

"The glass," I said to him, with urgency. "Give me your glass!"

He removed the sling from his shoulder, to which was attached the case which holstered the glass of the Builders.

At the high rail of the stern castle I saw, now far behind, the small motion in the water, now scarcely visible, even with the glass, in the swelling waves, which marked the point beyond which our mysterious companion could not proceed, that point which marked for it the end of a journey it could not complete.

I cast aside my sword and scabbard.

"Stop, Commander! Do not!" I heard the officer of the watch cry out, and then I saw the flash of the mighty rudder to my right, and entered the cold waters of gleaming Thassa.

Chapter Forty-Two

I Renew an Acquaintance

I encircled the mighty neck of the beast with my arm, and felt the throb of blood in the throat. It lived. I kicked my way to the surface, and was thrown yards to my right by the wash of water, and went under, and came up, again, and gasped for breath, half blinded by the water, still clinging to that massive, furred neck, and the beast's head was then, too, out of the water and I heard an explosive exhalation of air, and then I felt through the fur, the expansion of the throat, as massive lungs drew in a volume of air, and there was then an expellation of air and water, choking and eruptive, and the breath was like a burst of smoke in the cold air, and then, again, the beast breathed, and it seemed to rise from the water, pulling me upward, half out of the water, and breathed again, and was then beside me, and we were cast about, together, in the waves. In swells we would be lifted twenty or thirty feet into the air and would then swirl downward into the troughs, to be lifted again and slide downward again, and again. My body began to numb in the water, and my legs and arms began to lose feeling and stiffen, and my arm slipped from the neck of the beast and I was separated from it, surely for yards, and then I felt it beneath me, rising up, and my body was gripped, firmly, gently, in those wide jaws, and lifted up, and my head, gasping, my eyes lashed with wind and salt water, was above the surface, and I breathed. It seemed somehow, in these moments, the beast had renewed its vitality, and had come alive again. I did not think I could last long in waters of this temperature. My head above the water, the jaws released me, and I clung to the fur at its neck. My fingers seemed to stiffen and freeze, and lose their strength, but they were clenched in the fur, fastened there, like cold hooks in that cold, soaked fur. We would die together. It would be madness to put a longboat into that sea. I began, insanely, to count the Ihn, curious to know how long it would be until I lost consciousness, as though it might matter. Then I fought to feel, and to continue to feel, for all the torment and misery, to continue to feel. I determined to count to another Ehn, and then another. I lost consciousness and awakened, and again lost consciousness and again awakened. It seemed there was only the eternal rushing of the water, the lifting and falling, again and again, and the cold, and the large body beside me, to which I numbly clung. I caught sight of the sky over the water. I thought it beautiful. I lost consciousness, again. I do not know how long I was in the water. I awakened, again, in the misery and violence, and heard a low, vibratory rumble beside me, that odd emanation from a large thoracic cavity. My fingers began to slip from the fur. I could cling to it no longer.

"Commander!" I heard, as though from far off.

"Kill the beast!" I heard. "It is attacking the commander!"

"No!" I cried, hoarsely. I hoped they could hear me, if they were truly there. "No! No!"

I became dimly aware of the bulwarks of a pitching galley, her mast down, her oars outboard, about me.

I reached out with my right arm, and caught an oar. It was drawn inward, toward the thole port. I felt hands reach down, over the rail, and seize me, and was drawn inboard, over the rail.

"You went overboard," said Pertinax.

"Are you all right?" inquired Tajima.

One of the nested galleys had been launched.

"You are fortunate the officer of the watch saw you," said a man.

"Kill the sleen," said a mariner.

"Do not," I said. "Bring it aboard."

"No," said a man, "such beasts are dangerous."

"It is half dead," said another.

"Leave it," said an oarsman.

"No," I said.

"Stop!" cried Pertinax, reaching for me.

I went over the rail, and was in the water, making my way toward the sleen, now some yards abeam.

I caught it by the neck, and drew it toward the galley.

"Oars down!" I said. "Into the water, down!"

"Comply!" cried Tajima to the nearest oarsmen.

"Four oars went under the water, and I drew the body of the sleen over two of them. "Oars up!" I said, from the water. "Bring them inboard, blades out, close to the hull."

The body of the sleen then, though with difficulty, for its weight, was lifted from the water.

"Take it on board!" I cried.

"Surely not!" said an oarsman.

"Now!" I said.

"Comply," said Tajima, and he himself, followed by Pertinax, entered the water beside the hull, to roll the body of the sleen closer to the hull.

"See the size of it," said a mariner.

"It will tear your arm off!" said an oarsmen.

"Get ropes, lift," said a mariner.

I was aided aboard, again, and Tajima and Pertinax, in the freezing water, encircled the body of the sleen with ropes, and it was lifted aboard.

"Bring blankets," said Torgus, who had commanded the galley, adding, "for both."

"This thing, recovered, could kill everyone on board," said an oarsman.

"Yes," I said, shivering, "but it will not do so."

Tajima and Pertinax were then assisted in boarding.

"You did not fall overboard, did you?" said Pertinax.

"Perhaps not," I said.

With one blanket I tried, as I could, to dry the fur of the sleen, and put two others about it.

"So we have here," said Torgus, "three fools."

"And a beast brought on board," said an oarsman.

"Fitting for a voyage of madness," said a mariner.

Tajima, Pertinax, and I, shuddering and miserable, then availed ourselves of blankets.

"Put about," said Torgus. "Return to the ship."

"I could use a cup of kal-da," said an oarsman.

"So could we all," said another.

"This is a sleen," said Tajima, looking down.

A rumbling emanated from within its thoracic cavity. Then it closed its eyes, and slept.

"His name," I said, "is Ramar."

Chapter Forty-Three

The Recruit

"It was a very foolish thing you did, Tarl Cabot, tarnsman," said Lord Nishida.

"Perhaps," I said.

"We could have lost a galley," he said.

"I am pleased she is safe," I said.

"You brought a dangerous animal on board," he said.

"No more dangerous, surely," I said, "than ten larls."

"They are caged," he said.

"Not at Tarncamp," I said.

"The larl is large and noble," said Lord Nishida. "The sleen is sly and treacherous."

"It may one day save your life," I said.

"How is that?" he said.

"It is alert to menace, to deceit," I said.

"It is a beast," he said.

"An unusual beast," I said.

"It is a mystical thing," he smiled, "something magical, possessing a gift of divination?"

"Not at all," I said. "I think it has to do with scent, and with changes in a body, reticences, tensings, an incipient readiness to spring, restrained, such things."

"If it is to remain on board," he said. "It must be caged, or chained."

"It has spent much of its life in such imprisonments," I said. "It waits for the chain to be removed, the door of the cage opened."

"It is very large," he said. "It is not wild, I take it."

"No," I said. Ramar was the consequence of a long line of domestic breeding, on a Steel World, of generations of selection, designed to produce size, swiftness, agility, ferocity, and cunning. It had been bred, literally, for the hunt, and the arena.

"To what commands will it respond?" he asked.

"I do not know," I said. "And if I did, I could not pronounce them."

I was unable to produce the phonemes of Kur.

"That is strange," said Lord Nishida.

"They are in a different language," I said, "one spoken in a far place."

I observed lord Nishida closely, but he gave no sign of understanding me, of suspecting what might be the different language, or the far place.

I thought it well to change the course of our exchange.

"You might find such a beast of value," I said.

"Oh?" he said.

"It is an excellent tracker," I said. Indeed, the sleen was a tenacious, indefatigable tracker, the finest on Gor. Its tracking skills had doubtless been evolved for the pursuit of game, but, in the domesticated sleen, often carefully bred for generations, they often proved of great value to humans. It was not unusual for a sleen to locate and pursue a track which might have been laid down several days earlier. There have been documented cases of a sleen locating and following a trail put down more than a month earlier.

An obvious application of sleen is in hunting, say, tabuk, wild tarsk, and such. A related application of sleen is in tracking fugitives, slave girls foolish enough to think they might escape, and such. Depending on the commands issued, the sleen will either destroy and feed on the quarry, or drive it to a preappointed destination, usually a cage, the gate of which the quarry, if it wishes to live, must close, and swiftly, therewith locking itself within. There are also guard sleen, which guard granaries, storerooms, warehouses, and such. They may, too, patrol the perimeters of camps, to prevent intrusions and unauthorized departures. Many a slave girl has been turned back at a camp's periphery, sometimes to be hurried back to her master, by the fangs of a sleen to whom her value and beauty are a matter of utter indifference. Sleen may also be used to guard prisoners, holding them in place. Too, some sleen are used for herding. They may be used, for example, to herd stripped free women, not yet embonded, to whom the coffle might seem an indignity. Many such women are only too eager then to be permitted to seek refuge within a warrior's tent, within which they will serve as, and be used as, a slave. After a free woman has been used as a slave she is usually branded. After that, what else is she good for? She may then be coffled, without reservation. An interesting application, similar to the above, occurs when free women, in the hope of escaping looters, chains, and flames, hurry by postern gates and obscure exits from a fallen city into the surrounding countryside. Those who are not promptly taken into custody, running into the arms of enemy soldiers, fallen into fragilely roofed siege ditches, rather like capture pits, finding themselves unable to scale walls of circumvallation, caught in slave wire, taken in slave snares or slave traps, and such, may be sought by trained sleen. Each woman is likely to mean silver in the coffers of the conquerors. The sleen are trained then to round up, herd, and drive these women to the enclosures, say, corrals or pens, waiting for them. Some sleen are even trained to hold down and tear the garmenture from such women before starting them on their journey toward their readied facilities of incarceration. Recalcitrant quarry are eaten. In any event, there are numerous uses for domestic sleen, far more than it would be practical or convenient to enumerate. Some other uses, which might be mentioned in passing, for mere purposes of illustration, would be that of the bodyguard, and that of an animal used for sport, as in racing, or fighting. Ramar, for example, had been bred primarily as an arena animal, and, in his matches, had been a favorite amongst Kur gamblers.

"I am unfamiliar with such animals," he said.

"But you know something of them," I said.

"Of course," he said.

It was the day following Ramar's arrival on board. It was now toward the tenth Ahn, the Gorean noon, and Lord Nishida and I were met on the main deck, amidships. Ramar was below, caged in the same hold as Lord Nishida's larls. I had looked in on him several times. He had usually slept. Twice he had taken broth, and then slept again. How odd, I thought, had been that pursuit. I could not understand what might have been its motivation. Surely he could have died. Why should he, a mere beast, and a land beast, too, have essayed so long, dubious, and dangerous a journey? It made no sense. He could have lived in the forest on game, eventually made his way south, and such. Would that not have been best for him? Yet he had followed the great ship. How unaccountable, how inexplicable, I thought, had been that stubborn, single-minded, unremitting pursuit. It was absurd. Perhaps the beast was indeed mad, as a mariner had suggested. It made no sense. In four or five days, perhaps ten, I expected him to be muchly recovered from his ordeal. The heart was sound. It had not burst. He had not died in the freezing sea.

"It was not to reprimand you," said Lord Nishida, "that I suggested we meet."

I nodded.

A suggestion from Lord Nishida, of course, as might be an invitation from a high council or a Ubar, was not the sort of thing one would ignore.

Overhead, several of the tarns were being exercised.

"I have a recruit for the cavalry," said Lord Nishida, "one who has demonstrated his capacity to ride, and one whose sword is a welcome addition to our blades."

"I do not understand," I said. "I thought our contingents carefully formed, and complete."

"This remarkable individual," said Lord Nishida, "appeared in the river camp some five days before the launching of the ship."

"From where?" I inquired.

"From Ar, it seems," said Lord Nishida.

"I know of no new recruits," I said.

"He entered the camp, and slew two mercenaries, guards, before the tent of Lord Okimoto, as proof of prowess, and demanded to be presented to his Excellency. This was done. He proved his sword was of great value, for he then slew four, who were set against him."

This sort of thing is not unprecedented, when champions present themselves before generals, Ubars, and such. It is a way of proving skill, and their worthiness to replace lesser men. I have much frowned upon this. That one can kill is impressive, but seems to me to provide little assurance that one possesses properties of perhaps even greater importance to a leader, such as reliability, discipline, judgment, and fidelity.

"How can his sword be of great value," I asked, "if it has cost you six men?"

"Is such a sword not worth six men?" asked Lord Nishida.

"No," I said.

"Are you not of the Warriors?" inquired Lord Nishida.

"That is why," I said.

"He has taken fee with Lord Okimoto," said Lord Nishida.

"Lord Okimoto has made a serious mistake," I said.

"Lord Okimoto," said Lord Nishida, "is cousin to the *shogun*."

"What is the name of this recruit?" I asked.

"Rutilius, of Ar," said Lord Nishida.

"Not Anbar, of Ar?" I said.

"No," said Lord Nishida.

"May I meet this recruit?" I inquired.

"I have arranged it so," said Lord Nishida, and lifted his hand, and the wide, blue sleeve fell back from his wrist, as he signaled a group of men who were on the foredeck, below the stem castle.

One of the group, whose back had been to us, turned about, and approached, with a confident tread, and paused before us.

"Tal, Captain," said he to me.

"You know one another?" asked Lord Nishida.

"We have met," I said. "His name is not Rutilius, of Ar. He is Seremides, formerly captain of the Taurentians, the palace guard, in the time of the false Ubara, Talena, of Ar."

"Many of our mercenaries," said Lord Nishida, "have chosen names for convenience, to distance themselves from records of crime and blood, to elude pursuers, to escape justice, to begin new lives, such things."

"He is Seremides," I said, again, "formerly captain of the Taurentians, the palace guard, in the time of the false Ubara, Talena, of Ar."

It was important to me that Lord Nishida clearly understood this.

This was no ordinary recruit.

More was involved here than bladecraft. Much was involved here which might well give a leader pause. Not only the skill with which a blade might be used was relevant. Surely important, as well, were the uses to which it might be put. In such a case one should extend fee only with circumspection.

"It is clear then," said Lord Nishida, "why he might seek a different, safer name for himself, as doubtless many others with us, who were driven from Ar, either as former members of the party of the Ubara, or of the occupational forces."

Seremides bowed his head, briefly, appreciatively.

"And," said Lord Nishida, "should we not account ourselves fortunate to be successors to the skills of one who commanded such a guard?"

"Doubtless," I said.

"And one supposes," said Lord Nishida, "that one did not come easily to the captaincy of a palace guard."

"Undoubtedly not," I said.

"And thus his skills with the blade are less surprising."

"Doubtless," I said. Lord Nishida was certainly correct in suspecting that one who could rise to such a position would be wise with bladecraft. On the other hand, I had little doubt that such an elevation would not be bought by steel alone. One would expect, as well, cunning, astuteness, a will of implacable force, and, I supposed, given the nature of the traitorous party, remorseless ambition, and a useful lack of inhibitive scruples.

"We are greatly honored," said Lord Nishida, "that so high a personage, drawn from so remarkable a background, whose sword might purchase gold in a dozen cities, would present himself for our service."

Seremides inclined his head, briefly, acknowledging this compliment.

"He betrayed a Home Stone," I said. "He is a traitor. Do you expect more from him than those he betrayed?"

"I do not understand the matter of the Home Stone," said Lord Nishida, "though I have heard of such things. But I think we may suppose that Rutilius of Ar will act in his best interests, as he sees them, and that he will understand that his best interests are identical with ours, and more than this what can one expect?"

"Much," I said.

"I fear, Tarl Cabot, tarnsman," said Lord Nishida, "you do not know men."

"I am a simple warrior," I said. "I have never pretended to cultivate the subtleties of diplomacy nor to comprehend the wisdoms of politics."

"I fear," said Lord Nishida, "that you will never sit upon the mat of the *shogun* nor upon the throne of the Ubar."

"Not every man desires such things," I said.

"I see," said Lord Nishida. "Your business is a less ambitious, simpler one. It would be with the blade, and little more. The vocation of such as you is circumscribed narrowly, confined, so to speak, to a limited board."

"Perhaps," I said.

"Having to do with the kaissa of blood, the dark game."

"If you wish," I said.

The codes, of course, did not see things in this fashion. The board was set indeed, but amongst cities, always on a world. Its width was the width of worlds. The number and values of the pieces was uncertain, and the rules subject to convenient revision, or desuetude.

It is useful that the foe has rules. This puts him at your mercy.

Yet there was a hunt, a sport involved. All who have carried weapons are aware of this. Surely Lord Nishida was apprised of, and not unfamiliar with, scarlet allurements.

The fires of life burn brightly at the edge of death.

Few are the states which have not been born in blood.

"Lord Okimoto," said Lord Nishida, "desires that you accept our friend, Rutilius, of Ar, in the cavalry."

"I decline," I said.

"It is the wish of Lord Okimoto," said Lord Nishida.

"I do not accept him," I said.

"Lord Okimoto is cousin to the *shogun,*" said Lord Nishida.

"I do not accept him," I said.

I then drew my sword, and, smoothly, like the lifted head of an ost, so, too, did the blade of Seremides, as noiselessly as the menace of that venomous creature, leave its sheath.

"Hold!" said Lord Nishida. "He has killed six men."

"Let him try a seventh," I said.

"No," said Lord Nishida, "whatever the outcome seven men are lost."

I half sheathed my blade, watching Seremides from the side. He smiled, but did not move. He had not taken the bait. He had more in mind, I gathered, than another kill. Too, he understood the game. Lord Nishida smiled, too. He, too, understood what had occurred. Perhaps he thought that I was foolish to utilize so transparent a lure, but I had learned what I wanted. I had not expected Seremides to attack, but I had learned what I wanted, that he knew the game, that he was no fool, and that he would be extremely dangerous, patient and dangerous, not only if he were interested in me, but dangerous, too, to whoever or whatever might brook his ambition or projects. It seemed, given his rage and disappointment over the fruitlessness of our nocturnal interview, and the consequent collapse of his hope to secure a fugitive Talena, and thereby obtain both riches and a pardon, that he had had to reconcile himself to flight from known Gor and had accordingly sought both fee and refuge with the Pani. I hoped that Lords Okimoto and Nishida understood the nature of their new sword. I feared they did not.

"He is not with the cavalry," I said.

"Very well," said Lord Nishida. "His place then will be with the guard of Lord Okimoto."

"He will then have the ear of Lord Okimoto," I said.

"Yes," said Lord Nishida.

Chapter Forty-Four

I Use a Slave; I Walk the Deck Alone; The Sea Is Beautiful; The Ship Proceeds Apace

"Is Master troubled?" asked Cecily.

"Do not concern yourself," I said.

"Master conceals his thoughts from his girl," she said.

"Curiosity," I said, "is not becoming in a *kajira*."

"The slave is wholly the master's," she said.

"Yes," I said. "Every corpuscle, every hair, every trembling and shiver, every movement and expression, every feeling, every thought."

"Might I not conceal a thought?" she said.

"Certainly," I said, "as you might conceal a candy, but the thought is still his."

"Everything in me is his," she said.

"Everything," I said.

"But I want to give my thoughts to my master," she said. "I want him to know them. I want to offer them to him!"

"Then do so," I said.

"But what if he rejects them?" she said.

"Then they are rejected," I said.

"Of course," she whispered. "We are slaves."

One does not disparage a woman for her thriving in bondage, no more than one might denounce the tides, sunlight, wind, and rain, no more than one might denounce a flower for its blossoming, for the color, brightness, delicacy, and radiance of its petals.

No woman who wants a collar should be deprived of one.

Surely it is permissible for the slave to be herself.

By what authority is she to be denied this gift?

Let she who desires to submit submit.

Accept her submission.

She is then yours.

Let her beg to kiss the feet of her master, and let her rejoice, should she be given permission to do so.

Let her welcome the collar which encircles her neck, the thongs which, as she kneels with her head to the floor, lash her wrists behind her back.

On Gor such women are not castigated but coveted. They are not disparaged but sought. They adorn sales platforms as objects of value. They are bought and sold, bartered for, exchanged, traded about, and so on. Society is unwilling to do without them.

Are they not commodities of high regard, goods of high esteem?

They obey, and kneel, and serve, and kiss, and enrich a world.

They are beautiful, desirable, exquisite, and owned.

Surely the female slave is one of the loveliest and most valuable ingredients in a high culture.

Their presence, briefly and brightly tunicked, adds delight and charm to the markets, parks, and streets of a city, even to the remoter byways of rural areas.

The world is a thousand times richer and deeper for their existence.

And how pathetic and impoverished would be a puritanical and dictatorial culture, should any exist, which would permit them no place, which would deny them their most profound fulfillments.

I recalled Cecily, from when she had been fresh from Earth. How she had striven and struggled against the insistent whispers of her heart, as she had, even on Earth, for years, trying to deny her deepest needs. Yet, in a way, even on Earth, how clearly she had understood such things, even then, that she was, wanted to be, and should be a man's property, the abject, yielding, humbled slave of a powerful male, and yet, obedient to her background, education, training, and conditioning, how desperately she had struggled against such insights and truths, how frantically she had fought against them.

Indeed, reacting against the acute ambivalences she had felt concerning her own sexuality and men, products of the war between her genetic nature and needs and the provisional idiosyncratic enculturation prescribed by her current milieu, and hysterically attempting to counter the insistent claimancies of her dreams and fantasies, she had, on Earth, habitually, as though in a compensatory vengeance for her own unhappiness and bitter frustrations, delighted herself with leading on, and tormenting, men and boys, gratifying herself by the misery she could induce in culturally confused weaklings eager to impress, placate, and please her. Her greatest pleasure seemed to be flirting with, arousing, and then frustrating males, none of whom would take her in hand, strip her, and put her to their feet, teaching her she was a female.

Then, Priest-Kings, for their own purposes, had brought her to the Prison Moon. There, in fear of her life, in the midst of a Kur raid, she had proclaimed herself slave. The slave, of course, cannot unsay such words, for she is then a slave. At that moment, whether she had understood it or not, she had become a slave. Later, on a far world, far beyond the Prison Moon, a Steel World, as there were slavers there, and her attractions warranted this, she had been simply taken in hand, and branded and collared, routinely so, they not even understanding at that time that she was already a slave, not that that would have spared her the brand and collar, for such details are in order, and prescribed by merchant law. It had been done without thought, with indifferent and impersonal efficiency, precisely as it would have been done to any similar female in such circumstances. Indeed, had she not already been a slave, she would then, as thousands of other women, not self-proclaimed slaves, have become a slave. Branded and collared, of course, she is clearly identified, indisputably, publicly and legally, as what she is, a slave. And so what she was, from that time forth, was clearly displayed, for all to see.

She was marked and collared.

No longer would she frustrate men.

Her status and condition were now clear.

She was a female slave.

"Ohh," she said softly, suddenly.

It is pleasant to have a slave in one's arms.

She gasped. "You will give me no choice, will you, Master?" she said.

"No," I said. "You are not a free woman. You are a slave. You will be done with as a master pleases."

"I am content," she whispered.

"Would you have it another way?" I asked.

"No, my Master," she said. "No."

I looked down on her. "The collar is lovely on your neck," I said.

"It is yours," she said.

"And so, too, is its occupant," I said.

"Yes, Master," she said.

"Perhaps you should remove it," I said.

"I cannot, Master," she said. "I am a slave. It is locked on my neck."

It was late, past the eighteenth Ahn.

The small, glass-enclosed tharlarion-oil lamp, moving with the motion of the ship, provided a dim illumination in the cabin.

"Oh," said the slave, suddenly. "Oh!"

On a peg to the side hung the whip. I had seen to it that she had well pressed her lips to it.

"Does it amuse you to have me so in your arms?" she asked.

"How?" I asked.

"Helpless, and needful," she said, "begging, if you wish."

"It pleases me," I said.

"We are so at the mercy of our masters," she whispered.

"Men will have it so," I said.

"Yes, Master," she said.

"I love it," she whispered. "I love it!"

"This world," she said, "is a man's world."

"There are free women," I said.

"Even they must know," she said, "if they are not unutterably stupid, that their privileges and freedoms are a gift of men, perhaps temporarily accorded to them, revocable at will."

"Perhaps," I said.

"I do not envy them their freedom," she said.

"They may envy you your collar," I said.

"They may not have it," she whispered.

"Then perhaps another," I said.

"Each of them, somewhere," she said, "has her master."

"Perhaps," I said.

"Let us hope they meet," she said.

"I suppose you are right," I said.

"Master?" she said.

"That this world, Gor, is a man's world," I said.

"I would not have it otherwise," she said.

"Why is that?" I asked.

"Because," she said, "I am a woman."

"And a slave," I said.

"We are all slaves," she said. "We all hope to meet our masters."

"Perhaps," I said.

"Which of us does not wish to be sold off a block," she said, "into the arms of a master?"

"Perhaps you would like to choose the master," I said.

"Of course!" she laughed.

"But it is you who are chosen, you who are sold," I said.

"Yes, Master," she whispered.

I then reminded her of her vulnerability and bondage.

How pleasantly, in her collar, and how helplessly, unable to help herself, for I had denied her this option, she writhed, thrashed, and begged.

Slaves should be perfectly mastered, but not abused. They are lovely creatures to be owned and ruled, and worked, and put to the fullest of female uses, but are not to be treated with cruelty nor subjected, no more than any other animal one might own, to gratuitous pain. That is pointless, counterproductive, and irrational. The slave must strive to her utmost to be a good slave, to be pleasing, fully, to her master, but if she is honestly and sincerely, fervently and deferentially, doing her best, for what more could one ask? Relish her, and, if you wish, grant her a kind word, and, should it be your pleasure, a caress. From the body and mind of your slave extract the most exquisite and inordinate pleasures that a human male can know, the mastery of a female of his species.

Keep her in her collar, and enjoy her.

The finest of slaves knows the whip exists and that it will be used on her promptly if she is not pleasing, and that doubtless flavors the relationship, but, too, fear of the whip is much less likely to be her motivation than her desire to please her master. She is grateful to have a master, and grateful that he has seen fit to own and fulfill her.

When she had fallen asleep I covered her carefully with the blankets, arranging them about her, in the berth. I then dressed, and drew my sea cloak about me, left the cabin, ascended the stairs in the companionway, and went to the main deck, and thence to the stem castle. I stood there for a long time, watching the sea. The light of the three moons, visible together this night, shimmered on the water. I could occasionally hear the snap of the canvas of the three large, square sails, adjusting to the wind, and the creak of the yards from which they were suspended.

Our course, as I determined from the stars, would continue to take us south of Cos, and north of Tyros. Beyond these island ubarates would be some small, farther islands. It was not clear what might lie beyond those tiny islands.

Beyond them nothing was charted.

About the Author

John Norman, born in Chicago, Illinois, in 1931, is the creator of the Gorean Saga, the longest running series of adventure novels in science fiction history. Starting in December 1966 with *Tarnsman of Gor*, the series was put on hold after its twenty-fifth installment, *Magicians of Gor*, in 1988, when DAW refused to publish its successor, *Witness of Gor.* After several unsuccessful attempts to find a trade publishing outlet, the series was brought back into print in 2001. Norman has also produced a separate, three installment science fiction series, the Telnarian Histories, plus two other fiction works (*Ghost Dance* and *Time Slave*), a nonfiction paperback (*Imaginative Sex*), and a collection of thirty short stories, entitled Norman *Invasions*. The *Totems of Abydos* was published in spring 2012.

All of Norman's work is available both in print and as ebooks. The Internet has proven to be a fertile ground for the imagination of Norman's ever-growing fan base, and at Gor Chronicles (www.gorchronicles.com), a website specially created for his tremendous fan following, one may read everything there is to know about this unique fictional culture.

Norman is married and has three children.

www.ingramcontent.com/pod-product-compliance
Lightning Source LLC
Chambersburg PA
CBHW020242030726
47499CB00001B/29

* 9 7 8 1 4 9 7 6 4 8 7 4 6 *